JOHN WILLIS

THEATRE WORLD

2000-2001 SEASON

VOLUME 57

APPLAUSE
THEATRE & CINEMA BOOKS

THEATRE WORLD
Volume 57

Art Direction: Michelle Thompson
Book design: Kristina Rolander

ISBN: 1-55783-523-3 (cloth)
ISBN: 1-55783-521-7 (paper)
ISSN: 1088-4564

APPLAUSE THEATRE & CINEMA BOOKS
151 West 46th Street, 8th Floor
New York, NY 10036
PHONE: (212) 575-9265
FAX: (646) 562-5852
EMAIL: info@applausepub.com
INTERNET: www.applausepub.com

Sales & Distribution

NORTH AMERICA:
Hal Leonard Corp.
7777 West Bluemound Road
P. O. Box 13819
Milwaukee, WI 53213
PHONE: (414) 774-3630
FAX: (414) 774-3259
EMAIL: halinfo@halleonard.com
INTERNET: www.halleonard.com

UK:
Roundhouse Publishing Ltd.
Millstone, Limers Lane
Northam, North Devon Ex 39 2RG
PHONE: (0) 1237-474-474
FAX: (0) 1237-474-774
EMAIL: roundhouse.group@ukgateway.net

To Gerard Shoenfeld
Chairman of the Shubert Organization

For over fifty years of dedication to superlative theatrical productions, untiring efforts to revitalize the New York theatre district and Times Square, and the faithful preservation of our theatres in New York and throughout America.

CONTENTS

THEATRE WORLD
VOLUME 57

EDITOR
John Willis

ASSOCIATE EDITORS
Ben Hodges
Tom Lynch

ASSISTANTS
Jenny Berno
Alexander Dawson
Brad Hampton
Herbert Hayward, Jr.
Barry Monush
Eric Ort
John Stachniewicz
Laura Viade
Michael Viade
Rachel Werbel

STAFF PHOTOGRAPHERS
Gerry Goodstein
Michael Riordan
Michael Viade
Van Williams

APPLAUSE BOOKS STAFF
Production Editors: Matthew Callan, John J. O'Sullivan
Art Director: Michelle Thompson
Designer: Kristina Rolander

On June 2, 2001 at the 56th Annual Tony Awards ceremony held at Radio City Music Hall in New York, NY, John Willis, editor of *Theatre World*, was presented a Special Tony Honor for "Excellence in the Theatre," in recognition of *Theatre World* as the authoritative pictorial and statistical record of the Broadway and Off-Broadway seasons, touring companies, and professional regional companies throughout the United States.

INTRODUCTION

After completing my service in the U.S. Navy at the end of World War II, I returned to Manhattan from the Marshall Islands in 1946 and to prospects (like pounding the pavement in search of work as an actor) which were only slightly less daunting than what I had just lived through. One of my first auditions in New York was for the director Norman MacDonald, who was casting a season of summer stock on Long Island. Miraculously, I got the job, and while rehearsing one day, Norman told me that he and a friend had recently begun an annual chronicle of the Broadway theatre season and were in desperate need of a typist. He asked me if I could type, and I told him that it just so happened that I had been the assistant typing teacher at Milligan College in my home state of Tennessee. So, for $1 an hour, I was hired as an assistant to Daniel Blum, co-founder of *Theatre World*, and my 57-year career with *Theatre World* began. The three of us worked together out of Blum's West Village apartment, cranking out annual editions of *Theatre World* (which sold for $3.50 at the time). I was an assistant editor on *Theatre World* and its companion volume *Screen World* for 18 years, and unknowingly laid the foundation for one of the most important archives in the history of theatre and film. I assumed the editorship of both *Theatre World* and *Screen World* upon Daniel Blum's death in 1965.

In 1945, Daniel Blum also presented the first of his awards to "Promising Personalities," then conferred annually upon debut performers from the Broadway season by a committee that originally consisted of only Blum himself. Acknowledged with a loose piece of parchment and handed out by a giddy Daniel Blum at his apartment, I imagine many of those first "promising personalities" felt anything but. However uncertain the future of this awards "ceremony" was in the beginning, Blum had clearly hit on something magical with his passion for recognizing theatre's newcomers. Confirmation of his foresight came with the eventual success of those who emerged from the ranks of those first winners—Betty Comden, Judy Holiday, and John Raitt, joined the following year by Barbara Bel Geddes, Marlon Brando, and Burt Lancaster. These, and the many other actors and actresses who would follow them, have had careers which might have eventually eclipsed that first professional recognition, but the Theatre World Awards (as they became known in 1969), came to serve many of those same anointed performers as an early reminder of their potential in a sometimes unwelcoming profession. The Theatre World Awards are now voted on by New York theatre critics and presented annually to "Outstanding New Talent" in a Broadway or Off-Broadway debut.

Theatre World began 57 years ago as one man's love letter to Broadway and has evolved into the most comprehensive pictorial and statistical record of the American theatre. It includes the annual seasons of Broadway, Off-Broadway, Off-Off-Broadway, and regional and touring companies throughout the United States, and contains the most complete biographical records available of stage actors. The Theatre World Awards continue to be many actors' favorite awards presentation, maintaining a tradition of providing joy and camaraderie for an intimate gathering of friends.

In 2001, the Antoinette Perry (Tony) Award Committee recognized *Theatre World's* long run with a Special Tony Honor for "Excellence in the Theatre." It is my hope that the release of *Theatre World Volume 57* as a commemorative edition will serve as a reminder of the treasure of our theatrical history, and that it will also inspire a new generation of theatre lovers and artists to study, observe, and participate in what I hope will be a glowing future for the theatre. Whether it be the career progress of an established costume designer on Broadway or an actor's debut at the Mark Taper Forum, *Theatre World* is committed to the undiscriminating documentation of all of our careers and to the celebration and preservation of our shared legacy.

Special thanks to the countless volunteers who continue to commit their time and energy to ensure that the curtain never falls on *Theatre World*. But most importantly, neither *Theatre World* nor the Theatre World Awards would be capable of production without the cooperation and generosity of all of the New York and regional press agents and publicists who provide the crucial data and photographs on which we so greatly depend.

JOHN WILLIS
New York City
August 2003

MACBETH

By William Shakespeare; Director, Terry Hands; Set, Timothy O'Brien; Costumes, Timothy O'Brien; Lighting, Terry Hands; Sound, Tom Morse; Music, Colin Towns; Fights, B. H. Barry; General Manager, Abbie M. Strassler; Company Manager, Edward J. Nelson; Special Effects, Gregory Meeh; Fight Captain, Bruce A. Young; Casting, Jay Binder; Public Relations, Barlow-Hartman Public Relations; Production Stage Manager, John M. Galo; Stage Manager, Jenny Dewar; Presented by SFX Theatrical Group and Emanuel Azenberg; Press, John Barlow-Michael Hartman/ Wayne Wolfe; Previewed from Friday, June 9; Opened in the Music Box Theatre on Thursday, June 15, 2000*

Kelsey Grammer

Diane Venora

CAST

Seyton . . . . Peter Gerety
Witches . . . . Myra Lucretia Taylor, Starla Benford
Duncan . . . . Peter Michael Goetz
Malcolm . . . . Sam Breslin Wright
Ross . . . . Michael Gross
Macbeth . . . . Kelsey Grammer
Banquo . . . . Stephen Markle
Lennox . . . . Ty Burrell
Lady Macbeth . . . . Diane Venora
Fleance . . . . Jacob Pitts
A Porter . . . . Peter Gerety
Macduff . . . . Bruce A. Young
Donalbain . . . . Austin Lysy
An Old Man . . . . Peter Michael Goetz
Murderers . . . . John Ahlin, Mark Mineart
Lady Macduff . . . . Kate Forbes
Her Son . . . . Grant Rosenmeyer
Her Daughter . . . . Parris Nicole Cisco
An English Doctor . . . . Peter Michael Goetz
A Scottish Doctor . . . . John Ahlin
Gentlewoman . . . . Kelly Hutchinson
A Servant . . . . Jacob Pitts
Young Siward . . . . Austin Lysy
Siward . . . . Peter Michael Goetz

UNDERSTUDIES: John Ahlin (Duncan/English Doctor/Old Man/Porter/ Ross/Seyton/Siward), Starla Benford (Lady Macduff/Witch), Ty Burrell (Macduff), Kate Forbes (Lady Macbeth/Witch), Austin Lysy (Fleance/ Malcolm/Servant), Mark Mineart (Banquo/Lennox), Jacob Pitts (Donalbain/Malcolm/Siward)

A new production of Shakespeare's tragedy, performed without intermission.

Variety tallied 15 negative notices. *Times* (Brantley): "...stately actors planting themselves like trees at the edge of the stage and disclaiming fiercely and nobly. *News* (O'Toole): "...the determination to strip everything to the bone actually makes a nonsense of the drama." *Variety* (Isherwood): "...underpopulated, underdirected, and practically undersigned..."

*Closed June 25, 2000 after 13 performances and 8 previews.

Joan Marcus Photos

A THOUSAND CLOWNS

By Herb Gardner; Director, John Rando; Set, Allen Moyer; Costume Design, Martin Pakledinaz; Lighting Design, Brian MacDevitt; Sound Design, Peter Fitzgerald; Casting, Liz Woodman; Production Manager, Arthur Siccardi; General Management, Nina Lannan Associates; Stage Manager, Jane Grey; Press, Jeffrey Richards/Irene Gandy; Previewed from Wednesday, July 4; Opened in the Longacre Theatre on Wednesday, July 11, 2001*

CAST

Murray Burns . . . . Tom Selleck
Nick Burns . . . . Nicolas King
Albert Amundson . . . . Bradford Cover
Sandra Markowitz . . . . Barbara Garrick
Arnold Burns . . . . Robert LuPone
Leo Herman . . . . Mark Blum
UNDERSTUDIES: Ricky Ashley (Nick), Russ Anderson (Murray), Lauren Bone (Sandra), Eric Siegel (Albert/Arnold/Leo)

A new production of the 1962 comedy in three acts. The action takes place in New York City, 1962. For original Broadway production with Jason Robards Jr. and Sandy Dennis, see *Theatre World* Vol. 18.

Times (Weber): "...the remarkable societal changes wrought by the upheavals of the 1960s and the evolution of politics, culture, and technology in subsequent decades brought with them the expanded tolerance of (forgive me for the phrase) lifestyle choices beyond what used to be called 'The norm.' That there even is a perceived norm these days is a matter of debate." *News* (Kissel): "Selleck's Murray is laid-back, even bleary. Admittedly, it takes guts to emphasize the depressive quality inherent in the material, but you can't forgo the laughs." Post (Barnes): "It was to Herb Gardner's enormous credit that he came up with a modern character, Murray Burns, who convincingly embodied the ethos of the unmade bed with the philosophy of the Founding Fathers." *Variety* (Isherwood): "Eminently adorable TV star Tom Selleck has chosen a safe bet for his Broadway debut."

*Closed September 23, 2001 after 84 performances and 6 previews.

Carol Rosegg Photos

Nicolas King, Tom Selleck

THE MAN WHO CAME TO DINNER

By George S. Kaufman and Moss Hart; Director, Jerry Zaks; Set, Tony Walton; Costumes, William Ivey Long; Lighting, Paul Gallo; Sound, Peter Fitzgerald; Hair/Wigs, Paul Huntley; General Manager, Sydney Davolos; Company Manager, Jean Haring; Production Stage Manager, Andrea J. Testani; Stage Manager, Brendan Smith; Presented by Roundabout Theatre Company (Todd Haimes, Artistic Director; Ellen Richard, Managing Director; Julia C. Levy, Executive Director of External Affairs; Gene Feist, Founding Director); Previewed from Friday, June 30; Opened in the American Airlines (Selwyn) Theatre on Thursday, July 27, 2000*

CAST

Mrs. Stanley . . . . .Linda Stephens
Miss Preen . . . . .Mary Catherine Wright
Richard Stanley . . . . .Zach Shaffer
John . . . . .Jeffrey Hayenga
June Stanley . . . . .Mary Catherine Garrison
Sarah . . . . .Julie Boyd
Mrs. Dexter . . . . .Kit Flanagan
Mrs. McCutcheon . . . . .Julie Halston
Mr. Stanley . . . . .Terry Beaver
Maggie Cutler . . . . .Harriet Harris
Dr. Bradley . . . . .William Duell
Sheridan Whiteside . . . . .Nathan Lane
Harriet Stanley . . . . .Ruby Holbrook
Bert Jefferson . . . . .Hank Stratton
Professor Metz . . . . .Stephen DeRosa
Prison Guard . . . . .Hans Hoffman
Prisoners . . .Michael Bakkensen, Ian Blackman, André Steve Thompson
Expressmen (Act II) . . . . .Michael Bakkensen, Ian Blackman
Sandy . . . . .Ryan Shively
Lorraine Sheldon . . . . .Jean Smart
Beverly Carlton . . . . .Byron Jennings
Mr. Westcott . . . . .Ian Blackman
Radio Technicians . . . . .Hans Hoffman, André Steve Thompson
Choir Boys . . . . .Jack Arendt, Zachary Eden Bernhard,
Jozef Fahey, Brandon Perry, Matthew Salvatore, Ryan Torina
Banjo . . . . .Lewis J. Stadlen
Deputies . . . . .Michael Bakkensen, Hans Hoffman
Police Officer . . . . .Ian Blackman
Expressmen (Act III) . . . . .Ian Blackman, André Steve Thompson

UNDERSTUDIES: Michael Bakkensen (Sandy), Ian Blackman (John/ Professor Metz), Julie Boyd (Maggie Cutler), Stephen DeRosa (Banjo), Kit Flanagan (Harriet Stanley/Mrs. Ernest W. Stanley), Julie Halston (Lorraine Sheldon/Miss Preen), Jeffrey Hayenga (Mr. Stanley), Hans Hoffman (Expressman (Act II)/Expressman (Act III)/Mr. Westcott/Police Officer/Prisoner), Michael McKenzie (Bert Jefferson/Beverly Carlton/Dr. Bradley), Kathleen McKiernan (Mrs. Dexter/Mrs. McCutcheon/Sarah), Amelia Nickles (June Stanley), Brian Schreier (Deputy/Expressman (Act II)/Expressman (Act III)/Prison Guard/Prisoner/Radio Technician/ Richard Stanley)

Nathan Lane, Harriet Harris

Nathan Lane

Jean Smart

A new production of the 1939 comedy in three acts. The action takes place in a small town in Ohio during December. The restored Selwyn Theatre (1918) reopened under the name American Airlines Theatre with this production.

Variety tallied 12 favorable, 2 mixed, and 4 negative notices. *News* (Hinckley): "...loses none of its delectable sweetness...Nor could Roundabout find a better deliveryman than its latest star, Nathan Lane." *Post* (Lyons): "...a juicy assembly of the eccentric, the egomaniacal and the mad that keeps the comic fires burning..." *Variety* (Isherwood): "By happy happenstance, the Roundabout Theatre Co. gets to inaugurate its snazzy new restoration of a charming old theater with a snazzy new production of a charming old play."

*Closed October 8, 2000 after 85 performances and 32 previews.

Joan Marcus Photos

Gore Vidal's THE BEST MAN

By Gore Vidal; Director, Ethan McSweeny; Set, John Arnone; Costumes, Theoni V. Aldredge; Lighting, Howell Binkley; Music/Sound, David van Tieghem; Hair/Wigs, Bobby H. Grayson; Casting, Stuart Howard, Amy Schecter and Howard Meltzer; General Manager, Albert Poland; Company Manager, Rick Shulman; Production Stage Manager, Jane Grey; Stage Manager, Matthew Farrell; Presented by Jeffrey Richards, Michael B. Rothfeld, Raymond J. Greenwald, Jerry Frankel and Darren Bagert; Press, Jeffrey Richards/John Moreno, Irene Gandy, Michael Signer; Previewed from Tuesday, September 5; Opened in the Virginia Theatre on Sunday, September 17, 2000*

CAST

"THE CANDIDATES"
Secretary William Russell . . . . .Spalding Gray
Alice Russell, his wife . . . . .Michael Learned
Dick Jensen, his campaign manager . . . . .Mark Blum
Catherine, a campaign aide . . . . .Kate Hampton
Senator Joseph Cantwell . . . . .Chris Noth
Mabel Cantwell, his wife . . . . .Christine Ebersole
Don Blades, his campaign manager . . . . .Jordan Lage

"THE PARTY"
Ex-President Arthur Hockstader . . . . .Charles Durning
Mrs. Sue-Ellen Gamadge,
Chairman of the Women's Division . . . . .Elizabeth Ashley
Senator Clyde Carlin . . . . .Ed Dixon
Delegates . . . . .Joseph Culliton, Joseph Costa, Patricia Hodges, C.J. Wilson, Lee Mark Nelson

"THE VISITORS"
Dr. Artinian, a psychiatrist . . . . .Michael Rudko
Sheldon Marcus . . . . .Jonathan Hadary

"THE PRESS"
First Reporter . . . . .Joseph Culliton
Second Reporter . . . . .Joseph Costa
Third Reporter . . . . .Patricia Hodges
Fourth Reporter . . . . .C.J. Wilson
Fifth Reporter . . . . .Lee Mark Nelson
Additional Reporters and Hotel Staff . . .Kate Hampton, Michael Rudko
News Commentator . . . . .Walter Cronkite

STANDBYS: Joseph Costa (Dick Jensen/Dr. Artinian/Senator Clyde Carlin), Joseph Culliton (Dr. Artinian/Secretary William Russell), Ed Dixon (Ex-President Arthur Hockstader), Carol Halstead (Campaign Aide/Fifth Reporter/First Reporter/Fourth Reporter/Second Reporter/Third Reporter), Kate Hampton (Mabel Cantwell), Patricia Hodges (Alice Russell/Mabel Cantwell/Mrs. Sue-Ellen Gamadge), Lee Mark Nelson (Dick Jensen/Don Blades), Michael Rudko (Sheldon Marcus), C. J. Wilson (Don Blades/Senator Joseph Cantwell).

A new production of the 1960 play in two acts. The action takes place in Philadelphia during July 1960. For original Bdwy production with Melvyn Douglas, see *Theatre World* Vol. 16.

Variety tallied 4 favorable, 6 mixed, and 5 negative reviews. *Times* (Brantley): "The observations made here...have aged surprisingly well...the starry ensemble often gives off a frustratingly tentative quality." *News* (O'Toole): "...makes you pine for the time when Broadway was willing to expose politics to the scrutiny of wit, mockery and intelligence." *Post* (Barnes): "Vidal, appropriately, has not seen fit to amend a word or phrase."

*Closed December 31, 2000 after 121 performances and 15 previews.

Peter Cunningham Photos

Spalding Gray, Jonathan Hadary, Chris Noth

Charles Durning, Spalding Gray

Michael Learned, Spalding Gray, Mark Blum

THE DINNER PARTY

By Neil Simon; Director, John Rando; Set, John Lee Beatty; Costumes, Jane Greenwood; Lighting, Brian MacDevitt; Sound, Jon Gottlieb; Casting, Jay Binder and Amy Lieberman; General Manager, Abbie M. Strassler; Company Manager, Edward J. Nelson; Production Stage Manager, David O'Brien; Stage Manager, Lisa J. Snodgrass; Marketing, The Nancy Richards Group; Media Advisor, Alan Bernhard; Presented by Emanuel Azenberg, Ira Pittelman, Eric Krebs, Scott Nederlander, ShowOnDemand.com and Center Theatre Group/Mark Taper Forum/ Gordon Davidson; Press, Bill Evans/Jim Randolph, Jonathan Schwartz; Previewed from Tuesday, October 3; Opened in the Music Box Theatre on Thursday, October 19, 2000*

CAST

Claude Pichon .... John Ritter +1
Albert Donay .... Henry Winkler +2
Andre Bouville .... Len Cariou
Mariette Levieux .... Jan Maxwell +3
Yvonne Fouchet .... Veanne Cox
Gabrielle Buonocelli .... Penny Fuller
UNDERSTUDIES: John Boyle (Andre Bouville/Claude Pichon), Jennifer Harmon (Gabrielle Buonocelli/Mariette Levieux), Susie Spear (Yvonne Fouchet)

A comedy performed without intermission. The action takes place in a first-class restaurant in Paris.

Variety tallied 5 mixed and 8 negative reviews. *Times* (Brantley): "...exceedingly odd...hopes to invert a traditional comic form to reveal the truly absurd messes that so many people make of their marriages." *News* (Hinckley): "Simon forsakes the funny bone while never fully engaging the heartstrings." *Post* (Barnes): "...take *The Dinner Party* on its own frequently hilarious but also dangerously serious terms..."

*Closed September 1, 2001 after 366 performances and 20 previews.

+Succeeded by: 1. Larry Miller 2. Jon Lovitz 3. Carolyn McCormick

Carol Rosegg Photos

Henry Winkler, Penny Fuller, John Ritter

The Company of *The Dinner Party*

Jon Lovitz, Larry Miller, Len Cariou

PROOF

By David Auburn; Director, Daniel Sullivan; Set, John Lee Beatty; Costumes, Jess Goldstein; Lighting, Pat Collins; Music/Sound, John Gromada; General Manager, Stuart Thompson; Company Manager, James Triner; Production Stage Manager, James Harker; Stage Manager, Heather Cousens; Presented by Manhattan Theatre Club (Lynn Meadow, Artistic Director; Barry Grove, Executive Producer), Roger Berlind, Carole Shorenstein Hays, OSTAR Enterprises, Daryl Roth, Stuart Thompson; Press Representative, Chris Boneau-Adrian Bryan-Brown/ Steven Padla, Rachel Applegate; Previewed from Tuesday, October 10; Opened in the Walter Kerr Theatre on Tuesday, October 24, 2000*

CAST

Robert . . . . .Larry Bryggman
Catherine . . . . .Mary-Louise Parker
Hal . . . . .Ben Shenkman
Claire . . . . .Johanna Day
UNDERSTUDIES: Caroline Bootle (Catherine/Claire), Adam Dannheisser (Hal), Ron Parady (Robert)

A drama in two acts. The action takes place in Chicago. Winner of the 2001 "Tony" Award for Best Play, NY Drama Critics Circle (Best American Play), and the Pulitzer Prize. Winner of 2001 "Tony" Award for Best Actress in a Play (Mary Louise Parker), and Best Direction of a Play. This production originated last season Off Broadway, where it played 80 performances and 24 previews. For original OB production, see *Theatre World* Vol. 56.

Variety tallied 9 favorable, and 2 mixed reviews. *Times* (Weber): "...exhilarating and assured...as accessible and compelling as a detective story." *News* (O'Toole): "It proves that it's still possible for an intelligent new play by a young American dramatist to make it onto Broadway...Parker...an electrifying performance..." *Post* (Barnes): "All four actors are pitch-perfect, but the one you'll remember is Parker." *Variety* (Hofler): "...managed to improve upon this remarkable play in its transfer to Broadway from the Manhattan Theatre Club...Together Bryggman and Parker hit enough emotional highs to sustain a dozen lesser plays."

*Closed January 5, 2003 after 917 performances and 16 previews.

Joan Marcus Photos

Mary-Louise Parker

Mary-Louise Parker, Larry Bryggman

Johanna Day, Mary-Louise Parker

THE FULL MONTY

Music/Lyrics, David Yazbek; Book by Terrence McNally; Based on the 1997 British film; Director, Jack O'Brien; Choreography, Jerry Mitchell; Orchestrations, Harold Wheeler; Set, John Arnone; Costumes, Robert Morgan; Lighting, Howell Binkley; Sound, Tom Clark; Musical Director/Vocal/Incidental Arrangements, Ted Sperling; Dance Arrangements, Zane Mark; General Manager, The Charlotte Wilcox Company; Company Manager, Dave Harris; Production Supervisor, Gene O'Donovan; Production Stage Manager, Nancy Harrington; Stage Manager, Julie Baldauff; Conductor, Kimberly Grigsby; Casting, Liz Woodman; Cast Recording, RCA; Presented by Fox Searchlight Pictures, Lindsay Law and Thomas Hall; Press, John Barlow-Michael Hartman/Wayne Wolfe, Shellie Shovanec; Previewed from Monday, September 25; Opened in the Eugene O'Neill Theatre on Thursday, October 26, 2000*

CAST

Georgie Bukatinsky . . . . Annie Golden
Buddy "Keno" Walsh . . . . Denis Jones
Reg Willoughby . . . . Todd Weeks
Jerry Lukowski . . . . Patrick Wilson
Dave Bukatinsky . . . . John Ellison Conlee
Molcolm MacGregor . . . . Jason Danieley
Ethan Girard . . . . Romain Frugé
Nathan Lukowski . . . . Nicholas Cutro, Thomas Michael Fiss
Susan Hershey . . . . Laura Marie Duncan
Joanie Lish . . . . Jannie Jones
Estelle Genovese . . . . Liz McConahay
Pam Lukowski . . . . Lisa Datz
Teddy Slaughter . . . . Angelo Fraboni
Molly MacGregor . . . . Patti Perkins
Harold Nichols . . . . Marcus Neville
Vicki Nichols . . . . Emily Skinner
Jeanette Burmeister . . . . Kathleen Freeman
Noah "Horse" T. Simmons . . . . André De Shields
Police Sergeant . . . . C.E. Smith
Minister . . . . Jay Douglas
Tony Giordano . . . . Jimmy Smagula

UNDERSTUDIES: Jay Douglas (Jerry Lukowski/Malcolm MacGregor), Laura Marie Duncan (Estelle Genovese/Georgie Bukatinsky/Pam Lukowski/Vicki Nichols), Angelo Fraboni (Buddy "Keno" Walsh), Denis Jones (Ethan Girard), Jannie Jones (Georgie Bukatinsky), Liz McConahay (Vicki Nichols), Sue-Anne Morrow (Estelle Genovese/Georgie Bukatinsky/Pam Lukowski), Jason Opsahl (Ethan Girard/Malcolm MacGregor), Patti Perkins (Jeanette Burmeister), Jimmy Smagula (Dave Bukatinsky), C. E. Smith (Noah "Horse" T. Simmons), Matthew Stocke (Jerry Lukowski), Todd Weeks (Harold Nichols), Ronald Wyche (Noah "Horse" T. Simmons)

Patrick Wilson, Nicholas Cutro

MUSICAL NUMBERS: Overture, Scrap, It's A Woman's World, Man, Big-Ass Rock, Life With Harold, Big Black Man, You Rule My World, Michael Jordan's Ball, Entr'acte, Jeanette's Showbiz Number, Breeze Off the River, The Goods, You Walk with Me, You Rule My World (reprise), Let It Go

A musical comedy in two acts. The action takes place in Buffalo, NY.

Times (Brantley): "The Eugene O'Neill Theater won't have to look for a new tenant for a long, long time…With a winning, ear-catching pop score by David Yazbek and a lively gallery of performers who seem truly in love with the people they're playing…" *News* (Hinckley): "…delightful and more than occasionally poignant story of blue-collar pals who in desperation decide the only way to lift the crushing weight of unemployment and restore their dignity is to take their clothes off…a full-fledged dance musical…songs range from joyous to pensive…" *Post* (Barnes): "…the most daring, yet successful, Broadway adaptation of a movie script…masterly kind of book that gives the chance for a musical to slide to heaven…extraordinary, witty lyrics…" *Variety* (Isherwood): "A working-class musical aimed at an accordingly broad audience…"

*Closed September 1, 2002 after 769 performances and 36 previews.

Craig Schwartz Photos

John Ellison Conlee, Marcus Neville, Romain Frugé
Jason Danieley, André De Shields

The Company

Kathleen Freeman

Patrick Wilson, John Ellison Conlee

The Company

André De Shields

Denis Jones, John Ellison Conlee, Patrick Wilson

Romaine Frugé, Patrick Wilson, Jason Danieley

The Company

THE TALE OF THE ALLERGIST'S WIFE

By Charles Busch; Director, Lynne Meadow; Set, Santo Loquasto; Costumes, Ann Roth; Lighting, Christopher Akerlind; Sound, Bruce Ellman, Brian Ronan; Hairstylist, J. Roy Helland; Casting, Nancy Piccione, David Caparelliotis; General Manager, Stuart Thompson; Company Manager, Sean Free; Production Stage Manager, William Joseph Barnes; Stage Manager, Laurie Goldfeder; Presented by Manhattan Theatre Club (Lynn Meadow, Artistic Director; Barry Grove, Executive Producer), Carole Shorenstein Hays, Daryl Roth, Stuart Thompson and Douglas S. Cramer; Press Representative, Chris Boneau-Adrian Bryan-Brown/Jackie Green, Rachel Applegate; Previewed from Wenesday, October 11; Opened in the Ethel Barrymore Theatre on Thursday, November 2, 2000*

CAST

Mohammed . . . . .Anil Kumar
Marjorie . . . . .Linda Lavin
Ira . . . . .Tony Roberts
Frieda . . . . .Shirl Bernheim
Lee . . . . .Michele Lee
UNDERSTUDIES/STANDBYS: Rose Arrick (Frieda), Jana Robbins (Lee/Marjorie), Jamie Ross (Ira), Deep Katdare (Mohammed)

A comedy in two acts. The action takes place in New York City. This production originated last season at Off Broadway's Manhattan Theatre Club where it played 56 performances and 24 previews. For original OB production, see *Theatre World* Vol. 56.

Variety tallied 7 favorable, 1 mixed, and 2 negative reviews. *Times* (Brantley): "...Mr. Busch demonstrates a sure gift for turning gimlet-eyed social observation into hearty comedy." *News* (O'Toole): "...the theater has a long and brilliant history of high camp... *The Allergist's Wife* simply isn't in that league." *Post* (Barnes): "...the play is really all about Linda Lavin...And rightly so, for Lavin gives a performance that makes virtuosity into a natural human condition..." *Variety* (Isherwood): "The only bad news is...the second act is still muddled...But in Lavin's assured hands...the funniest play to be seen thereabouts in several seasons."

*Closed September 15, 2002 after 777 performances and 25 previews.

Joan Marcus Photos

Tony Roberts, Linda Lavin, Michele Lee

The Company of *The Tale of the Allergist's Wife*

Tony Roberts, Valerie Harper, Michele Lee

MATTERS OF THE HEART

Conceived/Directed by Scott Wittman; Musical Director/Arrangements, Dick Gallagher; Additional Dialogue, John Weidman; Lighting, John Hastings; Sound, Mark Fiore; Gowns, Vicki Tiel and Kleinfeld; Hair/Wigs, Danielle Vignjevich; General Manager, Steven C. Callahan; Company Manager, Adam Siegel; Produced by Lincoln Center Theater (André Bishop: Artistic Director; Bernard Gersten: Executive Producer); Press, Philip Rinaldi; Previewed from Sunday, October 15; Opened in the Vivian Beaumont Theatre on Monday, November 13, 2000*

CAST

PATTI LuPONE

A musical entertainment in two acts. The production played on Sunday and Monday evenings when *Contact* was dark.

Variety tallied 5 favorable and 2 mixed notices. *Times* (Weber): "Her voice has the capability of bringing down a Broadway house, but she is largely in delicate mode here…" *News* (Kissel): "…the best moments…are the theater songs—particularly those of Stephen Sondheim…" *Post* (Deffaa): "It is extremely rare to find a concert so filled with peak moments as this one."

*Closed December 17, 2000 after 11 performances and 8 previews.

Stephanie Berger Photos

Patti LuPone

Patti LuPone

BETRAYAL

By Harold Pinter; Director, David Leveaux; Set, Rob Howell; Costumes, Rob Howell; Lighting, David Weiner; Sound, Donald DiNicola; Casting, Jim Carnahan; General Manager, Sydney Davolos; Company Manager, Jean Haring; Production Stage Manager, Arthur Gaffin; Stage Manager, Bradley McCormick; Presented by The Roundabout Theatre Company (Todd Haimes, Artistic Director; Ellen Richard, Managing Director; Julia C. Levy, Executive Director of External Affairs; Gene Feist, Founding Director), Press Representative, Chris Bonneau-Adrian Bryan-Brown/ Amy Jacobs; Previewed from Friday, October 20; Opened in the American Airlines Theatre on Tuesday, November 14, 2000*

CAST

Emma . . . . Juliette Binoche
Jerry . . . . Liev Schreiber
Robert . . . . John Slattery
Waiter . . . . Mark Lotito
UNDERSTUDIES: Melissa Bowen (Emma), Ray Virta (Jerry/Robert/ Waiter)

A new production of the 1978 drama, performed without intermission. As the play progresses, the time period depicted goes chronologically backwards. For original 1980 Bdwy production with Blythe Danner, Roy Scheider, and Raul Julia, see *Theatre World* Vol. 36.

Variety tallied 10 favorable, 3 mixed, and 3 negative reviews. *Times* (Brantley): "Mr. Pinter has invested a well-worn formula with a gnawing, transforming sense of just how opaque people remain to one another." *News* (O'Toole): "If the search for meaning and a morality beyond the infliction of pain can make his plays seem dark and strange, it is a strangeness that comes from an all-too-familiar reality." *Post* (Barnes): "...dazzlingly enigmatic Juliette Binoche, the forcefully baffled Liev Schreiber, and the quietly commanding John Slattery...resourceful and subtle director, David Leveaux..."

*Closed February 4, 2001 after 91 performances and 28 previews.

Joan Marcus Photos

Juliette Binoche

Juliette Binoche, Liev Schreiber

THE ROCKY HORROR SHOW

Music/Lyrics/Book by Richard O'Brien; Director, Christopher Ashley; Musical Director/Vocal Arrangements, Henry Aronson; Orchestrations (new), Doug Katsaros; Orchestrations (original), Richard Hartley; Choreographer, Jerry Mitchell; Set, David Rockwell; Costumes, David C. Woolard, Sue Blane (original); Lighting, Paul Gallo; Sound, T. Richard Fitzgerald, Domonic Sack; Casting, Bernard Telsey; General Managers, Richard Frankel, David W. Caldwell; Company Manager, Eric Muratalla; Production Manager, Peter Fulbright; Production Stage Manager, Brian Meister; Stage Managers, Brendan Smith, Marisha Ploski; Video Design, Batwin & Robin Productions; Cast Recording, RCA; Presented by Jordan Roth by arrangement with Christopher Malcolm, Howard Panter, Richard O'Brien; Press, Judy Jacksina/Heather Prince, Maribel Aguilar; Previewed from Friday, October 20; Opened in the Circle in the Square Theatre on Wednesday, November 15, 2000*

CAST

Janet Weiss .... Alice Ripley +1
Brad Majors .... Jarrod Emick +2
Narrator .... Dick Cavett +3
Riff Raff .... Raúl Esparza +4
Magenta/Usherette .... Daphne Rubin-Vega
Columbia/Usherette .... Joan Jett +5
Frank 'N' Furter .... Tom Hewitt +6
Rocky .... Sebastian LaCause +7
Eddie/Dr. Scott .... Lea Delaria +8
Phantoms .... Kevin Cahoon, Deidre Goodwin, Aiko Nakasone, Mark Price, Jonathan Sharp, James Stovall

UNDERSTUDIES: Kevin Cahoon (Frank 'N' Furter/Narrator), Deidre Goodwin (Magenta), Kristen Lee Kelly (Columbia/Janet Weiss), John Jeffrey Martin (Brad Majors/Riff Raff/Rocky), Aiko Nakasone (Columbia/Janet Weiss/Magenta), Mark Price (Eddie/Dr. Scott/Riff Raff), Jonathan Sharp (Brad Majors/Rocky), James Stovall (Dr. Scott/Eddie/Frank 'N' Furter/Narrator)

MUSICAL NUMBERS: Science Fiction-Double Feature, Damn It Janet, Over at the Frankenstein Place, The Time Warp, Sweet Transvestite, The Sword of Damocles, I Can Make You a Man, Hot Patootie, I Can Make You a Man (Reprise), Touch-A-Touch-A-Touch Me, Once in a While, Eddie's Teddy, Planet Schmanet- Wise Up Janet Weiss, Floor Show/Rose Tint My World, I'm Going Home, Super Heroes, Science Fiction-Double Feature

A new production of the 1973 musical in two acts. The action takes place Here and There, Then and Now. For original 1975 Broadway production starring Tim Curry, see *Theatre World* Vol. 31.

Variety tallied 9 favorable and 5 negative notices. *Times* (Brantley): "A musical that deals with mutating identity and time warps becomes one of the most mutated, time-warped phenomena in show biz." *News* (O'Toole): "Leave behind any sense of decorum. And enjoy some good, wholesome filth." *Post* (Barnes): "...clearly believes that nothing succeeds like excess..."

*Closed January 6, 2002 after 437 performances and 30 previews. In the aftermath of the 9/11 attacks on New York, the production initially closed on September 23, 2001, but reopened on October 30, 2001.

+Succeeded by: 1. Kristen Lee Kelly 2. Luke Perry, Jarrod Emick 3. Kate Clinton (during vacation), rotating narrators: Jerry Springer, Sally Jesse Raphael, Penn & Teller, Dave Holmes, Cindy Adams, Robin Leach, Dick Cavett 4. Mark Price, Sebastian Bach 5. Kristen Lee Kelly, Ana Gasteyer, Liz Larsen 6. Terrence Mann 7. Jonathan Sharp 8. Jason Wooten

Carol Rosegg Photos

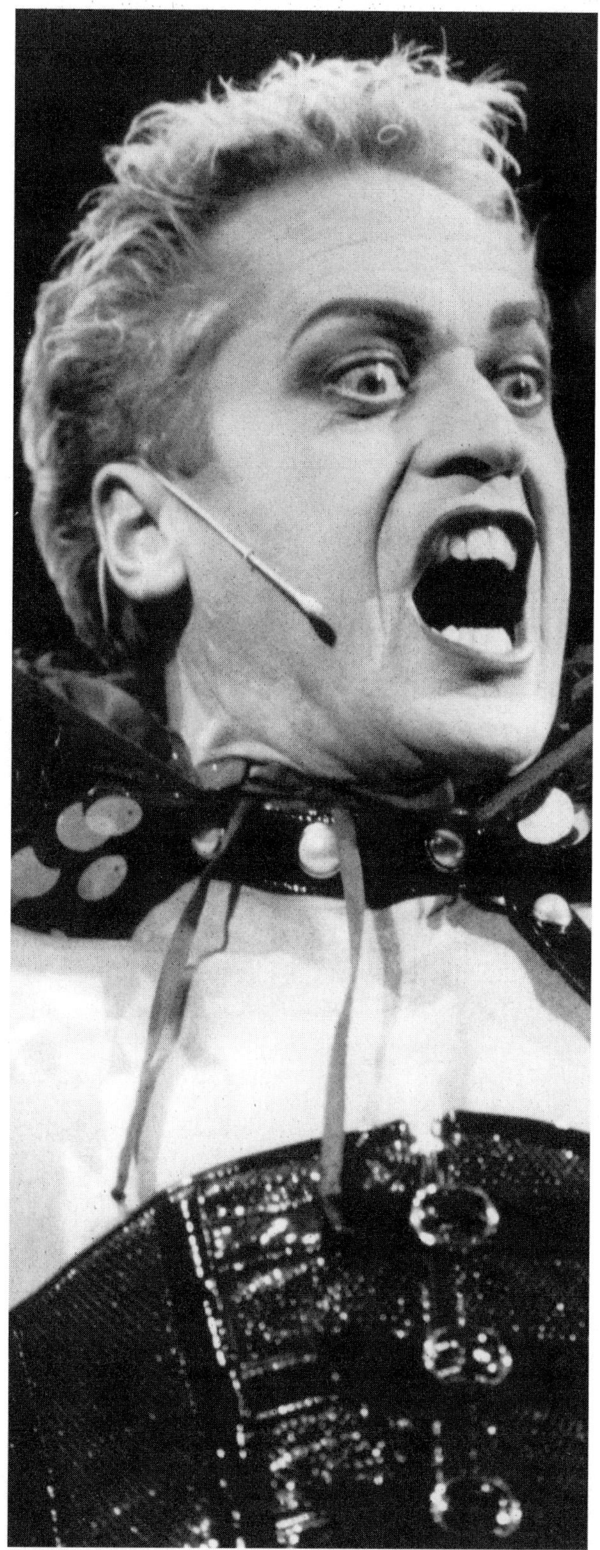

Tom Hewitt

Alice Ripley, Raúl Esparza, Joan Jett in *The Rocky Horror Show*

The Company of *The Rocky Horror Show*

Tom Hewitt and Company of *The Rocky Horror Show*

THE SEARCH FOR SIGNS OF INTELLIGENT LIFE IN THE UNIVERSE

By Jane Wagner; Director, Jane Wagner; Set, Klara Zieglerova; Lighting, Ken Billington; Sound, Tom Clark, Mark Bennett; General Management, EGS; Company Manager, Susan Sampliner; Production Supervisor, Janet Beroza; Stage Manager, Ilyse Bosch; Presented by Tomlin and Wagner Theatricalz; Press, John Barlow-Michael Hartman/Wayne Wolfe, Joseph Perrotta; Previewed from Saturday, November 11; Opened in the Booth Theatre on Thursday, November 16, 2000*

CAST

LILY TOMLIN

A new production of the 1985 one-woman play performed in two acts. The action takes place in NYC, Indiana, and LA. For original Bdwy production, see *Theatre World* Vol. 42.

Variety tallied 10 favorable and 5 mixed notices. *Times* (Weber): "...opened last night with its once-trenchant social commentary virtually unchanged..." *News* (O'Toole): "Far from being a mere vehicle for Tomlin's extraordinary virtuosity, it is a coherent and ambitious play in its right." *Post* (Barnes): "Tomlin is a clown of clowns. Her body moves like a dancer's, her face is as expressive as a mime's, and she controls the stage with a mix of self-deprecating charisma and ironic pain."

*Closed May 20, 2001 after 185 performances and 7 previews.

Lily Tomlin

Lily Tomlin

SEUSSICAL THE MUSICAL

Anthony Blair Hall, David Shiner

Kevin Chamberlin

Music/Vocal Arrangements, Stephen Flaherty; Lyrics, Lynn Ahrens; Book, Ahrens and Flaherty; Conceived, Ahrens, Flaherty and Eric Idle; Based on the works of Dr. Seuss; Director, Frank Galati, (Rob Marshall, uncredited); Orchestrations, Douglas Besterman; Musical Director, David Holcenberg; Dance Arrangements, David Chase; Choreography, Kathleen Marshall; Set, Eugene Lee, (Tony Walton, uncredited); Costumes, William Ivey Long, (Catherine Zuber, tryout run); Lighting, Natasha Katz; Sound, Jonathan Deans; Cast Recording, Decca Broadway; General Manager, Alan Wasser; Company Manager, Lizbeth Cone; Production Supervisor, Bonnie Panson; Production Manager, Juniper Street Productions, John H. Paull, III and Hillary Blanken; Stage Managers, Andrew Fenton, Joshua Halperin; Casting, Jay Binder, Sherry Dayton; Presented by SFX Theatrical Group, Barry & Fran Weissler, and Universal Studios; Press, John Barlow-Michael Hartman/Clint Bond Jr., Ash Curtis, Shellie Shovanec; Previewed from Wednesday, November 1; Opened in the Richard Rodgers Theatre on Thursday, November 30, 2000*

CAST

The Cat in the Hat . . . . .David Shiner +1
Horton the Elephant . . . . .Kevin Chamberlin
Gertrude McFuzz . . . . .Janine LaManna
Mayzie LaBird . . . . .Michele Pawk
JoJo . . . . .Anthony Blair Hall +2, Andrew Keenan-Bolger
Sour Kangaroo . . . . .Sharon Wilkins
The Mayor of Whoville . . . . .Stuart Zagnit
Mrs. Mayor . . . . .Alice Playten
Cat's Helpers . . . . .Joyce Chittick, Jennifer Cody, Justin Greer, Mary Ann Lamb, Darren Lee, Jerome Vivona
General Genghis Kahn Schmitz .Erick Devine
Bird Girls . . . . .Natascia Diaz, Sara Gettelfinger, Catrice Joseph
Wickersham Brothers . . . .David Engel, Tom Plotkin, Eric Jordan Young
The Grinch . . . . .William Ryall
Vlad Vladikoff . . . . .Darren Lee
Judge Yertle the Turtle . . . . .Devin Richards
Marshal of the Court . . . . .Ann Harada
Citizens of the Jungle of Nool, Whos, Mayor's Aides, Fish, Cadets, Hunters, Circus McGurkus Animals and Performers . . . . .Joyce Chittick, Jennifer Cody, Erick Devine, Natascia Diaz, David Engel, Sara Gettelfinger, Justin Greer, Ann Harada, Catrice Joseph, Eddie Korbich, Mary Ann Lamb, Darren Lee, Monique L. Midgette, Casey Nicholaw, Tom Plotkin, Devin Richards, William Ryall, Jerome Vivona, Sharon Wilkins, Eric Jordan Young

UNDERSTUDIES/STANDBYS: Bryan Batt, Eric Jordan Young (Cat in the Hat), Shaun Amyot (Cat's Helper/Vlad Vladikoff/Wickersham Brother), Sara Gettelfinger (Mayzie LaBird), Ann Harada (Mrs. Mayor), Jenny Hill (Bird Girl/Cat's Helper/Gertrude McFuzz/Marshal of the Court), Catrice Joseph (Sour Kangaroo), Michelle Kittrell (Bird Girl/Cat's Helper), David Lowenstein (Cat's Helper/Judge Yertle/ Turtle/The Grinch/Wickersham Brother), Monique Midgette (Sour Kangaroo), Casey Nicholaw (Horton the Elephant/Mayor of Whoville), William Ryall (General Genghis Kahn Schmitz)

MUSICAL NUMBERS: Overture, Oh, the Thinks You Can Think, Horton Hears a Who, Biggest Blame Fool, Here on Who, A Day for the Cat in the Hat, It's Possible (McElligot's Pool), How to Raise A Child, The Military, Alone in the Universe, The One Feather Tail of Miss Gertrude McFuzz, Amazing Mayzie, Amazing Gertrude, Monkey Around, Chasing the Whos, How Lucky You Are, Notice Me Horton, How Lucky You Are (Mayzie's Reprise), Horton Sits on the Egg/Act 1 Finale, Egg, Nest and Tree, Mayzie in Palm Beach, Alone in the Universe (Reprise), Solla Sollew, Havin' a Hunch, All for You, The People Versus Horton The Elephant, Finale/Oh, the Thinks You Can Think, Green Eggs and Ham (Curtain Call), (During Previews: Our Story Begins, Our Story Resumes)

Kevin Chamberlin and Company

The Company of *Seussical the Musical*

A musical in two acts.

Variety tallied 2 favorable, 3 mixed, and 12 negative reviews. *Times* (Brantley): "Somewhere in *Suessical* are the vestiges of a charming, unpretentious show, with a blithe hummable score, about the transforming powers of imagination." *News* (O'Toole): "The problem for Ahrens and Flaherty is that it's hard to add anything to Dr. Suess' books. They already function a bit like musicals." *Post* (Barnes): "It puts whimsy where talent should be...Kevin Chamberlin is quite adorable...Janine LaManna is enchanting."

*Closed May 20, 2001 after 197 performances and 34 previews.

+Succeeded by: 1. Rosie O'Donnell, Bryan Batt, Cathy Rigby 2. Aaron Carter

Joan Marcus Photos

Rosie O'Donnell

JANE EYRE

Music/Lyrics, Paul Gordon; Book/Additional Lyrics, John Caird; Directors, John Caird and Scott Schwartz; Based on the novel by Charlotte Brontë; Musical Director/Vocal Arrangements, Steven Tyler; Orchestrations, Larry Hochman; Sets, John Napier; Costumes, Andreane Neofitou; Lighting, Jules Fisher, Peggy Eisenhauer; Sound, Mark Menard, Tom Clark; Projections, John Napier, Lisa Podgur Cuscuna, Jules Fisher and Peggy Eisenhauer; Cast Recording, Sony; General Manager, Richards/Climan, Inc.; Company Manager, Diana L. Fairbanks; Production Stage Manager, Lori M. Doyle; Stage Manager, Debra A. Acquavella; Casting, Johnson-Liff Associates, Tara Rubin; Presented by Annette Niemtzow, Janet Robinson, Pamela Koslow and Margaret McFeely Golden, in association with Jennifer Manocherian and Carolyn Kim McCarthy; Press, Publicity Office/Bob Fennell, Marc Thibodeau; Previewed from Thursday, November 9; Opened in the Brooks Atkinson Theatre on Sunday, December 10, 2000*

CAST

Jane Eyre .... Marla Schaffel
Young Jane .... Lisa Musser
Young John Reed .... Lee Zarrett
Mrs. Reed .... Gina Ferrall
Mr. Brocklehurst .... Don Richard
Miss Scatcherd .... Marguerite MacIntyre
Marigold .... Mary Stout
Helen Burns .... Jayne Paterson
Schoolgirls .... Nell Balaban, Andrea Bowen, Elizabeth DeGrazia, Bonnie Gleicher, Rita Glynn, Gina Lamparella
Mrs. Fairfax .... Mary Stout
Robert .... Bruce Dow
Adele .... Andrea Bowen
Grace Poole .... Nell Balaban
Edward Fairfax Rochester .... James Barbour
Bertha .... Marguerite MacIntyre
Blanche Ingram .... Elizabeth DeGrazia
Lady Ingram .... Gina Ferrall
Mary Ingram .... Jayne Paterson
Young Lord Ingram .... Lee Zarrett
Mr. Eshton .... Stephen R. Buntrock
Amy Eshton .... Nell Balaban
Louisa Eshton .... Gina Lamparella
Colonel Dent .... Don Richard
Mrs. Dent .... Marguerite MacIntyre
Richard Mason .... Bill Nolte
The Gypsy .... Marje Bubrosa
Vicar .... Don Richard
St. John Rivers .... Stephen R. Buntrock

Swings: Sandy Binion, Bradley Dean, Erica Schroeder

Gina Ferrall, Lisa Musser, Don Richard

Marla Schaffel, James Barbour

Musical Numbers: The Orphan, Children of God, Forgiveness, The Graveyard, Sweet Liberty, Perfectly Nice, As Good As You, Secret Soul, The Finer Things, Oh, How You Look in the Light, The Pledge, Sirens, Things Beyond This Earth, Painting Her Portrait, In The Light Of The Virgin Morning, The Gypsy, The Proposal, Slip of a Girl, The Wedding, Wild Boy, Sirens (reprise), Farewell Good Angel, Forgiveness (reprise), The Voice Across the Moors, Poor Master, Brave Enough for Love

A musical in two acts. The action takes place in England during the 1840s.

Times (Weber): "What stands out in this production is the sense of scene-by-scene problem solving, a connect-the-dots approach to narrative that is particularly disappointing given the pedigree of the show's creators." *News* (O'Toole): "...a richly textured and superbly performed score." *Post* (Barnes): "...two legitimate, splendidly acted and robustly sung performances by a tremulous, yet bright-eyed, firm-jawed Maria Schaffel and a craggily, nobly, ruined James Barbour."

*Closed June 10, 2001 after 210 performances and 36 previews.

Joan Marcus Photos

A CLASS ACT

Music/Lyrics, Edward Kleban; Book, Linda Kline and Lonny Price; Director, Lonny Price; Orchestrations, Larry Hochman; Musical Director, David Loud; Incidental Music, Todd Ellison; Choreography, Marguerite Derricks; Set, James Noone; Costumes, Carrie Robbins; Lighting, Kevin Adams; Sound, Acme Sound Partners; General Manager, Donald Frantz; Company Manager, Richard Biederman; Production Stage Manager, Jeffrey M. Markowitz; Stage Manager, Heather Fields; Casting, Jay Binder; Marty Bell, Chase Mishkin and Arielle Tepper present the Manhattan Theatre Club Production; Press, Richard Kornberg/Don Summa, Tom D'Ambrosio, Bill Schelble, Carrie Freidman; Previewed from Wednesday, February 14; Opened in the Ambassador Theatre on Sunday, March 11, 2001*

CAST

Lucy . . . . .Donna Bullock
Bobby et al. . . . . .David Hibbard
Ed . . . . .Lonny Price
Felicia . . . . .Sara Ramirez
Lehman . . . . .Patrick Quinn
Charley et al. . . . . .Jeff Blumenkrantz
Mona . . . . .Nancy Anderson +1
Sophie . . . . .Randy Graff

Standbys: Danny Burstein (Ed/Lehman), Jamie Chandler-Torns (Mona), Jonathan Hadley (Bobby/Charley/Lehman), Ann Van Cleave (Felicia/Lucy/Sophie)

Musical Numbers: Light on My Feet*, The Fountain in the Garden, One More Beautiful Song, Fridays at Four, Bobby's A Song, Charm Song, Paris through the Window†, Mona, Under Separate Cover, Don't Do It Again (not in OB version), Gauguin's Shoes, Don't Do It Again, Follow Your Star, Better, Scintillating Sophie, The Next Best Thing to Love, Broadway Boogie Woogie, *A Chorus Line* excerpts, Better (reprise)‡, I Choose You, The Nightmare, Say Something Funny, I Won't Be There, Self Portrait, Self Portrait (reprise)
*Additional lyrics by Brian Stein
†Additional lyrics by Glenn Slater

A two-act musical biography of lyricist Edward Kleban. The action takes place on the stage of the Shubert Theatre and other locations, 1958–88.

Variety tallied 9 favorable, 3 mixed, and 3 negative reviews. *Times* (Weber): "In the confinement of the Manhattan Theater Club the show gave off a restiveness, an impatience to burst into greater view…At the Ambassador it feels more like the little show that could and…is far more welcoming." *News* (Kissel): "If you have ever imagined, as I once did, that musical theater was at the center of the universe, that nothing could do more for the happiness of mankind than an elegant lyric carefully wedded to a beautiful melody, then you will find, as I did, an almost unbearable poignancy…" *Post* (Barnes): "His lyrics were always admired. His music perhaps rather less so."

*Closed June 10, 2001 after 105 performances and 30 previews. Earlier in the season, the production gave 38 performances and 42 previews at OB's Manhattan Theatre Club.

+Succeeded by: 1. Michele Ragusa

Joan Marcus Photos

Donna Bullock, Lonny Price, Patrick Quinn, Nancy Anderson, Jeff Blumenkrantz, Dave Hibbard, Sara Ramirez

Lonny Price, Sara Ramirez

Jeff Blumenkrantz, Donna Bullock, Patrick Quinn, Nancy Anderson, Lonny Price, Sara Ramirez, David Hibbard

DESIGN FOR LIVING

By Noël Coward; Director, Joe Mantello; Sets, Robert Brill; Costumes, Bruce Pask; Lighting, James Vermeulen; Music/Sound, Douglas J. Cuomo; Casting, Jim Carnahan; General Manager, Sydney Davolos; Company Manager, Jean Haring; Production Stage Manager, Andrea J. Testani; Stage Manager, Bradley McCormick; Presented by Roundabout Theatre Company (Todd Haimes, Artistic Director; Ellen Richard, Managing Director; Julia C. Levy, Executive Director of External Affairs; Gene Feist, Founding Director); Press, Chris Boneau-Adrian Bryan-Brown/Matt Polk, Kel Christofferson; Previewed from Saturday, February 17; Opened in the American Airlines Theatre on Thursday, March 15, 2001*

Dominic West, Jennifer Ehle, Alan Cumming

CAST

Gilda ....Jennifer Ehle
Ernest ....John Cunningham
Otto ....Alan Cumming
Leo ....Dominic West
Miss Hodge ....Jenny Sterlin
Mr. Birbeck ....Saxon Palmer
Grace ....Marisa Berenson
Henry ....T. Scott Cunningham
Helen ....Jessica Stone

UNDERSTUDIES/STANDBYS: Patricia Hodges (Grace Torrence/Miss Hodge). Tina Benko (Gilda/Helen Carver/Matthew Birbeck), Saxon Palmer (Henry Carver/Otto).

Alan Cumming

A new production of the 1932 comedy, performed in two acts. The action takes place in Paris, London, and New York City. The original 1933 Bdwy staging, at the Ethel Barrymore Theatre, featured Alfred Lunt, Lynn Fontanne, and Noel Coward.

Variety tallied 6 favorable and 10 negative notices. *Times* (Brantley): "...apparently meant not only to bring out the play's homoerotic elements (which is an old game already) but also to reveal the crushing anxieties of the modern world." *News* (Kissel): "...the trio are very modern, because the main object of affection is themselves. They switch partners effortlessly..." *Variety* (Isherwood): "...a sensational show...the real achievement of Joe Mantello's production is to find the emotional grit in a play too often dismissed as a frivolous romp."

*Closed May 13, 2001 after 68 performances and 29 previews.

Joan Marcus Photos

Alan Cumming, Dominic West

Dominic West, Jennifer Ehle

JUDGMENT AT NUREMBERG

By Abby Mann; Based on his 1959 teleplay and 1961 screenplay; Director, John Tillinger; Set, James Noone; Costumes, Jess Goldstein; Lighting, Brian MacDevitt; Music/Sound, David van Tieghem; Projections, Elaine J. McCarthy; Hair/Wigs, Paul Huntley; Casting, Jay Binder; General Managers, Niko Associates/Manny Kladitis, Carl Pasbjerg; Company Manager, Bethanie Smith; Production Stage Manager, Anita Ross; Production Supervisor, Mitchell Erickson, Presented by National Actors Theatre (Tony Randall, Founder/Artistic Director; Fred Walker, Managing Director) in association with Earle I. Mack; Press, Gary Springer/Susan Chicoine/Joe Trentacosta; Previewed from Thursday, February 15; Opened in the Longacre Theatre on Monday, March 26, 2001*

CAST

Narrator .... Philip LeStrange
Colonel Parker .... Robert Foxworth
Judge Haywood .... George Grizzard
General Merrin .... Jack Davidson
Captain Byers .... Peter Francis James
Court Interpreter 1 .... Peter Hermann
Emil Hahn .... Peter Maloney
Court Interpreter 2 .... Jurian Hughes
Fredrich Hoffstetter .... Philip LeStrange
Werner Lammpe .... Reno Roop
Oscar Rolfe .... Michael Hayden
Ernst Janning .... Maximilian Schell +1
Judge Norris .... Henry Strozier
Judge Ives .... Fred Burrell
Guard .... Ty Jones
Dr. Wickert .... Joseph Wiseman
Mrs. Habelstadt .... Patricia Conolly
Mme. Bertholt .... Marthe Keller
Rudolf Peterson .... Michael Mastro
Geuter .... Peter Kybart
Maria Wallner .... Heather Randall
Thea .... Kellie Overbey
Waiter .... Peter Hermann
Elsa Lindnow .... Susan Kellermann

UNDERSTUDIES: Jack Davidson (Judge Haywood), Mitch Erickson (Emil Hahn/Fredrich Hoffstetter/Werner Lammpe), Peter Hermann (Captain Byers/Oscar Rolfe/Rudolf Peterson), Jurian Hughes (Elsa Lindnow/Maria Wallner/Mrs. Habelstadt), Ty Jones (Captain Byers/Court Interpreter 2/ Waiter), Peter Kybart (Court Interpreter 1/Dr. Wickert/General Merrin), Philip LeStrange (Colonel Parker), Peter Maloney (Ernst Janning), Reno Roop (Geuter/Judge Ives/Judge Norris)

A drama in two acts. The action takes place in Nuremberg, Germany, 1947. Mr. Schell appeared in both the 1959 television production and the 1961 film.

Variety tallied 4 favorable, 3 mixed, and 7 negative reviews. *Times* (Weber): "...a bit to brisk and trim for its own good...Mr. Schell is an imposing figure onstage...When he and Mr. Hayden are nose to nose...a palpable tremor..." *News* (Kissel): "Watching the beautiful production...I confess I was less caught up in its moral issues than in studying how the chemistry of individual actors can give the stage a vitality..." *Post* (Barnes): "...far more satisfying as a movie..." *Variety* (Isherwood): "...its sincerity, thoughtfulness and high-toned eloquence-are more or less intact, but its power is nevertheless dissipated on the stage, despite the fine work of a large cast..."

*Closed May 13, 2001 after 56 performances and 45 previews.

+Succeded by: 1. Peter Maloney (during illness)

Joan Marcus Photos

Maximilian Schell

Robert Foxworth, Philip LeStrange, Maximilian Schell, Peter Maloney

Joseph Wiseman, Michael Hayden

THE INVENTION OF LOVE

By Tom Stoppard; Director, Jack O'Brien; Set/Costumes, Bob Crowley; Lighting, Brian MacDevitt; Sound, Scott Lehrer; Music, Bob James; Hair/Wigs, David Brian Brown; ; Casting, Daniel Swee; General Manager, Steven C. Callahan; Company Manager, Gillian Roth; Stage Manager, Susie Cordon; Production Manager, Jeff Hamlin; Dialects, Elizabeth A. Smith; Presented by Lincoln Center Theater (André Bishop; Artistic Director; Bernard Gersten; Executive Producer); Press, Philip Rinaldi/Brian Rubin; Previewed from Thursday, March 1; Opened in the Lyceum Theatre on Thursday, March 29, 2001*

Robert Sean Leonard, David Harbour

CAST

A.E. Houseman, aged 77 .... Richard Easton
A.E. Houseman, aged 18 to 26 .... Robert Sean Leonard
Alfred William Pollard .... Michael Stuhlbarg
Moses John Jackson .... David Harbour
Charon .... Jeff Weiss
Mark Pattison/W.T. Stead .... Peter McRobbie
Walter Pater/Frank Harris .... Martin Rayner
John Ruskin/Jerome K. Jerome .... Paul Hecht
Benjamin Jowett/Henry Labouchère .... Byron Jennings
Robinson Ellis/John Percival Postgate .... Guy Paul
Katherine Houseman .... Mireille Enos
Chamberlain .... Mark Nelson
Chairman of Selection Committee .... Andrew McGinn
Oscar Wilde/Bunthorne .... Daniel Davis
Ensemble .... Neal Dodson, Brian Hutchison, Andrew McGinn, Matthew Floyd Miller, Peter A. Smith, David Turner

UNDERSTUDIES: Julian Gamble (Chairman/Charon/Jerome K. Jerome/John Ruskin/Oscar Wilde), Brian Hutchison (Moses John Jackson), Aaron Krohn (Ensemble), Andrew McGinn (Bunthorne/John Percival Postgate/Mark Pattison/Robinson Ellis/W.T. Stead), Matthew Floyd Miller (A.E. Houseman, aged 18 to 26), Caitlin Muelder (Katharine Houseman), Guy Paul (Benjamin Jowett/Frank Harris/Henry Labouchère/Walter Pater), Martin Rayner (A.E. Houseman, aged 77), Peter A. Smith (Chamberlain), David Turner (Alfred William Pollard)

A play that follows English poet and scholar A.E. Houseman (1859–1936) as he travels back in time at the end of his life to confront his younger self. Winner of "Tony" Awards for Best Actor in a Play (Richard Easton) and Best Featured Actor in a Play (Robert Sean Leonard).

Variety tallied 12 favorable, 1 mixed, and 1 negative notice. *Times* (Brantley) "Mr. Leonard...does it beautifully, capturing both the arrogance and awkwardness...Mr. Easton cannily finds the spark and color...Mark Nelson is superb in a sharply etched turn as a civil servant that speaks volumes about being gay in that time...deals in the uncertainties of memory and the impossibility of truly knowing anything..." *News* (Kissel): "The calisthenics Stoppard provides for the cerebrum leave you giddy and exhilarated." *Post* (Barnes): "...the most ambitious and even most complete of his plays...The staging is superb; director Jack O'Brien doesn't get a single nuance wrong." *Variety* (Isherwood): "Dazzling clouds of language come cascading from the stage...Less a drama than a densely layered meditation on life and its meanings...Leonard communicates the depth of Houseman's affection and the mixture of ecstacy and pain it causes him. Intelligence, craft, and that something greater—a kind of crystalline emotional clarity-that the greatest actors have are to be found in this performance."

*Closed June 30, 2001 after 108 performances and 31 previews.

Paul Kolnik Photos

Robert Sean Leonard, Richard Easton

Richard Easton

Robert Sean Leonard

Mireille Enos, Richard Easton in *The Invention of Love*

Michael Stuhlbarg, David Harbour, Robert Sean Leonard in *The Invention of Love*

STONES IN HIS POCKETS

By Marie Jones; Director, Ian McElhinney; Set, Jack Kirwan; Costumes, Jack Kirwan; Lighting, James C. McFetridge; Sound, Peter Fitzgerald; Casting, Jay Binder; General Manager, Abbie M. Strassler; Production Manager, Patrick Molony; Production Stage Manager, David O'Brien; Dialects, Lilene Mansell; Presented by Paul Elliott; Adam Kenwright, Pat Moylan, Ed and David Mirvish, Emanuel Azenberg/Ira Pittelman; Press, Chris Boneau-Adrian Bryan-Brown; Previewed from Friday, March 23; Opened in the John Golden Theatre on Sunday, April 1, 2001*

CAST

Jake Quinn . . . . .Seán Campion
Charlie Conlon . . . . .Conleth Hill
STANDBYS: Stevie Ray Dallimore (Jake Quinn), Declan Mooney (Charlie Conlon)

A comedy in two acts. The action takes place in County Kerry, Ireland

Variety tallied 8 favorable, 4 mixed, and 5 negative reviews. *Times* (Brantley): "The two human Etch-a-Sketches…offer overwhelming evidence that there are special effects the movies will never do that the theater does." *News* (Kissel): "…though they play several dozen roles between them, you always know who they are." *Post* (Barnes): "…not so mightily terrific as a play…but as a display of protean acting…" *Variety* (Isherwood): "…a simplistic swipe at Hollywood and a rather bigger insult to the Irish folks…"

*Closed September 23, 2001 after 201 performances and 11 previews.

Joan Marcus Photos

Conleth Hill, Seán Campion

Conleth Hill, Seán Campion

Seán Campion, Conleth Hill

FOLLIES

Music/Lyrics, Stephen Sondheim; Book, James Goldman; Director, Matthew Warchus; Orchestration (reduced from original charts), Jonathan Tunick; Musical Director, Eric Stern; Set, Mark Thompson; Costumes, Theoni V. Aldredge; Lighting, Hugh Vanstone; Sound, Jonathan Deans; Dance Arrangements, John Berkman, David Chase, General Manager, Sydney Davolos; Company Manager, Denys Baker; Production Stage Manager, Peter Hanson; Stage Manager, Karen Moore; Casting, Jim Carnahan; Presented by Roundabout Theatre Company (Todd Haimes, Artistic Director; Ellen Richard, Managing Director; Julia C. Levy, Executive Director of External Affairs; Gene Feist, Founding Director); Press, The Publicity Office/Bob Fennell, Marc Thibodeau, Candi Adams; Previewed from Thursday, March 8; Opened in the Belasco Theatre on Thursday, April 5, 2001*

CAST

Dimitri Weismann .... Louis Zorich
Showgirls .... Jessica Leigh Brown, Colleen Dunn, Amy Heggins, Wendy Waring
Sally Durant Plummer .... Judith Ivey
Sandra Crane .... Nancy Ringham
Dee Dee West .... Dorothy Stanley
Stella Deems .... Carol Woods
Sam Deems .... Peter Cormican
Solange La Fitte .... Jane White
Roscoe .... Larry Raiken
Heidi Schiller .... Joan Roberts
Emily Whitman .... Marge Champion
Theodore Whitman .... Donald Saddler
Carlotta Campion .... Polly Bergen
Hattie Walker .... Betty Garrett
Phyllis Rogers Stone .... Blythe Danner
Benjamin Stone .... Gregory Harrison
Buddy Plummer .... Treat Williams
Young Phyllils .... Erin Dilly
Young Sally .... Lauren Ward
Young Dee Dee .... Roxane Barlow
Young Emily .... Carol Bentley
Young Carlotta .... Sally Mae Dunn
Young Sandra .... Dottie Earle
Young Solange .... Jacqueline Hendy
Young Heidi .... Brooke Sunny Moriber
Young Stella .... Allyson Tucker
Young Roscoe .... Aldrin Gonzalez
Young Ben .... Richard Roland
Young Buddy .... Joey Sorge
Young Theodore .... Tod McCune
Kevin .... Stephen Campanella
"Margie" .... Roxane Barlow
"Sally" .... Jessica Leigh Brown
Ladies and Gentlemen of the Ensemble .... Roxane Barlow, Carol Bentley, Jessica Leigh Brown, Stephen Campanella, Colleen Dunn, Sally Mae Dunn, Dottie Earle, Aldrin Gonzalez, Amy Heggins, Jacqueline Hendy, Rod McCune, Kelli O'Hara, T. Oliver Reid, Alex Sanchez, Allyson Tucker, Matt Wall, Wendy Waring

Understudies/Standbys: Joan Barber (Dee Dee West/Heidi Schiller/ Sandra Crane), Don Correia (Benjamin Stone/Buddy Plummer/Theodore Whitman), Peter Cormican (Dimitri Weismann/Roscoe), Jeffrey Hankinson (Swing), Kelli O'Hara (Young Heidi/Young Phyllis/Young Sally), Nancy Ringham (Hattie Walker/Sally Durant Plummer/Solange LaFitte), Parisa Ross (Swing), Dorothy Stanley (Carlotta Campion/Emily Whitman/Phyllis Rogers Stone/Stella Deems), Matt Wall (Young Ben/ Young Buddy)

Judith Ivey, Treat Williams, Blythe Danner, Gregory Harrison

Musical Numbers: Prologue/Overture, Beautiful Girls, Don't Look at Me, Waiting for the Girls Upstairs, Rain on the Roof, Ah Paris!, Broadway Baby, The Road You Didn't Take, Danse d'Amour, In Buddy's Eyes, Who's That Woman, I'm Still Here, Too Many Mornings, The Right Girl, One More Kiss, Could I Leave You? *Follies*: *The Folly of Love*, Loveland; *The Folly of Youth*, You're Gonna Love Tomorrow, Love Will See Us Through; *Buddy's Folly*, The God-Why-Don't-You-Love-Me Blues; *Sally's Folly*, Losing My Mind; *Phyllis's Folly*, The Story of Lucy and Jessie; *Ben's Folly*, Live, Laugh, Love

A new production of the 1971 musical, performed in two acts. The action takes place in a decaying theatre about to be demolished. For original Bdwy production with Alexis Smith, Dorothy Collins, Gene Nelson, and John McMartin, see *Theatre World* Vol. 27.

Variety tallied 6 favorable, 3 mixed, and 8 negative notices. *Times* (Brantley): "The beauty we fell in love with 30 years ago isn't looking so good these days...She's turned all brittle and cynical, and she's thin to the point of emaciation...The magic of *Follies* was always in the music...The current incarnation shifts the emphasis to James Goldman's book..." *News* (Kissel): "When a certain number of elements in *Follies* work, the show is bathed in iridescent magic. The current production never reaches that critical mass." *Post* (Barnes): "...drab and unimaginative staging...which has little idea of the style needed..." *Variety* : "...its score is perhaps the greatest from the last great composer for the American musical theater...finely acted, directed with intelligence and craft, middlingly sung, minimally designed..."

*Closed July 14, 2001 after 116 performances and 31 previews.

Joan Marcus Photos

Blythe Danner and Company

Joan Roberts, Brooke Sunny Moriber

Company of *Follies*

ONE FLEW OVER THE CUCKOO'S NEST

By Dale Wasserman; Based on the novel by Ken Kesey; Director, Terry Kinney; Set, Robert Brill; Costumes, Laura Bauer; Lighting, Kevin Rigdon; Music/Sound, Rob Milburn and Michael Bodeen; Projections, Sage Marie Carter; Casting, Phyllis Schuringa, Pat McCorkle; General Managers, Robert Cole, Jennifer F. Vaughan; Executive Producer, Kristin Caskey; Company Manager, Lisa M. Poyer; Production Stage Manager, Robert H. Satterlee; Stage Manager, Michele A. Kay; The Steppenwolf Theatre Company Production presented by Michael Leavitt, Fox Theatricals, Anita Waxman and Elizabeth Williams, in association with John York Noble, Randall L. Wreghitt and Dori Berinstein; Press, Richard Kornberg/Don Summa; Previewed from Friday, March 16; Opened in the Royale Theatre on Sunday, April 8, 2001*

CAST

Chief Bromden . . . . .Tim Sampson
Aide Warren . . . . .Ron O.J. Parson
Aide Williams . . . . .Afram Bill Williams
Nurse Ratched . . . . .Amy Morton
Nurse Flinn . . . . .Stephanie Childers
Dale Harding . . . . .Ross Lehman
Billy Bibbit . . . . .Eric Johner
Scanlon . . . . .Alan Wilder
Cheswick . . . . .Rick Snyder
Martini . . . . .Danton Stone
Ruckly . . . . .Misha Kuznetsov
Colonel Matterson . . . . .Bill Noble
Patient #1 . . . . .Bruce McCarty
Patient #2 . . . . .Steven Marcus
Randle P. McMurphy . . . . .Gary Sinise
Dr. Spivey . . . . .K. Todd Freeman
Aide Turkle . . . . .John Watson Sr.
Candy Starr . . . . .Mariann Mayberry
Technician #1 . . . . .Bruce McCarty
Technician #2 . . . . .Jeanine Morick
Sandra . . . . .Sarah Charipar

UNDERSTUDIES: Sarah Charipar (Candy Starr/Nurse Flinn), K. Todd Freeman (Billy Bibbit), Misha Kuznetsov (Dr. Spivey), Steven Marcus (Cheswick/Colonel Matterson/Martini/Scanlon), Bruce McCarty (Dale Harding/Randle P. McMurphy), Jeanine Morick (Nurse Ratched/Sandra), Michael Nichols (Aide Warren/Aide Williams/Chief Bromden/Ruckly), John Watson, Sr. (Patient #1/Technician #1), Afram Bill Williams (Aide Turkle)

A new production of the 1963 drama in two acts. The action takes place in the day room of a state mental hospital in the Pacific Northwest. Winner of 2001 "Tony" Award for Best Revival of a Play. For original Bdwy production starring Kirk Douglas, see *Theatre World* Vol. 20.

Variety tallied 6 favorable, 4 mixed, and 6 negative notices. *Times* (Brantley): "...despite a full-throttle performance from Mr. Sinise and top-of-the-line production values, *Cuckoo's Nest* mostly feels just cute instead of confrontational." *News* (Kissel): "Much of the acting...verges on hysterical. This is the style we associate with Steppenwolf." *Post* (Barnes): "...this performance is fantastic, and for that matter the subject matter, at the very least, is intriguing." *Variety* (Isherwood): "The play is an emotional button-pusher, wringing tears and cheers with mechanical precision."

*Closed July 29, 2001 after 121 performances and 24 previews.

Tristram Kenton Photos

Gary Sinise, Mariann Mayberry

Gary Sinise

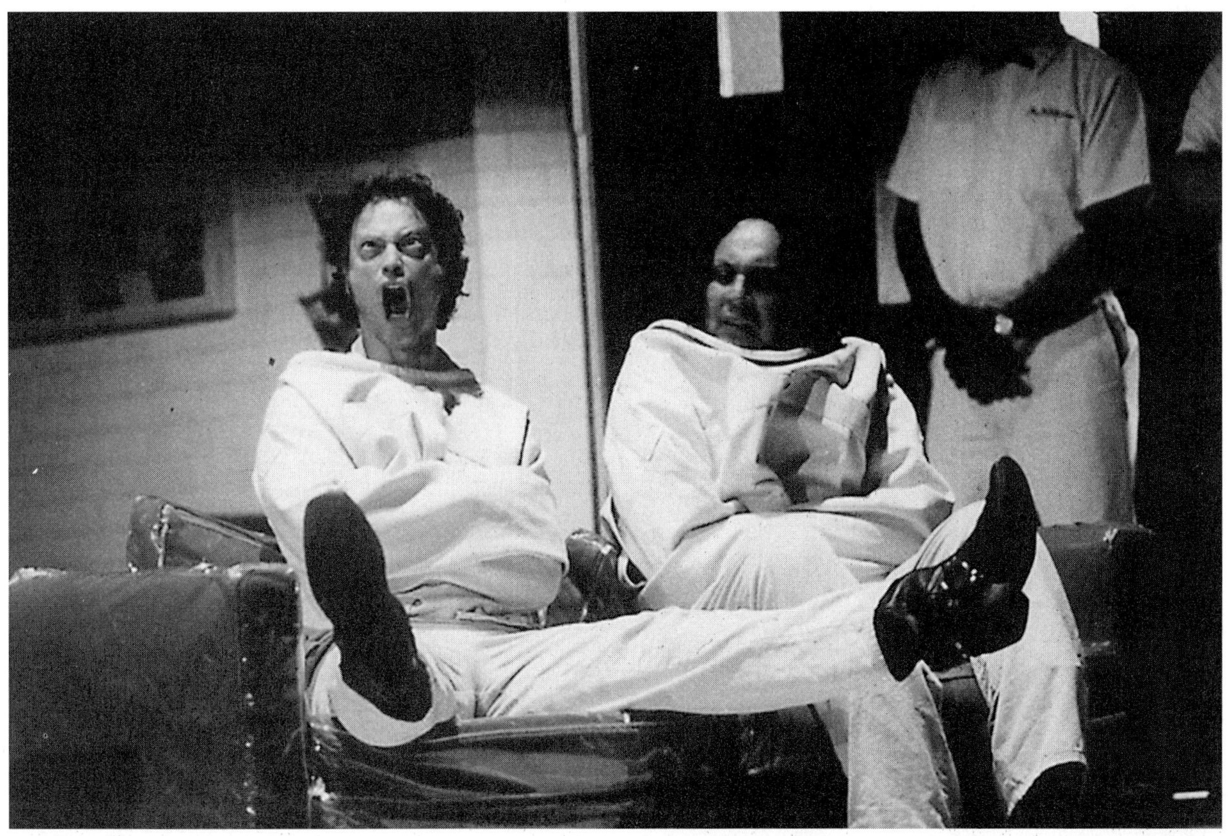

Gary Sinise, Tim Sampson

Amy Morton, Ron O.J. Parson, Gary Sinise

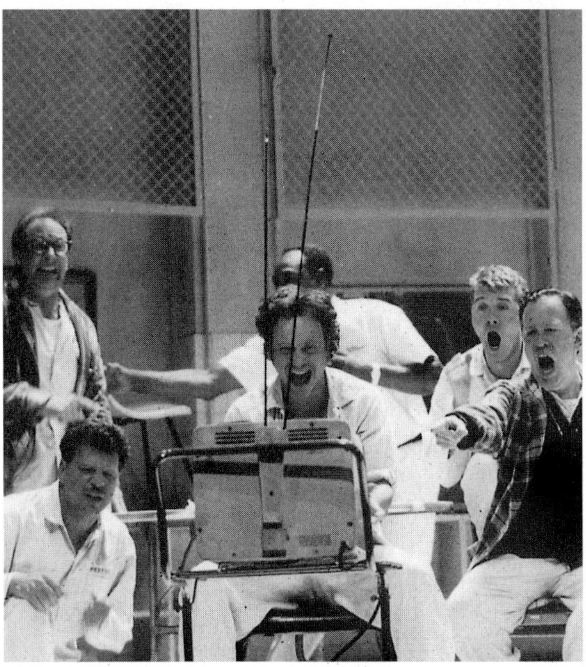

Foreground: Danton Stone, Gary Sinise, Ross Lehman;
Background: Rick Snyder, Afram Bill Williams, Eric Johner

BELLS ARE RINGING

Music, Jule Styne; Lyrics/Book, Betty Comden and Adolph Green; Director, Tina Landau; Choreography, Jeff Calhoun; Orchestrations, Don Sebesky; Musical Director, David Evans; Vocal Arrangements, David Evans; Incidental Music, David Evans, Mark Hummel; Dance Arrangements, Mr. Hummel; Set, Riccardo Hernandez; Costumes, David C. Woolard; Lighting, Donald Holder; Sound, Acme Sound Partners; Hair, David H. Lawrence; Cast Recording, Fynsworth Alley; General Manager, Robert V. Straus/Ellen Rusconi; Company Manager, Bruce Kagel; Production Stage Manager, Erica Schwartz; Stage Manager, James Latus; Video, Batwin & Robin; Casting, Stephanie Klapper; Presented by Mitchell Maxwell, Victoria Maxwell, Mark Balsam, Robert Barandes, Mark Goldberg, Anthony R. Russo and James L. Simon, in association with Fred H. Krones, Allen M. Shore and Momentum Productions, Inc.; Press, John Barlow-Michael Hartman/Ash Curtis, Jeremy Shaffer; Previewed from Tuesday, March 13; Opened in the Plymouth Theatre on Thursday, April 12, 2001*

Faith Prince

Faith Prince

CAST

TV Announcer ....Shane Kirkpatrick
Telephone Girls ...Caitlin Carter, Joan Hess, Emily Hsu, Alice Rietveld
Sue ....Beth Fowler
Gwynne ....Angela Robinson
Ella Peterson ....Faith Prince
Carl ....Julio Agustin
Inspector Barnes ....Robert Ari
Francis ....Jeffrey Bean
Sandor ....David Garrison
Jeff Moss ....Marc Kudisch
Larry Hastings ....David Brummel
Louie ....Greg Reuter
Ludwig Smiley ....Lawrence Clayton
Dr. Kitchell ....Martin Moran
Blake Barton ....Darren Ritchie
Joey ....Shane Kirkpatrick
Paddy, The Street Sweeper ....Roy Harcourt
Mrs. Simms ....Joan Hess
Olga ....Caitlin Carter
Corvello Mob Men ....David Brummel, Greg Reuter
Mrs. Mallet ....Joan Hess
Maid ....Linda Romoff
Paul Arnold ....Lawrence Clayton
Bridgette ....Joan Hess
Man on street ....Josh Rhodes
Madame Grimaldi ....Joanne Baum
Ensemble ....Julio Agustin, Joanne Baum, David Brummel, Caitlin Carter, Lawrence Clayton, Roy Harcourt, Joan Hess, Emily Hsu, Shane Kirkpatrick, Greg Reuter, Josh Rhodes, Alice Rietveld, Darren Ritchie, Angela Robinson, Linda Romoff
Dancers ....Caitlin Carter, Roy Harcourt, Joan Hess, Emily Hsu, Shane Kirkpatrick, Greg Reuter, Josh Rhodes
SWINGS: James Hadley, Stacey Harris, Marc Oka, Kelly Sullivan

MUSICAL NUMBERS: Overture, Bells Are Ringing, It's a Perfect Relationship, Independent, You've Got to Do It, It's a Simple Little System, Better Than a Dream, Hello Hello There, I Met a Girl, Is It a Crime?, Long Before I Knew You, Entr'Acte, Mu-Cha-Cha, Just in Time, Drop That Name, The Party's Over, Salzberg, The Midas Touch, I'm Going Back, Finale

A new production of the 1956 musical in two acts. The action takes place in New York City, late 1950s. For original Bdwy production with Judy Holliday, see *Theatre World* Vol. 13.

Variety tallied 8 favorable, 4 mixed, and 6 negative reviews. *Times* (Brantley): "Everything in this production, its leading lady aside, feels second- or thirdhand." *News* (Kissel): "...has always been one of my favorite shows. It defined New York for me in my adolescence in the provinces. The provinces, I'm afraid, are where this hopelessly misconceived revival belongs." *Post* (Barnes): "...staging by Tina Landau seems to make the least of its possibilities...Martin Moran has fun...Faith Prince is almost enough." *Variety* (Isherwood): "...affectionate homage to the breezy, bright musicals of the 1950s...alternately warm and bouncy score..."

*Closed June 10, 2001 after 69 performances and 35 previews.

Lois Greenfield Photos

BLAST!

Director, James Mason; Choreography, Jim Moore, George Pinney, Jonathan Vanderkolff; Orchestrations, James Prime; Set, Mark Thompson; Costumes, Mark Thompson; Lighting, Hugh Vanstone; Sound, Mark Hood, Bobby Aitken, Tom Morse; Company Manager, William Schaeffer; Production Supervisor, Tech Production Services; Production Stage Manager, William Coiner; Stage Manager, Victor Lukas; Special Effects, Flying by Foy; Presented by Cook Group Incorporated and Star of Indiana; Press, Chris Boneau-Adrian Bryan-Brown/Susanne Tighe, Amy Jacobs, Adriana Douzos; Previewed from Thursday, April 5; Opened in the Broadway Theatre on Tuesday, April 17, 2001*

CAST

Trey Alligood, III (Visual Ensemble, Voice), Rachel J. Anderson (French Horn, Mellophone, Voice), Nicholas E. Angelis (Snare Drum, Percussion, Voice), Matthew A. Banks (Tuba, Euphonium, Voice), Kimberly Beth Baron (French Horn, Mellophone, Keyboard, Voice), Wesley Bullock (Cornet, Trumpet, Didgerydoo, Voice), Mark Burroughs (Tuba), Jesus Cantu, Jr. (Trumpet, Cornet, Keyboard, Voice, Percussion), Jodina Rosario Carey (Visual Ensemble, Voice), Robert Carmical (Trombone, Bass Trombone, Baritone, Voice), Alan "Otto" Compton (Percussion, Voice), Dayne Delahoussaye (French Horn, Mellophone, Voice), Karen Duggan (Visual Ensemble, Voice), John Elrod (Trombone, Euphonium, Voice), Brandon J. Epperson (Trombone, Didgerydoo, Bass Trombone, Voice), Kenneth Frisby (Visual Ensemble, Voice), J. Derek Gipson (Trumpet, Piccolo Trumpet, Cornet, Voice), Trevor Lee Gooch (Tuba, Didgerydoo, Percussion, Voice), Casey Marshall Gooding (Trumpet, Piccolo Trumpet, Cornet, Didgerydoo, Voice), Bradley Kerr Green (Trombone, Conductor, Trombonium, Didgerydoo, Voice), Benjamin Taber Griffin (Trombone, Bass Trombone, Euphonium, Trombonium, Didgerydoo, Voice), Benjamin Raymond Handel (Percussion, Voice), Benjamin W. Harloff (Trumpet, Piccolo Trubpet, Flugelhorn, Cornet, Mellophone, Voice), Joe Haworth (Euphonium, Percussion, Voice), Darren M. Hazlett (Percussion, Didgerydoo, Voice), Tim Heasley (Trombone, Percussion, Voice), Freddy Hernandez, Jr. (Trumpet, Mellophone, Didgerydoo, Voice), George Hester (Trumpet, Cornet, Mellophone, Voice), Jeremiah Todd Huber (Visual Ensemble, Percussion, Voice), Martin A. Hughes (Visual Ensemble, Voice), Naoki Ishikawa (Persussion, Voice), Stacy J. Johnson (Visual Ensemble, Voice), Sanford R. Jones (Tuba, Didgerydoo, Voice), Anthony F. Leps (Trumpet, Cornet, Mellophone, Didgerydoo, Percussion, Voice), Ray Linkous (Conductor, Tuba, Didgerydoo, Voice), Jean Marie Mallicoat (Euphonium, Didgerydoo, Percussion, Voice), Jack Mansager (Percussion, Voice), Brian Mayle (Trombone, Trombonium, Didgerydoo, Percussion, Voice), Dave Millen (Trumpet, Voice), Jim Moore (Visual Ensemble, Voice), Westley Morehead (Trombone, Trombonium, Didgerydoo, Voice), David Nash (Percussion, Voice), Jeffrey A. Queen (Snare Drum, Percussion, Voice), Douglas Raines (Percussion, Didgerydoo, Voice), Chris Rasmussen (Percussion, Voice), Joseph J. Reinhart (Trumpet, Cornet, Voice), Jamie L. Roscoe (Visual Ensemble, Voice), Jennifer Ross (Visual Ensemble, Voice), Christopher Eric Rutt (French Horn, Mellophone, Didgerydoo, Percussion, Voice), Christopher J. Schletter (Trombone, Trombonium, Euphonium, Voice), Andrew Schnieders (Percussion, Voice), Jonathan L. Schwartz (Visual Ensemble, Voice), Greg Seale (Percussion, Voice), Andy Smart (Trumpet, Didgerydoo, Voice), Radiah Y. Stewart (Visual Ensemble, Voice), Bryan Anthony Sutton (Visual Ensemble, Voice), Sean Terrell (Trumpet, Didgerydoo, Voice), Andrew James Toth (Visual Ensemble, Voice), Joni Paige Viertel (French Horn, Mellophone, Didgerydoo, Voice), Kristin Whiting (Visual Ensemble, Voice)

Musical Numbers: Bolero (M. Ravel), Color Wheel (J. Lee), Split Complimentaries (J. Talbott), Everybody Loves the Blues (M. Ferguson/ N.Lane), Loss (D. Ellis), Simple Gifts/Appalachian Spring (A. Copeland), Battery Battle (T. Hannum/J. Lee/P. Rennick), Medea (S. Barber), The Promise of Living (A. Copland), Color Wheel Too (John Vanderkolff), Gee Officer Krupke (L. Bernstein/S. Sondheim), Lemontech (J. Vanderkolff), Tangerinamadidge (M. Mason/J. Vanderkolff), Land of Make Belive (C. Mangione), Spiritual of the Earth: Marimba Spiritual (M. Miki)/Earth Beat (M. Spiro), Malaguena (E. Lecuona), Added after 9/11 attacks on New York: Amber Waves

A musical entertainment in two acts. Winner of "Tony" Award for Special Theatrical Event.

Variety tallied 3 favorable, 1 mixed, and 5 negative reviews. *Times* (Weber): "...halftime show that has wandered onto the stage at the Broadway Theater as if it got lost on the way to the stadium." *News* (Kissel): "Everything is done with taste and intelligence, but what makes it such a winning evening is the cast, whose high spirits and enthusiasm are as great as their talent." *Post* (Barnes): "...not exactly theater, not exactly music, not exactly dance, not exactly anything but itself." *Variety* (Isherwood): "I half expected...I'd see the tireless kids following me into the subway, tubas and trombones still blaring."

*Closed September 23, 2001 after 176 performances and 13 previews.

The Company of *Blast!*

The Percussion Section of *Blast!*

THE PRODUCERS

Music/Lyrics, Mel Brooks; Book, Mr. Brooks and Thomas Meehan; Based on the 1967 film; Director/Choreography, Susan Stroman; Director, Patrick S. Brady; Musical Arrangements/Supervision, Glen Kelly; Orchestrations, Douglas Besterman, Larry Blank (uncredited); Musical Director/Vocal Arrangements, Patrick S. Brady; Set, Robin Wagner; Costumes, William Ivey Long; Lighting, Peter Kaczorowski; Sound, Steve Canyon Kennedy; Hair/Wigs, Paul Huntley; General Manager, Richard Frankel/Laura Green; Company Manager, Kathy Lowe; Production Stage Manager, Steven Zweigbaum; Stage Manager, Ira Mont; Cast Recording, Sony; Casting, Johnson-Liff Associates; Advertising, Serino Coyne, Inc.; Presented by Rocco Landesman, SFX Theatrical Group,The Frankel-Baruch-Viertel-Routh Group, Bob and Harvey Weinstein, Rick Steiner, Robert F.X. Sillerman and Mel Brooks, in association with James D. Stern/ Douglas L. Meyer; Press, John Barlow-Michael Hartman/Bill Coyle, Shellie Schovanec; Previewed from Wednesday, March 21; Opened in the St. James Theatre on Thursday, April 19, 2001*

Matthew Broderick and Company

Gary Beach, Roger Bart

CAST

The Usherettes .... Bryn Dowling, Jennifer Smith
Max Bialystock .... Nathan Lane +1
Leo Bloom .... Matthew Broderick +2
Hold-me Touch-me .... Madeleine Doherty
Mr. Marks .... Ray Wills
Franz Liebkind .... Brad Oscar
Carmen Ghia .... Roger Bart
Roger De Bris .... Gary Beach
Bryan/Judge/Jack Lepidus .... Peter Marinos
Scott/Guard/Donald Dinsmore .... Jeffry Denman
Ulla .... Cady Huffman
Lick-me Bite-me .... Jennifer Smith
Shirley/Kiss-me Feel-me/Jury Foreman .... Kathy Fitzgerald
Kevin/Jason Green/Trustee .... Ray Wills
Lead Tenor .... Eric Gunhus
Sergeant/Baliff .... Abe Sylvia
O'Rourke .... Matt Loehr
O'Houlihan .... Robert H. Fowler
Ensemble .... Jeffry Denman, Madeleine Doherty, Bryn Dowling, Kathy Fitzgerald, Robert H. Fowler, Ida Gilliams, Eric Gunhus, Kimberly Hester, Naomi Kakuk, Matt Loehr, Peter Marinos, Angie L. Schworer, Jennifer Smith, Abe Sylvia, Tracy Terstriep, Ray Wills

UNDERSTUDIES: Jim Borstelmann (Franz Liebkind/Roger De Bris), Jeffry Denman (Franz Liebkind/Leo Bloom), Ida Gilliams (Ulla), Jamie LaVerdiere (Carmen Ghia/Leo Bloom), Brad Musgrove (Carmen Ghia/ Roger De Bris), Brad Oscar (Max Bialystock/Roger De Bris), Angie L. Schworer (Ulla), Ray Wills (Max Bialystock). SWINGS: Jim Borstelmann, Adrienne Gibbons, Jamie LaVerdiere, Brad Musgrove, Christina Marie Norrup

Nathan Lane, Matthew Broderick

MUSICAL NUMBERS: Opening Night, The King of Broadway, We Can Do It, I Wanna Be a Producer, In Old Bavaria, Der Guten Tag Hop Clop, Keep it Gay, When You Got It Flaunt It, Along Came Bialy, Act One Finale, That Face, Haben Sie Gehoert Das Deutsche Band?, You Never Say 'Good Luck' On Opening Night, Springtime for Hitler, Where Did We Go Right?, Betrayed, 'Til Him, Prisoners of Love, Leo and Max, Goodbye!

Nathan Lane

A musical comedy in two acts. The action takes place in New York City, 1959. Winner of 2001 "Tony" Awards for Best Musical, Best Score, Best Book of a Musical, Best Actor in a Musical (Nathan Lane), Best Featured Actor in a Musical (Gary Beach), Best Featured Actress in a Musical (Cady Huffman), Best Director/Musical, Best Choreography, Best Sets, Best Costumes, Best Lighting, Best Orchestrations

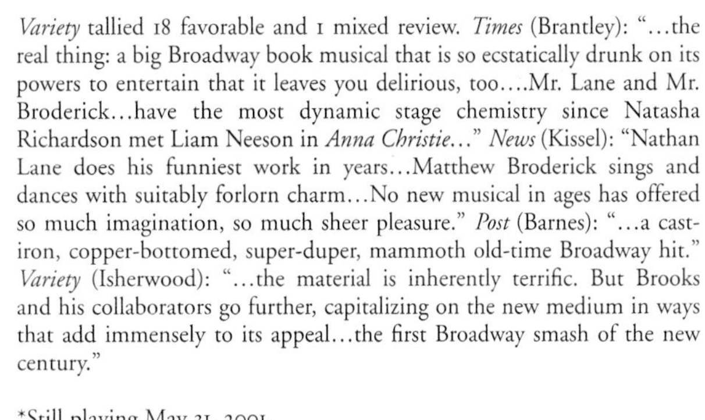

Variety tallied 18 favorable and 1 mixed review. *Times* (Brantley): "...the real thing: a big Broadway book musical that is so ecstatically drunk on its powers to entertain that it leaves you delirious, too....Mr. Lane and Mr. Broderick...have the most dynamic stage chemistry since Natasha Richardson met Liam Neeson in *Anna Christie*..." *News* (Kissel): "Nathan Lane does his funniest work in years...Matthew Broderick sings and dances with suitably forlorn charm...No new musical in ages has offered so much imagination, so much sheer pleasure." *Post* (Barnes): "...a cast-iron, copper-bottomed, super-duper, mammoth old-time Broadway hit." *Variety* (Isherwood): "...the material is inherently terrific. But Brooks and his collaborators go further, capitalizing on the new medium in ways that add immensely to its appeal...the first Broadway smash of the new century."

*Still playing May 31, 2001.

+Succeeded by: 1. Ray Wills (during illness) 2. Jamie LaVerdiere (during illness)

Paul Kolnik Photos

Matthew Broderick, Nathan Lane in *The Producers*

Nathan Lane and the Company of *The Producers*

THE GATHERING

By Arje Shaw; Director, Rebecca Taylor; Set, Michael Anania; Costumes, Susan Soetaert; Lighting, Scott Clyve; Sound, T. Richard Fitzgerald; Music, Andy Stein; Casting, Laurie Smith; General Manager, Roger Alan Gindi; Company Manager, Bobby Driggers; Production Stage Manager, Dom Ruggiero; Stage Managers, Betsy Herst, Robert Kellogg; Originally presented by The Jewish Repertory Theatre; Presented by Martin Markinson, Lawrence S. Toppall, Bruce Lazarus, Daniel S. Wise, Martha R. Gasparian, Steve Alpert and Robert Massimi, in association with Diaspora Productions; Press, Keith Sherman/Brett Oberman, Miller Wright; Previewed from Friday, April 13; Opened in the Cort Theatre on Tuesday, April 24, 2001*

CAST

Gabe . . . . .Hal Linden
Michael . . . . .Max Dworin
Diane . . . . .Deirdre Lovejoy
Stuart . . . . .Sam Guncler
Egon . . . . .Coleman Zeigen
Understudies/Standbys: Ru Flynn (Diane), Ben Hammer (Gabe), Myk Watford (Egon/Stuart) Ricky Ashley (Michael)

Sam Guncler, Deirdre Lovejoy, Hal Linden, Max Dworkin

Adam Rose, Hal Linden

A drama in two acts. The action takes place in New York City and Bitburg, West Germany, 1985.

Variety tallied 1 favorable, 1 mixed, and 11 negative reviews. *Times* (Weber): "...isn't a terribly good play, but it is an affecting sermon." *News* (Kissel): "It all falls under the heading of preaching to the choir..." *Post* (Barnes): "...the cast...is mostly very good, smoothly idiomatic, and capable of bringing a touch of originality to the expected." *Variety* (Isherwood): "...will...be embraced by audiences with strong sympathy for the material...neither subtle nor artful..."

*Closed May 13 after 24 performances and 12 previews.

Carol Rosegg Photos

Hal Linden

THE ADVENTURES OF TOM SAWYER

Music/Lyrics, Don Schlitz; Book, Ken Ludwig; Based on the novel by Mark Twain; Director, Scott Ellis; Musical Director, Paul Gemignani; Orchestrations, Michael Starobin; Dance/Incidental Music, David Krane; Choreography, David Marques; Sets, Heidi Ettinger; Costumes, Anthony Powell; Lighting, Kenneth Posner; Sound, Lew Mead; Hair, David Brian Brown; General Manager, Devin Keudell; Company Manager: Sean Free; Production Manager, Arthur Siccardi; Production Supervisor, Beverley Randolph; Stage Manager, David Hyslop; Fights, Rick Sordelet, Special Effects, Chic Silber; Dialects, Kate Wilson; Casting, Jim Carnahan, Bernard Telsey Casting, Inc.; Presented by James M. Nederlander, James L. Nederlander and Watt/Dobie Productions; Press, Chris Boneau-Adrian Bryan-Brown/Amy Jacobs, Rob Finn; Previewed from Tuesday, March 27; Opened in the Minskoff Theatre on Thursday, April 26, 2001*

The Company of *The Adventures of Tom Sawyer*

Jim Poulos

CAST

Tom Sawyer .... Joshua Park
Ben Rogers .... Tommar Wilson
George Bellamy .... Joe Gallagher
Lyle Bellamy .... Blake Hackler
Joe Harper .... Erik J. McCormack
Alfred Temple .... Pierce Cravens
Amy Lawrence .... Ann Whitlow Brown
Lucy Harper .... Mekenzie Rosen-Stone
Susie Rogers .... Élan
Sabina Temple .... Nikki M. James
Sally Bellamy .... Stacia Fernandez
Sereny Harper .... Donna Lee Marshall
Lucinda Rogers .... Amy Jo Phillips
Naomi Temple .... Sally Wilfert
Aunt Polly .... Linda Purl
Sid Sawyer .... Marshall Pailet
Doc Robinson .... Stephen Lee Anderson
Reverend Sprague .... Tommy Hollis
Lanyard Bellamy .... Richard Poe
Gideon Temple .... Ric Stoneback
Lemuel Dobbins .... John Christopher Jones
Muff Potter .... Tom Aldredge
Huckleberry Finn .... Jim Poulos
Injun Joe .... Kevin Durand
Judge Thatcher .... John Dossett
Becky Thatcher .... Kristen Bell
Widow Douglas .... Jane Connell
Pap .... Stephen Lee Anderson

UNDERSTUDIES: Stephen Lee Anderson (Lemuel Dobbins/Rev. Sprague), Patrick Boll (Doc Robinson/Gideon Temple/Injun Joe/Judge Thatcher/Lanyard Bellamy/Pap), Michael Burton (Ben Rogers/Joe Harper), Pierce Cravens (Sid Sawyer), Stacia Fernandez (Aunt Polly/Widow Douglas), Joe Gallagher (Huckleberry Finn), Blake Hackler (Tom Sawyer), John Herrera (Doc Robinson/Gideon Temple/Lanyard Bellamy/Lemuel Dobbins/Muff Potter/Pap/Sprague), Nikki M. James (Becky Thatcher), Erik J. McCormack (Tom Sawyer), Amy Jo Phillips (Widow Douglas), Richard Poe (Judge Thatcher), Kate Reinders (Amy Lawrence/Becky Thatcher), Sally Wilfert (Aunt Polly), Tommar Wilson (Huckleberry Finn)

SWINGS: Patrick Boll, Michael Burton, John Herrera, Kate Reinders, Elise Santora

Joshua Park

Joshua Park and Company

Kristen Bell, Joshua Park

Musical Numbers: Hey, Tom Sawyer, Here's My Plan, Smart Like That, Hands All Clean, The Vow, Ain't Life Fine, It Just Ain't Me, To Hear You Say My Name, Murrel's Gold, The Testimony, Ain't Life Fine (reprise), This Time Tomorrow, I Can Read, You Can't Can't Dance, Murrel's Gold, Angels Lost, Light, Angels Lost (reprise), Light (reprise), Finale

A musical in two acts. The action takes place in St. Petersburg, Missouri, 1844.

Variety tallied 5 mixed, and 10 negative notices. *Times* (Weber): "...a handful of winning tunes...It is primerlike theater..." *News* (Kissel): "If only all of *Tom Sawyer* were as fresh as Heidi Ettinger's sets...Joshua Park is a very appealing Tom...As a musicalization of a beloved book...unsatisfying." *Post* (Barnes): "It always sounds strangely disparaging to say that a show seems a good one for the children, but—very sorry—that is precisely what the new musical...seems to be." *Variety* (Isherwood): "It's not just the famous fence that gets whitewashed...sunny and handsome but deflatingly bland..."

*Closed May 13, 2001 after 21 performances and 34 previews.

Joan Marcus Photos

GEORGE GERSHWIN ALONE

By Hershey Felder; Music, George Gershwin; Lyrics, Ira Gershwin; Director, Joel Zwick; Set, Yael Pardess; Lighting, James F. Ingalls; Sound, Jon Gottlieb; Wardrobe, Kenneth Cole; General Managers, Steven Chaikelson and Snug Harbor Productions; Production Stage Manager, Arthur Gaffin; Presented by Richard Willis, Martin Markinson and HTG Productions; Press, Keith Sherman/Brett Oberman; Previewed from Tuesday, April 17; Opened in the Helen Hayes Theatre on Monday, April 30, 2001*

CAST

George Gershwin . . . . .Hershey Felder

A one-man play with music performed without intermission.

Variety tallied 2 favorable, 1 mixed, and 8 negative reviews. *Times* (Weber): "...Mr. Felder is neither writer enough nor actor enough to give his subject living charm..." *News* (Kissel): "...stunning piano technique..." *Post* (Barnes): "...the difference between George Gershwin alone and Hershey Felder alone is not inconsiderable." *Variety* (Isherwood): "...unilluminating and somewhat dull..."

*Closed July 24, 2001 after 96 performances and 16 previews.

Carol Rosegg Photos

Hershey Felder

KING HEDLEY II

By August Wilson; Director, Marion McClinton; Set, David Gallo; Costumes, Toni-Leslie James; Lighting, Donald Holder; Sound, Rob Milburn; Choreography, Dianne McIntyre; Fights, David S. Leong; Casting Barry Moss; General Manager, Roger Alan Gindi; Company Manager, Chris Morey; Production Stage Manager, Diane DiVita; Stage Manager, Cynthia Kocher; Presented by Sageworks, Benjamin Mordecai, Jujamcyn Theaters, 52nd Street Productions, Spring Sirkin, Peggy Hill, and Manhattan Theatre Club, in association with Kardana-Swinsky Productions; Press, John Barlow-Michael Hartman/Jeremy Shaffer; Previewed from Tuesday, April 10; Opened in the Virginia Theatre on Tuesday, May 1, 2001*

CAST

Stool Pigeon . . . . .Stephen McKinley Henderson
King . . . . .Brian Stokes Mitchell +1
Ruby . . . . .Leslie Uggams
Mister . . . . .Monté Russell
Tonya . . . . .Viola Russell
Elmore . . . . .Charles Brown
STANDBYS: Ron Dortch (Elmore/Stool Pigeon), Yvette Ganier (Tonya), Lynda Gravátt (Ruby), Keith Randolph Smith (King/Mister)

A drama in two acts. The action takes place in the Hill District, Pittsburgh, PA, 1985. This production continues August Wilson's cycle of plays (*Fences, Jitney, The Piano Lesson*) portraying the African-American experience through each decade of the 20th century. Winner of 2001 "Tony" Award for Best Featured Actress in a Play (Viola Davis).

Variety tallied 9 favorable, 4 mixed, and 2 negative reviews. *Times* (Brantley): "...grand, ungainly three-hour drama...you will hear some of the finest monologues ever written for the American stage..." *News* (Kissel): "For nearly 20 years, August Wilson has been writing operas cunningly disguised as plays...full of powerful images..." *Post* (Barnes): "...salty, ironic, often very funny dialogue...Mitchell...is splendid...as are the more rational Uggams and Davis..." *Variety* (Isherwood): "By any standard but the playwright's own...would probably rank as an impressive accomplishment...a disappointing entry in this ongoing literary landmark..."

*Closed July 1, 2001 after 72 performances and 24 previews.

+Succeeded by: 1. Keith Randolph Smith (during illness)

Joan Marcus Photos

Brian Stokes Mitchell

Charles Brown, Leslie Uggams

Leslie Uggams, Brian Stokes Mitchell

CINDERELLA

Music, Richard Rodgers; Lyrics/Book, Oscar Hammerstein II; Stage Adaptation by Tom Briggs, from teleplay by Robert L. Freedman; Director, Gabriel Barre; Musical Supervisor/Arrangements, Andrew Lippa; Musical Director, John Mezzio; Choreography, Ken Roberson; Orchestrations, (new) David Siegel, (original) Robert Russell Bennett; Set, James Youmans; Costume Design, Pamela Scofield; Lighting Design, Tim Hunter; Sound Design, Duncan Edwards; Special Effects, Gregory Meeh; Puppets, Integrity Designworks; Production Supervisor, Seth Wenig; General Management, Ken Davenport and Scott W. Jackson; Production Stage Manager, Daniel L. Bello; Presented by Radio City Entertainment; Opened in The Theatre at Madison Square Garden on Tuesday, May 1, 2001*

Jamie-Lynn Sigler

CAST

Fairy Godmother . . . . .Eartha Kitt
Cinderella . . . . .Jamie-Lynn Sigler
Prince Christopher . . . . .Paolo Montalban
Stepmother . . . . .Everett Quinton
Grace . . . . .NaTasha Yvette Williams
Joy . . . . .Alexandra Kolb
Lionel . . . . .Victor Trent Cook
Queen Constantina . . . . .Leslie Becker
King Maximillian . . . . .Ken Prymus
Ensemble . . . . .Joanne Borts, Natalie Cortez, Kip Driver, Kevin Duda, Jason Ma, Christy Morton, Monica Patton, Lyn Philistine, Christeena Michelle Riggs, Jason Robinson, Jessica Rush, Todd L. Underwood, Andre Ward, Patrick Wetzel

A stage version of the 1957 television musical. After the original 1957 TV production with Julie Andrews, later TV adaptations were done with Lesley Ann Warren (1965) and Brandy (1997). In addition to the original *Cinderella* score, this production interpolates "The Sweetest Sounds" from *No Strings* and "There's Music in You" from the 1953 film *Main Street to Broadway.*

*Closed May 13, 2001 after limited run of 13 performances.

Kate Levering and Company of *42nd Street*

42ND STREET

Music, Harry Warren; Lyrics, Al Dubin; Book, Michael Stewart and Mark Bramble; Based on a novel by Bradford Ropes; Director, Mark Bramble; Musical Staging/New Choreography, Randy Skinner; Musical Director, Todd Ellison; Musical Adaptation/Arrangements, Donald Johnston; Orchestrations (original), Philip J. Lang; Set, Douglas W. Schmidt; Costumes, Roger Kirk; Lighting, Paul Gallo; Sound, Peter Fitzgerald; Hair/Wigs, David H. Lawrence; Company Manager, Sandra Carlson; General Manager, Robert C. Strickstein, Sally Campbell Morse; Production Stage Manager, Frank Hartenstein; Stage Manager, Karen Armstrong; Casting, Jay Binder; Original Direction/Dances, Gower Champion; Presented by Dodger Theatricals, Joop Van Den Ende and Stage Holding; Press, Chris Boneau-Adrian Bryan-Brown/Susanne Tighe, Amy Jacobs, Adriana Douzos; Previewed from Wednesday, April 4; Opened in the Ford Center for the Performing Arts on Wednesday, May 2, 2001*

CAST

Andy Lee .... Michael Arnold
Maggie Jones .... Mary Testa
Bert Barry .... Jonathan Freeman
Mac .... Allen Fitzpatrick
Phyllis .... Catherine Wreford
Lorraine .... Megan Sikora
Diane .... Tamlyn Brooke Shusterman
Annie .... Mylinda Hull
Ethel .... Amy Dolan
Billy Lawlor .... David Elder
Peggy Sawyer .... Kate Levering
Oscar .... Billy Stritch
Julian Marsh .... Michael Cumpsty
Dorothy Brock .... Christine Ebersole
Abner Dillon .... Michael McCarty
Pat Denning .... Richard Muenz
Waiters .... Brad Aspel, Mike Warshaw, Shonn Wiley
Thugs .... Allen Fitzpatrick, Jerry Tellier
Doctor .... Allen Fitzpatrick
Ensemble .... Brad Aspel, Becky Berstler, Randy Bobish, Chris Clay, Michael Clowers, Maryam Myika Day, Alexander de Jong, Amy Dolan, Isabelle Flachsmann, Jennifer Jones, Dontee Kiehn, Renée Klapmeyer, Jessica Kostival, Keirsten Kupiec, Todd Lattimore, Melissa Rae Mahon, Michael Malone, Jennifer Marquardt, Meredith Patterson, Darin Phelps, Wendy Rosoff, Megan Schenck, Kelly Sheehan, Tamlyn Brooke Shusterman, Megan Sikora, Jennifer Stetor, Erin Stoddard, Yasuko Tamaki, Jonathan Taylor, Jerry Tellier, Elisa Van Duyne, Erika Vaughn, Mike Warshaw, Merrill West, Shonn Wiley, Catherine Wreford

UNDERSTUDIES/STANDBYS: Beth Leavel (Dorothy Brock/Maggie Jones). Brad Aspel (Andy Lee, Bert Barry), Becky Berstler (Annie), Randy Bobish (Andy Lee), Amy Dolan (Annie, Maggie Jones), Allen Fitzpatrick (Abner Dillon/Pat Denning), Renée Klapmeyer (Diane), Jessica Kostival (Dorothy Brock), Richard Muenz (Julian Marsh), Meredith Patterson (Peggy Sawyer), Darin Phelps (Doctor/Mac/Thug), Erin Stoddard (Lorraine/Peggy Sawyer), Jerry Tellier (Julian Marsh/Pat Denning), Elisa Van Duyne (Phyllis), Luke Walrath (Doctor/Mac/Thug), Shonn Wiley (Billy Lawlor)

MUSICAL NUMBERS: Overture, Audition, Young and Healthy, Shadow Waltz, Go into Your Dance, You're Getting to Be a Habit with Me, Getting Out of Town, Dames, Keep Young and Beautiful, Dames, I Only Have Eyes for You (not in orig production), We're in the Money, Keep Young and Beautiful (not in orig production), Entr'Acte, Sunny Side to Every Situation, Lullaby of Broadway, Getting Out of Town, Montage, About a Quarter to Nine, With Plenty of Money and You (not in orig. production), Shuffle Off to Buffalo, 42nd Street, Finale

Michael Arnold, David Elder, Michael Cumpsty, Mylinda Hull, and Company

Christine Ebersole

A new production of the 1980 musical in two acts. The action takes place in New York City and Philadelphia, 1933. Winnr of 2001 "Tony" Award for Best Revival/Musical and Best Actress in a Musical (Christine Ebersole). For original Bdwy production with Jerry Orbach and Tammy Grimes, see *Theatre World* Vol. 37.

Variety tallied 11 favorable, 1 mixed, and 4 negative reviews. *Times* (Brantley): "...premature revival...a faded fax of the last musical staged by the fabled Gower Champion..." *News* (Kissel) "...loaded with talent. And you know it as soon as the curtain rises on 24 pairs of tap-dancing feet." *Post* (Barnes): "...cast with exquisite care...everyone is superb..." *Variety* (Isherwood): "...gaudy, relentless production...pays tribute to the Gower Champion original..."

*Still playing May 31, 2001

Joan Marcus Photos

ENCORES! GREAT AMERICAN MUSICALS IN CONCERT

Eighth Season

Artistic Director, Jack Viertel; Musical Director, Rob Fisher; Director-in Residence, Kathleen Marshall; Orchestra, The Coffee Club Orchestra; Set, John Lee Beatty; Sound Design, Scott Lehrer; Casting, Jay Binder; Production Stage Manager, Bonnie L. Becker; Press, Philip Rinaldi/Barbara Carroll

A CONNECTICUT YANKEE

Music, Richard Rodgers; Lyrics, Lorenz Hart; Book, Herbert Fields, Adapted from *A Connecticut Yankee in King Arthur's Court* by Mark Twain, by David Ives; Director, Susan H. Schulman; Orchestrations, Don Walker; Choreography, Rob Ashford; Costume Design, Toni-Leslie James; Lighting Design, Natasha Katz; Presented in City Center on February 8-11, 2001 (5 performances)

CAST

Arthur Pendragos/King Arthur .Henry Gibson
Gerald Gareth/Sir Galahad . . . . .Seán Martin Hingston
Martin Barrett (The Yankee) . . . . .Steven Sutcliffe
Albert Kay/Sir Kay . . . . .Mark Lotito
Fay Morgan/Morgan Le Fay . . . . .Christine Ebersole
Evelyn Lane/Dame Evelyn . . . . .Nancy Lemenager
Alice Carter/Alisande (Sandy) . . . . .Judith Blazer
Angela/Maid Angela . . . . .Megan Sikora
Henry Merle/Merlin . . . . .Peter Bartlett
Sir Launcelot . . . . .Ron Liebman
Guinevere . . . . .Jessica Walter
Dancers . . . . .Robert M. Armitage, Vance Avery, David Eggers, Anika Ellis, Matt Lashey, Elizabeth Mills, Aixa M. Rosario Medina, Megan Sikora
Singers . . . . .Anne Allgood, Kate Baldwin, Tony Capone, Julie Connors, John Halmi, Chris Hoch, Robert Osborne, Frank Ream, Keith Spencer, Rebecca Spencer, J.D. Webster, Mimi Wyche

Musical Numbers: Overture, Here's Martin the Groom, This Is My Night to Howl, My Heart Stood Still, I Blush, Thou Swell, At the Round Table, On a Desert Island with Thee!, To Keep My Love Alive, Ye Lunchtime Follies, I Feel at Home with You, The Sandwich Men, You Always Love the Same Girl, The Camelot Samba, Can't You Do a Friend a Favor?, Finale Ultimo

A staged concert of a 1927 musical. This production utilizes the songs and orchestrations created for the 1943 revival.

Christine Ebersole

BLOOMER GIRL

Music, Harold Arlen; Lyrics, E.Y. Harburg; Book, Sig Herzig and Fred Saidy; Adaptation, David Ives; Director, Brad Rouse; Orchestrations, Robert Russell Bennett; Choreography, Rob Ashford; Costume Design, Toni-Leslie James; Lighting Design, Ken Billington; Presented in City Center on March 22-25, 2001 (5 performances)

CAST

Serena Applegate . . . . .Anita Gillette
Octavia . . . . .Michele Ragusa
Lydia . . . . .Joy Hermalyn
Julia . . . . .Ann Kittredge
Phoebe . . . . .Teri Hansen
Delia . . . . .Gay Willis
Daisy . . . . .Donna Lynne Champlin
Horatio Applegate . . . . .Philip Bosco
Gus . . . . .Ned Eisenberg
Evelina Applegate . . . . .Kate Jennings Grant
Joshua Dingle . . . . .Joe Cassidy
Herman Brasher . . . . .David de Jong
Ebenezer Mimms . . . . .Eddie Korbich
Wilfred Thrush . . . . .Tim Salamandyk
Hiram Crump . . . . .Roger DeWitt
Dolly Bloomer . . . . .Kathleen Chalfant
Jeff Calhoun . . . . .Michael Park
Pompey . . . . .Jubilant Sykes
Sheriff Quimby . . . . .Mike Hartman
Hamilton Calhoun . . . . .Herndon Lackey
Augustus . . . . .Todd Hunter
Alexander . . . . .Everett Bradley
Governor's Aide . . . . .Carson Church
Governor Newton . . . . .Merwin Goldsmith
Ballet Soloists . . . . .Karine Plantadit-Bageot, Nina Goldman, Todd Hunter, Robert Wersinger
Suffragettes/Deputies/Citizens.. . . . . . . .Deborah Allton, Kate Baldwin, Joe Cassidy, Carson Church, David de Jong, Susan Derry, Roger DeWitt, Donna Dunmire, John Halmi, Teri Hansen, Joy Hermalyn, Cherylyn Jones, Ann Kittredge, Eddie Korbich, Jason Lacayo, Mary Kate Law, Lori MacPherson, Michele Ragusa, Vale Rideout, Tim Salamandyk, Gay Willis

Musical Numbers: Overture, When the Boys Come Home, Evelina, Welcome Hinges, The Farmer's Daughter, Good Enough for Grandma, The Eagle and Me, Right as the Rain, T'morra T'morra, Rakish Young Man in the Whiskers, Pretty as a Picture, Sunday in Cicero falls, I Got a Song, Lullaby, Liza Crossing the Ice, Never Was Born, Man for Sale, Ballet, Finale

A staged concert of a 1944 musical. The action takes place in 1861.

Hair

HAIR

Music, Galt MacDermot; Lyrics/Book, Gerome Ragni and James Rado; Director/Choreography, Kathleen Marshall; Associate Choreographer, Joey Pizzi; Costume Design, Martin Pakledinaz; Lighting Design, Ken Billington; Presented in City Center on May 3-7, 2001 (6 performances)

CAST

Claude . . . . .Luther Creek
Berger . . . . .Tom Plotkin
Woof . . . . .Kevin Cahoon
Hud . . . . .Michael McElroy
Sheila . . . . .Idina Menzel
Jeanie/Buddhadalirama . . . . .Miriam Shor
Dionne . . . . .Brandi Chavonne Massey
Crissy . . . . .Jessica Snow-Wilson
Mother . . . . .Sheri Sanders, Kathy Deitch, Eric Millegan
Father/Principal . . . . .Kevin Cahoon, Gavin Creel, Miriam Shor
Tourist Couple . . . . .Jesse Tyler Ferguson, Billy Hartung
General Grant . . . . .Jesse Tyler Ferguson
Abraham Lincoln . . . . .Rosalind Brown
The Tribe . . . . .Rosalind Brown, Bryant Carroll, E. Alyssa Claar, Gavin Creel, Kathy Deitch, Jesse Tyler Ferguson, Jessica Ferraro, Stephanie Fittro, Billy Hartung, Todd Hunter, Eric Millegan, Sean Jeremy Palmer, Sheri Saunders, Carolyn Saxon, Michael Seelbach, Yuka Takara

Musical Numbers: Aquaris, Donna, Hashish, Sodomy, Colored Spade, Manchester England, Ain't Got No, Dead End, I Believe in Love, Air, I Got Life, Initials, Going Down, hair, My Conviction, Easy to Be Hard, Don't Put It Down, Frank Mills, Be In (Hare Krishna), Where Do I Go, Electric Blues, Oh Great God of Powers, Black Boys, White Boys, Walking in Space, Abie Baby, Three-Five-Zero-Zero, What a Piece of Work Is Man, Good Morning Sunshine, The Bed, The Flesh Failures (Let the Sun Shine In)

A staged concert of the 1967 musical. This production utilizes material from both the 1967 Off-Broadway and 1968 Broadway productions.

VOICES OF THE AMERICAN THEATER

Producer, Alec Baldwin; Artistic Director, Steve Lawson; Sound Design, Scott Lehrer; Lighting Design, Tricia Toliver; Press, Philip Rinaldi/Brian Rubin

ARSENIC AND OLD LACE

By Joseph Kesselring; Director, Steve Lawson; Stage Manager, Casey Aileen Rafter; Presented in City Center on Saturday, November 11, 2000 (1 performance only)

CAST

Abby Brewster . . . . .Celeste Holm
Rev. Dr. Harper/Lt. Rooney . . . . .Edmond Genest
Teddy Brewster . . . . .Tuck Milligan
Officer Brophy . . . . .John Hines
Officer Klein . . . . .John Rothman
Martha Brewster . . . . .Joanne Woodward
Elaine Harper . . . . .Jennifer Van Dyck
Mortimer Brewster . . . . .Alec Baldwin
Mr. Gibbs/Mr. Witherspoon . . . . .William Duell
Jonathan Brewster . . . . .Terrence Mann
Dr. Einstein . . . . .Lee Wilkof
Officer O'Hara . . . . .Joe Grifasi
Stage Directions . . . . .Ethan Sandler

A staged reading of the 1941 comedy in three acts. The action takes place in Brooklyn.

LITTLE MURDERS

By Jules Feiffer; Director, Steve Lawson; Projections, Jules Feiffer; Stage Manager, Kimberly Russel; Presented in City Center on Tuesday, January 30, 2001 (1 performance only)

CAST

Marjorie Newquist . . . . .Blythe Danner
Kenny Newquist . . . . .Christopher Fitzgerald
Carol Newquist . . . . .Joel Grey
Patsy Newquist . . . . .Polly Draper
Alfred Chamberlain . . . . .Patrick Breen
Judge . . . . .Louis Zorich
Rev. Henry Dupas . . . . .Mark McKinney
Lt. Miles Practice . . . . .Joe Morton
Stage Directions . . . . .Jules Feiffer

A staged reading of the 1967 black comedy.

THE DEVIL AND DANIEL WEBSTER

By Stephen Vincent Benet, based on his short story; Director, Steve Lawson; Stage Manager, Jill Cordle; Presented in City Center on Tuesday, March 13, 2001 (1 performance only)

CAST

Jabez Stone . . . . .James Naughton
Mary Stone . . . . .Jennifer Van Dyck
Daniel Webster . . . . .Harris Yulin
Mr. Scratch . . . . .Eric Bogosian
Fiddler/Clerk . . . . .William Duell
Judge Hathorne/Wedding Guest .Nick Wyman
Simon Girty/Wedding Guest . . . . .Nick Brooks
Walter Butler/Wedding Guest . . . . .Chris Hoch
King Philip/Wedding Guest .Stephen Mendillo
Blackbeard Teach/Wedding Guest . . . . .James Matthew Ryan
Violin . . . . .Julie Lyonn Lieberman

A staged reading of a 1939 play. The action takes place in New England, 1841.

Alec Baldwin

BROADWAY PRODUCTIONS FROM PAST SEASONS THAT PLAYED THROUGH THIS SEASON

AIDA

Music, Elton John; Lyrics, Tim Rice; Book, Linda Woolverton and Robert Falls and David Henry Hwang; Suggested by the opera; Director, Robert Falls; Choreography, Wayne Cilento; Set/Costumes, Bob Crowley; Lighting, Natasha Katz; Sound, Steve C. Kennedy; Music Produced and Musical Direction, Paul Bogaev; Music Arrangements, Guy Babylon, Paul Bogaev; Orchestrations, Steve Margoshes, Guy Babylon, Paul Bogaev; Casting, Bernard Telsey; Production Stage Manager, Clifford Schwartz; Cast Recording, Buena Vista; Presented by Hyperion Theatricals (Peter Schneider and Thomas Schumacher); Press, Chris Boneau-Adrian Bryan-Brown/Jackie Green, Steven Padla; Previewed from Friday, February 25, 2000; Opened in the Palace Theatre on Thursday, March 23, 2000*

CAST

Amneris . . . . .Sherie René Scott +1
Radames . . . . .Adam Pascal
Aida . . . . .Heather Headley
Mereb . . . . .Damian Perkins
Zoser . . . . .John Hickok
Pharaoh . . . . .Daniel Oreskes
Nehebka . . . . .Schele Williams
Amonasro . . . . .Tyrees Allen
Ensemble . . . . .Robert M. Armitage, Troy Allan Burgess, Franne Calma, Bob Gaynor, Kisha Howard, Tim Hunter, Youn Kim, Kyra Little, Kenya Unique Massey, Corinne McFadden, Phineas Newborn III, Jody Ripplinger, Raymond Rodriguez, Eric Sciotto, Samuel N. Thiam, Jerald Vincent, Schele Williams, Natalia Zisa

Understudies: Franne Calma, Kelli Fournier (Amneris), Bob Gaynor, Raymond Rodriguez, Eric Sciotto (Radames), Schele Williams (Aida), Tim Hunter, Phineas Newborn III (Mereb), Troy Allan Burgess (Zoser), Robert M. Armitage (Pharaoh), Kyra Little, Endalyn Taylor-Shellman (Nehebka), Samuel N. Thiam, Jerald Vincent (Amonasro)

Standbys: Thursday Farrar (Aida), Neal Benari (Zoser/Pharaoh)

Swings: Chris Payne Dupré, Kelli Fournier, Timothy Edward Smith, Endalyn Taylor-Shellman

Heather Headley and Company

Taylor Dayne

Musical Numbers: Every Story Is a Love Story, Fortune Favors the Brave, The Past is Another Land, Another Pyramid, How I Know You, My Strongest Suit, Enchantment Passing Through, The Dance of the Robe, Not Me, Elaborate Lives, The Gods Love Nubia, A Step Too Far, Easy as Life, Like Father Like Son, Radames' Letter, Written in the Stars, I Know the Truth

A musical in two acts. The action takes place in Egypt. Winner of 2000 "Tony" Awards for Original Score, Actress in a Musical (Heather Headley), Scenic Design, and Lighting Design.

*Still playing May 31, 2001.

+Succeeded by: 1. Taylor Dayne

Joan Marcus Photos

ANNIE GET YOUR GUN

Music/Lyrics, Irving Berlin; Original Book, Herbert and Dorothy Fields; Book Revisions, Peter Stone; Director, Graciela Daniele; Choreography, Ms. Daniele, Jeff Calhoun; Supervising Music Director/Vocal and Incidental Arranger, John McDaniel; New Orchestrations, Bruce Coughlin; Music Director, Dance Arrangements, Marvin Laird; Set, Tony Walton; Costumes, William Ivey Long; Lighting, Beverly Emmons; Sound, G. Thomas Clark; Production Manager, Arthur Siccardi; General Management, Nina Lannan Associates; Production Supervisor, Peter Lawrence; Stage Manager, Richard Hester; Cast Recording, Angel; Presented by Barry & Fran Weissler, in association with Kardana, Michael Watt, Irving Welzer, and Hal Luftig; Press, Pete Sanders/Miguel Tuason, Bill Coyle, Glenna Freedman; Previewed from Tuesday, February 2, 1999; Opened in the Marquis Theatre on Thursday, March 4, 1999*

CAST

Buffalo Bill . . . . .Dennis Kelly +1
Frank Butler . . . . .Patrick Cassidy +2
Dolly Tate . . . . .Michelle Blakely +3
Tommy Keeler . . . . .Randy Donaldson +4
Winnie Tate . . . . .Emily Rozek +5
Mac/Running Deer/Messenger .Tom Schmid
Charlie Davenport . . . . .Peter Marx
Foster Wilson . . . . .Gerry Vichi
Chief Sitting Bull . . . . .Kevin Bailey +6
Annie Oakley . . . . .Cheryl Ladd +7
Jessie Oakley . . . . .Jenny Rose Baker
Nelly Oakley . . . . .Laura M. Giberson +8
Little Jake . . . . .Eddie Brandt
Ballerina . . . . .Keri Lee
Hoop Dance Specialty . . . . .Adrienne Hurd +9
Eagle Feather . . . . .Carlos Lopez
Moonshine Lullaby Trio . . .Cleve Asbury, Brian O'Brien, David Villella
Pawnee Bill (Maj. Gordon Lillie) .Gerry Vichi
Band Leader . . . . .Marvin Laird
Mrs. Schyler Adams . . . . .Deanna Dys
Sylvia Potter-Porter . . . . .Kimberly Dawn Neumann
Ensemble . . . . .Madeleine Ehlert, Jason Gillman, Elisa Heinsohn, Hollie Howard, Desiree Parkman, Rommy Sandhu, Kelli Bond Severson, Patrick Wetzel, Kent Zimmerman

UNDERSTUDIES/STANDBYS: Kevin Bailey (Frank/Sitting Bull/Pawnee Bill/Foster), Michelle Blakely, Valerie Wright (Annie), Karyn Quackenbush (Dolly/Annie), David Hess (Frank), Deanna Dys (Dolly), Carlos Lopez (Tommy), Keri Lee, Hollie Howard, Kimberly Dawn Neumann (Winnie), Brad Bradley, Patrick Wetzel (Charlie/Sitting Bull/Pawnee Bill/Foster), Tom Schmid (Frank/Buffalo Bill) Ashley Rose Orr (Jessie/Nellie/Little Jake), Jennie Rose Baker, Blaire Restaneo (Little Jake), Jewel Restaneo (Jessie/Nellie) SWINGS: Leasen Beth Almquist, Rick Spaans, Kent Zimmerman

Cheryl Ladd, Patrick Cassidy

MUSICAL NUMBERS: There's No Business Like Show Business, Doin' What Comes Natur'lly, The Girl That I Marry, You Can't Get a Man with a Gun, I'll Share It All With You, Moonshine Lullaby, They Say It's Wonderful, My Defenses Are Down, The Trick, Entr'acte: European Tour, Lost in His Arms, Who Do You Love I Hope, I Got the Sun in the Morning, An Old Fashioned Wedding (written for 1966 revival), Anything You Can Do, Finale Ultimo Note: This production omits "Colonel Buffalo Bill", "I'm a Bad Bad Man," "I'm an Indian Too," and shifts the order of other numbers.

A revised version of the 1946 musical in two acts. For original Bdwy production with Ethel Merman, see *Theatre World* Vol. 2. For 1966 revival, also with Merman, see *Theatre World* Vol. 22

*Closed September 1, 2001 after 1,046 performances and 35 previews.

+Succeeded by: 1. Conrad John Schuck 2. Brent Barrett 3. Valerie Wright 4. Eric Sciotto 5. Claci Miller 6. Larry Storch 7. Reba McEntire 8. Blaire Restaneo 9. Kent Zimmerman

Jenny Rose Baker, Reba McEntire, Eddie Brandt, Blaire Restaneo

BEAUTY AND THE BEAST

Music, Alan Menken; Lyrics, Howard Ashman, Tim Rice; Book, Linda Woolverton; Director, Robert Jess Roth; Orchestrations, Danny Troob; Musical Supervision/Vocal Arrangements, David Friedman; Musical Director/Incidental Arrangements, Michael Kosarin; Choreography, Matt West; Set, Stan Meyer; Costumes, Ann Hould-Ward; Lighting, Natasha Katz; Sound, T. Richard Fitzgerald; Hairstylist, David H. Lawrence; Illusions, Jim Steinmeyer, John Gaughan; Prosthetics, John Dods; Fights, Rick Sordelet; Cast Recording, Walt Disney Records; General Manager, Dodger Productions; Production Supervisor, Jeremiah J. Harris; Company Manager, Kim Sellon; Stage Managers, James Harker, John M. Atherlay, Pat Sosnow, Kim Vernace; Presented by Walt Disney Productions; Press, Chris Boneau/Adrian Bryan-Brown, Amy Jacobs, Steven Padla; Previewed from Wednesday, March 9, 1994; Opened in the Palace Theatre on Monday, April 18, 1994*

CAST

Enchantress . . . . .Wendy Oliver
Young Prince . . . . .Tom Pardoe
Beast . . . . .Steve Blanchard
Belle . . . . .Andrea McArdle +1
Lefou . . . . .Gerard McIsaac
Gaston . . . . .Patrick Ryan Sullivan
Three Silly Girls . . . . .Lauren Goler-Kosarin, Pam Klinger, Linda Talcott Lee
Maurice . . . . .J. B. Adams
Cogsworth . . . . .Jeff Brooks
Lumiere . . . . .David deVries
Babette . . . . .Louisa Kendrick
Mrs. Potts . . . . .Barbara Marineau
Chip . . . . .Jonathan Andrew Bleicher, Joseph DiConcetto
Madame de la Grande Bouche . . . . .Judith Moore
Monsieur D'Arque . . . . .Gordon Stanley
Townspeople/Enchanted Objects . . . . .Anna Maria Andricain, Steven Ted Beckler, Kevin Berdini, Andrea Burns, Christophe Caballero, Sally Mae Dunn, Barbara Folts, Teri Furr, Gregory Garrison, Elmore James, Alisa Klein, Lauren Goler-Kosarin, Ellen Hoffman, Pam Klinger, Ken McMullen, Anna McNeely, Beth McVey, Bill Nabel, Wendy Oliver, Tom Pardoe, Raymond Sage, Joseph Savant, Sarah Solie Shannon, Matthew Shepard, Steven Sofia, Gordon Stanley, Linda Talcott Lee, David A. Wood, Wysandria Woolsey
Prologue Narrator . . . . .David Ogden Stiers

Musical Numbers: Overture, Prologue (Enchantress), Belle, No Matter What, Me, Home, Gaston, How Long Must This Go On?, Be Our Guest, If I Can't Love Her, Entr'acte/Wolf Chase, Something There, Human Again, Maison des Lunes, Beauty and the Beast, Mob Song, The Battle, Transformation, Finale

A musical in two acts. An expanded, live action version of the 1992 animated film musical with additional songs. Winner of 1994 "Tony" for Best Costume Design. Since the opening, the role of "Belle" has been played by Susan Egan, Sarah Uriarte, Christianne Tisdale, Kerry Butler, Deborah Gibson, Kim Huber, Toni Braxton, Andrea McArdle, and Sarah Litzsinger. The role of "The Beast" has been played by Terrence Mann, Jeff McCarthy, Chuck Wagner, James Barbour, and Steve Blanchard.

*Still playing May 31, 2001. The production moved to the Lunt-Fontanne Theatre on November 12, 1999.

+Succeeded by: 1. Sarah Litzsinger

Eduardo Patino Photos

Andrea McArdle, Steve Blanchard

CABARET

Music, John Kander; Lyrics, Fred Ebb; Book, Joe Masteroff; Based on the play *I Am a Camera* by John Van Druten and stories by Christopher Isherwood; Director, Sam Mendes; Co-Director/Choreography, Rob Marshall; New Orchestrations, Michael Gibson; Musical Director, Patrick Vaccariello; Set/Club Design, Robert Brill; Costumes, William Ivey Long; Lighting, Peggy Eisenhauer, Mike Baldassari; Sound, Brian Ronan; Dance Arrangements, David Krane, David Baker; Company Manager, Denys Baker; Stage Manager, Peter Hanson; Cast Recording, RCA; Presented by Roundabout Theatre Company (Todd Haimes, Artistic Director; Ellen Richard, General Manager; Gene Feist, Founding Director); Press, Chris Boneau-Adrian Bryan-Brown/Erin Dunn, Jackie Green, Andrew Palladino, Amy Nieporent; Previewed from Friday, February 13, 1998; Opened in the Kit Kat Club (the Henry Miller Theatre) on Thursday, March 19, 1998*

CAST

Emcee . . . . .Matt McGrath

Kit Kat Girls:
Rosie . . . . .Christina Pawl
Lulu . . . . .Victoria Lecta Cave
Frenchie . . . . .Nicole Van Giesen
Texas . . . . .Leenya Rideout
Fritzie . . . . .Victoria Clark
Helga . . . . .Kristin Olness

Kit Kat Boys:
Bobby . . . . .Michael O'Donnell
Victor . . . . .Brian Duguay
Hans . . . . .Richard Costa
Herman . . . . .Fred Rose

Sally Bowles . . . . .Joley Fisher +1
Clifford Bradshaw . . . . .Michael Hayden +2
Ernst Ludwig . . . . .Martin Moran +3
Customs Official/Max . . . . .Fred Rose
Fraulein Schneider . . . . .Carole Shelley
Fraulein Kost . . . . .Candy Buckley
Rudy . . . . .Richard Costa
Herr Schultz . . . . .Dick Latessa
Gorilla . . . . .Christina Pawl
Boy Soprano (recording) . . . . .Alex Bowen

UNDERSTUDIES: Linda Romoff, Victoria Lecta Cave (Sally), Brian Duguay, Michael O'Donnell (Cliff), Fred Rose, Manoel Felciano (Ernst), Vance Avery, Michael Arnold (Emcee), Maureen Moore (Schneider), Scott Robertson (Schultz), Leenya Rideout, Victoria Lecta Cave (Kost)
SWINGS: Linda Romoff, Penny Ayn Maas, Vance Avery, Manoel Felciano, Michael Arnold

A newly revised production of the 1966 musical in two acts. The action takes in Berlin, Germany, 1929–30. Winner of 1998 "Tony" Awards for Actor in a Musical (Alan Cumming), Actress in a Musical (Natasha Richardson), Featured Actor in a Musical (Ron Rifkin), and Best Revival of a Musical. For original Bdwy production with Joel Grey, Jill Haworth, and Lotte Lenya, see *Theatre World* Vol. 23.

+Succeeded by: 1. Lea Thompson, Katie Finneran, Gina Gershon 2. Matthew Greer 3. Peter Benson

*Still playing May 31, 2001. The production moved to Studio 54 on November 12, 1998.

Joan Marcus Photos

Gina Gershon

The Company

Matt McGrath

CHICAGO

Music, John Kander; Lyrics, Fred Ebb; Book, Mr. Ebb, Bob Fosse; Script Adaptation, David Thompson; Based on the play by Maurine Dallas Watkins; Original Production Directed and Choreographed by Bob Fosse; Director, Walter Bobbie; Choreography, Ann Reinking in the style of Bob Fosse; Music Director, Rob Fisher; Orchestrations, Ralph Burns; Set, John Lee Beatty; Costumes, William Ivey Long; Lighting, Ken Billington; Sound, Scott Lehrer; Dance Arrangements, Peter Howard; Cast Recording, RCA; General Manager, Darwell Associates and Maria Di Dia; Company Manager, Scott A. Moore; Stage Managers, Clifford Schwartz, Terrence J. Witter; Presented by Barry & Fran Weissler in association with Kardana Productions; Press, Pete Sanders/Helen Davis, Clint Bond Jr., Glenna Freedman, Bridget Klapinski; Previewed from Wednesday, October 23, 1996; Opened in the Richard Rodgers Theatre on Thursday, November 14, 1996*

CAST

Velma Kelly .... Sharon Lawrence +1
Roxie Hart .... Belle Calaway +2
Fred Casely .... Gregory Mitchell
Sergeant Fogarty .... Michael Kubala
Amos Hart .... P.J. Benjamin +3
Liz .... Michelle M. Robinson
Annie .... Mamie Duncan-Gibbs
June .... Donna Marie Asbury
Hunyak .... Mindy Cooper
Mona .... Caitlin Carter
Matron "Mama" Morton .... Roz Ryan +4
Billy Flynn .... Brent Barrett +5
Mary Sunshine .... R. Bean
Go-To-Hell-Kitty .... Mary Ann Hermansen
Harry .... Sebastian LaCause
Aaron .... David Warren-Gibson
Judge .... Gregory Butler
Martin Harrison/Doctor .... Denis Jones
Court Clerk .... John Mineo
The Jury .... Michael Kubala

UNDERSTUDIES/STANDBYS: Nancy Hess (Velma/Roxie), Caitlin Carter (Roxie), Amy Spanger, Donna Marie Asbury (Roxie/Velma), John Mineo (Amos), Mamie Duncan-Gibbs (Mama/Velma), Michael Berresse (Billy), Michael Kubala (Billy/Amos), J. Loeffelholz (Mary), Luis Perez (Billy/Fred), Denis Jones (Amos/Fred), Michelle M. Robinson (Mama), Eric L. Christian, Rocker Verastique (Fred), Randy Slovacek (Amos), Deidre Goodwin (Mama), Gregory Butler (Billy/Fred), Mark Anthony Taylor (Fred), Sebastian LaCause (Fred)

Brent Barrett and the Merry Murderesses (Carol Rosegg)

Bebe Neuwirth

MUSICAL NUMBERS: All That Jazz, Funny Honey, Cell Block Tango, When You're Good to Mama, Tap Dance, All I Care About, A Little Bit of Good, We Both Reached for the Gun, Roxie, I Can't Do It Alone, My Own Best Friend, Entr'acte, I Know a Girl, Me and My Baby, Mister Cellophane, When Velma Takes the Stand, Razzle Dazzle, Class, Nowadays, Hot Honey Rag, Finale

A new production of the 1975 musical in two acts. This production is based on the staged concert presented by City Center Encores. The action takes place in Chicago, late 1920s. Winner of 1997 "Tony" Awards for Revival of a Musical, Leading Actor in a Musical (James Naughton), Leading Actress in a Musical (Bebe Neuwirth), Direction of a Musical, Choreography, and Lighting. For original Bdwy production with Gwen Verdon, Chita Rivera, and Jerry Orbach, see *Theatre World* Vol. 32.

*Still playing May 31, 2000. Moved to the Shubert Theatre on February 12, 1997.

+Succeeded by: 1. Vicki Lewis, Jasmine Guy, Bebe Neuwirth, Donna Marie Asbury, Deidre Goodwin, Vicki Lewis 2. Charlotte d'Amboise, Belle Calaway, Nana Visitor 3. Tom McGowan 4. Marcia Lewis 5. Chuck Cooper, Clarke Peters

A CHRISTMAS CAROL

Music, Alan Menken; Lyrics, Lynn Ahrens; Book, Mike Ockrent, Lynn Ahrens; Based on the story by Charles Dickens; Director, Mike Ockrent; Choreography, Susan Stroman; Orchestrations, Michael Starobin, Douglas Besterman; Musical Director, Paul Gemignani; Set, Tony Walton; Costumes, William Ivey Long; Lighting, Jules Fisher, Peggy Eisenhauer; Sound, Tony Meola; Projections, Wendall K. Harrington, Flying by Foy; Dance Arrangements, Glen Kelly; Cast Recording, Columbia; Production Supervisor, Richard Bloom; Stage Managers, Steven Zweigbaum, Rolt Smith; Producers, Dodger Endemol Theatricals Productions; Presented by American Express; Press, Cathy Del Priore; Original Production opened in the Paramount Theatre on Thursday, December 1, 1994; Seasonal re-opening in The Theater at Madison Square Garden on Friday, November 24, 2000*

Frank Langella

PRINCIPAL CAST

Scrooge . . . . .Frank Langella
Ghost of Christmas Present . . . . .D'Ambrose Boyd
Ghost of Christmas Past . . . . .Ken Jennings
Ghost of Christmas Future .Christine Dunham
Bob Cratchit . . . . .Nick Corley

Musical Numbers: A Jolly Good Time, Nothing to Do with Me, You Mean More to Me, Street Song, Link by Link, Lights of Long Ago, God Bless Us Everyone, A Place Called Home, Mr. Fezziwig's Annual Christmas Ball, Abundance and Charity, Christmas Together, Dancing on Your Grave, Yesterday Tomorrow and Today, London Town Carol, Final Medley

Seventh annual return of a musical performed without intermission. The action takes place in London, 1880. Actors previously playing the lead role of Scrooge were Walter Charles ('94), Terrence Mann ('95), Tony Randall ('96), and Hal Linden/Roddy McDowall ('97), Roger Daltrey ('98), and Tony Roberts ('99).

*Closed December 31, 2000 after seasonal run.

The Company

CONTACT

By Susan Stroman (Director/Choreography) and John Weidman (Writer); Set, Thomas Lynch; Costumes, William Ivey Long; Lighting, Peter Kaczorowski; Sound, Scott Stauffer; Casting, Johnson-Liff Associates, Tara Rubin, Daniel Swee; Production Stage Manger, Thom Widmann; Recording, RCA; Presented by Lincoln Center Theater (André Bishop, Artistic Director; Bernard Gersten, Executive Producer); Press, Philip Rinaldi/Miller Wright, James A. Babcock; Previewed from Thursday, March 2, 2000; Opened in the Vivian Beaumont on Thursday, March 30, 2000*

Stephanie Michels, Seán Martin Hingston

Jason Antoon +1	Dana Stackpole	Angelique Ilo
Peter Gregus	Holly Cruikshank	Robert Wersinger
Stephanie Michels	Seán Martin Hingston	Steve Geary
John Bolton	Scott Taylor	David MacGillivray
Shannon Hammons	Pascale Faye	Deborah Gates
Mayumi Miguel	Stacey Todd Holt	Nina Goldman
Tomé Cousin	Rocker Verastique	Joanne Manning
Jack Hayes	Boyd Gaines	Karen Ziemba

CAST

Understudies: John Bolton, Steve Geary, Stacey Todd Holt, Robert Wersinger (Frenchmen), Holly Cruikshank, Shannon Hammons, Angelique Ilo, Joanne Manning (Girl on a Swing), Holly Cruikshank, Nina Goldman, Angelique Ilo (Wife), John Bolton, Peter Gregus, Stacey Todd Holt (Husband), Steve Geary, Scott Taylor, Rocker Verastique (Headwaiter), Scott Taylor (Michael Wiley), Joanne Manning (Girl in a Yellow Dress), John Bolton, Stacey Todd Holt (Bartender)
Standbys: John Bolton (Michael Wiley), Holly Cruikshank (Girl in a Yellow Dress)
Swings: Steve Geary, Stacey Todd Holt; Angelique Ilo, Joanne Manning

A dance play in three short parts: *Swinging, Did You Move?,* and *Contact.* Winner of 2000 "Tony" Awards for Best Musical, Featured Actor in a Musical (Boyd Gaines), Featured Actress in a Musical (Karen Ziemba), and Choreography.

*Closed September 1, 2002 after 1,009 performances. Prior to Bdwy, the production played in Off-Bdwy's Mitzi E. Newhouse Theatre from September 9, 1999–January 2, 2000.

+Succeeded by: 1. Danny Mastrogiorgio

Paul Kolnik Photos

The Company

DIRTY BLONDE

By Claudia Shear; Conceived by Claudia Shear and James Lapine; Director, Mr. Lapine; Musical Staging, John Carrafa; Sets, Douglas Stein; Costumes, Susan Hilferty; Lighting, David Lander; Sound, Dan Moses Schreier; Arrangements/Musical Direction, Bob Stillman; Production Stage Manager, Leila Knox; Presented by The Shubert Organization, Chase Mishkin, Ostar Enterprises, ABC, Inc. in association with New York Theatre Workshop; Press, Richard Kornberg/Don Summa; Previewed from Friday, April 14, 2000; Opened in The Helen Hayes Theatre on Monday, May 1, 2000*

Tom Riis Farrell, Claudia Shear

CAST

Frank Wallace, Ed Hearn, and others . . . . .Bob Stillman
Jo, Mae . . . . .Claudia Shear +1
Charlie and others . . . . .Kevin Chamberlin +2

UNDERSTUDIES: Nora Mae Lyng (Jo/Moe), Paul Amodeo (Frank Wallace/ Ed Hearn/Others), Kevin Carolan (Charlie/Others)

A play about a gal, a guy, and Mae West, performed without intermission. The production was seen earlier this season at Off-Bdwy's New York Theatre Workshop.

*Closed March 4, 2001 after 352 performances and 20 previews.

+Succeeded by: 1. Kathy Najimy 2. Tom Riis Farrell

Joan Marcus Photos

Kathy Najimy

FOSSE

Conceived by Richard Maltby Jr., Chet Walker, and Ann Reinking; Artistic Advisor, Gwen Verdon; Choreography, Bob Fosse; Director, Richard Maltby Jr.; Co-Director/Co-Choreographer, Ann Reinking; Choreography Recreated by Chet Walker; Orchestrations, Ralph Burns, Douglas Besterman; Musical Arrangements, Gordon Lowry Harrell; Musical Director, Patrick S. Brady; Sets/Costumes, Santo Loquasto; Lighting, Andrew Bridge; Sound, Jonathan Deans; Cast Recording, RCA; Company Manager, Steve Quinn; Stage Managers, Mary Porter Hall, Lori Lindquist, Mary Harwell; Presented by Livent (U.S.); Press, Mary Bryant/ Wayne Wolfe; Previewed from Saturday, December 26, 1998; Opened in the Broadhurst Theatre on Thursday, January 14, 1999*

CAST

Guest Principals . . . . .Ben Vereen, Anne Reinking, Bebe Neuwirth

Ken Alan
Greg Graham
Julio Monge
Brad Anderson
Kim Morgan Greene
Dana Moore
Mark Arvin
Francesca Harper
Sharon Moor
Ashley Bachner
Suzanne Harrer
Jill Nicklaus

Julio Boca
Anne Hawthorne
Elizabeth Parkinson
Bill Burns
Scott Jovovich
Valarie Pettiford
Lynne Calamia
James Kinney
Stephanie Pope
Marc Calamia
Dede LaBarre
Rachelle Rak
J.P. Christensen
Mary Ann Lamb
Mark C. Reis
Angel Creeks
Susan LaMontagne
Keith Richard
Dylis Croman
Jane Lanier
Desmond Richardson
Byron Easley
Lorin Latarro
Sergio Trujillo
Parker Esse
Robin Lewis
Christopher Windom
Eugene Fleming
Edwaard Liang
Scott Wise
Meg Gillentine
Mary MacLeod

Musical Numbers: Life Is Just a Bowl of Cherries, Fosse's World, Bye Bye Blackbird, From the Edge, Percussion 4, Big Spender, Crunchy Granola Suite, Hooray for Hollywood, From This Moment On, Alley Dance, I Wanna Be a Dancin' Man, Shoeless Joe from Hannibal Mo., Dancing in the Dark, I Love a Piano, Steam Heat, I Gotcha, Rich Man's Frug, Cool Hand Luke, Big Noise from Winnetka, Dancin' Dan (Me and My Shadow), Nowadays, Hot Honey Rag, Glory, Manson Trio, Mein Herr, Take Off with Us-Three Pas De Deux, Razzle Dazzle, Who's Sorry Now?, They'll Be Some Changes Made, Mr. Bojangles, Sing Sing Sing
During Tryout: Beat Me Daddy Eight to the Bar

A musical revue in three acts. The dances come from the varied career of choreographer/director Bob Fosse, including numbers originally created for television and films, as well as Mr. Fosse's stage works.

*Closed August 25, 2001 after 1,100 performances and 22 previews.

Joan Marcus Photos

The Company

The Company

Sharron Lewis (center) and Company

JEKYLL & HYDE

Music, Frank Wildhorn; Lyrics/Book, Leslie Bricusse; Conceived for the stage by Steve Cuden and Mr. Wildhorn; Based on the 1886 novella *The Strange Case of Dr. Jekyll and Mr. Hyde* by Robert Louis Stevenson; Director, Robin Phillips; Orchestrations, Kim Scharnberg; Musical Director, Jason Howland; Musical Supervisor, Jeremy Roberts; Set, Mr. Phillips, James Noone; Costumes, Ann Curtis; Lighting, Beverly Emmons; Choreography, Joey Pizzi; Sound, Karl Richardson, Scott Stauffer; Vocal Arrangements, Mr. Howland, Ron Melrose; Special Effects, Gregory Meeh; Wigs, Paul Huntley; Fights, J. Allen Suddeth; Cast Recording, Atlantic; General Manager, Niko Associates; Company Manager, Bruce Klinger; Stage Managers, Maureen F. Gibson, David Hyslop; Presented by PACE Theatrical Group and FOX Theatricals, in association with Jerry Frankel, Magicworks Entertainment and The Landmark Entertainment Group; Press, Richard Kornberg/Rick Miramontez, Don Summa, Jim Byk; Previewed from Friday, March 21, 1997; Opened in the Plymouth Theatre on Monday, April 28, 1997*

David Hasselhoff

Coleen Sexton, Sebastian Bach

CAST

John Utterson .George Merritt
Sir Danvers Carew .Barrie Ingram
Dr. Hanry Jekyll/Edward Hyde .Sebastian Bach +1 Joseph Mahowald (matinee)
Davie/Old Man/Manservant/Mr. Biset/Priest .David Chaney
Doctor/Lord G/Poole .Peter Johl
Kate .Christy Tarr
Alice/Maid/Whore/Bridemaid Corinne Melançon
Molly .Rebecca Baxter
Bet/Maid/Young Girl/Bridemaid .Kate Shindle
Polly/Whore .Bonnie Schon
Mike/Groom .John Treacy Egan
Albert/Gent/Priest .Craig Schulman
Ned/Patient/Tough .John Schiappa
Bill/Patient/Groom/Tough/Newsboy .Juan Betancur
Jack/Footman/Tough/Doorman/Curate .Russell B. Warfield
Simon Stride .Robert Jensen
Rupert/Sir Douglas/Police .Joel Robertson
Right Honorable Archibald Proops/Gent/Sir Peter .Brad Oscar
Lord Savage/The Spider .Martin Van Treuren
Lady Beaconsfield/Guinevere .Rebecca Spencer
Gen. Lord Glossop/Siegfried/Police .Stuart Marland
Emma Carew .Andrea Rivette
Lucy/Boy Soprano at Wedding .Coleen Sexton

UNDERSTUDIES: Robert Jensen (Jekyll/Hyde), Craig Schulman (Jekyll/Hyde/Utterson/Bishop), Whitney Allen (Lucy/Emma), Kate Shindle (Lucy), Christy Tarr (Emma), John Treacy Egan (Utterson), Stuart Marland (Utterson/Poole), Peter Johl, Martin Van Treuren (Danvers), Corinne Melançon, Bonnie Schon (Lady Beaconsfield/Guinevere), Brad Oscar (Poole), John Treacy Egan (Glossop), Douglas Ladnier (Glossop/Bishop/Savage/Spider/Stride), John Schiappa (Savage/Spider/Stride), Juan Betancur, Carmen Yurich (Proops)

SWINGS: Whitney Allen, Douglas Ladnier, Carmen Yurich, Rebecca Baxter

MUSICAL NUMBERS: Lost in the Darkness, Facade, Jekyll's Plea, Emma's Reasons, Take Me As I Am, Letting Go, No One Knows Who I Am, Good 'N' Evil, This Is the Moment, Alive, His Work and Nothing More, Someone Like You, Murder Murder, Once Upon a Dream, Obsession, In His Eyes, Dangerous Game, The Way Back, A New Life, Sympathy Tenderness, Confrontation, Dear Lord and Father of Mankind

PRE-BROADWAY: Board of Governors, Bring on the Men, Girls of the Night

A musical in two acts. The action takes place in London.

*Closed January 7, 2001 after 1,543 performances and 44 previews.

+Succeeded by: 1. David Hasselhoff

KISS ME, KATE

Music/Lyrics, Cole Porter; Book, Sam and Bella Spewack; Director, Michael Blakemore; Choreography, Kathleen Marshall; Musical Director, Paul Gemignani; Set, Robin Wagner, Costumes, Martin Pakledinaz; Lighting, Pete Kaczorowski; Sound, Tony Meola; Orchestrations, Don Sebesky; Dance Arrangements, David Chase; Casting, Johnson-Liff Associates; Fight Direction, B.H. Barry; Production Supervision, Steven Zweigbaum; Production Manager, Arthur Siccardi; Cast Recording, DRG; Presented by Roger Berlind and Roger Horchow; Press, Chris Boneau-Adrian Bryan-Brown/Amy Jacobs, Matt Polk; Previewed from Monday, October 25, 1999; Opened in the Martin Beck Theatre on Thursday, November 18, 1999*

CAST

Hattie . . . . .Mamie Duncan-Gibbs
Paul Stanley . . . . .Stanley Wayne Mathis
Ralph (Stage Manager) . . . . .Eric Michael Gillett
Lois Lane . . . . .Amy Spanger +1
Bill Calhoun . . . . .Michael Berresse +2
Lilli Vanessi . . . . .Marin Mazzie +3
Fred Graham . . . . .Brian Stokes Mitchell +4
Dance Captain . . . . .Vince Pesce
Harry Trevor . . . . .Herb Foster
Pops (Stage Doorman) . . . . .Robert Ousley
Cab Driver . . . . .Lee A. Wilkins
First Man . . . . .Lee Wilkof +5
Second Man . . . . .Michael Mulheren
Harrison Howell . . . . .Ron Holgate +6
"Taming of the Shrew" Players
Bianca (Lois Lane) . . . . .Amy Spanger +1
Baptista (Harry Trevor) . . . . .Herb Foster
Gremio (First Suitor) . . . . .Brad Andreson
Hortensio (Second Suitor) . . . . .Michael Gruber
Lucentio (Bill Calhoun) . . . . .Michael Berresse +2
Katharine (Lilli Vanessi) . . . . .Marin Mazzie +3
Petruchio (Fred Graham) . . . . .Brian Stokes Mitchell +4
Nathaniel . . . . .Lee A. Wilkins
Gregory . . . . .Vince Pesce
Philip . . . . .Kevin Ligon
Haberdasher . . . . .Michael X. Martin
Ensemble . . . . .Brad Anderson, Eric Michael Gillett, Patty Goble, Michael Gruber, Blake Hammond, Ashley Hull, JoAnn M. Hunter, Lorin Latarro, Nancy Lemenager, Darren Lee, Kevin Ligon, Michael X. Martin, Kevin Neil McCready, Carol Lee Meadows, Corinne Melançon, Elizabeth Mills, Linda Mugleston, Robert Ousley, Vince Pesce, Cynthia Sophiea, Jerome Vivona, Lee A. Wilkins

Understudies: Michael X. Martin (Fred/Petruchio), Patty Goble (Lilli/Katharine), JoAnn M. Hunter, Nancy Lemenager (Lois/Bianca), Kevin Neil McCready (Bill/Lucentio), Cynthia Sophiea (Hattie), Robert Ousley (Harry/Baptista), T. Oliver Reid (Paul), Blake Hammond (First Man), Blake Hammond, Michael X. Martin (Second Man), Michael X. Martin (Harrison Howell), Vince Pesce, T. Oliver Reid (Hortensio), Jerome Vivona, T. Oliver Reid (Gremio)
Swings: Paula Leggett Chase, Tripp Hanson, T. Oliver Reid
Standbys: Harrison Howell, Merwin Foard (Fred/Petruchio)

Musical Numbers: Another Op'nin' Another Show, Why Can't You Behave, Wunderbar, So in Love, We Open in Venice, Tom, Dick or Harry, I've Come to Wive it Wealthily in Padua, I Hate Men, Were Thine That Special Face, Cantiamo D'Amore, Kiss Me, Kate, Too Darn Hot, Where Is the Life That Late I Led?, Always True to You (In My Fashion), From This Moment On, Bianca, Brush Up Your Shakespeare, Pavane, I Am Ashamed That Women Are So Simple

Marin Mazzie, Brian Stokes Mitchell, Amy Spanger, Michael Berresse

Burke Moses, Carolee Carmello

A new production of the 1948 musical in two acts. The action takes place in the Ford Theatre, Baltimore, Maryland in June 1948. Winner of 2000 "Tony" Awards for Best Revival of a Musical, Director of a Musical, Actor in a Musical (Brian Stokes Mitchell), Costume Design, and Orchestrations. For original Bdwy production with Alfred Drake, Patricia Morrison, Lisa Kirk, and Harold Lang, see *Theatre World* Vol. 5

*Closed December 30, 2001 after 885 performances and 28 previews.

Succeeded by: 1. JoAnn Hunter, Janine LaManna 2. David Elder, Michael Berresse, Kevin Neil McCready 3. Carolee Carmello 4. Burke Moses 5. Michael McCormick
6. Walter Charles

Joan Marcus Photos

LES MISERABLES

By Alain Boublil and Claude-Michel Schonberg; Based on the novel by Victor Hugo; Music, Mr. Schonberg; Lyrics, Herbert Kretzmer; Original French Text, Mr. Boublil and Jean-Marc Natel; Additional Material, James Fenton; Direction/Adaptation, Trevor Nunn and John Caird; Orchestration Score, John Cameron; Musical Supervisor/Director, Dale Rieling; Executive Musical Director, David Caddick; Design, John Napier; Lighting, David Hersey; Costumes, Andreane Neofitou; Sound, Andrew Bruce/Autograph; Casting, Johnson-Liff & Zerman; Resident Director, Ron LaRosa, Jason Moore; Cast Recording, Geffen; General Manager, Alan Wasser; Company Manager, Robert Nolan; Production Supervisor, Marybeth Abel; Stage Managers, Karen Carpenter, Greg Kirsopp, Bryan Landrine, Tom Schilling, Brent Peterson; Associate Producer, Martin McCallum; Executive Producers, David Caddick, Peter Lawrence; Presented by Cameron Mackintosh; Press, Publicity Office/Marc Thibodeau, Bob Fennell, Michael S. Borowski, Brett Oberman; Previewed from Saturday, February 28, 1987; Opened in the Broadway Theatre on Thursday, March 12, 1987*

CAST

Prologue: J. Mark McVey +1(Jean Valjean), Greg Edelman +2 (Javert), Gary Moss, David McDonald, Paul Truckey, Christopher Eid, Chris Diamantopoulos, Joe Paparella, Stephen R. Buntrock, Peter Lockyer, Nick Wyman (Chain Gang), Mr. Paparella (Farmer), Kurt Kovalenko (Labourer), Ann Arvia (Innkeeper's Wife), Andrew Varela (Innkeeper), David Benoit (Bishop), Kevin Kern, Kevin Earley, Christopher Mark Peterson (Constables)
Montreuil-Sur-Mer 1823: Jane Bodle +3 (Fantine), Mr. McDonald (Foreman), Mr. Varela, Mr. Diamantopoulos (Workers), Dana Meller, Erika MacLeod, Gina Lamparella, Alexandra Foucard, Catherine Brunell (Women Workers), Holly Jo Crane (Factory Girl), Mr. Eid, Mr. Moss, Mr. Diamantopoulos (Sailors), Ms. Arvia , Ms. MacLeod, Ms. Foucard, Ms. Brunell, Ms. Meller, Ms. Crane, Megan Lawrence, Tobi Foster (Whores), Becky Barta (Old Woman), Ms. Lamparella (Crone), Mr. Peterson (Pimp), Mr. Truckey (Bamatabois), Mr. Kern (Fauchelevent), Mr. Moss (Champmathieu)
Montfermeil 1823: Christiana Anbri, Ashley Rose Orr, Cristina Faicco, Lisa Musser (Young Cosette/Young Eponine), Betsy Joslyn (Mme. Thenardier), Nick Wyman (Thenardier), Mr. Varela (Drinker), Mr. Eid, Ms. Foucard (Young Couple), Mr. Kern (Drunk), Mr. Benoit, Ms. MacLeod (Diners), Mr. Paparella, Mr. Peterson, Mr. Truckey (Drinkers), Mr. Moss (Young Man), Ms. Meller, Ms. Lamprella (Young Girls), Ms. Brunell, Mr. Diamantopoulos (Old Couple), Mr. McDonald, Mr. Kovalenko (Travelers)
Paris 1832: Patrick J.P. Duffey, Cameron Bowen (Gavroche), Ms. Barta (Beggar Woman), Ms. Meller (Young Prostitute), Mr. McDonald (Pimp), Catherine Brunell (Eponine), Mr. Benoit (Montparnasse), Mr. Kovalenko (Babet), Mr. Moss (Brujon), Mr. Paprella (Claquesous), Mr. Peterson (Enjolras), Peter Lockyer (Marius), Tobi Foster (Cosette), Mr. McDonald (Combeferre), Mr. Eid (Feuilly), Mr. Varela (Courfeyrac), Mr. Diamantopoulos (Joly), Mr. Truckey (Grantaire), Mr. Earley (Lesgles), Mr. Kern (Jean Prouvaire), Mr. Diamantopoulos (Major Domo)
Understudies: Mr. Moss, Mr. Varela (Valjean), Mr. McDonald, Mr. Truckey (Javert), Mr. Brandt, Mr.Watkins (Bishop), Ms. Crane, Ms. Foucard, Ms. MacLeod, Ms. Zimmerman (Fantine), Mr. Benoit, Mr. Colella, Mr. McDonald, Mr. Paparella (Thenardier), Ms. Arvia, Ms. Barta, Ms. Doherty, Ms. Glushak, Ms. Tolpegin (Mme. Thenardier), Ms. Brunell, Ms. (Sutton) Foster, Ms. Lawrence, Ms. Meller (Eponine), Diane DiCroce, Ms. Lamparella, Ms. Meller, Ms. Nichols (Cosette), Mr. Diamantopoulos, Mr. Foster, Mr. Kern (Marius), Mr. Brandt, Mr. Early, Mr. Kovalenko, Mr. Peterson, Mr. Thorn (Enjolras), Mr. Duffey (Gavroche), Ms. Kalehoff, Ms. Morton (Young Eponine)
Swings: Greggory Brandt, Angela DeCicco, Julia Haubner, Pete Herber, Dave Hugo, Cathy Nichols, Clif Thorn, Jeffrey Scott Watkins

The Company

Musical Numbers: Prologue, Soliloquy, At the End of the Day, I Dreamed a Dream, Lovely Ladies, Who Am I?, Come to Me, Castle on a Cloud, Master of the House, Thenardier Waltz, Look Down, Stars, Red and Black, Do You Hear the People Sing?, In My Life, A Heart Full of Love, One Day More, On My Own, A Little Fall of Rain, Drink with Me to Days Gone By, Bring Him Home, Dog Eats Dog, Soliloquy, Turning, Empty Chairs at Empty Tables, Wedding Chorale, Beggars at the Feast, Finale

A dramatic musical in two acts with four scenes and a prologue.

*Closed May 18, 2003 after 6,680 performances. Moved to the Imperial Theatre on October 18, 1990. At closing, the show was the second longest-running Bdwy show of all time (second only to *Cats*). Winner of 1987 "Tonys" for Best Musical, Best Score, Best Book, Best Featured Actor and Actress in a Musical (Michael Maguire, Frances Ruffelle), Direction of a Musical, Scenic Design, and Lighting.

+Succeeded by: 1. Ivan Rutherford 2. Shuler Hensley 3. Jacquelyn Piro

Joan Marcus Photos

THE LION KING

Music, Elton John; Lyrics, Tim Rice; Additional Music/Lyrics, Lebo M, Mark Mancina, Jay Rifkin, Julie Taymor, Hans Zimmer; Book, Roger Allers and Irene Mecchi adapted from screenplay by Ms. Mecchi, Jonathan Roberts and Linda Woolverton; Director, Julie Taymor; Choreography, Garth Fagan; Orchestrations, Robert Elhai, David Metzger, Bruce Fowler; Music Director, Joseph Church; Set, Richard Hudson; Costumes, Julie Taymor; Lighting, Donald Holder; Masks/Puppets, Julie Taymor and Michael Curry; Sound, Tony Meola; Vocal Arrangements/Choral Director, Lebo M; Cast Recording, Disney; Company Manager, Steven Chaikelson; Stage Manager, Jeff Lee; Presented by Walt Disney Theatrical Productions (Peter Schneider, President; Thomas Schumacher, Executive VP); Press, Chris Boneau-Adrian Bryan-Brown/Jackie Green, Patty Onagan, Colleen Hughes; Previewed from Wednesday, October 15, 1997; Opened in the New Amsterdam Theatre on Thursday, November 13, 1997*

Sheila Gibbs

CAST

Rafiki . . . . .Sheila Gibbs
Mufasa . . . . .Samuel E. Wright
Sarabi . . . . .Denise Marie Williams
Zazu . . . . .Tony Freeman
Scar . . . . .Derek Smith
Young Simba . . . . .Mykel Bath
Young Nala . . . . .Leovina Charles
Shenzi . . . . .Vanessa S. Jones +1
Banzai . . . . .Leonard Joseph
Ed . . . . .Timothy Gulan
Timon . . . . .John E. Brady
Pumba . . . . .Tom Alan Robbins
Simba . . . . .Christopher Jackson
Nala . . . . .Sharon L. Young
Ensemble Singers. . . . . .Eugene Barry-Hill, Gina Breedlove, Ntomb'khona Dlamini, Sheila Gibbs, Lindiwe Hlengwa, Christopher Jackson, Vanessa A. Jones, Faca Kulu, Ron Kunene, Anthony Manough, Philip Dorian McAdoo, Sam McKelton, Lebo M, Nandi Morake, Rachel Tecora Tucker
Ensemble Dancers . . . . .Camille M. Brown, Iresol Cardona, Mark Allan Davis, Lana Gordon, Timothy Hunter, Michael Joy, Aubrey Lynch II, Karine Plantadit-Bageot, Endalyn Taylor-Shellman, Levensky Smith, Ashi K. Smythe, Christine Yasunaga

UNDERSTUDIES/SWINGS: Sheila Gibbs, Lindiwe Hlengwa (Rafiki), Eugene Barry-Hill, Philip Dorian McAdoo (Mufasa), Camille M. Brown, Vanessa A. Jones (Sarabi), Kevin Cahoon, Danny Rutigliano (Zazu/Timon), Kevin Bailey (Scar), Kai Braithwaite (Young Simba), Jennifer Josephs (Young Nala), Lana Gordon, Vanessa A. Jones (Shenzi), Philip Dorian McAdoo, Levensky Smith (Banzai), Frank Wright II (Ed), Philip Dorian McAdoo, Danny Rutigliano (Pumba), Timothy Hunter, Christopher Jackson (Simba), Lindiwe Hlengwa, Sonya Leslie (Nala)

MUSICAL NUMBERS: Circle of Life, Morning Report, I Just Can't Wait to Be King, Chow Down, They Live in You, Be Prepared, Hakuna Matata, One By One, Madness of King Scar, Shadowland, Endless Night, Can You Feel the Love Tonight, King of Pride Rock/Finale

A musical in two acts. Winner of 1998 "Tony" Awards for Best Musical, Direction of a Musical, Scenic Design, Costume Design, Lighting, and Choreography.

*Still playing May 31, 2001.

+Succeeded by: 1. Lana Gordon

THE MUSIC MAN

Book/Music/Lyrics, Meredith Willson; Story, Meredith Willson and Franklin Lacey; Director, Susan Stroman; Set, Thomas Lynch; Costumes, William Ivey Long; Lighting, Peter Kaczorowski; Sound, Jonathan Deans; Production Supervisor, Steven Zweigbaum; Casting, Jay Binder; Musical Supervision and Direction, David Chase; Orchestrations, Doug Besterman; Cast Recording, Q Records; Presented by Dodger Theatricals, The John F. Kennedy Center for the Performing Arts, Elizabeth Williams/ Anita Waxman, Kardana-Swinsky Productions, Lorie Cowen Levy/Dede Harris; Press, Chris Boneau-Adrian Bryan-Brown/Susanne Tighe, Amy Jacobs, Matt Polk; Previewed from Wednesday, April 5, 2000; Opened in the Neil Simon Theatre on Thursday, April 27, 2000*

CAST

Conductor .... Andre Garner
Charlie Cowell .... Ralph Byers
Traveling Salesmen .... Liam Burke, Kevin Bogue, E. Clayton Cornelious, Michael Duran, Blake Hammond, Michael McGurk; Dan Sharkey, John Sloman
Harold Hill .... Craig Bierko +1
Olin Britt .... Michael-Leon Wooley
Amaryllis .... Jordan Puryear
Maud Dunlop .... Martha Hawley
Ewart Dunlop .... Jack Doyle
Mayor Shinn .... Paul Benedict +2
Alma Hix .... Leslie Hendrix
Ethel Toffelmier .... Tracy Nicole Chapman
Oliver Hix .... John Sloman
Jacey Squires .... Blake Hammond
Marcellus Washburn .... Max Casella +3
Tommy Djilas .... Clyde Alves +4
Marian Paroo .... Rebecca Luker
Mrs. Paroo .... Katherine McGrath
Winthrop Paroo .... Michael Phelan
Eulalie Mackecknie Shinn .... Ruth Williamson +5
Zaneeta Shinn .... Kate Levering +6
Gracie Shinn .... Ann Whitlow Brown
Mrs. Squires .... Ann Brown
Constable Locke .... Kevin Bogue
Residents of River City . . . Cameron Adams, Kevin Bogue, Sara Brenner, Chase Brock, Liam Burke, E. Clayton Cornelious, Michael Duran, Andre Garner, Ellen Harvey, Mary Illes, Joy Lynn Matthews, Michael McGurk, Robbie Nicholson, Ipsite Paul, Pamela Remler, Dan Sharkey, Lauren Ullrich, Travis Wall

UNDERSTUDIES: John Sloman (Harold Hill), Mary Illes, Cynthia Leigh Heim (Marion Paroo), Kevin Bogue (Marcellus Washburn), Ralph Byers, Jack Doyle (Mayor Shinn), Leslie Hendrix, Ellen Harvey (Eulalie Mackecknie Shinn), Martha Hawley, Ellen Harvey (Mrs. Paroo), Travis Wall, Lauren Ullrich (Winthrop Paroo), Lauren Ullrich, Sarah Brenner (Amaryllis), Jeff Williams (Charlie Cowell), Chase Brock, Michael McGurk (Tommy Djilas), Sara Brenner, Jennie Ford (Zaneeta Shinn), Cameron Adams, Sara Brenner (Gracie Shinn), Dan Sharkey, Kevin Bogue (Olin Britt), Michael Duran, Jeff Williams (Ewart Dulop), Jeff Williams, Dan Sharkey (Oliver Hix), Andre Garner, Michael Duran (Jacey Squires), Ellen Harvey, Joy Lynn Matthews (Maud Dunlop), Cynthia Leigh Heim, Ellen Harvey (Alma Hix), Cynthia Leigh Heim, Joy Lynn Matthews (Mrs. Squires), Joy Lynn Matthews, Ipsita Paul (Ethel Toffelmier)
STANDBYS: Jim Walton (Harold Hill/Marcellus Washburn/Charlie Cowell)
SWINGS: Jennie Ford, Cynthia Leigh Heim, Jason Snow, Jeff Williams

Rebecca Luker, Craig Bierko, Michael Phelan

Eric McCormack

MUSICAL NUMBERS: Rock Island, Iowa Stubborn, Trouble, Piano Lesson, Goodnight, My Someone, Seventy Six Trombones, Sincere, The Sadder-But-Wiser-Girl, Pickalittle, Goodnight Ladies, Marian the Librarian, Gary, Indiana, My White Knight, The Wells Fargo Wagon, It's You, Lida Rose, Will I Ever Tell You?, Shipoopi, Till There Was You, Finale

A new production of the 1957 musical in two acts. The action takes place in River City, Iowa, 1912. For original Bdwy production with Robert Preston and Barbara Cook, see *Theatre World* Vol. 14.

*Closed December 30, 2001 after 698 performances and 24 previews.

+Succeeded by: 1. Eric McCormack 2. Kenneth Kimmins 3. Joel Blum 4. Manuel Herrera 5. Ruth Gottschall 6. Cameron Adams

Joan Marcus Photos

THE PHANTOM OF THE OPERA

Music, Andrew Lloyd Webber; Lyrics, Charles Hart; Additional Lyrics, Richard Stilgoe; Book, Mr. Stilgoe, Mr. Lloyd Webber; Director, Harold Prince; Musical Staging/Choreography, Gillian Lynne; Orchestrations, David Cullen, Mr. Lloyd Webber; Based on the novel by Gaston Leroux; Design, Maria Björnson; Lighting, Andrew Bridge; Sound, Martin Levan; Musical Direction/Supervision, David Caddick; Conductor, Jack Gaughan; Cast Recording (London), Polygram/Polydor; Casting, Johnson-Liff & Zerman; General Manager, Alan Wasser; Company Manager, Michael Gill; Stage Managers, Steve McCorkle, Bethe Ward, Richard Hester, Barbara-Mae Phillips; Presented by Cameron Mackintosh and The Really Useful Theatre Co.; Press, Merle Frimark, Marc Thibodeau; Previewed from Saturday, January 9; Opened in the Majestic Theatre on Tuesday, January 26, 1988*

CAST

The Phantom of the Opera .Howard McGillin
Christine Daae . . . . .Sarah Pfisterer +2
Adrienne McEwan +2 (alternate)
Raoul, Vicomte de Chagny . . . . .Gary Maurer +3
Carlotta Giudicelli . . . . .Liz McCartney
Monsieur Andre . . . . .Jeff Keller
Monsieur Firmin . . . . .George Lee Andrews
Madame Giry . . . . .Leila Martin
Ubaldo Piangi . . . . .Larry Wayne Morbitt
Meg Giry . . . . .Geralyn Del Corso
M. Reyer . . . . .Richard Poole
Auctioneer . . . . .Richard Warren Pugh
Porter/Marksman . . . . .Maurizio Corbino
M. Lefevre . . . . .Kenneth H. Waller
Joseph Buquet . . . . .Joe Gustern
Don Attilio . . . . .John Kuether
Passarino . . . . .Thomas Sandri
Slave Master . . . . .Daniel Rychlec
Solo Dancer . . . . .Paul B. Sadler Jr.
Flunky/Stagehand . . . . .Jack Hayes
Hairdresser/Marksman . . . . .Gary Lindemann
Policeman . . . . .Thomas Sandri
Page . . . . .Patrice Pickering
Porter/Fireman . . . . .Maurizio Corbino
Spanish Lady . . . . .Wren Marie Harrington
Wardrobe Mistress/Confidante . . . . .Mary Leigh Stahl
Princess . . . . .Elizabeth Southard
Madame Firmin . . . . .Melody Johnson
Innkeeper's Wife . . . . .Johanna Wiseman
Ballet Chorus of the Opera Populaire . . .Emily Addona, Teresa DeRose, Nina Goldman, Elizabeth Nackley, Erin Brooke Reiter, Christine Spizzo, Kate Wray

UNDERSTUDIES: Jeff Keller (Phantom), James Romick (Phantom/Raoul/ Firmin/Andre), Elizabeth Southard (Christine), John Schroeder, Jim Weitzer (Raoul), Richard Warren Pugh (Firmin/Piangi), John Kuether (Firmin), Richard Warren Pugh (Firmin/Piangi), George Lee Andrews, Richard Poole (Andre), Wren Marie Harrington, Johanna Wiseman, Melody Johnson (Carlotta), Susan Russell, Patrice Pickering, Mary Leigh Stahl (Giry), Maurizio Corbino (Piangi), Teresa DeRose, Kate Wray (Meg), Paul B. Sadler, Jr.(Master), Daniel Rychlec (Dancer) SWINGS: Susan Russell, James Romick, Jim Weitzer

Howard McGillin

MUSICAL NUMBERS: Think of Me, Angel of Music, Little Lotte/The Mirror, Phantom of the Opera, Music of the Night, I Remember/Stranger Than You Dreamt It, Magical Lasso, Notes/Prima Donna, Poor Fool He Makes Me Laugh, Why Have You Brought Me Here?/Raoul I've Been There, All I Ask of You, Masquerade/Why So Silent?, Twisted Every Way, Wishing You Were Somehow Here Again, Wandering Child/Bravo Bravo, Point of No Return, Down Once More/Track Down This Murderer, Finale

A musical in two acts with nineteen scenes and a prologue. The action takes place in and around the Paris Opera house, 1881–1911.

*Still playing May 31, 2001. Winner of 1988 "Tonys" for Best Musical, Leading Actor in a Musical (Michael Crawford), Featured Actress in a Musical (Judy Kaye), Direction of a Musical, Scenic Design, and Lighting Design. The title role has been played by Michael Crawford, Timothy Nolen, Cris Groendaal, Steve Barton, Jeff Keller, Kevin Gray, Marc Jacoby, Marcus Lovett, Davis Gaines, Thomas J. O'Leary, Hugh Panaro, and Howard McGillin.

+Succeeded by: 1. Sandra Joseph 2. Lisa Vroman 3. Jim Weitzer

RENT

Music/Lyrics/Book by Jonathan Larson; Director, Michael Greif; Arrangements, Steve Skinner; Musical Supervision/Additional Arrangements, Tim Weill; Choreography, Marlies Yearby; Original Concept/Additional Lyrics, Billy Aronson; Set, Paul Clay; Costumes, Angela Wendt; Lighting, Blake Burba; Sound, Kurt Fischer; Cast Recording, Dreamworks; General Management, Emanuel Azenberg, John Corker; Company Manager, Brig Berney; Stage Managers, John Vivian, Crystal Huntington; Presented by Jeffrey Seller, Kevin McCollum, Allan S. Gordon, and New York Theatre Workshop; Press, Richard Kornberg/ Don Summa, Ian Rand; Previewed from Tuesday, April 16; Opened in the Nederlander Theatre on Monday, April 29, 1996*

CAST

Roger Davis . . . . Norbert Leo Butz +1
Richard H. Blake (alternate)
Mark Cohen . . . . Trey Ellett
Tom Collins . . . . Alan Mingo Jr. +2
Benjamin Coffin III . . . . Stu James
Joanne Jefferson . . . . Natalie Venetia Belcon
Angel Schunard . . . . Jai Rodriguez +3
Mimi Marquez . . . . Loraine Velez
Maureen Johnson . . . . Cristina Fadale
Mark's Mom/Alison/Others . . . . Maggie Benjamin
Christmas Caroler/Mr. Jefferson/Pastor/ Others . . . . Byron Utley
Mrs. Jefferson/Woman with Bags/Others . . . . Aisha de Haas
Gordon/The Man/Mr. Grey/Others . . . . Chad Richardson
Steve/Man with Squeegee/Waiter/Others . . . . Owen Johnston II
Paul/Cop/Others . . . . Robert Glean
Alexi Darling/Roger's Mom/Others . . . . Kim Varhola

UNDERSTUDIES: Dean Balkwill (Roger), Richard H. Blake, Will Chase (Roger/Mark), Calvin Grant (Tom/Benjamin), Byron Utley (Tom), Calvin Grant, Robert Glean (Tom/Benjamin), Darryl Ordell (Benjamin), Shelly Dickinson, Aisha de Haas (Joanne), Shayna Steele (Joanne/Mimi), Sharon Leal (Joanne/Mimi), Juan Carlos Gonzalez, Mark Setlock, Jai Rodriguez (Angel), Jessica Boevers, Maggie Benjamin (Maureen), Kristen Lee Kelly (Maureen), Owen Johnston II (Roger/Angel), Chad Richardson, Peter Matthew Smith (Roger/Mark), Yassmin Alers, Karen Olivo, Julie P. Danao (Mimi/Maureen)

SWINGS: Mr. Blake, Ms. Danao, Mr. Gonzalez, Mr. Grant, Ms. Leal, Ms. Steele

Manley Pope, Loraine Velez

MUSICAL NUMBERS: Tune Up, Voice Mail (#1–#5), Rent, You Okay Honey?, One Song Glory, Light My Candle, Today 4 U, You'll See, Tango: Maureen, Life Support, Out Tonight, Another day, Will I?, On the Street, Santa Fe, We're Okay, I'll Cover You, Christmas Bells, Over the Moon, La Vie Boheme/I Should Tell You, Seasons of Love, Happy New Year, Take Me or Leave Me, Without You, Contact, Halloween, Goodbye Love, What You Own, Finale/Your Eyes

A musical in two acts. The action takes place in New York City's East Village. Winner of 1996 "Tony" Awards for Best Musical, Best Original Score, Best Book of a Musical and Featured Actor in a Musical (Wilson Jermaine Heredia). *Rent* passed its 2,000th Bdwy performance during this season. Tragedy occurred when the 35-year-old author, Jonathan Larson, died of an aortic aneurysm after watching the final dress rehearsal of his show on January 24, 1996.

*Still playing May 31, 2001.

+Succeeded by: 1. Manley Pope 2. Mark Leroy Jackson 3. Andy Senor

RIVERDANCE ON BROADWAY

Director, John McColgan; Producer, Moya Doherty; Music/Lyrics, Bill Whelan; Set, Robert Ballagh; Lighting, Rupert Murray; Costumes, Joan Bergin; Sound, Michael O'Gorman; Orchestrations, Bill Whelan, Nick Ingman and David Downes; Cast Recording, Decca; Presented by Abhann Productions; Press, Merle Frimark; Previewed from Friday, March 3; Opened in the Gershwin Theatre on Thursday, March 16, 2000*

CAST

Brian Kenney +1
Tsidii Le Loka +2
Eileen Martin
Maria Pages
Pat Roddy

The Riverdance Irish Dance Troupe:

Dearbail Bates
Paula Goulding
David O'Hanlon
Natalie Biggs
Conor Hayes
Debbie O'Keeffe
Lorna Bradley
Gary Healy
Ursula Quigley
Martin Brennan
Matt Martin

Kathleen Ryan
Zeph Caissie
Tokiko Masuda
Anthony Savage
Suzanne Clearly
Sinéad McCafferty
Rosemarie Schade
Andrea Curley
Holly McGlinchy
Ryan Sheridan

Marty Dowds
Jonathan McMorrow
Claire Usher
Lindsay Doyle
Joe Moriarty
Leanda Ward
Shannon Doyle
Niall Mulligan
Margaret Williams
Susan Ginnety
Catherine O'Brien

The voice of Liam Neeson

UNDERSTUDIES: Martin Brennan, Suzanne Cleary, Susan Ginnety, Conor Hayes, Sinéad McCafferty, Joe Moriarty

The Company

MUSICAL NUMBERS: Invocation: Hear My Cry, Reel Around the Sun, The Heart's Cry, The Countess Cathleen, Caoineadh Chú Chulainn, Thunderstorm, Shivna, Firedance, At the Edge of the World, Slip Into Spring—The Harvest, Riverdance, American Wake, Lift the Wings, I Will Set You Free, Let Freedom Ring, Morning in Macedonia, The Russian Dervish, Heartbeat of the World—Andalucia, Rí Rá, Homecoming, Endless Journey, Heartland, Finale

A musical revue in two acts. *Riverdance* previously played Radio City Music Hall in 1996, 1997, and 1998.

*Closed August 26, 2001 after 605 performances and 13 previews.

+Succeeded by: 1. Michael Londra 2. Michel Bell

The Company (E.J. Camp)

SATURDAY NIGHT FEVER: THE MUSICAL

Music/Lyrics, The Bee Gees; Based on the Paramount/RSO Picture; Based on a story by Nik Cohn; Sceenplay by Norman Wexler; Stage Adaption, Nan Knighton, in collaboration with Arlene Philips, Paul Nicholas and Robert Stigwood; Director/Choreographer, Arlene Philips; Set, Robin Wagner; Costumes, Andy Edwards; Lighting, Andrew Bridge; Costumes, Suzy Benzinger; Dance and Vocal Arrangements, Phil Edwards; Sound, Mick Potter; Orchestrations, Nigel Wright; Musical Supervision, Phil Edwards; Musical Director, Martyn Axe; Production Supervision, Arthur Siccardi; Fight Director, J. Allen Suddeth; Casting, Bernard Telsey Casting; Production Stage Manager, Perry Cline; Presented by Robert Stigwood; Press, Bill Evans/Jim Randolph, Terry Lilly, Jonathan Schwartz; Previewed from Tuesday, September 28; Opened in the Minskoff Theatre on Thursday, October 21, 1999*

CAST

Tony Manero . . . . James Carpinello +1
Stephanie Mangano . . . . Paige Price
Annette . . . . Orfeh
Bobby C . . . . Paul Castree
Joey . . . . Sean Palmer
Double J . . . . Andy Blankenbuehler
Gus . . . . Richard H. Blake
Monty . . . . Bryan Batt +2
Frank Manero . . . . Casey Nicholaw
Flo Manero/Lucille . . . . Suzanne Costallos
Frank Junior . . . . Jerry Tellier
Fusco/Al . . . . Frank Mastrone
Jay Langhart/Becker . . . . David Coburn
Chester . . . . Andre Ward
Cesar . . . . Michael Balderrama
Vinnie . . . . Chris Ghelfi
Sal . . . . Danial Jerod Brown
Dino . . . . Brian J. Marcum
Lou . . . . Rick Spaans
Dom . . . . Miles Alden
Roberto . . . . Ottavio
Antonio . . . . Drisco Fernandez
Ike . . . . David Robertson
Shirley . . . . Karine Plantadit-Bageot
Maria . . . . Natalie Willes
Connie . . . . Jeanine Meyers
Doreen . . . . Angela Pupello
Linda Manero/Patti . . . . Aliane Baquerot
Gina . . . . Rebecca Sherman
Sophia . . . . Paula Wise
Donna . . . . Shannon Beach
Rosalie . . . . Deanna Dys
Lola . . . . Jennifer Newman
Inez . . . . Danielle Jolie
Lorelle . . . . Stacey Martin
Kenny . . . . Kristoffer Cusick
Nick . . . . Karl duHoffmann
Rocker . . . . Roger Lee Israel
Natalie . . . . Anne Nicole Biancofiore
Ann Marie . . . . Marcia Urani
Angela . . . . Gina Philistine

UNDERSTUDIES: Richard H. Blake, Sean Palmer (Tony Manero), Jeanine Meyers, Angela Pupello (Stephanie Mangano), Jeanine Meyers, Gina Philistine (Annette), Miles Alden, Rick Spaans (Bobby C), Chris Ghelfi, Rick Spaans (Joey), Danial Jerod Brown, Chris Ghelfi (Double J), Miles Alden, Danial Jerod Brown, Kristoffer Cusick (Gus), David Coburn, Jerry Tellier (Monty), David Coburn, Frank Mastrone (Frank Manero), Deanna Dys, Angela Pupello (Flo Manero/Lucille), Karl duHoffmann, Brian J. Marcum (Frank Junior), David Coburn, David Eggers, Brian J. Marcum (Fusco/Al), Karl duHoffmann, David Eggers (Jay Langhart/Becker)

SWINGS: Anne Nicole Biancofiore, Kristoffer Cusick, Karl duHoffmann, David Eggers, Roger Lee Israel, Gina Philistine, Amanda Plesa, Marcia Urani

MUSICAL NUMBERS: Stayin' Alive, Boogie Shoes, Disco Inferno, Night Fever, Disco Duck, More Than a Woman, If I Can't Have You, It's My Neighborhood, You Should be Dancing, Jive Talking, First & Last, Tragedy, What Kind of Fool, Nights on Broadway, Open Sesame, Salsation, Immortality, How Deep is Your Love

A musical in two acts. The action takes place in New York City in 1976.

*Closed December 30, 2000 after 500 performances and 27 previews.

+Succeeded by: 1. Sean Palmer 2. Michael Paternostro

Sean Palmer

Bryan Batt, Orfeh, Sean Palmer, Paige Price, Paul Castree

Joan Marcus Photos

OFF-BROADWAY PRODUCTIONS FROM PAST SEASONS THAT PLAYED THROUGH THIS SEASON

DE LA GUARDA: VILLA VILLA

Created/Directed by Pichon Baldinu and Diqui James; Music/Musical Director, Gabriel Kerpel; Presented by Kevin McCollum, Jeffrey Seller, David Binder and Daryl Roth; Press, Richard Kornberg/Don Summa; Opened in the Daryl Roth Theatre on Tuesday, June 9, 1998*

CAST

Valerie Alonso	Alejandro Garcia	Carlos Casella
Rafael Ferro	Martin Bauer	Gabriel Kerpel
Pichon Baldinu	Diqui James	Fabio D'Aquila
Ana Frenkel	Mayra Bonard	Maria Ucedo
Gabriela Barberio	Tomas James	Julieta Dentone

Performance art presented (in an old bank) without intermission. *Villa Villa* translates roughly, as "by the seat of your pants."

*Still playing May 31, 2001.

De La Guarda: Villa Villa

Julie White, Kevin Kilner, Lisa Emery, Matthew Arkin in *Dinner With Friends*

DINNER WITH FRIENDS

By Donald Margulies; Director, Daniel Sullivan; Set, Neil Patel; Costumes, Jess Goldstein; Lighting, Rui Rita; Sound, Peter Fitzgerald; Sound/Music, Michael Roth; Stage Manager, R. Wade Jackson; Presented by Mitchell Maxwell, Mark Balsam, Ted Tulchin, Victoria Maxwell, Mari Nakachi, Steven Tulchin; Press, John Barlow-Michael Hartman/Andy Shearer; Previewed from Friday, October 22, 1999; Opened in the Variety Arts Theatre on Thursday, November 4, 1999*

CAST

Gabe . . . . .Matthew Arkin
Karen . . . .Lisa Emery +1
Beth . . . . .Julie White +2
Tom . . . . .Kevin Kilner +3
UNDERSTUDIES: Felicity LaFortune (Karen/Beth), Michael Pemberton (Gabe/Tom)

A rueful comedy in two acts. The action takes place in Connecticut, Martha's Vineyard, and Manhattan. Winner of the 2000 Pulitzer Prize for Drama.

*Closed May 27, 2001 after 653 performances and 15 previews.

+Succeeded by: 1. Dana Delany, Sophie Hayden, Lisa Emery 2. Carolyn McCormick 3. Jonathan Walker, John Dossett, John Hillner

The Fantasticks

THE FANTASTICKS

Music, Harvey Schmidt; Lyrics/Book, Tom Jones; Director, Word Baker; Original Musical Director/Arrangements, Julian Stein; Design, Ed Wittstein; Musical Director, Dorothy Martin; Stage Managers, Ken Cook; Presented by Lore Noto; Associate Producers, Sheldon Baron, Dorothy Olim, Jules Field, Cast Recording, Decca; Opened in the Sullivan Street Playhouse on Tuesday, May 3, 1960*

CAST

The Boy (Matt) . . . . .Charles Hagerty
The Girl (Luisa) . . . . .Natasha Harper +1
The Girl's Father . . . . .William Tost
The Boy's Father . . . . .Richard P. Gang
Narrator/El Gallo . . . . .Paul Blankenship
Mute . . . . .Kim Moore
Old Actor . . . . .Bryan Hull
Man Who Dies . . . . .Joel Bernstein
UNDERSTUDIES: Kim Moore (Narrator), Heather Spore (Girl), William Tost (Boy's Father), Richard P. Gang (Girl's Father)

MUSICAL NUMBERS: Overture, Try to Remember, Much More, Metaphor, Never Say No, It Depends on What You Pay, Soon It's Gonna Rain, Abduction Ballet, Happy Ending, This Plumb Is Too Ripe, I Can See It, Plant a Radish, Round and Round, They Were You, Finale

A musical in two acts suggested by *Les Romanesques* by Edmond Rostand.

*Closed January 13, 2002 after 17,162 performances. The world's longest running musical played for 42 years at the 135-seat Sullivan Street Playhouse.

+Succeeded by: 1. Elizabeth Cherry

FORBIDDEN BROADWAY 2001: A SPOOF ODYSSEY

Created/Written/Directed by Gerard Alessandrini; Co-Director, Phillip George; Costumes, Alvin Colt; Set, Bradley Kaye; Musical Director, Brad Ellis; Choreography, Phillip George; Consultant, Pete Blue; General Manager, Jay Kingwell; Stage Manager, Jim Griffith; Cast Recordings, DRG; Presented by John Freedson, Harriet Yellin, Jon B. Platt; Press, Pete Sanders/Glenna Freedman, Clint Bond; This edition opened in the Stardust Theatre on Monday, October 30, 2000*

CAST

Felicia Finley
Danny Gurwin
Tony Nation
Christine Pedi

SUCCEEDING CAST: Carter Calvert, Robert Gallagher, Joel Carlton,
UNDERSTUDIES: William Selby, Gina Kreiezmar

CURRENT PROGRAM INCLUDES: Fake Opening, Forbidden Bdwy 2001, Stewardess, Trouble, Till There Was You & Winthrop, Judi Dench, Cole Porter, I Hate Ben, Cheryll Ladd, Saigon, Ann Reinking, Steam Heat, Stritch, Saturday Night Fever, Contact, Liza/Third Reich, Emcee Cabaret, Times Square, Merman/Elton, Phantom, Sarah Brightman, Copenhagen, Beauty & the Beast, Lion King/Rafreaky, Pain Tonight, Les Miz, Scars, Barbra Streisand, Jekyll & Hyde, Aida (Amneris, Cheesy, Elaborate Sets), 76 Hit Shows Bows & Ta Ta.

Performed in two acts. This season's edition of the parody revue whose first edition originated at Palssons on January 15, 1982. On May 10, 2001 the production moved to The Douglas Fairbanks Theatre.

*Still playing May 31, 2001.

Carol Rosegg Photos

FULLY COMMITTED

By Becky Mode; Based on characters developed by Becky Mode and Mark Setlock; Director, Nicholas Martin; Set, James Noone; Lighting, Frances Aronson; Sound, Bruce Ellman; Stage Manager, Bess Marie Glorioso; Casting, James Calleri; Press, Shirley Herz/Sam Rudy; Previewed from Thursday, September 16; Opened at the Vineyard Theatre on Thursday, September 30, 1999*

CAST

Sam/Others . . . . .Mark Setlock +1

A one-man comedy performed without intermission. The action takes place in the basement of a four star restaurant on the Upper East Side of Manhattan.

*Closed May 27, 2001 after 675 performances (total from both theatres). Moved to the Cherry Lane Theatre on December 14, 1999.

+Succeeded by: 1. Roger Bart, Christopher Fitzgerald

Mark Setlock in *Fully Committed*

Erin Leigh Peck, Cheryl Stern, Jordan Leeds, Kevin Pariseau in *I Love You, You're Perfect, Now Change*

I LOVE YOU, YOU'RE PERFECT, NOW CHANGE

Music/Arrangements, Jimmy Roberts; Lyrics/Book, Joe Dipietro; Director, Joel Bishoff; Musical Director, Tom Fay; Set, Neil Peter Jampolis; Costumes, Candice Donnelly; Lighting, Mary Louise Geiger; Sound, Duncan Edwards; Cast Recording, Varese Sarabande; Production Supervisor, Matthew G. Marholin; Stage Manager, William H. Lang; Presented by James Hammerstein, Bernie Kukoff, and Jonathan Pollard; Press, Bill Evans/Jim Randolph; Previewed from July 15, 1996; Opened in the Westside Theatre/Upstairs on Friday, August 1, 1996*

CAST

Jordan Leeds . . . . .Kevin Pariseau
Andrea Chamberlain . . . . .Cheryl Stern
SUCCEEDING CAST: Lori Hammel, Mylinda Hull, Bob Walton, Adam Hunter, Evy O'Rourke
SWINGS: Ray Roderick, Karyn Quackenbush

MUSICAL NUMBERS: Cantata for a First Date, Stud and a Babe, Single Man Drought, Why Cause I'm a Guy, Tear Jerk, I Will Be Loved Tonight, Hey There Single Guy/Gal, He Called Me, Wedding Vows, Always a Bridesmaid, Baby Song, Marriage Tango, On the Highway of Love, Waiting Trio, Shouldn't I Be Less in Love with You?, I Can Live with That, I Love You You're Perfect Now Change

A two-act musical revue for hopeful heterosexuals. On January 7, 2001, the production played it's 1,848th performance and became the longest running musical revue in Off-Broadway history (besting *Jacques Brel Is Alive and Well and Living in Paris*).

*Still playing May 31, 2001.

Carol Rosegg Photos

LATE NITE CATECHISM

By Vicki Quade and Maripat Donovan; Director, Patrick Trettenero; Design, Marc Silvia; Lighting, Tom Sturge; Stage Manager, Stephen Sweeney; Presented by Entertainment Events and Joe Corcoran Productions; Press, David Rothenberg/David Gersten; Opened in St. Luke's on Thursday, September, 26, 1996*

CAST

Sister . . . . .Patty Hannon
Fr. Martinez . . . . .George Bass

An interactive comedy in two acts. The setting is an adult catechism class.

*Still playing May 31, 2001.

Patty Hannon in *Late Night Catechism*

The Company of *Naked Boys Singing*

NAKED BOYS SINGING!

By Stephen Bates, Marie Cain, Perry Hart, Shelly Markham, Jim Morgan, David Pevsner, Rayme Sciaroni, Mark Savage, Ben Schaechter, Robert Schrock, Trance Thompson, Bruce Vilanch, Mark Winkler; Conceived/ Directed by Robert Schrock; Choreography, Jeffry Denman; Musical Direction/Arrangements, Stephen Bates; Set/Costumes, Carl D. White; Lighting, Aaron Copp; Stage Manager, Christine Catti; Presented by Jamie Cesa, Carl D. White, Hugh Hayes, Tom Smedes, and Jennifer Dumas; Press, Peter Cromarty; Previewed from Friday, July 2, 1999; Opened in the Actors' Playhouse on Thursday, July 22, 1999*

CAST

Glenn Allen +1
Jonathan Brody +2
Tim Burke +3
Daniel C. Levine +4
Sean McNally +5
Adam Michaels +6
Trance Thompson +7
Tom Gualtieri
Patrick Herwood

MUSICAL NUMBERS: Gratuitous Nudity, Naked Maid, Bliss, Window to Window, Fight the Urge, Robert Mitchum, Jack's Song, Members Only, Perky Little Porn Star, Kris Look What You've Missed, Muscle Addiction, Nothin' But the Radio On, The Entertainer, Window to the Soul, Finale/ Naked Boys Singing!

A musical revue in two acts.

*Still playing May 31, 2001.

+Succeeded by: 1. Trevor Richardson, Eric Dean Davis 2. Richard Lear, Steve Sparagen 3. Kristopher Kelly 4. George Livengood 5. Luis Villabon 6. Glen Allen, Patrick Herwood 7. Dennis Stowe, Ralph Cole Jr., Stephan Alexander, Eric Potter

Joan Marcus Photos

OUR SINATRA: A MUSICAL CELEBRATION;

Conceived by Eric Comstock, Christopher Gines, Hilary Kole; Director, Kurt Stamm; Production Supervisor, Richard Maltby Jr.; Set, Troy Hourie; Lighting, Jeff Nellis; Sound, Matt Berman; Stage Manager, Marian DeWitt; Presented by Jack Lewin and Scott Perrin; Press, Tony Origlio/David Lotz; Previewed from Wednesday, December 8, 1999; Opened in the Blue Angel on Sunday, December 19, 1999*

CAST

Eric Comstock +1 Christopher Gines Hilary Kole

Musical Numbers: These Foolish Things, Where or When, Come Rain or Come Shine, I Like to Lead When I Dance, A Lovely Way to Spend An Evening, I Fall in Love Too Easily, Time After Time, All the Way, The Tender Trap, Frome Here to Eternity, You're Sensational, Well Did You Evah?, My Kind of Town, As Long As There's Music, Nice 'n' Easy, I'm a Fool to Want You, Everything Happens to Me, Day In-Day Out, Ol' Man River, Without a Song, One for My Baby, Angel Eyes, In the Wee Small Hours, It Never Entered My Mind, Last Night When We Were Young, At Long Last Love, How Do You Keep the Music Playing, I've Got the World on a String, To Love and Be Loved, The One I Love Belongs to Somebody Else, I Have Dreamed, If You Are But a Dream, The Song Is You, Day by Day, Night and Day, The Way You Look Tonight, They Can't Take That Away, Guess I'll Hang My Tears Out to Dry, I'll Never Smile Again, Come Fly with Me, East of the Sun, Fly Me to the Moon, Lady Is a Tramp, Luck Be a Lady, Here's That Rainy Day, All or Nothing At All, I've Got You Under My Skin, High Hopes, Best Is Yet to Come, I've Got a Crush On You, All My Tomorrows, How Little We Know, Witchcraft, I Get a Kick Out of You, Saturday Night, Strangers in the Night, Come Dance with Me, I Won't Dance, Summer Wind, Second Time Around, Young at Heart, You Make Me Feel So Young, My Way, The Song Is You, Put Your Dreams Away

A two-act musical revue of songs associated with Frank Sinatra. Performed at the Algonquin Hotel's Oak Room prior to this Off-Bdwy engagement.

*Closed July 28, 2002 after 1,096 performances. Moved to The Reprise Room on August 13, 2000.

+Succeeded by: 1. Billy Stritch (during vacation)

James J. Kriegsmann Photo

Eric Comstock, Hilary Kole, Christopher Gines in *Our Sinatra: A Musical Celebration*

James Farrell, Catherine Russell in *Perfect Crime*

PERFECT CRIME

By Warren Manzi; Director, Jeffrey Hyatt; Set, Jay Stone, Mr. Manzi; Costumes, Nancy Bush; Lighting, Jeff Fontaine; Sound, David Lawson; Stage Manager, Julia Murphy; Presented by The Actors Collective in association with the Methuen Company; Press, Debenham Smythe/Michelle Vincents, Paul Lewis, Jeffrey Clarke; Opened in the Courtyard Playhouse on April 18, 1987*

CAST

Margaret Thorne Brent . . . . .Catherine Russell
Inspector James Ascher . . . . .Michael Minor
W. Harrison Brent . . . . .Don Leslie +1
Lionel McAuley . . . . .Chris Lutkin +2
David Breuer . . . . .Patrick Robustelli
Understudies: Lauren Lovett (Females), J. R. Robinson (Males)

A mystery in two acts. The action takes place in Windsor Locks, Connecticut.

*Still playing May 31, 2001. After opening at the Courtyard Playhouse, the production transferred to the Second Stage, 47th St. Playhouse, Intar 53 Theater, Harold Clurman Theatre, Theatre Four, and, currently, to The Duffy Theatre.

+Succeeded by: 1. Peter Ratray 2. Brian Hotaling

Joe Bly Photo

STOMP

Created/Directed by Luke Cresswell and Steve McNicholas; Lighting, Mr. McNicholas, Neil Tiplady; Production Manager, Pete Donno; General Management, Richard Frankel/Marc Routh; Presented by Columbia Artists Management, Harriet Newman Leve, James D. Stren, Morton Wolkowitz, Schuster/Maxwell, Galin/Sandler, and Markley/Manocherian; Press, Chris Boneau/Adrian Bryan-Brown, Jackie Green, Bob Fennell; Previewed from Friday, February 18, 1994; Opened in the Orpheum Theatre on Sunday, February 27, 1994*

CASTS

Taro Alexander	Maria Emilia Breyer	Mindy Haywood
Stephanie Marshall	Jason Mills	Raymond Poitier
R. J. Samson	Mario Torres	Sheilin Wactor
Morris Anthony	Marivaldo Dos Santos	Raquel Horsford
Keith Middleton	Mikel Paris	Ray Rodriguez Rosa
Henry W. Shead Jr.	Davi Vieira	Fiona Wilkes

An evening of percussive performance art. The ensemble uses everything but conventional percussion to make rhythm and dance.

*Still playing May 31, 2001.

Fiona Wilkes, Theseus Gerard in *Stomp*

Scott Bielecky, Kelly Cinnante in *Tony N' Tina's Wedding*

TONY N' TINA'S WEDDING

By Artificial Intelligence; Conception, Nancy Cassaro (Artistic Director); Director, Larry Pellegrini; Supervisory Director, Julie Cesari; Musical Director, Lynn Portas; Choreography, Hal Simons; Design/Decor, Randall Thropp; Costumes/Hairstyles/Makeup, Juan DeArmas; General Manager, Leonard A. Mulhern; Company Manager, James Hannah; Stage Manager, Larry S. Piscador; Presented by Joseph Corcoran & Daniel Cocoran; Press, David Rothenberg/Terence Womble; Opened in the Washington Square Church & Carmelita's on Saturday, February 6, 1988*

CAST

Valentia Lynne Nunzio, the bride . . . . .Domenica Cameron-Scorsese +1
Anthony Angelo Nunzio, the groom . . . . .Scott Bielecky
Connie Mocogni, maid of honor . . . . .Sophia Antonini
Barry Wheeler, best man . . . . .Joe Dallo
Donna Marsala, bridesmaid . . . . .Lisa Casillo
Dominick Fabrizzi, usher . . . . .Sal Marino
Marina Gulino, bridesmaid .Susan Ann Davis
Johnny Nunzio, usher/brother of groom . . . . .Michael Perri
Josephine Vitale, mother of the bride . . . . .Jacqueline Carol
Joseph Vitale, brother of the bride . . . . .Michael Gargani
Luigi Domenico, great uncle of the bride . . . . .Frankie Waters
Rose Domenico, aunt of the bride . . . . .Susan Varon
Sister Albert Maria, cousin of bride . . . . .Renae Patti
Anthony Angelo Nunzio, Sr., father of groom . . . . .Mark Nassar
Madeline Monroe, Mr. Nunzio's girlfriend . . . . .Denise Fennell
Grandma Nunzio, grandmother to groom . . . . .Letty Serra
Michael Just, Tina's ex-boyfriend . . . . .Patrick Holder
Father Mark, parish priest . . . . .James J. Hendricks
Vinnie Black, caterer . . . . .Henry Caplan
Loretta Black, wife of the caterer . . . . .Rebecca Weitman
Nikki Black, daughter of the caterer . . . . .Alyson Silverman
Pat Black, sister of the caterer . . . . .Joanne Newborn
Mikey Black, son of the caterer . . . . .Eric Gutman
Mike Black, brother of the caterer . . . . .Matthew Bonifacio
Rick Demarco, the video man . . . . .Anthony Barone
Sal Antonucci, the photographer . . . . .John DiBenedetto

An environmental theatre production. The action takes place at a wedding and reception.

*Closed May 18, 2003. After the opening, the production later transferred to St. John's Church & Vinnie Black's Coliseum (reception), and currently shows at St. Luke's Church and Vinnie Black's Vegas Room Coliseum in the Edison Hotel (reception).

+Succeeded by: 1. Kelly Cinnante

Carol Rosegg Photo

TUBES

Created and Written by Matt Goldman, Phil Stanton, Chris Wink; Director, Marlene Swartz and Blue Man Group; Artistic Coordinator; Caryl Glaab; Artistic/Musical Collaborators, Larry Heinemann, Ian Pai; Set, Kevin Joseph Roach; Costumes, Lydia Tanji, Patricia Murphy; Lighting, Brian Aldous, Matthew McCarthy; Sound, Raymond Schilke, Jon Weston; Computer Graphics, Kurisu-Chan; Stage Manager, Lori J. Weaver; Presented by Blue Man Group; Press, Manuel Igrejas; Opened at the Astor Place Theatre on Thursday, November 7, 1991*

BLUE MAN CASTS

Chris Bowen	Randall Jaynes	Jeffrey Doornbos
John Grady	Steve White	Pete Simpson
Pete Starrett	Wes Day	Matt Goldman
Michael Cates	Gen. Fermon Judd Jr.	Phil Stanton
	Chris Wink	

An evening of performance art presented without intermission.

*Still playing May 31, 2001.

Martha Swope Photo

Blue Man Group: Tubes

Eve Ensler in *The Vagina Monologues*

THE VAGINA MONOLOGUES

By Eve Ensler; Production Supervisor, Joe Mantello; Set, Loy Arcenas; Lighting, Beverly Emmons; General Management, EGS; Stage Manager, Barnaby Harris; Press, Publicity Office/Bob Fennell, Marc Thibodeau; Presented by David Stone, Willa Shalit, Nina Essman, Dan Markley/Mike Skipper, and The Araca Group; Previewed from Tuesday, September 21, 1999; Opened in the Westside Theatre/Downstairs on Sunday, October 3, 1999*

THIS SEASON'S CASTS

Joy Behar, Hazelle Goodman, and Holland Taylor; Linda Ellerbee, Calista Flockhart, and Lisa Gay Hamilton; Carol Kane, Melissa Joan Hart, and Phylicia Rashad; Teri Hatcher, Ricki Lake, Regina Taylor; Gloria Reuben, Julia Stiles, and Mary Testa; Brett Butler, Kimberly Williams, and Tonya Pinkins; Terri Garr, Sanaa Lathan, and Juliana Margulies; Brooke Shields, Mercedes Ruehl, and Ana Gasteyer; Kathleen Chalfant, Nell Carter, and Annabella Sciorra; Donna Hanover, Robin Givens, and Susie Essman; Erica Jong, Angelica Torn, and Lauren Velez; Ann Magnuson, Sarah Jones, and Lolita Davidovitch; Carolee Carmello, Roma Maffia, and Rue McClanahan; Julie Halston, Lisa Leguillou, and Lois Smith; Becky Ann Baker, Cynthia Garrett, and Ruthie Henshall; Kim Coles, Judy Gold, and Patricia Kalember; Katherine Helmond, Joie Lee, and Hayley Mills

Monologues based on interviews with a diverse group of women. Performed without intermission.

*Closed January 26, 2003.

PRODUCTIONS FROM PAST SEASONS THAT CLOSED DURING THIS SEASON

PRODUCTION	OPENED	CLOSED	PERFORMANCES
Bomb-itty of Errors	12/12/99	6/18/00	216 & 12 previews
Cats	10/7/82	9/10/00	7,485 & 16 previews
Copenhagen	4/11/00	1/21/01	326 & 21 previews
The Countess	3/13/99	12/30/00	634
Dame Edna: The Royal Tour	10/17/99	7/2/00	289 & 13 previews
Dinner with Friends	11/4/99	5/27/01	635 & 15 previews
Dirty Blonde	5/1/00	3/4/01	352 & 20 previews
Footloose	10/22/98	7/2/00	708 & 18 previews
Fully Committed	9/16/99	5/27/01	675
The Green Bird	4/18/00	6/4/00	56 & 16 previews
Jackie Mason: Much Ado About Everything	12/30/99	7/30/00	183 & 36 previews
Jekyll & Hyde	4/28/97	1/7/01	1,543 & 44 previews
Jesus Christ Superstar	4/16/00	9/3/00	161 & 28 previews
Jitney	4/25/00	1/28/01	311 & 20 previews
The Laramie Project	5/18/00	9/2/00	126 & 23 previews
Miss Saigon	4/11/91	1/28/01	4,097 & 19 previews
A Moon for the Misbegotten	3/19/00	7/2/00	120 & 15 previews
Over the River and Through the Woods	9/18/98	9/3/00	800 & 20 previews
The Real Thing	4/17/00	8/13/00	135 & 24 previews
The Ride Down Mt. Morgan	4/9/00	7/23/00	120 & 23 previews
Saturday Night Fever	10/21/99	12/30/00	500 & 27 previews
Swing	12/9/99	1/14/01	461 & 43 previews
Taller Than a Dwarf	4/24/00	6/11/00	56 & 37 previews
True West	3/9/00	7/29/00	154 & 21 previews
Uncle Vanya	4/30/00	6/11/00	49 & 29 previews
Wake Up and Smell the Coffee	5/4/00	6/11/00	45 & 10 previews
The Wild Party	4/13/00	6/11/00	68 & 36 previews

Over the River and Through the Woods

The Laramie Project

Footloose

(June 1, 2000–May 31, 2001)

ATLANTIC THEATER COMPANY

Sixteenth Season

Artistic Director, Neil Pepe; Managing Director, Hilary Hinckle; Casting, Marcia DeBonis, Susan Shopmaker; Production Manager, Kurt Gardner; General Manager, Andrew Loose; Fights, Rick Sordelet; Press, Chris Boneau-Adrian Bryan-Brown/Susanne Tighe, Rachel Applegate, Adriana Douzos

Tuesday, September 26–November 5, 2000 (30 performances and 17 previews)
THE BEGINNING OF AUGUST by Tom Donaghy; Director, Neil Pepe; Set, Scott Pask; Costumes, Ilona Somogyi; Lighting, Chris Akerlind; Sound, Janet Kalas; Music, David Carbonara; Stage Manager, Darcy Stephens CAST: Garret Dillahunt (Jackie), Jason Ritter (Ben), Mary Steenburgen (Joyce), Ray Anthony Thomas (Ted), Mary McCann (Pam)
A drama performed without intermission.

Wednesday, January 17–February 25, 2001 (19 performances and 22 previews)
FORCE CONTINUUM by Kia Corthron; Director, Michael John Garcés; Set, Alexander Dodge; Costumes, Mimi O'Donnell; Lighting, Kirk Bookman; Sound, Raymond D. Schilke; Stage Manager, Matthew Silver CAST: Chris McGarry (Flip/Cop1/Cop 2), Jordan Lage (Officer Hudson/Peter/Fuller), Chad L. Coleman (Dece), David Fonteno (Grandfather), Myra Lucretia Taylor (Homeless Woman/Mother/Tamara Jane), Ray Anthony Thomas (Father/Marley), Sean Squire (Dray/Dealer/Eric), Caroline S. Clay (Mrai/Cobbs/Margaret), Donovon Hunter McKnight (Young Dece/Kevin Martell/Quinton)
A drama in two acts. The action involves New York City policemen.

Tuesday, May 8–July 1, 2001 (31 performances and 33 previews)
THE DOG PROBLEM by David Rabe; Director, Scott Ellis; Set, Allen Moyer; Costumes, Michael Krass; Lighting, Brian Nason; Sound, Eileen Tague; Stage Manager, Darcy Stephens CAST: Joe Pacheco (Ronnie), Larry Clarke (Ray), David Wike (Joey), Victor Argo (Uncle Malvolio), Tony Cucci (Tommy Stones), Andrea Gabriel (Teresa), Robert Bella (Priest), Buddy (The Dog)
A dark comedy set mostly on the corner of Bowery and Grand Street in Manhattan.

Carol Rosegg Photos

The Company of *The Beginning of August*

Chris McGarry, Chad L. Coleman, Ray Anthony Thomas in *Force Continuum*

Larry Clark in *The Dog Problem*

Chairman of the Board, Bruce C. Ratner; President, Karen Brooks Hopkins; Executive Producer, Joseph V. Melillo; Publicity, Amy Hughes, Elena Park, Susan Yung

(Harvey Theatre) Wednesday, September 6–October 1, 2000 (14 performances)
RICHARD II by William Shakespeare; Director, Jonathan Kent; Design, Paul Brown; Lighting, Mark Henderson; Sound, John A. Leonard; Music, Jonathan Dove; Fights, Paul Benzing; Production Manager, James Crout; Company Manager, Maris Sharp; Stage Manager, Sophie Gabszewicz CAST: Ralph Fiennes (King Richard the Second), David Burke (John of Gaunt, Duke of Lancaster), Oliver Ford Davies (Edmund, Duke of York), Linus Roache (Henry Bolingbroke, Duke of Herford), Oliver Ryan (Duke of Aumerle/Earl of Rutland), Paul Moriarty (Thomas Mowbray, Duke of Norfolk), Emilia Fox (Queen Isabel), Danielle King (Lady), Barbara Jefford (Duchess of York), Angela Down (Duchess of Gloucester), Ian Barritt (Lord Marshall), Damian O'Hare (1st Herald/York's Man), Stephen Cambell Moore (2nd Herald/Harry Percy), Roger Swaine (Salisbury/Abbot of Westminster), Sean Baker (Bagot), David Fahm (Bushy/Exton's Man), Ed Waters (Green/2nd Gardener's Man), Bernard Gallagher (Bishop of Carlisle), Alan David (Capt. of Welsh Army/Gardener), Robert Swann (Henry Percy), Philip Dunbar (Lord Ross/Duke of Surrey/Groom), Stephen Finegold (Lord Willoughby/Lord Fitzwater), John Bennett (Exton), Paul Benzing (Prison Keeper), David Salter, Alex Sims, Marc Small (Attendants)
Performed by England's Almeida Theatre Company. In repertory with *Coriolanus.*

(Harvey Theatre) Saturday, September 9–30, 2000 (12 performances)
CORIOLANUS by William Shakespeare; Director, Jonathan Kent; Fights, William Hobbs; Other production credits the same as *Richard II* CAST: Ralph Fiennes (Caius Martius), Robert Swann (Titus Lartius), David Burke (Cominius), Oliver Ford Davies (Menenius Agippa), Barbara Jefford (Volumnia), Emilia Fox (Virgilia), Angela Down (Valeria), Danielle King (Gentlewoman), Gregg Prentice, Rowland Stirling, Dana Scarborough (Young Martius), Philip Dunbar (1st Roman Senator), Roger Swaine (2nd Roman Senator), Alan David (Sicinius Velutus), Bernard Gallagher (Junius Brutus), Paul Moriarty (1st Citizen), Sean Baker (2nd Citizen), Damian O'Hare (3rd Citizen), Stephen Finegold (4th Citizen), Ed Waters (5th Citizen), Paul Benzig (6th Citizen), Marc Small (7th Citizen), Oliver Ryan (Messenger/3rd Volsci), Linus Roache (Tullus Aufidius), John Bennett (1st Volsci Senator), Ian Barritt (2nd Volsci Senator), Stephen Campbell Moore (1st Volsci), David Fahm (2nd Volsci)
Performed by England's Almeida Theatre Company. In repertory with *Richard II.*

(Harvey Theatre) Wednesday, October 4–7, 2000
WAR OF THE WORLDS by Naomi Iizuka; Conception/Direction, Anne Bogart; Set, Neil Patel; Costumes, James Schuette; Lighting, Mimi Jordan Sherin; Sound, Darron L. West; Stage Manager, Megan Wanlass; Presented by The SITI Company CAST: Stephen Webber (Orson Welles), Akiko Aizawa (Beatrice Nelson), J. Ed Araiza (Thompson), Ellen Lauren (Leni Zadrov), Tom Nelis (Stratton), Barney O'Hanlon (Stephen Webber)
A meditation on Orson Welles's life, performed without intermission.

Sara Kestelman, Simon Russell Beale, Sylvester Morand in *Hamlet*

(Opera House) Friday, January 12–20, 2001
THE WHITE DEVIL by John Webster; Adapted/Directed by Gale Edwards; Set, Brian Thomson; Costumes, Roger Kirk; Lighting, Trudy Dalgleish; Sound, Paul Tilley; Music, Max Lambert, Martin Armiger; Fights, Steve Douglas-Craig; Stage Managers, R. Michael Blanco, Viv Rosman CAST: Marcus Graham (Brachiano), Angie Milliken (Vittoria Corombona), Bruce Spence (Camillo/Jailer), Jacqueline McKenzie, Jeanette Cronin (Isabella), Michael Siberry (Duke of Florence), John Gaden (Monticelso), Jeremy Sims (Flamineo), Matthew Newton (Marcello), Julia Blake (Cornelia), Paula Arundell (Zanche), William Zappa (Lodovico), Tony Poli (Antonelli), Mark Pegler (Gasparo/Lawyer), Keith Robinson (Dr. Julio), Brian Green (Hortensio), Joseph Manning (Jacques), Ryan Ottey (Giovanni)
A 1612 tragedy performed by Australia's Sydney Theatre Company.

(Harvey Theatre) Tuesday, April 24–May 6, 2001 (11 performances and 1 preview)
THE TRAGEDY OF HAMLET by William Shakespeare; Adapted/Directed by Peter Brook; Artistic Collaboration, Marie-Helene Estienne; Set/Costumes, Chloe Obolensky; Lighting, Philippe Vialatte; Music, Toshi Tsuchitori; Stage Manager, Philippe Mulon CAST: Scott Handy (Horatio), Jeffrey Kissoon (Claudius/Ghost), Adrian Lester (Hamlet), Bruce Myers (Polonius/Gravedigger), Natasha Parry (Gertrude), Naseeruddin Shah (Rosencrantz/1st Player), Shantala Shivalingappa (Ophelia), Rohan Siva (Guildenstern/Laertes/2nd Player)
A distillation of Shakepeare's play performed without intermission.

(Opera House) Wednesday, May 30–June 2, 2001 (4 performances)
HAMLET by William Shakespeare; Director, John Caird; Set/Costumes, Tim Hatley; Lighting, Paul Pyant; Sound, Christopher Shutt; Music, John Cameron; Fights, Terry King CAST: Simon Day (Horatio), Simon Russell Beale (Hamlet), Sylvester Morand (Ghost/Player King), Peter McEnery (Claudius), Sara Kestelman (Gertrude), Peter Blythe (Polonius/Gravedigger), Guy Lankester (Laertes), Cathryn Bradshaw (Ophelia), Edward Gower (Reynaldo/Francisco), Christopher Staines (Rosencrantz), Paul Bazely (Guildenstern), Janet Spencer-Turner (Player Queen), Chloe Angharad (Other Player), Ken Oxtoby (Barnardo/Priest), Martin Chamberlain (Marcellus), Michael Wildman (Osric/Other Player)
Performed by England's Royal National Theater.

Ivan Kyncl, John Nation Photos

CLASSIC STAGE COMPANY

Thirty-third Season

Artistic Director, Barry Edelstein; Producing Director, Beth Emelson; General Manager, Rachel M. Tischler; Production Manager, Ian Tresselt; Casting, Vince Liebhart/Tom Alberg; Press, Publicity Office/Marc Thibodeau, Bob Fennell, Candi Adams

Thursday, September 28–November 5, 2000 (20 performances and 18 previews)
TEXTS FOR NOTHING by Samuel Beckett; Directed/Performed by Bill Irwin; Set, Douglas Stein; Costumes, Anita Yavich; Lighting, Nancy Schertler; Sound, Aural Fixation; Stage Manager, Marci A. Glotzer
A prose work performed without intermission.

Thursday, February 8–March 11, 2001 (21 performances and 12 previews)
RACE by Ferdinand Bruckner; Adapted/Directed by Barry Edelstein; Set, Neil Patel; Costumes, Anglea Wendt; Lighting, Russell H. Champa; Projections, Jan Hartley; Sound, Robert Murphy; Stage Manager, Bryan Scott Clark CAST: Stephen Barker Turner (Peter Karlanner), Tommy Schrider (Tessow), Jeremy Shamos (Nathan Siegelmann/Vice Principal), C.J. Wilson (Hans Hinz Rosloh), Ronald Guttman (A. Marx/District Attorney), Jenny Bacon (Helene Marx), Mark H. Dold (Student Leader), Robert L. Devany (Magistrate/Student), Marc Palmieri (Rural Official/Student), Chris Stewart (Student), Kirsten Sahs (Teacher), Aaron Nutter (Boy), Colleen Corbett (Waitress), Gregory Porter Miller, Tom Nolan, Duncan Nutter (Others)
A 1933 Austrian drama performed in two acts. The action takes place in Western Germany, 1933.

Sunday, February 25–April 1, 2001 (20 performances and 6 previews)
I WILL BEAR WITNESS: *The Diaries of Victor Klemperer* by Victor Klemperer; Adaptation, Karen Malpede and George Bartenieff; Translation, Martin Chalmers; Director, Ms. Malpede; Set, Neil Patel; Costumes, Angela Wendt; Lighting, Tony Giovannetti; Stage Manager, Lisa Gavaletz CAST: George Bartenieff (Victor Klemperer)
A monologue in two acts. The action takes place in Dresden, Germany, 1942–45.

Dixie Sheridan Photos

George Bartenieff in *I Will Bear Witness*

Bill Irwin in *Texts for Nothing*

Stephen Barker Turner, Jenny Bacon in *Race*

DRAMA DEPT.

Artistic Director, Douglas Carter Beane; Managing Director, Michael S. Rosenberg; Production Head, Ilene Rosen; Production Manager, Christian Douglas Cargill; Press, Chris Boneau-Adrian Bryan-Brown/Steven Padla, Scott Yarbrough; Performances at Greenwich House Theatre

Tuesday, October 3–December 16, 2000 (61 performances and 16 previews)
LES MIZRAHI Written/Performed by Isaac Mizrahi; Director, Richard Move; Visual Director, Wendall K. Harrington; Musical Director, Ben Waltzer; Lighting, Kirk Bookman; Sound, Laura Grace Brown; Video Montage, Charles Atlas; Stage Managers, Sarah Bittenbender, Maria Ryan MUSICAL NUMBERS: Me & My Show, When You're Smiling, Baubles Bangles and Beads, I've Got a Little List, A Cup of Coffee a Sandwich and You, Lotus Blossom, Tea for Two, Doodling Song
A cabaret performance performed without intermission.

Monday, March 20–June 1, 2001 (68 performances and 14 previews)
THE BOOK OF LIZ by The Talent Family (David and Amy Sedaris); Director/Set, Hugh Hamrick; Costumes, Victoria Farrell; Lighting, Kirk Bookman; Sound, Laura Grace Brown; Music, Mark Levenson; Stage Manager, Jennifer Rae Moore CAST: Chuck Coggins (Rev. Tollhouse/Visil/Duncan Trask), Amy Sedaris (Sister Elizabeth Donderstock/Brother Hesikiah), David Rakoff (Brother Nathaniel Brightbee/Yvon/Donny Polk/Rudy Bruton), Jackie Hoffman (Sister Constance Butterworth/Oxana/Cecily Cole/Sophisticated Visitor/Dr. Barb Ginley/Ms. Yolanda Foxley)
A comedy set in Amish country.

Joan Marcus Photos

David Rakoff, Amy Sedaris, Jackie Hoffman, Chuck Coggins in *The Book of Liz*

David Rakoff, Jackie Hoffman, Amy Sedaris in *The Book of Liz*

Amy Sedaris in *The Book of Liz*

Artistic Director, Charlotte Moore; Producing Director, Ciarán O'Reilly; Sound Design, Murmod, Inc.; General Manager, Shelly A. Troupe; Press, John Barlow-Michael Hartman/Andy Shearer, Jeremy Shaffer

Tuesday, August 15–October 8, 2000 (50 performances and 6 previews)
DON JUAN IN HELL by George Bernard Shaw; Director, Ciarán O'Reilly; Costumes, David Toser; Lighting, Jason A. Cina; Sound, Murmod, Inc.; Stage Manager, John Handy CAST: Celeste Holm (Doña), Fritz Weaver (Don Juan), James A. Stephens (Statue), Donal Donnelly (Devil)
The famed third act sequence from Shaw's 1902 play, *Man and Superman.*

Friday, October 20–December 31, 2000 (64 performances and 9 previews)
THE HOSTAGE by Brendan Behan; Director, Charlotte Moore; Set, Eugene Lee, N. Joseph DeTullio; Costumes, Linda Fisher; Lighting, Gregory Cohen; Stage Managers, Casey Cook, John Handy CAST: Terry Donnelly (Meg), Mark Hartman (Piano Player), Jacqueline Kealy (Colette), John Martin Mconnell (IRA), Barry McNabb (Rio Rita), Fidelman Murphy (Ropeen), Anto Nolan (Pat), John O'Callaghan (Russian Sailor), Denis O'Neill (Volunteer), Ciarán O'Reilly (Mr. Mulleady), Derdriu Ring (Teresa), Ciaran Sheehan (Shaughnessy), Erik Singer (British Soldier), James A. Stephens (Monsewer), Steven X. Ward (Princess Grace), Elizabeth Whyte (Miss Gilchrist)
A dark comedy in two acts. The action takes place in an old house in Dublin, 1960.

Saturday, January 20–March 4, 2001 (29 performances and 16 previews)
THE IMPORTANCE OF BEING OSCAR by Micheál MacLiammóir; Director/ Design, Charlotte Moore; Costumes, David Tosier; Lighting, Jason A. Cina; Stage Manager, Thomas J. Gates CAST: Niall Buggy (Oscar Wilde)
A one-man portrait of Ireland's most popular playwright.

Tuesday, March 13–May 6, 2001 (47 performances and 9 previews)
THE PICTURE OF DORIAN GRAY Adaptation/Director, Joe O'Byrne; Based on the novel by Oscar Wilde; Set, Akira Yoshimura, Rebecca Vary; Costumes, David Tosier; Lighting, Brian Nason; Masks/Puppets, Bob Flanagan; Stage Manager, Elizabeth Larson CAST: Paul Vincent Black (Romeo/Adrian Singleton), Crispin Freeman (Dorian Gray), Nick Hetherington (James Vane/Francis), Tertia Lynch (Sybil Vane), Colleen Madden (Lady Henry/Gladys), Paul Anthony McGrane (Shadow One), Daniel Pearce (Lord Henry), Angela Pierce (Duchess of Harley/Mrs. Vane), Andrew Seear (Basil/Uncle George/Geoffrey), Timothy Smallwood (Thomas Burdon/Alan Campbell)
A drama in two acts. The action takes place in London, late 19th century.

Carol Rosegg Photos

Fritz Weaver, Celeste Holm, James A. Stephens, Donal Donnelly in *Don Juan in Hell*

Erik Singer, Derdriu Ring in *The Hostage*

Niall Buggy in *The Importance of Being Oscar*

JEAN COCTEAU REPERTORY

Thirtieth Season

Producing Artistic Director, David Fuller; Production Director, Ernest Johns; General Manager, Dona Lee Kelly; Stage Manager, Amy Wagner; Press, Jonathan Slaff; Spin Cycle/Ron Lasko, Shannon Jowett; Performances at Bouwerie Lane Theatre

Friday, June 2–25, 2000 (20 performances and 2 previews)
THE BUTTER AND EGG MAN by George S. Kaufman; Director, David Fuller; Set, Mark Fitzgibbons; Costumes, Irene Victoria Hatch; Lighting, Izzy Einsidler CAST: Christopher Black (Peter Jones), Craig Smith (Joe Lehman), Amy Fitts, Elise Stone, Harris Berlinsky, Angela Madden, Marc Diraison, Jolie Garrett, Neil Shah, Kathryn Savannah, Etya Dudko, Tim Deak
A 1925 comedy about show business.

Friday, August 18–November 16, 2000 (38 performances and 6 previews)
THE CRADLE WILL ROCK Music/Lyrics/Book by Marc Blitzstein; Director, David Fuller; Musical Director, Charles Berigan; Set, Mark Fitzgibbons; Costumes, Irene V. Hatch; Lighting, Izzy Einsidler; Choreography, Barbara Brandt CAST: Christopher Black (President Prexy/Junior Mister), Harris Berlinksky (Harry Druggist), Taylor Bowyer (Rev. Salvation/Steve), Jason Crowl (Larry Foreman), Tim Deak (Editor Daily), Jolie L. Garrett (Dauber/Buggs), Jennifer Herzog (Dick/Sister Mister/Sadie), Kyra Himmelbaum succeeded by Michele Goodson-Burnett (Yasha), Angela Madden (Mrs. Mister), Mark Rimer (Dr. Specialist), Craig Smith (Mr. Mister), "Blitz" Steinmark (Clerk/Attendant), Elise Stone (Moll/Ella Hammer), Mike Surabian (Cop)
A 1937 musical in two acts.

Friday, October 6–January 25, 2001 (26 performances and 5 previews)
THE MERCHANT OF VENICE by William Shakespeare; Director, Eve Adamson; Set, Robert Klingelhoefer; Costumes, Margaret McKowan; Lighting, Ms. Adamson, Harold A. Mulanix; Music, Charles Berigan CAST: Harris Berlinsky (Shylock), Elise Stone (Portia), Craig Smith (Antonio), Jolie Garrett (Bassanio), Jennifer Herzog, Mark Rimer, Christopher Black, Jason Crowl, Michael Surabian, Tim Deak, Neil Shah, Angela Madden, Taylor Bowyer

Angela Madden, Jolie Garrett in *Night and Day*

Craig Smith, Jason Crowl in *The Cradle Will Rock*

Friday, December 1, 2000–March 22, 2001 (30 performances and 8 previews)
NIGHT AND DAY by Tom Stoppard; Director, Ernest Johns; Set, Robert J. Martin; Costumes, Susan Soetaert; Lighting, Giles Hogya; Sound/Music, Ellen Mandel CAST: Tim Deak (George Guthrie), Angela Madden (Ruth Carson), Justin Spiegel (Alastair Carson), Jason Crowl (Richard Wagner), Taylor Bowyer (Jacob Milne), Harris Berlinsky (Geoffrey Carson), Jolie L. Garrett (President Mageeba), Irad Vanterpool (Francis)
A comedy set in the African nation of Kambawe, 1978.

Friday, February 9–May 3, 2001 (26 performances and 6 previews)
THE SUBJECT WAS ROSES by Frank D. Gilroy; Director, David Fuller; Set, Robert Klingelhoefer; Costumes, Gail Baldoni; Lighting, Izzy Einsidler CAST: Craig Smith (John Cleary), Elise Stone (Nettie Cleary), Christopher Black (Timmy Cleary)
A 1964 drama set in the Bronx.

Friday, April 6–May 27, 2001 (24 previews and 5 previews)
THE MISANTHROPE by Molière; Translation/Director, Rod McLucas; Set, Robert J. Martin; Costumes, Robin I. Shane; Lighting, David W. Kniep; Sound/Music, John Sandborn CAST: Christopher Black (Alceste), Tim Deak (Philinte), Jason Crowl (Oronte), Angela Madden (Célimène), Jennifer Herzog (Eliante), Elise Stone (Arsinoé), Jolie Garrett (Acaste), Harris Berlinsky (Clitandre), Taylor Bowyer (Basque/Du Bois), Craig Smith (Guard)
A new translation of the 1666 satire.

Jonathan Slaff Photos

Harris Berlinsky, Craig Smith in *The Merchant of Venice*

LA MAMA EXPERIMENTAL THEATRE CLUB

Thirty-ninth Season

Founder/Director, Ellen Stewart; Associate Director, Beverly Petty; Press, Jonathan Slaff; Gary Springer-Susan Chicoine

Thursday, October 26–November 19, 2000 (14 performances and 2 previews)
FAME TAKES A HOLIDAY by Cassandra Danz, Mary Fulham, and Warren Leight; Director, Mary Fulham; Musical Director, Mr. Gallagher; Music, Tracy Berg, Dick Gallagher, Cliff Korman, Marc Shaiman; Choreography, Barbara Allen; Set, Gregory John Mercurio; Costumes, Ramona Ponce; Lighting, David Adams; Sound, Tim Schellenbaum; Stage Manager, Kim Averett CAST: Abigail Gampel (Dee Dee), Deborah LaCoy (Lavender), Susan Murphy (Crystal), Mary Purdy (Polly), Kim Cea
MUSICAL NUMBERS: Girls Girls Girls, Dream Dream Dream, I Got the Music, Eleanor's Boogie, Just Another Jane, Je Ne Regrout Rien, Ballet for All Ages and Boys Too, Book Me Jesus, Kish Mir in Tuchas, Finale
A two-act comedy with music. The action takes place at New York's City's Copa nightclub, and the Masonic Lodge in Perth Amboy, NJ.

Thursday, January 4–21, 2001 (14 performances and 1 preview)
OPTIC FEVER Conceived/Designed/Written/Directed by Theodora Skipitares; Additional Text, David Adjami; Music, David First; Lighting, Pat Dignan; Video, Kay Hines CAST: Preston Foerder, Chris Maresca, Neil McNally, Alissa Mello, Sarah Provost (Puppeteers), Michael Moran (Narrator)
A miniaturist work on Renaissance art and science.

Abigail Gampel, Susan Murphy, Mary Purdy, Deborah LaCoy in *Fame Takes a Holiday*

LINCOLN CENTER THEATER

Sixteenth Season

Artistic Director, André Bishop; Executive Producer, Bernard Gersten; Casting, Daniel Swee; General Manager, Steven C. Callahan; Production Manager, Jeff Hamlin; Press, Philip Rinaldi/Brian Rubin; Off Broadway performances at Mitzi E. Newhouse Theater

Thursday, June 29–September 17, 2000 (61 performances and 31 previews)
SPINNING INTO BUTTER by Rebecca Gilman; Director, Daniel Sullivan; Set, John Lee Beatty; Costumes, Jess Goldstein; Lighting, Brian MacDevitt; Sound/Music, Dan Moses Schreier; Stage Manager, Michael Brunner CAST: Hope Davis (Sarah Daniels), Jai Rodriguez (Patrick Chibas), Daniel Jenkins (Ross Collins), Henry Strozier (Dean Burton Strauss), Brenda Wehle (Dean Catherine Kennedy), Matt DeCaro (Mr. Myers), Stephen Pasquale (Greg Sullivan)
A drama in two acts. The action takes place in Belmont College, Vermont.

Thursday, November 9, 2000–January 14, 2001 (45 performances and 32 previews)
OLD MONEY by Wendy Wasserstein; Director, Mark Brokaw; Set, Thomas Lynch; Costumes, Jane Greenwood; Lighting, Mark McCullough; Music, Lewis Flinn; Sound, Janet Kalas; Choreography, John Carrafa; Stage Manager, James FitzSimmons CAST: Charlie Hofheimer (Ovid Walpole Bernstein/Tobias Pfeiffer II), Mark Harelik (Jeffrey Bernstein/Arnold Strauss), Kathryn Meisle (Flinty McGee/Florence DeRoot), John Cullum (Tobias Vivian Pfeiffer III/Schuyler Lynch), Dan Butler (Sid Nercessian/Tobias Pfeiffer), Jodi Long (Penny Nercessian/Betina Brevoort), Emily Bergl (Mary Gallagher/Caroline Nercessian), Mary Beth Hurt (Saulina Webb/Sally Webster)
A drama in two acts. The action takes place at a party on Manhattan's Upper East Side.

Thursday, February 8–April 15, 2001 (45 performances and 32 previews)
TEN UNKNOWNS by Jon Robin Baitz; Director, Daniel Sullivan; Set, Ralph Funicello; Costumes, Jess Goldstein; Lighting, Pat Collins; Sound, Janet Kalas; Music, Robert Waldman; Stage Manager, Roy Harris CAST: Denis O'Hare (Trevor Fabricant), Donald Sutherland (Malcolm Raphelson), Justin Kirk (Judd Sturgess), Julianna Margulies (Julia Bryant)
A drama in two acts. The action takes place near a town in South Mexico, 1992.

Thursday, May 10–July 29, 2001 (61 performances and 32 previews)
CHAUCER IN ROME by John Guare; Director, Nicholas Martin; Set, Alexander Dodge; Costumes, Michael Krass; Lighting, Donald Holder; Sound/Music, Mark Bennett; Stage Manager, Michael Brunner CAST: Bruce Norris (Pete), Jon Tenney (Matt), Carrie Preston (Sarah), Lee Wilkof (Il Dottore/Fr. Shapiro/Joe/Charlie), Antonio Edwards Suarez (Il Tassinaro), Ümit Çelebi (Renzo), Polly Holliday (Dolo), Dick Latessa (Ron), Susan Finch, Mark Fish, Nancy McDoniel, Tim McGeever (Pilgrims/Fellows)
A drama performed without intermission. The action takes place in Rome, 2000.

For other Lincoln Center Theater productions, see *Patti LuPone: Matters of the Heart* and *The Invention of Love,* in the BROADWAY section.

Joan Marcus Photos

Jon Tenney, Carrie Preston in *Chaucer in Rome*

Hope Davis, Jai Rodriguez in *Spinning Into Butter*

Donald Sutherland, Julianna Margulies in *Ten Unknowns*

MANHATTAN THEATRE CLUB

Twenty-ninth Season

Artistic Director, Lynne Meadow; Executive Producer, Barry Grove; Associate Artistic Director, Michael Bush; Development Director, Andrew D. Hamingson; Director of Casting, Nancy Piccione; Other Casting, Jay Binder; Fight Director, Rick Sordelet; General Manager, Harold Wolpert; Production Manager, Michael R. Moody; Press, Chris Boneau-Adrian Bryan-Brown/Steven Padla, Rachel Applegate, Martine Sainvil

(Stage II) Tuesday, October 3–December 10, 2000 (38 performances and 42 previews)
A CLASS ACT Music/Lyrics, Edward Kleban; Book, Linda Kline and Lonny Price; Director, Mr. Price; Musical Director/Vocal Arrangements/Dance Music, Todd Ellison; Orchestrations, Larry Hochman; Choreography, Scott Wise; Set, James Noone; Costumes, Carrie Robbins; Lighting, Kevin Adams; Sound, Mark Menard/Geoff Zink; Cast Recording, RCA; Stage Manager, Heather Fields CAST: Nancy Kathryn Anderson (Mona, et al.), Carolee Carmello (Lucy, et al.), Jonathan Freeman (Lehman, et al.), Randy Graff (Sophie), David Hibbard (Bobby, et al.), Julia Murney (Felicia, et al.), Lonny Price (Ed), Ray Wills (Charley, et al.)
MUSICAL NUMBERS: Light on My Feet, Fountain in the Garden, One More Beautiful Song, Friday's at Four, Bobby's Song, Charm Song, Paris Through the Window, Mona, Making Up Ways, Under Separate Cover, Gauguin's Shoes, Follow Your Star, Better, Scintillating Sophie, Next Best Thing To Love, Broadway Boogie Woogie, "Chorus Line" excerpts, I Choose You, Say Something Funny, When the Dawn Breaks, Self Portrait, Finale
A musical in two acts. The action takes place on the stage of the Shubert Theatre and other locations, 1958–1988. The production resumed performances at Broadway's Ambassador Theatre on February 14, 2001 (see BROADWAY section).

(Stage I) Tuesday, October 24, 2000–January 7, 2001 (62 performances and 26 previews)
COMIC POTENTIAL by Alan Ayckbourn; Director, John Tillinger; Set, John Lee Beatty; Costumes, Jane Greenwood; Lighting, Brian MacDevitt; Sound, Bruce Ellman; Music, John Patterson; Choreography, Jeff Calhoun; Dialect Coach, Stephen Gabis; CAST: Alexander Chaplin (Adam Trainsmith), John Curless (Doctor/Farmer/Man in Dress Shop/Turkey), Janie Dee (Jacie Triplethree), MacIntyre Dixon (Lester Trainsmith/Hotel Clerk), Carson Elrod (Son/Marmion), Peter Michael Goetz (Chandler Tate), Mercedes Herrero (Tudi Floote/Girl in Dress Shop), Robin Mosely (Mother/Farmer's Wife/Prostitute), Kristine Nielsen (Carla Pepperbloom), Kellie Overbey (Prim Spring)
A black comedy in two acts. The action takes place in the not too distant future.

Lonny Price, Ray Wills in *A Class Act*

(Stage II) Tuesday, January 9–February 18, 2001 (24 performances and 24 previews)
TIME AND AGAIN Music/Lyrics, Walter Edgar Kennon; Book, Jack Viertel; Additional Story Material, James Hart; Based on the book by Jack Finney; Director, Susan H. Schulman; Musical Director, Kevin Stites; Choreography, Rob Asford; Set, Derek McLane; Costumes, Catherine Zuber; Lighting, Ken Billington; Sound, Brian Ronan; Stage Manager, Peggy Peterson CAST: Melissa Rain Anderson (Bessie), Ann Arvia (Mrs. Carmody), Laura Benati (Julia Charbonneau), Betsi Morrison (Julie during Laura Benati's illness), Lewis Cleale (Si Morley), Jeff Edgerton (Felix Tiltzer), Eric Michael Gillett (Edward Carmody), Gregg Goodbrod (Young Doctor), Christopher Innvar (Jake Pickering), Patricia Kilgarriff (Aunt Evie), Joseph Kolinski (Trolleyman), George Masswohl (Mr. Harriman), David McCallum (E.E. Danziger/Cyrus Hogue), Julia Murney (Kate Mancuso), Amy Walsh (Clarisse), Lauren Ward (Emily Hogue)
MUSICAL NUMBERS: Standing in the Middle of the Road, At the Theater, Who Would Have Thought It?, She Dies, The Lady in the Harbor, Carrara Marble, The Music of Love, Who Are You Anyway?, What of Love?, For Those You Love, The Marrying Kind, The Fire, Time and Time Again, The Right Look, I Know This House, Finale
A musical in two acts. The action takes place in New York City, 1880s and the present.

Alexander Chaplin, Janie Dee in *Comic Potential*

Laura Benanti, Lewis Cleale in *Time and Again*

(continued)

(Stage I) Tuesday, January 30–April 8, 2001 (56 performances and 24 previews)
BOY GETS GIRL by Rebecca Gilman; Director, Michael Maggio; Production Supervisor, Lynne Meadow; Set, Michael Philippi; Costumes, Nan Cibula-Jenkins; Lighting, John Culbert; Sound/Music, Rob Milburn, Michael Bodeen; Stage Manager, Ed Fitzgerald CAST: David Adkins (Mercer Stevens), Matt DeCaro (Howard Siegel), Shayna Ferm (Harriet), Mary Beth Fisher (Theresa Bedell), Ora Jones (Madeline Beck), Ian Lithgow (Tony), Howard Witt (Les Kennkat)
A drama in two acts. The action takes place in New York City.

(Stage II) Tuesday, February 27–April 8, 2001 (16 performances and 32 previews)
NEWYORKERS Music, Stephen Weiner; Lyrics, Glenn Slater; Director, Christopher Ashley; Musical Director/Vocal Arrangements, Robert Billig; Orchestrations, Robby Merkin; Choreography, Daniel Pelzig; Set, Derek Mclane; Costumes, David C. Woolard; Lighting, Ken Billington; Sound, Brian Ronan; Stage Manager, Kate Broderick CAST: Stephen DeRosa (Stephen), Jerry Dixon (Jerry), Jesse Tyler Ferguson (Jesse), Pamela Isaacs (Pamela), Liz Larsen (Liz), Priscilla Lopez (Priscilla)
A musical revue performed without intermission.

The Company of *Newyorkers*

(Stage II) Tuesday, April 24–June 24, 2001 (46 performances and 26 previews)
BLUR by Melanie Marnich; Director, Lynne Meadow; Set, Santo Loquasto; Costumes, James Schuette; Lighting, Brian MacDevitt; Sound/Music, David Van Tieghem CAST: Angela Goethals (Dot DiPrima), Polly Draper (Mom), Chris Messina (Joey D'Amico), Susan Pourfar (Francis Butane), Bill Raymond (Fr. O'Hara), Ken Marks (Doctor/Braille Student)
A drama performed without intermission.

(Stage I) Tuesday, May 1–July 8, 2001 (54 performances and 26 previews)
GLIMMER, GLIMMER AND SHINE by Warren Leight; Director, Evan Yionoulis; Set, Neil Patel; Costumes, Candice Donnelly; Lighting, Donald Holder; Sound, Jon Gottlieb; Music, Evan Lurie; Stage Manager, Richard Hester CAST: Scott Cohen (Jordan), Brian Kerwin (Daniel), Seana Kofoed (Delia), John Spencer (Martin)
A drama in two acts. The action takes place in New York City and Greenwich, CT, 1990.

Joan Marcus Photos

For other Manhattan Theatre Club Productions: *Proof, Tale of the Allergist's Wife* and *King Hedley II,* see BROADWAY section.

Brian Kerwin, John Spencer in *Glimmer, Glimmer and Shine*

MCC THEATRE (MANHATTAN CLASS COMPANY)

Fifteenth Season

Artistic Directors, Robert LuPone and Bernard Telsey; Associate Artistic Director, William Cantler; Fight Director, Rick Sordelet; General Manager, Barbara L. Auld; Production Managers, Obadiah Savage, Joshua Helman, Lester P. Grant; Press, Erin Dunn/Katie Miller

Tuesday, August 22–27, 2000 (6 performances)
SUMMER PLAY PARTY Play Party Director, James Bosley; Set, Beowulf Boritt; Lighting, Mike Riggs; Stage Manager, Anna Saggese; Press, Paula Mallino
EVENING A: *Family Peace* by Claudia De La Cruz; Director, Louis Moreno; Costumes, Liza Ziegler CAST: Marilyn Torres (Adrianna), Indio Melendez (Nelson)
Do Me a Favor by Jeremy Martinez; Director, Jeff Burchfield CAST: John Patrick Nord (Jay), Byron Castañeda (Tony), Mark D. Jackson (Mr. G.)
A Chance at Goodbye by Vilma Marte; Director, Katie Miller CAST: Melanie Murray (Faith), Walter Pagán (Fin)
The Tropical Fish of the Apocalypse by Esther Sapan; Director, Gregory Wolfe; Choreography, Jena Necrason CAST: Ata Dohrn-Melendez (Donna), Troy Hill (Tyler/Fish 1), Matt Higgins (Fish 2), James Wolfe (Fish 3)
EVENING B: *From Midnight 'Til Noon* by Cameron Crump; Director, Kevin Myers CAST: Brian McManamon (Estacado), Greta Rothman (Voice)
Goomba by Angel Flete; Director, Stephen Willems CAST: Dan Sarnelli (Ace), Chance Pinnell (Vinny)
Porcelain Baby by Danielle Wells; Director, Peter Dalto CAST: Cherita Armstrong (Lana), Vishnu (Joe), Laura Fois (Clarice)
Book 'Em by Kamar Anderson; Director, Justin Ross; Music, Michael Connolly CAST: J. Brandon Savage (Eric Johnson), Karl B. Stewart (Wayne Peterson), Domenica Cameron-Scorsese (Maria), Don Percassi (Joe Robinson), Malcolm Barrett
Eight plays by New York City public high school students.

Tuesday, October 17–November 11, 2000 (17 performances and 10 previews)
A PLACE AT THE TABLE by Simon Block; Director, Michael Sexton; Set, Jim Noone; Costumes, David Zinn; Lighting, John-Paul Szezepanski; Sound, David Van Tieghem; Stage Manager, Beth Stiegel-Rohr CAST: Zak Orth (Adam), Robin Weigert (Sarah), Jesse Pennington (Sammy), Jen Drohan (Rachel)
A comedy in two acts.

Thursday, February 1–March 25, 2001 (24 performances and 21 previews)
HIGH DIVE Written/Performed by Leslie Ayvazian; Director, David Warren; Set, Neil Patel; Lighting, Brian MacDevitt; Sound, Robert Murphy; Stage Manager, Anna Saggese
A comic monologue performed without intermission. The setting is a high dive in Greece.

Tuesday, April 10–May 19, 2001 (29 performances and 13 previews)
THE DEAD EYE BOY by Angus MacLachlan; Director, Susan Fenichell; Set, Christine Jones; Costumes, David Zinn; Lighting, Russell H. Champa; Stage Manager, Stacy P. Hughes CAST: Joseph Murphy (Billy), Lili Taylor (Shirley-Dianne), Aaron Himelstein (Soren)
A drama in two acts.

Joan Marcus, Dixie Sheridan Photos

Jen Drohan in *A Place at the Table*

Leslie Ayvazian in *High Dive*

Aaron Himelstein and Lili Taylor in *The Dead Eye Boy*

MINT THEATER COMPANY

Ninth Season

Artistic Director, Jonathan Bank; Associate Director, Jeni Mahoney; Artistic Assistants, David Carpenter, Yohei Suyama; Press, David Gersten

Friday, September 8–October 8, 2000 (30 performances)
WELCOME TO OUR CITY by Thomas Wolfe; Director, Jonathan Bank; Set, Vicki Davis; Costumes, Elly Van Horne; Lighting, Randy Glickman; Sound/Music, Ellen Mandel; Fights, Michael Chin; Stage Manager, Francis Eric E. Montesa CAST: Ward Asquith (McIntyre/Tyson), Sylver Gregory (Annie Johnson), John Lyndsay Hall (Picken Gaffney), Haakon Jepsen (Henry Sorrell), Michael LiDondici (Bull/Grimes), Bergin Michaels (Dan Reed), Gregory Mikell (Sykes), Lee Moore (Rutledge), Michael Moore (Lee Rutledge), Eric Moreland (Dr. Johnson), Robyne Parrish (Helen Neeley), Brocton Pierce (Slewfoot), Patrick Riviere (Bailey), Larry Swansen (Mr. Jordan), Frank Swingler (Amos), Jonathan Tindle (Prof. Hutching), Colleen Smith Wallnau (Mrs. Rutledge), Tommy Walsh (Bull/Grimes), T.D. White (Old Sorrell/Rev. Smallwood), Don Clark Williams (Sam Tipton), David Winton (Gov. Preston Carr)
A 1923 drama in two acts. The action takes place in Altamont, Summer 1922.

Friday, November 10–December 17, 2000 (37 performances)
THE FLATTERING WORD by George Kelly; and **FAREWELL TO THE THEATER** by Harley Granville-Barker; Director, Gus Kaikkonen; Set, Sarah Lambert; Costumes, Henry Shaffer; Lighting, William Armstrong; Stage Manager, Rachel R. Bush CASTS: *Flattering*: Sara Barnett (Lena), Allyn Burrows (Eugene Tesh), Sioux Madden (Mary Rigley), Michael Stebbins (Rev. Loring Rigley), Colleen Smith Wallnau (Mrs. Zooker), Sally Kemp (Mrs. Fox) *Farewell*: Sally Kemp (Dorothy), George Morfogen (Edward), Michael Stebbins (Clerk)
Two one-acts, both from 1916.

Thursday, February 15–March 11, 2001 (20 performances and 6 previews)
THE DOUBLE BASS by Patrick Süskind; Translation, Michael Hofmann; Director, Jonathan Bank; Set, Katerina Fiore; Lighting, Randy Glickman; Graphics, Jude Dvorak; Presented in association with the Working Theater CAST: Michael William Connors
A one-man drama about an obscure musician.

Friday, May 4–June 3, 2001 (19 performances and 4 previews)
DIANA OF DOBSON'S by Cicely Hamilton; Director, Eleanor Reissa; Set, Sarah Lambert; Costumes, Tracy Christensen; Lighting, Jeff Nellis; Sound, Ray Leslee; Dialects, Amy Stoller; Stage Manager, Joe Gladstone CAST: Caren Browning (Miss Smithers), Maitreya Friedman (Kitty Brant), Sara Barnett (Miss Jay), Rachel Sledd (Diana Massingberd), Jina Oh (Miss Morton), Danielle Delgado (Miss Pringle/Old Woman), Mikel Sarah Lambert (Mrs. Cantelupe), David Marantz (Waiter/Constable Fellowes), Glynis Bell (Mrs. Whyte-Fraser), John Plumpis (Sir Jabez Grinley), Karl Kenzler (Capt. Victor Bretherton)
A 1908 romantic comedy. The action takes place in England and Switzerland.

Carol Rosegg, Barry Burns Photos

Sioux Madden, Allyn Burrows in *The Flattering Word*

Sally Kemp, George Morfogen in *Farewell to the Theatre*

Patrick Riviere, Haakon Jepsen, Eric Moreland, David Winton, Lee Moore in *Welcome to Our City*

THE NEW GROUP

Seventh Season

Artistic Director, Scott Elliott; Producing Director, Elizabeth Timperman; Associate Artistic Director, Andy Goldberg; General Manager, Jill Bowman; Production Stage Manager, Valerie A. Peterson; Press, Craig Karpel/Bridget Klapinski; Performances at Theatre @ St. Clement's

Tuesday, October 31–December 31, 2000 (50 performances and 13 previews)
WHAT THE BUTLER SAW by Joe Orton; Director, Scott Elliott; Set, Derek McLane; Costumes, Mattie Ullrich; Lighting, James Vermeulen; Sound, Ken Travis CAST: Dylan Baker (Dr. Prentice), Chloë Sevigny (Geraldine Barclay), Lisa Emery (Mrs. Prentice), Karl Geary (Nicholas Beckett), Peter Frechette (Dr. Rance), Max Baker (Sgt. Match)
A comedy in two acts. The action takes place in England, 1960s.

Tuesday, January 16–February 25, 2001 (35 performances and 7 previews)
PARADISE ISLAND by Benjie Aerenson; Director, Andy Goldberg; Set, Rob Odorisio; Costumes, Mimi O'Donnell; Lighting, Russell H. Champa; Sound, Ken Travis CAST: Lynn Cohen (Emma), Adrienne Shelly (Terri)
A drama performed without intermission. The action takes place on Paradise Island, Bahamas, a few years ago.

Tuesday, March 13–April 22, 2001 (25 performances and 13 previews)
SERVICEMEN by Evan Smith; Director, Sean Mathias; Set, Derek McLane; Costumes, Catherine Zuber, Alejo Vietti; Lighting, Jeff Croiter; Sound, Fabian Obispo CAST: Eric Martin Brown (Gray), Olivia Birkelund (Cyn), William Westenberg (Doctor/Lieutenant/Waiter), Anthony Veneziale (Si/Soldier), Steven Polito (Glenn), Heather Matarazzo succeeded by Jessica Dunphy (Gloria)
A drama in two acts. The action takes place in New York City during WWII.

Carol Rosegg Photos

Adrienne Shelly, Lynn Cohen in *Paradise Island*

Chloë Sevigny, Dylan Baker in *What the Butler Saw*

Forty-sixth Season

Producer, George C. Wolfe; Artistic Producer, Rosemarie Tichler; Managing Director, Mark Litvin; Artistic Associate, Brian Kulick; Casting, Jordan Thaler/Heidi Griffiths; General Manager, Michael Hurst; Associate Producer, Bonnie Metzgar; Press, Carol Fineman/Tom Naro, Aimée Zygmonski

Keith David, Aunjanue Ellis in *The Winter's Tale*

(Delacorte/Central Park) Wednesday, June 21–July 16, 2000 (10 performances and 14 previews)

THE WINTER'S TALE by William Shakespeare; Director, Brian Kulick; Set, Riccardo Hernández; Costumes, Anita Yavich; Lighting, Kenneth Posner; Sound, Ken Travis; Music, Mark Bennett; Choreography, Naomi Goldberg; Stage Manager, James Latus CAST: Ema Bowers (Mopsa/Emilia), Bill Buell (Old Shepard), Randy Danson (Paulina), Keith David (Leontes), Kena Tangi Dorsey (Dorcas/2nd Lady), Aunjanue Ellis (Hermione), Jonathan Hadary (Antigonus), Francis Jue (1st Lord), Wayne Kasserman (Jailer/Servant), Jesse Pennington (Florizel), Bronson Pinchot (Autolycus), Daniel G. Pino (1st Officer/Gentleman), Gareth Saxe (Archidamus/Sheperd), Henry Stram (Camillo), Michael Stuhlbarg (Clown/Time), Erica N. Tazel (Perdita), Paul W. Tiesler (Mamillius), Michael Traynor (Mariner/Sheperd), Graham Winton (Polixenes), Lucia Brawley, Phyllis Johnson, Jenny Sandler (Ensemble)

The action takes place in Sicilia and Bohemia.

Bill Sims, Jr., Ruben Santiago-Hudson in *Lackawanna Blues*

(Delacorte/Central Park) Wednesday, August 9–September 3, 2000 (13 performances and 10 previews)

JULIUS CAESAR by William Shakespeare; Director, Barry Edelstein; Set, Narelle Sissons; Costumes, Angela Wendt; Lighting, Donald Holder; Sound, Ken Travis; Music, John Gromada; Fights, J. Steven White; Stage Manager, Martha Donaldson CAST: David McCallum (Julius Caesar), Jeffrey Wright (Marc Antony), Dennis Boutsikaris (Cassius), Nadia Bowers (Artemidorus), Ritchie Coster (Caska/Titinius), Keldrik Crowder (Caesar's Priest/Clitus), Peter Jay Fernandez (Decius Brutus/Messala), Clement Fowler (Cicero/Lepidus), Richard Frankfather (Dardanius), Judith Hawking (Calphurnia), Curt Hostetter (Trebonius/Strato), Jason Howard (Cinna the Poet), Wayne Kasserman (Lucius), Colette Kilroy (Portia/Poet), Ezra Knight (Metellus Cimber/Pindarus), Neal Lerner (Murellus/Publius), Sean McNall (Octavius/Carpenter), Larry Paulsen (Caius Ligarius/Volumnius), Jonathan Earl Peck (Flavius/Popilius Lena), Pablo T. Schreiber (Cobbler), James Shanklin (Cinna/Lucilius), Jamey Sheridan (Marcus Brutus), Ching Valdes-Aran (Soothsayer), Robert K. Wu (Antony's Servant), Sila Agavale, Dylan Carusona, Lizzy Davis, Holly Natwora, Lloyd C. Porter, Charles Daniel Sandoval, Christopher Sheller (Ensemble)

Performed with one intermission.

Steven Berkoff in *Shakespeare's Villains*

(Public/Newman) Tuesday, October 31–December 3, 2000 (17 performances and 23 previews)

KIT MARLOWE by David Grimm; Director, Brian Kulick; Set, Narelle Sissons; Costumes, Anita Yavich; Lighting, Mimi Jordan Sherin, D.M. Wood; Sound, Kurt B. Kellenberger; Music, Mark Bennett; Fights, Normand Beauregard; Stage Manager, Buzz Cohen CAST: Sam Trammell (Thomas Washington), Martin Rayner (Ingram Frizer), Bostin Christopher (Nicholas Skeres), Christian Camargo (Kit Marlowe), Richard Ziman (Edward Alleyn/Anthony Babington/Henry Percy), Jon DeVries (Sir Francis Walsingham), David Patrick Kelly (Robert Poley), Chris Kipiniak (French Merchant/Musician), Craig Bockhorn (Brother Auguste/Thomas Harriot), Robert Sella (Robert Deveraux), Keith David (Sir Walter Raleigh), Ned Stresen-Reuter (Young Actor)

A drama in two acts. The action takes place in England and France, 1586–93.

(continued)

Christian Camargo, Sam Trammell in *Kit Marlowe*

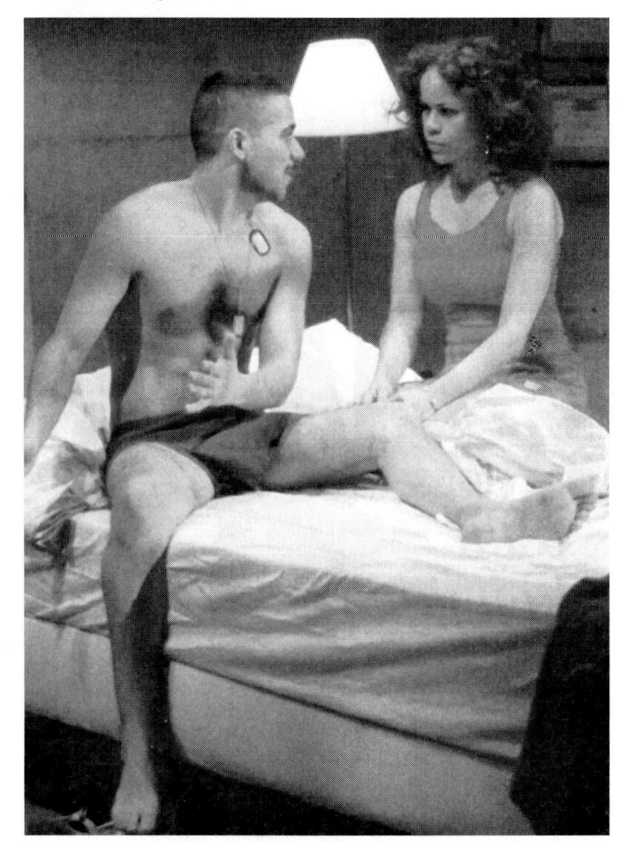

John Ortiz, Rosie Perez in *References to Salvador Dali Make Me Hot*

(Public/Joe's Pub) Thursday, November 9–18, 2000 (5 performances and 3 previews); Reopened at (Public/Anspacher) Wednesday, January 10–February 11, 2001 (29 performances)
SHAKESPEARE'S VILLAINS: *A Master Class in Evil* Created/Performed/ Directed by Steven Berkoff from some of Shakespeare's plays; Lighting, Martin Postmas; Stage Manager, Rick Steiger
Performed without intermission.

(Public/Martinson) Tuesday, November 14–December 17, 2000 (32 performances and 8 previews)
BOOK OF THE DEAD (SECOND AVENUE) Created/Set/Projections by John Moran; Costumes, James Schuette; Lighting, Jonathan Spencer; Sound, Andrew Keister; Masks/Puppets, Cabell Tomlinson; Stage Manager, Renée Lutz CAST: Theo Bleckmann (Singer), Patricia R. Floyd, Darryl Gibson, Anthony Henderson, Michael Huston, Laine Satterfield, David West, M. Drue Williams (Ensemble), Uma Thurman (Narrator)
A "theme park ride" through comparative religion, Ancient Egypt through New York City's Second Ave., performed without intermission.

(Public/Martinson) Tuesday, February 13–April 1, 2001 (33 performances and 23 previews)
DOGEATERS by Jessica Hagedorn; Based on her novel; Director, Michael Greif; Set, David Gallo; Costumes, Brandin Barón; Lighting, Michael Chybowski; Sound, Mark Bennett, Michael Creason; Projections, John Woo; Stage Manager, Lee J. Kahrs CAST: Arthur Acuña (Santos Tirador/ Lt. Pepe Carreon/Tito Alvarez), Raul Aranas (Freddie Gonzaga/Severo Alacran/Ka Edgar), Christopher Donahue (Fr. Jean Mallat/Rainer Fassbinder/Bob Stone), Rona Figueroa (Daisy Avila), Jojo Gonzalez (Waiter/Pedro/Gen. Ledesma), Hill Harper (Joey Sands), Christine Jugueta (Lolita Luna/Dolores Gonzaga), Mia Katigbak (Barbara Villanueva/Ka Lydia), Jonathan Lopez (Romeo Rosales/Ka Pablo), Alec Mapa (Perlita/BoomBoom/Steve Jacobs), Kate Rigg (Rio Gonzaga), Eileen Rivera (Pucha Gonzaga/Trinidad Gamboa), Ralph B. Peña (Nestor Noralez/Chiquitaing Moreno), Joel Torre (Sen. Domingo Avila/Uncle), Ching Valdes-Aran (Leonor Ledesma/Lola Narcisa/Imelda Marcos)
A drama in two acts. The action takes place in Manila, The Philippines, 1982.

(Public/Shiva) Tuesday, March 20–April 29, 2001 (25 performances and 24 previews)
REFERENCES TO SALVADOR DALI MAKE ME HOT by José Rivera; Director, Jo Bonney; Set, Neil Patel; Costumes, Clint E.B. Ramos; Lighting, David Weiner; Sound, Donald DiNicola, Obadiah Eaves; Music, Carlos Valdez; Stage Manager, Mike Schleifer CAST: Kevin Jackson (Coyote), Kristine Nielsen (Cat), Michael Lombard (Moon), Carlo Alban (Martin), Rosie Perez (Gabriela), John Ortiz (Benito)
A four act drama performed with one intermission. The action takes place in Barstow, CA, a few months after the Persian Gulf War.

(Public/LuEsther) Friday, April 6–May 27, 2001 (44 performances and 9 previews)
LACKAWANNA BLUES Written/Performed by Ruben Santiago-Hudson; Director, Loretta Greco; Set/Costumes, Myung Hee Cho; Lighting, James Vermeulen; Music/Guitarist, Bill Sims Jr.; Stage Manager, Buzz Cohen
A one-man play bringing to life the residents of a boarding house in Lackawanna, NY, then (1956) and now.

Michal Daniel Photos

NEW YORK THEATRE WORKSHOP

Twenty-first Season

Artistic Director, James C. Nicola; Associate Artistic Director, Linda S. Chapman; Artistic Associates, Charles Means, Michael Greif, Chiori Miyagawa; Artistic Assistant, Jeremy Kamps; Managing Director, Lynn Moffat; General Manager, Robert Marlin; Press, Richard Kornberg/Don Summa, Tom D'Ambrosio, Carrie Friedman, Jim Byk

Friday, August 25–October 15, 2000
STREET OF BLOOD Written/Performed by Ronnie Burkett
A solo performance with 34 puppets.

Thursday, October 26–December 9, 2000 (41 performances and 13 previews)
ALICE IN BED by Susan Sontag; Director, Ivo van Hove; Costumes, A.F. Vandevorst; Design, Jan Versweyveld; Videography, Runa Islam; Stage Manager, Martha Donaldson CAST: Joan MacIntosh (Alice James), Jorre Vandenbussche (Young Man) CAST OF VIDEO: Jeroen Krabbe (Father), Paul Rudd (Harry), Valda Setterfield (Mother), Elizabeth Marvel (Margaret Fuller), Arija Bareikis (Emily Dickinson), Constance Hauman (Kundry), Chris Nietvelt (Myrtha)
A dramatic fantasy performed without intermission.

Friday, January 5–February 25, 2001 (38 performances and 15 previews)
RESIDENT ALIEN by Tim Fountain; Director, Mike Bradwell; Set/Costumes, Neil Patel; Lighting, Brian MacDevitt; Sound, Jerry Yager; Stage Manager, Charles Means CAST: Bette Bourne (Quentin Crisp)
A one-man play on the life of "naked civil servant" Quentin Crisp. The action takes place in New York City, November 1999.

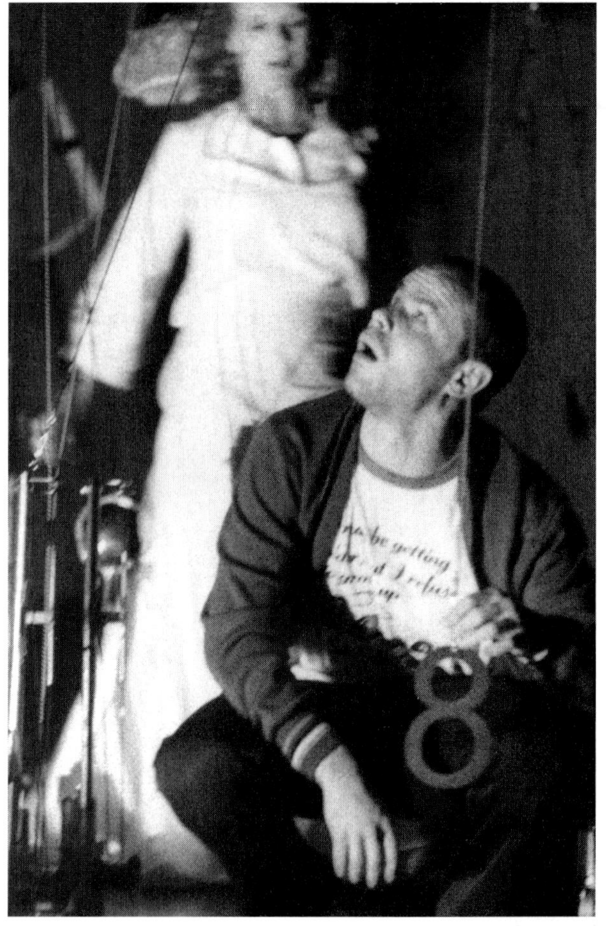

Joan MacIntosh, Jorre Vandenbussche in *Alice in Bed*

Anthony Mackie, Hazelle Goodman in *Up Against the Wind*

Dallas Roberts, Will LeBon in *Nocturne*

Friday, March 16–April 14, 2001 (15 performances and 21 previews)
UP AGAINST THE WIND by Michael Develle Winn; Director, Rosemary K. Andress; Set, Narelle Sissons; Costumes, Olu-Orondava Mumford; Lighting, Peter West; Sound, Jerry M. Yager; Music, Jonathan Sanborn; Stage Manager, Jason Scott Eagan CAST: Olubunmi Banjoko (The Girl/Lee Lee), David Brown Jr. (Record Store Clerk), Kevin Daniels (Suge Knight), Hazelle Goodman (Afeni Shakur), J.D. Jackson (Ed Gordon), Nashawn Kearse (Booker), Tracey A. Leigh (LaDonna), Anthony Mackie (Tupac Shakur), Jesse J. Perez (Jerome Perez), Christopher Rivera (Prison Guard), Joseph Siravo (Jimmy Lovine), Tracie Thoms (Sekyiwa Shakur), Isiah Whitlock Jr. (Lt. Dan)
A drama inspired by the life of rapper Tupac Shakur, in two acts.

Friday, May 4–June 17, 2001 (39 performances and 14 previews)
NOCTURNE by Adam Rapp; Director, Marcus Stern; Set, Christine Jones; Costumes, Viola Mackenthun; Lighting, John Ambrosone; Sound, Mr. Stern, David Remedios; Stage Manager, Jennifer Rae Moore CAST: Candice Brown (The Mother), Marin Ireland (The Red-Headed Girl with the Gray-Green Eyes), Will LeBow (The Father), Nicole Pasquale (The Sister), Dallas Roberts (The Son)
A drama in two acts.

Joan Marcus, Chris Van Der Burght Photos

PAN ASIAN COMPANY

Twenty-fourth Season

Artistic/Producing Director, Tisa Chang; Artistic Associate, Ron Nakahara; Press, Maya/Penny M. Landau, Michael Litchfield; Performances at Theatre Four and West End Theatre

Wednesday, June 21–July 23, 2000 (28 performances and 7 previews)
THE POET OF COLUMBUS AVENUE by Dennis Escobedo; Director, Ron Nakahara; Set, Peter Cabuay; Costumes, Kenneth Chu; Lighting, Victor En Yu Tan; Sound, Peter Griggs; Stage Manager, Elis C. Arroyo CAST: Charlee Chiv (Jay Yimou), Donna Leichenko (Mary Ling), Andrew Pang (Mark Li), Les J. N. Mau (Mr. Wong), Marcus Ho (Ethan Kwan)
A romantic comedy in two acts. The action takes place in San Francisco's Chinatown, 1990s.

Wednesday, January 17–27, 2001 (6 performances)
THE LEGEND OF THE WHITE SNAKE Adapted/Directed by Lu Yu; Martial Arts Choreography, Ding Mei-Kui CAST: Richard Chang (Xu Xian/ Guardian of the Magical Herb), Li Yiling (Bai Su Jen-White Snake), Li Jun (Xiao Qing-Blue Snake), Wang Fei (Boat Man/Fa Hai/Immortal of South Pole), Wang Xizo-Yen (Heavenly Soldier/Son of White Snake)
Dance theatre performed without intermission.

Tuesday, February 13–March 18, 2001 (25 performances and 7 previews)
RASHOMON by Fay and Michael Kanin; Based on novellas by Ryunosuke Akutagawa; Director, Tisa Chang; Set, Kaori Akazawa; Costumes, Molly Reynolds; Lighting, Victor En Yu Tan; Music, Shigeko Suga, Tom Matsusaka; Fights, Michael G. Chin; Stage Manager, James W. Carringer CAST: Orville Mendoza (Priest), Ron Nakahara (Woodcutter), Les J. N. Mau (Wigmaker), Tom Matsusaka (Deputy/Musician), Ken Park (Bandit), Marcus Ho (Husband), Rosanne Ma (Wife), Shigeko Suga (Mother/Shaman/Musician)
A drama in two acts. The action takes place in Kyoto, Japan, 1000 A.D.

Carol Rosegg, Corky Lee Photos

Donna Leichenko, Marcus Ho in *The Poet of Columbus Avenue*

Rosanne Ma, Marcus Ho in *Rashomon*

PEARL THEATRE COMPANY

Seventeenth Season

Artistic Director, Shepard Sobel; Development Director/Artistic Associate, Joanne Camp; Managing Director, Jessica Kroll; Casting Director, Rich Cole; Marketing/Press Director, Michelle Brandon; Fight Director, Rick Sordelet; Speech/Text Coach, Robert Neff Williams; Sound Design, Johnna Doty; Choreographer, Alice Teirstein

Thursday, August 31–October 22, 2000 (40 performances and 12 previews)
BLITHE SPIRIT by Noël Coward; Director, Stephen Hollis; Set, Harry Feiner; Costumes, Leslie Yarmo; Lighting, Stephen Petrilli; Stage Manager, Lisa Ledwich CAST: Elizabeth Ureneck (Edith), Joanne Camp (Ruth), Doug Stender (Charles), Dominic Cuskern (Dr. Bradman), Glynis Bell (Mrs. Bradman), Delphi Harrington (Madame Arcati), Hope Chernov (Elvira)
A comedy in three acts. The action takes place in Kent, England, 1941.

Thursday, November 2–December 17, 2000 (33 performances and 12 previews)
RICHARD III by William Shakespeare; Director, Shepard Sobel; Set, Beowulf Boritt CAST: Dan Daily (Richard), Glynis Bell (Elizabeth), Jonathan Peck (Buckingham), Rachel Botchan (Anne), Judith Roberts (Margaret), Edward Seamon (Edward), David Toney (Clarence), Albert Jones (Henry Tudor), Matthew J. Cody, Dominic Cuskern, Matthew Gray, Grant Hand, Robert Hand, Brent Harris, Anna Minot, Christopher Moore, Paul Niebanck

Thursday, January 11–February 25, 2001 (35 performances and 12 previews)
THE CHERRY ORCHARD by Anton Chekhov; Director, Joseph Hardy; Set, Beowulf Borritt; Costumes, Irene V. Hatch; Lighting, Stephen Petrilli; Stage Manager, Jane Siebels CAST: Mimi Bilinski (Varya), Rachel Botchan (Anya), Robin Leslie Brown (Carlotta), Arnie Burton (Trofimov), Joanne Camp (Ranevskaya), Dominic Cuskern (Yepichodov), Dan Daily (Lopachin), Robert Hock (Gaev), Christopher Moore (Yasha), Alex Roe (Vagrant/Stationmaster), Edward Seamon (Pishchick), Jennifer Lynn Thomas (Dunyasha), John Wylie (Feers)
Performed with one intermission. The action takes place on Lyubov's estate, which includes a once-famous cherry orchard, 1904.

Thursday, March 29–June 16, 2001 (31 performances and 12 previews)
A WILL OF HIS OWN by Jean-François Regnard; Translation, Michael Feingold; Director, Russell Treyz; Set, Beowulf Boritt; Costumes, E. Shura Pollatsek; Lighting, Chris Dallos; Stage Manager, Dale Smallwood CAST: Celeste Ciulla (Lisette), Arnie Burton (Crispin), Christopher Moore (Valere), John Wylie (Geronte), Andrew Firda (Geronte's Servant/Scruple), Valerie Leonard (Madame Argante), Rachel Botchan (Isabelle), Felice Yeh (Argante's Servant), Dominic Cuskern (Enema/Gaspard)
A comedy, set in Paris, performed with one intermission. Presented in rotating repertory with *Andromache.*

Thursday, April 26–June 17, 2001 (21 performances and 12 previews)
ANDROMACHE by Jean Racine; Translation, Earle Edgerton; Director, Shepard Sobel; For other production credits, see *A Will of His Own* CAST: Christopher Moore (Orestes), Dominic Cuskern (Pylades), Arnie Burton (Pyrrhus), John Wylie (Phoenix), Rachel Botchan (Andromache), Celeste Ciulla (Hermoine), Valerie Leonard (Cleone), Felice H. Yeh (Cephissa)
A tragedy, set in Epirus, performed with one intermission. Presented in rotating repertory with *A Will of His Own.*

Tom Bloom, Stephen Petrilli Photos

Arnie Burton, Celeste Ciulla in *A Will of His Own*

Hope Chernov, Joanne Camp in *Blithe Spirit*

Arnie Burton, Joanne Camp in *The Cherry Orchard*

PLAYWRIGHTS HORIZONS

Thirtieth Season

Artistic Director, Tim Sanford; Managing Director, Leslie Marcus; Casting Director, James Calleri; Director of Development, Jill Garland; General Manager, William Russo; Artistic and Management Assistant, Fell Ogden; Production Managers, Christopher Boll, Peter Waxdal, Joshua Helman; Press, Publicity Office/Bob Fennell, Michael S. Borowski, Marc Thibodeau, Candi Adams

(Mainstage) Friday, September 8–October 15, 2000 (16 performances and 28 previews)
THE BUTTERFLY COLLECTION by Theresa Rebeck; Director, Bartlett Sher; Set, Andrew Jackness; Costumes, Ann Hould-Ward; Lighting, Christopher Akerlind; Sound, Kurt B. Kellenberger; Stage Manager, Roy Harris CAST: Maggie Lacey (Sophie), Reed Birney (Frank), Marian Seldes (Margaret), Betsy Aidem (Laurie), James Colby (Ethan), Brian Murray (Paul)
A drama in two acts. The action takes place at a Connecticut country house during summer.

(Studio) Thursday, October 12–November 5, 2000 (17 performances and 12 previews)
OTHER PEOPLE by Christopher Shinn; Director, Tim Farrell; Set, Kyle Chepulis; Costumes, Mimi O'Donnell; Lighting, Andrew Hill; Sound, Ken Travis; Stage Manager, Lee J. Kahrs CAST: Kate Blumberg (Petra), Neal Huff (Stephen), Austin Lysy (Tan), Victor Slezak (Man), Pete Starrett (Mark), Philip Tabor (Darren)
A drama set in New York's East Village at Christmastime.

(Mainstage) Tuesday, December 12, 2000–January 21, 2001 (17 performances and 30 previews)
THE WAX by Kathleen Tolan; Director, Brian Kulick; Set, Walt Spangler; Costumes, Elizabeth Hope Clancy; Lighting, Kevin Adams; Sound, Jill B.C. Du Boff; Stage Manager, Pamela Edington CAST: Karen Young (Kate), Mary Testa (Angie), Robert Dorfman (Hal), Frank Wood (Christopher), Mary Schultz (Amelia), Gareth Saxe (Bert), Laura Esterman (Maureen), David Greenspan (Ben), Lola Pashalinsky (Lily)
A comedy performed without intermission. The action takes place in a New England hotel.

Marian Seldes, Brian Murray in *The Butterfly Collection*

Austin Lysy, Pete Starrett in *Other People*

Mary Testa, Karen Young in *The Wax*

(continued)

(Mainstage) Friday, February 16–April 15, 2001 (40 performances and 28 previews); Transferred to (John Houseman Theatre) Tuesday, May 8–September 2, 2001 (136 performances)
LOBBY HERO by Kenneth Lonergan; Director, Mark Brokaw; Set, Allen Moyer; Costumes, Michael Krass; Lighting, Mark McCullough; Sound, Janet Kalas; Stage Managers, James FitzSimmons, Thea Bradshaw Gillies; Producers, for Houseman transfer, Jenny Wiener, Jon Steingart, Hal Luftig
CAST: Glenn Fitzgerald (Jeff), Dion Graham (William), Heather Burns (Dawn), Tate Donovan (Bill)
A two-act play set in the lobby of a Manhattan high-rise apartment building.

(Mainstage) Friday, May 11–June 17, 2001 (16 performances and 28 previews)
THE CREDEAUX CANVAS by Keith Bunin; Director, Michael Mayer; Set, Derek McLane; Costumes, Michael Krass; Lighting, Keith Posner; Sound, Scott Myers; Fights, J. Steven White; Stage Manager, J. Philip Bassett
CAST: Annie Parisse (Amelia), Lee Pace (Winston), Glenn Howerton (Jamie), E. Katherine Kerr (Tess)
A drama in two acts. The action takes place in an attic apartment on East 10th St. in New York City.

(Studio) Thursday, May 31–July 1, 2001 (25 performances and 12 previews)
BREATH, BOOM by Kia Corthron; Director, Marion McClinton; Set/ Lighting, Michael Philippi; Costumes, Katherine Roth; Sound, Ken Travis; Fights, David Leong; Stage Manager, Jane Pole CAST: Yvette Ganier (Prix), Rosalyn Coleman (Angel), Kalimi A. Baxter (Malika/Socks), Heather Alicia Simms (Comet), Caroline Stefanie Clay (Mother), Russell Andrews (Jerome), Donna Duplantier (Cat/Girl with Pepper/Jo's Friend), Dena Atlantic (Shondra/Pepper/Jo), Abigail López (Fuego/Denise), Pascale Armand (Jupiter)
A drama in two acts.

Joan Marcus, Carol Rosegg Photos

Glen Fitzgerald, Dion Graham in *Lobby Hero*

Lee Pace, Annie Parisse in *The Credeaux Canvas*

Rosalyn Coleman, Yvette Ganier in *Breath, Boom*

PRIMARY STAGES

Sixteenth Season

Founder/Artistic Director, Casey Childs; Managing Director, Margaret Chandler; Associate Producer, Seth Gordon; Associate Artistic Directors, Janet Reed Ahearn, Tyler Marchant; Artistic/Administrative Associate, Anne Einhorn; Production Manager, Joshua Helman; Casting, Stephanie Klapper, Alan Filderman, Judy Henderson; Press, Jeffrey Richards/John Michael Moreno, Irene Gandy, Chloé Taylor, Jon Dimond

Wednesday, September 20–October 22, 2000 (21 performances and 13 previews)
STRAIGHT AS A LINE by Luis Alfaro; Director, Jon Lawrence Rivera; Set, Bob Phillips; Lighting, Deborah Constantine; Sound, Eric Shim; Stage Manager, Renee Lutz CAST: James Sie (Paulie), Natsuko Ohama (Mum)
A dark comedy performed without intermission.

Wednesday, January 17–February 18, 2001 (22 performances and 13 previews)
KRISIT by Y York; Director, Melia Bensussen; Set, James Noone; Costumes, Claudia Stephens; Lighting, Jeff Croiter; Sound, Charles T. Brastow; Stage Manager, Renee Lutz CAST: Scotty Bloch (Krisit), Jessica Stone (Lulu), Larry Pine (Peter)
A Hollywood satire performed without intermission. The action takes place in a grand bathtub in a grand bathroom, and a table in a grand bar.

Wednesday, March 21–April 22, 2001 (23 performances and 15 previews)
NO NIGGERS, NO JEWS, NO DOGS by John Henry Redwood; Director, Israel Hicks; Set, Michael Brown; Costumes, Christine Field; Lighting, Ann G. Wrightson; Sound, Eileen Tague; Stage Manager, Gretchen Knowlton CAST: Charis M. Wilson (Toke Cheeks), Rayme Cornell (Aunt Cora), Elizabeth Van Dyke (Mattie Cheeks), Marcus Naylor (Rawl Cheeks), Jack Aaron (Yaveni Aaronsohn), Adrienne Carter (Joyce Cheeks)
A drama in two acts. The action takes place in Halifax, NC, 1949.

Wednesday, May 30–July 1, 2001 (21 performances and 13 previews)
BYRD'S BOY by Bruce J. Robinson; Director, Arthur Masella; Set, Narelle Sissons; Costumes, Judith Dolan; Lighting, Peter West; Sound/Music, Donald DiNicola; Stage Manager, Douglas Shearer CAST: David McCallum (Byrd), Myra Lucretia Taylor (Birdie)
A two-act drama inspired by real events. The action takes place in a warehouse in Baltimore, 1988.

Samantha Morganville, Mark Garvin, Marvin Einhorn Photos

Marcus Naylor, Jack Aaron in *No Niggers, No Jews, No Dogs*

Larry Pine, Scotty Bloch in *Krisit*

David McCallum, Myra Lucretia in *Byrd's Boy*

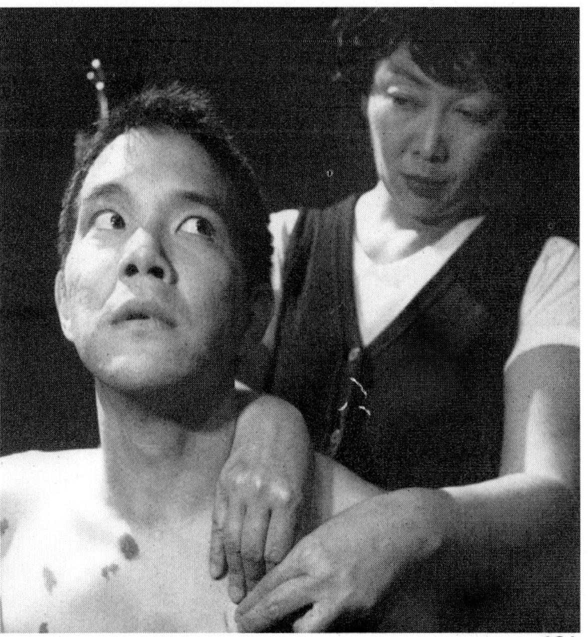

James Sie, Natsuko Ohama in *Straight as a Line*

Artistic Director, Todd Haimes; Managing Director, Ellen Richard; Executive Director/External Affairs, Julia C. Levy; Founding Director, Gene Feist; Associate Artistic Director, Scott Ellis; Artistic Development/ Director of Casting, Jim Carnahan; Fight Director, J. Steven White; Casting, Amy Christopher; Dialect Coach, Stephen Gabis; General Manager, Sydney Davolos; Production Stage Manager, Jay Adler; Press, Chris Boneau-Adrian Bryan-Brown/Matt Polk, Orlando Veras, Kel Christofferson; Off Broadway Performances at Gramercy Theatre

Friday, September 22–December 23, 2000 (76 performances and 32 previews)
JUNO AND THE PAYCOCK by Sean O'Casey; Director, John Crowley; Set/ Costumes, Rae Smith; Lighting, Brian MacDevitt; Sound/Music, Donald DiNicola CAST: Jason Butler Harner (Johnny Boyle), Gretchen Cleevely (Mary Boyle), Dearbhla Molloy (Juno Boyle), Norbert Leo Butz (Jerry Devine), Jim Norton (Capt. Jack Boyle), Thomas Jay Ryan (Joxer Daly), Edward James Hyland (Sewing Machine Man/Needle Nugent), John Keating (Coal Vendor/Furniture Man/Police), Liam Craig (Charles Bentham), Cynthia Darlow (Maisie Madigan), Roberta Maxwell (Mrs. Tancred), Kelly Mares (Neighbor), George Heslin (Mobilizer), Michael Lidondici (Irregular)
The 1924 three-act drama performed with one intermission. The action takes place in Dublin, August 1922.

Tuesday, January 30–May 20, 2001 (101 performances and 27 previews)
A SKULL IN CONNEMARA by Martin McDonagh; Director, Gordon Edelstein; Set, David Gallo; Costumes, Susan Hilferty; Lighting, Michael Chybowski; Sound, Stephen LeGrand; Music, Martin Hayes CAST: Kevin Tighe (Mick Dowd), Zoaunne LeRoy (Maryjohnny Rafferty), Christopher Carley (Martin Hanlon), Christopher Evan Welch (Thomas Hanlon)
A drama in two acts. The action takes place in rural Galway, Ireland. This is the second installment in Martin McDonagh's Leenane trilogy of plays. *The Beauty Queen of Leenane* and *The Lonesome West,* the other two plays in the trilogy, have received recent Broadway productions. See *Theatre World* Vol. 54 for *Beauty Queen,* and *Theatre World* Vol. 55 for *Lonesome West.*

For other Roundabout Theatre Company productions, *Betrayal, Design for Living,* and *Follies,* see BROADWAY section.

Joan Marcus Photos

Kevin Tighe, Christopher Evan Welch in *A Skull in Connemara*

Jason Butler Harner, Gretchen Cleevely, Dearbhla Molloy in *Juno and the Paycock*

SECOND STAGE THEATRE

Twenty-second Season

Artistic Director, Carole Rothman; 2001 Season Artistic Director, Mark Linn-Baker; Managing Director, Carol Fishman; Executive Director, Alexander Fraser; Associate Artistic Director, Christopher Burney; Fight Director, B.H. Barry; Casting, Bernard Telsey, James Calleri, Johnson-Liff Associates; General Manager, C. Barrack Evans; Production Manager, Peter J. Davis; Dialect Coach, Deborah Hecht; Press, Richard Kornberg/ Don Summa, Jim Byk, Tom D'Ambrosio, Carrie Friedman

Thursday, November 16, 2000–January 7, 2001 (41 performances and 24 previews)
TINY ALICE by Edward Albee; Director, Mark Lamos; Set, John Arnone; Costumes, Constance Hoffman; Lighting, Donald Holder; Sound, David Budries; Stage Manager, Lloyd Davis Jr. CAST: Stephen Rowe (Lawyer), Tom Lacy (Cardinal), Richard Thomas (Brother Julian), John Michael Higgins (Butler), Laila Robins (Miss Alice)
A mystery in three acts.

Wednesday, January 24–March 4, 2001 (25 performances and 23 previews)
CELLINI Written/Directed by John Patrick Shanley; Adapted from the *Autobiography of Benvenuto Cellini* translated by J. Addington Symonds; Set, Adrianne Lobel; Costumes, Martin Pakledinaz; Lighting, Brian Nason; Sound, David Van Tieghem; Stage Manager, Janet Takami CAST: Lucas Papaelias (Boy/Bernard/Giacamo), Reg Rogers (Cellini), Daniel Oreskes (Duke of Florence/Judge/Merchant), Lisa Bansavage (Duchess/ Gambetta/Serving Maid), Richard Russell Ramos (Pope Paolo/Riccio/ King Francois), Jennifer Roszell (Caterina/Mona Fiore), Gary Perez (Tasso/Judge), John Gould Rubin (Bandinello/Cardinal Cornaro/Judge), David Chandler (Pope Clement/Bargello/Gorini/Treasurer)
A drama in two acts. The action takes place in Italy, around 1558.

Tuesday, April 3–May 13, 2001 (33 performances and 16 previews)
CRIMES OF THE HEART by Beth Henley; Director, Garry Hynes; Set, Thomas Lynch; Costumes, Susan Hilferty; Lighting, Rui Rita; Music, Sound, Donald DiNicola; Stage Manager, Kelly Kirkpatrick CAST: Julia Murney (Chick), Enid Graham (Lenny), Talmadge Lowe (Doc), Amy Ryan (Meg), Mary Catherine Garrison (Babe), Jason Butler Harner (Barnett)
A comedy in two acts. The action takes place in Hazlehurst, Mississippi, five years after Hurricane Camille.

Joan Marcus, T. Charles Erickson Photos

Reg Rogers, Jennifer Roszell in *Cellini*

Amy Ryan, Enid Graham, Mary Catherine Garrison in *Crimes of the Heart*

Richard Thomas, John Michael Higgins in *Tiny Alice*

SIGNATURE THEATRE COMPANY

Tenth Season

Founding Artistic Director, James Houghton; Managing Director, Bruce E. Whitacre; Development Director, Kathryn M. Lipuma; Fight Director, B.H. Barry; General Manager, Karalee Dawn; Production Manager, Bill Kneissl; Casting, Jerry Beaver; Press, The Publicity Office/Marc Thibodeau, Bob Fennell, Candi Adams; All-Premiere Season (New Works from Signature's Past Playwrights-in-Residence)

Tuesday, September 5–October 22, 2000 (36 performances and 14 previews)
A LESSON BEFORE DYING by Romulus Linney; Based on the novel by Ernest J. Gaines; Director, Kent Thompson; Set, Marjorie Bradley Kellogg; Costumes, Alvin B. Perry; Lighting, Jane Cox; Sound, Don Tindall; Music, Chic Street Man; Stage Manager, Francys Olivia Burch CAST: Beatrice Winde (Emma Glenn), Aaron Harpold (Paul Bonin), Isiah Whitlock Jr. (Grant Wiggins), Stephen Bradbury (Sam Guidry), Jamahl Marsh (Jefferson), Tracey A. Leigh (Vivian Baptiste), John Henry Redwood (Rev. Moses Ambrose)
A drama set in Louisiana, 1948.

Isiah Whitlock, Jr., Beatrice Winde in *A Lesson Before Dying*

Tuesday, November 21, 2000–January 14, 2001 (43 performances and 13 previews)
THE LAST OF THE THORNTONS by Horton Foote; Director, James Houghton; Set, Christine Jones; Costumes, Elizabeth Hope Clancy; Lighting, Michael Chybowski; Sound, Kurt Kellenberger; Stage Manager, Tina M. Newhauser CAST: Alice Mclane (Miss Pearl Dayton), Estelle Parsons (Fannie Mae Gossett), Cherene Snow (Clarabelle Jones), Anne Pitoniak (Mrs. Ruby Blair), Mary Catherine Garrison (Ora Sue), Hallie Foote (Alberta Thornton), Mason Adams (Lewis Reavis), Jen Jones (Annie Gayle Long), Michael Hadge (Douglas Jackson), Timothy Altmeyer (Harry Vaughn Jr.)
A drama performed without intermission. The action takes place in a Harrison, Texas nursing home, 1970.

Estelle Parsons, Hallie Foote in *The Last of the Thorntons*

Tuesday, May 8–June 17, 2001 (29 previews and 13 previews)
THIEF RIVER by Lee Blessing; Director, Mark Lamos; Set, Marjorie Bradley Kellogg; Costumes, Jess Goldstein; Lighting, Pat Collins; Sound/Music, John Gromada; Stage Manager, Michael McGoff CAST: Jeffrey Carlson (Gil 1/Jody), Erik Sorensen (Ray 1/Kit), Neil Maffin (Gil 2/Harlow), Gregg Edelman (Ray 2/Reese), Remak Ramsay (Gil 3/Perry), Frank Converse (Ray 3/Anson)
A drama performed without intermission. The action takes place at an abandoned Midwest farmhouse during June of three different years: 1948, 1973, and 2001.

Susan Johann Photos

Neil Maffin, Gregg Edelman in *Thief River*

VINEYARD THEATRE

Twentieth Season

Artistic Director, Douglas Aibel; Executive Director/Founder, Barbara Zinn Krieger; Managing Director, Bardo S. Ramirez; External Affairs Director, Jennifer Garvey-Blackwell; Fight Director, Rick Sordelet; Artistic Associate, Sarah Stern; General Manager, Jodi Schoenbrun; Production Manager, Kai Brothers; Casting, Cindy Tolan; Press, Shirley Herz/Sam Rudy

Wednesday, September 27–November 19, 2000 (35 performances and 20 previews)
STRANGER by Craig Lucas; Director, Mark Brokaw; Set, Neil Patel; Costumes, Jess Goldstein; Lighting, Mark McCullough; Sound/Music, David Van Tieghem, Jill B.C. Du Boff; Stage Manager, Katherine Lee Boyer CAST: Kyra Sedgwick (Linda), David Strathairn (Hush), David Harbour (Steward/Frank/Pato), Julianne Nicholson (Stewardess/Linda's Mom/Girl)
A two-act drama about two strangers who meet on a plane.

Kyra Sedgwick, David Strathairn in *Stranger*

Friday, January 5–February 11, 2001 (22 performances and 17 previews)
MORE LIES ABOUT JERZY by Davey Holmes; Director, Darko Tresnjak; Set, Derek McLane; Costumes, Linda Cho; Lighting, Frances Aronson; Sound, Laura Grace Brown; Stage Manager, Katherine Lee Boyer CAST: Gretchen Egolf (Georgia Fischer), Jared Harris (Jerzy Lesnewski), Daniel London (Arthur Bausley), Lizbeth Mackay (Isabel Parris), Boris McGiver (Rysiek Zrupina), Betty Miller (Osucha Gruszka), Portia Reiners (Kasia Gruszka), Martin Shakar (Talk Show Host/Mr. Sorvillo/Jerzy's Father), Adam Stein (Brett Pearson/Mr. Kerry/Young Man), Gary Wilmes (Harry Frott/Witold Twarog)
A drama in two acts. The action takes place in New York City, 1972.

Gretchen Egolf, Jared Harris in *More Lies About Jerzy*

Wednesday, April 11–July 14, 2001 (70 performances and 26 previews)
ELI'S COMIN' Music/Lyrics, Laura Nyro; Created by Bruce Buschel and Diane Paulus; Director, Ms. Paulus; Musical Director, Joe Rubenstein; Vocal/Orchestral Arrangements, Diedre Murray; Set, G.W. Mercier; Costumes, Linda Cho; Lighting, Jane Cox; Sound, Brett Jarvis; Stage Manager, Christine M. Daly CAST: Judy Kuhn (Emmie), Mandy Gonzalez (The Young Girl), Anika Noni Rose (The Woman), Ronnell Bey (The Mother), Wilson Jermaine Heredia (Captain)
MUSICAL NUMBERS: Stoned Soul Picnic, New York Tendaberry, Captain Saint Lucifer, Luckie, Buy & Sell, Money, Eli's Comin', The Wind, Blowin' Away, Sweet Blindness, The Confession, Captain for Dark Mornings, I Am the Blues, Poverty Train, Been on a Train, Stoney End, Emmie, Mother's Spiritual, Brown Earth, And When I Die
A musical performed without intermission.

Carol Rosegg Photos

Ronnell Bey, Mandy Gonzalez, Anika Noni Rose, Judy Kuhn in *Eli's Comin'*

WOMEN'S PROJECT & PRODUCTIONS

Twenty-third Season

Artistic Director, Julia Miles; Managing Director, Patricia Taylor; Artistic Associate, Suzanne Bennett; Production Manager, B.D. White; Casting, Deborah Brown, Samuel D. Buggeln; Press, Gary Springer-Susan Chicoine/Joe Trentacosta

Wednesday, October 11–November 4, 2000 (26 performances and 8 previews)
HARD FEELINGS by Neena Beber; Director, Maria Mileaf; Set, Neil Patel; Costumes, Katherine Roth; Lighting, Russell Champa; Sound, Eileen Tague; Stage Manager, Becky Garrett CAST: Seana Kofoed (Selma Rogers), Guy Boyd (Dr. Disposio), Kate Jennings Grant (Finola Cornflakes), Mary Fogarty (Granny Gee), Pamela J. Gary (Irene)
A comedy in two acts.

Sunday, February 25–March 18, 2001 (20 performances and 4 previews)
LEAVING QUEENS Lyrics/Book, Kate Moira Ryan; Music/Orchestrations, Kim D. Sherman; Director, Allison Narver; Musical Director, Paul J. Ascenzo; Set, Anita Stewart; Costumes, Louisa Thompson; Lighting, Jennifer Tipton; Stage Manager, Jana Llynn CAST: Alice M. Vienneau (Megan Grant), Alexander Bonnin (Michael/Young Joseph), Barbara Tirrell (Anne/Mary), Cynthia Sophiea (Miss Cleaver Smith), Jim Jacobson (Thomas/Adult Joseph), Paul Niebanck (Ansel Adams/Edward Steichen)
MUSICAL NUMBERS: Let Me In, Reroute, The Song Nobody Hears, A Chair in the Dark, Paperless Office, Three A.M., Courage and Fire, Island of Hope, Art Is Not Useful, I Stay Until, Picture Show, Stay Oh, Spit and Polish, Family of Man, Break a Promise, Oh Give Me a Stout, At the Wild Rover, Leaving Queens, Dark Irish Men, Street Light, We Could Home, Newcomers Dawn
A musical in two acts. The action takes place in NYC and Kosovo.

Wednesday, March 28–April 29, 2001 (19 performances and 15 previews); Transferred to (Cherry Lane Theatre) Thursday, July 12–September 2, 2001 (61 performances)
SAINT LUCY'S EYES by Bridgette A. Wimberly; Director, Billie Allen; Set, Beowulf Borritt; Costumes, Alvin B. Perry; Lighting, Jane Reisman; Sound/Music, Michael Wimberly; Stage Manager, Susan D. Lange CAST: Ruby Dee (Old Woman), Toks Olagundoye (Young Woman), Willis Burks II (Bay), Sally A. Stewart (Woman)
A drama in two acts. The action takes place in Memphis, 1968–80.

Martha Holmes Photos

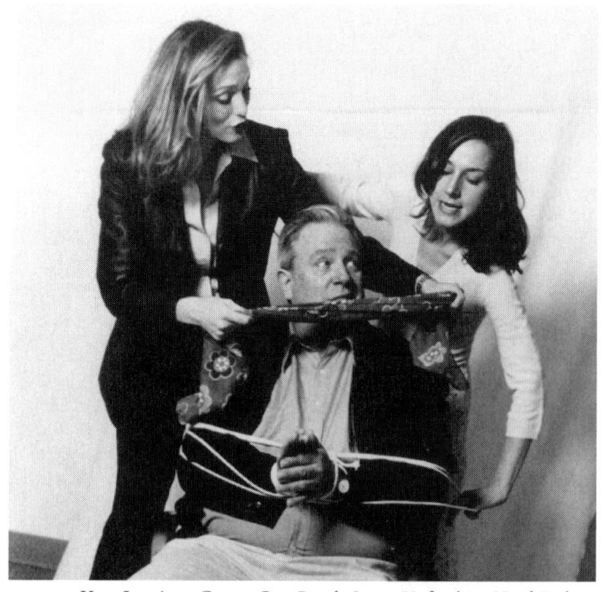

Kate Jennings Grant, Guy Boyd, Seana Kofoed in *Hard Feelings*

Alice Vienneau, Alexander Bonnin in *Leaving Queens*

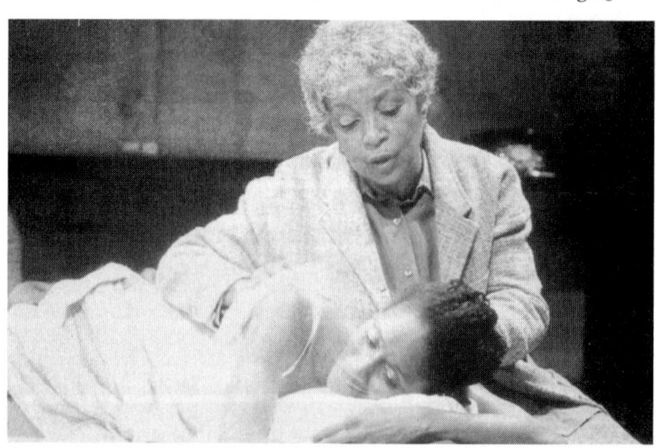

Toks Olagundoye, Rube Dee in *Saint Lucy's Eyes*

YORK THEATRE COMPANY

Thirty-second Season

Artistic Director, James Morgan; Managing Director, Clayton Phillips; Development Director, John L. Ruddock III; Casting, Norman Meranus; Press, Keith Sherman/Dan Fortune

Tuesday, November 21–December 31, 2000 (30 performances and 18 previews)
FERMAT'S LAST TANGO Music/Orchestrations, Joshua Rosenblum; Lyrics, Joanne Sydney Lessner and Mr. Rosenblum; Book, Ms. Lessner; Director, Mel Marvin; Musical Staging, Janet Watson; Music Director, Milton Granger; Set, James Morgan; Costumes, Lynn Bowling; Lighting, John Michael Deegan; Cast Recording, Original Cast Records; Stage Manager, Peggy R. Samuels CAST: Gilles Chiasson (Carl Friedrich Gauss/Reporter), Edwardyne Cowan (Anna Keane), Mitchell Kantor (Pythagoras/Reporter), Jonathan Rabb (Pierre de Fermat), Chris Thompson (Daniel Keane), Christianne Tisdale (Euclid/Reporter), Carrie Wilshusen (Sir Isaac Newton/Reporter)
MUSICAL NUMBERS: Prologue, Press Conference, You're a Hero Now, The Beauty of Numbers, Tell Me Your Secret, Sing We to Symmetry, Welcome to the AfterMath, Your Proff Contains a Hole, I Dreamed, My Name, All I Want for My Birthday, The Game Show, Math Window, I'll Always Be There (Fermat's Last Tango), The Relay Race, I'm Stumbling, Oh It's You, Finale
A musical, inspired by the achievements of Princeton University mathematics professor Andrew Wiles and French mathematician Pierre de Fermat, performed without intermission. The action takes place in a conference hall, Keane's attic, and points Heavenward, 1993–94.

Edwardyne Cowan, Chris Thompson, Jonathan Rabb in *Fermat's Last Tango*

Tuesday, February 13–March 25, 2001 (29 performances and 19 previews)
SUBURB Music, Robert S. Cohen; Lyrics, David Javerbaum; Book, Mr. Javerbaum and Mr. Cohen; Director, Jennifer Uphoff Gray; Music Director, Jeffrey R. Smith; Orchestrations, Lary Hochman; Choreography, John Carrafa; Music Supervisor, Steven Tyler; Set, Kris Stone; Costumes, Jan Finnell; Lighting, John Michael Deegan; Stage Manager, Peggy R. Samuels CAST: Jacquelyn Piro (Alison), James Ludwig (Stuart), Dennis Kelly (Tom), Alix Korey (Rhoda), Adinah Alexander, Ron Butler, Jennie Eisenhower, James Sasser
MUSICAL NUMBERS: Directions, Mow, Do It Yourself, Suburb, Not Me, Barbecue, The Girl Next Door, Ready Or Not, Commute, Mall, Duet, Handy, Walkin' to School, Bagel-Shop Quartet, Trio for Four, Everything Must Go, Someday
A musical in two acts.

James Ludwig, Jacquelyn Piro in *Suburb*

Tuesday, April 17–May 27, 2001 (29 performances and 19 previews)
THE IT GIRL Music/Orchestrations, Paul McKibbins; Lyrics/Director, BT McNicholl; Book, Michael Small, BT McNicholl; Music Director/Dance Arrangements, Albin Konopka, Charles Eversole; Choreography, Robert Bianca; Set, Mark Nayden; Costumes, Robin L. McGee; Lighting, Jeff Nellis; Projections, Elaine J. McCarthy; Silent Movie Sequences, Steve Smith; Cast Recording, Jay; Stage Manager, Peggy R. Samuels CAST: Jean Louisa Kelly (Betty Lou Spencer), Monte Wheeler (Mr. Hotting/Barker), Danette Holden (Jane/Mrs. Sullivan/Mrs. Van Norman), Susan M. Haefner (Daisy/Molly/Dancer), Jonathan Dokuchitz (Jonathan Waltham), Stephen DeRosa (Monty Montgomery), Jessica Boevers (Adela Van Norman)
MUSICAL NUMBERS: Black and White World, Why Not?, Stand Straight and Tall, It, Mama's Arms, What to Wear?, A Perfect Plan, Coney Island, Woman and Waif, Stay with Me/Left Hand Arrangement, Step into Their Shoes, Out at Sea, How Do You Say…?, You're the Best Thing That Ever Happened to Me, Finale
A two-act musical based on *It*, a 1927 Clara Bow film.

Carol Rosegg Photos

Jean Louisa Kelly, Jonathan Dokuchitz in *The It Girl*

OFF-BROADWAY PRODUCTIONS

(June 1, 2000-May 31 , 2001)

(Bessie Schönberg Theatre) Thursday, June 1–25, 2000 (13 performances and 9 previews); Transferred to (45 Bleeker Theatre) August 30–October 1, 2000 (30 performances) The Foundry Theatre presents:
AND GOD CREATED GREAT WHALES Written/Composed by Rinde Eckert; Director, David Schweizer; Set/Lighting, Kevin Adams; Costumes, Clint E.B. Ramos; Sound, James Rattazzi; Stage Manager, Scott Pegg; Press, Richard Kornberg/Tom D'Ambrosio CAST: Rinde Eckert (Nathan), Nora Cole (Olivia/Muse)
A musical theatre piece performed without intermission.

Nora Cole, Rinde Eckert in *And God Created Great Whales* (Carol Rosegg)

Dennis Paladino, Caryn Rosenthal in *Last of the Red Hot Lovers*

(Sande Shurin Theatre) Thursday, June 1–18, 2000 (12 performances) Highroad Productions present:
LAST OF THE RED HOT LOVERS by Neil Simon; Director, Christopher L. Bellis; Set, Emanuel Chionchio; Costumes, Mary O'Bradovich; Lighting, Phil Widmer; Stage Manager, James Israel; Press, James Gregory Collins CAST: Dennis Paladino (Barney Cashman), Alicia Sedwick (Elaine Navazio), Stacie Renna (Bobbi Michele), Caryn Rosenthal (Jeanette Fisher)
A comedy in three acts. The action takes place in New York City, 1969–70.

(Atlantic Theatre) Thursday, June 1–August 26, 2000 (70 performances and 18 previews) Patrick Blake, Andrew McTiernan, Beth Schacter, and Allyson Spellman present:
JOE FEARLESS (A FAN DANCE) Conceived/Written by Liz Tuccillo; Director, Craig Carlisle; Set/Lighting, Michael Brown; Costumes, Mattie Ullrich; Music, Keith Middletown; Basketball Choreography, Taro Alexander; Fearless Fly Girl Choreography, Danielle Flora, Laura Sheehy; Casting, Caroline Sinclair; Stage Manager, Jerry James; Press, Gary Springer-Susan Chicoine/Joe Trentacosta CAST: Michael Leydon Campbell (Joe Donnelly), Julie Dretzin (Linda Donnelly), Matthew Dawson (Tim), Callie Thorne (Meg/Saleslady), Michael Potts (Ray /Doctor), Nathan Dean (Announcers), Charlotte Colavin (Janine), Dan Folger (Ref), Danielle Flora (Fly Girl/Suzy), Laura Sheehy (Fly Girl /Cindy), Jessica Castro, Sundra Oakley (Fly Girls), Chris Stack (Drummer /Fan/Coach), Michael Ealy (Jo Jo Sharkey), Fred Benjamin (Pernell Evers), Blake Robbins (Cal Owens), Keith Tisdell (Chris Smalls), Eric Ingram (Erick Alvarez/Guard), Matthew McMurray (Jonesy Greenaway), Robert Manning (Renny Milton), Randy Ryan (Edward Vaclav/Benny the Blaster)
A sports play with music in two acts. There are two different endings, depending on Jo Jo's final shot.

(Connelly Theatre) Thursday, June 1–25, 2000 (12 performances and 11 previews) Moonwork presents:
ROMEO AND JULIET by William Shakespeare; Director, Gregory Wolfe; Set, Lowell Pettit; Costumes, June Wolfe; Lighting, Jen Acomb; Music, Andrew Sherman; Choreography, Jena Necrason; Stage Manager, Carla Rao; Press, Shirley Herz/Sam Rudy CAST: Gregory J. Sherman (Romeo /Fight Choreography), Monique Vukovic (Juliet), Mason Pettit (Friar Lawrence), Tom Shillue (Nurse), Anna Cody (Mercutio), Jennifer Carta (Benvolio), Gary Desbien (Capulet), James O'Connor (Peter), Mark Ellmore (Tybalt), Brina Bishop, Jenny Burleson, Todd Carlstrom, Michael Castellano, Michele Concha, David DelGrosso, Jay Gaussoin, Heather Hirardi, Tatiana Gomberg, Michael Gould, Bryan Grossbauer, Christopher Haas, Kevin Held, Kathleen Hunt, Hilary Ketchum, Molly Lloyd, Rhonda S. Musak, Kim Patton, Joshua Polenberg, Joe Reina, Sydney Rhoads, Stephen Michael Rondel, John Roque, Brent Rosenbaum, Justin J. Steeve, James Wolfe, Anna Zastrow

(Phil Bosakowski Theater) Thursday, June 1–24, 2000 (13 performances and 3 previews)
POOR FELLAS by Marc Palmieri; Director, Tony P. Pennino; Lighting, Curt Beach; Press, Brett Singer CAST: George Demas, Lee Dobson, Michael Lawrence, Marla Mervis, Brian Sloan, Carlo Trigiani, Christopher Wolk
Six short plays: *Prologue, Rocks, Tough Guys, The Departure of Brian O'Callahan, Makin' Sense of Nothin', Poor Fellas.*

(Gene Frankel Theatre) Friday, June 2–26, 2000 (16 performances); Transferred to (Phil Bosakowski Theatre) July 19–30, 2000 Lost City Productions present:
FIRST DATE by Stephen Tesher; Director, Laura Pierce; Press, Publicity Outfitters/Timothy J. Haskell, Christopher Joy CAST: Rachel Matz, Robert Steinman, Quince Marcum, Nicole Raphael, Sarah Paulding, Elizabeth Elinghaus, Aron Weidhorn
A comedy spanning 20 years.

(American Place Theatre) Tuesday, June 6–August 20, 2000 (81 performances and 7 previews) DIA Theatrical Inc., Nicholas C. Litrena, and Mary-Evelyn Card present:
FOR COLORED GIRLS WHO HAVE CONSIDERED SUICIDE/WHEN THE RAINBOW IS ENUF by Ntozake Shange; Director/Choreography, George Faison; Set, Walt Spanger; Costumes, Ann Marie Hould-Ward; Lighting, Robert Perry; Sound, Janet Kalas; Casting, Judy Dennis; Stage Manager, C. Renee Alexander; Press, Judy Jacksina CAST: Eleanor McCoy (woman in red), Novella Nelson (woman in brown), Lizan Mitchell (woman in purple), Jackée Harry (woman in blue), Carol-Jean Lewis (woman in green), Katherine J. Smith (woman in orange)
Twenty-fifth anniversary production of this choreopoem.

Eleanor McCoy, Carol-Jean Lewis, Jackée Harry in *for colored girls who have considered suicide/ when the rainbow is enuf*

The Company of *It Ain't Over 'Til The First Lady Sings*

(Douglas Fairbanks Theater) Tuesday, June 6–September 2, 2000 (92 performances and 12 previews) Erik Krebs, in association with Capitol Steps, presents:
IT AIN'T OVER 'TIL THE FIRST LADY SINGS Conceived/Written/Directed by Bill Strauss and Elaina Newport; Musical Director, Howard Breitbart; Set, R.J. Matson; Costumes, Linda Rose Payne; Sound, Jill B.C. Duboff; General Manager, Jonathan Shulman; Production Coordinator, Marina Bridges; Press, Jeffrey Richards/Rami Metal, Todd Emmett, John Michael Moreno CAST: Mike Carruthers, Andy Clemence, Janet Davidson Gordon, Toby Kemper, Mike Loomis, Elaina Newport, Linda Rose Payne, Ann Schmidt, Walker T. Smith, Bill Strauss, Mike Thornton, Mike Tilford, Brad Van Grack, Delores Williams, Jamie Zemarel
MUSICAL NUMBERS: Guns, Ten Grand, Just Like Bush, Do Shop, Libido Loca, Israelis, Lazio, Hillrita, Puttin on the Blitz, Pakistani Bang Bang, Fuel Am I, Who Will Buy, Lirty Dies, Nato, Serb War, Hebron, Smokey Mon, Janet Reno, Millionaire Candidate, Soccer Mom, Suture, Class of 2000, That's a Moron, Viagra, Census, Striking/Klan, Scottish Gourmet, Prequels, Very Good Years, Lity Dies-You Nork, Impossible Scheme
The musical comedy troupe Capitol Steps in a musical revue performed without intermission. Five members of the company perform at each show.

(CAP.21 Theatre) Wednesday, June 7–July 9, 2000 (25 performances and 2 previews) The Brave New Theatre Company, in association with Autumn Rain, Inc., presents:
THE GLASS MENAGERIE by Tennessee Williams; Director, Marjorie Ballentine; Set/Costumes, William F. Moser; Lighting, Jason Livingston; Music, Hui Cox; Stage Manager, Alice E. Einstman; Press, Max Eisen /Diane Masters CAST: Charles Sprinkle (Tom Wingfield), Patricia McAneny (Amanda), Sarah Jenkins (Laura Wingfield), George Macaluso (Jim O'Connor)
A drama in two acts. The action takes place in St. Louis.

(Metro Playhouse) Wednesday, June 7–30, 2000 (16 performances and 3 previews) Metro Playhouse presents:
LOVE'S POSTMAN (OR LOVE ON CRUTCHES) by Augustin Daly; Director, Scott Shattuck; Set, Christopher Holvenstot; Costumes, Fritz Masten; Lighting, John Demous; Sound, John Littig; Stage Manager, Brian Miller; Press, Publicity Outfitters/Timothy J. Haskell, Christopher Joy CAST: Paul Obedzinski (Podd), Karen Ryan (Netty), David L. Carson (Dr. Epenetus Quattles), Adam Smith (Sydney Austin), Erica Schmidt (Annis Austin), Mimi Stuart (Eudoxia Quattles), DeBanne Browne (Margery Gwynn), Kennedy Brown (Guy Roverly), Michael Surabian (Mr. Bitteridge), Myriam Blanckaert (Berta)
An 1884 comedy in three acts.

(Chicago City Limits) Wednesday, June 7, 2000–throughout season
CHICAGO CITY LIMITS TURNS 20: NOW AND FOREVER...AND WE MEAN IT! Artistic Director, Paul Zuckerman; Press, Keith Sherman/Alex DuBee CAST: Joe DeGise II, Carl Kissin, Denny Siegel, Victor Varnado, Frank Spitznagel
This season's offering from New York's longest running comedy/improvisation troupe.

Joe DeGise II, Denny Siegel, Carl Kissin in *Chicago City Limits Turns 20: Now and Forever...And We Mean It!* (Carol Rosegg)

(Altered Stages) Wednesday, June 7–August 13, 2000 (53 performances and 5 previews); Reopened at (American Place Theatre) May 25–October 7, 2001 (150 performances) Mefisto Theatre Company presents:
EAT THE RUNT by Avery Crozier; Director, Peter Hawkins; Producers, Matthew von Waaden, Weil Richmond, Matthew Richmond; Set, Jerome Martin; Costumes, Courtney McClain; Lighting, Michele Disco; Sound /Music, Will Pitts; Press, Pat Dale CAST: Kelli K. Barnett, Lora Chio, LaKeith Hoskin, Katrishka King, Myles O'Connor, Weil Richmond, Curtis Mark William, Jama Williamson SUCCEEDING CAST: Linda Cameron, Thom Rivera, Keesha Sharp
A comedy about a surreal interview.

The Company of *Eat the Runt*

(CHA) Wednesday, June 7–22, 2000 (25 performances and 4 previews) Sanctuary Theatre Workshop, in association with chashama, presents:
THE PICTURE by Eugene Ionesco; Translation, Abigail Sanders; Director, Ian Belton; Executive Producer, Rip Torn; Set/Costumes, Anduin Havens; Lighting, Rich Martin; Sound, Jeff Morey; Stage Manager, David Henderson CAST: Tony Torn (Large Gentleman), Tom Pearl (Painter), Laura Kachergus (Alice), Anita Durst, Molly Ward (Neighbor)
A new translation.

(Theater for the New City) Thursday, June 8–25, 2000 (12 performances) Theater for the New City, in association with The Frank Silvera Writers' Workshop, presents:
HOUSE ON FIRE by Jamal Williams; Director, Carmen Mathis; Press, LaQuita Henry CAST: Kamilah Autumn Brown, Randy Evans, Ebony Sunshine Jerido, Dominic Marcus, PhynJuar, Kenthedo Robinson, Tobias Trevillian, Erika Vaughn, Althea Vyfhuis, Erika Woods, Sundra Jean Williams
A play about black divas of Hollywood.

(Greenwich Street Theatre) Friday, June 9–July 8, 2000 (17 performances and 3 previews) Emerging Artists Theatre Company presents:
SYRIA, AMERICA by Lance Crowfoot-Suede; Director, Derek Jamison; Set, Warren Karp; Costumes, Rachel Lee Harris; Lighting, Annmarie Duggan; Stage Manager, Suzanne Menhart; Press, Peter Cromarty/Alice Cromarty, Sherri Jean Katz CAST: Max Ryan (Rob), Bob Bucci (Eli), Dan Fotou (Young Eli), Peter Macklin (Young Morris), J.T. Patton (Young Jackie), Matthew Rashid (Jackie), Michael Silva (Young Rob), Josh Jones (Morris)
A two-act drama about the Syrian Jews of Brooklyn. The action takes place in the present and the past.

Bob Bucci, Josh Jonas in *Syria, America* (Carol Rosegg)

(Blue Heron Arts Center) Friday, June 9–July 1, 2000 (15 performances) Blue Heron Theatre presents:

FANNY & WALT by Jewel Seehaus-Fisher; Director, Julia Murphy; Set /Lighting, Roman Tatarowicz; Costumes, Mary Wong; Stage Manager, J.P. Phillips; Press, Spin Cycle/Ron Lasko CAST: Charles Geyer (Walt Whitman), Dee Pelletier (Fanny Fern), Tom Hammond (Jemmy Parton), Gina Ojile (Mary Parton Rogers), Alan Semok (Samuel Wells)

A drama in two acts. The action takes place in New York City and nearby, 1856.

(HomeGrown Theatre) Saturday, June 10–July 15, 2000 (9 performances and 7 previews) New Directions Theater presents:

F-STOP by Olga Humphrey; Director, Eliza Beckwith; Set, John Walker; Costumes, Kim B. Walker; Lighting, Izzy Einsidler; Sound, Robert Gould; Fights, Heather Grayson; Stage Manager, Ilene Weintraub; Press, Shirley Herz/Sam Rudy CAST: Christopher Burns (Caleb Lawe), Rebekka Grella (Charlotte Wingate), Patricia Randell (Suzanne Ferrante), Vincent D'Arbouze (Ken Motuba), Charles Johnson (General), Heland Lee (Singapore Sling/Mr. Takimoto/Mee/One of the Two Dons), Bill McCarty, James Thomas (Shop Manager, One of the Two Dons)

A dark comedy in two acts. The action takes place in Africa.

Heland Lee, Patricia Randell, Christopher Burns in *F-Stop* (Carl Sturmer)

Robert Christophe in *Michigan Impossible* (Matthew Israel)

(John Houseman Studio) Saturday, June 10–August 18, 2000 (51 performances and 9 previews) Red Road Productions presents:

MICHIGAN IMPOSSIBLE Written/Performed by Robert Christophe; Co-Developed/Directed by Kim Waldauer; Press, Brett Singer

A one-man comedy.

(14th Street Y) Tuesday, June 13–25, 2000 (16 performances) Musicals Tonight!/Mel Miller presents:

GOLDILOCKS Music, Leroy Anderson; Lyrics, Walter Kerr, Joan Ford, Jean Kerr; Book, Walter and Jean Kerr; Director/Choreography, Thomas Mills; Music Director, Mark Hartman; Lighting, Rita Riddockl; Casting, Stephen DeAngelis; Stage Manager, Anthony Gallucio CAST: Georgia Vreighton (Bessie), Matthew Ellison (Pete), Gene Jones (J.C.), Jay Gould (Andy), Jen Celene Little (Lois), Michael McKenzie (Max), James Patterson (George), Cathy Trien (Maggie), Erin Malloy, Kelly Mealia, Fabio Monteiro, Joy E.T. Ross, Marc Smollin, Christopher Wisner (Ensemble)

MUSICAL NUMBERS: Lazy Moon, Give the Little Lady, Save a Kiss, No One'll Ever Love You, If I Can't Take It With Me (not in Bdwy original), Who's Been Sleeping in My Chair, There Never Was a Woman, The Pussy Foot, My Last Spring (not in Bdwy original), Act I Finale, Come To Me (not in Bdwy original), Opening, Lady in Waiting, The Beast in You, Shall I Take My Heart, I Can't Be in Love, Bad Companions, I Never Know When, Two Years in the Making, Heart of Stone, Finale

A new production of the 1958 musical in two acts. The action takes place in New York City, 1913.

(Hudson Guild Theatre) Wednesday, June 14–July 23, 2000 (33 performances and 8 previews) La Bave Du Crapaud Productions present:

OFF THE METER by Peter Zablotsky; Director, John Ahlers; Set, Walter Theodore; Costumes, Joseph La Court; Lighting, S. Ryan Schmidt; Press, David Rothenberg/David Gersten CAST: Gary Lowery (Eddie Davis), Kent Jackson (David Johnson), David Blackman, Tim Miller

A drama in two acts. The action takes place in New York City and the country.

Tim Miller, Gary Lowery, Kent Jackson in *Off the Meter* (Robert Maass)

(HERE) Friday, June 16–July 2, 2000 (12 performances) Upstart Theatre Company presents:
YOU LOOK FOR ME by Paul Harris; Director, Elowyn Castle; Lighting, Jason A. Cina; Press, Spin Cycle/Ron Lasko, Shannon Jowett CAST: Tom Foral (Christopher), Don Price (Jack)
A drama about a friendship spanning 35 years.

(Town Hall) Tuesday, June 20–26, 2000 (7 performances) Westbeth Theater Center presents:
CIRCLE Written/Performed by Eddie Izzard; Lighting, Josh Monroe; Music, Sarah McGuinness
A comic monologue. Previously performed at OB's Westbeth Theater Center April 4–8, 2000. Previous Izzard one-man shows performed in New York City include *Glorious* and *Dressed to Kill.*

(47th St. Theatre) Tuesday, June 20–September 18, 2000 (84 performances and 18 previews) The Wayne Howard Group presents:
THE FLAME KEEPER by Amos Kamil; Director, Charles Goforth; Set, Kenneth Foy; Costumes, Gail Cooper-Hecht; Lighting, Jason Kantrowitz; Sound, Peter Fitzgerald; Casting, Elissa Myers, Paul Fouquet; Stage Manager, Jana Llynn; Press, Kevin P. McAnarney/Grant Lindsey, Peter Cromarty/Sherri Jean Katz CAST: Lenny Mandel (Dr. Julius Reiter), Paul Whelihan (Ernst Gruber)
A drama performed without intermission. The action takes in Berlin, one year after the end of World War II.

Lenny Mandel, Paul Whelihan in *The Flame Keeper* (Carol Rosegg)

Gerald Downey, Mario Cantone in *The Crumple Zone* (Carol Rosegg)

(Context Studios) Thursday, June 22–July 2000 The Zanawa Theatre Company presents:
A REQUIEM OF THINGS PAST by David L. Williams; Director/Costumes, Tomi Tsunoda; Set/Lighting, Paul Paglia; Sound, Joe Vena; Press, Pete Sanders/Jim Mannino CAST: Sharon Eisman, Vanessa Longley-Cook, Preston Morgan, Paul Paglia, KaDee Strickland, Joe Vena

(Harry De Jur Playhouse) Thursday, June 22–July 30, 2000 (31 performances and 4 previews) New Federal Theatre presents:
THE DANCE ON WIDOWS' ROW Written/Directed by Samm-Art Williams; Set, Felix E. Cochren; Costumes, Evelyn Nelson; Lighting, Shirley Prendergast; Sound, Sean O'Halloran; Stage Manager, Jacqui Casto; Press, Max Eisen/Diane Masters CAST: Barbara Montgomery (Magnolia Ellis), Marie Thomas (Simone Jackson), Elizabeth Van Dyke (Annie Talbot), Elain Graham (Lois Miller), Adam Wade (Deacon Hudson), Jack Landron (Newly Benson), Ed Wheeler (Randolph Spears)
A comedy about four rich widows suspected of killing their husbands.

(HERE) Friday, June 23–July 2, 2000 Eleventh Hour Theatre Company presents:
RICHARD II by William Shakespeare; Director, Alexander Harrington; Design, Tom Sturge, Scott Aronow; Press, Tony Origlio/Mark Cannistraro CAST: Callum Keith-King (Richard), Lori Putnam (Queen), Ned Coulter (Henry Bolingbroke), Yaakov Sullivan (Gaunt), Richard Mawe (York), Frank Anderson (Bishop of Carlisle), Patricia Newcastle, Etain O'Malley

(78th St. Theatre Lab) Friday, June 23–July 16, 2000 Kaleidoscope Theatre Company, with the assistance of Bad Neighbors Ltd., presents:
THE STAIRWELL by Keith Merritt; Director, Marshall Mays; CAST: Tony Javed (Ethan), Todd Allen Durkin (Emerson), Sarah Saltzberg (Mary), Ned Butikofer (Father)
A drama performed without intermission. The setting is the stairwell of a hospital.

(Rattlestick Theatre) Friday, June 23–October 29, 2000 (125 performances and 5 previews) Marcus Kettles Productions present:
THE CRUMPLE ZONE by Buddy Thomas; Director, Jason Moore; Set, Dawn Robyn Petrlik; Costumes, David Mills; Lighting, Ed McCarthy; Sound, Laura Grace Brown; Choreography, Peter Kapetan; Fights, B.H. Barry; Casting, Paul Davis; Stage Manager, Gail Eve Malatesta; Press, Pete Sanders/Jim Mannino
A comedy in two acts about five very different men over one frantic holiday weekend. The action takes place in Staten Island, NY.

(Mint Space) Sunday, June 25–July 22, 2000 (13 performances and 3 previews) Judith Shakespeare Company presents:
JULIUS CAESAR by William Shakespeare; Director, Joanne Zipay; Set, Jason Ardizzone-West; Costumes, Rob Bevenger; Lighting, Jaie Bosse; Music, Shannon Ford; Movement, Elizabeth Mozer; Fights, Dan O'Criscoll; Stage Manager, Ci Herzog; Press, Shirley Herz/Sam Rudy CAST: Mary Andrews (Cicero/Cinna the Poet/Dardanius), Judith Annozine (Cinna/Lucilius), Laurie Bannister-Colon (Servant/Soldier), Naomi Barr (Metellus), Jennifer Chudy (Brutus), Antonio del Rosario (Calpurnia), Anthea Fane (Artemidorus/Young Cato), Alice M. Gatling (Mark Anthony), Eileen Glenn (Flavius/Ligarius/Pindarus), Jan Leslie Harding (Julius Caesar at certain performances), Sandy Harper (Citizen /Clitus), Terre L. Holmes (Soothsayer/Octavius Caesar), Ellen Lee, Jennifer Nadeau (Marcullus/Trebonius/Titinius), Leah Maddrie (Julius Caesar at certain performances), Rachel O'Neill (Lucius), Allie Rivenbark (Servant/Volumnius), Richard Simon (Portia), Laura Standley (Casca /Lepidus), Tanisha Thompson (Decius/Messala), Jane Titus (Cassius)
Performed in repertory with *Comedy of Errors.*

Ginny Hack, James Pinkowski, Kevin LeCaon in *Comedy of Errors* (Paula Court)

(Mint Space) Sunday, June 25–July 22, 2000 (11 performances and 3 previews) Judith Shakespeare Company presents:
COMEDY OF ERRORS by William Shakespeare; Director, Joanne Zipay; Set, Jason Ardizzone-West; Costumes, David Kaley; Lighting, Jaie Bosse; Music, Matthew Loren Cohen; Movement, Elizabeth Mozer; Fights, Dan O'Driscoll; Press, Shirley Herz/Sam Rudy CAST: Alegria Alcala (Newsboy), Susan Beyer (Courtesan), Mark Brey (Duke Solinus), Clark Carmichael (Antipholus of Ephesus), Kelli Cruz (Luciana), Jeannie Dalton (Dr. Pinch/Jailor), Ginny Hack (Adriana), Kate Konigisor (Angela the Goldsmith), Kevin LeCaon (Antipholus of Syracuse), Tom Lenaghen (Nell), Jennifer Nadeau (Reporter), Sherry Nehmer (Aemilia), Brooke Peterson (Merchant/Officer), James Pinkowski (Dromio of Syracuse), Jeffrey Shoemaker (Aegeon), Leese Walker (Dromio of Ephesus), Dov Weinstein (Balthazar)
Performed in repertory with *Julius Caesar.*

(Miranda Theatre) Monday, June 26–August 14, 2000 (7 performances and 1 preview) Miranda Theatre Company presents:
BIG KISS Hosted by Henry Alford CAST: Mr. Alford, Victoria Labalme, Vickie Schmidt, Greta Enszer, Joshua Lewis Berg, Hilary Howard, Matt Meyer, Alicia Velez, Micheline Auger, Andi Shrem
PROGRAM: Opening Remarks, Commercial Crack-Up, Cinderella, Animal Porn, Gay Bozo the Clown, Trampling Contempuously on Thy Disdain, My Day in Poultry, Little Girl Big Dreams, Poop, The Twins
Actors tell their most humiliating audition stories.

(P.S. 122) Wednesday, June 28–August 26, 2000 (54 performances) Danny Hoch presents:
SISTAH SUPREME Written/Directed by Liza Colón-Zayas; Developed /Directed by Stephen Adly-Guirgis; Lighting, Sarah Sidman; Sound, Eric De Armon; Press, Craig Karpel/Bridget Klapinski
An autobiographical monologue.

(Hemmerdinger Hall) Thursday, June 29–August 5, 2000 (18 performances) The Aquila Theatre Company presents:
COMEDY OF ERRORS by William Shakespeare; Adaptation/Director, Robert Richmond; Set, David Coleman, Owen Collins; Costumes, Lisa Martin Stuart; Lighting, Peter Meineck; Music, Anthony Cochrane; Press, Gary Springer-Susan Chicoine/Joe Trentacosta CAST: Alex Webb (Egeon), William Kwapy (Solinus/Angelo/Jailer), David Caron (Antipholus of Syracuse), John Butelli (Dromio of Syracuse), Lisa Carter (Adriana), Mira Kingsley (Luciana), Marci Adilman (Nell/Courtesan/Emilia), Tommy Caron (Antipholus of Ephesus), Louis Butelli (Dromio of Ephesus), Alex Webb (Balthasar/Pinch)
Performed in repertory with *Iliad: Book One.*

(Hemmerdinger Hall) Friday, June 30–August 6, 2000 (24 performances) The Aquila Theatre Company presents:
ILIAD: BOOK ONE by Homer; Translation, Stanley Lombardo; Director, Robert Richmond; Costumes, Christianne Myers; Lighting, Peter Meineck; Music, Anthony Cochrane; Press, Gary Springer-Susan Chicoine/Joe Trentacosta CAST: Alex Webb (Chryses/Nestor/Zeus /Hephaestus), Judy Hu (Chyseis), Louis Butelli (Agamemmnon), David Caron (Achilles), Mira Kingsley (Briseis/Athena/Hera), William Kwapy (Calchas/Odysseus), Lisa Carter (Thetis)
Performed in repertory with *Comedy of Errors.*

Lisa Carter, Marci Adilman, Mira Kingsley in *Comedy of Errors* (Aquila/Peter Meinick)

The Company of *Big Kiss* (Christopher Bierlein)

Sara Elizabeth Holliday, Brian Bartley, Chris Bock, Kathleen McClafferty in *Ernest* (James McNicholas)

(Jose Quintero Theatre) Friday, June 30–July 9, 2000 (7 performances) The New Punctuation Army presents:
ERNEST Music, Vance Lehmkuhl; Lyrics/Book/Director, Gayden Wren; Based on *The Importance of Being Earnest* by Oscar Wilde; Musical Director, Stephen O'Leary; Set, Daniel Z.S. Jagendorf; Costumes, Ms. Kennedy, Kate Monneyham, Sara Holliday; Lighting, Janette Kennedy; Press, Tony Origlio/Mark Cannistraro CAST: Randy Noak (Lane), Brian Bartley (Algernon Moncrieff), Chris Bock (Jack Worthing), Kathleen McClafferty (Gwendolen Fairfax), Annette Triquère (Lady Bracknell), Lorraine DeMan (Miss Prism), Simon Chaussé (Rev. Dr. Chasuble), Sara Elizabeth Holliday (Cecily Cardew), Jay Haddad (Merriman)
A musical in two acts. The action takes place in England, 1895.

William Westenberg, Martin Shakar, Shelley Williams in *Redfest 2000* (Josh Carter)

(Theatre 3) Wednesday, July 5–16, 2000 (13 performances) The Working Theatre Ensemble presents:
THE MANAGER by Darrin Shaughnessy; Director, Brian Hickey; Lighting, Michael Abrams; Stage Manager, Dan Kipp CAST: Jay Charan (Steven), Tracey Silver (Woman), Anna Van Etten (Shelly), Paul Van Etten (Manny)
A drama performed without intermission. The action takes place in Las Cruces, NM.

(Manhattan Theater Source) Wednesday, July 5–29, 2000 (19 performances) One Arm Red presents:
REDFEST 2000 by Douglas Mitchell; Directors, Chesley Krohn, William Hardy; Press, Brett Singer CAST: Bryan Carroll, Brian Corrigan, Bill Hardy, Tim Kirkpatrick, Mary Elaine Monti, Shaun Powers, Susan Scudder, Michael Linstroth, Martin Shakar, William Westenberg, Shelley Williams
Two programs of one-act plays: *Shatter the Golden Vessel, It's Got to Be Something, All Wrapped Up,* and *How to Sacrifice a Child.*

Kimberly Reiss, Toby Wherry in *Man in the Flying Chair* (Carol Rosegg)

(78th St. Theatre Lab) Thursday, July 6–August 12, 2000 (15 performances and 8 previews); Reopened October 12–November 18, 2000 (18 performances) 78th St. Theatre Lab presents:
MAN IN THE FLYING CHAIR Conceived/Directed/Sound by Eric Nightengale; Created by the Cast; Documented/Arranged by Allison Mattera; Set, Si Joong Yoon; Costumes, Diane Specioso; Lighting, Tyler Micoleau; Stage Manager, Julie Kessler; Press, Jim Baldassare CAST: Toby Wherry (Larry Walters), Kimberly Reiss (Carol), Carey Cromelin (Mrs. Van Deusen), Troy W. Taber (Tom), Monica Read (Belinda)
An ensemble-created piece performed without intermission. Based on the life of Larry Walters, who ascended to 16,000 feet in a lawn chair in 1982. The action takes place in West Hollywood and Manhattan, 1982–93.

Douglas Dickerman, Susan O'Connor, John Maria in *Never Swim Alone* (Jordan Hollender)

(Soho Playhouse) Thursday, July 6–September 2, 2000 (47 performances and 6 previews) Craig Garcia, Tim O'Brien, Britt Lafield, and Daryl Roth present:

NEVER SWIM ALONE by Daniel MacIvor; Director, Timothy P. Jones; Lighting, John Pinckard; Fights, Ian Marshall; Stage Manager, Monique Nottke; Press, Spin Cycle/Ron Lasko CAST: Susan O'Connor (Referee), John Maria (A. Francis Delorenzo), Douglas Dickerman (Bill Wade)
A drama ("in 13 rounds") about male relationships and rivalry.

(HERE) Friday, July 7–August 6, 2000 (15 performances) HERE presents:

THE LONG, SLOW DEATH OF LILA REMY Written/Designed/Performed by Toni Schlesinger; Director, Patrick Trettenero
A one-woman noir thriller.

(Washington Square Park) Friday, July 7–23, 2000 (11 performances and 4 previews) Gorilla Repertory Theatre Company presents:

UBU IS KING! Written/Designed/Directed by Christopher Carter Sanderson; Freely adapted from *Ubu Roi* by Alfred Jarry; Puppets, Elizabeth Margulies; Press, Brett Singer CAST: Tracy Appleton, Reginald Austin, David Blasher, Matthew Freedman, Rachel Jackson, Adria Long, André-Phillippe Mistier, Aedín Moloney, Eric Dean Scott, Josie Whittlesey
An outdoor performance.

(Bessie Schönberg Theatre) Saturday, July 8–August 13, 2000 (34 performances and 2 previews); Transferred to (American Place Theatre) October 19–December 31, 2000 (72 performances and 13 previews) The Working Theatre presents:

TABLETOP by Rob Ackerman; Director, Connie Grappo; Producers for transfer, Amy Danis, Dr. Richard Firestone, Mark Johannes, Joan D. Firestone, Ellen M. Krass, in association with Karen Davidov; Set, Dean Taucher; Costumes, Ilona Somogyi; Lighting, Jack Mehler; Casting, Jerry Beaver; Stage Managers, Neveen Mahmoud, Doanld Fried; Press/Publicity Outfitters/Timothy J. Haskell, Christopher Joy, Peter Cromarty/Sherri Jean Katz CAST: Harvy Blanks (Oscar), Jeremy Webb (Ron), Dean Nolen (Jeffrey), Jack Koenig (Dave), Elizabeth Hanley Rice (Andrea), Rob Bartlett (Marcus)
A comedy performed without intermission. The action takes place at the filming of a television commercial.

(New York Performance Works) Monday, July 10–August 7, 2000 (5 performances) Cold Productions, All Seasons Theatre Group, New York Performance Works, and Karen Hauser present:

E.V. by Patrick Blake; Directors, David Elliott and Carlo Vogel CAST: Joe Ardizzone (Esteban), Jessica Faller (Dom), Linda Halaska (Brigit), Bradford Olson (BJ/Gangster)
A "soap opera" set in New York City.

(Vital Theatre) Thursday, July 13–30, 2000 (12 performances) Vital Theater Company, in association with Cicada Film Group Ltd., presents:

DEATH OF ENGLAND by Sam Bobrick; Director, Scott C. Embler; Set, Katie Levey; Costumes, Nestelynn Gay, Stefanie Sowa; Lighting/Sound, Martin Miller; Fights, David Sitler; Choreography, Michael Schloegl; Stage Manager, Christine Nicole; Press, Sun/Stephen Sunderlin CAST: Todd Butera (Inspector Mirabelle), Polly Humphreys (Jane), Marianna Kulukundis (Constance Lawson), Joe McClean (Alfie Crown), Robert Meksin (Jonathan Pike), Kenny Morris (Michael Hedges), Todd Wilson (Death), Karin Wolfe (Irene Hedges)
A mystery farce set at a British sanitarium.

Joe McClean in *Death of England* (Anne Czichos)

(Currican Theatre) Thursday, July 13–30, 2000 (16 performances) Mark Marques and The Attic Show present:

PRICE'S RIGHT: *The Adventures of Jack Price and Gordon. A Circus in Six Parts* Written/Directed by Tom Ellis; Set, Elisha Nameri; Lighting, Ed Miller; Sound, Jeff Subik; Music, Steve Goldberger; Orchestrations, Bryan Schimmel; Choreography, Rommy Sandhu; Stage Manager, Wai-Yee Lee; Press, Scott Tucker CAST: Rufus Collins (Jack Price), David Tirosh (Gordon), Melissa Darling (Reena/Anna), Ken Mason (Kenny/Chip), Marjan Dor'e (Julie/Hilly), Phillip Cruise (Keith/Dan), Lauren Volkmer (Patty/Mary), Rik Sansone (Kevin/Robby), Jennifer Voss (Selma), Tara Radcliffe (Candice), William O'Donnell (DJ/Snake Rivers)
A satire performed with one intermission. The action takes place in New York City.

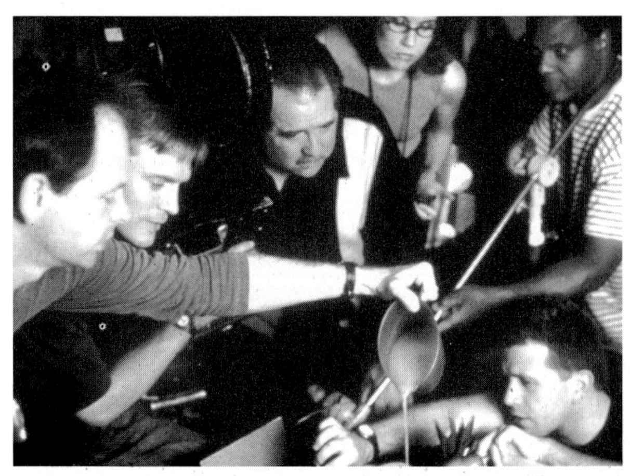

The Company of *Tabletop* (Louis Mullen-Leray)

Kaipo Schwab, Arthur Acuña, Manuel Terrón in *Santos & Santos* (Carol Rosegg)

(Studio Theatre) Friday, July 14–August 5, 2000 (14 performances and 3 previews) Imua! Theatre Company presents:
SANTOS & SANTOS by Octavio Solis; Director, Michael John Garcés; Set, Antje Ellermann; Costumes, Mimi O'Donnell; Lighting, Shawn K. Kaufman; Sound, David Margolin Lawson; Press, Shirley Herz/Michael Goldfried CAST: Kaipo Schwab (Tomas), Jose Febus (Don Miguel), Manuel Terrón (Michael), David Anzuelo (Fernie), Nilaja Sun (Pamela), Maite Bonilla (Nena), Arthur Acuña (Camacho), Sturgis Warner (Judge Benton), Dacyl Acevedo (Vicky), Yvonne Jung (Peggy), Donald Silva (Casper T. Willis), Dorothea Harahan (Felecia Lee), Jesse Ontiveros (Gonzalez)
A drama in three acts. The action takes place in El Paso, TX.

(Tribeca Performing Arts Center) Friday, July 14–26, 2000 (12 performances) Indo-American Arts Council presents:
DANCE LIKE A MAN by Mahesh Dattani; Director, Lillete Dubey; Lighting, Lynne Fernandez; Sound, Rajju Chandiramani; Press, Terence Womble CAST: Suchitra Pillai (Lata/Young Ratna), Joy Sengupta (Viswas/Young Jaiaj), Vijay Crishna (Jairaj/Amrilal Preekh), Lillette Dubey (Ratna)
An Indian drama centered around two generations of dancers. Performed in English.

(Promenade Theatre) Friday, July 14–September 3, 2000 (15 performances and 43 previews) Jennifer Smith Rockwood presents:
HIGH INFIDELITY by John Dooley; Director, Luke Yankee; Set, Harrison Williams; Costumes, Carrie Robbins; Lighting, Jack Mehler; Sound, Catherine D. Mardis; Casting, Alan Filderman; Stage Manager, Christine Catti; Production Supervisor, Anita Ross; Press, Keith Sherman/Tom Chiodo CAST: Neil Maffin (Dr. Edward Finger), John Davidson (Charles Gordon), Morgan Fairchild (Ellen Gordon), J.C. Wendel succeeded by Jennifer Roszell (Jane McAlpin), Dan Ziskie (Bill Brennan), Deborah Latz (Singer)
A comedy in two acts. The action takes place on the Jersey shore, mid-1970s.

(Century Center for the Performing Arts) Friday, July 14–August 20, 2000 (29 performances and 16 previews) Janet Robinson, MJM Productions, Leonard Soloway, and Steven M. Levy present:
AVOW by Bill C. Davis; Director, Jack Hofsiss; Set, David Jenkins; Costumes, Julie Weiss; Lighting, Ken Billington; Sound, Peter J. Fitzgerald; Music, Stephen Hoffman; Casting, Julie Hughes and Barry Moss; Stage Manager, Lee J. Kahrs; Press, Peter Cromarty/Sherri Jean Katz CAST: Scott Ferrara (Tom), Christopher Sieber (Brian), Alan Campbell (Father Raymond), Sarah Knowlton (Irene), Kathleen Doyle (Julie), Jane Powell (Rose), Reatheal Bean (Father Nash)
A drama in two acts. The action takes place in an American city.

(Center Stage) Tuesday, July 18–August 12, 2000 (20 performances) transferred to (East 13th Street Theater) Tuesday, November 21–December 31, 2000 (39 performances and 9 previews) LAByrinth Theater Company, Ron Kastner, Roy Gabay, and John Gould Rubin present:
JESUS HOPPED THE A TRAIN by Stephen Adly Guirgis; Director, Philip Seymour Hoffman; Set, Narelle Sissons; Costumes, Mimi O'Donnell; Lighting, Sarah Sidman; Sound/Music, Eric DeArmon; Casting, Heidi Marshall; Stage Managers, Iva Hacker-Delany, Babette Roberts; Production Manager, Andrew Baldwin-Merriweather; Press, Chris Boneau~Adrian Bryan-Brown/Erin Dunn CAST: Elizabeth Canavan (Mary Jane Hanrahan), Salvatore Inzerillo (D'Amico), Ron Cephas Jones (Lucius Jenkins), John Ortiz (Angel Cruz), David Zayas (Valdez)
A prison-courtroom-comic drama in two acts. The action takes place in New York City's Dept. of Corrections system, largely at Rikers Island.

John Davidson, Morgan Fairchild in *High Infidelity* (Carol Rosegg)

Scott Ferrara, Christopher Sieber, Jane Powell, Alan Campbell, Sarah Knowlton in *Avow* (Carol Rosegg)

Chad Kimball, Barrett Foa, Leslie Kritzer in *Godspell* (Carol Rosegg)

(Theatre at Saint Peter's) Tuesday, July 18–October 7, 2000 (77 performances and 18 previews) NET Theatrical Productions presents:
GODSPELL Music/New Lyrics, Stephen Schwartz; Book, John-Michael Tebelak; Director, Shawn Rozsa; Co-Director, RJ Tolan; Music Director, Dan Schachner; Set, Keven Lock; Costumes, William Ivey Long, Bernard Grenier; Lighting, Herrick Goldman; Choreography, Ovi Vargas; Cast Recording, Fynsworth Alley; Casting, Dave Clemmons/Rachel Hoffman; Stage Manager, Samuel-Moses Jones; Press, Keith Sherman/Tom Chiodo CAST: Shoshana Bean, Tim Cain, Catherine Carpenter, Will Erat, Barrett Foa, Lucia Giannetta, Capathia Jenkins, Chad Kimball, Leslie Kritzer, Eliseo Roman
MUSICAL NUMBERS: Prologue, Prepare Ye, God Save the People, Day by Day, Learn Your Lessons Well, Bless the Lord, All for the Best, All Good Gifts, Light of the World, Turn Back O Man, Alas for You, By My Side, We Beeseech Thee, Beautiful City, On the Willows, Finale
A contemporary interpretation of the 1971 musical in two acts. This production originated last season at Third Eye Repertory.

(Westbeth Theatre Center) Wednesday, July 19–September 30, 2000 (39 performances and 6 previews) Westbeth Theatre Center presents:
JERUSALEM SYNDROME Written/Performed by Marc Maron; Directed /Developed by Kirsten Ames; Set, Jessica Krause; Lighting, Roy Trejo; Sound, Gregory Kostroff; Music, Mark Nilson; Video, Kevin Scott; Press, Tony Origlio/Karen Greco
A bio-comedy.

(New York Performance Works) Thursday, July 27–August 12, 2000 (10 performances and 5 previews) Cold Productions, New York Performance Works, and All Seasons Theatre Group present:
THE PERPETUAL PATIENT by Keith Reddin; Adapated from Molière's *The Imaginary Invalid*; Director, Billy Hopkins; Set, Jason Kirschner; Costumes, Sarah Edwards; Lighting, Matthew Staniec; Songs, Jeffrey Lunden and Art Perlman; Stage Manager, Adrienne Willis; Press, Gary Springer-Susan Chicoine/Joe Trentacosta CAST: David Thornton succeeded by Keith Reddin (Argan), Leslie Lyles (Bridget), Nile Lanning (Angelique), Anna Thomson (Beline), Tom O'Brien (Clutter), Matthew Nelson (Cleatis), Matthew Sussman (Dr. Purge), Marc Ardito (Thomas), Ean Sheehy (Bernard), Linda Halaska (Dr. Flea), Foss Curtis, Annie MacRae (Maids)
A comedy in two acts. The action takes place in a large American city, early 1900s.

(Flea Theater) Thursday, July 27–December 16, 2000 The Bat Theater Company presents:
BAAL by Bertolt Brecht; Translation, Peter Mellencamp; Director, Jim Simpson; Musical Director, David Geist; Set, Clayton Binkley; Costumes, Mimi O'Donnell; Lighting/Sound, Ben Struck; Stage Manager, Jenny Kusner; Press, Spin Cycle/Ron Lasko CAST: Kate Benson, Joanie Ellen, Michael J.X. Gladis, Gordon Holmes, Andrew Ledyard, Alfredo Narcisco, Jack O'Neill, Meredith Perlman, Tamar Schoenberg, Paul Siemens, Leah Smith, Kristin Stewart, Siobhan Towey, Irene Walsh
This production sets the action in the beatnik jazz world of urban America, 1947.

(Tribeca Performing Arts Center) Friday, July 28–August 2, 2000 (6 performances) Indo-American Arts Council presents:
ONCE UPON A FLEETING BIRD by Vijay Tendulkar; Director, Akash Khurana; Design, Sabas Mascarenhas; Press, Terence Womble CAST: Kaykay Krishna Menon (Arun), Dilip Prabhavalkar (Baba), Tara Deshpande (Saru), Hidayat Sami (Vishwas), Inaayat Sami (Banda), Vidula Mungekar (Aaie)
An Indian love story set in Bombay during the 1990s. Performed in English.

(Mint Space) Saturday, July 29–August 20, 2000 (15 performances and 2 previews) The Queen's Company presents:
MACBETH by William Shakespeare; Director, Rebecca Patterson; Set, Louisa Thompson; Lighting, Mark Barton; Fights, Deborah S. Keller, DeeAnn Weir; Press, Brett Singer CAST: Karen Pruis (Macbeth), Aysan Çelik (Lady Macbeth), DeeAnn Weir (Macduff), Virginia Baeta, Sheila Lynn Buckley, Heather Grayson, Jacqueline Gregg, Stacie Hirsch, Lisette Merenciana, Jina Oh, Ami Shukla, Katlan Walker, Tessa Zugmeyer
Performed by an all-female cast.

Karen Pruis, Aysan Çelik in *Macbeth*

(Mint Space) Tuesday, August 1–17, 2000 (9 performances) Scenic Route Productions and The Queen's Company present:
SHE KEEPS TIME Director, Allison Eve Zell; Costumes, Lauren Cordes; Lighting/Stage Manager, Hidehiro Usui; Sound/Visual Consultant, Greg King; Press, Publicity Outfitters, Timothy J. Haskell, Christopher Joy
Come To Leave by Allison Eve Zell CAST: Lethia Nall
Pickling by Suzan-Lori Parks CAST: Jaye Austin-Williams
Two one-act plays.

(Gershwin Hotel) Thursday, August 3–September 7, 2000 (14 performances and 2 previews) Skypie Productions presents:
WHY WE DON'T BOMB THE AMISH Written/Performed by Casey Fraser; Musicians, Jeff Peretz, Mark Robohm, Daniel Fabricatore; Press, Tony Origlio/Karen Greco
A one-woman show examining strange hypocrisies.

(Central Park) Thursday, August 3–27, 2000 (16 performances) New York Classical Theatre presents:
A MIDSUMMER NIGHT'S DREAM by William Shakespeare; Director, Stephen Burdman; Costumes, Derek Nye Lockwood; Lighting, Nicole Pearce; Music, Amy Kohn; Choreography, Terry Berliner; Press, Philip Thurston CAST: Jon Shaver (Oberon/Theseus), Patricia Marie Kelly (Titania/Hippolyta), Amy Groeschel (Hermia), Jocelyn Rose (Helen), Philip Tabor (Demetrius), Paul West (Lysander), Kael Kuster (Puck), Fred Berman (Bottom/Pyramus)

Ernesto Altamirano in *Beggar on Horseback*

(Bank Street Theatre) Thursday, August 3–27, 2000 (14 performances and 2 previews) The Peccadillo Theater Company presents:
BEGGAR ON HORSEBACK by George S. Kaufman and Marc Connelly; Director, Dan Wackerman; Set/Costumes, Anne Lommel; Lighting, Mark Simpson; Sound, Robert Auld; Choreography, Bev Brown; Stage Manager, Paul A. Powell; Press, Tony Origlio/Karen Greco CAST: Ernesto Altamirano (Georgie/Club Goer), Robert Arcaro (Mr. Cady), Tracee Beazer (Miss Hey/Miss You/Art Factory Poet), Todd Allen Durkin (Neil McRae), James T. Hall (Juror/Diva), Gerard Heintz (Steve/Butler), Alicia Minshew (Cynthia Mason), Amy Maluno (Worker/Tourist), Simon Petrie (Homer Cady), Tara Sands (Gladys Cady), Patrick Thorbourne (Cousin Harry/A Kiss in Xanadu), Robert Tyree (Dr. Albert Rice/Preacher /Executioner), Colleen Smith Wallnau (Mrs. Cady), Chio Yamada (Alf /Candy Vendor)
An updated interpretation of a 1924 comedy set in New York City.

Ralph Waite, Daniel McDonald in *The Personal Equation*

(Provincetown Playhouse) Friday, August 4–19, 2000 (9 performances and 5 previews) Playwrights Theater of New York presents:
THE PERSONAL EQUATION by Eugene O'Neill; Director, Stephen Kennedy Murphy; Set, Roger Hanna; Costumes, Meganne George; Lighting, Matthew E. Adelson; Sound, Jill B.C. Du Boff; Stage Manager, Elis C. Arroyo; General Manager, Dominick Balletta; Press, Richard Kornberg /Jim Byk CAST: Ralph Waite (Thomas Perkins), Daniel McDonald (Tom), Jaime Sanchez (Henderson), Kristin Taylor (Olga Tarnoff), Steve Brady (Hartmann), Jack O'Connell (Enwright), Don Wallace (Whitely), Barbara Poitier (Mrs. Allen), Con Horgan (O'Rourke), Lawrence Levy (Cocky), Howard Garner (Harris), Taylor Ruckel (Schmidt), Michael McMonagle (Hogan), Stephen Payne (Murphy), Rory Mallon (Jack), Alfred Hyslop (Doctor), Tanya Jackson (Miss Brown), Joe Byrnes, Michael Dee (Stokers)
Written in 1915 while O'Neill was at Harvard, this play has never previously been staged. A four-act drama performed with one intermission. The action takes place in Hoboken, NJ and Liverpool, England.

(Peking/South St. Seaport) Friday, August 4–28, 2000 (14 performances and 2 previews) Gorilla Repertory Theatre Company presents:
THE PIRATES OF PENZANCE by Gilbert and Sullivan; Adaptation/Director, Michael Scheman; Musical Director, Steven Gross; Costumes, Terry Leong; Choreography, Tony Parise; Press, Brett Singer CAST: David Joseph (Frederic), Patrick McCarthy (Ruth), Michael Colby Jones (Pirate King), Gordon Stanley (Major General), Annette Cortes (Mabel), John P.F. Moore (Sergeant), Brett Colby, Alison Renee Foster, Joseph Greene, Stephen Kaplan, Rebecca Kendall, Kent LeVan, Kenny Marshall, Brenda McEldowney, Kristy L. Merola, Jessica Polsky, Heather Jane Rolff, Amy Shure, Colin Stokes, Gretchen Weigel, J. Michael Zally
Performed onboard a three-mast sailing ship.

(Pulse Ensemble Courtyard) Wednesday, August 9–September 17, 2000 (30 performances) Pulse Ensemble Theatre presents:
MACBETH and **A MIDSUMMER NIGHT'S DREAM** by William Shakespeare; Director, Alexa Kelly; Set, Rubén Arana-Downs; Costumes, Terry Leong; Lighting, Herrick Goldman; Press, Shirley Herz/Michael Goldfried CASTS: *Macbeth* Brian Richardson (Macbeth), Natalie Wilder (Lady Macbeth), Bryan Brendle, Jayne Corey, Amanda Corey, Amanda Dubois, Aaron J. Fili, Nicole Godino, Milly Harrington, Jaccyne Howell, Tom Jasorka, Mark Vaughn, Nathan M. White, Pamela Wild, Jim Wizniewski *Midsummer* Kolawole Ogundiran (Puck), Gretchen Greaser (Titania), David DelGrosso (Lysander), Michael Birch (Bottom) Becky Leonard, Danielle Stille, Jim Wiznieweski, Steve Abbruscato, Jospeh Capone, Jay Colligan, Oscar de la Colon, Christian Desmond, Linda Past
Outdoor productions presented in repertory.

(John Montgomery Theater) Thursday, August 10–24, 2000 John Montgomery Theatre Company presents:
ICONS AND OUTCASTS Written/Directed by Suzanne Bachner; Costumes, Orna Jackson, Iran, Manny's Closet; Lighting, John Tees III; Sound, Patrick Hillan; Press, Shirley Herz/Michael Goldfried CAST: Barbara Hentscher (Candy Box), Alex McCord (HP), Felicia Scarangello (Arkansas Jack/Bobby Ray), Liz Sullivan (Jennifer Monroe), Sarah E. Shively (Clark Parker), Anthony Giangrande (Anthony), Rebecca Doerr, Trish Minskoff, Cara Pontillo, Stacey Tomassone, Margaret Stockton, Alexander R Warner, Elizabeth Reeves, Francis O'Flynn, Danny Wiseman, David E. Liedholdt, Mark Diaz

(Triad Theater) Friday, August 11–December 3, 2000 (121 performances and 10 previews) Laura Heller, Carol Ostrow, and Edwin W. Schloss present:
BERLIN TO BROADWAY WITH KURT WEILL Music, Kurt Weill; Lyrics, Maxwell Anderson, Marc Blitzstein, Bertolt Brecht, Jacques Deval, Michael Feingold, Ira Gershwin, Paul Green, Langston Hughes, Alan Jay Lerner, Ogden Nash, George Tabori, Arnold Weinstein; Text/Format by Gene Lerner; Director/Choreography, Hal Simons; Musical Direction /Arangements, Eric Stern; Set, William Barclay; Costumes, Suzy Benzinger; Lighting, Phil Monat; Stage Manager, Richard Costabile; Press, Media Blitz/Beck Lee CAST: Lorinda Lisitza, Veronica Mittenzwei, Björn Olsson, Michael Winther
MUSICAL NUMBERS: How to Survive, Barbara Song, Useless Song, Jealousy Duet, Pirate Jenny, Mack the Knife, March Ahead/Don't Be Afraid, Surabaya Johnny, Bilbao Song/Mandalay Song, Alabama Song, Deep in Alaska, As You Make Your Bed, I Wait for a Ship, Sailor's Tango, Hymn to Peace, Johnny's Song, How Can You Tell an American?, September Song, It Never Was You, Saga of Jenny, My Ship, Speak Low, That's Him, Progress, Ain't It Awful the Heat, Lonely House, Train to Johannesburg, Cry the Beloved Country Country, Lost in the Stars, Love Song, Happy Ending
A new production of the 1972 musical revue in two acts.

Björn Olsson, Veronica Mittenzwei, Lorinda Lisitza, Michael Winther in *Berlin to Broadway with Kurt Weill*

Glen Williamson, Brian Patrick Mooney in *Memorial Days* (Carl Sturmer)

(HomeGrown Theater) Saturday, August 12–September 18, 2000 (10 performances and 4 previews) New Directions Theater presents:
MEMORIAL DAYS by John Attanas; Director, John Gaines; Set, Mark Hankla; Costumes, Tara E. Waugh; Lighting, Beth Turomsha; Stage Manager, Nicole Press; Press, Shirley Herz/Sam Rudy CAST: Melissa Wolff (Carol Crewdson), Jensen Wheeler (Lynette Desantis), Brian Patrick Mooney (David Oxley), Glen Williamson (Greg Oxley), T.J. Mannix (Leif Anderson), Kate Downing (Shawn Leslie), Cory Bonvillain (Tara-Lynn Baxter), Karen Krantz (Strength)
A two-act play unfolding in the Adirondack Mountains over a series of Memorial Day weekends.

(Raw Space) Thursday, August 12-13 (2 performances) BrazenHeart Productions present:
LOVE, ETC. by Edward Musto; based on a book by Charles Webb; Director, Abbe Levin, Lighting/Sound Design, Chagrin da Largo CAST: D. James Reynolds (Roger), Anitra Frasier (Mrs. Becker), Bill Dante (Customer/Sal /Policeman/Game Show Host), Don Creeche (Mr. Becker/Bartender /Announcer/Psychiatrist), Chandra Jesse (Melinda), Amy Soucy (Joanna), Jadah Carroll (Operator), Jaimi B. Williams (Beth)
A comedy in two acts. The action takes place in Boston, 1977.

(Duplex) Sunday, August 13–October 22, 2000 BGH Productions present:
WHERE'S ROSE? Written/Directed by Daniel Logan; Press, Mark Cannistraro CAST: Daniel Logan, Sarah Bierstock, Jim Eigo, Brett Owen
A drama about a television interview between a young journalist and a veteran of the Stonewall riots.

(Joyce Theatre) Monday, August 14–27, 2000 (15 performances)
LES BALLETS TROCKADERO DE MONTE CARLO General Director, Eugene McDougle; Artistic Director, Tory Dobrin; Press, Bob Johnson PRINCIPALS: Colette Adae, Fifi Barkova, Sylphia Belchick, Maria Clubfoot, Tanya Doumiafeyva, Svetlana Lofatkina, Anya Marx, Margeaux Mundeyn, Ida Nevasayneva, Maria Paranova, Nadia Rombova, Olga Supphozova, Maya Thickenthighya, Gerd Törd, Iona Trailer, Vanya Verikosa COMPANY: Bernd Burgmaier, Kenneth Busbin, Matthew Carter, Robert Carter, Carlos Garcia, Paul Ghiselin, Jason Hadley, Raymell Jamison, Yonny Manaure, Fernando Medina Gallego, Brian Millet, Manolo Molina, Brian Norris, Mark Rudzitis, Jai Williams
PROGRAM: Les Sylphides, Go for Borocco, Pas de Deux (Grand Pas Classique, Le Corsaire, Don Quixote, Diana and Aceton), Dying Swan, Raymonda's Wedding, Swan Lake, Cross Currents, Russian Dance, Pas de Quatre, Paquita, Legend
The comic all-male ballet troupe.

(Theatre 3) Monday, August 14–October 14, 2000 (55 performances and 8 previews) Herkimer Entertainment present:

THE SOUL OF AN INTRUDER by Steve Braunstein; Director, Frank Cento; Set/Costumes, Chas W. Roeder; Lighting, Ed McCarthy; Sound, Bart Fasbender; Casting, Pratt/Moarefi; Stage Manager, Adam Grosswirth; Press, Tony Origlio/Mark Cannistraro CAST: Sylva Kelegian (Mable Codd), Stephen Beach (Jack Amsterdam), Cliff Diamond (Eddie Dixon)
A drama in two acts. The action takes place in a suburban Connecticut home.

(Minetta Lane Theatre) Tuesday, August 15–October 1, 2000 (46 performances and 10 previews) Back to Back Productions presents:

IMPERFECT CHEMISTRY Music/Story, Albert Tapper; Lyrics/Book, James Racheff; Director/Choreography, John Ruocco; Musical Director /Orchestrations, August Eriksmoen; Set, Rob Odorisio; Costumes, Curtis Hay; Lighting, John-Paul Szczepanski; Sound, Robert Kaplowitz; Casting, Cindi Rush; Stage Manager, Renée Rimland; Press, Pete Sanders/Jim Mannino CAST: John Jellison (Dr. Goodman/Dr. Bubinski), Brooks Ashmanskas (Harry Lizzarde), Ken Barnett (Dr. Alvin Rivers), Amanda Watkins (Dr. Elizabeth Gibbs), Joel Carlton, Michael Greenwood, Deirdre Lovejoy, Sara Schmidt
MUSICAL NUMBERS: Avalon, Dream Come True, Serious Business, I Love Problems, It's All Written in Your Genes, Ahhhh, St. Andrews, Leave Your Fate to Fate, Hell to Pay, Loxagane, Big Hair, E-Mail Love Notes, Bub's Song, Chaos Ballet, Finale
A musical comedy performed without intermission.

Ken Barnett, Amanda Watkins in *Imperfect Chemistry* (Carol Rosegg)

Cyrus Farmer, Sherri Pullum, Andrew Stewart Jones, Andrew Oswald, Renée Bucciarelli in *A Midsommer Nights Dreame* (Jonathan Slaff)

(Founders Hall Theatre) Tuesday, August 15–September 2, 2000 (7 performances and 2 previews) Kings County Shakespeare Company presents:

A MIDSOMMER NIGHTS DREAME by William Shakespeare; Director, Liz Shipman; Set/Lighting, Dan Nicholas; Costumes, Deborah Hertzberg; Sound, Alex Roe, Mr. Ryan; Music, Joe Ryan; Choreography, Amy Schwartzman Brightbill; Fights, Lucie Chin; Press, Jonathan Slaff CAST: Andrew Oswald (Demetrius), Cyrus Farmer (Lysander), Sherri Pullum (Hermia), Renée Bucciarelli (Helena), John Flaherty (Nick Bottom), John McCarthy (Francis Flute), Jon Fordham (Oberon), Andrew Stewart-Jones (Puck), Deborah Wright (Titania)
Performed in repertory with *The Rivals*.

(Founders Hall Theatre) Wednesday, August 16–September 3, 2000 (8 performances and 2 previews) Kings County Shakespeare Company presents:

THE RIVALS by Richard Brinsley Sheridan; Director, Deborah Wright Houston; Set/Lighting, Dan Nichols; Costumes, Cathy Maguire; Press, Jonathan Slaff CAST INCLUDES: Joseph Small (Anthony Absolute), Alex Roe (Capt. Absolute), Bev Lacy (Lydia Languish), Donald Bledsoe (Bob Acres), Frank Smith (Faulkland), Sherri Pullum (Julia), Vicki Hirsch (Mrs. Malaprop), John Flaherty (Lucius O'Trigger), Ian Gould (Fag)
The 1775 comedy of manners.

(Charas/El Bohio) Wednesday, August 16–26, 2000 (7 performances) Theater Et Al presents:

I DIDN'T ASK FOR BARE-CHESTED MEN SINGING DOO-WOP by Ann Warren; Songs, Fred Converse and Ms. Warren; Director, Fabienne Bouville; Set, Tamar Gadish; Costumes, Amy Clark; Lighting, David Moodey; Stage Manager, Jennifer Brainsky CAST: Marissa Copeland, Alan Cove, Darren Fouse, Nadine George, Dennis Horvitz, Robin Poley, Joe Rejeski, James A. Walsh

James Heatherly in *Life With Jeem* (Nigel Teare)

(Collective Unconscious) Thursday, August 17–26, 2000 (7 performances) Company Q, in association with Fringe NYC, presents:
LIFE WITH JEEM by Jimmy O'Neill; Director, Michael Hyman; Stage Manager, Jeannine L. Jones; Press, David Gersten CAST: James Heatherly (Jimmy Jimmers)
A play about a gay man and the top of a Macy's mannequin. The action takes place in New York City, 1993.

(Clark Studio) Thursday, August 17–September 17, 2000 (25 performances and 5 previews) The Auila Theatre Company presents:
CYRANO DE BERGERAC by Edmond Rostand; Adaptation/Director, Robert Richmond; Design, Peter Meineck, Mr. Richmond; Costumes/Puppets, Justine Scherer; Lighting, Mr. Meineck; Music, Anthony Cochrane; Press, Gary Springer-Susan Chicoine/Joe Trentacosta CAST: Daniel Rappaport (Ragueneau), Noah Trepanier (Ligniere), Alvaro Heinig (Christian /Valvert), Jennie Israel (Buffet Girl/Pickpocket/Minder), William Kwapy (Le Bret/The Bore), Noah Trepanier (Mountfluery/Monk), Anthony Cochrane (Cyrano), Lisa Carter (Roxanne/Lise), Sean Fri (De Guiche /Musketeer)
Performed with one intermission.

Lisa Carter, Anthony Cochrane in *Cyrano de Bergerac* (Peter Meineck/Aquila)

(Henry St. Settlement) Friday, August 18–20, 2000 (7 performances) New York Fringe Festival presents:
ALL'S WELL THAT ENDS WELL by William Shakespeare; Director, David Gaard; Press, Philip Thurston CAST: Randi Helle (Countess of Rossillion), Demos Tsilikoudis (Bertram), Allison Quinn (Helena), Mike Durell (Layfew), Robert Steffen (Parolles), George Trahanis (King of France), David Sochet (Lavatch), Brett Caruso (Dumain the Older), Jeremy Brena (Dumain the Younger), Jonathan Calindas (Duke of Florence), Trish Balbert (Widow of Florence), Monika Ramnath (Diana)

(B.B. King Blues Club) Sunday, August 20–November 12, 2000 (37 performances and 11 previews) Eric Krebs presents:
IT AIN'T NOTHIN' BUT THE BLUES by Charles Bevel, Lita Gaithers, Randal Myler, Ron Taylor, Dan Wheetman; Based on an original idea by Mr. Taylor; Director, Mr. Myler; Musical Director, Jim Ehinger; Costumes, Enid Turnbull; Casting, Stephanie Klapper; Press, Richard Kornberg/Tom D'Ambrosio, Jim Byk, Don Summa CAST: Cheryl Alexander, "Mississippi" Charles Bevel, Carter Calvert, Debra Laws, Michael Mandell, Gregory Porter
MUSICAL NUMBERS: Let the Good Times Roll, I've Been Living with the Blues, I'm a Blues Man, Sweet Home Chicago, Wang Dang Doodle, Someone Else Is Steppin' In, Please Don't Stop Him, I'm Your Hoochie Coochie Man, Crawlin' King Snake, Mind Your Own Business, Walkin' After Midnight, I Can't Stop Lovin' You, The Thrill Is Gone, I Put a Spell on You, Fever, Walkin' Blues, Come On in My Kitchen, Crossroad Blues, Goodnight Irene, Strange Fruit, Someday We'll All Be Free, Members Only, Finale
A revised version of the 1999 Broadway production, now staged for an intimate club. Now performed without intermission. For original Bdwy production, see *Theatre World* Vol. 55.

Carter Calvert, Gretha Boston, Eloise Laws in the Broadway production of *It Ain't Nothin' But the Blues* (Joan Marcus)

(Curricán Theatre) Friday, August 25–September 10, 2000 Inertia Productions present:
LIFE DURING WARTIME by Keith Reddin; Director, Kevin Kittle; Set, Eric Walton; Costumes, Frank Chavez; Lighting, Michael A. Reese; Sound, Susan Williams CAST: Aaron Stanford (Tommy), Danielle Liccardo (Gale), Eric Walton (Heinrich), Nathan Flower (John Calvin), Eric Alperin (The Young Men), Missy Thomas, Calvin Gladen
A dark comedy.

The Company of *4 Guys Named José* (Carol Rosegg)

(Blue Angel Theatre) Friday, August 25, 2000–March 4, 2001 Enrique Iglesias and Dasha Epstein present:

4 GUYS NAMED JOSÉ...*and Una Mujer Named Maria* Conceived by David Coffman and Dolores Prida; Book, Ms. Prida; Director, Susana Tubert; Musical Supervision/Arrangements, Oscar Hernandez; Choreography, Maria Torres; Set, Mary Houston; Costumes, Tania Bass; Lighting, Aaron Spivey; Sound, T. Richard Fitzgerald; Cast Recording, DRG; Casting, Elsie Stark; Stage Manager, Joe Witt; Press, Keith Sherman/Dan Fortune CAST: Philip Anthony (José Dominicano), Henry Gainza (José Mexicano), Lissette Gonzalez (Maria), Allen Hidalgo (José Boriqua), Ricardo Puente (José Cubano)

Four guys dream of staging a musical show to counteract Latino stereotypes. Performed in two acts.

(Dixon Place) Wednesday, August 30–September 23, 2000 (7 performances and 7 previews) Dixon Place presents:

THE PROPAGANDA PLAYS by Micah Schraft; Director, Trip Cullman; Set, Sandra Goldmark; Costumes, Georgia Lee; Lighting, Matt Richards; Sound, Fitz Patton; Press, Shirley Herz/Sam Rudy CAST: Sheri Graubert, David Hornsby, Adrian La Tourelle, Tatyana Yassukovich

A drama following characters interconnected by time and circumstance over 25 years.

(New York Performance Works) Wednesday, August 30–October 14, 2000 (34 performances and 4 previews) CBT Productions, in association with Greg Trautman and Cold Productions, presents:

WHERE EVERYTHING IS EVERYTHING Written/Directed by Stephen Spoonamore; Set, Sean Patrick Anderson; Costumes, Charlene Alexis Gross; Lighting, Robert Williams; Sound, Michael Wrobleyski; Stage Manager, Rebecca Wilson; Press, Gary Springer-Susan Chicoine/Joe Trentacosta CAST: Daisy Eagan (Traveler Tracy/Tracy Cochran/Carla), Paul Sparks (Main Man Dan/Dan Kurlingham/Renée)

A romance set in New York City.

(78th St. Theatre Lab) Thursday, August 31–October 8, 2000 (16 performances and 8 previews) 78th St. Theatre Lab, in association with Curt and Katherine Welling, presents:

WYOMING by Catherine Gillet; Director, Eric Nightengale; Set, Lenore Doxsee; Lighting, Allison Brummer; Costumes, Julie Fischoff; Stage Manager, Julie Kessler; Press, Jim Baldassare CAST: Mary Louise Burke (Sheila), Rosalyn Coleman (Jasmine), Camilla Enders (Annie), George R. Sheffey (Man)

A drama performed without intermission.

(Red Room) Wednesday, September 6–17, 2000 (10 performances) Spellbound Theatreworks, in association with Horse Trade Theater Group, presents:

HAIR by Galt MacDermot, James Rado, and Gerome Ragni; Director, Genevieve Williams; Musical Director, Jack Aaronson; Musical Staging, Ryan Duncan; Costumes, Barry Brown, Kevin Roback, Chuck Stanley; Lighting, Ms. Williams and Karen Currie CAST: Jim Bray (Claude), Salvador Navarro (Berger), David Solomon (Woof), Ceora Hoxsey (Hud), Allison Cipris (Sheila), Kate Pazakis (Jeanie), Annette Powers, K'Dara Korin, Leslee Warren, Jeremy Manta, Kevin Robak, Samantha Franco, Lisa Margaroli, Barry Brown, Anna Carbonell, Frank Galgano, Candice Harper, Mark Hickman

(Wings Theatre) Wednesday, September 6–16, 2000 (10 performances) Playwrights/Actors Contemporary Theater, in association with Wings Theatre, presents:

NOT WITH A BANG, BUT... by Paul Knowles and Lacy J. Thomas; Director, Phillip Filiato; Press, Sun/Stephen Sunderlin CAST: Paul Nicholas, Jerome Weinstein, Gloria Suavé, Jane Petrov, Jim Ireland, Sarah Ireland

A drama set in a mountain home over the Christmas holidays.

Sarah and Jim Ireland in *Not With a Bang, But...* (Paul Knowles)

Mary Louise Burke, Rosalyn Coleman, Camilla Enders in *Wyoming* (Dave Cross)

Dee Dee Friedman, Timothy Harris in *Order Up Watch TV* (Mark Lang)

(Grove St. Playhouse) Wednesday, September 6–30, 2000 (14 performances and 2 previews) The Harbor Theatre presents:
ORDER UP WATCH TV by Stephanie Lehmann; Director, Harry Bouvy; Set, Richard Dennis; Costumes, Martha Bromelmeier; Lighting, Douglas Filomena; Sound, Robert Auld; Stage Manager, Bruce Greenwood; Press, Philip Thurston CAST: Dee Dee Friedman (Ella Moore), Timothy Harris (Henry), Michael Anderson (Miles Moore), Michael Gnat, Carol Todd (TV Voices), Lisa DeSimone (Theme Song)
A comedy in two acts. The action takes place in Manhattan, and New Jersey.

Pamela Gien in *The Syringa Tree* (Michael Lamont)

(Playhouse 91) Wednesday, September 6, 2000–June 2, 2002 (586 performances and 8 previews) Matt Salinger present:
THE SYRINGA TREE by Pamela Gien; Director, Larry Moss; Set, Kenneth Foy; Costumes, William Ivey Long; Lighting, Jason Kantrowitz; Sound, Tony Suraci; Stage Manager, Frederick H. Orner; Press, Bill Evans/Jim Randolph, Jonathan Schwartz CAST: Pamela Gien (All 28 Characters)
A drama performed without intermission. The action takes place in Johannesburg, South Africa, beginning in 1963.

(Present Company Theatorium) Wednesday, September 6–30, 2000 New York City Players present:
BOXING 2000 Written/Directed by Richard Maxwell; Set, Stephanie Nelson CAST INCLUDES: Robert Torres (Freddie), Gladys Perez (Marissa), Benjamin Tejeda (Father), Lakpa Bhutia (Referee), Jim Fletcher, Candido Rivera, Chris Sullivan
A drama about a pair of half-brothers in New York City.

(Westbeth Theatre Center) Thursday, September 7–30 (19 performances and 3 previews); Reopened November 8, 2000–January 27, 2001 (56 performances) TWEED Theater Works and Russel Scott Lewis present:
LYPSINKA! THE BOXED SET Director, Kevin Malony; Set, Jim Boutin; Lighting, Mark T. Simpson Press, Publicity Office/Bob Fennell CAST: John Epperson (Lypsinka)
Musical performance art.

John Epperson as *Lypsinka* (Michael Childers)

(Blue Heron Arts Center) Friday, September 8–October 1, 2000 (19 performances and 6 previews) Ma-Yi Theatre Company presents:
MIDDLE FINGER by Hans Org; Director/Set, Loy Arcenas; Costumes, Gino Gonzales; Lighting, James Vermeulen; Sound/Music, Fabian Obispo; Press, Gary Springer-Susan Chicoine CAST: Ramon De Ocampo (Jacob), Orlando Pabotoy (Benjamin), Michi Barall, Jojo Gonzales, Mia Katigbak, Seth Michael May, Harvey Perr, Shawn Randall, Brian Webster, B. Martin Williams, Rebecca Wisocky, Ching Valdes-Aran, Marty Zantz
A drama set in a repressive Catholic boys school.

(Greenwich St. Theatre) Friday, September 8–October 1, 2000 26 Film Productions present:
BEIRUT by Alan Bowne; Director, Richard Scanlon; Set, Mark Dowey, Danielle LoDuca; Lighting, Drew Scott CAST: Matthew Walton (Torch), Jennifer Raye (Blue), Graham Anderson (Guard)
A drama set in the not-so-distant future.

(Hudson Guild Theater) Friday, September 8–October 21, 2000 (36 performances and 11 previews) Grimalkyn Ltd. presents:
THAT ILK by Nancy Dean; Director, Jere Jacob; Set, Matthew Maraffi; Costumes, Leslie Nuss; Lighting, Michael Gottlieb; Music, Craig Brandwein; Press, Tony Origlio/Emily Lowe CAST: Annie Montgomery (Lisa), Susan Izatt (Julia), Lorina Parker (Iris), Kathleen Garrett (Eleanor), James Nugent (Michael Aaron), Steven Gibbons, Sandra Kazan, Jennifer Sternberg
A family drama spanning 1938–56.

(Blue Heron Arts Center) Friday, September 8–17, 2000
PIECES Written/Performed by Zohar Tirosh; Director, Kathleen Powers; Press, Publicity Outfitters/Timothy J. Haskell, Christopher Joy
The true story of a female soldier in the Israeli army, 1994–96.

Chris Payne Gilbert, Maria Thayer, Black-Eyed Susan in *Eloise & Ray* (Dave Cross)

(Sanford Meisner Theater) Friday, September 8–24, 2000 (12 performances and 4 previews) Tangent Theatre Company, in association with Apple Blossom Productions, presents:
WANDERERS by Michael Rhodes; Director, Keith Teller; Press, Shirley Herz/Sam Rudy CAST: Michael Rhodes (Paul), Heather Dilly (Rose), Michael Campion, Martha Millan, Paul Molnar, Elissa Piszel, Caise Rode
A drama about contemporary dating and relationships.

(Connelly Theatre) Saturday, September 9–October 1, 2000 (15 performances and 3 previews) Chain Lightning Theatre presents:
WHEN REAL LIFE BEGINS by Karen Sunde; Director, Ken Marini; Set /Costumes, Dorothea Brunialti; Lighting, Scott Clyve; Sound, Sheree Sano; Stage Manager, B.D. White; Press, Shirley Herz/Michael Goldfried CAST: Raye Lankford
A one-woman drama based on the experiences of Kricker James and Claire Higgins, the founders of Chain Lightning Theatre.

(Ohio Theatre) Sunday, September 10–30, 2000 (14 performances and 2 previews) New Georges presents:
ELOISE & RAY by Stephanie Fleischmann; Director, Alexandra Aron; Set, Marsha Ginsberg; Costumes, Moe Schell; Lighting, Diane D. Fairchild; Sound, David A. Arnold; Music, Miki Navazio; Video, Sue-Ellen Stroum; Stage Manager, Sarah Thomas; Press, Jim Baldassare CAST: Maria Thayer (Eloise), Chris Payne Gilbert (Ray), Black-Eyed Susan (Actress), In Video: James Stanley (Jed), Louis London (Young Jed), Jacob Kizer (Young Ray)
A drama performed without intermission. The action takes place in Colorado, a couple of years back.

(Don't Tell Mama) Sunday, September 10–October 1, 2000 (4 performances) Flip Productions presents:
7 HABITS OF HIGHLY EFFECTIVE MISTRESSES Written/Performed by Lisa Faith Phillips; Musical Director, Ellen Mandel
A one-woman show. Previously performed at Cornelia Street Café in April 2000.

(Cherry Lane Alternative) Monday, September 11–30, 2000 (16 performances and 3 previews) Young Playwrights Inc. presents:
YOUNG PLAYWRIGHTS FESTIVAL 2000 Artistic Director, Sheri M. Goldhirsch; Managing Director, Brett W. Reynolds; Sets, Narelle Sissons; Costumes, Kitty-Leech; Lighting, Pat Dignan; Sound, David A. Gilman; Casting, Cindi Rush; Stage Managers, Thomas J. Gates and Linda Marcello; Press, Terence Womble
Woof by Caroline Noble Whitbeck; Director, Jeremy Dobrish CAST: Carolann Page (Mother), Jen Drohan (Girl)
A Mind of Its Own by Adam Feldman; Director, Beth Milles CAST: Brad Malow (Danny Rosenberg), Ann Hu (Rena Chung), Chaz Mena (Dr. Phallus), Todd Lawson (Simon), Carolann Page (Mother/Justine), Martin LaPlatney (Father)
Fish-Eye View by Sherry Ou-yang; Director, Richard Caliban CAST: An Hu (Daughter), Karen Tsen Lee (Mother), Suzen Murakoshi (Grandmother)
I'm Coming In Soon by Gemma Cooper-Novack; Director, Lynn M. Thomson CAST: Todd Lawson (Brian Sanders), Erika Thomas (Nina Cassidy), Susan Pellegrino (Catherine Voigt Cassidy), Martin LaPlatney (Jerome Cassidy)
Four plays by writers age 18 or younger.

Stella Duffy, Niall Ashdown in *Lifegame* (Russell Caldwell)

(Jane Street Theatre) Tuesday, September 12–December 3, 2000 (78 performances and 19 previews) David Stone, Markley Skipper, Nina Essman, and Julian Schlossberg present The Improbable Theatre Production of:

LIFEGAME Created by Keith Johnstone; Artistic Direction/Design, Phelim McDermott, Lee Simpson, Julian Crouch; Lighting, Colin Grenfell; Stage Manager, Jason Scott Eagan; Guest Coordinator, MacKenzie Cadenhead; Press, Publicity Office/Bob Fennell, Candi Adams CAST: Niall Ashdown, Angela Clerkin, Guy Dartnell, Stella Duffy, Phelim McDermott, Toby Park, Lee Simpson, and Guests

Improvisational theatre in which the cast interviews a guest and dramatizes scenes from his or her own life.

(14th Street Y) Tuesday, September 12–24, 2000 (16 performances) Musicals Tonight!/Mel Miller presents:

I MARRIED AN ANGEL Music, Richard Rodgers; Lyrics, Lorenz Hart; Book, Rodgers and Hart; Director/Choreography, Thomas Mills; Music Director, Mark Hartman; Lighting, Shuhei Seo; Casting, Stephen DeAngelis; Stage Manager, Anthony Gallucio CAST: Courtney Blythe (Seronella), Kathy Fitzgerald (Peggy), Richard Grayson (Gen. Lucash), Brad Little (Willy), Jayne Ackley Lynch (Modiste), Kenny Morris (Harry), Nanne Puritz (Angel), Andrea Quinn (Lucinda), Larry Raben (Peter), Ritta Rehn (Anna Murphy), Lois Saunders (Duchess), Jennifer Scheer (Clarinda), Stacy Lee Tilton (Arabella), Al Gillespie, Andrew Gitzy

MUSICAL NUMBERS: Did You Ever Get Stung?, I Married an Angel, The Modiste, I'll Tell the Man in the Street, How Was I To Know?, How to Win Friends and Influence People, Spring Is Here, Angel Without Wings, A Twinkle in Your Eye, At the Roxy Music Hall, Finale

A 1938 musical in two acts. The action takes place in Budapest, Hungary, 1938.

(Fifth Avenue Presbyterian Church) Tuesday, September 12–16, 2000 (5 performances) Theatre Fellowship presents:

ANCESTRAL VOICES by A.R. Gurney; Director, John Rowell; Lighting, Sharon Shuford; Stage Manager, Aileen Whiteside CAST: Richard G. Cottrell, Vincent F. Dowling, Jayne Heller, Jeanne Lehman, John Rowell

A family drama.

(CAP21 Theatre) Wednesday, September 13–October 8, 2000 (21 performances and 6 previews) Collaborative Arts Project 21 presents:

THE IMMIGRANT Music, Steven M. Alper; Lyrics, Sarah Knapp; Book, Mark Harelik based on his play; Director, Randal Myler; Musical Director, Albert Ahronheim; Set, Beowulf Boritt; Costumes, C. David Russell; Lighting, Jane Cox; Sound, Randy Hansen; Stage Manager, Vienna Hagen; Press, Peter Cromarty/Sherri Jean Katz CAST: Evan Pappas (Haskell Harelik), Cass Morgan (Ima Perry), Walter Charles (Milton Perry), Jacqueline Antaramian (Leah Harelik)

MUSICAL NUMBERS: The Stars, A Stranger Here, Simply Free, Changes, Travel Light, Through His Eyes, People Change Hard, I Don't Want It, Take the Comforting Hand of Jesus, Padadooly, The Sun Comes Up, Candlesticks, Safe and Sound, Where Would You Be?, No Place to Go, The Comforting Hand, Finale

A musical in two acts. The action takes place in Hamilton, TX, 1909–42.

(Chelsea Playhouse) Wednesday, September 13–October 8, 2000 The Riverside Stage Company presents:

WHERE DID VINCENT VAN GOGH Written/Performed by Dan Castellaneta; Press, Pete Sanders/Jim Mannino

A one-man comedy.

(Irish Arts Center) Thursday, September 14–October 1, 2000 Hand Rubbed Productions present:

LOCATING THE PLANT by Tim Marks; Director, Paula D'Alessandris CAST: Laura James-Flynn, Mark Hankla, Daniel Haughey, Sean Heeney, Matthew Hennessey, Richard Lester, Trish McGettrick

Cass Morgan, Walter Charles, Jacqueline Antaramian, Evan Pappas in *The Immigrant* (Carol Rosegg)

Lindel Sandlin, Thomas F. Walsh in *My Ass* (Shon Little)

Nick Gomez, Anthony DiMaria, Irene Glezos in *Big Cactus* (Gerry Goodstein)

(Bank Street Theatre) Friday, September 15–October 1, 2000 (13 performances) Shon Little and Jodi Shilling present:
MY ASS Written/Directed by Shon Little; Costumes, Melanie Wehrmacher; Lighting, Cindy Shumsey; Stage Manager, Marty Joyce; Press, Carolyn M. Nivling CAST: Tiffany D. Jones (Kelly), Sarah Jane Wytko (Brenda), Larry Giantonio (Tim), Jodi Shilling (Sandy), Shon Little (Rich), Joshua Koehn (Rich), Thomas F. Walsh (Clark), Lindel Sandlin (Angel), Paula Ehrenberg (Noel), Lee Blair (John), Ashley Trimble (Gail), Vickie Schmitt (Lucy)
A comedy in two acts. The place is here, the time is now.

(Curican Theatre) Saturday, September 16–October 7, 2000 (15 performances and 4 previews) The Flock Theater Company and Josh Liveright present:
BIG CACTUS by David T. King; Director, Victoria Pero; Set, Jesse Poleshuck; Costumes, Daniel Lawson; Lighting, Edward Pierce, Jonathan Spencer; Sound, Jeffrey Yoshi Lee; Stage Manager, Mary Bernardi; Press, Shirley Herz/Sam Rudy CAST: Anthony DiMaria (Bob), Nick Gomez (Edgar), Irene Glezos (Darlene), Fred Burrell (Old Jim), Mark Hofmaier (Claxton)
An edgy comedy in two acts. The action takes place in LA and the Sonoran Desert.

(The Duke) Tuesday, September 19–October 1, 2000 (10 performances and 2 previews) New Professional Theatre presents:
THE IN-GATHERING Music, Daryl Waters; Lyrics, Mr. Waters, John Henry Redwood; Book, Mr. Redwood; Director/Choreography, Hope Clarke; Set, Ruben Arana-Downs; Costumes, Evelyn Nelson; Lighting, Bridget K. Welty; Casting, Alaine Alldaffer; Stage Manager, Jacqui Casto; Press, Shirley Herz/Sam Rudy CAST: Carl Cofield (Sweeper), Ann Duquesnay (Cozy), Vinson German (Rufus/Spirits/Juice), Darryl Reuben Hall (Jasper), Rosena M. Hill (Sofi/Old Woman), Kimberly Jajuan (Annie Jewel), Janice Lorraine (Ola), Derrick McGinty (Giant), Frederick Owens (January), Nancy Ringham (Shirley Mordecai), Richard White (Silas Mordecai/Marue), Dathan B. Williams (Aristede Drambuie)
MUSICAL NUMBERS: Dawn, Don't Answer Me, Do You Remember, Heaven Right Here on Earth, Lead Me, Movin', A Boy, Gather Togther, Dance of Congo Square, There's a Chill in the Air January, Do You Remember, Life Is a Party, I Knew a Girl, What's Wrong with You?, I'm My Own Woman
A musical in two acts. The action takes place in the Carolinas, Mississippi, and Louisiana, 1862–65.

(Douglas Fairbanks Theater) Tuesday, September 19–December 31, 2000 (97 performances and 23 previews) Eric Krebs and Chase Mishkin present:
TALLULAH HALLELUJAH! by Tovah Feldshuh (with Larry Amoros and Linda Selman); Music/Lyrics, Van Alexander, Maxwell Anderson, Jean Barry, Nat Burton, Dick Charles, J. Fred Coots, Noël Coward, Henry Creamer, Mort Dixon, Ella Fitzgerald, Haven Gillespie, Ray Henderson, Jimmy Johnson, Walter Kent, Cecil Mack, Geoffrey Mack, Ray Noble, Cole Porter, Max Steiner, Leah Worth, Kurt Weill; Director, William Wesbrooks; Musical Direction/Arrangements, Bob Goldstone; Set, Michael Schweikardt; Costumes, Carrie Robbins; Lighting, Jeff Croiter; Sound, Jill B.C. Du Boff; Stage Manager, Babette Roberts; Kevin P. McAraney/Grant Lindsey CAST: Tovah Feldshuh (Tallulah Bankhead), Bob Goldstone (Meredith Wilson), Mark Deklin (Corp. Chapman)
An imagination of the life of actress Tallulah Bankhead performed without intermission. The setting is a USO show, 1956.

(Gloria Maddox Theatre) Wednesday, September 20–October 15, 2000 (21 performances) T. Schreiber Studio presents:

SWEENEY TODD: THE DEMON BARBER OF FLEET STREET by C.G. Bond; Director, Marc Geller; Set, Nathan Heverin; Costumes, Tracy Christensen; Lighting, Frank DenDanto III; Music, Daniel T. Denver; Stage Manager, John Henry Watson; Press, Kevin P. McAnarney CAST: Edwin Sean Patterson (Sweeney Todd), Zoey O'Toole (Mrs. Lovett), David Paterson (Tobias Ragg), J.M. McDonough (Judge Turpin), Tom Kulesa (The Beadle), Ellen Lindsay (Johanna), Charlie Romanelli (Anthony Hope), Mary Beth Lowalski (Beggar Woman), Gabriel Hernandez (Alfredo), Michael Edgar Murphy (Joans Fogg)

A macabre tale set in London, 1845.

(29th Street Rep) Wednesday, September 20–December 17, 2000 (97 performances) 29th Street Rep presents:

CHARLES BUKOWSKI'S SOUTH OF NO NORTH (*Stories of the Buried Life*) Adapted/Directed by Leo Farley and Jonathan Powers; Set, Mark Symczak; Sound, Gerard Drazba; Lighting, Stewart Wagner; Stage Manager, Cesar Malantic; Press, Tom Stanton CAST: Stephen Payne (Charles Bukowski), Tim Corcoran, Paula Ewin, Elizabeth Elkins, Gordon Holmes, Moira MacDonald, Charles Willey

PROGRAM: *Guts, You and Your Beer and How Great You Are, Stop Staring at My Tits Mister, Loneliness, Love for $17.50, The Devil Was Hot, A Man, Hit Man, Class*

Nine stories. Previously performed last season (February 24–March 26, 2000) at 29th St. Rep.

(Producer's Club) Thursday, September 21–October 1, 2000 (11 performances) Stage Right Productions present:

BEDLAM! by Dan Remmes; Director, Paula D'Alessandris; Set, Dan Martin; Lighting, Chris Rossiter; Sound, Jose Cruz; Stage Manager, Josh Knapp; Press, Brett Singer CAST: Duncan Lee (Yule), Sherikay Perry (Emily), Wende O'Reilly (Georgia), Susan Cameron (Angela), Chuck Powers (Guy), Amir Arison (Bud), Daniel B. Martin (Louis), Kathy Searle (Monica), Maitely Weismann (Susan), Collette Porteous (Paula), Dan Remmes (Dwight), Charlotte Dooling (Doctor), Eric Giancoli (Jack)

A one-act play of scenes about beds.

The Company of *Bedlam!* (Chris Rossiter)

(Lark Studio) Thursday, September 21–25, 2000 (6 performances) The Lark Theatre Company presents:

KNEPP by Jorge Goldenberg; Translated/Adapted by Judith Leverone; Director, Steven Williford; Costumes, Joseph LaCorte; Sound, Marco Joachim; Stage Manager, Valerie A. Peterson; Press, Todd Rosen CAST: Thom Christopher (Knepp), Meg Gibson (Maria Elena), Jeff Swarthout (Police), Lois Markle (Mother), Robert Montano (Luis), Matthew Conlon (Voice of Raul)

A drama performed without intermission. The action takes place in the old family home.

David Heckel, Jamie Marrs, Eddie Weiss in *The Four Corners of Suburbia* (Yahel Herzog)

(30th St. Theatre) Thursday, September 21–October 8, 2000 (15 performances and 1 preview) Double Helix Productions present:

THE FOUR CORNERS OF SUBURBIA by Elizabeth Puccini; Director, Alan Langdon; Set, Yoon Jin Kim; Lighting, Michael L. Kimmel; Video, Joanne Nerenberg; Stage Manager, Nicole Friedman; Press, Peter Cromarty CAST: Eddie Weiss (Walt), Jamie Watkins (Fiona), Jamie Marrs (Rachel), David Heckel (Benjamin), Emily Brannen (Susan), Brian Letscher (Doug)

A drama set at a New England summer house, July 1992.

(Wings Theatre) Thursday, September 21–October 21, 2000 (20 performances and 5 previews) Wings Theatre Company presents:

COWBOYS! Music, Paul L. Johnson; Lyrics/Book, Clint Jefferies; Director, Jeffery Corrick; Choreography, Kate Swan; Set, Sam Sommer; Costumes, Tom Claypool; Lighting, Aaron Spivey; Fights, Kymberli E. Morris; Stage Managers, Judy DeSantis, Kristen Leigh Grant; Press, Tony Origlio/Joel Treick CAST: John Lavin (Ranger Rick Rowdy), Steve Hasley (Buck), Steven Baker (Sidewinder), Andrew Phelps (Colt), Judy Kranz (Aunt Rosie Ritter), Stephen Cabral (Judge Sassafras Devine), Daniel Carlton (Boston Bart Black), Laura Sechelski (Lovely Lilly Luscious), Jim Gaddis (Injun Bob), Winnie the Wonder Horse (Lightning)

MUSICAL NUMBERS: Where Men Are Men, One Thing I Can Do Good, War Dance, I Fall to Faded Pieces After Midnight When Your Sweet Dreams Drive Me Crazy, Nothin' at All, Lonesome Cowpoke, Everything's Bigger in Texas, Gringo's Lament, Girl from Texarkana, Ain't Never Had a Kiss Like His, Make the Switch, I Ain't No Good for You, Apache Dance, Cloggin' Onto Broadway, Always Get My Man

A musical comedy in two acts. The action takes place on the Straight Arrow Ranch.

Vivien Landau, Ted Zurkowski in *King Richard III* (Dave Cross)

(West-Park Church) Thursday, September 28–October 22, 2000 (16 performances) Frog & Peach Theatre Company presents:
KING RICHARD III by William Shakespeare; Director, Lynnea Benson; Fights, Ian Marshall; Stage Manager, Christopher Currie; Press, Jim Baldassare CAST: James Aaron (Brakenbury), Martin Carey (Richmond), Rhonda Cole (Prince/Tyrrel), Joe Corey (Buckingham), Peter J. Coriaty (Ling Edward IV), Brian de Benedictis (Hastings), Carl Fischer (Lord Cardinal), Peter Hess Friedland (Rivers), Roland Johnson (Stanley), Vivien Landau (Elizabeth), Andrea Leigh (Lady Anne), Tom Marsden (Catesby), John Steinfels (Dorset), Stewart Walker (Ratcliffe), John David West (Clarence), Carolyn Sullivan-Zinn (Duchess of York), Ted Zurkowski (King Richard III)

(Intar53 Theater) Thursday, September 28–October 29, 2000 (24 performances) The Aulis Collective for Theater and Media presents:
KING LEAR by William Shakespeare; Director, Bernice Rohret; Music /Musical Director, Carl Schimmel; Set, Mary Houston; Costumes, Andrea Huelse; Lighting, Aaron Spivey; Fights, Samantha Phillips; Stage Manager, Scott F. DelaCruz; Press, Tony Origlio/Karen Greco, Emily Lowe CAST: Ralph Waite (Lear), Julie Campbell (Gonerill), Shirley Roeca (Regan), Natily Blair (Cordelia), Joe Hickey (Duke of Albany), Gregory Ivan Smith (Duke of Cornwall/Captain), Samuel Frederick Reynolds (King of France /Doctor), Todd Weldon (Duke of Burgundy), Kathryn Graybill (Earl of Kent), Mary Jane Wells (Earl of Gloucester), David Logan Rankin (Edgar), Suzanne Savoy (Edmund), Ashton Crosby (Oswald/Old Man), Christie Spain-Savage (Lear's Fool)
A production re-envisioned with an emphasis on contemporary issues relating to violence.

(John Houseman Studio) Friday, September 29–October 15, 2000 (16 performances) The Saints Theatre Company presents:
TWO SMALL BODIES by Beal Bell; Director, Carl Andress; Press, Publicity Outfitters/Timothy J. Haskell, Christopher Joy CAST: Jeffrey Guyton, Marianna Romalis
A drama exploring a love/hate relationship.

(Kaye Playhouse) Friday, September 29–October 5, 2000 (6 performances) International Cultural Productions present:
BOONAH, COME DOWN by Tsutomu Mizukami; Translation, David W. Griffith, Tanakka Keishi, Hori Mariko; Director, Kanichiro Suzuki; Set, Ueda Junko; Costumes, Ito Sachiko; Lighting, Nakagawa Ryuichi; Press, Gary Springer-Susan Chicoine/Joe Trentacosta CAST: Hitoshi Oya (Boonah), Yuko Haraguchi, Hiromi Inaba, Hiroshi Iwasaki, Ippei Kanie, Yoko Koyanagi, Hiroshi Nagahata, Yoshinobu Ota, Shino Oyamada, Yushi Sato, Wataru Takase, Mihoko Tsuchiya, Hiroko Uchiyama, Fumiya Yazaki
A philosophical Buddist fable.

(Century Center for the Performing Arts) Tuesday, October 3–December 10, 2000 (65 performances and 16 previews) Ken Hoyt and Kevin McDermott, in association with Brent Peek, present:
THE GOREY DETAILS: *A Musicale* by Edward Gorey; Music/Orchestrations, Peter Matz; Direction/Staging, Daniel Levans; Musical Director, Bruce W. Coyle; Set, Jesse Poleshuck; Costumes, Martha Bromelmeier; Lighting, Craig Kennedy; Sound, Johnna Doty; Stage Manager, Kenneth J. McGee; Press, Keith Sherman/Brett Oberman CAST: Alison Crowley, Allison DeSalvo, Matt Kuehl, Daniel C. Levine, Kevin McDermott, Ben Nordstrom, Liza Shaller, Clare Stollak, Christopher Youngsman
MUSICAL NUMBERS: The Narrator, Q.R.V., The Frozen Man, The Disrespectful Summons, The Weeping Chandelier, The Doubtful Guest, The Forty-Seven Questions, The Deranged Cousins, The Woeful Waking, The Blue Aspic, The Nursery Frieze, The Object Lesson, The Wuggly Ump, Gin, The Insect God, The Unknown Vegetable, The Inanimate Tragedy, The Admonitory Hippopotamus, Finale
A two-act "musicale" from the published and unpublished works of author-illustrator Edward Gorey.

Kevin McDermott in *The Gorey Details* (Brad Fowler)

Ralph Waite, Julie Campbell, Shirley Roeca in *King Lear* (Tom Bloom)

(City Center) Wednesday, October 4–8, 2000 (6 performances) The National Theater of Greece presents:

OEDIPUS REX by Sophocles; Director/Translation, Vassilis Papassileiou; Set /Costumes, Yorgas Ziakas; Lighting, Antonis Panayotopoulos; Music, Dimitris Kamarotos; Choreography, Vasso Barbousi; Press, Richard Kornberg/Jim Byk CAST: Grigoris Valtinos (Oedipus), Manos Stalakis (Priest), Stephanos Kyriakidis (Creon), Costas Galanakis (Teiresias), Jenny Gaitanopolou (Jocasta), Yannis Rozakis (Messenger), Iakovos Psarras (Attendant), Themis Panou (Domestic Messenger), Nini Vosniakou, Costas Basis, Manos Stalakis, Alexandros Panagou, Christos Papas, Petros Petrakis, Christos Sapountzis, Manolis Seiragakis, Yorgos Psychoyios (Chorus), Efstathios Nikolaidis (Guard), Emilia Vassilakai, Olga Liatiri (Daughters)
Performed in Greek with English supertitles.

(Storm Theatre) Wednesday, October 4–28, 2000 (18 performances and 2 previews) The Storm Theatre, in association with East End Productions, presents:

MONEY by Edward Bulwer-Lytton; Director, John S. Davies; Set, Mary Houston; Costumes, E. Shura Pollatsek; Lighting, Charles Cameron; Choreography, Maryanne Chaney; Stage Manager, Jean Klepka; Press, Shirley Herz/Nancy Khuu CAST: Stephen Logan Day (Sir John Vesey), Colleen Crawford (Georgina Vesey), Suzanna Geraghty (Lady Franklin), Elizabeth Roby (Clara Douglas), Peter Dobbins (Alfred Evelyn), Brett Hemmerling (Sir Frederick Blount), Grant McKeown (Charles Lord Glossmore), John Regis (Benjamin Stout/Tabouret), Laurence Drozd (Sir Henry Graves/MacFinch), William Joseph Brookes (Sharp/Old Member), Hugh Brandon Kelly (Capt. Dudley Smooth), Colleen Beakey, Cedric O'Gorman (Servants)
An 1840 comedy performed in two acts.

(Rude Room) Wednesday, October 4–29, 2000 (21 performances and 7 previews) Rude Mechanicals, in association with Ego Po Productions, -presents:

COMPANY by Samuel Beckett; Conceived/Directed by Lane Savadove; Sound, Glen Tarachow; Press, Spin Cycle/Ron Lasko, Shannon Jowett CAST: David Fitzgerald, Omar Metwally, Sara Bakker, Jessica Claire, Melanie Flood, Connie Hall, Diane Landers, Kristin Ketterer, Zachary Knower, Hilary Redmon, Kelly Van Zile, Tessa Zugmeyer
An adaptation of Beckett's late prose work.

(Tribeca Playhouse) Thursday, October 5–29, 2000 (13 performances and 3 previews) The Worth Street Theater Company presents:

SNAPSHOTS 2000 Director, Jeff Cohen; Producer/Press, Carol R. Fineman; Costumes, Allyson Lapidus; Lighting, Matthew Piercy
Stars by Romulus Linney CAST: Jim Hazard (Man), Diane Love (Woman)
Scene with Celery by Peter Hedges CAST: Adam Hirsch (Man), Noel True (Woman)
Bea's Legacy by Jeff Cohen CAST: Keira Naughton (Bea Miller), Gerald Anthony (Interviewer), Paul Whitthorne (Ned Tripplett), Adam Hirsch (Police), Diane Love (NPR Announcer), Queen Esther (Toni Martin), Jim Hazard (Sen. Joe Dryden)
Dreamin' in Church by Robert O'Hara CAST: Derek Lively (Rev. Benson)
Genitalia by Robert O'Hara CAST: Queen Esther (Eudarrie), Heather Alicia Simms (Adella), Noel True (Big Shirley), Derek Lively (Voice 4)
Bagging Groceries by Mark Novom CAST: Paul Whitthorne (A), Derek Lively (B), Karen Traynor (C), Gerald Anthony (D)
The Age of Pie by Peter Hedges CAST: Derek Lively (Clark), Jim Hazard (Stan), Heather Alicia Simms (Betty O), Noel True (Joy), Adam Hirsch (Stuart), Karen Traynor (Ruth), Keira Naughton (Connie), Paul Whitthorne (Skip)
Seven one-act plays.

(Theater for the New City) Thursday, October 5–21, 2000 (16 performances) The Lady Cavaliers presents:

GLORIA by Peter Hilton; Director, Alexandra Ornitz; Costumes, Christianne Myers; Lighting, Diane D. Fairchild; Sound/Music, Robert Kaplowitz; Fights, David Dean Hastings; Stage Manager, Leslie Klug; Press, Laura Davis CAST: Carrie Brewer (Gloria), Bevin Kaye (Maladie), Kittson O'Neill (Stepmother), Jennifer Loia Alexander (Abbess), Amanda Barron (Sapphire/Willow/Ariel), Denise Alessandria Hurd (Donnabella /Birch/Gothica), Judi Lewis (Carmella), Kittson O'Neill (Queen Convolvula/Dendrophelia), Alexandra Ornitz (Jade), Barbara J. Spence (Nurse), Dayna Steinfeld (Opal/Hawthorn/Romana), Carey Van Driest (Ruby/Oak/Italica)
An all-female swashbuckling fantasy in verse.

(Blue Heron Arts Center) Thursday, October 5–29, 2000 (19 performances) Blue Heron Theatre presents:

SACRED JOURNEY by Matt Witten; Director, Michael Warren Powell; Set /Lighting, Roman Tatarowicz; Costumes, Martha Louise Bromelmeier; Sound, Samuel C. Tresler; Press, Pete Sanders/Bill Coyle CAST: Gregory Zaragoza (Indian John)
A solo play about a Native American living on the streets on New York City.

(Center Stage) Friday, October 6–22, 2000 (13 performances) New Moon Rising Productions presents:

NOT WAVING... by Gen LeRoy; Director, K. Lorrel Manning; Press, Stephen Sunderlin CAST: Sheila Saunders (Gabby), Janis Schodowski (Nicole), Jacqueline Bowman, David Fraioli
A drama about a widow and her daughter.

Laurence Drozd, Suzanna Geraghty in *Money*

Brian Belovitch in *Boys Don't Wear Lipstick*

(Players Theatre) Friday, October 6–November 2000 Steve Asher, David W. Unger, and Avalon Entertainment present:
BOYS DON'T WEAR LIPSTICK Written/Performed/(And Lived) by Brian Belovitch; Director, Keith Greer; Set, Scott Pask; David C. Woolard; Lighting, James Vermeulen; Sound, Robert Murphy; Projections, Elaine J. McCarthy; Stage Manager, Julia P. Jones; Press, Craig Karpel/Brian Carmody, Bridget Klapinski
A one-man show about a journey from boyhood to manhood, by way of a 15-year detour through womanhood.

(Connelly Theatre) Saturday, October 7–29, 2000 (18 performances and 3 previews) Synapse presents:
THE ELEPHANT MAN by Bernard Pomerance: Director, David Travis; Set, Adrian W. Jones; Costumes, Miguel Angel Huidor; Lighting, Alistair Wandesforde-Smith; Press, Shirley Herz/Sam Rudy CAST: Tony Ward (Frederick Treves), Angus Hepburn (Carr Gomm), David Caton (Ross), Timothy McCracken (John Merrick), Glenn Peters (Pinhead Manager), Jeff Burchfield (Snork/Will/Lord John), Jamie Jones (Mrs. Kenda), Nina Hellman (Miss Sandwich), Hillary Keegin (Princess/Countess)
A drama based on the life of John Merrick, a deformed young man. The action takes place in Victorian London.

(Dixon Place) Tuesday, October 10–28, 2000 (6 performances and 3 previews) Dixon Place presents:
PARTY DEVIL Written/Performed by Ken Bullock; Developed/Directed by Eric Silberman; Music, Roger Pauletta; Lyrics, Mr. Bullock; Press, Shirley Herz/Sam Rudy, Nancy Khuu
A one-man show with music in which Mr. Bullock portrays Princess Sahara and the characters she encounters.

(Theatre 22) Tuesday, October 10–22, 2000 (12 performances) Terese Hayden presents:
ALL OVER by Edward Albee; Director, Terese Hayden; Design, Fred Kolo; Lighting, Sidney Armus; Press, Max Eisen/Caraid O'Brien CAST: Jacqueline Brookes (The Wife), Elizabeth Nafpaktitis (The Mistress), Charles D. Cissel (The Son), Jill Van Note (The Daughter), James Stevenson (The Best Friend), Richard Durham (The Doctor), Terese Hayden (The Nurse), Jeremie Adkins (The Photographer), Patrick Buonaiuto (The Reporter)
A drama in two acts. The action takes place in a bed/sitting room, 1971.

(Promenade Theatre) Tuesday, October 10, 2000–January 28, 2001 (112 performances and 16 previews) Julian Schlossberg, Ben Sprecher, Ted Tulchin, William P. Miller in association with Aaron Levy and Morton Wolowitz present:
THE UNEXPECTED MAN by Yasmina Reza; Translation, Christopher Hampton; Director, Matthew Warchus; Set/Costumes, Mark Thompson; Lighting, Hugh Vanstone; Sound, Mic Pool, David Bullard; Music, Gary Yershon; Casting, Stephanie Klapper; Stage Manager, Michael Brunner; Press, Jeffrey Richards/John Moreno CAST: Alan Bates (The Man), Eileen Atkins (The Woman)
A drama performed without intermission. The action takes place on a train from Paris to Frankfurt.

Alan Bates, Eileen Atkins in *The Unexpected Man*

Tony Ward, Timothy McCracken in *The Elephant Man*

Michael McGrath and members of the audience in *Game Show* (Joan Marcus)

(45 Bleecker) Tuesday, October 10–December 31, 2000 (78 performances and 17 previews) Jeffrey Finn Productions presents:
GAME SHOW by Jeffrey Finn and Bob Walton; Based on an idea by Mr. Finn; Director, Mark Waldrop; Set, James Youmans; Costumes, Theresa Squire; Lighting, Jeffrey S. Koger; Sound, One Dream/Kurt B. Kellenberger; Music, Mr. Walton; Stage Manager, Brian Rardin CAST: Joel Blum (Joe McGuire/Tyler Scott), Jeb Brown (Steve Fox), Jeremy Ellison-Gladstone (Johnny Wilderman/Cliff Andrews), Dana Lynn Mauro (Penny /Erica Singer), Michael McGrath (Troy Richards), Cheryl Stren (Ellen Ryan)
A comedy performed without intermission. The action takes place during a live broadcast of a TV game show.

(The Duke) Tuesday, October 10–November 5, 2000 (17 performances and 15 previews) The Jewish Repertory Theatre presents:
BIG POTATO by Arthur Laurents; Director, Richard Sabellico; Set, James Noone; Costumes, Carrie Robbins; Lighting, Richard Latta; Stage Manager, Judith Schoenfeld; Press, John Barlow-Michael Hartman /Jeremy Schaffer CAST: Dylan Chalfy (Sonny), Elzbieta Czyzewska (Nessa), David Margulies (Itzhak), Joanna Glushak (Rochelle), Paul Hecht (Julius)
A drama in two acts. The action takes place in Kew Gardens, Queens, 1975.

(Gramercy Arts Theatre) Wednesday, October 11–May 2, 2001 (29 performances and 1 preview) Repertorio Español presents:
VIEQUES by Juan González; Director, Alfredo Galván; Design, Robert Weber Federico; Sound, Mr. Miranda; Voice-Overs, Nancy Millán and Frankie Miranda; Video, Carlos (Abi) Torres and Eduardo Rosado; Press, Gary Springer-Susan Chicoine/Joe Trentacosta CAST: Ricardo Barber (Julio), Tatiana Vecino (Lola), Miriam Cruz (Marta), Bettina Mercado (Silvia), Indio Meléndez (Miguel), Milena Pérez (Josefina), Lucio Fernández (Roberto)
A drama set on the island of Vieques, Puerto Rico, during the 1950s.

(Ohio Theatre) Wednesday, October 11–November 18, 2000 (20 performances and 7 previews) adobe theatre company presents:
ORPHEUS AND EURYDICE Written/Directed by Jeremy Dobrish; Set, Matthew Maraffi; Lighting, Michael Gottlieb; Costumes, Meganne George; Sound, Chriss Todd; Music, Lewis Flinn; Stage Manager, Jacqueline Terbay; Press, Jeffrey Richards CAST: Arthur Aulisi (Aristaeus), Jeremy Brisiel (Hercules/Sissyphus), Vin Knight (Homelessius/Teiresias /No. 2), Kathryn Langwell (Eurydice), Andrew Elvis Miller (Orpheus), Erin Quinn Purcell (Atalanta/Death), Adam Smith (Jason/Tantalus), Jennifer Ward (Andrea/Bacche/No.1)
A 21st century take on the popular myth.

(Washington Square Church) Wednesday, October 11–28, 2000 (11 performances and 1 preview) NaCL Theatre (North American Cultural Laboratory) presents:
ACRA NOVA Director, Brad Krumholz; Press, Brett Singer CAST: Randall Kent Cohn, Benedetta Ferrario, Lidy Lopez Gonzalez, Tannis Kowalchuk, Jill Samuels, Pamela Samuelson, Allison Waters, Megan Wyler
A performance piece based on the Book of Genesis.

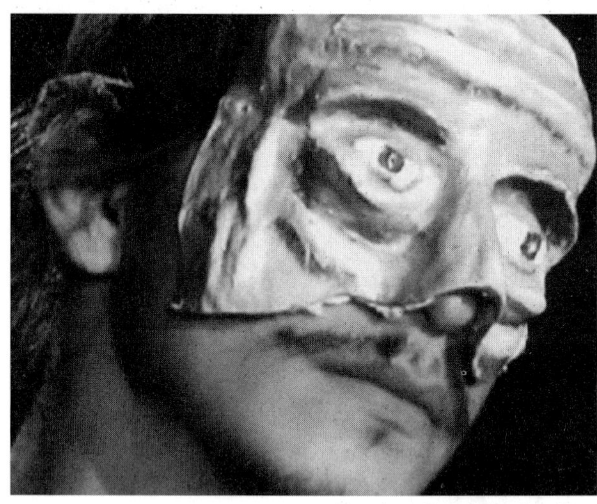

Benedetta Ferrario in *Arca Nova*

(Producer's Club) Thursday, October 12–21, 2000 (6 performances)
THE SIX MILLION DOLLAR MUSICAL by John Cecil CAST: Jeromy Barber, Doreen Barnard, John Carlton, John Cecil, Denise Clark, Jamie Smith, John Wake
A musical comedy set in the 1970s.

(Access Theatre) Thursday, October 12–29, 2000 (18 performances) The Key Theatre presents:
BOSTON PROPER by Edward Musto; Director, Nathan Halvorson; Set /Lighting, Katie Hefel; Costumes, Carolyn Humphrey; Press, Spenser-Addison/Angela Toomsen CAST: Brian Ach (Ted), Steven Camarillo (Brian), Angie Den Adel (Michelle), Tiffany May (Candy), Matt Mullin (Rusty)
A comedy set in Boston on July 4, 1976.

Andrew Elvis Miller in *Orpheus and Eurydice* (Richie Fahey)

(78th St. Theatre Lab) Thursday, October 12–29, 2000 (9 performances and 5 previews) 78th Street Theatre Lab, in association with The Notorious James Sisters, presents:
DEER SEASON by Pamela Cuming; Director/Set, Del Matthew Bigtree; Costumes, Andee Kinzy; Stage Manager, Susan Lange; Press, Gary Springer-Susan Chicoine/Joe Trentacosta CAST: Delyn Hall (Billy), Keith Perry (Vern), Debra Kay Anderson (Madge), Abra Bigham (Angel), George Brouillette (Chester)
A two-act drama set in a run-down Vermont farmhouse.

Debra Kay Anderson in *Deer Season* (David Monderer)

(Curricau Theatre) Friday, October 13–November 18, 2000 (17 performances and 5 previews) Empire Theatre Company presents:
ROBERTO ZUCCO by Bernard Marie Koltes; Translation, Martin Krimp; Director, Daniel Safer; Set/Costumes, Ruth Ponstaphone; Lighting, Jay Ryan; Music, Douglas Wagner; Press, Shirley Herz/Sam Rudy CAST: Peter Bisgaier (Roberto Zucco), Jessma Evans, Wendy Allegaert, Emmitt C. George, Kevin Mambo, Cecil MacKinnon, Fred Tietz, Laura Avery, Justin Barrett, John McCausland, Raina Von Waldenburg
A French play about a serial killer.

(Duplex) Saturday, October 14–28, 2000 (3 performances) SourceWorks presents:
THE VELOCITY OF GARY (NOT HIS REAL NAME) by James Still; Director, Mark Cannistraro; Set, Michael Dion; Costumes, David Kaley; Press, Tony Origlio/Phil Geoffrey Bond CAST: Danny Pintauro (Gary)
A return engagement of last season's production of a solo play performed without intermission. The action takes place in the past, the present, and in the infinity of Gary's mind.

Anne Bobby and Anne Newhall in *Strictly Personal* (Carol Rosegg)

(Soho Playhouse) Tuesday, October 17, 2000–March 11, 2001 (141 performances and 25 previews) Strictly Productions present:
STRICTLY PERSONAL by Jake Feinberg; Director, Donna Drake; Set, George Xenos, Robert Bissinger; Costumes, Caroline Birks; Lighting, Michael Gilliam; Casting, Jessica Gilburne, Ed Urban; Stage Manager, Brian Klevan Schneider; Press, Tony Origlio/Karen Greco, Emily Lowe CAST: Angela Roberts (Darlene/Mike), Daniel Cantor (Dan), Hayden Adams (James), Steven Arvanites succeeded by Chris Tomaino, Mike Bachmann (Freddy), Lucy Martin succeeded by Celia Tackaberry (Mom), Kimberly Farrell succeeded by Denise Wilbanks (Billie), Anne Newhall succeeded by Andrea Powell (Louise), Anne Bobby succeeded by Laurie Dawn (Lori)
A comedy in two acts. The action takes place in New York City.

(Irish Arts Center) Tuesday, October 17–December 10, 2000 (37 performances and 12 previews) Georganne Alrich Heller and The Irish Arts Center present:
RED ROSES & PETROL by Joseph O'Connor; Director, Neal Jones; Set, Niall Walsh; Costumes, Hilary O'Connor; Lighting, David Higham; Design, John Dib; Casting, Aria Alpert; Stage Manager, Byron Hartman; Press, Shirley Herz/Nancy Khuu CAST: Dara Coleman (Johnny Doyle), David Costelloe (Tom Ivers), Fiona Gallagher (Catherine Doyle), Julie Hale (Medbh Doyle), Aideen O'Kelly (Moya Doyle), Frank McCourt (Enda Doyle)
A drama set in Dublin.

David Costelloe, Aideen O'Kelly in *Red Roses & Petrol* (Carol Rosegg)

(Danny's Skylight Cabaret) Thursday, October 19–December 31, 2000
George Gordon presents:
OIL CITY SYMPHONY by Mike Craver, Debra Monk, Mark Hardwick and Mary Murfitt; Director, Ms. Murfitt; Set, Shelly Barclay; Costumes, Michael Krass; Lighting/Sound, Bobby Kneeland; Press, Laura Davis
CAST: Mike Craver, John DePinto, Mary Ehlinger, Mary Murfitt
A "replugged" version of the popular 1987 OB musical performed in a cabaret room. The action involves a zany high school class reunion set in an imaginary town in Middle America.

(Greenwich St. Theatre) Thursday, October 19–22, 2000 (5 performances) Emerging Artists Theatre Company presents:
NOONER by Erik Attias; Director, Blake Lawrence; Set, Larry Brown; Lighting, Daniel Ordower; Costumes, Alejo Vietti; Sound, Joanna Staub
CAST: Benim Foster, Patrick Frederic, Jamie Heinlein, David Nevell, Jeff Wiens
A romantic comedy.

(The Flea Theater) Thursday, October 19–December 16, 2000 (24 performances and 11 previews) The Bat Theater Company presents:
THE LIGHT OUTSIDE by Kate Robin; Director, Jim Simpson; Set/Lighting, Kyle Chepulis; Costumes, Moe Schell; Sound, Joel Douecek; Stage Manager, Simon Hammerstein; Press, Erin Dunn CAST: Elizabeth Bunch, Robert LuPone, Chris Messina, Karen Silas
A dark cautionary tale of narcissistic New Yorkers.

Nan Schmid, Andrew Oswald in *Dahling* (Darren Setlow)

Mal Z. Lawrence, Bruce Adler, David (Dudu) Fisher in *Borscht Belt Buffet on Broadway* (Battman)

(Red Line Theatre) Thursday, October 19–November 13, 2000 (8 performances) Cold Productions and Andrew McTiernan present:
WRONG WAY UP Music/Lyrics/Book, Robert Whaley and Tony Grimaldi; Director, Trent Jones; Press, Gary Springer-Susan Chicoine/Joe Trentacosta CAST: Robert Whaley (Arthur), Tony Grimaldi (Arthur's Conscience), Rachael Stern, Jeff Wells
A rock tragicomedy about coming of age. The action takes place in Syracuse, NY, and New York City. This production was forced to close early because the theatre itself was shut down.

(Grove Street Playhouse) Thursday, October 19–November 25, 2000
DAHLING: *The Life and Times of Tallulah Bankhead* by Nan Schmid; Director, Gareth Hendee; Set, Steve Johnson; Costumes, Linda Ross; Lighting, Cris Dopher; Sound, Catherine Mardis; Stage Manager, Lisa Latendresse; Press, Richard Kornberg/Don Summa CAST: Lee Blair, Tracey Gilbert, Elizabeth London, Janice O'Rourke, Andrew Oswald, Andy Rapoport, Nan Schmid, Kathy Schmidt
A play about the life of the famed actress. The cast of eight portrays 55 characters.

(Town Hall) Tuesday, October 24–November 6, 2000 (16 performances) NYK Productions present:
BORSCHT BELT BUFFET ON BROADWAY Director/Choreography, Dan Siretta; Associate Director, Nikki Sahagen; Music Directors, Gil Nagel, Michael Tornick; Lighting, Tom Sturge; Sound, Emient Productions; Stage Manager, Dom Ruggiero; Press, Les Schecter CAST: Bruce Adler, David (Dudu) Fisher, Mal Z. Lawrence
Performed without intermission.

(Triad Theatre) Wednesday, October 25, 2000–May 27, 2001 (232 performances) Louise Westergaard, Stephen Downey, and Peter Martin, in association with Linda Wadsong, present:
AMERICAN RHAPSODY Continuity by KT Sullivan, Mark Nadler and Ruth Leon; Director, Ms. Leon; Musical Staging, Donald Saddler; Arrangements, Mr. Nadler; Set, William Barclay; Lighting, Phil Monat & John Tees III; Stage Manager, DC Rosenberg; Press, Pete Sanders/Jim Mannino CAST: KT Sullivan, Mark Nadler
MUSICAL NUMBERS: Fascinatin' Rhythm/Sweet and Low Down/Real American Folk Song, Love Is Here to Saty, By Strauss/Little Jazz Bird, Isn't It a Pity, But Not for Me, Blah Blah Blah, Vodka, American in Paris /Mademoiselle in New Rochelle/Embraceable You, Man I Love, Medley, Summertime/Bess You Is My Woman, It Ain't Necessarily So, Lorelei, Slap That Bass, Beginner's Luck, They All Laughed, They Can't Take That Away from Me, Shall We Dance, S'Wonderful/Rhapsody in Blue, Swanee, Who Cares
A two-act musical revue of songs of the Gershwins.

Adam Simmons, Russell Scott Lewis in *End of the World Party* (Carol Rosegg)

(47th St. Theatre) Wednesday, October 25, 2000–February 25, 2001 (108 performances and 16 previews) Kings Road Entertainment, in association with Tim Ranney, presents:
END OF THE WORLD PARTY by Chuck Ranberg; Director, Matthew Lombardo; Set, Christopher Pickart; Lighting, Michael Gilliam; Costumes, Raymond Dragon; Sound/Music, Michael Sottile; Stage Manager, Denise Yaney; Press, David Gersten CAST: Jim J. Bullock (Hunter), Christopher Durham (Roger), Brian Cooper (Phil), Anthony Barrile (Will), David Drake (Travis), Russell Scott Lewis (Nick), Adam Simmons (Chip)
A comedy in two acts. The action takes place at a beach house on Fire Island Pines, last summer.

(HERE) Wednesday, October 25–November 19, 2000 (15 performances and 5 previews) Elevator Repair Service presents:
HIGHWAY TO TOMORROW by the ERS Company; Based on Euripides' *The Bacchae*; Directors, John Collins and Steve Bodow; Set, Jula Tüllmann; Costumes, Carson Kreitzer; Lighting, Eric Dyer; Sound, Michael Kraskin; Press, Richard Kornberg CAST: Randolph Curtis Rand (Dionysus), Rinne Groff, James Hannaham, Paul Boocock, Susie Sokol, Katherine Profeta
Fuses found-object puppets, mid-century Afropop, sound effects and fractured choreography.

(Chelsea Playhouse) Wednesday, October 25–December 10, 2000 (39 performances and 9 previews) David Young and Norma Langworth, in association with Riverside Stage Company, present:
THE HEAD by William S. Leavengood; Director, Brian Feehan; Set, Dan Kuchar; Costumes, Mira Goldberg; Lighting, Chad McArver; Music, Jay Spadone; Stage Manager, JP Phillips; Press, Pete Sanders/Jim Mannino CAST: Branislav Tomich (Izzy), Aaron J. Fill (Dr. Perry Hess), Andrew Coleman (Dr. Lester Raymer), Heather Anne McAllister (Deyla Hess), Jay Rosenbloom (Harley), Kaleo Griffith (Harris), Jay Rodgers (Pooley), Leotomas Judge (Reza)
A disembodied comedy in two acts. The action takes place in a secret dungeon laboratory somewhere outside London, late 1930s.

(413 W. 44th) Thursday, October 26–November 19, 2000 (16 performances) Gorilla Rep presents:
STORY OF AN UNKNOWN MAN by Anthony Pennino; Adapted from Anton Chekhov's novel *An Anonymous Story*; Director, Christopher Carter Sanderson; Press, Brett Singer CAST: Tracy Appleton, Kina Bermudez, Michael Colby Jones, Sean Elias-Reyes, Matt Freeman, Clayton Hodges, Lynda Kennedy, Brian O'Sullivan, Greg Petroff, Tom Staggs, John Walsh
A drama set in war-torn Chechnya.

Susie Sokol in *Highway to Tomorrow* (Greg Weiner)

Heather Anne McAllister, Jay Rodgers in *The Head* (Brian Feehan)

(Abingdon Theater) Thursday, October 26–November 18, 2000 (15 performances and 5 previews) The Women's Shakespeare Company presents:

ROSENCRANTZ AND GUILDENSTERN ARE DEAD by Tom Stoppard; Director, Brian PJ Cronin; Costumes, Mary Margaret O'Neil; Lighting, Owen Hughes; Press, Brett Singer CAST: Clayton Dowty (Guildenstern), Kate Sandberg (Rosencrantz), Missy Bonaguide, Cheryl Dennis, Gwyneth Dobson, Sarah Gilbert, Ginny Hack, Ellen Lee, Heather Mieko, Diane Neal, Kelly Ann Sharman
An all-female production.

Clayton Dowty, Kate Sandberg in *Rosencrantz and Guildenstern Are Dead* (Matthew Israel)

(Duplex) Thursday, October 26–November 10, 2000 (6 performances) The Genesius Guild, in association with Gargantuan Productions, presents:

THE GLASS MENDACITY by Maureen Morley & Tom Willmorth; Story by Doug Armstrong, Keith Cooper, Ms. Morley & Mr. Willmorth; Director, Thomas Morrissey; Set/Costumes, Jayde Chabot; Lighting/Sound, Thomas Honeck; Stage Manager, Rich Delia; Press, Laura Davis CAST: Joey Landwehr (Mitch O'Connor), Jennifer Doctorovich (Maggie the Cat), Harold Slazer (Amanda Dubois/Big Momma), Manny Kenn (Brick Dubois), Roslyn Cohn (Blanche Kowalski), Tom Huston (Stanley Kowalski), John Ellis (Big Daddy Dubois), Jessica Calvello (Laura Dubois)
A parody of a Tennessee Williams drama.

(Lucille Lortel Theatre) Thursday, October 26, 2000–February 11, 2001 (93 performances and 16 previews) The Melting Pot Theatre Company, by arrangement with Trigger Street Productions and Kevin Spacey, presents:

COBB by Lee Blessing; Director, Joe Brancato; Set, Matthew Maraffi; Costumes, Daryl A. Stone; Lighting, Jeff Nellis; Sound, Jerry Yager, One Dream; Casting, Paul Russell; Stage Manager, Richard A. Hodge; Press, John Barlow-Michael Hartman/Ash Curtis CAST: Michael Cullen (Mr. Cobb), Matthew Mabe (The Peach), Michael Sabatino (Ty), Clark Jackson (Oscar Charleston)
A drama performed without intermission. The action takes place in Georgia and elsewhere, 1886–1961 and later. Originally performed last season at The Melting Pot Theatre.

(Harry De Jur Playhouse) Friday, October 27–November 26, 2000 (22 performances and 5 previews) New Federal Theatre presents:

CONFLICT OF INTEREST Written/Directed by Jay Broad; Press, Jeffrey Richards CAST: Al Freeman Jr. (Justice Joe Balding), Ellen Holly (Liz Balding), Earle Hyman (Sen. Thaddeus Jones), John Wilkerson (President William Maxwell), Count Stovall, Lisa Bostnar, William Cain, Harold Scott, Greg Jackson
A revision of an early-1970s political thriller.

(Mazer Theatre) Saturday, October 28–December 31, 2000 (52 performances and 5 previews) Yiddish Public Theatre presents:

GREEN FIELDS by Peretz Hirschbein; Director, Bryna Turetsky; Music, Vladimir Heifetz and Sholem Secunda; Set, Rachel Nemec; Costumes, Anthony Braithwaite; Lighting, Nicole Pearce; Stage Manager, Wendy Ouellette; Press, Max Eisen/Caraid O'Brien CAST: Norman Kruger (David Noakh), Zypora Spaisman (Rokhl), Hy Wolfe (Hersh Ber), Roni Neuman (Tsine), Felix Fibich (Alkone), Shifra Lerer (Gitl), Julie Alexander (Stere), Joad Kohn (Levi Yitshok)
A 1919 Yiddish comedy.

(Wings Theatre) Saturday, October 28–December 2, 2000 (17 performances and 3 previews) Idle Hands and Wings Theatre Company present:

THE WITCHES' TRIPTYCH by Lillian Ann Slugocki; Director, Erica Gold; Set, Molly Hughes; Costumes, Meghan Healy; Lighting, David Lander; Press, Erin Dunn CAST: David Bennett, Christian Clifford, Joshua Gordon, Lisa Levy, Dee Pellestier, John Daggett, Dennis Fox, Bradley Goodwill, Gretchen Lee Krich, Mark Leydorf, Annie McAdams
A play drawing on original letters, trial transcrips and death warrants of victims accused of witchcraft. The action takes place in 17th century Germany, England, and Salem, MA.

Matthew Mabe, Michael Sabatino, Michael Cullen, Clark Jackson in *Cobb* (Joan Marcus)

Nathan Hinton, Keesha Sharp in *Living in the Wind* (Martha Holmes)

(Century Center) Saturday, October 28–November 18, 2000 (13 performances and 5 previews) Century Center Theatre First Foundation presents:

THE LADY FROM THE SEA by Henrik Ibsen; Translation, Rolf Fjelde; Director, Alfred Christie; Set, Tim Goodmanson; Costumes, Sydney Maresca; Lighting, Peter Petrino; Sound, John Littig; Press, Shirley Herz /Sam Rudy CAST: Laurena Mullins (Ellida Wangel), Larry Peterson (Dr. Wangel), Jennifer E. Corby (Bolette), Steve Witting (Arnholm), Tina Jones (Hilda), Jay Gould (Hans Lyngstrand), Christopher Burns (The Stranger), Eleanor Madrinan

Ibsen's 1888 drama.

(American Place Theatre) Sunday, October 29, 2000–February 25, 2001 (105 performances and 15 previews) The American Place Theatre presents:

LIVING IN THE WIND by Michael Bradford; Director, Regge Life; Set, Beowulf Boritt; Costumes, Helen L. Simmons; Lighting, Chad McArver; Sound, David D. Wright; Casting, Pat Golden; Stage Manager, Jacqui Casto; Press, Peter Cromarty/Alice Cromarty CAST: Nathan Hinton (JoJo), Keesha Sharp (Mary), Arthur French (Vance), Lizann Mitchell (Hattie), Cheryl Freeman succeeded by Sally Stewart-Coleman (Sarah Maddox), Chad L. Coleman succeeded by David Damane (Isaiah Maddox)

A drama in two acts. The action takes place in Georgia circa 1875.

(45 Bleeker) Monday, October 30–November 13, 2000 (3 performances) The Culture Project presents:

THE EXONERATED by Eric Jensen and Jessica Blank; Press, Richard Kornberg CASTS: (October 30) Susan Sarandon, Tim Robbins, Edie Falco, David Morse, Sarah Jones (November 6) Richard Dreyfuss, Steve Buscemi, Vincent D'Onofrio, Hazelle Goodman, Ruben Santiago-Hudson (November 13) Martha Plimpton, Cherry Jones, Ben Vereen, Paul Butler

A drama based on interviews with wrongly acused death row inmantes.

(Connelly Theatre) Wednesday, November 1–16, 2000 (8 performances) EB&C presents:

GULL Adapted from Chekhov's *The Seagull*; Director, Ellen Beckerman; Press, Shirley Herz CAST: Robert Barcia, C. Andrew Bauer, Lilly Blue, Margot Ebling, Shawn Fagan, Elliott Kennerson, Colleen Madden, James M. Saidy

Part of the Chekhov NOW festival.

(Looking Glass Theater) Wednesday, November 1–18, 2000 (12 performances) RubyRose Lovechild Productions presents:

THE BASTARD LOVE CHILD OF AUNT JEMIMA & UNCLE BEN Written /Performed by Ron Stroman; Director, Jeffrey Collins-Harper; Music, Kerry Prep; Lyrics, Prep and Stroman

A one-man show.

(14th Street Y) Wednesday, November 1–December 3, 2000 (21 performances and 4 previews); Reopened January 9–February 4, 2001 (28 performances) The Hypothetical Theatre Company present:

BUYING TIME by Michael Weller; Director, Amy Feinberg; Set, Mark Symczak; Costumes, T. Michael Hall; Lighting, Jeff Croiter; Sound, Tim Cramer; Stage Manager, Margaret A. Flanagan; Press, Jonathan Slaff, Peter Cromarty/Sherri Jean Katz CAST: Nathan M. White (Carter Van Sant), David Ari (Lane Scotto/Waiter), Jeff Kronson (Hal Gold), Jennifer Trimble (Margot Buonavecchio), Michael Oberlander (Peter Water), Lee Sellars (Bennett Traub), Tibor Feldman (Del Gregorian), Chuck Montgomery (Max Lasker/Laird Sutter), Evan Thompson (Abe Einhorn), Monique Fowler (Jobeth Traub), Jennifer Gibbs (Christine Martel), Antonio del Rosario (Carlos), Irene McDonnell (Becky Sutter), Andy Powers (Troy Sutter) Patrick Boll

A two-act drama based on a true story. The action takes place in Mesa, a fictional city in the Southwest, 1991.

(Axis Theatre) Wednesday, November 1–December 23, 2000 (28 performances and 4 previews) Axis Company presents:

CRAVE by Sarah Kane; Director, Randy Sharp; Set, David Ramirez; Costumes, Mark Spada; Lighting, David Zeffren; Sound, Steve Fontaine; Stage Manager, Kate Aronsson; Press, Spin Cycle/Ron Lasko CAST: Brian Barnhardt (A), David Guion (B), Kristin Disaltro (C), Deborah Harry (M)

A non-linear drama examining the disintegration of four characters. The playwright commited suicide in 1999.

Jennifer Trimble, Jeff Kronson, Nathan M. White, David Ari, Patrick Boll in *Buying Time* (Carol Rosegg)

(47th St. Theatre) Thursday, November 2–18, 2000 (16 performances) sage/girl friday productions presents:
ALMOST ASLEEP by Julie Hébert; Director, Jennifer Kagen; Press, Publicity Outfitters/Timothy J. Haskell, Christopher Joy CAST: Heather Ann Barclay, Emily Cline, Shauna Lewis, Abigail Rose Solomon, Denise Wilbanks
A drama in which five women play different aspects on one woman's mind.

(Access Theatre) Thursday, November 2–18, 2000 (12 performances -and 3 previews) Karalee Dawn, Margaret Perry, and Greg Schaffert, in association with Access Theatre present:
FORSAKING ALL OTHERS by Brian Dykstra; Director, Margarett Perry; Set /Lighting, Thom Weaver; Costumes, Krista Mangano; Sound, Ken Hypes; Press, David Gersten/Karalee Dawn CAST: Brian Dykstra (David), Sarah Baker (Cloe), Rob Sedgwick (Alan), Cynthia Babak (Jenifer)
A drama about the boundaries between friendship and sexual conquest.

(Clark Studio Theatre) Thursday, November 2–19, 2000 (9 performances and 3 previews) Starfish Theatreworks presents:
THE ST. NICOLA CYCLE Director, Gail Noppe-Brandon; Set, Regina Garcia; Costumes, Valerie Marcus; Lighting, Peter Nigrini; Music, Bradford R. Ross; Choreography, Daniel Ponickly
Pusong Babe (Heart of a Woman) by Linda Faigo-Hall CAST: Lydia Gaston, Arthur T. Acuna, Roxanne Baisas, Ron Trenouth
Double-Cross by Gail Noppe-Brandon CAST: Susan Peters, June Squibb, Jose M. Aviles
Two one-acts inspired by photographer Andrea Sperling's photo of St. Nicola Catherdral in Italy.

(Sande Shurin Studio) Thursday, November 2–18, 2000 (9 performances) Grunt Productions present:
A JERSEY CANTATA by Bill Mesce Jr.; Director, Ken Dashow; Set, Elizabeth Wunsch; Lighting/Sound, Jack Russoniello; Stage Managers, Hallie Wynn, Krista Sarubbi; Press, Publicity Outfitters/Timothy J. Haskell, Christopher Joy CAST: Joseph Pacillo (Caruso), Ken Dashow (Albie), Joseph Prussak (Billy Bones), Jonathan Sang (John), Frank Lombardi (Francis), Craig McNulty (Daniel), Nat Habib (Big Sal), Lethia Nall (Michelle)
The action takes place in the North Ward of Newark, NJ.

(Bank Street Theatre) Friday, November 3–19, 2000 (13 performances and 1 preview) Vagabond Productions present:
BEYOND THERAPY by Christopher Durang; Director, Amanda Charlton; Lighting, Joshua Briggs CAST: Scott Roberts (Bruce), Katie Atcheson (Prudence), Bart Vanlaere (Stuart), Louise Seyffert (Charlotte), John Bundrick (Bob), Michael Wallace (Andrew)
A comedy in two acts.

(Gene Frankel Theatre) Friday, November 3–19, 2000 (9 performances) Nosedive Productions present:
ALLSTON by James Comtois; Director, Peter Boisvert; Press, James Comtois CAST: Christopher Bujold, Sharon Eisman, Mike Gilpin, Adam Heffernan, Rosa Luo, Lyndon Salas, Jim Ward, Jim Yue, Christopher Yustin
A black comedy/drama set in Boston.

(Theatre 3) Friday, November 3–19, 2000 (11 performances and 5 previews) Reckless Theatre Company presents:
RAIN FROM HEAVEN by S.N. Behrman; Director, Julie Hamberg; Set, Chris Jones; Costumes, Moira Shaughnessy; Lighting, Christian Methot; Stage Manager, Michael Wilhoite; Press, Tony Origlio/Joel Treick CAST: Nell Mooney (Joan Eldridge), Jane Shepard (Madame Jurin), Wendell Laurent (Rand Eldridge), Jon Krupp (Hobart Eldridge), Donna Jean Fogel (Lady Lael Wyngate), Bruce Ross (Hugo Willens), Richard Swan (Sascha Barashaev), Andrea Maulella (Phoebe Eldridge)
A 1934 four-act drama performed with one intermission. The action takes place near London.

(Musical Theatre Works) Friday, November 3–12, 2000 (6 performances) Risk Ensemble presents:
HEDDA GABLER by Henrik Ibsen; Director, Michael Cruz Sullivan; Press, Leslie Hunt CAST: Leslie Ann Loye (Hedda), Liz Stanton (Thea), Kennedy Brown (Eilert Lovborg), Patrick S. McCullough (George Tessman), Marcus Powell (Judge Brack), Ruth Kulerman (Aunt Julie), Julia Kristeller (Berte)

(American Globe Theatre) Saturday, November 4–December 3, 2000 (15 performances and 1 preview) American Globe Theatre presents:
HAMLET by William Shakespeare; Director, John Basil; Set, Vincent A. Masterpaul; Costumes, Terry Leong; Lighting, Reid Farrington; Music, Scott O'Brien; Press, Brett Singer CAST: Dennis Turney (Hamlet), Elizabeth Keefe (Gertrude), Michael Bachmann, Robert Chaney, Tim Cooper, Jonathan Dewberry, Kathleen Early, Scott Eck, Stanley Harrison, Justin Lewis, Dan Matisa, H.T. Snowday, Graham Stevens, Rusty Tennant

Elizabeth Keefe, Dennis Turney in *Hamlet* (Brett Singer)

Wendell Laurent, Donna Jean Fogel, Bruce Ross in *Rain From Heaven*

(Present Company Theatorium) Sunday, November 5–28, 2000 (14 performances) Matching Productions, in association with The Present Company, presents:

LOOKING TOWARD HALF DOME by Robert Duxbury; Director, Bob McDonald; Set, Tony Andrea; Costumes, Jayde Chabot; Lighting, Daniel D.Z. Jagendorf; Press, Spin Cycle/Ron Lasko CAST: Kathleen Huber, Heather McGonigal, Adenrele Ojo, Nancy Walsh, Rik Walter
A comedy set in the art world.

(Flatiron Playhouse) Wednesday, November 8–December 2, 2000 (16 performances and 5 previews) Bill Miller and Stanley Steinberg present:

AUTO-TRAINS, FIRE ANTS AND LESBIANS Written/Performed by Michael Garin; Director, Jeremy Dobrish; Set, Steve Capone; Lighting, Michael Gottlieb; Sound, Chris Todd; Press, Kevin P. McAnarney
A musical performance.

(Tenement Theatre) Wednesday, November 8–19, 2000 (9 performances and 1 preview) Immigrant Theatre Project and the Lower East Side Tenement Museum present:

LOOKING FOR LOUIE Written/Performed by Stacie Chaiken; Music, Ian Walker
A one-woman show about a second-generation Russian Jewish American.

Anne Jackson, Eli Wallach in *Down the Garden Paths* (Miguel Pagliere)

Charlie Shanian, Shari Simpson in *Maybe Baby, It's You* (Gerry Goodstein)

Brian Townes, Christian Macchio in *Michael's #1 Fan* (Bernard Doyle)

(Producers Club II) Wednesday, November 8–19, 2000 (13 performances) The New Cockpit Ensemble presents:

MICHAEL'S #1 FAN Written/Directed by Frank J. Avella; Set, Phil Devine; Sound, David Frost; Press, David Gersten CAST: Kristi Elan Caplinger, Michael P. Ciminera, Jami Coogan, Jessica Faller, Christian W. Macchio, Jeanine Tolve, Brian Townes, Greta Thyssen
A drama about a fan of actor Michael Sarrazin.

(Minetta Lane Theatre) Thursday, November 9, 2000–January 14, 2001 (65 performances and 12 previews) Elliot Martin, Max Cooper, Ron Shapiro, and Sharon Karmazin present

DOWN THE GARDEN PATHS by Anne Meara; Director, David Saint; Set, James Youmans; Costumes, David Murin; Lighting, Michael Lincoln; Sound, Chris Bailey; Video, Stan Open Productions; Casting, Pat McCorkle; Stage Manager, Thomas Clewell; Press, Jeffrey Richards/Irene Gandy/Chloe Taylor CAST: Angela Pietropinto (Prof. Cramer), John Shea (Arthur Garden), Anne Jackson (Stella Dempsey Garden), Eli Wallach (Sid Garden), Leslie Lyles (Liz Garden), Adam Grupper (Max Garden), Amy Stiller (Sharon Garden/Jodie Garden), Roberta Wallach (Claire Shayne/Claire Garden), On Video: Jerry Stiller (Herschel Strange)
A comedy performed without intermission. The action takes place at the Herschel Strange Awards Ceremony and in Arthur Garden's apartment.

(Theatre at St. Luke's) Thursday, November 9, 2000–June 30, 2001 (163 performances) Entertainment Events presents:

MAYBE BABY, IT'S YOU Written/Performed by Charlie Shanian and Shari Simpson; Lighting, Greg Cohen; Costumes, Emily Straka; Sound, Christopher Todd; Stage Manager, Paul Hovis; Press, David Gersten
A comedy about finding your soul mate. Performances rotate around the schedules of *Late Nite Catechism* and *Tony n' Tina's Wedding*.

Susan Matús, Jeff Berry in *The Trials of Martin Guerre* (Matthew Israel)

(42nd Street Theatre) Thursday, November 9–December 17, 2000 (22 performances and 12 previews) The Deptford Players present:
THE TRIALS OF MARTIN GUERRE by Frank Cossa; Director, Mark Blum; Design, Mark Bloom; Costumes, Billye Roberts; Music, Archoolie Productions; Stage Manager, Judith Scher; Press, Brett Singer CAST: Thomas McCann (Francois de Ferrieres), Joseph Kamal (Jean de Coras), H. Clark Kee (Pierre Guerre), Jeff Berry (Martin), Dudley Stone (Jaques Boeri), Loree True (Jeanne de Guerre), Susan E. Matús (Bertrande de Rols), Eric Hanson (Crippled Man), Peter J. Coriarty, Rachel Lyerla, Christian Todd (Villagers)
A drama in two acts. The action takes place in the French village of Artigat.

(Ensemble Studio Theatre) Thursday, November 9–December 10, 2000 (21 performances and 4 previews) The Ensemble Studio Theatre presents:
THE SHANEEQUA CHRONICLES Written/Performed by Stephanie Berry; Director, Talvin Wilks; Set, Evan Alexander; Costumes, Sydney Kai Inis; Sound, Robert Gould; Choreography, Amparo Santiago; Stage Manager, Jim Ring
An African-American woman's journey to adulthood in late 20th century America.

Deana Barone, Shira Flam, Steve Sterner, Yelena Shmulenson, Raquel Polite in *An American Family* (Carol Rosegg)

(Phil Bosakowski Theatre) Thursday, November 9–December 10, 2000 (19 performances and 4 previews) Allyson Spellman and Tounge in Cheek Productions present:
SPINE by Jessie McCormack; Director, Craig Carlisle; Set/Lighting, Michael Brown; Costumes, Rebecca Wimmer; Sound, Jesse Bayer; Music, Keith "Wild Child" Middleton; Stage Manager, Eleza Kort; Press, Gary Springer-Susan Chicoine/Joe Trentacosta CAST: Aliza Waksal (Gwynn /Claire/Dr. Sanders), Jessie McCormack (Julie/Brittany/Dr. Sanders), Chris Stock (Man on Tape/Billy/Chad)
A comedy performed without intermission.

Jessie McCormack, Aliza Waksal in *Spine*

(Red Room) Thursday, November 9–December 10, 2000 (20 performances) Horse Trade Theater Group and Alberto Orso present:
STAGE BLOOD by Charles Ludlam; Director, Michael Goldfried; Set, Heidi Meisenhelder; Costumes, T. Michael Hall; Lighting, Steven Shelly; Sound, Adam Brown; Press, Spin Cycle/Ron Lasko CAST: Tim Cusack (Stage Manager), Marshall Correro (Carlton Stone), Michael Nathanson (Carl Stone Jr.), Dara Seitzman, Jessica Chandlee Smith, Bob Yarnell, Nate Levine
A 1975 backstage comedy about a traveling theater family.

(Sargeant Theatre) Friday, November 10–18, 2000 (10 performances) Active Drive/The Active Theater presents:
INDEPENDENCE by Lee Blessing; Director, David Belisle; Set, John Felty; Costumes, Annie-Laurie Wheat CAST: Carol Mennie (Evelyn), Andrea Miskow (Kess), Sonda Staley (Jo), Karma Tiffany (Sherry)
The action takes place in Independence, IA, 1983.

(Theatre Four) Sunday, November 12, 2000–January 21, 2001 (64 performances and 7 previews) The Folsbiene Yiddish Theatre presents:
AN AMERICAN FAMILY by Miriam Kressyn; Director, Eleanor Reissa; Musical Director, Zalmen Mlotek; Set, Vicki Davis; Costumes, Terry Leong; Lighting, Jeff Nellis; Sound, Henry Sapoznik; Press, Keith Sherman /Brett Oberman CAST INCLUDES: Deana Barone, Spencer Chandler, I.W. Firestone, Shira Flam, Murray Nesbitt, Sheila Rubell, Raquel Polite, Yelena Shmulenson, Steve Sterner, Cary Woodworth, Mina Bern
A play with music. The action takes place on New York City's Lower East Side, from the turn of the century through the Great Depression.

(Miranda Theatre) Monday, November 13–December 11, 2000 (5 performances) Miranda Theatre Company presents:
WE CAN'T ALL BE MATT LAUER *or Bobby Rivers' Misadventures in Broadcasting* Written/Performed by Bobby Rivers; Director, Matt Lenz; Stage Manager, Margaret Bodriguian; Press, John Barlow-Michael Hartman/Shellie Schovanec
A comic monologue.

Michael Moschen in *Michael Moschen in Motion* (Bachrach Photography)

(Joyce Theater) Tuesday, November 14–26, 2000 (16 performances) Micocco Productions present:
MICHAEL MOSCHEN IN MOTION: *Touching the Kinetics Continuum* Conceived/Choreographed/Performed by Michael Moschen; Director, Janis Brenner; Set, Mr. Moschen, John Kahn, Anne Patterson; Costumes, Mei-Ling Louie; Lighting, Dave Feldman; Music, David Van Tieghem; Co-Choreographer/Movement Stage Manager, Heather Miller; Press, Peter Cromarty/Alice Cromarty
Conceptual juggling performed in two acts.

(Ensemble Studio Theatre) Tuesday, November 14–December 19, 2000 (11 performances) The Ensemble Studio Theatre presents:
ARMONK: *Strange Tales from a Strange Town* by Sean Sutherland; Director, Eileen Myers; Press, Jim Baldassare CAST: Paul Bartholomew, Derrick McGinty, Heather Robinson, Sonya Rokes, Sarah Rose, Eric Scott, Kevin Shinick, Sean Sutherland
Eleven short comedies.

(Miranda Theatre) Tuesday, November 14–December 17, 2000 (27 performances and 7 previews) Urban Stages presents:
MOTHER LOLITA by Guillermo Reyes; Director, T.L. Reilly; Set/Lighting, Roman Tatarowitz; Costumes, Markas Henry; Sound, Marc Gwinn; Casting, Stephanie Klapper, Susan Lovell; Stage Manager, Ken Hall; Press, Brett Singer CAST: Matt Skollar (Tristerio), Brigitte Viellieu-Davis (Lola), Piter Fattouche (Capo), Debora Rabbai, Mary Bacon (Sister Ellie), Rana Kazkaz (Santa), Carlos Molina (Franco), Caesar Samayoa (Xavier)
A comedy in two acts. The action takes place in The Hollywood Pit Garden Apartments, 1994.

Reed Birney, Susan Pellegrino, Susan Knight in *Sightseeing* (Nick Andrews)

(Jose Quintero Theatre) Wednesday, November 15, 2000–January 7, 2001 (46 performances and 6 previews) Come Along Productions present:
SIGHTSEEING by Margaret Dulaney; Director, Julie Boyd; Set, Abigail Kinney; Costumes, Linda Ross; Lighting, Chad McArver; Sound, Matt Balitsaris; Stage Manager, Michael McGoff; Press, Publicity Outfitters /Timothy J. Haskell, Christopher Joy CAST: Susan Pellegrino (Lilith), Reed Birney (Will), Susan Knight (Myra), Tony Carlin (Howard), Chris Clavelli (Bob/Enrique Enriquez)
A comedy in two acts. The action takes place in New York City and South America.

(Performing Garage) Wednesday, November 15–December 9, 2000 (15 performances) Big Dance Theater, Performing Garage Visiting Artist Series, and DTW Around present:
ANOTHER TELEPATHIC THING Written/Directed by Annie-B Parson and Paul Lazar; Set, Joanne Howard and Sky Lanigan; Costumes, Stacy Dawson; Lighting, Jay Ryan; Sound/Music, Cynthia Hopkins and Jane Shaw; Press, Spin Cycle/Ron Lasko CAST: Tymberly Canale, Stacy Dawson, Molly Hickok, Cynthia Hopkins, Paul Lazar, David Neumann
Inspired by Mark Twain's story *The Mysterious Stranger.*

Brigitte Viellieu-Davis, Piter Fattouche, Caesar Samayoa in *Mother Lolita* (Gerry Goodstein)

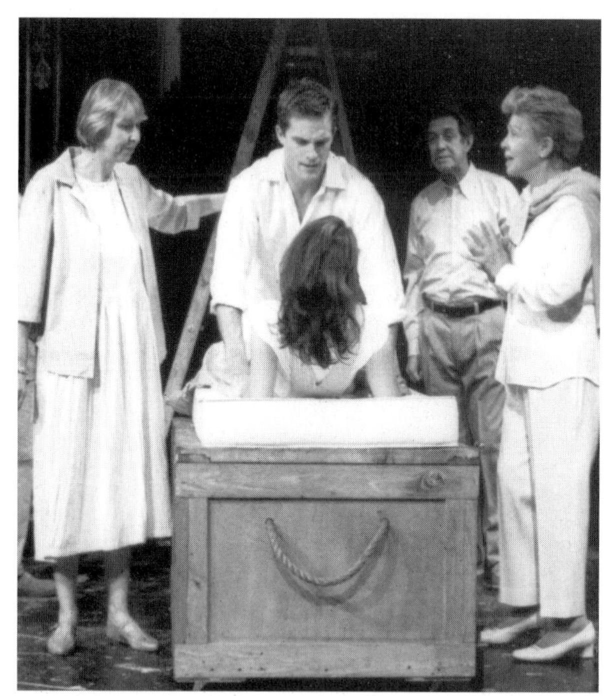

Julie Halston, Michael Doyle, Michi Barall, Larry Pine, Scotty Bloch in *Saved or Destroyed* (Carol Rosegg)

(Rattlestick Theatre) Wednesday, November 15–December 3, 2000 (11 performances and 5 previews) Rattlestick Productions present:
SAVED OR DESTROYED by Harry Kondoleon; Director, Craig Lucas; Set, John McDermott; Costumes, David Zinn; Lighting, Jeffrey Lowney; Sound, Laura Grace Brown; Press, David Gersten CAST: Michi Barall (Karin), Scotty Bloch (Anne), Michael Doyle (Vincent), David Greenspan (Harry Kondoleon), Julie Halston (Lucille), Larry Pine (Ivan), Ray Anthony Thomas (Maurice)
A comedy about a group of actors performing along the coast of Maine. The premiere production of Mr. Kondoleon's final play.

(Hudson Guild Theatre) Thursday, November 16–December 17, 2000 (28 performances and 5 previews) The Overture Theatre Company presents:
LONG ROAD HOME Music/Arrangements, Kathy Sommer; Lyrics/Book /Direction, Barry Harman; Music Director, Wendy Bobbitt-Cavett; Music Supervisor, Karl Jurman; Musical, DJ Salisbury; Set, Merope Bachlioti; Costumes, Toni-Leslie James; Lighting, Kenneth L. Schutz; Sound, Bernard Fox; Casting, Matt Messinger; Stage Manager, Eileen Haggerty; Press, Les Schecter CAST: Brenda Braxton (Cybele), Charles Gray (Virgil), Jamie Danielle Jackson (Merle), Saundra McClain (Mama), Joseph Siravo (Walker)
MUSICAL NUMBERS: Take a Look at My Heart, Ask Him, Virgil and Me, Come-Back-to-Bed-Babe Eyes, A Bottle to Remind Me, I Want This Tomorrow, Twelve Steppin' Out, Call Patty, So I Think I Might Have Lied, Sure As Christmas, Dump Another Load on Me, Walk in My Shoes, I Know Myself Better, Life Slipping Away, Long Road Home
A musical in two acts. The action takes place in a small chuech south of Memphis, TN.

(Soho Playhouse) Monday, November 20, 2000–March 5, 2001 (13 performances and 4 previews) Boy in the Drain Productions, in association with Arlin Seville Productions, presents:
CARY AND GALLO: WHAT IF WE DID THIS? by Josh Cary, Patrick Gallo, Dan Cronin, Chris DeLuca, Julius Sharpe, Brian Tucker; Director, Ted Sullivan; Films, Paul Sullivan; Press, Karen Greco CAST: Josh Cary and Patrick Gallo
A blend of comedy sketches and short films.

(47th St. Theater) Wednesday, November 22, 2000–February 2001 The Jewish Theater of New York and Earle I. Mack present:
THE DIARY OF ADOLF EICHMANN Adapted/Directed by Tuvia Tenenbom; Translation, Hana Gross, Melanie Vollmert and the JTNY; Set, Mark Symczak; Lighting, David Comstock; Music, Phil Rubin; Press, Sam Singer CAST: Ron Palillo
Based on Eichmann's prison memoirs released by Israel in 2000.

(St. Mark's Studio) Friday, November 24–26, 2000 (4 performances) Bon Bock Productions in association with Horse Trade Theatre Group presents:
ARTURRO THE ARMLESS; Written/Designed by Alex Dawson; Director, Amy Parlow; Producer, Gareth Smith; Sound, Flynn Hundhausen CAST: Charles Laine (Arturro), Chad Brown (park), Dave Dwyer (Circus Owner), Jane Hardy (The Gypsy), Jake Jordan (El Bruto), Amy Parlow (La Tormenta), Lee Rosen (Kev), Marvin Schwartz (Angelo), Joe Romeo, Mike Denkowycz
A drama loosely suggested by the 1924 film *The Unknown.*
and
THE FINE DINING ACID TEST by Joe Taverney; Director/Design, Michael Nathanson CAST: Jonathan Kandel succeeded by Michael Nathanson (Tim), Tamela Stevens succeeded by Jeanine Bartel (Tara), Jake Jordan succeeded by Marshall Correro (Mr. Steemzma), Lori Marcus succeeded by Sadie Jones (Mrs. Steezma), Risshan Leak succeeded by Mike Durell (Bartender), Joe Azzarello (Waiter)
A comedy set in a dive bar and a four star restaurant. Reopened May 3–27, 2001 at the Red Room theatre featuring succeeding cast.

(Ohio Theater) Saturday, November 25–December 10, 2000 (10 performances) Ping Chong & Company present:
SECRET HISTORY by Ping Chong & Company; Press, Jonathan Slaff CAST: Tinket Monsod, Hiromi Sakamoto, Tania Salmen, Vaimoana Niumeitolu, Patrick Ssenjovu, Cherry Lou Sy
Personal testimonies of foreign-born New Yorkers.

The Company of *Secret History* (Jonathan Slaff)

(Pulse Ensemble Theatre) Tuesday, November 28–December 17, 2000 (13 performances and 3 previews) Pulse Ensemble presents:
MISALLIANCE by George Bernard Shaw; Director, Ann Bowen; Set, Roger Mooney; Costumes, Terry Leong; Lighting, Herrick Golman; Press, Shirley Herz/Nancy Khuu CAST: Michael Gilpin (John Tarleton), Maureen Hayes (Mrs. Tarleton), Natalie Wilder (Hypatia), Bryan Grosbauer (Bentley), Stephen Aloi (Johnny Tarleton), Julie Hera DeStefano (Lina Schepanowska), Steve Abbruscato (Lord Summerhays)

(Clark Studio) Tuesday, November 28–December 23, 2000 (24 performances and 1 preview) Aquila Theatre Company London/New York presents:
JULIUS CAESAR by William Shakespeare; Director, Robert Richmond; Design, Peter Meineck, Mr. Richmond; Lighting, Mr. Meineck; Music, Anthony Cochrane; Press, Gary Springer-Susan Chicoine/Joe Trentacosta CAST: Louis Butelli (Cassius), David Caron (Mark Anthony), Lisa Carter (Portia/Octavius), Anthony Cochrane (Brutus), Robert Richmond (Caesar), Shirleyann Kaladjian (Calpurnia), Alex Webb (Casca), Jessica Perlmeter (Soothsayer), Noah Trepanier

Anthony Cochrane, Robert Richmond in *Julius Caesar* (Ken Howard)

(McGinn/Cazale Theatre) Tuesday, November 28–December 30, 2000 (26 performances and 9 previews) Blue Light Theater Co. presents:
PRINCESS TURANDOT Written/Directed by Darko Tresnjak; Set, David P. Gordon; Costumes, Linda Cho; Lighting, Christopher J. Landy; Sound /Music, Robert Murphy; Stage Manager, Janet Takami; Press, Gary Springer/Susan Chicoine/Joe Trentacosta CAST: Jeffrey Binder (Pantalone), Wes Day (Imperial Judge), Crispin Freeman (Altoum), Roxanna Hope (Princess Turandot), Christopher K. Morgan (Imperial Executioner), Leith Burke, Ron Nahass, Aaron Michael Norris (Imperial Guards), Gregor Paslawsky (Barach), Carolyn Pasquantonio (Third Eunuch/Dorma), Susan Pourfar (Zelina/Queen Almaze), Josh Radnor (Brighella), Maria Elena Ramirez (Adelma), Mark Shunock (Second Eunuch/Nessun), James Stanley (Prince Calaf), Andrew Weems (Truffaldino/Ishmael)
A fable in two acts. The action takes place in the city of Peking during China's highly improbable past.

(MAP Penthouse) Wednesday, November 29–December 16, 2000 William C. Lane, in associtiion with McGuffin Productions, presents:
PSYCHO/DRAMAS Conceived/Directed by Chuck Noell; Press, Tony Origlio/Emily Lowe CAST: Nancy Lipper (Michaela), Lawrence C. Daly (Mike), Robert Ierardi (Steve), Susan J. Jacks (Rebecca), Alex Bond (Leigh), Bill Tatum (Christian), Jay Alvarez, Dominic Marcus
Mixes experimental and improvisational theatre through the elements of a traditional psychodrama workshop.

Jack Green, Jennifer Jiles, Rick Bank in *The Arrangement* (Vital Theatre Company)

(Vital Theatre) Thursday, November 30–December 17, 2000 (10 performances and 3 previews) Vital Theatre Company presents:
THE ARRANGEMENT by Eric Eisenberg; Director, Laura M. Stevens; Set /Lighting, Obadiah Savage; Costumes, Staci Shember; Sound, Bill Grady; Stage Manager, Fran Rubenstein; Press, Brett Singer CAST: Rick Bank (Tom Marigold), Jack Green (Bill Flynn), Jennifer Jiles (Amy Reynolds), Peter Waldren (Isaac Baldusaar)
A drama set in the high-stakes world of a Wall Street public relations agency.

James Stanley, Roxanna Hope in *Princess Turnadot*

(Henry Miller's Theatre) Thursday, November 30, 2000–February 17, 2001 (79 performances and 14 previews) David Henderson and P. Jennifer Dana present:

THE BITTER TEARS OF PETRA VON KANT by Rainer Werner Fassbinder; Translation, Dennis Calandra; Adaptation, Barbara Saurman and Ian Belton; Director, Mr. Belton; Press, Richard Kornberg CAST: Rebecca Wisocky (Petra), Anita Durst (Marlene), Rosalyn Coleman (Sidonie), Tami Dixon (Karin/Gabi), Joy Franz (Valerie)
A drama about a lesbian love affair, performed without intermission.

(Bank Street Theatre) Friday, December 1–23, 2000 (15 performances and 2 previews) The Fourth Unity Theatre Company presents:

ICARUS by Edwin Sánchez; Director, Dennis Smith; Set, Andris Krumkains; Lighting, Renée Molina; Choreography, Leah Gray; Stage Manager, Shuhei Seo; Press, Karen Greco CAST: Marlène Ramírez-Camcio (Altagracia), Ivan Davilla (Primitivo), Tony Hamilton (Mr. Ellis), Ann Chandler (The Gloria), Matthew Gorrek (Beau)
A surreal drama.

(Studio Theater) Friday, December 1–23, 2000 (15 performances and 5 previews) The Working Theatre Ensemble presents:

A TASTE OF HONEY by Shelagh Delaney; Director, John Gould Rubin; Set, Nancy Thun; Costumes, Mimi O'Donnell; Lighting, Sarah Sidman; Sound, Joanna Park; Stage Manager, Dawn Wagner; Press, Erin Dunn CAST: M.J. Karmi (Helen), Marina Nichols (Jo), Charles Goforth (Peter), Malcolm Barrett (Jimmie), T.J. Kenneally (Geof)
A 1958 drama in two acts. The action takes place in Manchester, England, 1958.

(Intar 53 Theater) Friday, December 1–23, 2000 (19 performances and 5 previews) The National Asian American Theatre Company presents:

THE HOUSE OF BERNARDA ALBA by Federico García Lorca; Adapted /Directed by Chay Yew; Design, Gabriela Lopez; Set, Sarah Lambert; Costumes, Elly Van Horne; Lighting, Stephen Petrilli; Sound, Laura Brown; Music, Fabian Obispo; Choreography, Kristin Jackson; Press, Shirley Herz/Sam Rudy CAST INCLUDES: Ching Valdes Aran (Bernarda Alba), Natsuko Ohama, Michi Barall, Eunice Wong, Kati Kuroda, Gusti Bogard, Jo Yang, Sophia Morae, Julienne Kim, Julyana Soelistyo
A new adaptation of a 1936 drama.

Sally Mayes, George Dvorsky in *Pete 'N' Keely* (Carol Rosegg)

Joey Arias and Jason Scott in *Christmas With the Crawfords* (Pate Eng)

(John Houseman Theater) Saturday, December 2, 2000–March 11, 2001 (101 performances and 13 previews) Steve Asher, David W. Unger, and Avalon Entertainment present:

PETE 'N' KEELY by James Hindman; Director, Mark Waldrop; Musical Director/Arrangements, Patrick S. Brady; Choreography, Keith Cromwell; Set, Ray Klausen; Costumes, Bob Mackie; Lighting, F. Mitchell Dana; Sound, Jon Weston; Stage Manager, Julia P. Jones; Press, Pete Sanders/Jim Mannino CAST: Sally Mayes (Keely), George Dvorsky (Pete) GUEST STARS: Jo Ann Worley, Phyllis Diller, Charo, Cousin Brucie
MUSICAL NUMBERS: Battle Hymn of the Republic, Bernice I Don't Believe You, Besame Mucho, Black Coffee, But Beautiful, Cross Country Tour, Daddy, Fever, Have You Got a Lot to Learn, Hello Egypt!, It's Us Again, Kid Stuff, Love, Lover, Secret Love, Swell Shampoo Song, That's All, This Could Be the Start of Something Big, Tony & Cleo, Too Fat to Fit, Wasn't It Fine, What Now My Love
A musical comedy set during the live broadcast of a television variety special in 1968.

(Grove Street Playhouse) Saturday, December 2–30, 2000 (24 performances and 2 previews) Artful Circle Theatre presents:

CHRISTMAS WITH THE CRAWFORDS Created by Richard Winchester; Written by Wayne Buidens and Mark Sargent; Director/Choreography, Donna Darks; Musical Director, Joe Collins; Set, Sacha Troxler; Costumes, Chris March, Dana Peter Porras, Richard Sanchez; Lighting, Jenny B/Shady Lady; Press, Maya/Penny M. Landau, Michael Litchfield CAST: Joey Arias (Joan Crawford), Jason Scott (Christina Crawford), Max Grenyo (Christopher Crawford), Chris March (Shirley Temple/Hedda Hopper), Matthew Martin (Baby Jane Hudson-Bette Davis/Katherine Hepburn/Ann Miller), Connie Champagne (Judy Garland/Maxine Andrews), Mark Sargent (LaVerne Andrews/Edith Head/Carmen Miranda/Ethel Merman), Trauma Flintstone (Patty Andrews/Gloria Swanson)
A comedy set at the Crawford's Brentwood Mansion, Christmas Eve, 1944.

(14th Street Y) Tuesday, December 5–17, 2000 (16 performances)
Musicals Tonight!/Mel Miller presents:
FOXY Music, Robert Emmett Dolan; Lyrics, Johnny Mercer; Book, Ian McLellan Hunter and Ring Lardner Jr.; Suggested by Ben Johnson's *Volpone*; Director/Choreography, Thomas Mills; Musical Director, Robert Felstein; Lighting, Shuhei Seo; Stage Manager, Shih-hui Wu Cast: Marvin Einhorn (Rottingham), Jessica Frankel (Brandy), Andrew Gitzy (Buzzard), Natasha Harper (Celia), Rob Lorey (Doc), Michael Mendiola (Stirling), George Pellegrino (Ben), Rudy Roberson (Foxy), David Sabella (Bedrock), Jay Brian Winnick (Shortcut), Amy Barker, Brian Cooper, Lawrence Cummings, James Flynn, Jason Levinson, Juliette Morgan, Marni Raab, Jennifer Scheer (Ensemble)
Musical Numbers: Prologue, Respectability (not in Bdwy version), Many Ways to Skin a Cat, Rollin' in Gold, Money Isn't Everything, Larceny and Love, S.S. Commodore Ebenezer McAfee III, The Honeymoon Is Over (not in Bdwy version), Talk to Me Baby, My Night to Howl, Bon Vivant, It's Easy When You Know How, Run Run Cinderella, I'm Way Ahead of the Game, The Letter of the Law (not in Bdwy version), In Loving Memory, Finale
A new production of the 1964 musical in two acts. The action takes place in The Yukon, Canada, 1896.

Tony Torn in *Now That Communism Is Dead My Life Feels Empty!*

(Phil Bosakowski Theatre) Thursday, December 14–30, 2000 (8 performances and 5 previews) The Protean Theatre Company, in association with The Fanfare Theatre Ensemble, presents:
THE DOCTOR IN SPITE OF HIMSELF by Molière; Translation, Guylaine Laperriere; Director, Owen Thompson; Set/Lighting, Rych Curtiss; Costumes, Jennifer Moeller; Press, Shirley Herz/Nancy Khuu Cast: Gregory Couba, Lisa Ann Goldsmith, John Grace, David H. Hamilton, Matt Cooney, Cynthia Enfield, Tristana Gonzalez, John Grace, Brian Voelcker, Mather Zickel
A new adaptation of the classic comedy.

(Producer's Club) Friday, December 15–16, 2000 (2 performances)
LatinoWorld/MundoLatino, in assocition with Baez Entertainment, presents:
NUDE IN NY Written/Performed by Jonisha; Director, Jesse Mojica
A comic monologue about making it in New York City.

(Soho Rep) Friday, December 15, 2000–January 20, 2001 (17 performances and 3 previews) Soho Rep and Theodore C. Rodgers present:
CAT'S PAW by Mac Wellman; Director, Daniel Aukin; Set, Kyle Chepulis; Costumes, Robin I. Shane; Lighting, Michael O'Connor; Sound, Colin Hodges; Music, Cynthia Hopkins; Stage Manager, Scott Dela Cruz; Press, Shirley Herz/Sam Rudy Cast: Nancy Franklin (Hildegard Bub), Alicia Goranson (Lindsay Rudge), Ann Talman (Jo Rudge), Laurie Williams (Jane Bub)
A mediation of the "Don Juan Theme," minus Don Juan. Performed without intermission.

(Ontological Theater) Thursday, January 4–April 29, 2001 (69 performances and 10 previews) Ontological-Hysteric Theater presents:
NOW THAT COMMUNISM IS DEAD MY LIFE FEELS EMPTY! Written/Directed /Designed/Scored by Richard Foreman; Costumes, Sarah Beadle and Laura Angotti; Stage Manager, Evan Cabnet Cast: Jay Smith (Fred), Tony Torn (Freddie)
A drama performed without intermission.

(Neighborhood Playhouse) Thursday, January 4–20, 2001 (14 performances and 1 preview) The Colleagues Theatre Company presents:
SECOND SUMMER by Gary Richards; Director, Roy B. Steinberg; Set, Drew Francis; Costumes, Louis Valantasis; Lighting, Jeff Fontaine; Sound, David Gilman; Stage Managers, Angela Adams, Ajit Anthony, Elizabeth Block, Sharika Niles, Lisa-LeClaire Taylor; Press, Susan L. Schulman Cast: Gil Rogers (Reginald Herring), Catherine Wolf (Doris Cabella), Joel Rooks (Ernie Cabella), Joan Copeland (Sheila Haskett), Margery Beddow (Bev Perkins), Jerry Rockwood (Murray Abrams), Carolyn Younger (Esther Lishansky)
A play in two acts. The action takes place in Brooklyn and Florida.

(Blue Heron Arts Center) Friday, January 5–28, 2001 (12 performances and 3 previews) Golden Squirrel Theatre presents:
AUTOEROTICISM IN DETROIT by Steven Somkin; Director, James B. Nicola; Press, Naomi Spatz Cast: Ariane Brandt, Collen Clinton, Peter Husovsky, Dennis Jordan, Jill Kotler, Lianne Kressin, Stu Richel, J.R. Robinson
A comedy based on the creation of the first electric car.

(Flamboyan Theatre) Friday, January 5–April 14, 2001 (110 performances and 6 previews)
THEATER OF LIGHT Conceived/Directed/Produced by Rudi Stren; Technical Director, Jerry Culligan; Puppetry Direction, Erik Blanc; Puppetry Developed/Performed by Matthew Lavin, Robin Snow and Mr. Blanc; Puppet Design/Staging Consultant, Barbara Pollitt; Sound, Ben Struck; Dancer, Akim Ndlovu; Press, Shirley Herz/Sam Rudy
A virtual fantasia of light, painting, music and movement. Previously performed at the Flea Theater (1999) and LaMama (2000).

Chris Messina, Robert Walden, Erica Leehrsen, Michael Mastro, Betsy Aidem in *Tamicanfly* (Carol Rosegg)

Kenneth Wilson-Harrington in *Gemini* (Timothy Haskell)

Annie Meisels, Stephen Speights in *My Mother's a Baby Boy* (Jason Louth)

(McGinn/Cazale Theater) Tuesday, January 9–February 4, 2001 (20 performances and 8 previews) Weissberger Theater Group presents:
TAMICANFLY by Scott Marshall Taylor; Director, Ethan McSweeny; Set, Neil Patel; Costumes, Michael Sharpe; Lighting, Howell Binkley; Sound, Aural Fixation; Fights, Rick Sordelet; Casting, Bernard Telsey; Stage Manager, Jana Llynn; Press, Richard Kornberg CAST: Robert Walden (Oscar), Chris Messina (C.J.), Erica Leerhsen (Maggie), Betsy Aidem (Charlotte), Michael Mastro (Steven)
A comedy set somewhere outside of Yakima, WA.

(78th St. Theatre Lab) Thursday, January 11–February 3, 2001 (16 performances and 3 previews) 78th St. Theatre Lab, in association with Monkey Damage Theatre and David Kennedy & Kenneth Wilson-Harrington, presents:
GEMINI by Edward Manning; Director, David Kennedy; Set/Projections, Craig Siebels; Costumes, Montague Everett Melville; Lighting, Matthew Richards; Sound, Ken Travis; Stage Manager, Julie Kessler; Press, Publicity Outfitters/Timothy J. Haskell, Christopher Joy CAST: Kenneth Wilson-Harrington (Joe), Shannon Emerick (Ajax), Marina Celander (Thumper)
A comical rant set in a mental hospital, and then the world.

(present Company Theatorium) Thursday, January 11–February 3, 2001 (12 performances) The Neo-Futurists and Theater Oobleck present:
THE COMPLETE LOST WORKS OF SAMUEL BECKETT AS FOUND IN AN ENVELOPE (PARTIALLY BURNED) IN A DUSTBIN IN PARIS LABELED "NEVER TO BE PERFORMED. NEVER. EVER. EVER! OR I'LL SUE! I'LL SUE FROM THE GRAVE!!!" by Greg Allen, Danny Thompson, and Ben Schneider; Director, Mr. Allen; Press, Spin Cycle/Shannon Jowett CAST: Danny Thompson, Ben Schneider, Umit Celebi, Greg Allen
Parodies of the works of Samuel Beckett.

(Kraine Theatre) Thursday, January 11–February 3, 2001 (9 performances and 3 previews) Jack Pierson presents:
MY MOTHER'S A BABY BOY Written/Directed by Chris Burns; Lighting, Farley Whitfield; Stage Manager, Cameron Wright; Press, Gary Springer-Susan Chicoine/Joe Trentacosta CAST: Chris Burns (Ben), Jane Casserly (Moviegoer), Andrea Cirie (Mathilda), Helen Coxe (Claire), Caroline Ficksman (Scorned Armed Woman), David Haugen (Moviegoer), Tim McGee (Bill), Annie Meisels (Kieley), Charlotte Patton (Mom), Stephen Speights (Richard), Baylen Thomas (Forgetful Man)
Three modern urban relationships.

(Henry St. Settlement) Thursday, January 11–February 11, 2001 (25 performances and 4 previews) New Federal Theater/Woodie King Jr. presents:
THE CONJURE MAN DIES: *A Mystery Tale of Dark Harlem* by Rudolph Fisher; Director, Clinton Turner Davis; Set, Kent Hoffman; Costumes, Evelyn Nelson; Lighting, Shirley Prendergast; Sound, Sean O'Halloran; Stage Manager, Ken Hall; Press, Max Eisen/Caraid O'Brien CAST: Peggy Alston (Landlady/Entertainer/Girl), Christine Campbell (Aramintha Snead/Patron), Rafeal Clements (Bubber Brown), Marcuis Harris (Sam Crouch/Easley Jones), Cat Jagar (Martha Crouch/Waitress), Everton Lawrence (Frimbo/Smalls), Curtis McClarin (Perry Dart), Eric McLendon (Dr. John Archer), Justice Pratt (Dr. Winkler/Club Patron/Tynes), Esau Pritchett (Jinx Jenkins), Edward Washington (Doty/Hicks/Hanks), Tee C. Williams (Spider Webb/Brady), Kevin R. Free
A 1937 mystery set in Harlem.

(Alice Tully Hall) Friday, January 12–12, 2001 (2 performances) Lincoln Center's American Songbook presents:
SOMETHING TO REMEMBER HIM BY Artistic Director, Jonathan Schwartz; Music Director, Paul Schwartz; Press, Eileen McMahon CAST: Davis Gaines, Bill Irwin, Rebecca Luker, Maureen McGovern, Jane Monheit
A tribute to composer Arthur Schwartz.

Mark McDonough, Linda Ewing, Michael Scelle, Michael Medeiros in *Code of the West* (Carol Rosegg)

(Mint Space) Friday, January 12–February 11, 2001 (26 performances and 6 previews); Transferred to (McGinn/Cazale Theatre) Saturday, March 24–April 29, 2001 (33 performances and 4 previews) MJT Productions, in association with Alces Productions, present:
CODE OF THE WEST Written/Directed by Mark R. Giesser; Set, John C. Scheffler; Costumes, Melanie Ann Schmidt; Lighting, Aaron Meadow; Stage Manager, Marcos Dinnerstein; Press, Peter Cromarty/Alice Cromarty CAST: Bradley Cole (Frank Tremont), Mark McDonough (T. Preston Booth), Linda Ewing (Claire Greeleaf), Jordan Charney (Joshua A. Norton), Elizabeth Ziambetti (Violet Allerton)
A comedy in two acts. The action takes place in San Francisco, 1867.

Rinde Eckert in *An Idiot Divine* (Marion Gray)

(45 Bleeker Theatre) Friday, January 12–February 18, 2001 (31 performances and 5 previews) The Culture Project @ 45 Bleeker presents:
AN IDIOT DIVINE Written/Composed/Performed by Rinde Eckert; Director, Ellen McLaughlin; Set/Lighting, Giselda Beaudin; Sound, James Rattazzi; Stage Manager, Erik Sniedze
Two music theatre pieces: *Dryland Divine* and *The Idiot Variations.*

(Abingdon Theatre) Thursday, January 18–21, 2001 (5 performances) Abingdon Theatre Company presents:
THE PARKER FAMILY CIRCUS by Jan Buttram; Director, Taylor Brooks; Set, Elizabeth Chaney; Costumes, Ingrid Maurer; Lighting, Kim T. Sharp; Stage Manager, Ernest Delli Santi III CAST: Lori Gardner, Rita Gardner, Debbie Jaffe, Carole Monferdini, David Newer, Brian Schany

Beverly Bartlett, Elsie James in *The Shadow Box*

(Hudson Guild Theatre) Thursday, January 18–28, 2001 (10 performances) Paper Moon Theatre Company presents:
THE SHADOW BOX by Michael Cristofer; Director/Set/Costumes, Marc Geller; Lighting, Frank DenDanto III CAST: Kevin Villers (Joe), Daniel Balboni (Steve), Eve Alexander (Maggie), B. Simeon Goldstein (Brian), Jason Howell (Mark), Sarah Green (Beverly), Elsie James (Felicity), Beverly Bartlett (Agnes)
A drama in two acts. The action takes place in and around three cabins at the City of Hope hospice in Mendocino, CA.

(HERE) Friday, January 9–28, 2001 (8 performances) HERE presents:
THE FOX by Carne Ross; Director, Royston Coppinger; Set/Costumes, Meganne George; Video, Rych Curtis; Press, Gary Springer-Susan Chicoine/Joe Trentacosta CAST: Mason Phillips, Martin Hillier, Simona Morecroft
A contemporary tragedy of extremist idealism set in London.

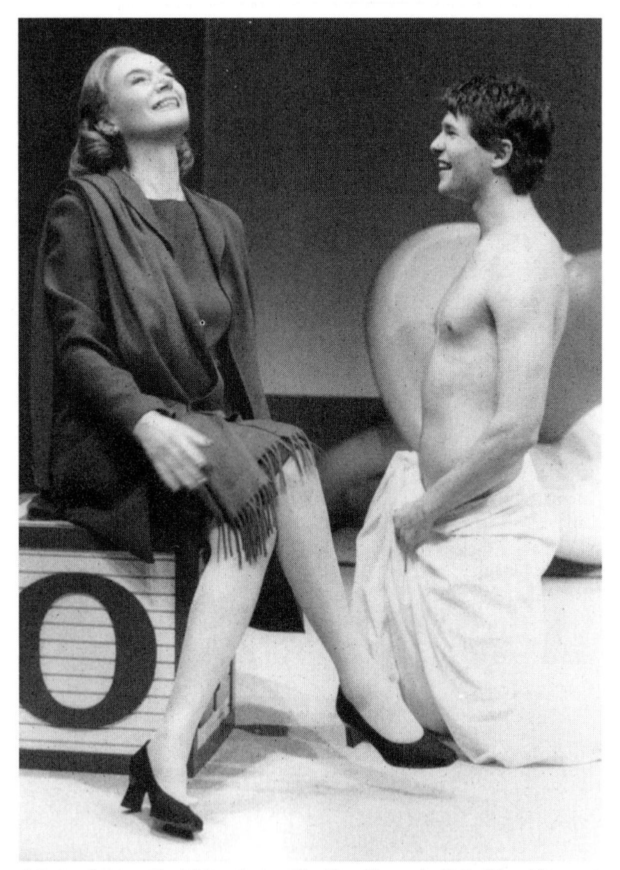
Marian Seldes, David Burtka in *The Play About the Baby* (Carol Rosegg)

Salome Jens in *Embers* (Catherine Gropper)

(Century Center for the Performing Arts) Tuesday, January 17–September 1, 2001 (245 performances and 18 previews) Elizabeth Ireland McCann, Daryl Roth, Terry Allen Kramer, Fifty-Second Street Productions, Robert Bartner, and Stanley Kaufelt, in association with The Alley Theatre, present:
THE PLAY ABOUT THE BABY by Edward Albee; Director, David Esbjornson; Set, John Arnone; Costumes, Michael Krass; Lighting, Kenneth Posner; Sound, Donald DiNicola; Casting, Jerry Beaver; Stage Manager, Mark Wright; Press, Shirley Herz/Sam Rudy CAST: David Burtka (Boy), Kathleen Early (Girl), Brian Murray (Man), Marian Seldes (Woman)
A play in two acts.

(Ohio Theater) Wednesday, January 17–February 24, 2001 (31 performances and 8 previews) Target Margin Theater presents:
DIDO, QUEEN OF CARTHAGE by Christopher Marlowe; Director, David Herskovits; Set, David Zinn; Costumes, Kaye Voyce; Lighting, Lenore Doxsee; Sound, Tim Schellenbaum; Stage Manager, Brenna St. George Jones; Press, Shirley Herz/Sam Rudy CAST: Rinne Groff (Venus/Anna), Nicole Halmos (Dido), Adrian LaTourelle (Aeneas), Mary Neufeld (Juno /Nurse), Greig Sargeant (Iarbus), William Badgett, Abigail Savage, Rizwan Manji, Steven Rattazzi, Douglas Stewart
A 1580 drama, believed to be Christopher Marlowe's first play.

(Rattlestick Theatre) Wednesday, January 17–February 18, 2001 (22 performances and 3 previews) Rattlestick presents:
KILLERS AND OTHER FAMILY by Lucy Thurber; Director, John Lawler; Set, Charles Kirby; Costumes, David M. Barber; Lighting, Bobby Harrell; Sound, Jason Mills; Press, David Gersten CAST: Ana Reeder (Elizabeth), Tessa Auberjonois (Claire), Dan Snook (Danny), Jason Weinberg (Jeff)
A drama performed without intermission. The action takes place in New York City.

(St. Peter's Church) Monday, January 22–27, 2001 (7 performances) Artistic Stage Productions and Saint Peter's Church present:
EMBERS by Catherine Gropper; Director, Mark Bloom; Set, Katerina Fiore; Costumes, Lorree True; Lighting, Izzy Einsiedler; Stage Manager, Constance George; Press, Brett Singer CAST: Salome Jens (Louise), Peter J. Coriaty (Richard), Michael Graves (Will), David Katz (Syd), Scott Klavan (Nick), Melissa Wolff (Dede)
A three-act drama inspired by the story of sculptor Louise Nevelson. Nevelson designed the chapel at the church where the production is housed.

(Looking Glass Theatre) Tuesday, January 23–February 24, 2001 (22 performances and 3 previews) Loca Productions presents:
SOMEWHERE IN BETWEEN by Craig Pospisil; Director, Alexander Zalben; Lighting, Sheldon Senek; Sound, Joel Stigliano; Stage Manager, Tarja Parssinen; Press, Brett Singer CAST: Dale Ho (Jasper), Vanessa Longley-Cook (Holly/Lawyer), Alex Miller (Rick/Homeless Man), Lawrence Feeney (Chris/Robert), Julie Thaxter-Gourlay (Ms. Sanders/Valerie), Nick Janik (Mary/Tourist)
A comedy in ten scenes.

(American Theatre of Actors) Wednesday, January 24–February 4, 2001 (12 performances) StageRight presents:
CAFÉ ENCOUNTERS Director, Paula D'Alessandris CAST: Eddie Goines, Susan Estes, Trevor Jones, Joshua Knapp, Jennifer Lorch, Daniel Martin, Kristy Maynard, Marsha Maynard, Marsha McGogney, Andrea Miskow, Wende O'Reilly, Sherikay Perry, Chuck Powers, Melissa Quirk, Dan Remmes, Kathy Searle, Richard Thompkins, Maitely Weissmann, Carrie Yaeger
PROGRAM: *Christmas Breaks* and *Counting Rita* by Patrick Gabridge, *Karmic Café* by Teresa Sullivan, *Menstruating Waitress from Hell* by Mary Lathrop, *Liver for Breakfast* by Lindsay Price, *Cognito* by P.S. Lorio
Six one-act comedies.

(Blue Heron Arts Center) Thursday, January 25–February 18, 2001 (16 performances and 4 previews) Blue Heron Theatre presents:
MEDAL OF HONOR RAG by Tom Cole; Director, Jim Pelegano; Set/Lighting, Roman Tatarowicz; Costumes, Robert J. Martin; Stage Manager, Paige Handler; Press, Peter Cromarty/Alice Cromarty CAST: Thomas James O'Leary (Doctor), Reginald James (Dale Johnson-DJ), Adam Brown (Military Guard)
A 1976 drama performed without intermission. The action takes place at the Valley Forge Army Hospital, PA, on April 23, 1971.

(HERE) Thursday, January 25–February 17, 2001 (16 performances and 1 preview) The Salt Theatre presents:
STAGE DOOR by Edna Ferber and George S. Kaufman; Director, Emma Griffin; Set, David Korins; Costumes, Jenny Chappelle Fulton; Lighting, Mark Barton; Sound, Noah Scalin; Stage Manager, Rachel Fachner CAST: Maria Striar (Judith Canfield), Linda Donald (Mrs. Orcutt), Tonya Canada (Kaye Hamilton), Christina Kirk (Terry Randall), Sheila Mitchell (Louise Mitchell), Ryan Shogren (Keith Burgess), Lisa Yonker (Mrs. Shaw), Suzi Takahashi (Linda Shaw), Yuri Skujins (David Kingsley), Stephanie Failing, Maggie Bofill, Mercedes Vasquez, Julia Prud'homme, Lily Koster, Megan Morrison, Danielle Delgado, Sarah K. Lippman, Linda Donald, Tonya Canada, Billie James, Melanie Martinez, Tara Taylor, Elena Beja, Jonathan Hyland, John McClure, Jan-Peter Pedross, Yuri Skujins, Erin McCormack, Christina Pollak, Henry Steele
A 1936 play set at The Footlights Club, a boardinghouse for young actresses.

(HomeGrown Theater) Friday, January 26–March 5, 2001 (16 performances and 2 previews) The Snow White Co. presents:
THE FIRST JEWISH BOY IN THE KU KLUX KLAN Written/Directed by Lionel Kranitz; Set/Lighting, Peter Lach; Costumes, Ellen Robertson Moynihan; Stage Manager, Nicole Press; Press, Brett Singer CAST: Mary Round (Sylvia), Brad Surosky (Arthur), Peter Stadlen (Sonny), Richard Springle (Sam)
The action takes place in suburbia, mid-1950s.

Miche Braden in *The Devil's Music* (Anastasia Courtney)

(Theatre 3) Friday, January 26–March 3, 2001 (28 performances and 6 previews) Melting Pot Theatre Company presents:
THE DEVIL'S MUSIC *The Life and Blues of Bessie Smith* by Angelo Parra; Director, Joe Brancato; Set, Matthew Maraffi; Costumes, Curtis Hay; Lighting, Jeff Nellis; Arrangements, Miche Braden; Stage Manager, Alicia Edwards; Press, Publicity Outfitters/Timothy J. Haskell, Christopher Joy CAST: Miche Braden (Bessie Smith), Terry Walker (Pickle), Jimmy Hankins, Pierre Andre
A play with music about the great blues singer.

(Greenwich Street Theatre) Friday, January 26–February 18, 2001 (16 performances and 10 previews) A Word Productions presents:
THE "A" WORD by Latife Mardin; Director, Melamie Martin Long; Set, Troy Hourie; Costumes, Melissa Schlactmeyer; Lighting, Randy Glickman; Sound, Seth Guterman; Stage Manager, Lori Ann Zepp; Press, Shirley Herz/Nancy Khuu CAST: Defne Halman (Sally Ward), Jennifer Dorr White (Marian Ward), Lara Agar Stoby (Tracy Ward), Becky London (Arlene Bonelli), Babs Winn (Liz Allen)
A drama about the effects of teenage pregnancy on a suburban family, 1968.

(Walker Space) Thursday, February 1–25, 2001 (14 performances and 2 previews) transferred to (Theatre-Studio) Thursday, March 8–April 29, 2001 (32 performances) Asen-Fulham Productions presents:
P.S. 69 by Susan Jeremy and Mary Fulham; Director, Ms. Fulham; Press, Gary Springer-Susan Chicoine/Joe Trentacosta CAST: Susan Jeremy
A comic monologue about a gay subsitute teacher who moonlights as an exotic dancer.

(Red Room) Thursday, February 1–25, 2001 Bon Bock Productions, in association with Horse Trade Theatre Group, presents:
BARMAN Written/Designed by Alex Dawson; Director, Jane Hardy; Producers, Gareth Smith, Joe Taverney; Sound, Flynn Hundhausen CAST: Morgan Baker (George), Bruce Borman (College Kid/Rich), Dave Dwyer (Angelo), Jake Jordan (Bouncer Wes), Joseph Pacillo (Mower Mike), Amy Parlow (Grace), Joseph Prussak (Skippy), Jonathan David Sang (Jack), Marvin W. Schwartz (Billy)
A memoir in two acts. The action takes place in a New Jersey gin mill and a Park Avenue apartment.

(135 Space) Friday, February 2–April 29, 2001 (41 performances and 11 previews) Faux-Real Theatre Company and Chashama present:
FUNBOX TIMES SQUARE by Mark Greenfield and the Company; Director, Mr. Greenfield; Set, Michael Casselli; Costumes, Carrie Dubois, Constance Tarbox; Lighting, Sarah Sidman; Sound, Jeremy X. Halpern; Press, Peter Cromarty/Sherri Jean Katz CAST: Corey Carthew, Lamar Davenport, Tom Day, Josh Dibb, Don Downie, Emily Doubilet, Carrie DuBois, Brie Jonti Eley, Layna Fisher, Mark Frankos, Jenni Graham, Lisa Hargus, Susan Hyon, Cerris Morgan-Moyer, Brian Simons, Nakia Syvonne, Constance Tarbox, Mike Urdaneta, Ben Wilson, Jen Wineman
Performance art with audience participation.

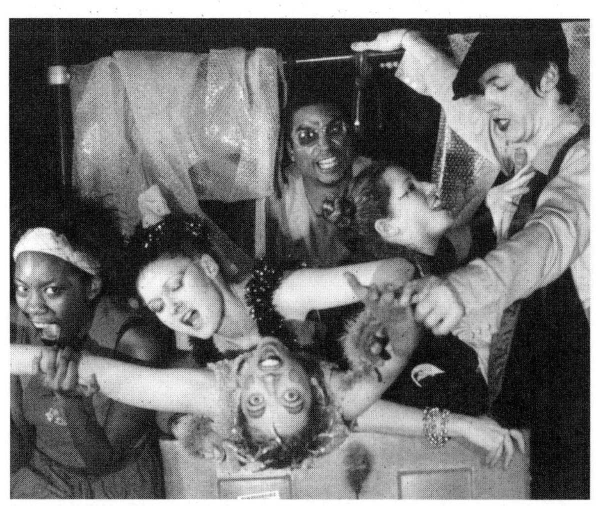
Brie Jonti Eley, Cerris Morgan-Moyer, Layna Fisher, Tom Day, Jen Wineman, Josh Dibb in *FUNBOX Times Square* (Mariya Lipunova)

Susie Cover, Maddie Corman in *Isn't It Romantic* (Kate Raudenbush)

(Tribeca Playhouse) Friday, February 2–March 25, 2001 (30 performances and 8 previews) Carol R. Fineman and The Worth Street Theater Company present:

ISN'T IT ROMANTIC by Wendy Wasserstein; Director, Jeff Cohen; Set, Lauren Helpern; Costumes, Veronica Worts; Lighting, Traci Klainer; Sound, Paul Adams; Music, Dan Rosengard; Casting, Vince Leibhart/Tom Alberg; Stage Manager, Michael V. Mendelson; Press, Carol R. Fineman CAST: Maddie Corman (Janie Blumberg), Susie Cover (Harriet Cornwall), Hillel Meltzer (Marty Sterling), Barbara Speigel (Tasha Blumberg), Peter Van Wagner (Simon Blumberg), Jennifer Bassey (Lillian Cornwall), Tom Wiggin (Paul Stuart), Adam Hirsch (Vladimir)

A two-act comedy set in New York City, 1983.

(78th St. Theatre Lab) Thursday, February 8–March 4, 2001 (16 performances) 78th Street Theatre Lab presents:

A LESSON FROM ALOES by Athol Fugard; Director, Thomas A. Bullard; Set, John Scheffler; Costumes, Allison Galker; Lighting, Ji-Youn Chang; Stage Manager, Phil Kasper CAST: Judylee Vivier (Gladys), Harrison Long (Piet), Todd Anthony-Jackson (Steve)

A drama set in Port Elizabeth, South Africa, 1963.

(present Company Theatorium) Saturday, February 10–March 4, 2001 (16 performances) Reverie Productions, in association with the present Company, presents:

VALERIE SHOOTS ANDY by Carson Kreitzer; Director, Randy White; Set, Elizabeth Chaney; Costumes, Lauren Cordes; Lighting, Colin D. Young; Sound, Stefan Jacobs; Stage Manager, Julie Blumenthal; Press, Spin Cycle /Tron Lasko CAST: Lynne McCollough (Valerie Solanas), Heather Grayson (Young Valerie), Walter Magnuson (Andy Warhol), Jeff Burchfield (Alan Midgette/Andy), Christy Marie Moore (Edie Sedgwick), Laura Rush (Viva), Anushka Carter, Christopher Briggs, Noah Brody, Ayelet Kaznelson, Jessica Claire, Carla Harting, Ean Sheehy, Daniel Harnett, Beth Tapper, Gary Brownlee, Mark Leydorf

A drama based on the 1968 shooting of artist Andy Warhol.

(New York Comedy Club) Sunday, February 11–March 11, 2001 (5 performances) The Live Theatre Gang presents:

THE PRINTZ OF POETS: *The Legend of a Loose Lipped Lunatic* Produced /Directed by Reed McCants CAST: Brother Natural, Jay-Sun, Jomo, Nacinimod, Shakespeare

One man's fight for clarity through the conflicting personalities in his head.

(Pulse Ensemble) Tuesday, February 13–March 11, 2001 (18 performances and 3 previews) Pulse Ensemble Theatre presents:

TOWARDS ZERO by Agatha Christie; Director, Alexa Kelly; Set, Jennifer Varbalow; Press, Shirley Herz/Nancy Khuu CAST: Julie Hera DeStefano (Kay), Stephen Aloi (Neville), Neil Steward (Superintendent Battle), Marianne Mathews, Steve Abbruscato, Jo Ann Tolassi, Mar McClain Wilson, Adam Green

A mystery set in Cornwall, England, 1956.

Kim Lindsay, Jennifer Piech in *As You Like It* (Charles Cameron)

(Studio Theatre) Wednesday, February 14–March 10, 2001 (18 performances and 2 previews) The Storm Theatre, in association with East End Productions, presents:

AS YOU LIKE IT by William Shakespeare; Director, Peter Dobbins; Set, Mary Houston; Costumes, E. Shura Pollatsek; Lighting, Charles Cameron; Choreography, Maryanne Chaney; Music, Laura Flynn; Stage Manager, Jean Klepka; Press, Shirley Herz/Nancy Khuu CAST: Eric Alperin (Orlando), Dan Berkey (Jacques), William Joseph Brookes (Duke Frederick/Sir Oliver Martext), Maryanne Chaney (Hymen), Brian J. Coffey (Duke Senior), Colleen Crawford (Phebe), Antony Ferguson (Le Beau/Corin), Kim Lindsay (Celia), Carmit Levitè (Audrey), Gavin Moore (Charles the Wrestler), Cedric O'Gorman (Dennis/Amiens/William), William Peden (Oliver), Jennifer Piech (Rosalind), John Regis (Touchstone), Bill Roulet (Adam), Eric Thorne (Lord/Jacques de Boys), Brian Whisenant (Silvius)

Performed with one intermission.

(Raw Space) Wednesday, February 14–24, 2001 (12 performances) The Bits Players, in association with Freefall Productions, presents:

THE GAME by Danny Zyne; Director, David Calafiore; Set, Brian Lynch; Costumes, Cindy Heney; Sound, Josh Sherman CAST: Jay Billiet (Johnny), Matt Stevens (Phil), Eryc Whiteley (Al), Jim Bray (Pizza Boy), Vickie Varnuska (Ms. Betty), Jen Daum (Georgia Rose)

Five guys get snowed-in with the woman of their dreams on New Year's Eve.

Steven McElroy, Michael Irby, Grant-James Varjas in *Let a Hundred Flowers Bloom* (David Gochfeld)

(Center Stage) Wednesday, February 14–March 10, 2001 (16 performances and 2 previews) The New Ensemble Theatre Company presents:

LET A HUNDRED FLOWERS BLOOM by David Zellnik; Director, Dave Mowers; Set, Murker54; Costumes, Charles Schoonmaker; Lighting, John Finen and Guy Smith; Sound, Ian Murphy; Stage Manager, Amy Podgurski; Press, Publicity Outfitters/Timothy J. Haskell and Christopher Joy CAST: Steven McElroy (Puppy), Grant-James Varjas (Jake), Andy Paris (Samson/Al), Michael Irby (Addison/Rod/Carmine)
A comedy about a disabled writer of gay, Marxist pornography.

(14th Street Y) Wednesday, February 14–March 11, 2001 (20 performances) The Hypothetical Theatre Company presents:

SITTING PRETTY by Amy Rosenthal; Director, Amy Feinberg; Set, Mark Symczak; Costumes, Melissa Schlachtmeyer; Lighting, Rych Curtiss; Sound, Tim Cramer; Stage Manager, Kimberly Palomo; Press, Jonathan Slaff CAST: Aviva Jane Carlin (Nancy), Tanny McDoanld succeeded by Maurren Lipman, John O'Creagh (Max), Mark Jacoby (Philip), Lina Roessler, Jo Haney (Zelda), Nathan M. White (Luka), Dannah Chaifetz (Josie), Kate Konigisor (Bridget), Marilyn Bernard (Sylvia), Charles Major (Martin)
A drama in two acts. The action takes place in London over the course of six months.

(Theatre 22) Thursday, February 15–March 4, 2001 (12 performances) Marina Levitskaya and Sonia Kozlova present:

OH MY DEAR ANDERSON Based on fairy tales by Hans Christian Anderson; Adapted/Directed by Aleksey Burago; Set, Matthew Wright; Costumes, Uta Bekaia, Nadia Fadeeva, Nora Heart; Music, Colm Clark; Puppets, Rachel Kramer, David Gochfeld CAST: Snezhana Chernova, Cordis Head, Amanda Jones

(The Producers Club) Thursday, February 15–March 4, 2001 (10 performances and 2 previews) The Writers Group presents:

DOWN THE LOFT and **THE TANNING SALON** by Patrick Hurley; Director, Glyn O'Malley; Set, Fritz Faulhaber; Costumes, David Moyer; Lighting, Futz; Sound, David Gilman; Stage Manager, Arielle Segal; Press, Shirley Herz/Nancy Khuu CASTS: *Loft* Anthony Moore (Shorts), Donna Svennevik (Suit), Eric Friedman (JQ) *Tanning* Diane Landers (Jane), Sean Harris (Clark), Scott Miller (Joe), Donna Svennevik (Magnifique), Ryohei Hoshi (General)
A tandem of one-acts.

(Douglas Fairbanks Theater) Thursday, February 15–April 1, 2001 (30 - performances and 23 previews) Stellar Productions Intl. and James M. Nederlander present:

"IF IT WAS EASY..." by Stewart F. Lane and Ward Morehouse III; Director, Mr. Lane; Set, Michael Anania; Costumes, Steven Epstein; Lighting, Phil Monat; Sound, Peter Fitzgerald; Casting, Stephanie Klapper; Stage Manager, Alan Fox; Press, Keith Sherman/Brett Oberman CAST: Bonnie Comley (Randi Lester), John Jellison (Steve Gallop), Vicki Van Tassel (Lucy Handover), William Marshall Miller succeeded by Stewart F. Lane (Joey Fingers), Brad Bellamy (Charlie), Gustave Johnson (Wilbur/Waiter), Christian Kauffmann (Lars/Mailman), Martin LaPlatney (Papa)
A backstage comedy in two acts. The action takes place in Producer Steve Gallop's New York City office in the recent past.

Vicki Van Tassel, William Marshall Miller, John Jellison in *"If It Was Easy..."*

(Arclight Theatre) Thursday, February 15–April 9, 2001 (41 performances and 14 previews) Laine Valentino, in association with MakePeace Theater, presents:

BOBBI BOLAND by Nancy Hasty; Director, Evan Bergman; Set, John Farrell; Costumes, Jill Kliber; Lighting, Steve Rust; Sound, Cynthia Tuohy; Casting, Judy Henderson; Stage Manager, Jim Ring; Press, Judy Jacksina CAST: Rose McGuire succeeded by Nancy Hess (Bobbi Boland), Holiday Segal (Susan Johnson), Gregg Henry (Roger Boland), Byron Loyd (Sam White), David Little (George McGowan), Tanya Clarke (Kim McGowan)
A drama in two acts. The action takes place in Crestview, FL, 1967.

Sean Harris, Donna Svennevik in *The Tanning Salon*

Amy Ryan, Norbert Butz, Pete Starrett in *Saved* (Ken Howard)

(American Place Theatre) Saturday, February 17–March 18, 2001 (22 performances and 8 previews) Theatre for a New Audience presents:
SAVED by Edward Bond; Director, Robert Woodruff; Set, Douglas Stein; Costumes, Catherine Zuber; Lighting, David Weiner; Sound, Leah Gelpe; Music, Douglas Wieselman; Dialects, Deborah Hecht, Charmian Hoare; Casting, Deborah Brown; Stage Manager, Judith Schoenfeld; Press, Gary Springer-Susan Chicoine/Joe Trentacosta CAST: Pete Starrett (Len), Norbert Butz (Fred), Terence Rigby (Harry), Justin Hagan (Pete), David Barlow (Colin), Joey Kern (Mike), Justin Campbell (Barry), Amy Ryan (Pam), Randy Danson (Mary), Wendy Allegaert (Liz)
A 1965 drama in two acts. The action takes place in South London.

(Century Center/Ballroom) Tuesday, February 20–March 17 (13 performances and 4 previews) Century Center Ibsen Series presents:
ROSMERSHOLM by Henrik Ibsen; Translation, Rolf Fjelde; Costumes, Sydney Maresca; Lighting, Jason Cina; Sound, John Littig; Press, Shirley Herz/Sam Rudy CAST: William Broderick (Rector Kroll), Dean Harrison (Pastor John Rosmer), Kelly Overton (Rebecca West), Bruce Edward Barton, Tamara Daniel, David Jones
A rarely performed 1886 drama.

(Manhattan Ensemble Theater) Wednesday, February 21–March 25, 2001 (27 performances and 7 previews) Manhattan Ensemble Theater presents:
THE IDIOT by Fyodor Dostoyevsky; Dramatized/Directed by David Fishelson; Set, Richard Hoover; Costumes, Susan L. Soetaert; Lighting, Brian Aldous; Casting, Deborah Brown; Stage Manager, Gail Eve Malatesta; Press, Shirley Herz/Sam Rudy CAST: Carl Bradford (Footman /Gang), Christian Conn (Prince Sherbatsky/Gang), Gibson Frazier (Ganya), Peter Goldfarb (Gen. Yepanchin/Gen. Ivolgin), Karl Herlinger (Gen. Denisov/Gang), Roxanna Hope (Nastasya Filipovna), John Kinsherf (Lededev/Col. Levitsky), Jerusha Klemperer (Adelaida/Darya), John Lenartz (Myshkin), Abigail López (Aglaya), Tricia Norris (Mrs. Ivolgin /Princess Belokonsky), Kevin Orton (Radomsky/Totsky/Conductor), Triney Sandoval (Rogozhim), April Sweeney (Varya/Maid), Angela Vitale (Mrs. Yepanchin)
The inaugural production of M.E.T.'s new theatre in Soho.

(Ensemble Studio Theatre) Wednesday, February 21–March 18, 2001 (18 performances and 5 previews) Ensemble Studio Theatre, in association with Youngblood, presents:
SUMMER CYCLONE by Amy Fox; Director, Nela Wagman; Set, George Xenos, Dorothea Brunialti; Costumes, Amela Baksic; Lighting, Greg MacPherson; Sound, Dean Gray; Music, David Rothenberg; Stage Manager, Carolyn M. Bennett; Press, Erin Dunn/Katie Miller CAST: Jenna Stern (Lucia), Christine Farrell (Julie), Chris Ceraso (Jeremy), Johnny Giacalone (Eugene), William Wise (Milton), Amy Staats (Reena)
A drama set in New York City.

(Vital Theatre) Thursday, February 22–March 18, 2001 (13 performances and 4 previews) Vital Theatre Company presents:
HORSEY PEOPLE by Brent Askari; Director, Laura M. Stevens; Set /Lighting, Obadiah Savage; Costumes, Staci Shember; Sound, Bill Grady; Fights, Laurie Miller, Edward J. Wheller; Stage Manager, Fran Rubenstein; Press, Stephen Sunderlin/Shannon Golub, Anne Czichoz CAST: Colin Ficks (Cyril), Diane Grotke (Sydney), Bolen High (Horace), Jeff Patterson (Jake), Leigh Pittard (Brittany), Ted Rodenborn (Morning Sparkle)
A comedy set among Virginia's exclusive horse-and-hunt crowd.

(Metro Baptist Church) Thursday, February 22–25, 2001 (4 performances) Heartbeat Productions present:
W.E.B. DUBOIS, PROPHET IN LIMBO by Dan Snow and Alexa Kelly; Set, Ruben Arana-Downs; Costumes, Terry Leong; Lighting, Herrick Goldman; Press, Shirley Herz/Nancy Khuu CAST: Dan Snow (W.E.B. Dubois), Brian Richardson

(Hudson Guild Theatre) Friday, February 23–March 18, 2001 (20 performances and 4 previews) Abingdon Theatre Company presents:
LITTLE FISHES by Steven Haworth; Director, Kim T. Sharp; Set, Elizabeth Chaney; Costumes, Melissa Richards; Lighting, David Castaneda; Fights, Rick Sordelet; Stage Manager, Lisa Elena Nelson; Press, Brett Singer CAST: Nicholas Piper (Brad), John Tardibuono (Pipe), Frank J. O'Donnell (Joe), Paul Barry (Nels)
A drama performed without intermission. The action takes place in a Minneapolis nursing home.

(45 Bleeker Theatre) Wednesday, February 28–April 15, 2001 (36 performances and 4 previews) The Culture Project presents:
CARTAS: *Love Letters of a Portugese Nun* Based on *Les Lettres d'une Religieuse Portugaise*, Translated by Myriam Cyr; Director, Lisa Forrell; Set, Richard Hsu; Costumes, Luca Mosca and Marco Cattoretti; Lighting, Rick Martin; Sound, Nancy Allen; Stage Manager, Erik Sniedze; Press, Richard Kornberg/Tom D'Ambrosio CAST: Myriam Cyr (Marianne Alcoforado), Liev Schreiber-Voice (Claude Barbin)
The setting is a 17th century convent in Portugal.

Myriam Cyr in *Cartas* (Aimee Toledano)

(Don't Tell Mama) Thursday, March 1–12, 2001 (3 performances) Flip Productions presents:
7 HABITS OF HIGHLY EFFECTIVE MISTRESSES Written/Performed by Lisa Faith Phillips; Musical Director, Ellen Mandel; Press, Clair Clarke
A one-woman show.

Caroline Ficksman, Jeff Gurner in *The London Cuckolds*
(James McClure)

(Blue Heron Arts Center) Thursday, March 1–24, 2001 (15 performances and 5 previews) The Protean Theatre Company presents:
THE LONDON CUCKOLDS by Edward Ravenscroft; Adaptation, John Byrne; Director, Owen Thompson; Set, Tony Andrea; Costumes, Hilary Oak; Lighting, Beth Amanda Hoare; Fights, David Dean Hastings; Stage Manager, Michael Biondi; Press, Shirley Herz/Nancy Khuu Cast: Michael Cone (Alderman Dashwell), Jerry Jerger (Alderman Doodle), Jenny Deller (Arabella), Caroline Ficksman (Engine), Jeff Gurner (Ned Ramble), Michael Daly (Frank Townly), Lance Windish (Roger), Eva Kaminsky (Evgenta), Lisa Ann Goldsmith (Jane), Jeffrey M. Bender (Valentine Loveday), John Grace, Mark Cajigao (Sweeps/Watchmen), Kate Kenney (Linkboy)
A 1681 comedy set in London society.

(Raw Space) Thursday, March 1–9, 2001 (6 performances) 2001: A Spotlight on Festival Odyssey and Frank Calo, in association with 2B Theatre Company and Wholly Terror, present:
THE STATUE, THE CORPSE AND ME and **LADY BY THE SEA** by Andrès J. Wrath; Director, Brenda D. Cook; Press, Steven Thornburg Cast: Dinah Marina Geiger, Caroline Goldrick, Matthew Hammond, Christopher Kann, Cornelia Lorentzen, W. Allen Wrede
Two one-acts.

(HERE) Friday, March 2–11, 2001 (10 performances) Vortex Theater presents:
DESPAIR'S BOOK OF DREAMS AND THE SOMETIMES RADIO by Kirk Smith; Director, Bonnie Cullman; Press, Spin Cycle/Ron Lasko Cast: Kirk Smith, Patricia Wappner, David Sangalli, Elizabeth Doss, Ellen Kolsto, Matthew Patterson
A musical theatre piece.

(Kraine Theatre) Saturday, March 3–August 4, 2001 Saturday Players presents:
CANNIBAL! THE MUSICAL by Trey Parker; Adaptation, Lisa Gardner; Director, Joan Eileen Murray; Set/Lighting, David Hein; Costumes, Wendy R. Seyb; Choreography, Wendy R. Seyb and Jennifer MacQueen; Press, Spin Cycle/Ron Lasko Cast: Ryan Brack (Alfred Packer), Kasey Daley (Polly Pry), Nadine Klein (Lianne), Matt Parson (Bell), Yoshi Amao, Lisa Gardner, Joshua Gilliam, Paul Lang, Jeremy Manta, Rob McDonald, Elizabeth Quinn, Mark Ramsey, Scott Sanborn, John David West
A musical comedy adaptation of a 1996 independent film.

(Union Square Theatre) Saturday, March 3–December 2, 2001 (257 performances and 21 previews) Nancy Nagel Gibbs, Riot Entertainment, Robyn Goodman, Michael Alden, Jean Doumanian, and The Producing Office present:
BAT BOY: *The Musical* Music/Lyrics, Laurence O'Keefe; Story/Book, Keythe Farley and Brian Flemming; Licensed under agreement with Weekly World News; Director, Scott Schwartz; Musical Director, Alex Lacamoire; Orchestrations, Mr. O'Keefe, Mr. Lacamoire; Musical Staging, Christopher Gattelli; Sets, Richard Hoover & Bryan Johnson; Costumes, Fabio Toblini; Lighting, Howell Binkley; Sound, Sunil Rajan; Casting, Dave Clemmons; Cast Recording, RCA; Stage Manager, Renee Lutz; Press, Craig Karpel/Bridget Klapinski Cast: Deven May (Bat Boy), Kaitlin Hopkins (Meredith), Sean McCourt (Parker), Kerry Butler (Shelley), Kathy Briar (Maggie/Ron), Daria Hardeman (Ruthie/Ned), Trent Armand Kendall (Rev. Hightower/Mrs. Taylor/Roy), Jim Price (Bud/Daisy/Pan), Richard Prueitt (Sheriff), Doug Storm (Rick/Lorraine), John Treacy Egan, Stephanie Kurtzuba, J.P. Potter, Charles Gray
Musical Numbers: Hold Me Bat Boy, Christian Charity, Another Dead Cow, Ugly Boy, Watcha Wanna Do?, A Home for You, Dance with Me Darling, Ruthie's Lullaby, Show You a Thing or Two, Comfort and Joy, A Joyful Noise, Let Me Walk Among You, Three Bedroom House, Children Children, More Blood, Inside Your Heart, Apology to a Cow, Revelations, I Imagine You're Upset, Finale
A musical comedy in two acts. The action takes place in Hope Fall, West Virginia.

Deven May, Kerry Butler in *Batboy: The Musical*
(Joan Marcus)

(Ohio Theatre) Sunday, March 4–25, 2001 (17 performances and 2 previews) Synapse Productions present:
MACHINAL by Sophie Treadwell; Director, Ginevra Bull; Set/Lighting, Adrian Jones; Costumes, Miguel Angel Huidor; Sound, Jane Shaw; Stage Manager, Jennifer Conley Darling; Press, Shirley Herz/Sam Rudy CAST: Jessica Claire (Helen Jones), Richard Kohn (George Jones/Bartender /Judge), Allison Cimmet (Telephone Girl), Jack O'Neill (Richard Roe), Jacqueline Sydney (Mother/Nurse/Court Reporter), Jerry Della Salla, David Lapkin, Michael Doyle, David B. Martin, Dina Comolli
A 1928 drama based loosely on a 1927 love triangle murder in urban America.

(Curtican Theatre) Tuesday, March 6–22, 2001 (11 performances) Queen's Company, in association with Good Bones, presents:
MILES BELOW ZERO; Written/Directed by Tessa Leigh Defner; Press, Publicity Outfitters/Timothy J. Haskell, Christopher Joy CAST: Barbara Pitts (Charlotte Perkins Gilman)
An examination of the life of a feminist author during the Victorian era.

Brian d'Arcy James in *The Good Thief* (Josh Bradford)

(Jose Quintero Theatre) Wednesday, March 7–25, 2001 (11 performances and 4 previews); Transferred to (45 Bleeker) Wednesday, April 4–May 26, 2001 (47 performances) Keen Company presents:
THE GOOD THIEF by Conor McPherson; Director, Carl Forsman; Set, Nathan Heverin; Costumes, Theresa Squire; Lighting, Josh Bradford; Sound, Stefan Jacobs; Stage Manager, Kara Bain; Press, Karen Greco CAST: Brian d'Arcy James
A one-man drama performed without intermission.

(West-Park Church) Thursday, March 8–April 1, 2001 (13 performances and 3 previews) Frog & Peach Theatre Company presents:
RICHARD II by William Shakespeare; Director, Lynnea Benson; Fights, Ian Marshall; Press, Jim Baldassare CAST: Austin Pendleton (Richard), Ted Zurkowski (Bolingbroke), Martin Carey, Rhonda Cole, Joe Corey, Letty Ferrer, Matthew Freeman, Peter Hess Friedland, Charlotte Hampden, Roland Johnson, William Laney, Stewart Walker

Austin Pendleton, Ted Zurkowski in *Richard II* (Dave Cross)

(Dixon Place) Friday, March 9–24, 2001 (8 performances and 1 preview) Dixon Place presents:
BREAKER: AN AERIAL FAIRIE TALE Written/Directed/Choreographed by Chelsea Bacon; Co-Director, Patricia Buckley; Design, Kyle Chepulis, Costumes, Kiva Kahl; Music, Rachelle Garniez, Franz Nicolay; Press, Shirley Herz/Sam Rudy CAST: Chelsea Bacon, Katie Baldwin, K. Olness, Sabine Lathrop, Britt Nhi Sarah, Aurelia Thierree, Carl Van Vechten
An arial (trapeze) theatre dance piece.

(Raw Space) Sunday, March 10–17, 2001 (4 performances) 2001: A Spotlight on Festival Odyssey and Frank Calo, in association with 2B Theatre Company and Wholly Terror, present:
CELTIC CROSS: SOLO STORIES INTO HOMOPHOBIA Written/Directed by Richard Morell; Press, Steven Thornburg CAST: Anthony Ciccotelli, Brenda D. Cook, Tony Hamilton, Susan Barnes Walker

(Tribecca Performing Arts Center) Sunday, March 11–25, 2001 (3 performances) The Vineyard Theatre and Tribecca Performing Arts Center present:
APPELEMANDO'S DREAMS Music, James Kurtz; Libretto, Barbara Zinn Krieger; Based on a book by Patricia Polacco; Director/Choreography, Reed Farley; Musical Director, Jana Zielonka; Set, Rob Odorisio; Lighting, John Paul Szczepanski; Costumes, Curtiss Hay; Press, Shirley Herz/Sam Rudy CAST: Asher Monroe Book, Michele Ariele Cobham, Ellie Grosso, Carol Linnea Johnson, Raphael Nash-Thompson, Samantha Takosi, Matthew Gasper, Colin Stokes
A return engagement for a family musical first performed at the Vineyard in 1994.

Nicole Leach, Craig Bonacorsi in *Starmites 2001* (Carol Rosegg)

(Theatre 3) Wednesday, March 14–April 8, 2001 (17 performances and 7 previews) Amas Musical Theatre, in association with Mary Kei and Jim Steinman, presents:
STARMITES 2001 Music/Lyrics, Barry Keating; Book, Stuart Ross and Mr. Keating; Director, Mr. Keating; Musical Director, Wendy Bobbitt Cavett; Choreography, Dominick DeFranco; Puppet Design, Richard Druther, Michael Duffy, Jeffrey Wallach; Set, Beowulf Boritt; Costumes, John Russell; Lighting, Aaron Spivey; Sound, David Gilman, Ray Shilke, Ins & Outs Sound; Casting, Gilburne & Urban; Stage Manager, Brenda Arko; Press, Tony Origlio CAST: Nicole Leach (Eleanor/Bizarbara), Gwen Stewart (Eleanor's Mother/Diva), Larry Purifory (Trinkulus), Craig Bonacorsi (Space Punk), Jason Wooten (Dismo Razzle Dazzle), Adam Fleming (Ack Ack Hackeraxe), Eric Millegan (S'up S'up Sensaboi), Pegg Winter (Shotzi/Oragala), Darlene Bel Grayson (Maligna), Valerie A. Hawkins (Ballbraka), Kim Cea (Canibelle), Rob Del Colle, Michael Duffy (Puppeteers)
MUSICAL NUMBERS: Superhero Girl, Starmites, Trink's Narration, Afraid of the Dark, Little Hero, Attack of the Banshees, Hard to Be Diva, Love Duet, Sance of Spousal Arousal, Finaletto, Bizarbara's Wedding, Milady, Beauty Within, The Cruelty Stomp, Reach Right Down, Immolation, Starmites/Diva, Finale
A revised version of the 1989 musical in two acts. The action takes place on Earth and Innerspace.

(Raw Space) Thursday, March 15–24, 2001 (6 performances) also performed at (HERE) June 18, 2001 The John Montgomery Theatre Company and Frank Calo present:
CIRCLE by Suzanne Bachner; Director, Trish Minskoff; Set, Anthony Bishop; Lighting, John Tees III; Costumes, Nadia Volvic, Deborah Alves; Slides, Danny Wiseman; Press, Shirley Herz/Nancy Khuu CAST: Thaddeus Daniels, Felicia Scarangello, Bob Celli, Judy Turkisher
A modern day adaptation of Arthur Schnitzler's *La Ronde.*

(Flatiron Theatre) Thursday, March 15–April 1, 2001 (11 performances and 5 previews) Butch Brady/Tontagram Shmulewitz presents:
BEARDED IRIS by David Stein; Director, David Calafiore; Press, Stephen Sunderlin CAST: Kelly Mizell (Iris), Kevin Varner (Gerald), Rahti Gordien (Mother), Joel Briel (Roger), Michael Rhodes (Gary)
A two-act comedy about two lovers trying to co-write a play.

(Raw Space) Friday, March 16–18, 2001 (3 performances) 2001: A Spotlight on Festival Odyssey presents:
THE CALLBACK by Robert C. Boston Jr. and **LEAVING TAMPA** by Edward Crosby Wells; Directors, Frank Calo and Ellen Sandberg; Design, Louis Lopardi; Press, S. Thornburg CASTS: Doc Fletcher, Richard Brundage, Robert C. Boston Jr., Ellen Sandberg, Sue Marticek
Two one-acts.

(HomeGrown Theater) Friday, March 16–April 21, 2001 (15 performances and 2 previews) The Homegrown Theater presents:
RUMBA Written/Directed/Choreographed by Wally Strauss; Press, Brett Singer CAST: Larry Bell (Victor Riesel), Asaaf Ben Shetrit, Jason McDermott, Petranella Jefferson, Maria Medina
A drama set in New York City, 1956.

(HERE) Friday, March 16–April 1, 2001 (12 performances) proto-type presents:
BUNNY'S LAST NIGHT IN LIMBO Written/Directed by Peter Petralia; Set, Betsy Ayer; Lighting, Rebecca Makus; Video, MGB; Costumes, Michelle Shaffer; Music, Max Giteck Duykers; Press, Spin Cycle/Shannon Jowett CAST: Tom Pilutik, David Sochet, Stephanie Sanditz, Lu Chekowsky, Dan Sherman
A dark comedy about a boy named Bunny.

Kevin Varner in *Bearded Iris* (Jeffrey Hornstein)

(Atlantic 453) Friday, March 16–April 8, 2001 (16 performances and 3 previews) The Women's Shakespeare Company presents:
LOVE'S LABOUR'S LOST by William Shakespeare; Director, Christopher Briggs; Set/Lighting, Jay Ryan; Costumes, Alejo Vietti; Press, Brett Singer CAST: Dorothy Abrahams, Laura Benedict, Melissa Bonaguide, Emily Mitchell, Rachel diCerbo, Clayton Dowty, Jillian Hahn, Kelli Lynn Harrison, Kate Hess, Ellen Lee, Catherine McNelis, Amy Rhodes, Kelly Ann Sharman, Karen Sternberg, Constance Zaytoun
An all-female production.

(American Globe Theatre) Saturday, March 17–April 8, 2001 (14 performances) The American Globe Theatre presents:
HEDDA GABLER by Henrik Ibsen; Director, John Basil; Set/Lighting, J. Reid Farrington and Morgan von Prelle Pecelli; Costumes, Terry Leong; Music, Scott O'Brien CAST: Richard Fay, Maureen Hayes, Melissa Hill, Elizabeth Keefe, Kelley McKinnon, David Munnell, Charles Tucker

(14th Street Y) Tuesday, March 20–April 1, 2001 (16 performances) Musicals Tonight!/Mel Miller presents:
LEAVE IT TO ME Music/Lyrics, Cole Porter; Book, Bella & Samuel Spewack; Director/Choreography, Thomas Mills; Musical Director/Vocal Arrangements, Mark Hartman; Lighting, Shuhei Seo; Casting, Stephen DeAngelis; Stage Manager, Shih-hui Wu CAST: Robin Baxter (Mrs. Goodhue), Keith Benedict (Grainger), Gordon Connell (J.H. Brody), Jamie Day (Dolly), J. Michael McCormack (Latvian Ambassador), Barbara McCulloh (Colette), Kenny Morris (Mr. Goodhue), Lois Saunders (Princess), Michael Scott (Buck Thomas), Ed Smit (French Ambassador), John Wasiniak (British Ambassador), Courtney Blythe, Liz Casasola, Christine Gonzales, Blythe Gruda, L.J. Mitchell, Seth Muse, Kurt Robbin, Will Woodrow
MUSICAL NUMBERS: How Do You Spell Ambassador, When the Hen Stops Laying, We Drink to You J.H. Brody, Vite Vite Vite, Taking the Steppes to Russia, Get Out of Town, Most Gentlemen Don't Like Love, Information Please, When All Is Said and Done, Comrade Alonzo, From Now On, I Want to Go Home, My Heart Belongs to Daddy, Tomorrow, Far Away, From the USA to the USSR, Wild Wedding Bells
A 1938 musical set in Russia.

Simon Jones, John Curless, Natacha Roi, Leslie Lyles, Maureen Anderman in *Passion Play* (Carol Rosegg)

Kelly Ann Sharman, Clayton Dowty, Karen Sternberg, Catherine McNelis in *Love's Labour's Lost* (Matthew Israel)

(Minetta Lane Theatre) Tuesday, March 20–May 6, 2001 (39 performances and 17 previews) Louise and Stephen Kornfeld, Kardana /Swinsky Productions, Karen Adler, and Teri Solomon Mitze, in association with Roy Gabay, Lawrence Roman present:
PASSION PLAY by Peter Nichols; Director, Elinor Renfield; Set, Narelle Sissons; Costumes, Christine Field; Lighting, Jeff Croiter; Sound, Ken Travis; Casting, Ilene Starger; Stage Manager, Allison Sommers; Press, Richard Kornberg/Tom D'Ambrosio CAST: Natacha Roi (Kate), Simon Jones (James), Maureen Anderman (Eleanor), Lucy Martin (Agnes), John Curless (Jim), Leslie Lyles (Nell), Peter Bradbury, Rosemarie DeWitt, Cynthia Hood, Claywood Sempliner
A 1981 two-act drama set in London. In 1983 the play was performed on Broadway as *Passion*.

(Cap 21 Theater) Tuesday, March 20–April 29, 2001 (35 performances and 7 previews) transferred to (Players Theater) Thursday, May 10–December 9, 2001 (243 performances) Gardenia Productions presents:
SIX GOUMBAS AND A WANNABE by Vincent M. Gogliormella; Director, Thomas G. Waites; Set/Lighting, Mark Bloom; Costumes, Lorree True; Sound, David Gilman; Stage Manager, Duff Dugan; Press, Media Blitz /Beck Lee CAST: George Bamford (Sonny Rigatoni), David Cera (Mike), Dan Grimaldi (Danny), Sian Heder (Rose/Cathy), Joe Iacovino (Tommy /Hotel Clerk), Tara Kapoor (Angela/Jen), Joe Maruzzo (Vinny), Annie McGovern (Gina), Ernest Mingione (Tony), Katherine Narducci (Anna), Sal Petraccione (Richie), Howard Spiegel (Wayne), Charles E. Wallace (Charles) SUCCEEDING CAST: James Lorenzo

(Center Stage NY) Wednesday, March 21–April 14, 2001 (13 performances and 5 previews) LAByrinth Theater Company presents:
THE TRAIL OF HER INNER THIGH by Erin Cressida Wilson; Director, John Gould Rubin; Set, Michelle Malavet; Costumes, Mimi O'Donnell; Lighting, David Lander; Sound, Elizabeth Rhodes; Music, Joseph Diebes; Choreography, Jill DeArmon; Video, Mariana Hellmund and Ernesto Solo; Stage Manager, Dawn Wagner; Press, Erin Dunn/Katie Miller CAST: Quincy Tyler Bernstine (Kymmie/Bunny/Stephanie), Jennifer Hall (Jolene), Laura Hughes (Patricia), Gina Maria Paoli (Maria), Johnny Sánchez (Kasper)
A multi-lingual erotic tale, performed without intermission.

Tannis Kowalchuk in *The Passion According to G.H.* (James Wengler)

(Access Theatre) Wednesday, March 21–April 14, 2001 (14 performances and 2 previews) North American Cultural Laboratory presents:

THE PASSION ACCORDING TO G.H. Adapted from the Brazilian novel by Claire Lispector; Director, Brad Krumholz; Press, Brett Singer CAST: Tannis Kowalchuk (G.H.)
A solo performance piece.

Thomas Toner, William H. Andrews in *Boss Grady's Boys* (Dave Cross)

(78th St. Theatre Lab) 78th Street Theatre Lab, in association with Organic Theater Company, presents:

BOSS GARDY'S BOYS by Sebastian Barry; Director, Ina Marlowe; Set /Lighting/Sound, Eric Nightengale; Costumes, Moira Shaughnessy; Casting, Josie Abady; Stage Manager, Kimberly Reiss; Press, Jim Baldassare CAST: William H. Andrews (Mick), Thomas Toner (Josey), Margo Skinner (Mrs. Malloy), Kay Michaels (Mrs. Swift), Alfred Cherry (Mr. Reagan), Bob Sonderskov (Father), Corliss Preston (Mother), Meghan Wolf (Girl)
A drama in two acts. The action takes place on a 40-acre hill farm on the Cork/Kerry border, Ireland.

(Walkerspace) Thursday, March 22–April 1, 2001 (10 performances)

FRANKIE'S WEDDING Created/Performed by Gabrielle Lansner; Set, Dean Taucher; Lighting, Jeff Croiter; Press, Grant Lindsey
A performance piece based on the character of Frankie Addams from Carson McCuller's *The Member of the Wedding.*

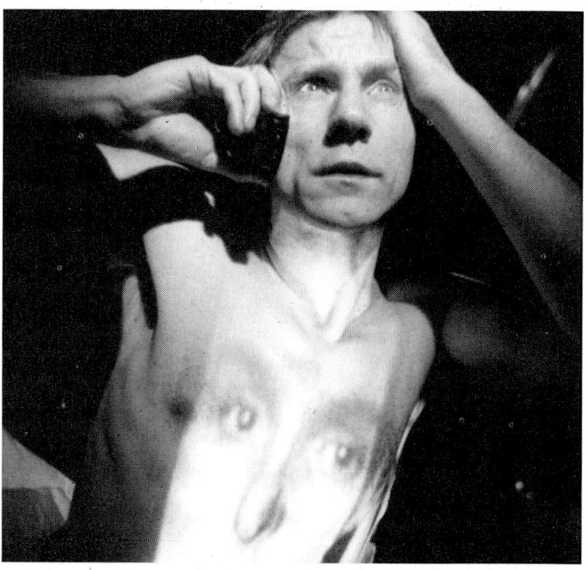

Simon McBurney in *Mnemonic* (Alastair Muir)

(John Jay College Theater) Thursday, March 22–May 24, 2001 (67 performances and 7 previews) Thomas Viertel, Steven Baruch, Marc Routh, Richard Frankel, Dede Harris/Lorie Cowen Levy, Timothy Childs, Herb Goldsmith, Libby Adler Mages/Mari Glick, and Margo Lion present:

MNEMONIC Conceived/Directed by Simon McBurney; Devised by the Theatre de Complicite Company; Design, Michael Levine; Costumes, Christina Cunningham; Lighting, Paul Anderson; Puppets, Simon Auton; Sound, Christopher Shutt; Stage Managers, Anita Ashwick, Arabella Powell; Press, Philip Rinaldi CAST: Katrin Cartlidge (Alice), Simon McBurney (Virgil), Tim McMullan (Prof. Spindler/Capsoni), Eric Mallet (BBC Correspondant/Innsbruck), Kostas Philippoglou (Greek Taxi Driver /Italian), Catherine Schaub Abkarian (Chambermaid in Brlin/Polish Half-Sister), Daniel Wahl (Piano Student/Swiss Doctor)
Two parallel stories: the discovery of an unidentified body in the Alps, and a woman's quest through Eastern Europe in search of the father she never knew.

(P.S. 122) Thursday, March 22–April 14, 2001 (15 performances) P.S. 122 presents:

THE GATHERING Written/Performed by Will Power; Press, Spin Cycle /Shannon Jowett
A hip-hop journey to meeting places of black men.

(Theater for the New City) Thursday, March 22–April 6, 2001 (10 performances) Theater for the New City presents:
THE OPEN GATE by David Willinger; Based on the novel *The Manor* by Isaac Bashevis Singer; Music, Arthur Abrams; Musical Director, Chris Cherney; Set, Mark Symzcak; Costumes, Terry Leong; Lighting, Aaron Meadow; Choreography, Shelia Kaminsky; Stage Manager, Erin Grayson CAST: Barbara Bleier, Darby Dizard, David Dotterer, Morgan Faro, Gary Hess, Erica Hanrahan, Kevin Hughes, Nicole Kaplan, Josh Kreitzman, Katherine Mester, Larry Picard, Matthew Reese, Primy Rivera, Bruce Sabath, Carolyn Seiff, Robert Silber, Sherie Weinstein
The action takes place in Poland during the 19th century.

(American Globe Theatre) Monday, March 26–April 10, 2001 (10 performances) The American Globe Theatre presents:
THE IMPORTANCE OF BEING EARNEST by Oscar Wilde; Director, Nathaniel Merchant; Set/Lighting, J. Reid Farrington and Morgan von Prelle Pecelli; Costumes, Melissa Richards; Music, Scott O'Brien; Press, Brett Singer CAST: Peter Parks Husovsky (Algernon), Julia McLaughlin (Lady Bracknell), Kathryn Savannah (Cecily), Anna Stone (Gwendolyn), David Wilcox (Jack), Rick Fortsmann, Julia Levo, Philip "Pip" Rogers
Performed in repertory with the company's *Hedda Gabler*.

(Producer's Club) Tuesday, March 27–April 1, 2001 (8 performances) Pemberton Productions present:
DON JUAN by Molière; Adaptation, Christopher Hampton; Directors, Gina Bonati and Dunsten J. Cormack; Costumes, Rosemary Ponzo; Press, Michelle Olofson CAST: Robert Lin Pemberton (Don Juan), Dunsten J. Cormack (Sganarelle)
A drama set in Sicily during the late 1600s.

(HERE) Tuesday, March 27–April 21, 2001 (15 and 5 previews) HERE presents:
POSSESSED Adapted by Robert Lyons and Kristin Marting from Fyodor Dostoevesky's novel; Director/Choreography, Ms. Marting; Set, David Morris; Costumes, Kay Voyce; Lighting, Christian Methot; Puppets, Kevin Augustine; Music, Matthew Pierce; Press, Richard Kornberg/Don Summa CAST: Paul Boocock, Thomas Shaw, Richard Toth, Cezar Williams (Nikolai Stavrogin), Mariana Newhard (Maria), Molly Ward (Liza Tishin)
A dramatic adaptation, with music and dance, of an 1872 novel. Each male actor plays some aspect of the main character.

(Connelly Theatre) Thursday, March 29–April 21, 2001 (17 performances and 7 previews) Moonwork Theater Company presents:
WHAT YOU WILL by William Shakespeare; Music, Andrew Sherman & Rusty Magee; Director, Gregory Wolfe; Musical Director, Mr. Magee; Set, Lowell Pettit; Costumes, Oana Botez-Ban; Lighting, David Sherman; Choreography, Lars Rosager; Fights, Chris Burmester; Casting, Rossmon; Stage Manager, Laura Fenton; Press, Shirley Herz/Sam Rudy, James Shubert CAST: Mason Pettit (Orsinio), Brandy Zale (Viola), Craig D. Pearlberg (Sebastian), Margaret Nichols (Olivia), Jason Cicci (Malvolio), Julie Dingman (Maria), Rusty Magee (Feste), Ron McClary (Sir Toby Belch), Tom Shillue (Sir Andrew Aguecheek), Chad Jacobson (Sir Topaz /Cesario), Isaiah DiLorenzo (Officer Leonardo), Erik Hayden (Officer Launce), Jeffrey Stephens (Valentine), Timothy Quinlan (Curio), Jena Necrason (Lucille), Robin Levine (Loretta), Michelle Nessie Fernandez (Lorraine), John Roque (Antonio), Joe Reina (Bartender)
A two-act musical adaptation. The action takes place at Club Illyria during World War II.

Paul Boocock, Richard Toth, Molly Ward in *Possessed* (Carol Rosegg)

The Company of *What You Will* (Peter Benson)

Chuck Richards in *Eula Mae* (Chuck Morgan)

(Jose Quintero Theatre) Friday, March 30–still playing May 31, 2001 Ninth Runner-Up Productions presents:
EULA MAE'S BEAUTY, BAIT & TACKLE by Frank Blocker and Chuck Richards; Director, Linda A. Patton; Set, William C. Landolina; Lighting, V.C. Fuqua, Chris Mahlmann; Stage Manager, Jana Llynn; Press, Publicity Outfitters/Timothy J. Haskell, Christopher Joy CAST: Helen Bessette (Eula Mae), Frank Blocker (Rev. Lester Burkett/Anna Mae/Carl Joe/Sue Sue Daniels), Chuck Richards succeeded by Tony Braswell (Eva Mae Raspberry/Rita Mae Raspberry)
A comedy in two acts. The action takes place in Odeopolis, AL.

(Urban Stages) Friday, March 30–April 21, 2001 (15 performances and 2 previews) The Women's Expressive Theatre presents:
BOLD GIRLS by Rona Munro; Director, Hayley Finn; Press, Publicity Outfitters/Timothy J. Haskell, Christopher Joy CAST: Sasha Eden, Denise Lute, Sally Wheeler, Marian Tomas Griffin
A drama set in Belfast, Ireland, 1991.

The Company of *Urinetown* (Joan Marcus)

(American Theater of Actors) Sunday, April 1–June 25, 2001 (58 performances and 40 previews); Transferred to Broadway's Henry Miller Theatre on Monday, August 27, 2001 The Araca Group and Dodger Theatricals, in association with TheatreDreams Inc. and Lauren Mitchell, present:
URINETOWN; Music/Lyrics, Mark Hollmann; Book/Lyrics, Greg Kotis; Director, John Rando; Musical Director, Edward Strauss; Musical Staging, John Carrafa; Orchestrations, Bruce Coughlin; Set/Environmental Design, Scott Pask; Costumes, Jonathan Bixby, Gregory Gale; Lighting, Brian MacDevitt; Sound, Jeff Curtis; Fights, Rick Sordelet; Cast Recording, RCA: Casting, Jay Binder, Cindi Rush, Laura Stanczyk; Stage Manager, Julia P. Jones; Press, Chris Boneau-Adrian Bryan-Brown/Jim Byk, Kel Christofferson CAST: Jeff McCarthy (Officer Lockstock), Spencer Kayden (Little Sally), Nancy Opel (Penelope Pennywise), Hunter Foster succeeded by Marcus Lovett (Bobby Strong), Jennifer Laura Thompson (Hope Cladwell), David Beach (Mr. McQueen), John Deyle (Senator Fipp), Ken Jennings (Old Man Strong/Hot Blades Harry), Rick Crom (Tiny Tom/Dr. Billeaux), Rachel Coloff (Soupy Sue/Cladwell's Secretary), Megan Lawrence succeeded by Jennifer Cody (Little Becky Two Shoes /Mrs. Millennium), Victor W. Hawks (Robbie the Stockfish/Business Man #1), Lawrence Street (Billy Boy Bill/Business Man #2), Kay Walbye (Old Woman/Josephine Strong), Daniel Marcus (Officer Barrel), John Cullum (Caldwell B. Cladwell)
MUSICAL NUMBERS: Overture, Urinetown, Privilege to Pee, Mr. Cladwell, Cop Song, Follow Your Heart, Look at the Sky, Don't Be the Bunny, Act One Finale, What Is Urinetown?, Snuff That Girl, Run Freedom Run, Why Did I Listen to That Man?, Tell Her I Love Her, We're Not Sorry, I See a River
A musical comedy in two acts. The action takes place in Urinetown, a city where it's no longer free to pee.

Tricia Paoluccio, Tony Church, Joey Kern in *Troilus & Cressida* (Ken Howard)

(American Place Theatre) Tuesday, April 3–May 13, 2001 (30 performances and 13 previews) Theatre for a New Audience presents:
TROILUS & CRESSIDA by William Shakespeare; Director, Sir Peter Hall; Set, Douglas Stein; Costumes, Martin Pakledinaz; Lighting, Scott Zielinski; Music, Herschel Garfein; Fights, B.H. Barry; Casting, Deborah Brown; Stage Manager, Alexis Shorter; Press, Gary Springer-Susan Chicoine/Joe Trentacosta CAST: Vivienne Benesch (Cassandra), Jordan Charney (Alexander/Menelaus), Tony Church (Pandarus), David Conrad (Hector), Idris Elba (Achilles), Philip Goodwin (Ulysses), Thomas M. Hammond (Aeneas), Earl Hindman (Ajax), Cindy Katz (Helen), Nicholas Kepros (Nestor), Joey Kern (Troilus), Luke Kirby (Deiphobus/Patroclus), Andrew Elvis Miller (Helenus), Tricia Paoluccio (Cressida), Lorenzo Pisoni (Paris), Frank Raiter (Priam/Calchas), Terence Rigby (Agamemnon), Michael Rogers (Diomedes), Matt Semler (Antenor), Tari Signor (Andromache), Andrew Weems (Thersites)
Performed with one intermission.

A singer in *Dralion* (Al Seib)

(Liberty State Park) Wednesday, April 4–June 10, 2001 (86 performances and 7 previews) Cirque Du Soleil presents:
DRALION Director, Guy Caron; Creative Director, Gilles Ste-Croix; Acrobatic Designs, Li Xi Ning; Costumes, François Barbeau; Sets, Stéphane Roy; Lighting, Luc Lafortune; Music, Violaine Corradi; Choreography, Julie Lachance; Sound, Guy Desrochers; Press, Publicity Office/Marc Thibodeau CAST: Viktor Kee, Geneviève Bessette, Han Yan, Li Qin, Wang Dongguo, Zhang Hongwei, Blas Villalpando, Guto Vasconcelos, John Gilkey, Gonzalo Muñoz
The lateste edition of the theatrical circus troupe features 56 artists from eight countries.

(Ensemble Studio Theatre) Thursday, April 5–29, 2001 (18 performances and 4 previews) The Alfred P. Sloan Foundation and Ensemble Studio Theatre present:
LOUIS SLOTIN SONATA by Paul Mullin; Director, David Moore; Set, Rachel Hauck; Costumes, Amela Baksic; Lighting, Greg MacPherson; Sound, Robert Gould; Stage Manager, James W. Carringer; Press, Erin Dunn /Katie Miller CAST: William Salyers (Dr. Louis Slotin/Joseph Mengele), Amy Love (Nurse Dickie), Patrick Cleary (Robert Oppenheimer), Joel Rooks (Albert Einstein/Israel Slotin), Allyn Burrows (Philip Morrison), Bill Cwikowski, Richmond Hoxie, Ezra Knight, Matthew Lawler
A drama inspired by a scientist's accident in 1946.

(Village Theater) Tuesday, April 10, 2001–January 5, 2003 (713 performances and 13 previews) Jennifer Dumas, Jack Cullen, Patricia Watt, and Jeff Rosen, in association with Laura Joplin and Michael Joplin, present:
LOVE, JANIS Conceived/Adapted/Directed by Randal Myler; Based on the book by Laura Joplin; Musical Director/Arrangements, Sam Andrew; Design, Jules Fisher & Peggy Eisenhauer; Costumes, Robert Blackman; Projections, Bo G. Eriksson; Sound, Tony Meola; Creative Consultant, Scooter Weintraub; Casting, Jessica Gilburne & Ed Urban; Stage Manager, Jack Gianino; Press, Gary Springer-Susan Chicoine/Michelle Moretta CAST: Catherine Curtin (Janis-private), Andrea Mitrovich and Cathy Richardson (Janis Joplin-public), Seth Jones (Interviewer)
A musical biography in two acts.

(Promenade Theatre) Tuesday, April 10–June 24, 2001 Madame Melville Producing Partners, in association with Sonny Everett, Tel Tulchin, Darren Bagert and Aaron Levy, present:
MADAME MELVILLE Written/Directed by Richard Nelson; Set, Thomas Lynch; Costumes, Susan Hilferty; Lighting, Jennifer Tipton; Sound, Scott Myers; Casting, Mark Bennett; Stage Manager, Matthew Silver; Press, Publicity Office/Bob Fennell CAST: Macaulay Culkin (Carl), Joely Richardson (Claudie Melville), Robin Weigert (Ruth)
A drama performed without intermission. The action takes place in Paris, 1966.

Macaulay Culkin, Joely Richardson in *Madame Melville* (Joan Marcus)

Andra Mitrovich and band in *Love, Janis*

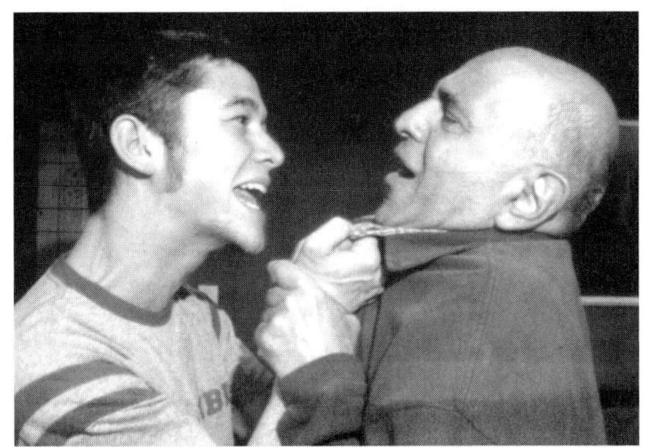

Joseph Gordon-Levitt, George Morfogen in *Uncle Bob* (Yasuyuki Takagi)

(Soho Playhouse) Wednesday, April 11–July 1, 2001 (78 performances and 15 previews) Rebellion Theatre Company presents:

UNCLE BOB by Austin Pendleton; Director, Courtney Moorehead; Set, Matt Corsover, Andrew Sendor; Costumes, Pamela Snider; Lighting, Jason A. Cina; Fights, Lee Willet; Stage Manager, Jason Sutton; Press, Tony Origlio CAST: George Morfogen (Bob), Gale Harold succeeded by Joseph Gordon-Levitt

A new production of the 1995 drama in two acts. The action takes place in the West Village.

(Gershwin Hotel) Thursday, April 12–30, 2001 (16 performances) Moibus Group Productions presents:

JITTERBUGGING: SCENES OF SEX IN A NEW SOCIETY by Richard Nelson; Freely adapted from Arthur Schnitzler's *La Ronde* as translated by Helga Ciulei; Director, Paul Uricioli; Set/Costumes, Rick Gradone; Lighting, Tyler Micoleau; Sound, Stefan Jacobs; Stage Manager, Kara Bain; Press, Spin Cycle/Ron Lasko, Shannon Jowett CAST: Paul Marcarelli (G.I. /Husband), Jen Davis (Whore/Young Married Woman), Cynthia Carroll (Maid/Sweet Young Singer), Douglas Mancs (Hotel Manager/Mayor)

The action takes place in and around a small New England city on the Atlantic Ocean, 1947.

Paul Marcarelli in *Jitterbugging*

Naava Piatka in *Better Don't Talk*

(Blue Heron Arts Center) Tuesday, April 17–22, 2001 (8 performances) Blue Heron Arts Center presents:

BETTER DON'T TALK Written/Performed by Naava Piatka; Press, Peter Cromarty/Alice Cromarty

A one-woman show about a daughter discovering her mother's hidden past.

(Puerto Rican Traveling Theatre) Wednesday, April 18–May 27, 2001 (34 performances and 8 previews) Puerto Rican Traveling Theatre presents:

THE HOUSE MUST BE DISMANTLED by Sebastian Junyent; Translation, Asa Zatz; Director, Alba Oms; Set, Regina Garcia; Lighting, Sarah Sidman; Costumes, Barbara Kent; Press, Max Eisen/Corinne Hall CAST: Fulvia Vergel, Georgina Corbo

A drama about two sisters who come together to settle their parents' estate. performances in English and Spanish.

(Altered Stages) Friday, April 20–May 6, 2001 (14 performances) Ergo Theatre Company presents:

PERSONALS Book/Lyrics, David Crane, Seth Friedman, Marta Kauffman; Music, William K. Dreskin, Joel Phillip Friedman, Seth Friedman, Alan Menken, Stephen Schwartz, Michael Skyloff; Director/Choreography, Robert Jay Cronin; Musical Director/Arrangements, Charles Alterman; Costumes, David Kaley; Lighting, Martin E. Vreeland; Stage Manager, Jeffrey Landman; Press, Jennifer Johnson CAST: Jedidiah Cohen (Louis et al.), Todd Alan Crain (Richard et al.), Joe Farrell (Sam et al.), Anika Larsen (Claire et al.), Johanna Pinzler (Patty et al.), Hazel Anne Raymundo (Kim et al.)

MUSICAL NUMBERS: Nothing to Do with Love, After School Special, Mama's Boys, A Night Alone, I Think You Should Know, Second Grade, Imagine My Surprise, I'd Rather Dance Alone, Moving in with Linda, I Could Always Go to You, Michael, The Guy I Love, A Little Happiness, Picking Up the Pieces, Some Things Don't End

A 1985 musical revue in two acts.

The Company of *Personals* (Greg Gorman)

(Theater for the New City) Wednesday, April 25–May 26, 2001 (16 performances and 4 previews) Irondale Ensemble Project presents:
IN THE JUNGLE OF THE CITY by Bertolt Brecht; Translation, Philip Boehm; Director, Jim Niesen; Set, Ken Rothchild; Costumes, Christine Myers; Lighting, Randy Glickman; Music, Walter Thompson; Choreography, Sarah Adams; Stage Manager, Maria Knapp; Press, Tony Origlio/Joel Treick CAST: Sarah Adams, Christian Brandjes, Carolyn Fischer, Michael-David Gordon, Terry Greiss, Jack Lush, Sven Miller, Patrena Murray, Damen Scranton
A new translation of a drama set in Chicago, 1912.

(Abrons Art Center) Wednesday, April 25–May 20, 2001 (10 performances and 2 previews) The National Black Touring Circuit presents:
BEAUTIFUL THINGS Written/Directed by Selaelo Maredi; Set, Terry Chandler; Costumes, Anita D. Ellis; Lighting, Antoinette Tynes; Sound, David Wright; Press, Max Eisen/Corinne Hall CAST: Selaelo Maredi (Muzi), Ramadumetja Rasebotsa (Noni)
A drama set in South Africa.

Brigitte Barnett, Blair Singer in *Goodnight Irene* (Jonathan Slaff)

(14th Street Y) Wednesday, April 25–May 20, 2001 (17 performances and 3 previews) Hypothetical Theatre Company presents:
GOODNIGHT IRENE by Ari Roth; Director, David Mowers; Set, Mark Symczak; Lighting, Kevin Hardy; Costumes, T. Michael Hall; Sound, Tim Cramer; Press, Jonathan Slaff CAST: Blair Singer (Ethan Goodman), Brigitte Barnett, Lona Leigh, Tammy Meneghini, Leopold Lowe
A serious comedy about a liberal troublemaker.

(Hudson Guild Theatre) Friday, April 27–May 20, 2001 (19 performances and 5 previews) Abingdon Theatre Company presents:
THE APPOINTMENT by Bob Clyman; Director, Wendy Liscow; Set, Jeremy Douchette; Costumes, Karen Ledger; Stage Manager, Ernest Delli Santi III; Press, Brett Singer CAST: Robert Arcaro, Joey Collins, Dan Cordle, Kit Flanagan, Rohana Kenin, Pamela Paul
A murder myster and dark comedy set in New York City.

(The Duke) Saturday, April 21–May 13, 2001 (16 performances and 10 previews) The Jewish Repertory Theatre presents:
THE GARDENS OF FRAU HESS by Milton Frederick Marcus; Director, Rhoda R. Herrick; Set, Richard Ellis; Costumes, Gail Cooper-Hecht; Lighting, Richard Latta; Sound, Steve Shapiro; Stage Manager, Marci A. Glotzer; Press, Pete Sanders/Jim Mannino CAST: Lisa Bostnar (Ilse), Joel Leffert (Isaac)
A drama in two acts. The action takes place in Germany, 1944.

(Ohio Theatre) Wednesday, May 2–June 10, 2001 (33 performances and 8 previews) The Foundry Theatre presents:
LIPSTICK TRACES: *A Secret History of the Twentieth Century* Conceived /Directed by Shawn Sides; Adapted by Kirk Lynn from a book by Greil Marcus; Lighting, Heather Carson; Sound, Darron L. West; Stage Manager, Sarah Richardson; Press, Chris Boneau-Adrian Bryan-Brown /Jim Byk CAST: Lana Lesley (DR. Narrator), Jason Liebrecht (Johnny Rotten), David Greenspan (Malcolm McLaren), James Urbaniak (Guy Debord/Steve Jones/Hugo Ball), T. Ryder Smith (Richard Huelsenbeck /Glen Matlock), Ean Sheehy (John of Leyden/Tristan Tzara/Michael Mourre)
An alternative history of the 20th century. Originally created/presented by Austin, TX theatre company Rude Mechs.

Dan Cordle, Rohana Kenin, Pamela Paul in *The Appointment* (Tom Bloom)

Joel Leffert, Lisa Bostnar in *The Gardens of Frau Hess* (Carol Rosegg)

(Women's Project Theatre) Wednesday, May 2–13, 2001 (12 performances and 1 preview) The Acting Company, in association with Women's Project & Productions, presents:

O PIONEERS! From the novel by Willa Cather; Adaptation/Lyrics, Darrah Cloud; Music/Orchestrations, Kim D. Sherman; Director, Richard Corley; Musical Director, Kimberly Grigsby; Set, Loy Arcenas; Costumes, Murrell Dean Horton; Lighting, Dennis Parichy; Sound, David A. Arnold; Stage Manager, Cole P. Bonenberger; Press, Gary Springer-Susan Chicoine/Joe Trentacosta, Judy Katz CAST: Matt Hoverman (Oscar), Grace Hsu (Marie), Gregory Jackson (Carl), Royden Mills (Lou), Evan Robertson (Emil), Todd Cerveris (Amadée), Michael Thomas Holmes (Frank), Jonathan Uffelman (Ivar), Erica Rolfsrud)

A play with music based on a 1913 novel. The action takes place on the plains of Nebraska, 1890s.

(Red Room) Thursday, May 3–26, 2001 (13 performances) Bon Bock Productions, in association with Horse Trade Theatre Group, presents:

ROOM TO SWING AN AXE Written/Directed/Designed by Alex Dawson CAST: Craig McNulty (Gaz), Joseph Pacillo (Jack)

A story of friendship performed as a series of dueling monologues.

and

SLIGHT OF HAND by Gareth Smith; Director, Eric Werner CAST: Robin Dawn Arocha (Marissa), Hollis Doherty (Allison), Michael Healey (Bob), David Law (Derek), Terence Patrick Schappert (Jack), Ellen Thompson (Dori)

The action takes place in the backyard of a New England B&B.

(Currican Theatre) Thursday, May 3–26, 2001 (18 performances) Grass Arena, in association with The Tennessee Project, presents:

ARMITAGE SHANKS: *(a play about piss and vinegar in an age of anxiety)* Written/Directed by Kirk Marcoe; Set, David Markowitz; Costumes, Tina Nigro; Lighting, Dave Overcamp; Sound, Recorded Books; Press, Spin Cycle/Shannon Jowett CAST: D.J. Mendel (Carl), Tim McGee (Jospeh), Jessma Evans (Laura), Raquel Cion (Mrs. Tendreese)

A dark comedy about four would-be terrorists.

(Theatre 3) Saturday, May 5–20, 2001 (12 performances and 4 previews) Judith Shakespeare Company presents:

THE TEMPEST by William Shakespeare; Director, Joanne Zipay; Set, Luke Cantarella; Costumes, One Choi; Lighting, Joel Moritz; Music, Kathy Devine; Movement, Elizabeth Mozer; Press, Shirley Herz/Sam Rudy, James Shubert CAST: Jane Titus (Prospero), Hilary Ward (Miranda), Antonio del Rosario (Caliban), Dacyl Acevedo (Ariel), Steven Fales (Ferdinand), Michael Shattner (Stephano), Suzanne Hayes (Trinculo), Peter Zazzali (Antonio), Ivanna Cullinan (Sebastian), Bill Galarno (Gonzalo), Joseph Primavera (Alonso), Laurie Bannister-Colon, Christiana Blain, Lea C. Franklin, Jennifer Jonassen, Richard Kass, Michelle Kovacs, Angie Moore, Kevin Till

This production sets the action in the modern era.

(Producers Club II) Wednesday, May 9–26, 2001 (23 performances)

DAN BREDEMANN-1 MAN IN REP Written/Performed by Dan Bredemann; Press, Brett Singer

Two one-man plays: *The Museum of Cures* and *Pictures of Me, Actually-An Evening of Stand-Up with Lewis Carroll.*

(St. Clement's) Wednesday, May 9–June 2, 2001 (27 performances) The Chekhov Theater Ensemble presents:

THE VOCAL LORDS by Eric Winick; Director, Floyd Rumohr; Musical Director, Kelly Ellenwood; Musical Supervisor, David Andrews Rogers; Set, Russell Michael Schramm; Costumes, Andrea Huelse; Lighting, Dominic Housiaux; Sound, Stefan Jacobs; Stage Manager, Janine Vanderhoff CAST: Joseph Ragno (Marty), Philip Levy (Steve), Ethan James Duff (Butchie), Fred Berman (Tudie)

A play with doo-wop music. The action takes place in Brooklyn and Manhattan, flashing between the late 1950s and late 1990s.

Livia Newman, Scott C. Reeves in *Historic Times* (Jamie Santos)

(78th St. Theatre Lab) Thursday, May 10–June 3, 2001 (13 performances and 3 previews) 78th Street Theatre Lab presents:

HISTORIC TIMES by Andrew Case; Director, Carolyn Rendell; Set, Jane Mancini; Costumes, Deanna Berg; Lighting/Sound, Eric Nightengale; Choreography, Tesha Busse; Fights, Dan O'Driscoll; Press, Jim Baldassare CAST: Scott C. Reeves (Adorno), Livia Newman (Parker), Evan Zes (Schoenberg), Zander Teller (Stravinsky), Kate Cordaro (Dorothy Chandler), Christian Pedersen (Goldwyn), Keri Setaro (Valerie Vail), Jeremy Alan Richards (Police), Richard Abrams

A drama set in Los Angeles during two different time periods: World War II and 1999.

(Pulse Theatre) Friday, May 11–26, 2001 (15 performances) Lightning Strikes Theatre Company presents:

IN THE PARLANCE by Richard Harland Smith; Director, Keith Oncale; Press, Brett Singer CAST: Stephen Aloi, Rozie Bacchi, Roy Bacon, Annmarie Benedict, Tom Bolster, Jeff Buckner, Tom Cappadona, Nicholas Coleman, Julie Hera DeStefano, Martin Everall, Larry Fleischman, Jay Aubrey Jones, Lou Kylis, Michelle Maryk, J. Richey Nash, Robyn Parsons, Mikhail Pogul, D.L. Shroder

An intellectual comedy.

(Altered Stages) Friday, May 11–June 2, 2001 (12 performances) New Avenue Theatre Project presents:

FOUR NOTES AND A BLENDER by Larry Bell; Director, Robert McCaskill; Set, Zeke Leonard; Lighting, Jason Livingston CAST: Larry Bell, Lisa Lyons, Tyagi Schwartz, Celia Schaefer

A comedy of marital mixups.

(Blue Heron Arts Center) Friday, May 11–27, 2001 (14 performances and 6 previews) The Development Wing, Robert Kravitz, Evangeline Morpphos, Karen Davidov, Noel Ashman, Jason Kahan, Richard Rothenberg, Adam Ernster, Vlaire Kelly, and Up and Coming present:

BLOOD ORANGE by David Weiner; Director, Anders Cato; Set, John McDermott; Costumes, Richard Pierce; Lighting, Justin Burleson; Sound, Roger Raines; Fights, Paul Molnar; Stage Manager, Paul A. Kochman CAST: Jonathan Hova (Ernie-BoBo), Julienne Hanzelka Kim (The Girl), Ilene Kristen (Linda), Susan Pellegrino (Jill), Brian Sacca (Ray-Ray), Pablo T. Schreiber (Clinton), Wendy vanden Heuvel (Angela)

A drama performed without intermission. The action takes place in California in the summer of 1980.

(P.S.122) Wenesday, May 16–June 2, 2001 (12 performances and 2 previews) reopened Tuesday, July 24–August 25, 2001 Performance Space 122 presents:

SHUT UP AND LOVE ME; Written/Performed by Karen Finley; Lighting, Frank Den Danto III; Press, Spin Cycle/Ron Lasko

A collection of pieces about sex.

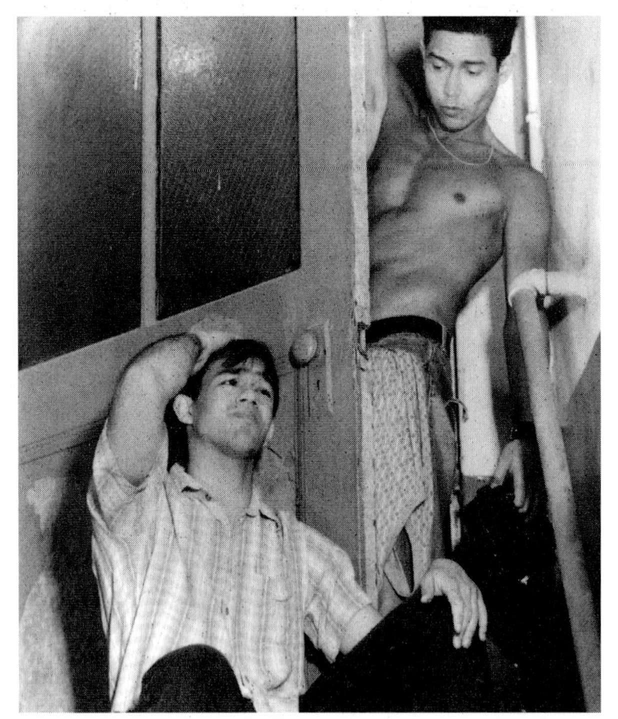

Orlando Pabotoy, Anthony Ruivivar in *Watcher* (Nigel Teare)

(Cap 21 Theatre) Friday, May 18–June 17, 2001 (23 performances and 6 previews) Ma-Yi Theatre Company presents:
WATCHER by Han Ong; Director/Set, Loy Arcenas; Costumes, Clint E.B. Ramos; Lighting, James Vermeulen; Sound/Music, Fabian Obispo; Stage Manager, Cristina Sison; Press, Peter Cromarty/Alice Cromarty CAST: Mia Katigbak (Loretta), Marty Zentz (Man/Boy), Orlando Pabotoy (Angelo), Gilbert Cruz (Cinquenta), Virginia Wing (Bessie), Jojo Gonzalez (Jun), Anthony Ruivivar (Nestor), Ching Valdes Aran (Tia Maria), Harvey Perr (Johnson)
A drama in two acts. The action takes place in Times Square.

(New Victory Theatre) Friday, May 18–June 3, 2001 (18 performances) The New 42nd Street presents:
ANTIGRAVITY'S CRASH TEST DUMMIES Director/Choreography, Christopher Harrison; Original Concept, Duncan Pettigrew and Mr. Harrison; Set, Jonah Logan; Costumes, Shelly Bomb; Lighting, Herrick Goldman; Sound, Mr. Weir; Music, Sxip Shirey and Paul Weir; Stage Managers, Jenifer A. Sheniker, Keith England; Press, Kevin P. McAnarney CAST: Amy Gordon, Jonah Logan, Jonathan Nosan, Colt Sandberg, Kamila Zapytowski, Tatyana Petruk
The Antigravity troupe, an urban aerial performance company, in a new performance piece.

(HERE) Saturday, May 19–June 9, 2001 (15 performances and 2 previews) New Georges and HERE present:
THE RIGHT WAY TO SUE by Ellen Melaver; Director, Anne Kauffman; Set, Susan Zeeman Rogers; Costumes, Michael Krass; Lighting, Gwen Grossman; Sound, Samuel C. Tresler; Stage Manager, Terry Dale; Press, Jim Baldassare CAST: Jennifer Morris (Maggie), Kelly AuCoin (Tom), Stephanie Brooke (Sue), T.R. Knight (Franklin/Jersey Moms), Caitlin Miller (Trina), Robert English (Walter)
A comedy set in New York City and New Jersey.

(The Duke) Sunday, May 20–June 17, 2001 (17 performances and 16 previews) The Jewish Repertory Theatre presents:
A NAUGHTY KNIGHT Music/Lyrics, Chuck Strand; Book/Director, William Martin; Musical Director, Steven Silverstein; Choreography, Dennis Dennehy; Set/Costumes, Frank J. Boros; Lighting, Jason Kankel; Sound, Randy Hansen; Stage Manager, D.C. Rosenberg; Press, Pete Sanders/Jim Mannino CAST: Rebecca Kupka (Lady Constance), Mark Manley (Gerber), Christopher J. Hanke (Jervis), Gordon Joseph Weiss (King Berger), Rebecca Rich (Lady Esther), Kurt Domoney, Paul Romero, John Michael Coppola (Guards), Mark Manley
A musical comedy loosely based on Mark Twain's fable *A Medieval Romance.*

(present Company Theatorium) Wednesday, May 23–June 9, 2001 (12 performances) The Key Theatre presents:
TWO GIRLS FROM VERMONT by John Kaufmann; Director, Liesl Tommy; Music Director, Doug Brandt; Costumes, Carolyn Humphrey; Lighting, Faye Armon; Sound, Nick Micozzi; Choreography, Brent Smith; Press, Spencer-Addison/Cara Moore CAST: Doug Brandt, Drew Frady, James Garver, Michael Giese, Stephanie Goldman, Nathan Halvorson, Carolyn Humphrey, Jeff Long, Jim Taylor McNickle, Tiffany May, Molly Mullin, Braden Joy Poposil, Alex Staggs, Doug Thoms
A "dirty pop extravaganza."

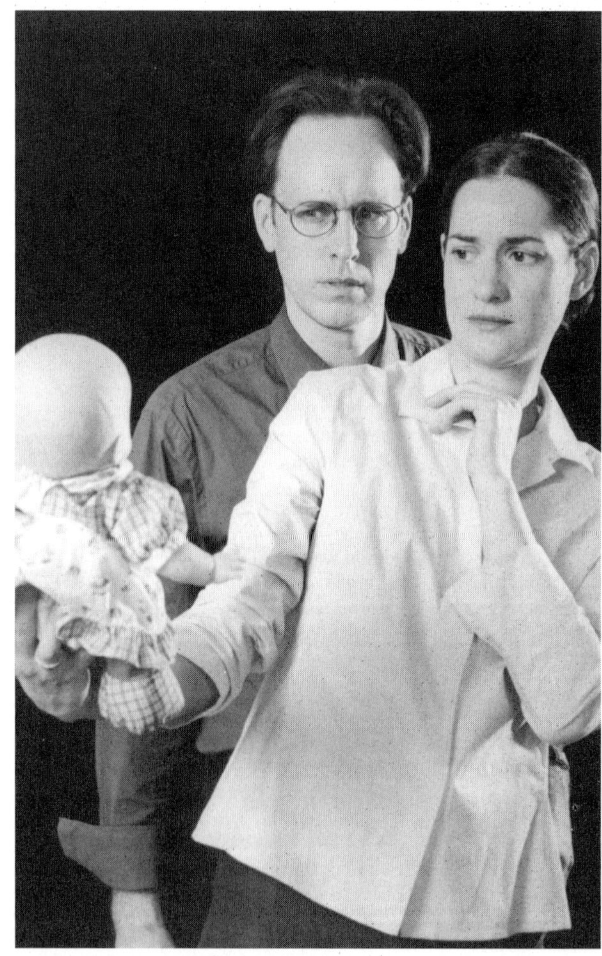

Kelly AuCoin, Jennifer Morris in *The Right Way to Sue* (Richard Termine)

(McGinn/Cazale Theatre) Thursday, May 24–July 1, 2001 (23 performances and 12 previews) New Federal Theatre/Woodie King Jr presents:

EVERY DAY A VISITOR by Richard Abrons; Director, Arthur Strimling; Set, Robert Joel Schwartz; Costumes, Dawn Robyn Petrlik; Lighting, Shirley Prendergast; Casting, McCorkle Casting; Stage Manager, Kim M.T. Jones; Press, Max Eisen/Corinne Hall CAST: Lisa Bostnar (Dr. Robinson), Tom Brennan (Feltenstein/Henry Kissinger), John Friemann (Stoopak), Sylvia Gassell (Mrs. Fanny Levy/EPA Administrator), Kenneth Gray (Bob), Helen Hanft (Mrs. Tillie Marcus/Bella Abzug), Joe Jamrog (Leon Davidowitz), Jerry Matz (Albert Grossman/Alan Greenspan), Anthony Spina (Figliozo/Mayor La Guardia), Fiona Walsh (Nurse Riley/Mrs. Lowenstein)

A comedy in two acts. The action takes place in a Jewish seniors home in the Upper Bronx.

Keither Baxter, Jared Reed in *The Woman in Black* (Craig Schwartz)

(Minetta Lane Theatre) Tuesday, May 29–July 8, 2001 (40 performances and 8 previews) Don Gregory presents:

THE WOMAN IN BLACK Adapted by Stephen Mallatratt; From the book by Susan Hill; Director, Patrick Garland; Set, James Noone; Costumes, Noel Taylor; Lighting, Ken Billington, Brian Monahan; Sound, Chris R. Walker; Stage Manager, J.P. Elins; Press, Bill Evans CAST: Keith Baxter (Arthgur Kipps), Jared Reed (The Actor), Leslie Kalarchian (Woman in Black)

A ghost story performed without intermission. The action takes place in a small Victorian theatre. This play has been a long-running success in London's West End.

(Blue Heron Arts Center) Thursday, May 31–June 2001 Verse Theatre Manhattan presents:

KINGS by Christopher Logue; Based on Samuel Butler's translation of the books of Homer's *Iliad*; Director, James Milton; Set/Lighting, Melissa Parrish; Press, Shirley Herz/Nancy Khuu CAST: James Doherty, Michael T. Ringer

Part II of Christopher Logue's adaptation of Homer's *Illiad. War* is part I and *The Husbands* is part III.

PROFESSIONAL REGIONAL COMPANIES

Highlights

ALLEY THEATRE

Houston, Texas
Nineteenth Season

Artistic Director, Gregory Boyd; Managing Director, Paul R. Tetreault

ARSENIC AND OLD LACE by Joseph Kesselring; Set Design, Kevin Rigdon; Costume Design, Jeanne Button; Lighting Design, Paulie Jenkins; Sound Design, Malcolm Nicholls; Friday, June 30–July 16, 2000 CAST: James Belcher (Teddy Brewster), James Black (Jonathan Brewster), Kevin Cooney (Mr. Gibbs/Officer O'Hara/Mr. Witherspoon), Bettye Fitzpatrick (Abby Brewster), Lillian Evans (Martha Brewster), Elizabeth Heflin (Elaine Harper), Paul Hope (Officer Brophy), Charles Krohn (Rev. Dr. Harper/Lieutenant Rooney), Ty Mayberry (Officer Klein), John Tyson (Dr. Einstein), Todd Waite (Mortimer Brewster)

TOWARDS ZERO by Agatha Christie; Set Design, Kevin Rigdon; Costume Design, Jeanne Button; Lighting Design, Paulie Jenkins; Sound Design, Malcolm Nicholls; Friday, July 21–August 6, 2000 CAST: James Belcher (Superintendent Battle), Michelle Federer (Audrey Strange), Lillian Evans (Lady Tressilian), Elizabeth Heflin (Mary Aldin), Paul Hope (Thomas Royde), Julia Krohn (Kay Strange), Charles Krohn (Matthew Treves), Ty Mayberry (Ted Latimer), Michael Tisdale (Neville Strange), John Tyson (Inspector Leach)

A MIDSUMMER NIGHT'S DREAM by William Shakespeare; Set Design, Vincent Mountain; Costume Design, Judith Anne Dolan; Lighting Design, Chris Parry; Sound Design, Malcolm Nicholls; Large Stage Friday, October 6–November 4, 2000 CAST: James Belcher (Egeus/Snout), James Black (Bottom), Chris Henry Coffey (Lysander), Elizabeth Heflin (Hippolyta/Titania), Laura Heisler (Hermia), Paul Hope (Starveling), Charles Krohn (Quince), Teri Lamm (Helena), Ty Mayberry (Demetrius), David Rainey (Snug), Jonathan Scarfe (Puck/Philostrate), John Tyson (Flute), Todd Waite (Theseus/Oberon)

CLOSER by Patrick Marber; Director, Stephen Rayne; Set Design, Kevin Rigdon; Costume Design, Esther Marquis; Lighting Design, Michael Lincoln, Sound Design, Malcolm Nicholls; Neuhaus Arena Stage Friday, October 20–November 19, 2000 CAST: Michelle Federer (Alice), John Wojda (Dan), Russ Anderson (Larry), Jenna Stern (Anna)

A CHRISTMAS CAROL adaptation from book by Charles Dickens; Director, Stephen Rayne; Set Design, Doug Schmidt; Costume Design, Esther Marquis; Lighting Design, Rui Rita; Sound Design, Malcolm Nicholls; Large Stage Monday, November 20–December 31, 2000 CAST: James Belcher (Ebenezer Scrooge), Bettye Fitzpatrick (Miss Goodleigh/Mrs. Dilber), Elizabeth Heflin (Spirit of Christmas Past/Mrs. O'Malley), Paul Hope (Coutts/Fezziwig), Charles Krohn (Marley/Priest/Old Joe), Ty Mayberry (Phizz/Belle's Husband), David Rainey (Spirit of Christmas Present/Poor Man), John Tyson (Bob Cratchit), Todd Waite

EQUUS by Peter Shaffer; Director, Gregory Boyd; Set and Lighting Design, Kevin Rigdon; Costume Design, Jeanne Button and Andrea Lauer, Sound Design, Malcolm Nicholls; Large Stage Friday, January 12–February 10, 2001 CAST: James Belcher (Frank Strang), James Black (Martin Dysart), Elizabeth Heflin (Hesther Salomon), Laura Heisler (Nurse), Teri Lamm (Jill Mason), Ty Mayberry (Young Horseman/Nugget), Ben Nordstrom (Alan Strang), David Rainey (Harry Dalton), Jeanne Ruskin (Dora Strang), Todd Waite (Horse)

SYNERGY by Keith Reddin; World Premiere; Set Design, Kevin Rigdon; Costume Design, Karyl Newman; Lighting Design, Michael Lincoln; Sound Design, Malcolm Nicholls; Neuhaus Arena Stage Friday, February 2–March 4, 2001 CAST: Jenny Maguire (Deb), Eric Sheffer Stevens (Marc), Edmond Genest (Devil), Christopher Duva (Roland), Callum Keith-King (Otto), Fay Ann Lee (Jade/Michelle), Reathel Bean (Sidney)

A FLEA IN HER EAR by Georges Feydeau; Director, Gregory Boyd; Set Design, Tony Straiges, Costume Design, Jeanne Button, Lighting Design, Kevin Rigdon; Sound Design, Malcolm Nicholls; Large Stage Friday, February 23–March 24, 2001 CAST: James Belcher (Finache), James Black (Victor-Emmanuel Chandebise/Poche), Bettye Fitzpatrick (Olympe), Elizabeth Heflin (Lucienne), Paul Hope (Etienne), Charles Krohn (Feraillon), Ty Mayberry (Rugby), David Rainey (Baptistin), Todd Waite (Romain Tournel), Laura Heisler (Eugenie), Kimberly King (Raymonde Chandebise), Teri Lamm (Antoinette), Noble Shropshire (Don Homenides de Histangua), Jamison Stern (Camille)

DINNER WITH FRIENDS by Donald Margulies; Set Design, Neil Patel; Costume Design, Jess Goldstein and Daryl Stone; Lighting Design, Rui Rita; Music and Sound, Michael Roth; Large Stage Friday, April 6–May 5, 2001 CAST: Claudia Fielding (Beth), Gregory Northrop (Tom), Andrew Polk (Gabe), Lynne Wintersteller (Karen)

THE DEVIL'S DISCIPLE by George Bernard Shaw; Director, Gregory Boyd; Set Design, Vincent Mountain, Lighting Design, Robert Wierzel; Costume Design, Sam Fleming; Sound Design, Malcolm Nicholls; Friday, May 18–June 8, 2001 CAST: James Belcher (Lawyer Hawkins), James Black (Anthony Anderson), Bettye Fitzpatrick (Mrs. Anne Dudgeon), Elizabeth Heflin (Aunt William Dudgeon), Paul Hope (Major Swindon), Charles Krohn (Uncle William Dudgeon/Reverend Brudenell), Ty Mayberry (Dick Dudgeon), David Rainey (Sergeant), Todd Waite (General Burgoyne/Uncle Titus Dudgeon), Laura Heisler (Essie), Teri Lamm (Judith Anderson), John Raymond Barker (Christopher Dudgeon)
Please note that *The Devil's Disciple* was intended to run from May 18–June 17, 2001 but was cut short by Tropical Storm Allison on June 8, 2001

ALLEY THEATRE

(continued)

THE CARPETBAGGER'S CHILDREN by Horton Foote; World Premiere; Set Design, Jeff Cowie; Costume Design, David Woolard; Lighting Design, Rui Rita; Sound and Orginal Music, John Gromada; Neuhaus Arena Stage Friday, June 1–July 1, 2001 Cast: Roberta Maxwell (Cornelia), Jean Stapleton (Grace Anne), Hallie Foote (Sissie)

AMERICAN CONSERVATORY THEATRE

San Francisco, California
Thirty-fourth Season

Artistic Director, Carey Perloff; Managing Director, Heather M. Kitchen

HANS CHRISTIAN ANDERSON Music and Lyrics, Frank Loesser; Book, Sebastian Barry; Based on the Samuel Goldwyn Motion Picture; Director and Choreography, Martha Clarke; Musical Adaption and Arrangements, Richard Peaslee; Orchestrations, Michael Starobin; Musical Director, Constantine Kitsopoulos; Scenic Design, Robert Israel; Costume Design, Jane Greenwood; Lighting Design, Paul Gallo; Sound Design, Garth Hemphill; Flying Systems, Flying by Foy; Animal Trainer, Bill Berloni; World Premiere; Thursday, August 31–September 7, 2000 Cast: John Glover (Hans Christian Anderson), Galina Alexandrova, Rob Besserer, Jarlath Conroy, Katie Green, George Hall, Teri Hansen, John Christopher Jones, Julia Mattison, Jenny Sterlin, Karen Trott, Ian Wolff Ensemble: Felix Blaska, Dashiell Eaves, Marie-Christine Mouis, Alexander Proia, Erica Stuart, Paola Stryron, Shen Wei

THE MISANTHROPE by Molière; Adaption, Constance Congdon from a new translation by Virginia Scott; Director, Carey Perloff; Scenic Design, Kate Edmunds; Costume Design, Beaver Bauer; Lighting Design, Rui Rita; Sound Design, Garth Hemphill; Thurdsay, October 19–November 19, 2000 Cast: David Adkins (Alceste), René Augesen (Celimine), Kimberly King (Arsinoe), Anthony Fusco (Oronte), Steven Anthony Jones, Gregory Wallace, Chris Ferry, Kathleen Kaefer, Patrick McNulty, David Mendelsohn

GLENGARRY GLEN ROSS by David Mamet; Director, Les Waters; Scenic Design, Ly Arcenas, Costume Design, Ann Bruice-Aling; Lighting Design, James F. Ingalls; Sound Design, Garth Hemphill; Thursday, January 4–February 4, 2001 Cast: Tony Amendola (Levene), John Apicella (Moss), Marco Barricelli (Roma), James Carpenter (Lingk), Rod Gnapp (Williamson), Matt Gottlieb (Aaronow), Brian Keith Russell (Baylen)

Gregory Wallace, Steven Anthony Jones in *"Master Harold"...and the Boys* (Kevin Berne)

Heather Goldenhersh, Jesse Pennington in *Goodnight Children Everywhere* (Ken Friedman)

Kimberly King, René Augesen in *The Misanthrope* (Kevin Berne)

GOODNIGHT CHILDREN EVERYWHERE Writer and Director, Richard Nelson; Scenic Design, Thomas Lynch; Costume Design, Susan Hilferty; Lighting Design, James F. Ingalls; Sound Design, Garth Hemphill; Thursday, February 15–March 18, 2001 Cast: Rachel Black (Rose), Jon De Vries (Mike), Heather Goldenhersh (Vi), Jesse Pennington (Peter), Charles Shaw Robinson (Hugh), Robin Weigert (Betty), Yvonne Woods (Ann)

ENRICO IV by Luigi Pirandello; Translation, Richard Nelson; Director, Carey Perloff; Scenic Design, Ralph Funicello; Costume Design, Deborah Dryden; Lighting Design, Peter Maradudin; Sound Design, Garth Hemphill; Thursday, March 29–April 29, 2001 Cast: Felicity Jones (Matilda), Anthony Fusco (Belcredi), Claire Winters (Frida), David Mendelsohn (Di Nolli), Charles Lanyer (Doctor Genoni), Scott Asti, Marco Barricelli, Tom Blair, Chris Ferry, Samuel Gates, Tommy A. Gomez, Benton Greene, Douglas Nolan

"MASTER HAROLD"... AND THE BOYS by Athol Fugard; Director, Laird Williamson; Scenic Design, Ralph Funicello; Costume Design, Claudia Everett; Lighting Design, Peter Maradudin; Sound Design, Garth Hemphill; Friday, May 4–June 3, 2001 Cast: Steven Anthony Jones (Sam), Gregory Wallace (Willie), Jonathan Sanders

TEXTS FOR NOTHING by Samuel Beckett; Director, Bill Irwin; Set Design, Douglas Stein; Lighting Design, Nancy Schertler; Costume Design, Anita Yavich; Sound Design, Aural Fixation; Wednesday, June 14–July 15, 2001 Cast: Bill Irwin

Kevin Berne, Ken Friedman, Dixie Sheridan Photos

AMERICAN REPERTORY THEATRE

Cambridge, Massachusetts

Artistic Director, Robert Brustein; Managing Director, Robert J. Orchard

THE KING STAG by Carlo Gozzi; English Version, Albert Bermel; Director, Andrei Serban; Set Design, Michael H. Yeargan; Lighting Design, John Ambrosone; Music, Elliot Goldenthal; Sound Adaption, Christopher Walker; Movement, Masks and Puppetry, Julie Taymor; Production Restaged by Abbie H. Katz; Stage Manager, Martin Lechner; Assistant Stage Manager, Victoria Sewell; Tour Lighting Supervisor, Stephen Hills; Tour Audio Engineer, Denise Eberly; Movement Consultant, Thomas Derrah; Puppeteer Coordinator, Kelli Edwards; Thursday, September 14–September 28, 2000 CAST: Jeremy Rabb (Cigolotti), Sean Runnette (Durandarte), Douglas Goodenough (Brighella), Sophia Fox-Long (Smeraldina), Kevin Bergen (Truffaldino), Dmetrius Conley-Williams (Tartaglia), Kristine Goto (Clarice), William Church (Pantalone), Sarah Howe (Angela), Antonio Suarez (Leandro), Jay Boyer (Deramo), Russ Gold (Multi-percussionist), Movement of Puppets, Shadow Puppets, Kites/Understudies: Mark Fortin, Maura Nolan Henry, Todd Thomas Peters, Jeremy Proctor, Naeemah A. White-Peppers

NOCTURNE by Adam Rapp; Director, Marcus Stern; Set Design, Christine Jones; Costume Design, Viola Mackenthun; Lighting Design, John Ambrosone; Sound Design, David Remedios; Stage Manager, Jennifer Rae Moore; Assistant Stage Manager, Chris De Camillis; Production Associate, Jennifer Grutza; Dramaturg, Kathy White; Voice and Speech Coach, Patricia Delorey; Fight Captain, Marin Ireland; Friday, October 13, 2000 CAST: Dallas Roberts (The Son), Nicole Paquale (The Daughter), Candice Brown (The Mother), Will LeBow (The Father), Marin Ireland (The Redheaded Girl)

ANTIGONE by Sophocles; Translation, Robert Fagles; Director, François Rochaix; Set Design, Jean-Claude Maret; Costume Design, Catherine Zuber; Lighting Design, Michael Chybowski; Sound Design, David Remedios; Movement, Margaret Eginton; Stage Manager, Deborah Vandergrift; Assistant Stage Manager, Chris De Camillis; Production Assistant, Jennifer Grutza; Production Dramaturgs, Gideon Lester and Walter Valeri; Voice and Speech Coach, Nancy Houfek; Projection Designer, J. Michael Griggs; Friday, November 24, 2000 CAST: Aysan Çelik (Antigone), Rachael Warren (Ismene), John Douglas Thompson (Creon), Thomas Derrah (Sentry), Sean Dugan (Haemon), Alvin Epstein (Tiresias), Benjamin Evett (Messenger), Jodi Lin (Eurydice) CHORUS: Jack Atamian, Darrin Browne, Tenelle Cadogan, Scott Draper, Sean Dugan, Benjamin Evett, Sean Kelly, Jodi Lin, Nick Newell, Trevor Oswalt, Jonathon Roberts, James Spencer, Marguerite Stimpson, Peggy Trecker, Children: Robbine Eginton, Gabe Goodman, Ezra Lichtman Percussionist: Vessela Stoyanova

Karen MacDonald in *Mother Courage and her Children* (Richard Feldman)

The Company of *Mother Courage and her Children* (Richard Feldman)

THREE FARCES & A FUNERAL by Robert Brustein; adapted from the life and works of Anton Chekhov; Director, Yuri Yeremin; Set Design, Riccardo Hernandez; Costume Design, Catherine Zuber; Lighting Design, John Ambrosone; Sound Design, David Remedios; Stage Manager, Chris De Camillas; Assistant Stage Manager, Deborah Vandergrift; Production Associate, Amy James; Production Dramaturg, Misha Aster; Translator, Alex Tetradze; Voice and Speech Coach, Nancy Houfek; Movement Coach, Margaret Eginton; Friday, December 8, 2000 CAST: Jeremy Geidt (Stefan Chubukov/Doctor Schwoerer), Mirjana Jokovic (Natasha/Olga Knipper), Jeremiah Kissel (Lomov/Anton Chekhov), Tim Kang (Vanya/Gregory Smirnoff/Kharlampy Marshmalopolis), Sarah Isenberg (Masha/Yelena Popova/1st Lady), Gerardo Rodriguez (Tracker/Gregory Smirnoff/Dribbelov), Jennifer Black (Treasure/Yelena Popova/Anna Martinovna Snakina), Karen MacDonald (Yelena Popova/Nastasya), Myriam Cyr (Yelena Popova/Anna Martinovna Snakina), Roslyn S. Ruff (Yelena Popova/Anna Martinovna Snakina), Frances Chewning (Yelena Popova/Masha), Anna Goldfeld (Yelena Popova/2nd Lady), Will LeBow (Gregory Smirnoff/Gonov), Ken Cheeseman (Gregory Smirnoff/Zetz), Trey Burvant (Gregory Smirnoff/Marinin), Douglass Bowen Flynn (Gregory Smirnoff/Master of Ceremonies), Gladdy Matteosian (Gregory Smirnoff/3rd Lady), Remo Airaldi (Luka/Epaminodas Pomponov), Alvin Epstein (Fyodor Nautikin-Keelov), Misha Aster (Man in Black, 12/8-21, 1/10 forward), Darrin Browne (Man in Black, 12/22–1/3) UNDERSTUDIES: Amber Allison, Jon Bernthal, Hannah Bos, Samrat Chakrabarti, Ian Collet Barr, Harry Crane, Craig Doescher, Sarah Douglas, David Gravens, Dana Gotlieb, Philip Graeme, Sandro Isaack, Sydney Kohn, Jason Pugach, Chelsey Rives, Jennifer Shirley, Ayça Varlier, Michael Wheeler

THE DOCTOR'S DILEMMA by George Bernard Shaw; Director, David Wheeler; Set Design, Riccardo Hernandez; Costume Design, Catherine Zuber; Lighting Design, John Ambrosone; Sound Design, David Remedios; Stage Manager, Thomas M. Kauffman; Assistant Stage Manager, Chris De Camillis; Production Associate, Jennifer Grutza; Production Dramaturg, Jennifer Roberts; Voice and Speech Coach, Nancy Houfek; Movement Coach, Margaret Eginton; Monday, January 26, 2001 CAST: Sarah deLima (Emmy), Scott Draper (Redpenny), John Feltch (Sir Colenso Ridgeon), Remo Airaldi (Leo Schutzmacher), Jeremy Geidt (Sir Patrick Cullen), Ken Cheeseman (Culter Walpole), Will LeBow (Sir Ralph Bloomfield Bonington), Alvin Epstein (Dr. Blekinsop), Rachael Warren (Jennifer Dubedat), Sean Dugan (Louis Dubedat), Laura Napoli (Minnie Tinwell), Frederick Hood (Waiter), Nick Newell (The Newspaper Man), Frederick Hood (Mr. Danby) UNDERSTUDIES: Jack Atamian, Jennifer Black, Darrin Browne, Trey Burvant, Frances Chewning, Scott Draper, Sean Kelly, Nick Newell, Gerardo Rodriguez, James Spencer, Peggy Trecker

MOTHER COURAGE AND HER CHILDREN by Bertolt Brecht; Adaption, János Szász, Erzsébet Rácz, and Gideon Lester; Translation, Gideon Lester; Music, Paul Dessau and Hannis Eisler; Director, János Szász; Set Design, Csaba Antal; Costume Design, Edit Szücs; Lighting Design, John Ambrosone; Sound Design and Original Song, David Remedios; Movement, Csaba Horváth; Stage Manager, Chris De Camillis; Assistant Stage Manager, Thomas M. Kauffman; Production Associate, Amy James; Production Dramatug, Gideon Lester; Voice and Speech Coach, Nancy Houfek; Friday, February 9, 2001 CAST: Amos Lichtman (Bertolt Brecht), Benjamin Evett (General), Graham Sack (Sergeant), Trey Burvant (Recruiting Officer), Karen MacDonald (Mother Courage), Mirjana Jokovic (Kattrin), Jonathan Roberts (Eilif), Tim Kang (Swiss Cheese), John Douglas Thompson (Cook), Thomas Derrah (Chaplain), Paula Plum (Yvette Pottier), Trevor Oswalt (Man with One Eye), Edwin Thurston (An Old Colonel), Gilbert Owuor (Corporal), Tenelle Cadogan (Young Prostitute), Darrin Browne (Regimental Clerk), Jodi Lin (Peasant Women), Joseph Pearlman (Soldier), Edward Tournier (Soldier), Erin Breen (Soldier) UNDERSTUDIES: Jack Atamain, Jennifer Black, Darrin Browne, Trey Burvant, Scott Draper, Sean Kelly, Nick Newell, Gerrardo Rodriguez, Roslyn Ruff, James Spencer, Marguerite Stimpson

ANIMALS & PLANTS by Adam Rapp; Director, Scott Zigler; Set Design, J. Michael Griggs; Costume Design, Jane Alois Stein; Lighting Design, John Ambrosone; Sound Design, David Remedios; Stage Manager, M. Pat Hodge; Production Associate, Jennifer Grutza; Production Dramaturg, Gideon Lester; Assistant Dramaturg, Jennifer Roberts; Voice and Speech Coach, Nancy Houfek; Hasty Pudding Theatre Friday, March 30, 2001 CAST: Benjamin Evett (Burris), Will LeBow (Dantly), Frances Chewning (Cassandra), Scott A. Albert (A Man); Karen MacDonald (Weather Reporter)

RICHARD II by William Shakespeare; Director, Robert Woodruff; Set Design, David R. Gammons; Costume Design, Catherine Zuber; Lighting Design, Stephen Strawbridge; Sound Design, Darron L. West; Movement, Saar Magal; Stage Manager, Chris De Camillis; Assistant Stage Manager, Luke Peters; Production Associate, Amy James; Production Dramaturg, Gideon Lester; Voice and Speech Coach; Nancy Houfek; Sunday, May 11, 2001 CAST: Thomas Derrah (King Richard II), Jonno Roberts (Young Man/Lord Willoughby), John Feltch (Duke of Gloucester/Earl of Northumberland), Alvin Epstein (John of Gaunt), Karen MacDonald (Duchess of Gloucester/Duchess of York), Jodi Lin (Queen to Richard), Darrin Browne (Richard's Attendant), Remo Airaldi (Bishop of Carlisle), Benjamin Evett (Thomas Mowbray/Sir Stephen Scroope), Bill Camp (Henry Bolingbroke), Sean Dugan (Aumerle), Trevor Oswalt (Bagot), Jim Spencer (Green/Prison Keeper), Tim Kang (Bushy/Sir Piers Exton), John Douglas Thompson (Duke of York), Robert Ross (Lord Ross) ENSEMBLE: Jason Beaubier, James Dittami, Seth Reich, Kieran Smiley, Chris Starr UNDERSTUDIES: Jennifer Black, Robert Brustein, Trey Burvant, Tenelle Cadogan, Frances Chewning, Scott Draper, Jeremy Geidt, Nancy Houfek, Sean Kelly, Nick Newell, Gerardo Rodriguez, Roslyn Ruff, Jim Spencer, Marguerite Stimpson, Peggy Trecker, Scott Zigler

The Company of *Richard II*

The Company of *Richard II*

The Company of *Richard II*

ARIZONA THEATRE COMPANY

Tucson and Phoenix, Arizona
Seventeenth Season

Artistic Director, David Ira Goldstein; Associate Artistic Director, Samantha Wyer; Artistic Associates, Jay Rabins, Trudy Shaylor; Assistant to the Artistic Director, David Morden; Playwright in Residence, Elaine Romero; Company Manager, Robyn Waterman; Artistic Intern, Todd Loyd

INVENTING VAN GOGH by Steven Dietz; Saturday, April 7–April 29, 2001 Tucson, AZ May 3–May 20, 2001 Phoenix, AZ CAST: Peter Van Norden (Dr. Jonas Miller/Dr. Paul Gachet), Lee Sellars (Patrick Stone), Tom Ramirez (Rene Bouchard/Paul Gaugin), Jennifer Erin Roberts (Hallie Miller/Marguerite Gachet), Dan Donohue (Vincent van Gogh)

Tim Fuller Photos

Lee Sellars, Dan Donohue in *Inventing Van Gogh* (Tim Fuller)

Dan Donohue, Jennifer Erin Roberts in *Inventing Van Gogh* (Tim Fuller)

AURORA THEATRE

Berkeley, California

TOUGH! by George F. Walker Friday, January 26–March 4, 2001 CAST: Amanda Duarte, Danny Wolohan

David Allen Photos

Amanda Duarte, Danny Wolohan in *TOUGH!* (David Allen)

BARTER THEATRE

Abingdon, Virginia

Producing Artistic Director, Richard Rose; Business Manager, Joyce Phillips

FAIR AND TENDER LADIES Adaption, Quinn Hawkesworth from the book by Lee Smith; Director, Tom Celli; Sets and Lighting Design, Todd Wren; Properties Designer, Cheri L. Prough; Production Stage Manager, Karen Rowe; Assistant Stage Manager, John Keith Hall; Stage II Thursday, February 3–March 16, 2000 Cast: Quinn Hawkesworth

SLEEPING BEAUTY Music, Jerome Kern; Lyrics, Oscar Hammerstein II, Otto Harbach, P.G. Wodehouse, and Ira Gershwin; Book and Additional Lyrics, Paul Blake; Director, Charles Repole; Musical Director, Michael Horsley; Choreography, Gemze de Lappe; Assistant Choreography, Suzanne Hawe; Scenic Design, Daniel Ettinger; Costume Design, Amanda Aldridge; Lighting Design, Todd Wren; Vocal Arrangements, Hugh Martin; Sound Design, Bobby Beck; Dance Arrangements, Bruce Pomahac; Stage Manager, Christopher Halpin; Assistant Stage Manager, John Keith Hall; Dance Captain, Dannul Dailey; Production Manager, Kelly Terrell; Production Associate, Tim Johnson; Main Stage Wednesday, February 9–March 11, 2000 Cast: Catherine Brunell (Sunny), Jeff Edgerton (Maxwell), Joel Carlton (Wendell), Ellen Horst (Madame Sophie), Sandy Binion (Francine), John Freimann (King Leo), Cara Johnston (Queen Lizzie), Tony Freeman (Barry), Colby Foytik (Tommy), John Long (The Cow - front), Polly Morrow (The Cow - back) Ensemble: Dannul Dailey, Amy Barker, Tina McGhee, Nik Rocklin, Rachel Lafer, Britt Freund

BRIGADOON Book and Lyrics, Alan Jay Lerner; Music, Frederick Loewe; Director, Tom Celli; Musical Director, William Perry Morgan; Choreography, Amanda Aldridge; Scenic Design, Daniel Ettinger; Costume Design, Amanda Aldridge; Lighting Design, Wendy Luedtke; Sound Design, Bobby Beck; Properties Manager, Cheri L. Prough; Production Stage Manager, Christopher Halpin; New York Casting, Paul Russell; Assistant Stage Manager, John Keith Hall; Main Stage Thursday, March 16–May 20, 2000 Cast: William Sanders (Mr. Lundie), Michael Ostroski (Tommy Aldright), Jim Van Valen (Jeff Douglas), Will Bigham (Sandy Dean), Christa Germanson (Meg Brockie), John Hardy (Archie Beaton), Josephine Hall (Fiona McClaren), Catherine Gray (Jean McClaren), John Hedges (Andrew McClaren), Will Hines (Harry Beaton), Scott Westerman (Angus McGuffie), Happy Mahaney (Charlie Dalrymple), Don Bodie (Stuart Dalrymple), Tina McGhee (Maggie Anderson), Andreas Lopez (Macgregor/Frank the Bartender), Polly Morrow (Mary McGuffie), Karen Sabo (Molly Dean/Jane Ashton)

CHILDREN OF THE SUN by N. Scott Momaday; Director and Choreography, Katy Brown; Scenic Design, George Chavatel; Costume Design, Madison Tyler; Sound Design, Bobby Beck; Properties Manager, Cheri L. Prough; Production Stage Manager, Karen Rowe; New York Casting, Paul Russell; Stage II Tuesday, March 21–May 21, 2000 Cast: Virginia Wing (Grandma Spider), Kalani Queypo (Male Actor), Derrick Alipio (Male Dancer), Shammen McCune (Woman), Susanne Trani (Female Dancer)

A MIDSUMMER NIGHT'S DREAM by William Shakespeare; Director, John Hardy; Musical Director, William Perry Morgan; Choreography, Debra Gillingham; Scenic Design, Daniel Ettinger; Costume Design, Vicki Davis; Lighting Design, Wendy Luedtke; Sound Design, Bobby Beck; Properties Manager, Cheri L. Prough; Production Stage Manager, Karen Rowe; New York Casting, Paul Russell; Assistant Stage Manager, John Keith Hall; Main Stage Wednesday, March 29–May 20 2000 Cast: Kalani Queypo (Theseus), Tina McGhee (Philostrate/Cobweb/Fairy), Polly Morrow (Hippolyta), William Sanders (Eqeus), Christa Germanson (Hermia), Lysander (Will Bigham), Will Hines (Demetrius), Josephine Hall (Helena), Jim Van Valen (Peter Quince), Michael Ostroski (Nick Bottom), Scott Westerman (Francis Flute), Don Bodie (Tom Snout), Catherine Gray (Snug), Quinn Hawkesworth (Robin Starveling), Tom Celli (Puck), Shammen McCune (Titania), John Hedges (Oberon), Susanne Trani (Peaseblossom), Happy Mahaney (Mustardseed)

THE TURN OF THE SCREW Adaptation, Robert Anglin from the novel by Henry James; Director, Robert Anglin; Scenic Design, D.R. Mullins; Costume Design, Amanda Aldridge; Sound Design, Bobby Beck; Properties Manager, Cheri L. Prough; Production Stage Manager, Christopher Halpin; New York Casting, Paul Russell; Stage II Thursday, March 30–May 20, 2000 Cast: Andreas Lopez (Douglas), Karen Sabo (Governess), Derrick Alipio (Peter Quinn), Virginia Wing (Mrs. Gross), Stephanie DeMaree (Flora), Katy Brown (Miss Jessel), Davis Sweatt (Miles)

MY FAIR LADY Book and Lyrics, Alan Jay Lerner; Music, Frederick Loewe; Director, Richard Rose; Musical Director, William Perry Morgan; Scenic Design, Daniel Ettinger; Costume Design, Amanda Aldridge; Choreography, Amanda Aldridge; Technical Designer, Mark DeVol; Lighting Design, Todd Wren; Sound Design, Bobby Beck; Properties Manager, Cheri L. Prough; Stage Manager, John Keith Hall; New York Casting, Paul Russell; Assistant Stage Managers, John Hardy, Stephen Vess; Stage Management Interns, Toya Profit, Yoko Yamada; Main Stage Thursday, May 25–August 20, 2000 Cast: Dennis Creaghan (Henry Higgins); Christa Germanson (Eliza Doolittle), Quinn Hawkesworth (Mrs. Higgins), Mike Ostroski (Freddy Eynsford-Hill), Laura Morton (Mrs. Eynsford-Hill/Servant), Tom Celli (Colonel Pickering), Don Bodie (A Man from Selsey/Cockney/Bartender/Servant/Lord Boxington), Andreas Lopez (A Man from Hoxton/Cockney/Angry Resident/Butler/Guest Attending Ascot), Catherine Gray (Cockney/Angry Resident/Servant/Lady Boxington/Maid), Will Hines (Cockney/Harry/Guest Attending Ascot), Karen Sabo (Cockney/Mrs. Pearce/Guest Attending Ascot), Jim VanValen (Cockney/Jamie/Guest Attending Ascot), Katy Brown (Cockney/Mrs. Hopkins/Servant/Guest Attending Ascot), Jennifer Katz (Cockney/Angry Resident/Servant/Flower Girl), John Hedges (Alfred Doolittle/Guest Attending Ascot)

THE BEAUTY QUEEN OF LEENANE by Martin McDonagh; Director, John Hardy; Technical Director, Mark DeVol; Scenic Design, Madison Tyler; Costume Design, Madison Tyler; Lighting Design, Erica Kissam; Sound Design, Bobby Beck; Properties Manager, Cheri L. Prough; Stage Manager, Karen N. Rowe; New York Casting, Paul Russell; Assistant Stage Managers, John Hardy, Chad Singleton; Stage II Thursday, June 1–August 20, 2000 Cast: Darcy Pulliam (Mag Folan), Josephine Hall (Maureen Folan), Scott Hamilton Westerman (Ray Dooley), Will Bigham (Pato Dooley)

HARVEY by Mary Chase; Director, Tom Celli; Scenic Design, Lynn Pecktal; Costume Design, Martha Hally; Lighting Design, Todd Wren; Technical Design, Mark DeVol; Sound Design, Bobby Beck; Properties Manager, Cheri L. Prough; Stage Manager, Karen N. Rowe; New York Casting, Paul Russell; Assistant Stage Managers, John Hardy, Chad Singleton; Stage Management Interns, Toya Profit, Yoko Yamada; Main Stage Wednesday, June 7–August 19, 2000 CAST: Laura Morton (Myrtle Mae Simmons), Quinn Hawkesworth (Veta Louise Simmons), Jim VanValen (Elwood P. Dowd), Darcy Pulliam (Mrs. Ethel Chauvenet), Catherine Gray (Ruth Kelly, R.N.), Scott Hamilton Westerman (Duane Wilson), Will Bigham (Lyman Sanderson, M.D.), Dennis Creaghan (William R. Chumley, M.D.), Josephine Hall (Betty Chumley), Will Hines (Judge Omar Gaffney), Andreas Lopez (E.J. Lofgren)

FALSETTOS Music and Lyrics, William Finn; Book, William Finn and James Lapine; Director, William Perry Morgan; Choreography, Katy Brown; Scenic Design, Daniel Ettinger; Costume Design, Martha Hally; Technical Director, Mark DeVol; Lighting Design, Erica Kissam; Sound Design, Bobby Beck; Properties Design, Cheri L. Prough; Stage Manager, John Keith Hall; New York Casting, Paul Russell; Assistant Stage Managers, Tom Celli, Stephen Vess; Stage II Thursday, June 15–August 27, 2000 CAST: John Hedges (Marvin), Christa Germanson (Trina), Ryan Curry (Jason), Josey Montana McCoy (Jason), John Hardy (Mendel), Mike Ostroski (Whizzer), Karen Sabo (Charlotte), Katy Brown (Cordelia)

IDOLS OF THE KING by Ronnie Claire Edwards and Allen Crowe; Director, John Briggs; Musical Director, William Perry Morgan; Scenic/Lighting Director, Daniel Ettinger; Costume Designer, Amanda Aldridge; Technical Director, Mark DeVol; Sound Design, Bobby Beck; Properties Manager, Cheri L. Prough; Stage Manager, Karen N. Rowe; Main Stage Monday, August 24–September 30, 2000 CAST: Scot Bruce (Elvis), Will Bigham (All Men Parts), Catherine Gray (All Women Parts)

WIT by Margaret Edson; Director, Richard Rose; Scenic Design, Daniel Ettinger; Costume Design, Amanda Aldridge; Lighting Design, David G. Friedl; Sound Design, Bobby Beck; Properties Manager, Cheri L. Prough; Technical Director, Mark J. DeVol; Assistant Director, Katy Brown; Stage Manager, John Keith Hall; Assistant Stage Manager, John Hardy; Stage II Wednesday, September 27–November 12, 2000 CAST: Christa Germanson (Vivian Bearing), Tom Celli (Harvey Kelekian/Mr. Bearing), Christina Murdock (E.M. Ashford), Mike Ostroski (Jason Posner), Jennifer Blevins (Susie Monahan), Technicians: Katy Brown, Jennifer Katz, Eugene Sumlin, Stephen Vess

HOUND OF THE BASKERVILLES Adapted and Directed by Richard Rose, from a story by Sir Arthur Conan Doyle; Scenic Design, Daniel Ettinger; Costume Design, Amanda Aldridge; Lighting Design, David G. Friedl; Sound Design, Bobby Beck; Properties Manager, Cheri L. Prough; Technical Director, Mark J. DeVol; Stage Manager, John Keith Hall; Original Music, Rene Kempler; Designer of the Hound, Karen Brewster; New York Casting, Paul Russell; Assistant Stage Manager, Will Bigham; Main Stage Thursday, October 5–November 18, 2000 CAST: Jim VanValen (Sir Hugo Baskerville/Mr. Stapleton), Catherine Gray (The Maiden/Miss Stapleton), Andreas Lopez (The Shephard/Seldon), John Hardy (Sherlock Holmes), Will Hines (Doctor Watson), Mike Ostroski (Dr. Jones Mortimer), John Hedges (Sir Henry Baskerville), Tom Celli (Mr. Frankland of Lafter Hall), Scott Hamilton Westerman (Mr. Barrymore), Christa Germanson (Mrs. Laura Lyons), Eugene Sumlin (The Hound)

THE FOREIGNER by Larry Shue; Director, John Hardy; Scenic Design, Daniel Ettinger; Costume Design, Amanda Aldridge; Lighting Design, David G. Friedl; Sound Design, Bobby Beck; Properties Design, Cheri L. Prough; Technical Director, Mark J. DeVol; Stage Manager, Karen Rowe; New York Casting, Paul Russell; Assistant Stage Manager, John Hardy; Main Stage Thursday, October 12–November 19, 2000 CAST: Will Hines (Froggy LeSueur), John Hedges (Charlie Baker), Quinn Hawkesworth (Betty Meeks), Will Bigham (Rev. David Marshall Lee), Catherine Gray (Catherine Simms), Jim VanValen (Owen Musser), Scott Hamilton Westerman (Ellard Simms)

LITTLE HOUSE ON THE PRAIRIE CHRISTMAS Adapted and Directed by John Hardy, from the book by Laura Ingalls Wilder; Scenic Design, Sean Arnold; Costume Design, Amanda Aldridge; Lighting Design, David G. Friedl; Sound Design, Bobby Beck; Properties Manager, Technical Director, Mark J. DeVol; Stage Manger, Karen Rowe; Assistant Stage Manager, John Hardy; Stage II Tuesday, November 21–December 23, 2000 CAST: Christine Murdock (Ma), Scott Hamilton Westerman (Pa), Lindsey Fields (Laura), Stephanie Demaree (Carrie), Andreas Lopez (Man #1), Quinn Hawkesworth (Woman #1), Eugene Sumlin (Man #2), Jennifer Katz (Woman #2)

SHE LOVES ME Musical Book, Joe Masteroff; Music, Jerry Bock; Lyrics, Sheldon Harnick; Director, Tom Celli; Choreography, Amanda Aldridge; Musical Director, William Perry Morgan; Scenic Design, Daniel Ettinger; Costume Design, Amanda Aldridge; Sound Design, Bobby Beck; Properties Design, Cheri L. Prough; Technical Director, Mark J. DeVol; Stage Manager, John Keith Hall; Assistant Stage Manager, Tom Celli; Main Stage Friday, November 24–December 23, 2000 CAST: Will Hines (Ladislav Sipos), Brandon Roberts (Arpad Laszlo), Christa Germanson (Ilona Ritter), Will Bigham (Steven Kodaly), Jim VanValen (Georg Nowack), John Hedges (Mr. Maraczek/Ensemble), Catherine Gray (Amalia Balash), Mike Ostroski (Keller/Ensemble), Roy Fisher (Street Santa Claus) ENSEMBLE: Jennifer Blevins, Katy Brown, Karen Sabo, Eugene Sumlin

BAY STREET THEATRE

Sag Harbor, New York

Executive Director, Stephen Hamilton; General Manager, Norman Kline; Artistic Directors, Sybil Christopher and Emma Walton

THE WOMAN IN BLACK Adaption, Stephen Mallatratt, from the novel by Susan Hill; Director, Leonard Foglia; Casting, Judy Henderson; Set Design, Michael McGarty; Costume Design, Nan Young; Lighting Design, Brian Nason; Sound Design, Randall Freed; Projections, Elaine McCarthy; Production Stage Manager, Linda Barnes; Production Manager, Gary N. Hygom; Wednesday, May 24–June 11, 2000 CAST: Jason Butler Harner (Actor), Josef Sommer (Kipps)

HEDDA GABLER by Henrik Ibsen; New version by Jon Robin Baitz; Director, Nicholas Martin; Casting, Amy Christopher; Set Design, Alexander Dodge; Costume Design, Michael Krass; Lighting Design, Kevin Adams; Sound Design, Randall Freed; Wig Design, Paul Huntley; Production Stage Manager, Laura Brown MacKinnon; Production Manager, Gary N. Hygom; Wednesday, June 21–July 9, 2000 CAST: Kathryn Hahn (Berta), Angela Thornton (Miss Julia Tesman), Michael Emerson (George Tesman), Kate Burton (Hedda Tesman), Katie Finneran (Mrs. Elvsted), Harris Yulin (Judge Brack), David Lansbury (Eilert Lovborg)

Hedda Gabler (Gary Mamay)

YOU CAN'T TAKE IT WITH YOU by Moss Hart and George S. Kaufman; Director, Jack Hofsiss; Set Design, Michael McGarty; Costume Design, Ann Hould-Ward; Lighting Design, Beverly Emmons; Sound Design, Randall Freed; Casting, Judy Henderson; Production Stage Manager, Chris Clark; Production Manager, Gary Hygom; Wednesday, August 16–September 3, 2000 CAST: John Fiedler (Mr. De Pinna), Roger Bart (Ed Carmichael), Mason Adams (Martin Vanderhof), Tom Gustin (Wilbur C. Henderson/Man), Robert Meehan (Man), Michael DeSanti (Man)

Gary Mamay Photos

Hedda Gabler (Gary Mamay)

Hedda Gabler (Gary Mamay)

The Company of *You Can't Take It With You* (Gary Mamay)

CAPITOL REPERTORY THEATRE

Albany, New York

Producing Artistic Director, Maggie Mancinelli-Cahill; Managing Director, Jeff Dannick

NIXON'S NIXON by Russell Lees; Directed by Charles Towers; Scenic Design, Bill Clarke; Costume Design, Gordon DeVinney; Lighting Design, Dan Kotlowitz; Production Stage Manager, Beth Cuthbertson CAST: Keith Jochim (President Richard M. Nixon), Tim Donoghue (Secretary of State Henry Kissinger)

KING O' THE MOON (OVER THE TAVERN PART II) by Tom Dudzik; Scenic Design, Doug Huszti; Costume Design, Martha Hally; Lighting Design, Tom Sturge; Sound Design, Tom Gould; Production Stage Manager, John Godbout; Fight Director, William A. Finlay; Directed by Terence Lamude CAST: Nicholas Joy (Rudy), Ryan Patrick Bachand (Georgie), Derek Phillips (Eddie), Stacey Branscombe (Maureen), Judith K. Hart (Ellen), Amanda Ronconi (Annie), Joe Phillips (Walter)

TERRA NOVA by Ted Tally; Scenic Design, Donald Eastman; Lighting Design, Stephen Quandt; Costume Designer, Thom Heyer; Composer/Sound Design, Steve Stevens; Dialect Coach, Julie Nelson; Production Stage Manager, Beth Cuthbertson; Casting Director, Stephanie Klapper, CSA; Directed by Maggie Mancinelli-Cahill CAST: James Hallett (Captain Scott), Mark Elliot Wilson (Amundsen), Molly Pietz (Kathleen), Paul Taviani ("Birdie" Bowers), Nick Plakias (Wilson), Tom Martin (Oates), Daniel Stewart Sherman (Evans)

HAVING OUR SAY: THE DELANY SISTERS' FIRST 100 YEARS Adaptation by Emily Mann, from the book by Sarah L. Delany and A. Elizabeth Delany with Amy Hill Hearth; Scenic Design, Patrice Andrew Davidson; Lighting Design, Deborah Constantine; Costume Design, Isabel Rubio; Sound Design, Jane Shaw; Production Stage Manager, John Godbout; Directed by Edris Cooper-Anifowoshe CAST: Gammy L. Singer (Sadie Delany), Betty Vaughn (Bessie Delany)

STEVE MARTIN'S PICASSO AT THE LAPIN AGILE Directed by Ron Bashford; Scenic Design, Steven Capone; Costume Design, Nanzi Adzima; Lighting Design, Jeffrey S. Koger; Sound Design, Christopher St. Hilaire; Production Stage Manager, Beth Cuthbertson; Casting Director, Stephanie Klapper, CSA CAST: Guiesseppe Jones (Freddy), John Field Wood (Gaston), Carine Montbertrand (Germaine), Paul Taviani (Albert Einstein), Kat Auster (Suzanne), Jay Brian Winnick (Sagot), Cody Nickell (Pablo Picasso), Kris Anderson (Charles Dabernow Schmendiman), Kat Auster (The Countess), Kat Auster (Female Admirer), Charlton David James (Visitor)

MARK TWAIN'S THE DIARIES OF ADAM AND EVE Adapted for the stage and directed by David Birney; Set Design, Tracy Strickfaden; Lighting Design, Robert Mumm; Music by Jac Redford; Additional Music by Scott Joplin; Stage Manager, Tracy Strickfaden; Produced by Grail Productions in association with Michele Roberge CAST: David Birney (Adam), Clarinda Ross (Eve)

I LOVE YOU, YOU'RE PERFECT, NOW CHANGE Book and Lyrics by Joe DiPietro; Music by Jimmy Roberts; Directed by Maggie Mancinelli-Cahill; Musical Direction, Mark Gionfriddo; Choreography, Cailin Heffernan; Scenic Design, Donald Eastman; Costume Design, Austin Sanderson; Lighting Design, Deborah Constantine; Sound Designer, Steve Stevens; Production Stage Manager, Beth Cuthbertson COMPANY: Tony Freeman, Michael Thomas Holmes, Christine Kienzle, Diana Pappas; Chamber Trio: Mark Gionfriddo (Pianist), Michael Wicks (Bass), Elaine Gervais (Violinist)

Joseph Schuyler Photos

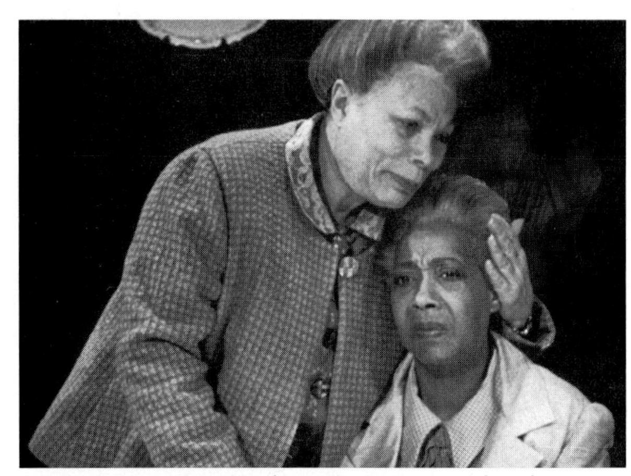

Gammy L. Singer, Betty Vaughn in *Having Our Say: The Delany Sisters' First 100 Years* (Schuyler Photography)

Keith Jochim, Tim Donoghue in *Nixon's Nixon* (Schuyler Photography)

Kat Auster, Cody Nickell in *Steve Martin's Picasso at the Lapin Agile* (Schuyler Photography)

CENTER THEATRE GROUP/MARK TAPER FORUM

Los Angeles, California
September 5, 2000–September 16, 2001
Thirty-fourth Season

Artistic Director, Gordon Davidson; Managing Director, Charles Dillingham; Producing Director, Robert Egan; General Manager, Douglas C. Baker; Associate Artistic Director, Corey Madden; Development Director, Yvonne Bell; Production Supervisor, Frank Bayer; Production Manager, Jonathan Barlow Lee; Casting Director, Amy Lieberman; Press Director, Nancy Hereford; Press Senior Associate, Phyllis Moberly; Press Associate, Jason Martin; Marketing Director, Jim Royce

AUGUST WILSON'S KING HEDLEY II Director, Marion McClinton; Choreography, Dianne R. McIntyre; Scenic Design, David Gallo; Costume Design, Toni-Leslie James; Lighting Design, Donald Holder; Sound Design, Rob Milburn; Casting, Amy Lieberman; Fight Director, Payson Burt; Producing Associate, Benjamin Mordecai; Production Stage Manager, Tami Toon; Stage Manager, Robin Veith CAST: Charles Brown (Elmore), Jerome Butler (King Hedley II - October 17-22 only), Juanita Jennings (Ruby), Harry Lennix (King Hedley II), Lou Myers (Stool Pigeon), Monte Russell (Mister), Mone Walton (Tonya) UNDERSTUDIES: Jerome Butler, John Eddins, Abdul Salaam El Razzac, Lisagig Tharps

CLOSER by Patrick Marber; Director, Robert Egan; Original Music, Karl Fredrik Lundeberg; Additional Music, Nathan Birnbaum; Set Design, David Jenkins; Costume Design, Deborah Nadoolman; Lighting Design, Amy Appleyard; Sound Design, Jon Gottlieb; Casting, Amy Lieberman; Production Stage Manager, James T. McDermott; Stage Manager, Susie Walsh CAST: Rebecca De Mornay (Anna), Maggie Gyllenhaal (Alice), Randle Mell (Larry), Christopher Evan Welch (Dan) UNDERSTUDIES: Matt McKenzie, Liann Pattison, Jennifer Tighe

Charles Brown, Harry Lennix in *August Wilson's King Hedley II* (Craig Schwartz)

FOR HERE OR TO GO? Cornerstone Theater Company's Presentation by Allison Carey; World Premiere; Songs Composed by Michael Abels and Shishir Kurup; Director, Bill Ranch; Music Direction, Michael Abels; Choreography, Jessica Wallenfels; Set Design, Lynn Jeffries; Costume Design, Christopher Acebo; Lighting Design, Geoff Korf; Sound Design, Paul James; Fight Direction, Randy Kovitz; Stage Manager, Paula Donnelly; Stage Manager, Susie Walsh CAST: (Equity members) Ahmad Enani, Omar Gomez, Peter Howard, Shishir Kurup, Page Leong, Armando Molina

Maggie Gyllenhaal, Randy Mell in *Closer* (Craig Schwartz)

Page Leong, Emily Hong in *For Here or To Go?* (Craig Schwartz)

Alexa Fischer, Jonathan Silverman in *Glimmer, Glimmer and Shine* (Craig Schwartz)

GLIMMER, GLIMMER AND SHINE by Warren Leight; West Coast Premiere; Director, Evan Yionoulis; Set Design, Neil Patel; Costume Design, Candice Donnelly; Lighting Design, Donald Holder; Original Music, Evan Lurie; Sound Design, Jon Gottlieb; Casting, Amy Lieberman; Production Stage Manager, James T. McDermott; Stage Manager, David S. Franklin CAST: Alexa Fischer (Delia), Jonathan Silverman (Jordan), John Spencer (Martin), Nicolas Surovy (Daniel) UNDERSTUDIES: Allison Barcott, Christian Casper, Kenneth Ryan.

QED by Peter Pamell, inspired by the writings of Richard Feynman and Ralph Leighton's *Tuva or Bust!*; World Premiere; Director, Gordon Davidson; Creative Consultant, Ralph Leighton; Set Design, Ralph Funicello; Costume Design, Marianna Elliott; Lighting Design, D. Martyn Bookwalter; Sound Design, Jon Gottlieb; Movement, Donald McKayle; Drumming Consultant, Tom Rutishauser; Casting, Amy Lieberman; Associate Producer, Susan Obrow; Production Stage Manager, Mary K. Klinger; Stage Manager, Robin Veith CAST: Alan Alda (Richard Feynman), Allison Smith (Miriam Field) UNDERSTUDY: Sue Cremin.

THE BODY OF BOURNE by John Belluso; World Premiere; Director, Lisa Peterson; Set Design, Rachel Hauck; Costume Design, Candice Cain; Lighting Design, Geoff Korf; Sound Design, Darron L. West; Projection Design, Christopher Komuro; Casting, Amy Lieberman; Wigs and Hair Design, Carol F. Doran; Production Stage Manager, James T. McDermott; Stage Manager, Susie Walsh. CAST: Stephen Caffrey (Carl Zigrosser, et al.), Nicolas Coster (Uncle Halsey, Ellery Sedgwick, et al.), Mitchell Edmonds (Chorus), Heather Ehlers (Beulah Amidon, Yvonne, Agnes de Lima et al.), Clark Middleton (Randolph Bourne), Lisa Lovett-Mann (Chorus), Michele Marsh (Chorus), Jenny O'Hara (Sara Bourne, et al.), Jill Remez (Chorus), Ann Stocking (Helen Hummel, Emmy, et al.), Michael Eric Strickland (Chorus), Jodi Thelen (Ruth Bourne, Lilja, et al.), Christopher Thomton (Chorus) UNDERSTUDIES: Mitchell Edmonds, Lisa Lovett-Mann, Michele Marsh, Jill Remez, Michael Eric Strickland, Christopher Thornton

Clark Middleton, Ann Stocking, Stephen Caffrey in *The Body of Bourne* (Craig Schwartz)

Alan Alda in *QED* (Craig Schwartz)

CENTER THEATRE GROUP/MARK TAPER FORUM

(continued)

IN REAL LIFE Written and performed by Charlayne Woodard; World Premiere; Director, Dan Sullivan; Set Design, John Lee Beatty; Costume Design, James Berton Harris; Lighting Design, Kathy A. Perkins; Original Music, Daryl Waters; Sound Design, Chris Walker; Production Stage Manager, Mary K. Klinger; Stage Managers, Robin Veith and David Franklin.

ANOTHER AMERICAN: ASKING AND TELLING Written and performed by Marc Wolf; Director, Joe Mantello; Set Design, Robert Brill; Lighting Design, Brian MacDevitt; Sound Design, David Van Tieghem; Production Stage Manager, Mary K. Klinger; Stage Managers, David Franklin and Robin Veith.

Craig Schwartz Photos

Charlayne Wood in *In Real Life* (Craig Schwartz)

Marc Wolf in *Another American: Asking and Telling* (Craig Schwartz)

CINCINNATI PLAYHOUSE IN THE PARK

Cincinnati, Ohio
Forty-first Season

Producting Artistic Director, Edward Stern

INHERIT THE WIND Jerome Lawrence and Robert E. Lee; Director, Edward Stern; Casting Director, Rich Cole; Executive Director, Buzz Ward; Set Design, Karen TenEyck; Costume Design, Kristine A. Kearney; Lighting Design, Peter E. Sargent; Production Stage Manager, Bruce E. Coyle; Stage Manager, Suann Pollock; Stage Management Intern, Alicia Spain; Robert S. Marx Theatre; Tuesday, September 5–October 6, 2000 CAST: Andrea Backscheider (Melinda), Joe Sofranko (Howard), Allison Krizner (Rachel Brown), Whit Reichert (Meeker), Jason Bowcutt (Bertram Cates), Bill Hartnett (Mr. Goodfellow/Dr. Keller), Debra Watassek (Mrs. Krebs), Robert Elliot (Reverend Jeremiah Brown), Wm. Daniel File (Sillers), Tim Perrino (Krebs), Ric Young (Bollinger), Matthew Francisco Morgan (Cooper/Photographer), Jerry Vogel (Bannister), Drew Fracher (Dunlap), Patrick Toon (Hot Dog Man), Sandy Harper (Mrs. McLain), Susie Wall (Mrs. Blair), Michael Blankenship (Elijah/Radio Man), David Haugen (E.K. Hornbeck), Joneal Joplin (Matthew Harrison Brady), Jill Tanner (Mrs. Brady), Paul Hebron (Mayor), Mark Mocahbee (Tom Davenport), Philip Pleasants (Henry Drummond), Dane Knell (Judge), David Johnson (Reuters Reporter), Collin Worster (Phil/Eskimo Pie Hawker), Jane Schrantz (Mrs. Loomis), A. Jackson Ford (Organ Grinder), Gene Wolters (Doc Kimble/Dr. Page), Tom Caruso (Reporter), Branan Whitehead (Reporter), Rob Jansen (Reporter), Leslie Dock (Court Reporter/Townsperson), John Marshall (Dr. Aaronson), Aransas Thomas (Townsperson) Jurors: Clint Bramkamp, Don Frimming, Jerry Lowe, Burt McCollom, Michael L. Morehead, Tom Murphy, Jim Racster, Arnie Shayne, Aaron Simms, Gary Wettengel UNDERSTUDIES: Collin Worster, Angela Odom

SHAKESPEARE'S R & J Adapted by Joe Calarco; Director, Alan Bailey; Set Design, Ursula Belden; Costume Design, Gordon DeVinney; Lighting Design, James Sale; Casting Directors, Rich Cole and Richard Hicks; Executive Director, Buzz Ward; Stage Manager, Emily F. McMullen; Assistant Stage Manager, Stephanie M. Snodgrass; Stage Management Intern, Andrea L. Shell; Movement Coach, Charlie Oates; Dialect Coach/Text Consultant, Laura Parrotti; Saturday, September 23–October 22, 2000 CAST: Christopher Baker (Student #1), Liam Christopher O'Brien (Student #2), Randy Reyes (Student #3), Crispin Freeman (Student #4) UNDERSTUDIES: David Johnson, Matthew Francisco Morgan, Shannon Michael Wamser, Collin Worster

EVERYTHING'S DUCKY Book, Bill Russell and Jeffrey Hatcher; Lyrics, Bill Russell; Music, Henry Krieger; Director, Gip Hoppe; Musical Director, Shawn Gough; Orchestrator, Harold Wheeler; Choreography, Linda Goodrich; Set Design, Robert Bissinger; Costume Design, Beaver Bauer; Lighting Design, Jeff Croiter; Sound Design, David B. Smith; Vocal Arrangements, David Chase; Additional Arrangements, Shawn Gough; Puppet Design, Erminio Pinque; Casting, Johnson-Liff Associates; Executive Director, Buzz Ward; Robert S. Marx Theatre; Tuesday, October 17–November 17, 2000 CAST: Tracey Conyer Lee (Mrs. Bovine/Galinda), John Herrera (Mr. Lambkins/Wolf), Tony Capone (Mayor Mule/Drake), Mark Chmiel (Rooster Bob/King/Police Dog/Armand Dillo/Giorgio Grouse), Jonathan Brody (Free-Range Chicken/Sheep/Clem Coyote/Pig 2/Runway Model), Bobby Daye (Free-Range Chicken/Sheriff Goat/Carl Coyote/Pig 1/Runway Model), Alicia Irving (Mrs. Mallard/Aunt Leda/Queen), J.B. Wing (Millicent Mallard/Sally/Wren/Stylist/Ruta/Guard/Assistant), Angela Pupello (Mildred Mallard/Daphne/Pig 3/Make-up Artist/Verblinka), Natalie Toro (Serena), Facilitators: Alex Domeyko/Shannon Faith, Sara Frank, Dylan Shelton

(continued)

I LOVE YOU, YOU'RE PERFECT, NOW CHANGE Book and Lyrics, Joe DiPietro; Music, Jimmy Roberts; Director/Choreography, Dennis Courtney; Musical Director, Louis F. Goldberg; Casting Director, Rich Cole; Executive Director, Buzz Ward; Set Design, Felix E. Cochren; Costume Design, David Kay Mickelsen; Lighting Design, Betsy Adams; Stage Manager, Emily F. McMullen; Stage Management Intern, Alicia Spain; Thompson Shelterhouse Theatre; Saturday, November 4–December 31, 2000 CAST: Heather Ayers (Woman #1), Jamison Stern (Man #1), Ginette Rhodes (Woman #2), Brad Little (Man #2)

A CHRISTMAS CAROL Adaptation by Howard Dallin from book by by Charles Dickens; Director, Michael Evan Haney; Musical Director, Carol Walker; Casting Director, Rich Cole; Executive Director, Buzz Ward; Choreography, Dee Anne Bryll; Set Design, James Leonard Joy; Costume Design, David Murin; Lighting Design, Kirk Bookman; Sound Design/Composer, David B. Smith; Costume Coordinator, Cindy Witherspoon; Lighting Contractor, Jim Fulton; Production Stage Manager, Bruce E. Coyle; Second Stage Manger, Jenifer Morrow; Stage Management Intern, Matthew Sayre; Robert S. Marx Theatre; Friday, December 1–December 30, 2000 CAST: Joneal Joplin (Ebenezer Scrooge), Mark Mocahbee (Mr. Cupp/Percy), Larry Bates (Mr. Sosser/Dick Wilkens/Topper/Man with Shoe Shine), Bruce Cromer (Bob Cratchit/Schoolmaster Oxlip), Jake Storms (Fred), Gregory Procaccino (Jacob Marley/Old Joe), Celeste Ciulla (Ghost of Christmas Past/Patience), A.J. Grubbs (Boy Scrooge/Boy at Fezziwig's/Bootblack), Äna Starr Gilmore (Fan/Guest at Fezziwig's/Streets), Mark Mineart (Mr. Fezziwig/Ghost of Christmas Present), Regina Pugh (Mrs. Fezziwig/Mrs. Cratchit), Jason Bowcutt (Young and Mature Scrooge/Ghost of Christmas Future), Eva Kaminsky (Belle/Catherine Margaret), Katie Johanningman (Belinda Cratchit/Guest at Fezziwig's/Streets), Mary Jesse Price (Martha Cratchit/Guest at Fezziwig's), Dustin M. Hicks (Peter Cratchit/Gregory/Apprentice at Fezziwig's), Adam Weinel (Tiny Tim), Dale Hodges (Rose/Laundress at Fezziwig's/Mrs. Peake), Andrea Auten (Rich Caroler/Guest at Fezziwig's), Chuck DuSablon (Poor Caroler/Tailor at Fezziwig's/Streets), Amber K. Browning (Poor Caroler/Rich Wife at Fezziwig's), Shannon Michael Wamser (Rich Caroler/Rich Father at Fezziwig's/Man with Pipe/Streets), Nathan Wallace (Matthew/Rich Son at Fezziwig's/Ignorance), Matthew L. Taylor (Charles/Apprentice at Fezziwig's/George/Streets), Ali Breneman (Want/Guest at Fezziwig's/Streets), Aransas Thomas (Guest at Fezziwig's/Mrs. Dilber/Streets), Jane Schrantz (Scrubwoman at Fezziwig's/Streets), Leslie Dock (Guest at Fezziwig's/Streets), Angela Odom (Guest at Fezziwig's/Streets/Caroler), David Johnson (Lawyer at Fezziwig's/Poulterer/Streets), Matthew Francisco Morgan (Constable at Fezziwig's/Streets/Caroler), Collin Worster (Baker at Fezziwig's/Undertaker/Streets)

CLOSER by Patrick Marber; Director, Charles Towers; Casting Director, Rich Cole; Set Design, Klara Zieglerova; Costume Design, Martha Hally, David Lander; Dialect Coach, Philip Thompson; Executive Director, Buzz Ward; Stage Manager, Suann Pollock; Stage Management Intern, Tara Swadley; Thompson Shelterhouse Theatre Tuesday, January 9–February 4, 2001 CAST: Caitlin Muelder (Alice), Kyle Fabel (Dan), T. Ryder Smith (Larry), Judith Lightfoot Clarke (Anna), UNDERSTUDY: Aransas Thomas

DARK PARADISE: THE LEGEND OF THE FIVE POINTED STAR by Keith Glover; Director, Keith Glover; Casting Director, Rich Cole; Fight Director, Drew Fracher; Special Effects Director, Jim Steinmeyer; Set Design, David Gallo; Costume Design, Ann Hould-Ward; Sound Design, David B. Smith; Dramaturg, Maxine Kern; Executive Director, Buzz Ward; Production Stage Manager, Bruce E. Coyle; Stage Manager, Jenifer Morrow; Stage Management Intern, Andrea L. Shell; Robert S. Marx Theatre Thursday, February 1–March 3, 2001 CAST: Tony Todd (Chiron), Sean Haberle (Colonel Jeddadiah Crate), Leland Gantt (William LaRue/Ty LaRue), Kim Brockington (Sura Rise), James Horan (Wyatt Earp), Gary Sloan (John Henry Holliday), Elena Aaron (Bessatura), Ron Riley (Cole Regert), Mike Hartman (Packard Tate)

AVENUE X Book and Lyrics, John Jiler; Music, Ray Leslee; Director/Choreography, John Ruocco; Music Director, Georgia Stitt; Fight Director, K. Jenny Jones; Casting Director, Rich Cole; Executive Director, Buzz Ward; Set Design, Narelle Sissons; Costume Design, Curtis Hay; Lighting Design, John-Paul Szczepanski; Stage Manager, Emily F. McMullen; Stage Management Intern, Matthew Sayre; Thompson Shelterhouse Theatre Saturday, February 17–March 18, 2001 CAST: Jon Stewart (Pasquale), Roy Chicas (Chuck), Michael Sharon (Ubazz), Leenya Rideout (Barbara), Kevin R. Free (Milton), Jeffrey V. Thompson (Roscoe), Virginia Ann Woodruff (Julia), Corey Reynolds (Winston)

ART by Yasmina Reza; Translation, Christopher Hampton; Director, Charles Towers; Casting Director, Rich Cole; Executive Director, Buzz Ward; Set Design, Bill Clarke; Costume Design, David Zinn; Lighting Design, Dan Kotlowitz; First Stage Manager, Suann Pollock; Second Stage Manager, Bruce E. Coyle; Stage Management Intern, Alicia Spain; Robert S. Marx Theatre Sunday, March 18–April 20, 2001 CAST: Christopher McHale (Marc), Tim Donoghue (Serge), Bill Kux (Yvan)

THE MYSTERY OF IRMA VEP by Charles Ludlam; Director, Michael Evan Haney; Casting Director, Rich Cole; Executive Director, Buzz Ward; Set Design, Paul Shortt; Costume Design, David R. Zyla; Lighting Design, Kirk Bookman; Stage Manager, Jenifer Morrow; Stage Management Intern, Andrea Shell; Thompson Shelterhouse Theatre Saturday, April 7–May 20, 2001 CAST: Greg McFadden (Jane Twisden/Lord Edgar Hillcrest/An Intruder), Remi Sandri (Nicodemus Underwood/Lady Enid Hillcrest/Alcazar)

TALLEY'S FOLLY by Lanford Wilson; Director, Marshall W. Mason; Casting Director, Rich Cole; Executive Director, Buzz Ward; Set Design, John Lee Beatty; Costume Design, Laura Crow; Lighting Design, Dennis Parichy; Sound Design, Chuck London; Production Stage Manager, Bruce E. Coyle; Second Stage Manager, Suann Pollock; Stage Management Intern, Matthew Sayre; Robert S. Marx Theatre Sunday, April 29–June 1, 2001 CAST: Geoffrey Cantor (Matt Friedman), Kelly McAndrew (Sally Talley)

CLARENCE BROWN THEATRE

Knoxville, Tennessee

Department Head and Producing Artistic Director, Blake Robinson; General Manager, Thomas A. Cervone

ARCADIA by Tom Stoppard; Director, David Kennedy; Set Design, Craig Siebels; Costume Design, Bill Black; Lighting Design, Robert Perry; Sound Design, Mike Ponder; Choreography, Kathy Moore; Dramaturg, Dr. Klaus van den Berg; Stage Manager, Jennifer C. Kennedy; Friday, September 1–September 17, 2000 CAST: Shannon Emerick (Thomasina Coverly), Nick Merritt (Septimus Hodge), Dan Owenby (Jellaby), David Melville (Ezra Chater), Tony Cedeño (Richard Noakes), Dee Pelletier (Lady Croom), Darren Matthias (Captain Brice, R.N.), Bonne Gould (Hannah Jarvis), Angela Church (Chloe Coverly), Craig Wroe (Bernard Nightingale), Terry Weber (Valentine Coverly), Chad Ervin (Gus Coverly/ Augustus Coverly)

DHA-FUSION Director, Nancy Prebilich; Set Design, Ryan Gill; Sound Design, Mike Ponder; Costume Design, Jessica Wegener; Lighting Design, Josh Hamrick; Videography, Adam Choa; Stage Manager, Marta Stout; Technical Director, James Peliwo; Friday, October 13–October 28, 2000 CAST: Akim Funk Buddha, Brother Neel, Chikado Cat Dragon, Edward Alsiva, Father Laraaji, Felix Bass Mantra, Jason Sarubbi, Sister Mami, Vincent Van Trigger Man, Uzuri Awolowo (Homegirl/Monk), Flow (Homeboy/Monk/Straightjacket), Kristin A. Lewis (Opera Singer), Zakiyyah Modeste (Homegirl/Monk), Latausha Renne Mose-Jones (Cop/ Monk), Michael "Pitt" Pittman (Homeboy/Straightjacket)

CINDERELLA by Richard Rogers and Oscar Hammerstein II; Direction and Musical Staging, Abigail Crabtree; Musical Director, James Brimer; Choreography, Michelle Colvin; Scenic Design, Michael Heil; Costume Design, Bill Black; Lighting Design, John Horner; Sound Design, Mike Ponder; Stage Manager, Jennifer Kennedy; Assistant Stage Managers, Holly Anderson, Eleanor Eggers, Jennifer Bingham; Friday, November 17–December 9, 2000 CAST: Thomas Adkins (Steward/Company), Joseph Beuerlein (Herald/Company), Nancy Dinwiddie (Queen), Quinn Fortune (Fairy Godmother), Ashley Kemp (Portia), Linda Libby (Stepmother), Samantha Miller (Dream Cinderella/Company/Horse), Dan Owenby (King), Leigh Price (Joy), John Ramsey, Jr. (Pierrot Clown), Jennifer Richmond (Cinderella), Stephen J. Smith (Prince Christopher), Thomas Webb (Chef/Company) COMPANY: Lindsey Andrews, Katy Baker, Michael Boris, Adam Cox, John Curtis, Olivia Lott Edge, Joshua Eleazer, Frances Hamrick, Michael Harmon, Ryan Haynes, Meghan McCoy, Deanna McGovern, James W. Morris III, Keiana Richard, Friesia Schuil, Stephanie Webb, Thomas Webb, Kasey Williams, Elizabeth Wilson, Horses: Deanna McGovern, Kasey Williams, Katy Baker, Mice: Elizabeth Wilson, Ryan Haynes, John Curtis, Meghan McCoy

INHERIT THE WIND by Jerome Lawrence and Robert E. Lee; Director, Jay Dysart; Set, Craig Siebels; Costume Design, Bill Black; Lighting Design, Michael Barnett; Sound Design, Masha Kamyshkova; Stage Manager, Eleanor Eggers; February 2 through February 17 CAST: David Bryan Alley (Hornbeck), Thomas DeMarcus (Cates), Michael Harmon (Meeker), Gay Harrison (Reverend Brown), Ali O'Hern (Melinda), Richard Remine (Mayor), Barbara Stasiw (Mrs. Brady), Stewart Steinberg (Matthew Harrison Brady), Evan Thompson (Henry Drummond), Elizabeth Urello (Rachel), Jarron Vosberg (Howard), Matthew Wilson (Davenport) COMPANY: Joseph Beuerlein, Rusty Birdwell, Garrett Brown, Sarah Byrd, Lynn Cooley, Ian Dunn, Joshua Eleazer, Colin Fisher, Scott Hooper, Justin Ipock, Steve Louis, Susan Love, Amy Loyd, Jay Morris, Dustin Parrott, Jessie Risola, Friesia Schuil, Jessica Scott, Abby Shoemaker, Joshua Shuter, Daniel Stewart, Tara Taylor, Lora Wilson

THE BRECHT FILE by George Tabori; script adaptation with additional translations by Klaus van den Berg; Director, Veronika Nowag-Jones; Composer/Musical Director, Sirone; Set, Michael Heil; Costume Design, Marianne Custer; Lighting Design, L.J. DeCuir; Sound Design, Mike Ponder; Stage Manager, Jennifer Kennedy; Fights, David Heuvelman; Technical Director, Jim Peliwo; March 2 – March 17, 2001 CAST: Chevy Anz (Mrs. Finnegan/Mamma/Buzzard); Ethan T. Bowen (Referee/Bella Lugosi/The Chief/Boxer/Buzzard); Tony Cedeno (Boxer/Charlie Chaplin/ Gallagher); Bonnie K.A. Gould (Greta Garbo/Mrs. Applebaum/Helene Weigel/Buzzard); David Heuvelman (Boxer/Brecht); Dan Owenby (Boris Karloff/Mr. Applebaum/Buzzard); Andrew Sellon (MC/Peter Lorre/Father Mulligan/Fleishman/Tattleman); Thomas Webb (Trainer/Charles Laughton/Shine) ENSEMBLE: Brigette Harless (Barbara/Funnyface/Sign Girl); Mandi Lawson (Big Ramona/Trainer); Leigh Price (Sign Girl/ Secretary/Blondie) MUSICIANS: Piano, Steve Clements, Ben Dockery, Emil Harris, Andrea Link; Bass, Preston Davis, Tommy Sauter; Drums, Dave Ohmer, Josh Wolter; Reeds, Chad Bailey, Willem Learn, Dave King, Jason Thompson.

THE GLASS MENANGERIE by Tennessee Williams; Director, Blake Robison; Set, Britt Lynn; Lighting Design, John Horner/Joshua Hamrick; Sound Design, Mike Ponder; Stage Manager, Robin Lee; April 13 – April 28 CAST: Carol Mayo Jenkins is the Bob and Margie Parrott Visiting Artist; David Brian Alley (Tom Wingfield), Thomas DeMarcus (Jim O'Conner), Carol Mayo Jenkins (Amanda Wingfield), Jessica Scott (Laura Wingfield)

PICASSO AT THE LAPIN AGILE by Steve Martin; Director, Elizabeth Craven; Set, Rex Heuschkel; Costume Design, Christianne Myers; Lighting Design, Joshua Hamrick; Sound Design, Mike Ponder; Stage Manager, Jennifer C. Kennedy; June 1 – June 16 CAST: Chris Burns (Freddy), John Forrest Ferguson (Gaston), Amy Russel (Germaine), Jon Wesley Burnett (Albert Einstein), Elizabeth Baron (Suzanne/Countess), Dan Owenby (Sagot), Tim Kniffin (Pablo Picasso), Tony Cedeño (Charles Dabernow Schmendiman), Leigh Price (A Female Admirer), Drew Starlin (A Visitor)

THE CLEVELAND PLAYHOUSE

Cleveland, Ohio

Artistic Director, Peter Hackett; Managing Director, Dean R. Gladden

ELIOT NESS IN CLEVELAND Book by Peter Ullian; Music and Lyrics by Robert Lindsey Nassif; Based on the play *In The Shadow of the Terminal Tower* by Peter Ullian; Directed by David Esbjornson; Musical Director, Lee Stametz; Musical Staging by Lynne Taylor-Corbett; Scene Design, Christine Jones; Costume Design, Elizabeth Hope Clancy; Lighting Design, Jane Cox; Sound Design, Richard Ingraham; Stage Manager, Dawn Fenton; Casting, Elissa Myers/Paul Fouquet; Bolton Theatre Tuesday, September 26–November 5, 2000 CAST: Burke Moses (Eliot Ness), Alison Fraser (Hildy Lincoln), Ray DeMattis (Al Capone), Jay Stuart (Thurgood Stoneham), Polly Penn (Hobo Woman), Wally Dunn (Seeley), Richard Pruitt (Marlo), Tory Schaefer (Sidney), Marva Hicks (Saloon Singer), Kimberly Breault, Marva Hicks, Randi Megibow (Trio), Ric Stoneback (Mayor), Barry Finkel (Frank Dolezal), Tom Titone (Karpis), Newsboys: Michael Cappetta, Mathew Langenhop ENSEMBLE: Kimberly Breault, Tina Cannon, James Doberman, Randi Megibow, Ric Stoneback, Tom Titone EXTRAS: Norman Berry, Crystal Krosec, Susan Lucier, Shannon MacNamara, Makeba Tounsend, James Workman

THE GUARDSMAN by Ferenc Molnar; Directed by Hegyi Arpad Jutocsa; Scene Design, Vicki Smith; Costume Design, Elizabeth A. Novak; Lighting Design, Lap-Chi Chu; Sound Design, Richard Ingraham; Stage Manager, Bruno Ingram; Dramaturg, John Orlock; Casting, Elissa Myers/Paul Fouquet; Drury Theatre Tuesday, October 31–November 26, 2000 CAST: Andrew May (The Actor), Crista Moore (The Actress), William Meisle (The Critic), Johanna Morrison (Mama), Golde (Liesl), Ron Wilson (A Creditor), Harriet DeVeto (An Usher)

HARVEY by Mary Chase; Directed by David Colacci; Scene Design, Robert N. Schmidt; Costume Design, Elizabeth A. Novak; Lighting Design, Tracy Odishaw; Sound Design, Richard Ingraham; Stage Manager, Dawn Fenton; Assistant Stage Manager, Maryann Morris; Casting, Elissa Myers/Paul Fouquet; Bolton Theatre Tuesday, November 28, 2000–January 7, 2001 CAST: Brandy McClendon (Myrtle Mae Simmons), Darrie Lawrence (Veta Louise Simmons), Mike Hartman (Elwood P. Dowd), Sherri Britton (Mrs. Ethel Chauvenet), Tess Hartman (Ruth Kelly, R.N.), Brian Anthony Wilson (Duane Wilson), Sean Dougherty (Lyman Sanderson, M.D.) Chuck Patterson (William R. Chumley, M.D.), Lauren Klein (Mrs. Betty Chumley), Allen Leatherman (Judge Omar Gaffney), Doug Jewell (E.J. Lofgren)

THE SEAGULL by Anton Chekhov; Translated by Paul Schmidt; Directed by Edward Payson Call; Scene Design, Ariel Goldberger; Costume Design, Rose Pederson; Lighting Design, Rick Paulson; Sound Design, Jeff Ladman; Composer, Larry Delinger; Dramaturg, Park Goist; Stage Manager, Bruno Ingram; Casting, Elissa Myers/Paul Fouquet; Drury Theatre Tuesday, January 9–February 4, 2001 CAST: Elizabeth Hess (Irina Nikolayevna Arkandina), Max T. Moore (Konstantin Gavrilovich Treplev), Maury Cooper (Pyotr Nikolayevich Sorin), Julie Lund (Nina Mikhailovna Zarechnaya), John Tillotson (Ilya Afanasyevich Shamrayev), Donna David (Paulina Andreyevna), Christine Apathy (Masha), Jason Culp (Boris Alexeyevich Trigorin), Kenneth Gray (Yevgeny Sergeyevich Dorn), Karl Kenzler (Semyon Semyonovich Medvedenko), John Kolibab (Yakov), Meg Kelly (The Maid), Christine McBurney (The Cook), Andrew Towler (A Farm Hand)

Vivan Reed, Alvin Keith in *Blues for an Alabama Sky* (Roger Mastroianni)

BLUES FOR AN ALABAMA SKY by Pearl Cleage; Directed by Chuck Patterson; Scene and Costume Design, Felix E. Cochren; Lighting Design, William H. Grant III; Sound Design, Richard Ingraham; Stage Manager, Dawn Fenton; Dramaturg, Matthew Korahias; Casting, Elissa Myers/Paul Fouquet; Bolton Theatre Tuesday, February 6–March 11, 2001 CAST: Vivian Reed (Angel Allen), Stanley Wayne Mathis (Guy Jacobs), Kena Tangi Dorsey (Delia Patterson), Wiley Moore (Sam Thomas), Alvin Keith (Leland Cunningham)

JERUSALEM by Seth Greenland; Directed by Peter Hackett; Scene Design, Michael Ganio; Costume Design, David Kay Mickelsen; Lighting Design, Richard Winkler; Composer, Lewis Flinn; Sound Design, Robin Heath; Stage Manager, Bruno Ingram; Fight Choreography, Ron Wilson; Assistant Director, Thom Bowers; Drury Theatre Tuesday, March 13–April 8, 2001 CAST: Stephen Kunken (Will Soloman), Ben Lipitz (Guberman), Sue-Anne Morrow (Meg Soloman), Susan Ericksen (Glory Matthews-Daniels), Ann Guilbert (Mary Matthews), Steve McCue (Bing Daniels), David Alan Novak (Fisher/Saladin/Cop Voice/Yitz)

(continued)

SIDE SHOW Book and Lyrics by Bill Russell; Music by Henry Krieger; Vocal and Dance Arrangements by David Chase; Orchestrations by Harold Wheeler; Original Broadway Production Produced by Emanuel Azenberg, Joseph Nederlander, Herschel Waxman, Janice McKenna, Scott Nederlander; Original Broadway Production Directed and Choreographed by Robert Longbottom; Directed by Victoria Bussert; Music Director, Larry Delinger; Choreography, Janiece Kelley-Kiteley; Assistant Music Director, David Williams; Conductor, Lee Stametz; Scene Design, Karen TenEyck; Costume Design, Russ Borski; Lighting Design, Mary Jo Dondlinger; Sound Design, Jeremy J. Lee; Stage Manager, Carrie Purdum; Casting, Elissa Myers/Paul Fouquet; Bolton Theatre Tuesday, April 17–May 13 2001 CAST: Hunter Bell (Buddy Foster), Pierre-Jacques Brault (Geek/Ensemble), Craig Bennett (Roustabout/Browning), Jodi Capeless (Dolly Dimples/Ensemble), Derrick Cobey (Sheik/Ensemble), David Colacci (The Boss), Peter Connelly (Reptile Man/Ensemble), Carol Dunne (Daisy Hilton), Mary Klaehn (Harem Girl/Ensemble), Devin Settles (Roustabout/Ensemble), Michael Levesque (Roustabout/Ensemble), C. Mingo Long (Jake), Roland Rusinek (Bearded Lady/Ensemble), Lori Scarlett (Harem Girl/Ensemble), Sandra Simon (Violet Hilton), Carol Schuberg (Harem Girl/Ensemble), Greg Violand (Terry Connor), Natasha Williams (Fortune Teller/Ensemble)

ART by Yasmina Reza; Translated by Christopher Hampton; Directed by Peter Hackett; Scene Design, Karen TenEyck; Costume Design, Jeffrey Van Curtis; Lighting Design, Derek Duarte; Sound Design, Robin Heath; Composer, Lewis Flinn; Stage Manager, Bruno Ingram; Drury Theatre Tuesday, May 15–June 10, 2001 CAST: Andrew May (Serge), Murphy Guyer (Marc), Mike Hartman (Yvan)

Roger Mastroianni Photos

Stephen Kunken, Susan Ericksen, Sue-Anne Morrow, Steve McCue in *Jerusalem* (Roger Mastroianni)

COLONIAL THEATRE

Boston, Massachusetts

SEUSSICAL THE MUSICAL Book, Lynn Ahrens and Stephen Flaherty; Music, Stephen Flaherty; Lyrics, Lynn Ahrens; Conceived by Lynn Ahrens, Stephen Flaherty and Eric Idle; Director, Frank Galati; Choreography, Kathleen Marshal; Scenic Design, Eugene Lee; Costume Design, Catherine Zuber; Lighting Design, Natasha Katz; Sound Design, Jonathan Deans; Orchestrations, Doug Besterman; Music Director, David Holcenberg; Dance Arranger, David Chase; Vocal Arranger, Stephen Flaherty; General Management, Alan Wasser Associates; Casting, Jay Binder and Sherry Dayton; Music Coordinator, John Miller; Production Management, Juniper Street Productions; Press Representative, Barlow - Hartman Public Relations; Executive Producers, Gary Gunas and Alecia Parker; Presented in Association with Kardana/Swinsky Productions, Hal Luftig and Michael Watt; Production Supervisor, Bonnie Panson; Associate Director, Stafford Arima; Associate Choreographys, Rob Ashford and Joey Pizzi CAST: David Shiner (The Cat in the Hat), Kevin Chamberlin (Horton the Elephant), Janine LaManna (Gertrude McFuzz), Michele Pawk (Mayzie La Bird), Andrew Keenan-Bolger (JoJo), Anthony Blair Hall (JoJo - matinees), Sharon Wilkins (Sour Kangaroo), Stuart Zagnit (The Mayor of Whoville), Alice Playten (Mrs. Mayor/The Lorax), Erick Devine (General Genghis Kahn Schmitz), Natascia A. Diaz (Bird Girl), Sara Gettelfinger (Bird Girl), Catrice Joseph (Bird Girl), David Engel (Wickersham Brother), Tom Plotkin (Wickersham Brother), Eric Jordan Young (Wickersham Brother), William Ryall (The Grinch), Joyce Chittick (The Cat in the Hat's Helper), Jennifer Cody (The Cat in the Hat's Helper), Justin Greer (The Cat in the Hat's Helper), Jerome Vivona (The Cat in the Hat's Helper), Monique L. Midgette (JoJo's Teacher), Darren Lee (Vlad Vladikoff), Eddie Korbich (The Once-ler), Devin Richards (Judge Yertle the Turtle), Ann Harada (Marshal of the Court), Mary Ann Lamb (Everythingable), Casey Nicholaw (Hummingfish) SWINGS: Shaun Amyot, Jenny Hill, Michelle Kittrell, David Lowenstein

GUMBOOTS Director, Zenzi Mbuli; Choreography, Rishile Gumboot Dancers of Soweto and Zenzi Mbuli; Designer, Nigel Triffitt; Lighting Design, Gavin Norris; Sound Design, Andy Jackson; Projections, Michael Clark; Creative Advisor, Wayne Harrison; General Management, 101 Productions, Ltd.; Technical Supervisor, Gene O'Donovan; Press Representative, TMG-The Marketing Group CAST: Vincent Ncabashe, Mfana "Jones" Hlophe, Samuel "K.K." Nene, Nicholas Nene, Sipho Ndlela, Lloyd Rathebe, Brian Muzi Nkosi, Thabiso Setlhatlole, Thulu Mkhize, Thabo Mathiba, Darryl G. Ivey (Musical Director and Keyboards), Basi Mahlasela (Percussion), Dari "Lucky" Thobela (Drums), Mabeleng Moholo (Swing Percussionist)

DALLAS THEATER CENTER

Dallas, Texas

Artistic Director, Richard Hamburger; Managing Director, Edith Love; General Manager, Mark Hadley; Production Manager, Al Franklin; Director of Finance, Kelly Lamport; Director of Marketing, David Hadlock; Director of Development, Scott Warren; Director of Education and Community Programs, Jennifer King

CRUMBS FROM THE TABLE OF JOY by Lynn Nottage; Director, Reggie Montgomery; Set Design, Donald Eastman; Costume Design, Claudia Stephens; Stage Manager, Elizabeth Lohr; Wednesday, September 6–October 1, 2000 CAST: Erica N. Tazel (Ernestine Crump), Nomsa L. Mlambo (Ermina Crump), Alex Morris (Godfrey Crump), Portia Johnson (Lily Ann Green), Sally Nystuen Vahle (Gerte Schulte)

Crumbs from the Table of Joy (Amy Lacy)

AN EXPERIMENT WITH AN AIR PUMP by Shelagh Stevenson; Stage Manager, Christy Weikel Wednesday, October 18–November 12, 2000 CAST: Sam Tsoutsouvas (Fenwick/Tom), Caitlin O'Connell (Susannah/Ellen), Mary Bacon (Harriet/Kate), Joanna Schellenberg (Maria), Adrian LaTourelle (Roget), Kevin Henderson (Armstrong/Phil), Kate Goehring (Isobel)

A CHRISTMAS CAROL Adaptation from the novel by Charles Dickens; Friday, November 24–December 24, 2000 CAST: Reggie Montgomery (Scrooge), Chamblee Ferguson (Bob Cratchit/Joe the Keeper), Chris Carlos (Fred/Ali Baba/Young Scrooge/Ensemble), James Crawford (Charitable Gentleman/Debtor/Rich Man/Ensemble), Kaitlin O'Neal (Charitable Gentlewoman), Akin Babatunde (Marley/Mr. Fezziwig/Rich Gentleman), Tony Delgado (The Spirit of Chirstmas Past), Alexander Ferguson (Child Scrooge/Tiny Tim/Ignorance), Ian Flanagan (Adolescent Scrooge/James Cratchit), Julie Ann Williams (Fan/Martha Cratchit), David Novinski (Dick Wilkins/Topper/Rich Gentleman), Liz Mikel (The Spirit of Christmas Present/Charwoman), Joanna Schellenberg (Belle/Lily), Dolores Godinez (Mrs. Cratchit/Mrs. Dilber), Hunter Tharp (Peter Cratchit/Turkey Boy), Charlotte Gruber (Belinda Cratchit), Mackenzie Ferguson (Sarah Cratchit), Elizabeth Rothan (Cynthia/Debtor's Wife), Sanaya Stuart-Robles (Want), Erin Nishimura (Ensemble)

An Experiment with an Air Pump (Amy Lacy)

THE NIGHT OF THE IGUANA by Tennessee Williams; Stage Manager, Christy Weikel; Wednesday, January 17–February 11, 2001 CAST: Paul Lima (Pedro), Geraldine Librandi (Maxine), Al Castro (Pancho), Christopher Burns (Reverend Shannon), Heidi-Marie Ferren (Hilda), Craig Bridger (Wolfgang), Kevin Paul Hofeditz (Herr Farenkopf), Elizabeth Rothan (Frau Farenkopf), James Crawford (Hank), Gail Cronauer (Judith Fellowes), Monique Fowler (Hannah), Erin Neal (Charlotte), Michael Bradshaw (Nonno), Mark Waltz (Jake Latta)

TWELTH NIGHT by William Shakespeare; Stage Manager, Amber Wedin; Wednesday, February 28–March 25, 2001 CAST: Mary Bacon (Viola), Mark Waltz (Sea Captain/Priest), Jeremiah Wiggins (Orsino), Craig Bridger (Curio/Officer), John Patrick (Valentine/Officer), Richard Ziman (Sir Toby Belch), Elizabeth Rothan (Maria), Chamblee Ferguson (Sir Andrew Aguecheek), Jesse Lenat (Feste), Krista Hoeppner (Olivia), Robin Chadwick (Malvolio), James Crawford (Antonio), T.J. Kenneally (Sebastian), Scott Phillips (Fabian), Kat Field (Servant), Summer Powell (Sevant)

WIT by Margaret Edson; Stage Manager, Christy Weikel; Wednesday, April 11–May 6, 2001 CAST: Brenda Thomas (Vivian Bearing), Mark Waltz (Harvey Kelekian), Perry Laylon Ojeda (Jason Posner), Nicole Halmos (Susie Monahan), Mary Fogarty (E.M. Ashford), Lab Technicians/Students/Residents: Paul Lima, Nomsa Mlambo, John Patrick, Jamie Richards

Wit (Amy Lacy)

GEORGIA SHAKESPEARE FESTIVAL

Atlanta, Georgia

Producing Artistic Director, Richard Garner; Managing Director, Philip J. Santora; Education Director, Kathleen McManus

TWELFTH NIGHT by William Shakespeare; Director, Sabin Epstein; Scenic Design, Charlie Caldwell; Costume Design, Leslie Taylor; Lighting Design, Mike Post; Dramaturg/Assistant Director, Andrew Hartley; Composer, Laura Karpman; Musical Director, Michael Monroe; Vocal/Speech Coach, Elisa Hurt-Lloyd; Wig/Hair Design, J. Montgomery Schuth; Stage Manager, Karen S. Martin; Friday, June 16–August 13, 2000 CAST: Brad Sherrill (Orsino), Janice Akers (Olivia), Carolyn Cook (Viola), Damon Boggess (Sebastian), Mark Kincaid (Antonio), Hudson Adams (Sea Captain), Todd Denning (Valentine), Allen Read (Curio), Bruce Evers (Sir Toby Belch), Chris Kayser (Sir Andrew Aguecheek), Tim McDonough (Malvolio), Richard Garner (Fabian), Allen O'Reilly (Feste), Megan McFarland (Maria), Hudson Adams (Priest), Johnell Easter (Officer #1), Jeff Galfer (Officer #2/Sailor), Jim Butz (Attendant to Orsino), Danielle Grabianowski (Olivia's Attendant)

Damon Boggess, Megan Cramer in *A Midsummer Night's Dream* (Kim Kenney)

TARTUFFE by Molière; Translation, Ranjit Bolt; Director, Karen Robinson; Scenic Design, Kathryn Conley; Costume Design, Christine Turbitt; Lighting Design, Mike Post; Dramaturg, Julia Matthews; Music Composed and Performed by Klimchak; Vocal/Speech Coach, Elisa Hurt-Lloyd; Wig/Hair Design, J. Montgomery Schuth; Stage Manager, Margo Kuhne; Friday, June 30–August 12, 2000 CAST: Megan McFarland (Mme. Pernelle), Tim McDonough (Orgon), Janice Akers (Elmire), Damon Boggess (Damis), Danielle Grabianowski (Marianne), Brad Sherrill (Valère), Allen O'Reilly (Claénte), Chris Kayser (Tartuffe), Carolyn Cook (Dorine), Hudson Adams (Laurent), Joe Knezevich (M. Loyal), James Andrew Butz (Loyal's Agent), Johnell Easter (Loyal's Agent), Mark Kincaid (Officer), Jeff Galfer (Policeman), Allen Read (Policeman), Tricia Beigh (Flipote), UNDERSTUDIES: Jim Butz, Todd Denning, Johnell Easter, Bruce Evers, Jeff Galfer, Elisa Hurt, Mark Kincaid, Allen Read

KING RICHARD II by William Shakespeare; Director, Tom Ocel; Scenic Design, Leslie Taylor; Costume Design, B Modern; Lighting Design, Mike Post; Dramaturg, Alice Bentson; Composer, Gregg Coffin; Vocal/Speech Coach, Elisa Hurt-Lloyd; Wig/Hair Designer, J. Montgomery Schuth; Stage Manager, Karen S. Martin; Sunday, July 14–August 11, 2000 CAST: Chris Kayser (King Richard, the Second), Allen O'Reilly (Edmund, Duke of York), Jim Butz (The Duke of Aumerle), Hudson Adams (Thomas Mowbray/Abbot of Westminster/A Groom), Brad Sherrill (Sir William Bagot), Allen Read (Sir John Bushy/Gardener's Servant/Guard), Damon Boggess (Sir Henry Green/Gardener's Servant/Guard), Greg Isaac (Bishop of Carlisle), Johnell Easter (Earl of Salisbury/Guard), Joe Knezevich (Duke of Surrey/Welsh Captain), Tim McDonough (John of Gaunt/A Gardener), Mark Kincaid (Henry Bolingbroke), Bruce Evers (Earl of Northumberland), Jeff Galfer (Harry Percy), Scott Cowart (Lord Ross), Todd Denning (Sir Pierce of Exton), Neal Hazard (Lord Fitzwater), Janice Akers (Queen Isabella), Megan McFarland (Duchess of Gloucester), Elisa Hurt (Duchess of York), Danielle Grabianowski (Lady in Waiting/The Keeper)

A MIDSUMMER NIGHT'S DREAM by William Shakespeare; Director, Richard Garner; Scenic Design, Rochelle Barker; Costume Design, Mark Pirolo; Lighting Design, Mike Post; Composer, Klimchak; Dramaturg, Andrew Hartley; Vocal/Speech Coach, Elisa H. Lloyd; Assistant Director, Tim Conley; Stage Manager, Karen S. Martin; Friday, October 13–November 5, 2000 CAST: Mark Kincaid (Theseus/Oberson), Thalia Baudin (Hippolyta/First Fairy), Saxon Palmer (Philostrate/Puck), Janice Akers (Titania), Allen O'Reilly (Egeus/Quince), Megan Cramer (Hermia), Joe Knezevich (Demetrius), Damon Boggess (Lysander), Tara Ochs (Helena), Bruce Evers (Snug/Mustardseed), Scott Cowart (Flute/Cobweb), Hudson Adams (Snout/Moth), Neal Hazard (Starveling/Peaseblossom), Jonathan Davis (Bottom), UNDERSTUDIES: Courtney Patterson, Tim Conley

Brad Sherrill, Carolyn Cook in *Twelfth Night* (Kim Kenney)

GOODSPEED OPERA HOUSE

East Haddam, Connecticut

Executive Director, Michael P. Price; Associate Producer, Sue Frost; Music Director, Michael O'Flaherty

MAN OF LA MANCHA by Dale Wasserman; Music, Mitch Leigh; Lyrics, Joe Darion; Director, Gerald Gutierrez; Orchestrations, Christopher Jahnke; Choreography, Ramón Oller; Scenic Design, John Lee Beatty; Costume Design, Catherine Zuber and Fabio Toblini; Lighting Design, Pat Collins; Assistant Musical Director, F. Wade Russo; Assistant Choreography, Aixa M. Rosario Medina; Sound Consultant, Tony Meola; Production Manager, R. Glen Grusmark; Stage Manager, Donna Cooper Hilton; Casting, Alan Filderman and Warren Pincus; Assistant Stage Manager, Bradley G. Spachman; Friday, April 7–July 1, 2000 CAST: Shawn Elliott (Cervantes), Stephen Mo Hanan (Sancho), Nancy Ticotin (Aldonza), Don Mayo (The Innkeeper), Amy Jo Phillips (Maria/Ensemble), Joseph Dellger (The Padre), Brent Black (Dr. Carrasco), Michelle Carr (Antonia), Kristine Zbornik (The Housekeeper), Michael Cone (The Barber), Shaun R. Parry (Pedro/Ensemble), William Thomas Evans (Anselmo/Ensemble) ENSEMBLE: Lori Alexander, Deborah Crocker, Roy Harcourt, Bruce Harris, Cristin J. Hubbard, Bobby Pestka, David Rosales, Christopher Snow

DORIAN Book, Music, and Lyrics by Richard Gleaves; Director, Gabriel Barre; Musical Direction, Stephen Oremus; Scenic Design, James M. Youmans; Costume Design, Pamela Scofield; Lighting Design, Timothy Hunter; Sound Design, J.W. Hilton, Jr.; Casting Director, Warren Pincus; Assistant Musical Director; William J. Thomas; Stage Manager, Ruth E. Kramer; Production Manager, R. Glen Grusmark; Technical Director, Jason W. Harshaw; The Norma Terris Theatre Thursday, May 11–June 4, 2000 CAST: Sutton Foster (Sister Claire), Tom Stuart (Dorian Gray), Vince Trani (Mr. Longraves/Mr. Isaacs/Sir Thomas/Mr. Singleton/ Lord Boxington/Victor/Ensemble), Steve Routman (Lawyer/Parker/Alan Campbell/Ensemble), Verna Pierce (Mrs. Leaf/Lady Gwendolyn/ Ensemble), Tom Souhrada (Basil Hallward), Nancy Anderson (Sybil Vane), Tom Flynn (Lord Henry Wotten), Tina Stafford (Lady Campbell/ Ensemble), Sam Zeller (James Vane/Dorian's Manservant/ Ensemble), Barbara Tirrell (Mrs. Vane/Lady Narborough/Ensemble)

GEORGE M! Music and Lyrics, George M. Cohan; Book, Michael Stewart and John and Francine Pascal; Lyrics and Musical Revisions, Mary Cohan; Director, Greg Ganakas; Choreography, Randy Skinner; Produced for Goodspeed Opera House by Michael P. Price; Scenic Design, Howard Jones; Costume Design, John Carver Sullivan; Lighting Design, Kirk Bookman; Orchestrations, Dan DeLange; Assistant Musical Director, William J. Thomas; Associate Choreography, Kelli Barclay; Production Manager, R. Glen Grusmark; Stage Manager, Donna Cooper Hilton; Casting Director, Warren Pincus; Friday, July 7–October 7, 2000 CAST: John Scherer (George M. Cohan), Frank Root (Jerry Cohan), Dorothy Stanley (Nellie Cohan), Liz Pearce (Josie Cohan), Dale Hensley (Albee/ Sam Harris), Nancy Johnston (Madame Grimaldi/Ma Templeton/ Ensemble), Jennifer Smith (Ethel Levey), Tom Demenkoff (Behman/ Ensemble), Tia Speros (Agnes Nolan), Jennifer Goode (Fay Templeton/ Ensemble), Casey Hushion (Rose/Ensemble), Branch Woodman (Freddie/ Ensemble), Shonn Wiley (Walt/Ensemble) ENSEMBLE: Jennifer Lee Crowl, Jeremy Davis, Dontee Kiehn, Joel Newsome, Rosie North, John Simpkins, Jason Sirois, Adam Souza, Jennifer Taylor

SUMMER OF '42 Book, Hunter Foster; Music and Lyrics, David Kirshenbaum; Based upon the novel and motion picture by Herman Raucher; Director and Choreography, Gabriel Barre; Musical Director, Lynne Shankel; Scenic Design, James M. Youmans; Costume Design, Pamela Scofield; Lighting Design, Timothy Hunter; Sound Design, J.W. Hilton, Jr.; Casting Director, Warren Pincus; Orchestrations and Vocal Arrangements, Lynne Shankel; Stage Manager, Gail Eve Malatesta; Production Manager, R. Glen Grusmark; Technical Director, Jason W. Harshaw; The Norma Terris Theatre Thursday, August 10–September 3, 2000 CAST: Ryan Driscoll (Hermie), Idina Menzel (Dorothy), Megan Walker (Miriam), Celia Keenan Bolger (Aggie), Jeanne Goodman (Gloria), Brett Tabisel (Oscy), Jason Marcus (Benjie), Bill Kux (Mr. Sanders/Walter Winchell); Matt Farnsworth (Pete)

Shawn Elliot, Nancy Ticotin in *Man of La Mancha* (Diane Sobolewski)

Frank Root, John Scherer in *George M!* (Diane Sobolewski)

(continued)

RED, HOT AND BLUE! Music and Lyrics, Cole Porter; Book, Howard Lindsay and Russel Crouse; Revised by Michael Leeds; Director, Michael Leeds; Orchestrations, Dan DeLange; Choreography, Andy Blankenbuehler; Produced for Goodspeed Opera House by Michael P. Price; Scenic Design, Kenneth Foy; Costume Design, Ann Hould-Ward; Lighting Design, Ken Billington; Dance Music Arrangements and Additional Vocal Arrangements, David Loud; Assistant Musical Director, F. Wade Russo; Production Manager, R. Glen Grusmark; Stage Manager, Donna Cooper Hilton; Casting Director, Warren Pincus; Assistant Stage Manager, Bradley G. Spachman; Artistic Associate, John Pike Friday, October 13–December 31, 2000 CAST: Debbie Gravitte (Nails O'Reilly Duquesne), Peter Reardon (Bob Hale), Ben Lipitz (Policy Pinkle), Jessica Kostival (Grace), Billy Hartung (Fingers), Robin Baxter (Peaches), Brian Barry (Rats Dugan), Randy Bobish (Bugs Metelli), Steve Luker (Eagle-Eye O'Roarke), Matt Williams (Coyote Johnson), Kevin Covert (Leonard), Trish Reidy (Vivian), Dianna Bush (Olive), Darlene Wilson (Barbara), Stephanie Kurtzuba (Jane), Kristin Maloney (Helen), Paul Carlin (Senator Craig/Warden), Beth Glover (Senator Johnson/Woman #2), Vince Trani (Senator O'Shaughnessy/Guard), Lesley Blumenthal (Senator Del Grasso/ Woman #1), Jody Madaras (Sergeant-at-Arms/Servant/Minister) UNDERSTUDIES: Beth Glover, Randy Bobish, Vince Trani, Paul Carlin, Kristin Maloney

DEAR WORLD Music and Lyrics, Jerry Herman; Book, Jerome Lawrence and Robert E. Lee; Adaption, David Thompson; Director, Richard Sabellico; Musical Direction and Arrangements, Darren R. Cohen; Choreography, Jennifer Paulson Lee; Scenic Design, James Morgan; Costume Design, Suzy Benzinger; Lighting Design, Mary Jo Dondlinger; Sound Design, Jay Hilton; Casting Director, Warren Pincus; Orchestrations and Additional Arrangements, Christopher Jahnke; Stage Manager, Gail Eve Malatesta; Production Manager, R. Glen Grusmark; Technical Director, Jason W. Harshaw; The Norma Terris Theatre Thursday, November 16–December 10, 2000 CAST: Sally Ann Howes (Countess Aurelia), Adam Barruch (Deaf Mute), Frank Moran (Waiter), Kristin Carbone (Nina), Kirby Ward (The Prospector), Richard Bell (President La Farge), Warren Kelley (President La Frec), Jeff Talbott (President La France), Ben Sheaffer (Julian), Jon Vandertholen (Sergeant), Guy Stroman (Sewer Man), Diane J. Findlay (Constance), Georgia Engel (Gabrielle)

Ben Lipitz, Debbie Gravitte, Peter Reardon in *Red, Hot and Blue!* (Diane Sobolewski)

Artistic Director, Nicholas Martin; Managing Director, Michael Maso

DEAD END by Sidney Kingsley; Director, Nicholas Martin; Music Composer, Mark Bennett; Scenic Design, James Noone; Costume Design, Michael Krass; Lighting Design, Kenneth Posner; Sound Design, Kurt B. Kellenberger; Fight Director, Rick Sordelet; Casting Director, James Calleri; Production Stage Manager, Kelley Kirkpatrick; Assistant Stage Manager, Printha K. McCallum CAST: Jon Patrick Walker (Gimpty), Lucas Papaelias (T.B.), Charlie Day (Tommy), Keith Elijah (Dippy), Rollin Carlson (Angel), Dennis Staroselsky (Spit), George Pendleton III (Doorman), Claire Gregoire (Wealthy Lady), William Young (Wealthy Gentleman), Dominic Fumusa ("Baby-face" Martin), Diego Arciniegas (Hunk), Matthew Bretchneider (Philip Griswald), Bobbie Steinbach (Governess), Jack Ferver (Milty), Kathryn Hahn (Drina), Will Lyman (Mr. Griswald), Bob Colonna (Mr. Jones), Jennifer Van Dyck (Kay), Bill Mootos (Jack Hilton), Alice Duffy (Lady with Dog), Robert St. Laurence (Boy #1/Philip Alternate), Adam Howe (Boy #2), Gabriel Goodman (Boy #3), Eric Anderson (2nd Ave. Boy #1), Seth Decker (2nd Ave. Boy #2), Alexander Maso (2nd Ave. Boy #3), Nancy E. Carroll (Mrs. Martin), Rod McLachlan (Patrolman Mulligan), Amy Van Nostrand (Francey), Gene Farber (G-Man #1), Bill Moontos (G-Man #2), Jason Schuchman (G-Man #3), Michael Kaye (Policeman), Richard Auguste (Intern), Bob Colonna (Medical Examiner), Ed Sorrell (Ed), Abby Huston (Young Girl #1), Rachel Neuman (Young Girl #2), Jessica Dickey (Tenement Girl), Eric Rubb (Young Man), Peg Saurman Holzemer (Lady with Broom), Ray McDavitt (Mr. Tranche) UNDERSTUDIES: Aron Epstein, John P. Herring, Tim O'Neil, Gloria Stanton, Robert St. Lawrence, Daniel Stowell, John Yarwood

ILLINOIS THEATRE CENTER

Park Forest, Illinois
Twenty-fifth Season

Producing Director, Etel Billig; Associate Director, Jonathan R. Billig; Administrative Associate, Alexandra Murdoch; Technical Director, James Corey; Business Manager, Howard Hahn; Graphic Design,Sean Garza; Resident Costumer, Mary Ellen O'Meara;

ALL MY SONS by Arthur Miller; Directed by Etel Billig Friday, September 29–October 15, 2000 Cast: Gary Rayppy, Marilyn Bogetich, Peter Robel, Melissa Carlson, Jeff Segall, Alexandra Murdoch, Sam Nykaza-Jones, Jacquelyn Flaherty, Jeff Grafton, Sam Sullivan

SHMULNIK'S WALTZ by Allan Knee; Directed by Judy Rossignuolo-Rice Friday, October 27–November 12, 2000 Cast: David Frutkoff, Jennifer Hall, Genevieve Lynch, Johnny Dark, Jeanne T. Arrigo, Howard Hahn, Michael Rothschild

STARS IN YOUR EYES by Chip Meyrelles; Directed by Pete Thelen Friday, December 1–17, 2000 Cast: Bill Scharpen, John Librizzi, Carmen Severino, K.J., Gina Torrecilla, Marci Medwed

Lisa Fontana, Marco Verna in *The Princess of President Street* (Warren Skalski)

TRAVELER IN THE DARK by Marsha Norman; Directed by Etel Billig Friday, January 12–28, 2001 Cast: Tim Rezash, Cathy Bieber, Gary Rayppy, Tom Carreras

FLYIN' WEST by Pearl Cleage; Directed by Paulette McDaniels Friday, February 16–March 4, 2001 Cast: Alma Washington, James Meredith, Emilie Byron, Shelia-Marie Robinson, Paulette McDaniels, Phillip Sanchez

THE PRINCESS OF PRESIDENT STREET by Adam Kraar; World Premiere; Directed by Pete Thelen Friday, March 23–April 8, 2001 Cast: Lisa Fontana, Deborah Goldstein, Marci Medwed, Lawrence Gamer, Marco Verna, Jeff Segall, Judy Rossignuolo-Rice

AS THOUSANDS CHEER by Irving Berlin and Moss Hart; Directed by Pete Thelen Friday, April 27–May 13, 2001 Cast: Jane Brewer, Makeba Pace, Candace Thomas, Robert Browning, Peter Robel, Pete Thelen

Warren Skalski Photos

Candace Thomas, Robert Browning in *As Thousands Cheer* (Warren Skalski)

Melissa Carlson, Peter Robel in *All My Sons* (Warren Skalski)

Cathy Bieber, Tom Carreras in *Traveler in the Dark* (Warren Skalski)

JOHN LANE'S OGUNQUIT PLAYHOUSE

Ogunquit, Maine

Producing Artistic Director, Roy M. Rogosin; General Manager, Henry J. Weller

ART by Yasmina Reza; Translation, Christopher Hampton; Director, Judd Hirsch; Scenic Design, Ani Blackburn; Costume Design, Amy Handy; Lighting Design, Richard Latta; Original Music and Lyrics, Jude Ciccolella; Sound Design, John Giles; Production Stage Manager, Marlene Mancini; Resident Stage Manager, Alan Fox Tuesday, July 31–August 12, 2000 CAST: David Dukes (Marc), William Atherton (Serge), Jack Willis (Yvan)

NEW HARMONY THEATRE

Evansville, Indiana
Thirteenth Season

Producer, James R. Blevins; Artistic Director, Scott LaFeber; Managing Director, Steven Renner

NOISES OFF by Michael Frayn; Director, Michael Unger; Set Design, Todd Rosenthal; Costume Design, Shan Jensen; Lighting Design, Nelson R. Downend, Jr.; Sound Design, Andrew M. Timko; Production Stage Management, T.R. Martin; Friday, June 9–June 25, 2000 CAST: Susan Cella (Dottie Otley), Craig Dudley (Lloyd Dallas), Paul Witthorne (Garry LeJeune), Allison Nega (Brooke Ashton) Stacey Branscum (Poppy Norton-Taylor), Jeb Brown (Frederick Fellowes), Janet Metz (Belinda Blair), Nick Toren (Tim Allgood), Tom Roland (Selsdon Mowbray), Kevin Lottes (Electrician)

THE PHILADELPHIA STORY by Philip Barry; Director, Scott LaFeber; Set Design, Vladimir Shpitalnik; Costume Design, Shan Jensen; Lighting Design, Matthew McCarthy; Sound Design, Andrew M. Timko; Production Stage Management, T.R. Martin; Friday, July 7–July 23, 2000 CAST: Kirsti Carnahan (Tracy Lord), Jackie Angelescu (Dinah Lord), Alice White (Margaret Lord), Sam Mossler (Alexander Lord), Steve Small (William Tracy), Elizabeth Raetz (Elizabeth Imbrie), Larry Gleason (Macaulay Connor), Marc Moritz (George Kittredge), Robert Gallagher (C.K. Dexter Haven), Tom Markus (Seth Lord), Jennifer Baxter (Elsie), Kevin Lottes (Mac)

ALWAYS...PATSY CLINE by Ted Swindley; Director, Scott LaFeber; Musical Direction, Jose C. Simbulan; Settings, Ron Naversen; Costumes, Shan Jensen; Lighting, Mark Varns; Sound, Andrew M. Timko; Production Stage Management, T.R. Martin; Friday, July 28–August 13, 2000 CAST: Terri Dixon (Patsy Cline), Jane Labanz (Louise Segar) MUSICIANS: Jose C. Simbulan (Conductor/Piano), Russ Wever (Pedal Steel), Steve Miles (Guitar), Vy Wickam (Fiddle), Jonathan Lutz (Bass), David Ritterskamp (Drums)

Terri Dixon in *Always...Patsy Cline* (Studio B–Daniel Knight)

Craig Dudley in *Noises Off* (Studio B–Daniel Knight)

The Philadelphia Story (Studio B–Daniel Knight)

OLD GLOBE THEATRE

San Diego, California
Sixty-sixth Season

Artistic Director, Jack O'Brien; Managing Director, Douglas C. Evans; Executive Director, Craig Noel

THE FULL MONTY Music and Lyrics by David Yazbek; Book by Terrence McNally; Directed by Jack O'Brien; Music Director, Ted Sperling; Orchestrations, Harold Wheeler; Choreography, Jerry Mitchell; Scenic Design, John Arnone; Costume Design, Robert Morgan; Lighting Design, Howell Binkley; Sound Design, Jeff Ladman; Dance Arranger, Zane Mark; Stage Managers, Julie Baldauff, Nancy Harrington and Joel Rosen; World Premiere Tuesday, May 23–July 2, 2000 CAST: John Ellison Conlee (Dave Bukatinski), Adam Covalt (Nathan Lukowski, on alternate performance), Jason Daniely (Malcolm Macgregor), Lisa Datz (Pam Lukowski), André De Shields (Noah "Horse" T. Simmons), Jay Douglas (Minister), Laura Marie Duncan (Susan Hershey), Thomas Michael Fiss (Nathan Lukowski, on alternate performances), Angelo Fraboni (Teddy Slaughter), Romain Frugé (Ehtan Girard), Annie Golden (Georgie Bukatinski), Denis Jones (Buddy "Keno" Walsh), Jannie Jones (Joanie Lish), Liz McConahay (Estelle Genovese), Marcus Neville (Harold Nichols), Patti Perkins (Molly Mcgregor), Emily Skinner (Vicki Nichols), Jimmy Smagula (Tony Giordano), C.E. Smith (Police Sergeant/Moving Man), Kathleen Freeman (Jeanette Burmeister), Todd Weeks (Carol Crosby), Patrick Wilson (Jerry Lukowski)

The Company of *The Full Monty* (Craig Schwartz)

HENRY V by William Shakespeare; Director, Dakin Matthews; Scenic Design, Ralph Funicello; Costume Design, Lewis Brown; Lighting Design, Peter Maradudin; Composer, James Legg; Sound Design, Jeff Ladman; Fight Choreography, Steve Rankin; Stage Manager, D. Adams Sunday, July 2–August 12, 2000 CAST: Gigi Bermingham (Catherine of France), Bix Bettwy (Boy), Mark Capri (Chorus/Harfleur/Exeter), Kandis Chappell (Chorus/Quickly/Alice/Ely/Mountjoy), J. Michael Flynn (Cambridge/Constable), Amanda Henkel (Queen of France), Ben Hopkin (Bourbon/Sir Thomas Grey), Hal Landon, Jr. (Nym), Henri Lubatti (Dauphin/Scrope), Jonathan McMurtry (Chorus/King of France/ Erpingham/Cantebury), Ted Matthews (Duke of York), Paul Vincent O'Connor (Westmoreland), Tom Ramirez (Pistol), Norman Snow (Fluellen), Don Sparks (Bardolph), Michael Eric Strickland (Henry V), Dierk Torsek (Gower), Scott Wood (Duke of Bedford), Brian Hutchinson (MacMorris/John Bates), Scott Wood (Jamy/Michael Williams)

GOD'S MAN IN TEXAS by David Rambo; Director, Leonard Foglia; Scenic Design, Robin Sanford Roberts; Costume Design, Lewis Brown; Lighting Design, Ann Archbold; Sound Design, Jeff Ladman; Stage Manager, Raúl Moncada; Cassius Carter Centre Stage; Monday, July 16–August 26, 2000 CAST: Robert Pescovitz (Rev. Jeremiah Mears), Robert Symonds (Dr. Philip Gottschall), Andy Taylor (Hugo Taney)

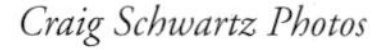

Craig Schwartz Photos

Robert Pescovitz, Robert Symonds in *God's Man in Texas* (Craig Schwartz)

Thomas Michael Fiss, Patrick Wilson in *The Full Monty* (Craig Schwartz)

Michael Eric Strickland in *Henry V* (Craig Schwartz)

PAPER MILL PLAYHOUSE

Millburn, New Jersey

Executive Producer, Angelo Del Rossi; Artistic Director, Robert Johanson; Associate Producer, Roy Miller; Press, Charlie Siedenburg; Casting, Jessica Donovan, Alison Franck; Stage Managers, Eric Sprosty, Catherine Doherty, Becky Miller, Marlene Mancini, Gary Mickelson, Gail P. Luna

MAME; Music/Lyrics, Jerry Herman; Book, Jerome Lawrence and Robert E. Lee; Director, Robert Johanson; Musical Director, Jim Coleman; Choreography, Michael Lichtenfeld; Sets, Michael Anania; Costumes, David Murin; Lighting, F. Mitchell Dana; CAST: Paul S. Iacono (Patrick, age 10), Sandy Rosenberg (Agnes Gooch), Kelly Bishop (Vera Charles), Christine Ebersole (Mame Dennis), Jeffrey Broadhurst (Ralph Devine), Stanley Bojarski (M. Lindsay Woolsey), Tony Romero (Ito), Peter Huck (Doorman), Mark MacKay Lusk (Elevator Boy), Hayes Bergman (Messenger), William McCauley (Dwight Babcock), Peter Cormican (Uncle Jeff/Stage Manager), Susan Cella (Madame Branislowski), Jody Reynard (Gregor), Dan Schiff (Beauregard Jackson Pickett Burnside), Marian Steiner (Cousin Fan), Erika Greene (Sally Cato), D. Titus (Mother Burnside), Ken Barnett (Patrick, age 19-29), Eric H. Kaufman (Junior Babcock), Regina O'Malley (Mrs. Upson), David Titus (Mr. Upson), Danette Holden (Gloria Upson), Melissa Rae Mahon (Pegeen Ryan), Frank Winters (Peter Dennis), Jennifer Howard, Matt Lashey, Sara Lepere, Marianne Martin, Laurie Sondermeyer, Erin Swanson

RAGS; Music, Charles Strouse; Lyrics, Stephen Schwartz; Book, Joseph Stein; Director, Jeffrey B. Moss; Choreography, Barbara Siman; Musical Director, John Mulcahy; Sets, James Morgan; Costumes, Carrie Robbins; Lighting, Stuart Duke CAST: Hunter Bell (Mikhel/Irish Tenor), Jonathan Andrew Bleicher (David Hershkowitz), Marilyn Caskey (Rebecca Hershkowitz), Peter Cormican (Big Tim/Mr. Bronstein), M. Kathryn Quinlan (Bella Cohen), Christopher Bishop (Avram Cohen/Rosenkrantz), Darin De Paul (Rosen/Jack), Caesar Samayoa (Ben/Hamlet), Tia Speros (Anna/Gertrude), Maureen Silliman (Social Worker/Rachel/Ophelia), Wayne LeGette (Nathan Hershkowitz/Laertes), William Whitefield (Ivan), Angela DeCicco (Rosa), Raymond Jaramillo McLeod (Saul), Jayme McDaniel (Man)

NOISES OFF by Michael Frayn; Director, James Brennan; Sets, Michael Anania; Costumes, Jan Finnell; Lighting, Jack Mehler CAST: Anne Rogers (Dotty Otley), Brian Murray (Lloyd Dallas), Edward Staudenmayer (Garry Lejeune), Fiona Gallagher (Brooke Ashton), Blair Sams (Poppy Norton-Taylor), Frederick Fellowes (Graeme Malcolm), Lisby Larson (Belinda Blair), Jonathan F. McClain (Tim Allgood), Leo Leyden (Selsdon Mowbray)

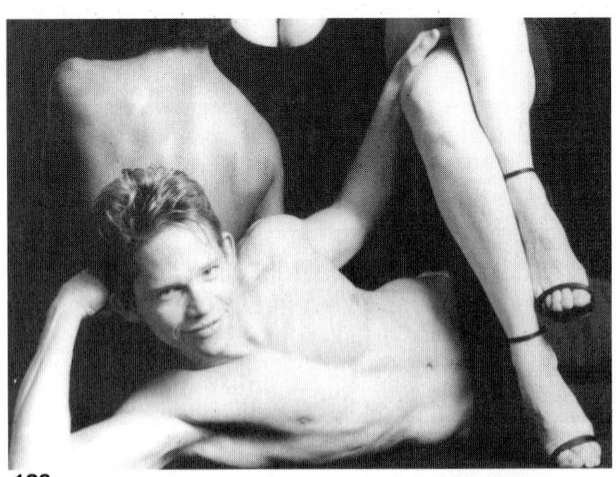

Jack Noseworthy in *Pippin* (Joan Marcus)

Christine Ebersole, Kelly Bishop in *Mame* (Gerry Goodstein)

DEATHTRAP by Ira Levin; Director, Leonard Foglia; Sets, Michael Anania; Costumes, David C. Woolard; Lighting, Jack Mehler; CAST: Jonathan Hadary (Sidney Bruhl), Amy Hohn (Myra Bruhl), Adrian Rieder (Clifford Anderson), Marilyn Sokol (Helga Ten Dorp), Lewis Alt (Porter Milgrim)

THE STUDENT PRINCE; Music, Sigmund Romberg; Lyrics/Book, Dorothy V. Donnelly; Revised Book, Jerome Chodorov; Revised Lyrics, Forman Brown; Revised Arrangements, Harper Mackay; New Lyrics/Musical Arrangements, Albert Evans; Adaptation/Director, Robert Johanson; New Musical Arrangements/Musical Director, Tom Helm; Choreography, Mr. Johanson, Jayme McDaniel; Sets, Michael Anania; Costumes, David Murin; Lighting, Kirk Bookman CAST: Bill Bateman (Herr Lutz), Bill Bowers (Hubert), William McCauley (Count Von Mark), Jerome Hines (DR. Engel), Brandon Jovanovich (Prince Karl Franz), Susan Speidel (Gretchen), Charles Goff (Herr Ruder), Eddie Bracken (Old Josef), Benjamin Brecher (Lucas), William Whitefield (Detleff), Steve Hogle (Von Asterberg), Christiane Noll (Kathie), Jane Connell (Grand Duchess), Glory Crampton (Princess Margaret), Robert Longo (Capt. Tarnitz), Tom Hafner, Chris Pucci, Brian Charles Rooney, Craig Weidner, Stephanie Fredricks, Kristin Huffman, Cara Johnston, Tara Lynne Khaler, Colleen Marcello, Glenn Seven Allen, Todd Almond, Gregory Eichelzer, Brian Frutiger, James Patterson, Michael Pesce, Daniel Pruyn, Dana Steer, Scott Tucker, Lois Hageman, Lynn Bodarky Kronengold, Connie Pearson, Sharon Sandbach

PIPPIN; Music/Lyrics, Stephen Schwartz; Book, Roger O. Hirson; Director, Robert Johanson; Choreography, Rob Ashford; New Orchestrations, David Siegel; Musical Director, Danny Kosarin; Sets, Michael Anania; Costumes, Greg Barnes, (opening number) Gene Meyer; Lighting, Kirk Bookman CAST: Jack Noseworthy (Pippin), Jim Newman (Leading Player), Charlotte Rae (Berthe), Timothy J. Alex (Beggar), Matt Allen (Noble/Head), Roxanne Barlow (Fire Goddess), Natascia A. Diaz (Catherine), Ed Dixon (Charlemagne), Sara Gettelfinger (Fastrada), Gregg Goodbrod (Treasurer), Ramzi Khalaf (Theo), Davis Kirby (Lewis), Clifton Oliver (Field Marshall), Ivan Quintanilla (Peasant), Julie Connors, Amy Heggins, Aixa M. Rosario Medina, Wendy Waring

ANYTHING GOES; Music/Lyrics, Cole Porter; Book, (original) Guy Bolton & P.G. Wodehouse and Howard Linsay & Russel Crouse, (new) Timothy Crouse and John Weidman; Director, Lee Roy Reams; Choreography, Michael Lichtefeld; Musical Director, Tom Helm; Sets, Michael Anania; Costumes, Liz Covey, David F. Shapiro; Lighting, F. Mitchell Dana CAST: Chita Rivera (Reno Sweeney), Ryan Hilliard (Elisha J. Whitney), Peter Cormican (Fred), George Dvorsky (Billy Crocker), Dimitiri Christy (Captain), Don Stitt (Purser), Mark MacKay Lusk (Photographer), James Darrah (Rev. Henry Dobson), Keong Sim (Luke), Randy B. Ballesteros (John), Yasuko Tamaki (Purity), Tara Radcliffe (Chastity). Melissa Hillmer (Charity), Mia Price (Virtue), Stacey Logan (Hope Harcourt), Patrick Quinn (Lord Evelyn Oakleigh), Eleanor Glockner (Evangeline Harcourt), Eric Gunhus, Matthew LaBanca (FBI Agents), Bruce Adler (Moonface Martin), Colleen Hawks (Erma), Melodie Wolford (Old Lady), Becky Berstler (Attendant), Danea Lee Polise

VICTOR/VICTORIA; Music, Henry Mancini; Lyrics, Leslie Bricusse; Book, Blake Edwards; Director, Mark S. Hoebee; Choreography, Arte Phillips; Musical Director, Tom Helm; Sets, Robin Wagner; Costumes, Willa Kim, Jimm Halliday; Lighting, Bob Bonniol CAST: Judy McLane (Victoria), Allen Lewis Rickman (Sal Andretti) Lee Roy Reams (Carroll Todd), Felix Montano (Richard DiNardo), Ellen Sowney (Simone), Martina Vidmar (Company President), Steven Bogard (Deviant Husband/Clam), Roy Harcourt (Gregor), Davis Hall (Henri Labisse), Greta Martin (Piano), Betsy Craig (Madame Roget), Matthew Ellison (Choreographer/Juke), Betsy Craig (Miss Selmer), Dale Hensley (Andre Cassell), Tara O'Brien (Norma Cassidy), Robert Cuccioli (King Marchan), Jody Ashworth (Squash-Mr. Bernstein), Leisa Mather (Street Singer), Jason L. Carroll, Keith Coughlin, David Hyland, Mark MacKay Lusk (Les Boys), Jean Marie, Karen Lifshey, Greta Martin, Vanessa McMahan, Ellen Sowney, Amy Vincent (Norma's Girls)

ART by Yasmina Reza; Translation, Christopher Hampton; Director, Judd Hirsch; Set, Ani Blackburn; Lighting, Cletus Karamon CAST: Judd Hirsch (Marc), Cotter Smith (Serge), Jack Willis (Yvan)

AN IDEAL HUSBAND by Oscar Wilde; Director, James Warwick; Sets, Michael Anania; Lighting, Paul Miller; Costumes, David Murin CAST: Laura Leopard (Mrs. Marchmont), Libby Christophersen (Lady Basildon), Peter Cormican (Mason), Denis Holmes (Duke of Maryborough), Colleen Smith Wallnau (Duchess of Maryborough), George S. Irving (Earl of Caversham), Fiona Hutchison (Lady Chiltern), Stephanie Cozart (Miss Mabel Chiltern), Kathleen Huber (Lady Markby), Stephanie Beacham (Mrs. Cheveley), Rob Breckenridge (Vicomte de Nanjac), David Ledingham (Sir Robert Chiltern), Daniel McDonald (Lord Goring), Michael Mendelson (Mr. Montford), Denis Holmes (Phipps), T.S. Joseph, Nicholas F. Starace II, Jonathan Wentz (Footmen)

FUNNY GIRL; Music, Jule Styne; Lyrics, Bob Merrill; Book, Isobel Lennart; Director, Robert Johanson; Choreography, Michael Lichtefeld; Musical Director, Tom Helm; Sets, Michael Anania; Costumes, David Murin; Lighting, Mark Stanley CAST: Leslie Kritzer (Fanny Brice), Steven Bogard (John), Lori Alexander (Emma), Diane J. Findlay (Mrs. Brice), Marie Lillo (Mrs. Strakosh), Sandy Rosenberg (Mrs. O'Malley), Marian Steiner (Mrs. Meeker), Ray Friedeck (Tom Keeney), Robert Creighton (Eddie Ryan), Matt Lashey (Piano), Mark MacKay Lusk (Snub Taylor), Mia Price (Bubbles), Nicole Batalias (Maude/Mrs. Nadler), Katie Rayle (Polly), Robert Cuccioli (Nick Arnstein), Bob Dorian (Ziegfeld), Jean Marie (Mimsey), Christopher Pucci (Tenor), Drew Taylor (Adolph/Renaldi), Anthony Frisina (Paul), Susan Paige Henderson (Vera), Hayes Bergman, Keith Coughlin, Jennifer Clippinger Dudik, Jaclyn Ford, Melissa Hillmer, Tari Kelley, Michael Taylor, Adriene Thorne

Cotter Smith, Jack Willis, Judd Hirsch in *Art* (Joan Marcus)

Brandon Jovanovich, Christiane Noll in *The Student Prince* (Gerry Goodstein)

CAROUSEL; Music, Richard Rodgers; Lyrics/Book, Oscar Hammerstein II; Director, Robert Johanson; Choreography, Robert La Fosse; Musical Directors, Tom Helm, Vicki Carter; Sets, Michael Anania; Costumes, Gregory A. Poplyk; Lighting, F. Mitchell Dana CAST: Christiane Noll (Carrie), Glory Crampton (Julie), Betsy Craig (Mrs. Mullin), Matt Bogart (Billy Bigelow), Michael Hunsaker (Police), Ray Friedeck (David Bascombe), Marsha Bagwell (Nettie), Brandon Jovanovich (Enoch Snow), Jeb Brown (Jigger), Ilene Bergelson (Hannah), Sean Kelly (Boatswain), Alisa Klein (Arminy), Matthew Scott (Police), Dante A. Sciarra (Captain), Blake Segal, Allison Siko (Heavenly Friends), Eddie Bracken (Starkeeper/Dr. Seldon), Geralyn Del Corso (Louise), Mark Myars (Carnival Boy), Robert McClure (Enoch Snow Jr.), Jessica Goldyn (Snow Girl), Seth Malkin (Principal), Timothy W. Bish, Gabriela Garcia, Jessica Goldyn, Deena Goodman, Bruce Harris, Joy Hermalyn, Michael Hunsaker, Brian Letendre, Mark Myars, Holly Rone, Desiree Sanchez, Alexandra Sawyier, Blake Segal, Laura Shoop, Bret Shuford, Courtney Steven, Jenna Steven

Gerry Goodstein

THE PASADENA PLAYHOUSE

Pasadena, California

Artistic Director, Sheldon Epps; Interim Executive Director, Lyla White

THE GLASS MENAGERIE by Tennessee Williams; Director, Andrew J. Robinson; Scenic Design, John Iacovelli; Costume Design, Dione H. Lebhar; Lighting Design, J. Kent Inasy; Sound Design, Mitch Greenhill; Hair, Wig, and Make-up Design, Judi Lewin; Casting, Amy Lieberman; Production Stage Manager, Jill Johnson Gold; Stage Manager, Lea Chazin Friday, May 5–June 18, 2000 CAST: Susan Sullivan (Amanda Wingfield), Tony Crane, Rachel Robinson, Raphael Sbarge

THE GOOD DOCTOR by Neil Simon; Director, Stephanie Shroyer; Scenic Design, Gary Wissmann; Costume Design, Dana Woods; Lighting Design, Michael Gilliam; Sound Design, Stafford Floyd; Casting Director, Julia Flores; Production Stage Manager, Jill Gold; Stage Manager, Annie Gilbert; Friday, July 7–August 20, 2000 CAST: Harry Groener, Michael Learned, Raye Birk, Marita Geraghty, Time Winters

BLITHE SPIRIT by Noël Coward; Director, Douglas C. Wager; Scenic Design, Roy Christopher; Costume Design, Jean-Pierre Dorleac; Lighting Design, D Martyn Bookwalter; Associate Sound Design, Francois Bergeron; Associate Sound Design, Martin Carrillo; Hair, Wig, and Make-up Design, Judi Lewin; Casting, Julia Flores; Production Stage Manager, Heidi Swartz; Stage Manager, Lea Chazin; Friday, November 3–December 17, 2000 CAST: Shirley Knight, Kaitlin Hopkins, Sara Botsford, Megan Cavanagh, Francois Giroday, Charles Lanyer, Carol Mansell

HOW THE OTHER HALF LOVES by Alan Ayckbourn; Director, Larry Arrick; Scenic Design, Ursula Belden; Costume Design, Diane Eden; Lighting Design, Michael Zinman; Sound Design, Stafford Floyd; Casting Director, Julia Flores; Production Stage Manager, Jill Johnson Gold; Stage Manager, Annie Gilbert Friday, January 5–February 18, 2001 CAST: Jeanie Hackett (Teresa Phillips), Jamison Jones (Bob Phillips), Lily Knight (Mary Detweiler), Keith Langsdale (William Detweiler), Brian Reddy (Frank Foster), April Shawhan (Fiona Foster)

SIDE MAN Director, Andrew J. Robinson; Friday, May 4–June 17, 2001 CAST: Mare Willingham, Dennis Christopher, J.D. Cullum, Daniel Reichert

Craig Schwartz Photos

Susan Sullivan, Raphael Sbarge, Rachel Robinson in *The Glass Menagerie* (Craig Schwartz)

Harry Groener, Michael Learned, Raye Birk in *The Good Doctor* (Craig Schwartz)

Jamison Jones, April Shawhan in *How the Other Half Loves* (Craig Schwartz)

Carol Mansell, Francois Giroday, Shirley Knight, Sara Botsford, Charles Lanyer in *Blithe Spirit (Craig Schwartz)*

THE SHUBERT THEATRE

Operated by the Wang Center for the Performing Arts
President and Chief Executive Officer, Josiah A. Spalding, Jr.; Vice President and Chief Operating Officer, William C. Taylor; Director of Human Resources, Paul M. Looby; Executive Assistant to the President, Anne Taylor; Assistant to the V.P. & C.O.O., John Grendon; Web Director, Joyce A. Spinney; Information Systems Manager, Kyriakos Kalaitzidis; Receptionist, Maritza Franklin

DEATH OF A SALESMAN by Arthur Miller; Director, Robert Falls; Scenic Design, Mark Wendland; Costume Design, Birgit Rattenborg Wise; Lighting Design, Michael Philippi; Original Sound/Music Design, Richard Woodbury; Associate Producer, SFX Theatrical Group; Casting, Bernard Telsey Casting/Tara Lonzo; Technical Supervision, Gene O'Donovan; Company Manager, Lisa M. Poyer; Production Stage Manager, Mary K. Klinger; Press Representative, Richard Kornberg and Associates; General Management, Robert Cole Productions; The Shubert Theatre, Operated by The Wang Center for the Performing Arts, David Richenthal, Jujamcyn Theaters, Allan S. Gordon and Fox Theatricals, in association with Jerry Frankel and Robert Cole present a Goodman Theatre Production; Tuesday, November 28–December 10, 2000 CAST: Brian Dennehy (Willy Loman), Elizabeth Franz (Linda), Ted Koch (Biff), Steve Cell (Happy), Richard Thompson (Bernard), Kate Buddeke (The Woman), Howard Witt (Charley), Allen Hamilton (Uncle Ben), Steve Pickering (Howard Wagner), Barbara Eda-Young (Jenny), Kent Klineman (Stanley), Nina Landey (Miss Forsythe), Laura Moss (Letta), UNDERSTUDIES: Steve Cell, Barbara Eda-Young, Philip LeStrange, Patrick Boll, Kent Klineman, Nina Landey, Allison Barcott

THE ADVENTURES OF TOM SAWYER Based on the novel by Mark Twain; Book, Ken Ludwig; Music and Lyrics, Don Schlitz; Director, Scott Ellis; Musical Direction, Paul Gemignani; Orchestrations, Michael Starobin; Choreography, David Marques; Scenic Design, Heidi Ettinger; Costume Design, Anthony Powell; Lighting Design, Kenneth Posner; Sound Design, Lew Mead; Hair Design, David Brian Brown; Dance and Incidental Music, David Krane; Production Manager, Arthur Siccardi; Fight Director, Rick Sordelet; Production Supervisor, Beverley Randolph; General Management, Devin Keudell; Press Representative, Boneau/Bryan-Brown; Marketing, The Marketing Group; Casting, Jim Carnahan, CSA Tuesday, February 27–March 11, 2001 CAST: Joshua Park (Tom Sawyer); Tommar Wilson (Ben Rogers), Joe Gallagher (George Bellamy), Blake Hackler (Lyle Bellamy), Erik J. McCormack (Joe Harper), Pierce Cravens (Alfred Temple), Ann Whitlow Brown (Amy Lawerence), Mekenzie Rosen-Stone (Lucy Harper), Èlan (Susie Rogers), Nikki M. James (Sabina Temple), Stacia Fernandez (Sally Bellamy), Donna Lee Marshall (Sereny Harper), Amy Jo Phillips (Lucinda Rogers), Sally Wilfert (Naomi Temple), Linda Purl (Aunt Polly), Stephen Lee Anderson (Doc Robinson/Pap), Tommy Hollis (Reverend Sprague), Richard Poe (Lanyard Bellamy), Ric Stoneback (Gideon Temple), John Christopher Jones (Lemuel Dobbins), Marshall Pailet (Sid Sawyer), Kristen Bell (Becky Thatcher), Jim Poulos (Huckleberry Finn), Tom Aldredge (Muff Potter), Kevin Serge Durand (Injun Joe), John Dossett (Judge Thatcher), Jane Connell (Widow Douglas) UNDERSTUDIES: Blake Hackler, Erik J. McCormack, Joe Gallagher, Tommar Wilson, Nikki M. James, Kate Reinders, Stacia Fernandez, Sally Wilfert, Richard Poe, Patrick Boll, John Herrera, Amy Jo Phillips, Pierce Cravens, Stephen Lee Anderson, Swings: Patrick Boll, Michael Burton, John Herrara, Kate Reinders, Elise Santora

THE THREE MUSKETEERS Choreography, André Provosky; Music, Giuseppe Verdi; Arrangements and Additional Music, Guy Woolfenden; Decor and Costumes, Alexandre Vassiliev; Lighting Design, Jaak Van de Velde Friday, March 24, 2001 CAST: Leslie Pierce (Milady), Aki Saito (Constance), Olga Voloboueva (The Queen), Lars Van Cauwenbergh (D'Artagnan), Ilia Belitchkov (Aramis), Artur Lill (Porthos), Alain Honorez (Athos), Guiseppe Nocera (Lord Buckingham), Emre Sokmen (Rochefort), Gideon Louw (Cardinal Richelieu), Wim Vanlessen (King Louis XIII), Sanny Kleef (Cardinal's Guard), Howard Quintero (Cardinal's Guard), Frederick Deberdt (Cardinal's Guard), Kevin Durwael (Cardinal's Guard), Tom Colin (Cardinal's Guard), Jesse Jacobs (Cardinal's Guard)

STAMFORD CENTER FOR THE ARTS

Executive Director, George E. Moredock, III; Artistic Director, George E. Moredock, III; Executive Assistant, Gail Mason; Director of Special Projects, John Hiddlestone; Director of Finance and Administration, Frank K. Thiel; Director of Operations, Felicia Bettini; Director of Development and Communications, Jenny Ober; Assistant to the Director, Helen Rocco; Production Manager, Onis McHenry; Media Manager, Richard P. Pheneger; Systems Administrator, C.J. Currier; Production Stage Manager, Leisah Swensen, Marketing Manager, Steve Blair; Manager, Box Office services, Michael E. Moran, Jr.; Facilities Manager, Tom Corbett; Senior House Manager, Vicki Keiffer-Rinkerman; Manager of Development, Lisa Caporizzo

BELLS ARE RINGING Book and Lyrics, Betty Comden and Adolph Green; Music, Jule Styne; Director, Tina Landau; Choreography, Jeff Calhoun; Associate Choreography, Patti D'Beck; Scenic Design, Riccardo Hernandez; Costume Design, David C. Woolard; Lighting Design, Donald Holder; Sound Design, Acme Sound Partners; Production Stage Manger, Erica Schwartz; Casting, Stephanie Klapper, CSA; Technical Supervision, Larry Morley; Video, Batwin and Robin Productions; Musical Direction and Vocal Arrangements, David Evans; Orchestrations, Don Sebesky; Musical Coordinator; Seymour Red Press; Dance Music Arrangements, Mark Hummel; Press Representative, Barlow-Hartman Public Relations; General Management, Robert V. Straus Productions Inc., Robert V. Straus/Ellen Rusconi; Director of Marketing, Tracey Mendelsohn; Marketing/Promotions, Leanne Schanzer Promotions, Inc.; Associate Producers, Alan S. Kopit, Richard Berger; Palace Theatre Tuesday, February 20–February 25, 2001 CAST: Shane Kirkpatrick (TV Announcer/Ella's Dream Jeff/Joey/Dancer), Caitlin Carter (Telephone Girl/Olga/Dancer), Joan Hess (Telephone Girl/Bridgette/Mrs. Mallet/Dancer), Emily Hsu (Telephone Girl/Dancer), Alice Rietveld (Telephone Girl), Beth Fowler (Sue), Angela Robinson (Gwynne), Faith Prince (Ella), Julio Agustin (Carl/Ensemble), Roy Harcourt (Ella's Dream Jeff/Padie/Dancer), Greg Reuter (Ella's Dream Jeff/Louie/Carvello Mob Man/Dancer), Josh Rhodes (Ella's Dream Jeff/Charlie Bessemer/Waiter/Man on Street/Dancer), Robert An (Inspector Barnes), Jeffrey Bean (Francis), David Garrison (Sandor), Marc Kudisch (Jeff Moss), David Brummel (Larry Hastings/Carvello Mob Man), Lawrence Clayton (Ludwig Smiley/Paul Arnold), Martin Moran (Dr. Kitchell), Darren Ritchie (Blake Burton), Linda Romoff (Maid/Ensemble), Joanne Baum (Madame Grimaldi), Alice Rietveld (Ensemble) SWINGS: James Hadley, Stacey Harris, Kelly Sullivan

TALLULAH Rich Forum Tuesday, March 13–March 18, 2001 CAST: Kathleen Turner

SYRACUSE STAGE

Syracuse, NY
Twenty-eighth Season

Artistic Director, Robert Moss; Producing Director Jim Clark

BORN YESTERDAY by Garson Kanin; Director, Robert Moss; Set Design, Rick Dennis; Costume Design, Michael Krass; Lighting Design, Phil Monat; Sound Design, Jonathan Herter; Stage Manager, Stuart Plymesser; John D. Archbold Theatre Wednesday, September 20–October 14, 2000 CAST: Kelly AuCoin (Paul Verrall), Tim Barrett (Eddie Brock), Mimi Bensinger (Mrs. Hedges), Malachi Cleary (Ed Devery), Suzanne Grodner (Helen), Taylor Hooper (Assistant Manager), Paul Stolarsky (Senator Hedges) Vicki Van Tassel (Billie Dawn), Timothy Wheeler (Harry Brock)

ELEANOR: HER SECRET JOURNEY by Rhoda Lerman; Director, John Tillinger; Costume Design, Noel Taylor; Sound Design, Aural Fixation; Wig Design, Paul Huntley; Production Supervisor/Lighting Design, Ron Nash. John D. Archbold Theatre Tuesday, October 17–November 12, 2000 CAST: Jean Stapleton (Eleanor Roosevelt)

PETER PAN based on the play by James M. Barrie; Lyrics by Carolyn Leigh; Music by Mark Charlap; Additional Music by Jule Styne; Additional lyrics by Betty Comden and Adolph Green; A Syracuse Stage and the S. U. Drama Department collaboration; Director and Choreography, Anthony Salatino; Musical Direction, Dianne Adams McDowell; Set Design, Beowulf Boritt; Costume Design, Soonwha Choi; Lighting Design, A. Nelson Ruger IV; Sound Design, Jonathan Herter; Stage Manager, Stuart Plymesser; John D. Archbold Theatre Tuesday, November 28–December 30, 2000 CAST: Amanda Butterbaugh (Peter Pan), Izetta Fang (Tiger Lily), Rodney Scott Hudson (Mr. Darling/Captain Hook), Marie Kemp (Mrs. Darling), Tom Richter (Smee), Sandy Rustin (Wendy) NON-EQUITY CAST: Ross Berman (Michael), Brian Caccopola (Tootles), Kyle Davies (Nibs), Matt Dengler (John), Michael DiLiberto (Noodler), Alex Friedman (Michael), Patrick Garrigan (Slightly), Taylor Hooper (Cookson), Spencer Murphy (John), Tiffany Quist (1st Twin), Erin Race (Curly), Heather Rachel Rosenfeld (Nana/Crocodile), Russ Salmon (Starkey), Stephanie Schweitzer (2nd Twin), Wesley Thornton (Cecco), Kevin C. Wanzor (Jukes), Emily Agy, Nikki Coble, Lauren Fruchter, Deborah Joffee, Patti Murin, Shelley Thomas, Kate Vallee (Indians)

BLUES FOR AN ALABAMA SKY by Pearl Cleage; Director, Timothy Douglas; Set Design, Tony Cisek; Costume Design, Randall E. Klein; Lighting Design, Michael Gilliam; Sound Design, Jonathan Herter; Stage Manager, Sarah Pickett; John D. Archbold Theatre, Thursday, January 11–February 3, 2001 CAST: Pascale Armand (Delia), Tyrone Mitchell Henderson (Guy), Charles Parnell (Leland), Godfrey L. Simmons, Jr. (Sam), Kelly Taffe (Angel).

WIT by Margaret Edson; Director, Kevin Moriarty; Sets, Matthew Maraffi; Lights, Jeff Croiter; Costumes, Jared B. Leese; Sound, Jonathan Herter; Stage Manager, John M. Atherlay; John D. Archbold Theatre Wednesday, February 14–March 1, 2001 CAST: Tawanna Benbow (Susie Monahan), Mark Boyett (Jason Posner), Joseph Costa (Dr. Kelekian, Mr. Bearing), Susanne Marley (Vivian Bearing), Peg Small (E.M. Ashford), Brett Glazer, Pegge Johnson and Kevin Merrill-Wilson (Lab Technicians, Students, and Clinical Fellows).

ROMEO AND JULIET by William Shakespeare; Director, Robert Moss; Set Design, Erhard Rom; Costume Design, Michael Krass; Lighting Design, Robert Williams; Sound Design, Jonathan Herter; Dance and Fight Choreography, Anthony Salatino; Stage Manager, Stuart Plymesser; John D. Archbold Theatre Thursday, March 29–April 28, 2001 CAST: Elizabeth Arnold (Nurse), Rick Bank (Paris), Stephen Bradbury (Capulet), Matt Golden (Benvolio), Jonathan Hammond (Mercutio), Malcolm Ingram (The Prince), Paul James (Peter), Corinna May (Lady Capulet), Gerard Moses (Montague), Devon Sorvari (Juliet), PJ Sosko (Tybalt), Rob A. Wilson, (Romeo), Joe Wilson, Jr. (Friar Laurence), Matt Benson, Elias Christeas, Nikki Coble, Teanna DiMicco, Jenn Doerr, Sarah Easterling, Taylor Hooper, Laura Jeanne Ingalls, William Kuhrt, Michael Patrick Mattie, Sarah Novikoff, Evan Salama (Citizens of Verona)

ART by Yasmina Reza; Translated by Christopher Hampton; Director, Melissa Kievman; Set Design, Michael Fagin; Costume Design, Lora LaVon; Lighting Design, Matthew Frey; Sound Design, Jonathan Herter; Stage Manager, John M. Atherlay; John D. Archbold Theatre Wednesday, May 9–May 27, 2001 CAST: Patrick Husted (Marc), Gary Sloan (Serge), Jim True-Frost (Yvan)

THE WILBUR THEATRE

Boston, Massachusetts

DAME EDNA: THE ROYAL TOUR Devised and Written by Barry Humphries; Additional Material by Ian Davidson; Keyboards, Wayne Barker; Scenic Design, Kenneth Foy; Costume Design, Stephen Adnitt; Lighting Design, Jason Kantrowitz; Sound Design, Peter Fitzgerald; Production Manger, Arthur Siccardi; Production Stage Manager, James W. Gibbs; General Management, Soloway/Levy; Press Representative/Marketing; TMG-The Marketing Group; Artistic Associate, Cynthia Onrubia; Associate Producers, Skylight Productions, Adam Friedson, David Friedson, Allen Spivak/Larry Magid, Richard Martini Tuesday, February 20–March 11, 2001 CAST: Dame Edna (Barry Humphries), Teri Digianfelice (Gorgeous Ednaette), Michelle Pampena (Gorgeous Ednaette)

Juliette Binoche of *Betrayal*

Macaulay Culkin of *Madame Melville*

Janie Dee of *Comic Potential*

Raul Esparza of *The Rocky Horror Show*

Kathleen Freeman of *The Full Monty*

Deven May of *Bat Boy*

Reba McEntire of *Annie Get Your Gun*

Chris Noth of *Gore Vidal's The Best Man*

Joshua Park of *The Adventures of Tom Sawyer*

Rosie Perez of *References to Salvador Dalí Make Me Hot*

Joely Richardson of *Madame Melville*

John Ritter of *The Dinner Party*

Seán Campion of *Stones in His Pockets*

Conleth Hill of *Stones in His Pockets*

THEATRE WORLD AWARDS

PRESENTED AT STUDIO 54

(May 14, 2001)

Mary-Louise Parker

Host Peter Filichia

Rosie Perez

Chris Noth

Raul Esparza

Reba McEntire

Daphne Rubin-Vega

Joely Richardson, Rosemary Harris

Juliette Koka

Juliette Binoche

John Ritter

Brian Stokes Mitchell, Leslie Uggams

Alec Baldwin

2001 THEATRE WORLD AWARDS ENDOWMENT DONORS

ANGELS ($1000 AND OVER)

Lucie Arnaz
1979 Theatre World Award
They're Playing Our Song

Jane Alexander
Fat Chance Productions, Inc.
Alec Baldwin
Chase Mishkin
Anonymous
Charlotte Moore & John McMartin

Patricia Elliott
1973 Theatre World Award
A Little Night Music

PATRONS ($500-$999)

Anonymous
Laurence Guittard
Billy Crudup
Peter & Marsue MacNicol
Joan Cullman
Audra McDonald
Roy & Evan

SPONSORS ($100-$499)

Anonymous
Linda Hart
Jordan Baker & Kevin Kilner
Ernestine Jackson
David Birney
Stephen James
Kate Burton
Elaine Joyce
Maxwell Caufield
Laura Dean Koch
Thom & Judith Christopher
Juliette Koka
Kathy B. Combs
Dr. Raymond & Suzy Lowry
Barbara Cook
Spiro & Marlena Malas
Dennis J. Cooney
Andrea Martin
David Cryer
James Mitchell
Dr. Brenda Dean
Bill Moor
Bambi Linn DeJesus
Morristown-Hamblen H.S. East
Leslie Denniston
James Naughton
Nancy Dussault
Kip Osborne
Shirley W. Epstein
Louise B. Owens
Giancarlo Esposito
Estelle Parsons
Harvey Evans
Michael Pober
Brian Farrell
David A. Powers
Tovah Feldshuh
Daryl Roth
Harvey Fierstein
Bill Schelble
Bonnie Franklin
Sheila A. Smith
James Frasher
Jane Sell Trese
Julie Garfield
Joan Van Ark
Nancy Giles
Beatrice Winde
Marlene J. Gould
Eli Wallach

FRIENDS ($99 AND UNDER)

Anonymous
David Keith
Howard & Barbara Atlee
Laurie Kennedy
Maureen Brennan
Lizbeth Mackay
Leonard Crofoot
Crista Moore
Lindsay Duncan

Leonard Crofoot

Mary Murfitt
Craig Dudley
Eddie & Elaine Overholt
Jim Hollifield
Roger Rathburn
Katherine Houghton
Charles Repole
Mark Jacoby
Joseph Urla

THEATRE WORLD AWARDS, INC. ENDOWMENT FUND
c/o Peter Filichia, Treasurer
1 Star-Ledger Plaza
Newark, NJ 07102-1200

PREVIOUS THEATRE WORLD AWARD RECIPIENTS

Everett Bradley

Len Cariou

Daphne Rubin-Vega

1944–45: Betty Comden, Richard Davis, Richard Hart, Judy Holliday, Charles Lang, Bambi Linn, John Lund, Donald Murphy, Nancy Noland, Margaret Phillips, John Raitt
1945–46: Barbara Bel Geddes, Marlon Brando, Bill Callahan, Wendell Corey, Paul Douglas, Mary James, Burt Lancaster, Patricia Marshall, Beatrice Pearson
1946–47: Keith Andes, Marion Bell, Peter Cookson, Ann Crowley, Ellen Hanley, John Jordan, George Keane, Dorothea MacFarland, James Mitchell, Patricia Neal, David Wayne
1947–48: Valerie Bettis, Edward Bryce, Whitfield Connor, Mark Dawson, June Lockhart, Estelle Loring, Peggy Maley, Ralph Meeker, Meg Mundy, Douglass Watson, James Whitmore, Patrice Wymore
1948–49: Tod Andrews, Doe Avedon, Jean Carson, Carol Channing, Richard Derr, Julie Harris, Mary McCarty, Allyn Ann McLerie, Cameron Mitchell, Gene Nelson, Byron Palmer, Bob Scheerer
1949–50: Nancy Andrews, Phil Arthur, Barbara Brady, Lydia Clarke, Priscilla Gillette, Don Hanmer, Marcia Henderson, Charlton Heston, Rick Jason, Grace Kelly, Charles Nolte, Roger Price
1950–51: Barbara Ashley, Isabel Bigley, Martin Brooks, Richard Burton, Pat Crowley, James Daley, Cloris Leachman, Russell Nype, Jack Palance, William Smithers, Maureen Stapleton, Marcia Van Dyke, Eli Wallach
1951–52: Tony Bavaar, Patricia Benoit, Peter Conlow, Virginia de Luce, Ronny Graham, Audrey Hepburn, Diana Herbert, Conrad Janis, Dick Kallman, Charles Proctor, Eric Sinclair, Kim Stanley, Marian Winters, Helen Wood
1952–53: Edie Adams, Rosemary Harris, Eileen Heckart, Peter Kelley, John Kerr, Richard Kiley, Gloria Marlowe, Penelope Munday, Paul Newman, Sheree North, Geraldine Page, John Stewart, Ray Stricklyn, Gwen Verdon
1953–54: Orson Bean, Harry Belafonte, James Dean, Joan Diener, Ben Gazzara, Carol Haney, Jonathan Lucas, Kay Medford, Scott Merrill, Elizabeth Montgomery, Leo Penn, Eva Marie Saint
1954–55: Julie Andrews, Jacqueline Brookes, Shirl Conway, Barbara Cook, David Daniels, Mary Fickett, Page Johnson, Loretta Leversee, Jack Lord, Dennis Patrick, Anthony Perkins, Christopher Plummer
1955–56: Diane Cilento, Dick Davalos, Anthony Franciosa, Andy Griffith, Laurence Harvey, David Hedison, Earle Hyman, Susan Johnson, John Michael King, Jayne Mansfield, Sara Marshall, Gaby Rodgers, Susan Strasberg, Fritz Weaver
1956–57: Peggy Cass, Sydney Chaplin, Sylvia Daneel, Bradford Dillman, Peter Donat, George Grizzard, Carol Lynley, Peter Palmer, Jason Robards, Cliff Robertson, Pippa Scott, Inga Swenson
1957–58: Anne Bancroft, Warren Berlinger, Colleen Dewhurst, Richard Easton, Tim Everett, Eddie Hodges, Joan Hovis, Carol Lawrence, Jacqueline McKeever, Wynne Miller, Robert Morse, George C. Scott
1958–59: Lou Antonio, Ina Balin, Richard Cross, Tammy Grimes, Larry Hagman, Dolores Hart, Roger Mollien, France Nuyen, Susan Oliver, Ben Piazza, Paul Roebling, William Shatner, Pat Suzuki, Rip Torn
1959–60: Warren Beatty, Eileen Brennan, Carol Burnett, Patty Duke, Jane Fonda, Anita Gillette, Elisa Loti, Donald Madden, George Maharis, John McMartin, Lauri Peters, Dick Van Dyke
1960–61: Joyce Bulifant, Dennis Cooney, Sandy Dennis, Nancy Dussault, Robert Goulet, Joan Hackett, June Harding, Ron Husmann, James MacArthur, Bruce Yarnell
1961–62: Elizabeth Ashley, Keith Baxter, Peter Fonda, Don Galloway, Sean Garrison, Barbara Harris, James Earl Jones, Janet Margolin, Karen Morrow, Robert Redford, John Stride, Brenda Vaccaro
1962–63: Alan Arkin, Stuart Damon, Melinda Dillon, Robert Drivas, Bob Gentry, Dorothy Loudon, Brandon Maggart, Julienne Marie, Liza Minnelli, Estelle Parsons, Diana Sands, Swen Swenson
1963–64: Alan Alda, Gloria Bleezarde, Imelda De Martin, Claude Giraud, Ketty Lester, Barbara Loden, Lawrence Pressman, Gilbert Price, Philip Proctor, John Tracy, Jennifer West

1964–65: Carolyn Coates, Joyce Jillson, Linda Lavin, Luba Lisa, Michael O'Sullivan, Joanna Pettet, Beah Richards, Jaime Sanchez, Victor Spinetti, Nicolas Surovy, Robert Walker, Clarence Williams III
1965–66: Zoe Caldwell, David Carradine, John Cullum, John Davidson, Faye Dunaway, Gloria Foster, Robert Hooks, Jerry Lanning, Richard Mulligan, April Shawhan, Sandra Smith, Leslie Ann Warren
1966–67: Bonnie Bedelia, Richard Benjamin, Dustin Hoffman, Terry Kiser, Reva Rose, Robert Salvio, Sheila Smith, Connie Stevens, Pamela Tiffin, Leslie Uggams, Jon Voight, Christopher Walken
1967–68: David Birney, Pamela Burrell, Jordan Christopher, Jack Crowder (Thalmus Rasulala), Sandy Duncan, Julie Gregg, Stephen Joyce, Bernadette Peters, Alice Playten, Michael Rupert, Brenda Smiley, Russ Thacker
1968–69: Jane Alexander, David Cryer, Blythe Danner, Ed Evanko, Ken Howard, Lauren Jones, Ron Leibman, Marian Mercer, Jill O'Hara, Ron O'Neal, Al Pacino, Marlene Warfield
1969–70: Susan Browning, Donny Burks, Catherine Burns, Len Cariou, Bonnie Franklin, David Holliday, Katharine Houghton, Melba Moore, David Rounds, Lewis J. Stadlen, Kristoffer Tabori, Fredricka Weber
1970–71: Clifton Davis, Michael Douglas, Julie Garfield, Martha Henry, James Naughton, Tricia O'Neil, Kipp Osborne, Roger Rathburn, Ayn Ruymen, Jennifer Salt, Joan Van Ark, Walter Willison
1971–72: Jonelle Allen, Maureen Anderman, William Atherton, Richard Backus, Adrienne Barbeau, Cara Duff-MacCormick, Robert Foxworth, Elaine Joyce, Jess Richards, Ben Vereen, Beatrice Winde, James Woods
1972–73: D'Jamin Bartlett, Patricia Elliott, James Farentino, Brian Farrell, Victor Garber, Kelly Garrett, Mari Gorman, Laurence Guittard, Trish Hawkins, Monte Markham, John Rubinstein, Jennifer Warren, Alexander H. Cohen (Special Award)
1973–74: Mark Baker, Maureen Brennan, Ralph Carter, Thom Christopher, John Driver, Conchata Ferrell, Ernestine Jackson, Michael Moriarty, Joe Morton, Ann Reinking, Janie Sell, Mary Woronov, Sammy Cahn (Special Award)
1974–75: Peter Burnell, Zan Charisse, Lola Falana, Peter Firth, Dorian Harewood, Joel Higgins, Marcia McClain, Linda Miller, Marti Rolph, John Sheridan, Scott Stevensen, Donna Theodore, Equity Library Theatre (Special Award)
1975–76: Danny Aiello, Christine Andreas, Dixie Carter, Tovah Feldshuh, Chip Garnett, Richard Kelton, Vivian Reed, Charles Repole, Virginia Seidel, Daniel Seltzer, John V. Shea, Meryl Streep, A Chorus Line (Special Award)
1976–77: Trazana Beverley, Michael Cristofer, Joe Fields, Joanna Gleason, Cecilia Hart, John Heard, Gloria Hodes, Juliette Koka, Andrea McArdle, Ken Page, Jonathan Pryce, Chick Vennera, Eva LeGallienne (Special Award)
1977–78: Vasili Bogazianos, Nell Carter, Carlin Glynn, Christopher Goutman, William Hurt, Judy Kaye, Florence Lacy, Armelia McQueen, Gordana Rashovich, Bo Rucker, Richard Seer, Colin Stinton, Joseph Papp (Special Award)
1978–79: Philip Anglim, Lucie Arnaz, Gregory Hines, Ken Jennings, Michael Jeter, Laurie Kennedy, Susan Kingsley, Christine Lahti, Edward James Olmos, Kathleen Quinlan, Sarah Rice, Max Wright, Marshall W. Mason (Special Award)
1979–80: Maxwell Caulfield, Leslie Denniston, Boyd Gaines, Richard Gere, Harry Groener, Stephen James, Susan Kellermann, Dinah Manoff, Lonny Price, Marianne Tatum, Anne Twomey, Dianne Wiest, Mickey Rooney (Special Award)
1980–81: Brian Backer, Lisa Banes, Meg Bussert, Michael Allen Davis, Giancarlo Esposito, Daniel Gerroll, Phyllis Hyman, Cynthia Nixon, Amanda Plummer, Adam Redfield, Wanda Richert, Rex Smith, Elizabeth Taylor (Special Award)
1981–82: Karen Akers, Laurie Beechman, Danny Glover, David Alan Grier, Jennifer Holliday, Anthony Heald, Lizbeth Mackay, Peter MacNicol, Elizabeth McGovern, Ann Morrison, Michael O'Keefe, James Widdoes, Manhattan Theatre Club (Special Award)
1982–83: Karen Allen, Suzanne Bertish, Matthew Broderick, Kate Burton, Joanne Camp, Harvey Fierstein, Peter Gallagher, John Malkovich, Anne Pitoniak, James Russo, Brian Tarantina, Linda Thorson, Natalia Makarova (Special Award)
1983–84: Martine Allard, Joan Allen, Kathy Whitton Baker, Mark Capri, Laura Dean, Stephen Geoffreys, Todd Graff, Glenne Headly, J.J. Johnston, Bonnie Koloc, Calvin Levels, Robert Westenberg, Ron Moody (Special Award)
1984–85: Kevin Anderson, Richard Chaves, Patti Cohenour, Charles S. Dutton, Nancy Giles, Whoopi Goldberg, Leilani Jones, John Mahoney, Laurie Metcalf, Barry Miller, John Turturro, Amelia White, Lucille Lortel (Special Award)
1985–86: Suzy Amis, Alec Baldwin, Aled Davies, Faye Grant, Julie Hagerty, Ed Harris, Mark Jacoby, Donna Kane, Cleo Laine, Howard McGillin, Marisa Tomei, Joe Urla, Ensemble Studio Theatre (Special Award)
1986–87: Annette Bening, Timothy Daly, Lindsay Duncan, Frank Ferrante, Robert Lindsay, Amy Madigan, Michael Maguire, Demi Moore, Molly Ringwald, Frances Ruffelle, Courtney B. Vance, Colm Wilkinson, Robert DeNiro (Special Award)
1987–88: Yvonne Bryceland, Philip Casnoff, Danielle Ferland, Melissa Gilbert, Linda Hart, Linzi Hately, Brian Kerwin, Brian Mitchell, Mary Murfitt, Aidan Quinn, Eric Roberts, B.D. Wong, Special Awards: Tisa Chang, Martin E. Segal.
1988–89: Dylan Baker, Joan Cusack, Loren Dean, Peter Frechette, Sally Mayes, Sharon McNight, Jennie Moreau, Paul Provenza, Kyra Sedgwick, Howard Spiegel, Eric Stoltz, Joanne Whalley-Kilmer, Special Awards: Pauline Collins, Mikhail Baryshnikov
1989–90: Denise Burse, Erma Campbell, Rocky Carroll, Megan Gallagher, Tommy Hollis, Robert Lambert, Kathleen Rowe McAllen, Michael McKean, Crista Moore, Mary-Louise Parker, Daniel von Bargen, Jason Workman, Special Awards: Stewart Granger, Kathleen Turner
1990–91: Jane Adams, Gillian Anderson, Adam Arkin, Brenda Blethyne, Marcus Chong, Paul Hipp, LaChanze, Kenny Neal, Kevin Ramsey, Francis Ruivivar, Lea Salonga, Chandra Wilson, Special Awards: Tracey Ullman, Ellen Stewart
1991–92: Talia Balsam, Lindsay Crouse, Griffin Dunne, Larry Fishburne, Mel Harris, Jonathan Kaplan, Jessica Lange, Laura Linney, Spiro Malas, Mark Rosenthal, Helen Shaver, Al White, Special Awards: Dancing at Lughnasa Company, Plays for Living.
1992–93: Brent Carver, Michael Cerveris, Marcia Gay Harden, Stephanie Lawrence, Andrea Martin, Liam Neeson, Stephen Rea, Natasha Richardson, Martin Short, Dina Spybey, Stephen Spinella, Jennifer Tilly. Special Awards: John Leguizamo, Rosetta LeNoire.
1993–94: Marcus D'Amico, Jarrod Emick, Arabella Field, Adam Gillett, Sherry Glaser, Michael Hayden, Margaret Illman, Audra Ann McDonald, Burke Moses, Anna Deavere Smith, Jere Shea, Harriet Walter.
1994–95: Gretha Boston, Billy Crudup, Ralph Fiennes, Beverly D'Angelo, Calista Flockhart, Kevin Kilner, Anthony LaPaglia, Julie Johnson, Helen Mirren, Jude Law, Rufus Sewell, Vanessa Williams, Special Award: Brooke Shields
1995–96: Jordan Baker, Joohee Choi, Karen Kay Cody, Viola Davis, Kate Forbes, Michael McGrath, Alfred Molina, Timothy Olyphant, Adam Pascal, Lou Diamond Phillips, Daphne Rubin-Vega, Brett Tabisel, Special Award: An Ideal Husband Cast
1996–97: Terry Beaver, Helen Carey, Kristin Chenowith, Jason Danieley, Linda Eder, Allison Janney, Daniel McDonald, Janet McTeer, Mark Ruffalo, Fiona Shaw, Antony Sher, Alan Tudyk, Special Award: Skylight Cast
1997–98: Max Casella, Margaret Colin, Ruaidhri Conroy, Alan Cumming, Lea Delaria, Edie Falco, Enid Graham, Anna Kendrick, Ednita Nazario, Douglas Sills, Steven Sutcliffe, Sam Trammel, Special Awards: Eddie Izzard, Beauty Queen of Leenane Cast
1998–99: Jillian Armenante, James Black, Brendan Coyle, Anna Friel, Rupert Graves, Lynda Gravatt, Nicole Kidman, Ciaran Hinds, Ute Lemper, Clarke Peter, Toby Stephens, Sandra Oh, Special Award: Jerry Herman
1999–2000: Craig Bierko, Everett Bradley, Gabriel Byrne, Ann Hampton Callaway, Toni Collette, Henry Czerny, Stephen Dillane, Jennifer Ehle, Philip Seymour Hoffman, Hayley Mills, Cigdem Onat, Claudia Shear

MAJOR THEATRICAL AWARDS

2000-2001 ANTOINETTE PERRY "TONY" AWARDS

Awards and winners are listed in bold face type.

BEST PLAY (award goes to both author and producer)
The Invention of Love by Tom Stoppard, produced by Lincoln Center Theater under the direction of Andre Bishop and Bernard Gersten
King Hedley II by August Wilson, produced by Stageworks, Benjamin Mordecai, Jujamcyn Theaters, 52nd Street Productions, Spring Sirkin, Peggy Hill, Manhattan Theatre Club, Kardana-Swinsky Productions
***Proof* by David Auburn, produced by Manhattan Theatre Club, Roger Berlind, Carole Shorenstein Hays, Jujamcyn Theaters, Ostar Enterprises, Daryl Roth, Stuart Thompson**
The Tale of the Allergist's Wife by Charles Busch, produced by Manhattan Theatre Club, Lynne Meadow, Barry Grove, Carole Shorenstein Hays, Daryl Roth, Stuart Thompson, Douglas S. Cramer

BEST MUSICAL (award goes to the producer)
A Class Act, produced by Marty Bell, Chase Mishkin, Arielle Tepper, Manhattan Theatre Club
The Full Monty, produced by Fox Searchlight Pictures, Lindsay Law, Thomas Hall
Jane Eyre, produced by Annette Niemtzow, Janet Robinson, Pamela Koslow, Margaret McFeeley Golden, Jennifer Manocherian, Carolyn Kirn McCarthy
***The Producers,* produced by Rocco Landesman, SFX Theatrical Group, The Frankel-Baruch-Viertel-Routh Group, Bob and Harvey Weinstein, Rick Steiner, Robert F.X. Sillerman, Mel Brooks, James D. Stern/Douglas Meyer**

BEST BOOK OF A MUSICAL
A Class Act by Linda Kline and Lonny Price
The Full Monty by Terrence McNally
Jane Eyre by John Caird
***The Producers* by Mel Brooks and Thomas Meehan**

BEST ORIGINAL SCORE (music and lyrics)
A Class Act, music and lyrics by Edward Kleban
The Full Monty, music and lyrics by David Yazbek
Jane Eyre, music by Paul Gordon, lyrics by Paul Gordon and John Caird
***The Producers,* music and lyrics by Mel Brooks**

BEST REVIVAL OF A PLAY (award goes to the producer)
Betrayal, produced by Roundabout Theatre Company, Todd Haimes, Ellen Richard, Julia C. Levy
Gore Vidal's The Best Man, produced by Jeffrey Richards/Michael B. Rothfeld, Raymond J. Greenwald, Jerry Frankel, Darren Bagert
***One Flew Over the Cuckoo's Nest,* produced by Michael Leavitt, Fox Theatricals, Anita Waxman, Elizabeth Williams, John York Noble, Randall L. Wreghitt, Dori Berinstein, The Steppenwolf Theatre Company**
The Search for Signs of Intelligent Life in the Universe, produced by Tomlin and Wagner Theatricalz

BEST REVIVAL OF A MUSICAL (award goes to the producer)
Bells Are Ringing, produced by Mitchell Maxwell, Mark Balsam, Victoria Maxwell, Robert Barandes, Mark Goldberg, Anthony R. Russo, James L. Simon, Fred H. Krones, Allen M. Shore, Momentum Productions, Inc.
Follies, produced by Roundabout Theatre Company, Todd Haimes, Ellen Richard, Julia C. Levy
***42nd Street,* produced by Dodger Theatricals, Joop van den Ende, Stage Holding**
The Rocky Horror Show, produced by Jordan Roth, Christopher Malcolm, Howard Panter, Richard O'Brien, The Rocky Horror Company Ltd.

BEST PERFORMANCE BY A LEADING ACTOR IN A PLAY
Sean Campion, *Stones in His Pockets*
Richard Easton, *The Invention of Love*
Conleth Hill, *Stones in His Pockets*
Brian Stokes Mitchell, *King Hedley II*
Gary Sinise, *One Flew Over the Cuckoo's Nest*

BEST PERFORMANCE BY A LEADING ACTRESS IN A PLAY
Juliette Binoche, *Betrayal*
Linda Lavin, *The Tale of the Allergist's Wife*
Mary-Louise Parker, *Proof*
Jean Smart, *The Man Who Came to Dinner*
Leslie Uggams, *King Hedley II*

BEST PERFORMANCE BY A LEADING ACTOR IN A MUSICAL
Matthew Broderick, *The Producers*
Kevin Chamberlin, *Seussical*
Tom Hewitt, *The Rocky Horror Show*
Nathan Lane, *The Producers*
Patrick Wilson, *The Full Monty*

BEST PERFORMANCE BY A LEADING ACTRESS IN A MUSICAL
Blythe Danner, *Follies*
Christine Ebersole, *42nd Street*
Randy Graff, *A Class Act*
Faith Prince, *Bells Are Ringing*
Maria Schaffel, *Jane Eyre*

BEST PERFORMANCE BY A FEATURED ACTOR IN A PLAY
Charles Brown, *King Hedley II*
Larry Bryggman, *Proof*
Michael Hayden, *Judgment at Nuremberg*
Robert Sean Leonard, *The Invention of Love*
Ben Shenkman, *Proof*

BEST PERFORMANCE BY A FEATURED ACTRESS IN A PLAY
Viola Davis, *King Hedley II*
Johanna Day, *Proof*
Penny Fuller, *The Dinner Party*
Marthe Keller, *Judgment at Nuremberg*
Michele Lee, *The Tale of the Allergist's Wife*

BEST PERFORMANCE BY A FEATURED ACTOR IN A MUSICAL
Roger Bart, *The Producers*
Gary Beach, *The Producers*
John Ellison Conlee, *The Full Monty*
Andre De Shields, *The Full Monty*
Brad Oscar, *The Producers*

BEST PERFORMANCE BY A FEATURED ACTRESS IN A MUSICAL
Polly Bergen, *Follies*
Kathleen Freeman, *The Full Monty*
Cady Huffman, *The Producers*
Kate Levering, *42nd Street*
Mary Testa, *42nd Street*

BEST DIRECTION OF A PLAY
Marion McClinton, *King Hedley II*
Ian McElhinney, *Stones in His Pockets*
Jack O'Brien, *The Invention of Love*
Daniel Sullivan, *Proof*

BEST DIRECTION OF A MUSICAL
Christopher Ashley, *The Rocky Horror Show*
Mark Bramble, *42nd Street*
Jack O'Brien, *The Full Monty*
Susan Stroman, ***The Producers***

BEST SCENIC DESIGN
Bob Crowley, *The Invention of Love*
Heidi Ettinger, *The Adventures of Tom Sawyer*
Douglas W. Schmidt, *42nd Street*
Robin Wagner, *The Producers*

BEST COSTUME DESIGN
Theoni V. Aldredge, *Follies*
Roger Kirk, *42nd Street*
William Ivey Long, *The Producers*
David C. Woolard, *Rocky Horror Show*

BEST LIGHTING DESIGN
Jules Fisher and Peggy Eisenhauer, *Jane Eyre*
Paul Gallo, *42nd Street*
Peter Kaczorowski, *The Producers*
Kenneth Posner, *The Adventures of Tom Sawyer*

BEST CHOREOGRAPHY
Jerry Mitchell, *The Full Monty*
Jim Morgan, George Pinney and John Vanderkloff, *Blast!*
Randy Skinner, *42nd Street*
Susan Stroman, *The Producers*

BEST ORCHESTRATIONS
Doug Besterman, *The Producers*
Larry Hochman, *A Class Act*
Jonathan Tunick, *Follies*
Harold Wheeler, *The Full Monty*

SPECIAL TONY AWARDS
Special theatrical event: Blast!

Lifetime achievement in the theater:
Paul Gemignani, musical director

TONY HONORS for excellence in theater:
Betty Corwin and the Theatre on Film and Tape Archive at the New York Public Library for the Performing Arts at Lincoln Center

New Dramatists, playwright's workshop

***Theatre World*, the definitive pictorial and statistical annual record of the American theatre.**

REGIONAL THEATRE
To a regional theater company that has displayed a continuous level of artistic achievement contributing to the growth of the theater nationally, recommended by the American Theatre Critics Association:
Victory Gardens Theater, Chicago, IL

AMERICAN THEATRE WING ANTOINETTE PERRY (TONY) PAST AWARD WINNING PRODUCTIONS

1948–Mister Roberts, 1949–Death of a Salesman, Kiss Me, Kate, 1950–The Cocktail Party, South Pacific, 1951–The Rose Tattoo, Guys and Dolls, 1952–The Fourposter, The King and I, 1953–The Crucible, Wonderful Town, 1954–The Teahouse of the August Moon, Kismet, 1955–The Desperate Hours, The Pajama Game, 1956–The Diary of Anne Frank, Damn Yankees, 1957–Long Day's Journey into Night, My Fair Lady, 1958–Sunrise at Campobello, The Music Man, 1959–J.B., Redhead, 1960–The Miracle Worker, Fiorello! tied with The Sound of Music, 1961–Becket, Bye Bye Birdie, 1962–A Man for All Seasons, How to Succeed in Business without Really Trying, 1963–Who's Afraid of Virginia Woolf?, A Funny Thing Happened on the Way to the Forum, 1964–Luther, Hello Dolly!, 1965–The Subject Was Roses, Fiddler on the Roof, 1966–The Persecution and Assassination of Marat as Performed by the Inmates of the Asylum of Charenton under the Direction of the Marquis de Sade, Man of La Mancha, 1967–The Homecoming, Cabaret, 1968– Rosencrantz and Guildenstern Are Dead, Hallelujah Baby!, 1969–The Great White Hope, 1776, 1970–Borstal Boy, Applause, 1971–Sleuth, Company, 1972–Sticks and Bones, Two Gentlemen of Verona, 1973–That Championship Season, A Little Night Music, 1974–The River Niger, Raisin, 1975–Equus, The Wiz, 1976–Travesties, A Chorus Line, 1977–The Shadow Box, Annie, 1978–Da, Ain't Misbehavin', Dracula, 1979–The Elephant Man, Sweeney Todd, 1980–Children of a Lesser God, Evita, Morning's at Seven, 1981–Amadeus, 42nd Street, The Pirates of Penzance, 1982–The Life and Adventures of Nicholas Nickleby, Nine, Othello, 1983–Torch Song Trilogy, Cats, On Your Toes, 1984–The Real Thing, La Cage aux Folles, 1985–Biloxi Blues, Big River, Joe Egg, 1986–I'm Not Rappaport, The Mystery of Edwin Drood, Sweet Charity, 1987–Fences, Les Misérables, All My Sons, 1988–M. Butterfly, The Phantom of the Opera, 1989–The Heidi Chronicles, Jerome Robbins' Broadway, Our Town, Anything Goes, 1990–The Grapes of Wrath, City of Angels, Gypsy, 1991–Lost in Yonkers, The Will Rogers' Follies, Fiddler on the Roof, 1992–Dancing at Lughnasa, Crazy For You, Guys & Dolls, 1993–Angels in America: Millenium Approaches, Kiss of the Spider Woman, 1994–Angels in America: Perestroika, Passion, An Inspector Calls, Carousel, 1995–Love! Valour! Compassion! (play), Sunset Boulevard (musical), Show Boat (musical revival), The Heiress (play revival), 1996–Master Class (play), Rent (musical), A Delicate Balance (play revival), King and I (musical revival), 1997–Last Night of Ballyhoo (play), Titanic (musical), Doll's House (play revival), Chicago (musical Revival) 1998–Art (play), Lion King (musical), View from the Bridge (play revival), Cabaret (musical revival), 1999–Side Man (play), Fosse (musical), Death of a Salesman (play revival), Annie Get Your Gun (musical revival), 2000–Copenhagen (play), Contact (musical), The Real Thing (play revival), Kiss Me, Kate (musical revival), 2001–Proof (play), The Producers (play), One Flew Over the Cuckoo's Nest (play revival), 42nd Street (musical revival)

46th ANNUAL VILLAGE VOICE OBIE AWARDS

For outstanding achievement in Off and Off-Off Broadway theater

PERFORMANCE
George Bartenieff, *I Will Bear Witness*
Stephanie Berry, *The Shaneequa Chronicles*
Ronnell Bey, Mandy Gonzalez,
Judy Kuhn and Anika Noni Rose, *Eli's Comin'*
Bette Bourne, *Resident Alien*
Brian d'Arcy James, *The Good Thief*
Janie Dee, *Comic Potential*
Jackie Hoffman, *The Book of Liz*
Pamela Isaacs, *Newyorkers*
Brian Murray, *The Play About the Baby*
John Ortiz, *References to Salvador Dali Make Me Hot*
Mary-Louise Parker, *Proof*

DIRECTION
Michael Greif, *Dogeaters*
Craig Lucas, *Saved or Destroyed*
Bob McGrath, *Jennie Richee*

SET DESIGN
Neil Patel for *I Will Bear Witness, Race, Resident Alien, and War of the Worlds*
Douglas Stein, *Saved and Texts for Nothing*

MUSIC
Diedre Murray, *Eli's Comin'*
Bill Sims Jr., *Lackawanna Blues*

CHOREOGRAPHY
John Carrafa, *Urinetown*

PLAYWRITING
Jose Rivera, *References to Salvador Dali Make Me Hot*

BEST PLAY
Pamela Gien, *The Syringa Tree*

SUSTAINED ACHIEVEMENT
Marian Seldes

SPECIAL CITATIONS
Justin Bond and Kenny Mellman, *Kiki and Herb: Jesus Wept*
Kirsten Childs, *The Bubbly Black Girl Sheds Her Chameleon Skin*
Rinde Eckert, *And God Created Great Whales*
Mark Holhnann and Greg Kotis, *Urinetown: The Musical*
Edward Kleban, *A Class Act*
Cynthia Hopkins, Pilar Limosner, Bill Morrison, Laurie Olinder, Ruth Pongstaphone, Tim Schellenbaum, Howard S. Thies, Matthew Tierney, Fred Tietz and Julia Wolfe, *Jennie Richee*
Ruben Santiago-Hudson, *Lackawanna Blues*

GRANTS:
Classical Theatre of Harlem
Clubbed Thumb
Mint Theater Company
Soho Rep

ROSS WETZSTEON AWARD:
Theatre for a New Audience

OBIE AWARDS – BEST NEW PLAY AWARD WINNING PRODUCTIONS

1956–Absalom, Absalom, 1957–A House Remembered, 1958–no award given, 1959–The Quare Fellow, 1960–no award given, 1961–The Blacks, 1962–Who'll Save the Plowboy?, 1963–no award given, 1964–Play, 1965–The Old Glory, 1966–The Journey of the Fifth Horse, 1967–no award given, 1968–no award given, 1969– no award given, 1970–The Effect of Gamma Rays on Man-in-the-Moon Marigolds, 1971–House of Blue Leaves, 1972–no award given, 1973–The Hot l Baltimore, 1974–Short Eyes, 1975–The First Breeze of Summer, 1976–American Buffalo, Sexual Perversity in Chicago, 1977–Curse of the Starving Class, 1978–Shaggy Dog Animation, 1979–Josephine, 1980–no award given, 1981–FOB, 1982–Metamorphosis in Miniature, Mr. Dead and Mrs. Free, 1983–Painting Churches, Andrea Rescued, Edmond, 1984–Fool for Love, 1985–The Conduct of Life, 1986–no award given, 1987–The Film, Film is Evil Radio is Good, 1988–Abingdon Square, 1989–no award given, 1990–Prelude to a Kiss, Imperceptible Mutabilities in the Third Kingdom, Bad Benny, Crowbar, Terminal Hip, 1991–The Fever, 1992–Sight Unseen, Sally's Rape, The Baltimore Waltz, 1993–no award given, 1994–Twilight: Los Angeles 1992, 1995–Cyrptogram, 1996–Adrienne Kennedy, 1997–One Flea Spare, 1998–Pearls for Pigs and Benita Canova, 1999–no award given, 2000–no award given

46th ANNUAL DRAMA DESK AWARDS

For outstanding achievement in the 2000-2001 season, voted by an association of New York drama reporters, editors and critics from nominations made by a committee

New play: *Proof*
New musical: *The Producers*
Revival of a play: *Gore Vidal's The Best Man*
Revival of a musical: *42nd Street*
Book: Mel Brooks and Thomas Meehan, *The Producers*
Composer: David Yazbek, *The Full Monty*
Lyricist: Mel Brooks, *The Producers.*
Actor in a play: Richard Easton, *The Invention of Love*
Actress in a play: Mary-Louise Parker, *Proof*
Featured actor in a play: Charles Brown, *King Hedley II*
Featured actress in a play: Viola Davis, *King Hedley II*
Actor in a musical: Nathan Lane, *The Producers*
Actress in a musical: Maria Schaffel, *Jane Eyre*
Featured actor in a musical: Gary Beach, *The Producers*
Featured actress in a musical: Cady Huffman, *The Producers*
Solo performance: Pamela Gien, *The Syringa Tree*
Direcotor of a play: Jack O'Brien, *Proof*
Director of a musical: Susan Stroman, *The Producers*
Choreography: Susan Stroman, *The Producers*
Orchestrations: Doug Besterman, *The Producers*
Set design of a play: Bob Crowley, *The Invention of Love*
Set design of a musical: Robin Wagner, *The Producers*
Costume design: William Ivey Long, *The Producers*
Lighting design: Paul Anderson, *Mnemonic*
Sound design: Christopher Shutt, *Mnemonic*
Outstanding musical revue: *Forbidden Broadway 2001: A Spoof Odyssey*
Unique theatrical experience: *Mnemonic*
Special awards: RebaMcEntire, *Annie Get Your Gun*; Sean Campion and Conleth Hill, *Stones in His Pockets.*
Ensemble performance: *Cobb* (Michael Cullen, Clark Jackson, Matthew Mabe, Michael Sabatino); *Tabletop* (Rob Bartlett, Harvy Blanks, Jack Koenig, Dean Nolen, Elizabeth Hanly Rice, Jeremy Webb)

51st ANNUAL OUTER CRITICS CIRCLE AWARDS

For outstanding achievement in the 2000-2001 season, voted by critics on out-of-town periodicals and media

Broadway play: *Proof*
Off-Broadway play: Jitney
Revival of a play (tie): *Gore Vidal's The Best Man, One Flew Over the Cuckoo's Nest*
Actor in a play: Richard Easton, *The Invention of Love*
Actress in a play: Mary-Louise Parker, *Proof*
Featured actor in a play: Robert Sean Leonard, *The Invention of Love*
Featured actress in a play: Viola Davis, *King Hedley II*
Director of a play: Jack O'Brien, *The Invention of Love*
Broadway musical: *The Producers*
Off-Broadway musical: *Bat Boy: The Musical*
Revival of a musical: *42nd Street*
Actor in a musical: Nathan Lane, *The Producers*
Actress in a musical (tie):
Christine Ebersole, *42nd Street*; Maria Schaffel, *Jane Eyre*
Featured actor in a musical (tie): Gary Beach, *The Producers*; Andre De Shields, *The Full Monty*
Featured actress in a musical: Cady Huffman, *The Producers*
Director of a musical: Susan Stroman, *The Producers*
Choreography: Susan Stroman, *The Producers*
Scenic design: Robin Wagner, *The Producers*
Costume design: William Ivey Long, *The Producers*
Lighting design: Brian MacDevitt, *The Invention of Love*
Solo performance: Pamela Gien, *The Syringa Tree*
John Gassner Playwriting Award: David Auburn, *Proof*
Special Achievement Award:
Sean Campion and Conleth Hill, *Stones in His Pockets*; Henry Winlder, John Ritter, Len Cariou, Penny Fuller, Veanne Cox and Jan Maxwell, *The Dinner Party*; Reba McEntire, *Annie Get Your Gun*

PULITZER PRIZE AWARD WINNING PRODUCTIONS

1918–Why Marry?, 1919–no award, 1920–Beyond the Horizon, 1921–Miss Lulu Bett, 1922–Anna Christie, 1923–Icebound, 1924–Hell-Bent fer Heaven, 1925–They Knew What They Wanted, 1926–Craig's Wife, 1927–In Abraham's Bosom, 1928–Strange Interlude, 1929–Street Scene, 1930–The Green Pastures, 1931–Alison's House, 1932–Of Thee I Sing, 1933–Both Your Houses, 1934–Men in White, 1935–The Old Maid, 1936–Idiot's Delight, 1937–You Can't Take It with You, 1938–Our Town, 1939–Abe Lincoln in Illinois, 1940–The Time of Your Life, 1941–There Shall Be No Night, 1942–no award, 1943–The Skin of Our Teeth, 1944–no award, 1945–Harvey, 1946–State of the Union, 1947–no award, 1948–A Streetcar Named Desire, 1949–Death of a Salesman, 1950–South Pacific, 1951–no award, 1952–The Shrike, 1953–Picnic, 1954–The Teahouse of the August Moon, 1955–Cat on a Hot Tin Roof, 1956–The Diary of Anne Frank, 1957–Long Day's Journey into Night, 1958–Look Homeward, Angel, 1959–J.B., 1960–Fiorello!, 1961–All the Way Home, 1962–How to Succeed in Business without Really Trying, 1963–no award, 1964–no award, 1965–The Subject Was Roses, 1966–no award, 1967–A Delicate Balance, 1968–no award, 1969–The Great White Hope, 1970–No Place to Be Somebody, 1971–The Effect of Gamma Rays on Man-in-the-Moon Marigolds, 1972–no award, 1973–That Championship Season, 1974–no award, 1975–Seascape, 1976–A Chorus Line, 1977–The Shadow Box, 1978–The Gin Game, 1979–Buried Child, 1980–Talley's Folly, 1981–Crimes of the Heart, 1982–A Soldier's Play, 1983–'night, Mother, 1984–Glengarry Glen Ross, 1985–Sunday in the Park with George, 1986–no award, 1987–Fences, 1988–Driving Miss Daisy, 1989–The Heidi Chronicles, 1990–The Piano Lesson, 1991–Lost in Yonkers, 1992–The Kentucky Cycle, 1993–Angels in America: Millenium Approaches, 1994–Three Tall Women, 1995–Young Man from Atlanta, 1996–Rent, 1997–no award, 1998–How I Learned to Drive, 1999–Wit, 2000–Dinner With Friends, 2001–Proof

NEW YORK DRAMA CRITICS AWARD WINNING PRODUCTIONS

1936–Winterset, 1937–High Tor, 1938–Of Mice and Men, Shadow and Substance, 1939–The White Steed, 1940–The Time of Your Life, 1941–Watch on the Rhine, The Corn Is Green, 1942–Blithe Spirit, 1943–The Patriots, 1944–Jacobowsky and the Colonel, 1945–The Glass Menagerie, 1946–Carousel, 1947–All My Sons, No Exit, Brigadoon, 1948–A Streetcar Named Desire, The Winslow Boy, 1949–Death of a Salesman, The Madwoman of Chaillot, South Pacific, 1950–The Member of the Wedding, The Cocktail Party, The Consul, 1951–Darkness at Noon, The Lady's Not for Burning, Guys and Dolls, 1952–I Am a Camera, Venus Observed, Pal Joey, 1953–Picnic, The Love of Four Colonels, Wonderful Town, 1954–Teahouse of the August Moon, Ondine, The Golden Apple, 1955–Cat on a Hot Tin Roof, Witness for the Prosecution, The Saint of Bleecker Street, 1956–The Diary of Anne Frank, Tiger at the Gates, My Fair Lady, 1957–Long Day's Journey into Night, The Waltz of the Toreadors, The Most Happy Fella, 1958–Look Homeward Angel, Look Back in Anger, The Music Man, 1959–A Raisin in the Sun, The Visit, La Plume de Ma Tante, 1960–Toys in the Attic, Five Finger Exercise, Fiorello!, 1961–All the Way Home, A Taste of Honey, Carnival, 1962–Night of the Iguana, A Man for All Seasons, How to Succeed in Business without Really Trying, 1963–Who's Afraid of Virginia Woolf?, 1964–Luther, Hello Dolly!, 1965–The Subject Was Roses, Fiddler on the Roof, 1966–The Persecution and Assassination of Marat as Performed by the Inmates of the Asylum of Charenton under the Direction of the Marquis de Sade, Man of La Mancha, 1967–The Homecoming, Cabaret, 1968–Rosencrantz and Guildenstern Are Dead, Your Own Thing, 1969–The Great White Hope, 1776, 1970–The Effect of Gamma Rays on Man-in-the-Moon Marigolds,Borstal Boy, Company, 1971–Home, Follies, The House of Blue Leaves, 1972–That Championship Season, Two Gentlemen of Verona, 1973–The Hot l Baltimore, The Changing Room, A Little Night Music, 1974–The Contractor, Short Eyes, Candide, 1975–Equus, The Taking of Miss Janie, A Chorus Line, 1976–Travesties, Streamers, Pacific Overtures, 1977–Otherwise Engaged, American Buffalo, Annie, 1978–Da, Ain't Misbehavin', 1979–The Elephant Man, Sweeney Todd, 1980–Talley's Folley, Evita, Betrayal, 1981–Crimes of the Heart, A Lesson from Aloes, Special Citation to Lena Horne, The Pirates of Penzance, 1982–The Life and Adventures of Nicholas Nickleby, A Soldier's Play, (no musical), 1983–Brighton Beach Memoirs, Plenty, Little Shop of Horrors, 1984–The Real Thing, Glengarry Glen Ross, Sunday in the Park with George, 1985–Ma Rainey's Black Bottom, (no musical), 1986–A Lie of the Mind, Benefactors, (no musical), Special Citation to Lily Tomlin and Jane Wagner, 1987–Fences, Les Liaisons Dangereuses, Les Misérables, 1988–Joe Turner's Come and Gone, The Road to Mecca, Into the Woods, 1989–The Heidi Chronicles, Aristocrats, Largely New York (Special), (no musical), 1990–The Piano Lesson, City of Angels, Privates on Parade, 1991–Six Degrees of Separation, The Will Rogers Follies, Our Country's Good, Special Citation to Eileen Atkins, 1992–Two Trains Running, Dancing at Lughnasa, 1993–Angels in America: Millenium Approaches, Someone Who'll Watch Over Me, Kiss of the Spider Woman, 1994–Three Tall Women, Anna Deavere Smith (Special), 1995–Arcadia, Love! Valour! Compassion!, Special Award: Signature Theatre Company, 1996- Seven Guitars, Molly Sweeny, Rent, 1997-HowI Learned to Drive, Skylight, Violet, Chicago (special) 1998- Pride's Crossing, Art, Lion King, Special: Cabaret, 1999-Wit, Parade, Closer, David Hare (special), 2000–Jitney, James Joyce's The Dead, Copenhagen, 2001–The Invention of Love, The Producers, Proof

THE LONGEST RUNNING SHOWS ON BROADWAY

(Through May 31, 2001)

When the musical or play version of a production is in question, it is so indicated, as are revivals.
(PLAYS IN BOLDFACE WERE STILL PLAYING AS OF MAY 31, 2001)

PRODUCTION	PERFORMANCES	OPENING DATE
Cats	7,485	October 7, 1982
A Chorus Line	6,137	July 25, 1975
Oh! Calcutta (revival)	5,959	September 24, 1976
Les Miserables	5,859	March 12, 1987
The Phantom of the Opera	5,570	January 26, 1988
Miss Saigon	4,097	April 11, 1991
42nd Street	3,486	August 25, 1980
Grease	3,388	February 14, 1972
Fiddler on the Roof	3,242	September 22, 1964
Life With Father	3,224	November 8, 1939
Tobacco Road	3,182	December 4, 1933
Beauty and the Beast	2,891	April 18, 1994
Hello, Dolly!	2,844	January 16, 1964
My Fair Lady	2,717	March 15, 1956
Annie	2,377	April 21, 1977
Man of La Mancha	2,328	November 22, 1965
Abie's Irish Rose	2,327	May 23, 1922
Oklahoma!	2,212	March 31, 1943
Rent	2,125	April 29, 1996
Smokey Joe's Café	2,036	March 2, 1995
Pippin	1,944	October 23, 1972
South Pacific	1,925	April 7, 1949
The Magic Show	1,920	May 28, 1974
Chicago (musical, revival)	1,894	November 14, 1996
Deathtrap	1,793	February 26, 1978
Gemini	1,788	May 21, 1977
Harvey	1,775	November 1, 1944
Dancin'	1,774	March 27, 1978
La Cage aux Folles	1,761	August 21, 1983
Hair	1,750	April 29, 1968
The Wiz	1,672	January 5, 1975
Born Yesterday	1,642	February 4, 1946
The Best Little Whorehouse in Texas	1,639	June 19, 1978
Crazy for You	1,622	February 19, 1992
Ain't Misbehavin'	1,604	May 9, 1978
Mary, Mary	1,572	March 8, 1961
Evita	1,567	September 25, 1979
The Voice of the Turtle	1,557	December 8, 1943
Jekyll & Hyde	1,543	April 28, 1997
Barefoot in the Park	1,530	October 23, 1963
Brighton Beach Memoirs	1,530	March 27, 1983
Dreamgirls	1,522	December 20, 1981
Mame (musical)	1,508	May 24, 1966
Grease (revival)	1,503	May 11, 1994
The Lion King	1,482	November 13, 1997
Same Time, Next Year	1,453	March 14, 1975
Arsenic and Old Lace	1,444	January 10, 1941

The Sound of Music	1,443	November 16, 1959
Me and My Girl	1,420	August 10, 1986
How to Succeed in Business Without Really Trying	1,417	October 14, 1961
Hellzapoppin'	1,404	September 22, 1938
The Music Man	1,375	December 19, 1957
Funny Girl	1,348	March 26, 1964
Mummenschanz	1,326	March 30, 1977
Angel Street	1,295	December 5, 1941
Cabaret (revival)	1,292	March 19, 1998
Lightnin'	1,291	August 26, 1918
Promises, Promises	1,281	December 1, 1968
The King and I	1,246	March 29, 1951
Cactus Flower	1,234	December 8, 1965
Sleuth	1,222	December 8, 1965
Torch Song Trilogy	1,222	June 10, 1982
1776	1,217	March 16, 1969
Equus	1,209	October 24, 1974
Sugar Babies	1,208	October 8, 1979
Guys and Dolls	1,200	November 24, 1950
Amadeus	1,181	December 17, 1980
Cabaret	1,165	November 20, 1966
Mister Roberts	1,157	February 18, 1948
Annie Get Your Gun	1,147	May 16, 1946
Guys and Dolls (revival)	1,144	April 14, 1992
The Seven Year Itch	1,141	November 20, 1952
Bring in 'da Noise, Bring in 'da Funk	1,130	April 25, 1996
Butterflies Are Free	1,128	October 21, 1969
Pins and Needles	1,108	November 27, 1937
Plaza Suite	1,097	February 14, 1968
They're Playing Our Song	1,082	February 11, 1979
Grand Hotel (musical)	1,077	November 12, 1989
Kiss Me, Kate	1,070	December 30, 1948
Don't Bother Me, I Can't Cope	1,065	April 19, 1972
The Pajama Game	1,063	May 13, 1954
Shenandoah	1,050	January 7, 1975
The Teahouse of the August Moon	1,027	October 15, 1953
Damn Yankees	1,019	May 5, 1955
Never Too Late	1,007	November 26, 1962
Big River	1,005	April 25, 1985
Fosse	1,001	January 14, 1999
The Will Rogers Follies	983	May 1, 1991
Any Wednesday	982	February 18, 1964
Sunset Boulevard	977	November 17, 1994
A Funny Thing Happened on the Way to the Forum	964	May 8, 1962
The Odd Couple	964	March 10, 1965
Anna Lucasta	957	August 30, 1944
Kiss and Tell	956	March 17, 1943
Show Boat (revival)	949	October 2, 1994
Annie Get Your Gun (revival)	938	March 4, 1999
Dracula (revival)	925	October 20, 1977
Bells Are Ringing	924	November 29, 1956
The Moon Is Blue	924	March 8, 1951
Beatlemania	920	May 31, 1977
The Elephant Man	916	April 19, 1979
Kiss of the Spider Woman	906	May 3, 1993
Luv	901	November 11, 1964
The Who's Tommy	900	April 22, 1993
Chicago (musical)	898	June 3, 1975
Applause	896	March 30, 1970
Can-Can	892	May 7, 1953
Carousel	890	April 19, 1945
I'm Not Rappaport	890	November 19, 1985
Hats Off to Ice	889	June 22, 1944
Fanny	888	November 4, 1954

Children of a Lesser God	887	March 30, 1980
Follow the Girls	882	April 8, 1944
City of Angels	878	December 11, 1989
Camelot	873	December 3, 1960
I Love My Wife	872	April 17, 1977
The Bat	867	August 23, 1920
My Sister Eileen	864	December 26, 1940
No, No, Nanette (revival)	861	January 19, 1971
Ragtime	861	January 18, 1998
Song of Norway	860	August 21, 1944
Chapter Two	857	December 4, 1977
A Streetcar Named Desire	855	December 3, 1947
Barnum	854	April 30, 1980
Comedy in Music	849	October 2, 1953
Raisin	847	October 18, 1973
Blood Brothers	839	April 25, 1993
You Can't Take It With You	837	December 14, 1936
La Plume de Ma Tante	835	November 11, 1958
Three Men on a Horse	835	January 30, 1935
The Subject Was Roses	832	May 25, 1964
Black and Blue	824	January 26, 1989
The King and I (revival)	807	April 11, 1996
Inherit the Wind	806	April 21, 1955
Anything Goes (revival)	804	October 19, 1987
Titanic	804	April 23, 1997
No Time for Sergeants	796	October 20, 1955
Fiorello!	795	November 23, 1959
Where's Charley?	792	October 11, 1948
The Ladder	789	October 22, 1926
Forty Carats	780	December 26, 1968
Lost in Yonkers	780	February 21, 1991
The Prisoner of Second Avenue	780	November 11, 1971
M. Butterfly	777	March 20, 1988
Oliver!	774	January 6, 1963
The Pirates of Penzance (revival, 1981)	772	January 8, 1981
Woman of the Year	770	March 29, 1981
My One and Only	767	May 1, 1983
Sophisticated Ladies	767	March 1, 1981
Bubbling Brown Sugar	766	March 2, 1976
Into the Woods	765	November 5, 1987
State of the Union	765	November 14, 1945
Starlight Express	761	March 15, 1987
The First Year	760	October 20, 1920
Broadway Bound	756	December 4, 1986
You Know I Can't Hear You When the Water's Running	755	March 13, 1967
Two for the Seesaw	750	January 16, 1958
Joseph and the Amazing Technicolor Dreamcoat (revival)	747	January 27, 1982
Death of a Salesman	742	February 10, 1949
for colored girls who have considered suicide/when the rainbow is enuf	742	September 15, 1976
Sons o' Fun	742	December 1, 1941
Candide (musical version, revival)	740	March 10, 1974
Gentlemen Prefer Blondes	740	December 8, 1949
The Man Who Came to Dinner	739	October 16, 1939
Nine	739	May 9, 1982
Call Me Mister	734	April 18, 1946
Victor/Victoria	734	October 25, 1995
West Side Story	732	September 26, 1957
High Button Shoes	727	October 9, 1947
Finian's Rainbow	725	January 10, 1947
Claudia	722	February 12, 1941
The Gold Diggers	720	September 30, 1919
Jesus Christ Superstar	720	October 12, 1971
Carnival	719	April 13, 1961
The Diary of Anne Frank	717	October 5, 1955

Show	Performances	Opening
A Funny Thing Happenedon the Way to the Forum (revival)	715	April 18, 1996
I Remember Mama	714	October 19, 1944
Tea and Sympathy	712	September 30, 1953
Junior Miss	710	November 18, 1941
Footloose	708	October 22, 1998
Last of the Red Hot Lovers	706	December 28, 1969
The Secret Garden	706	April 25, 1991
Company	705	April 26, 1970
Seventh Heaven	704	October 30, 1922
Gypsy (musical)	702	May 21, 1959
The Miracle Worker	700	October 19, 1959
That Championship Season	700	September 14, 1972
Da	697	May 1, 1978
Cat on a Hot Tin Roof	694	March 24, 1955
Li'l Abner	693	November 15, 1956
The Children's Hour	691	November 20, 1934
Purlie	688	March 15, 1970
Dead End	687	October 28, 1935
The Lion and the Mouse	686	November 20, 1905
White Cargo	686	November 5, 1923
Dear Ruth	683	December 13, 1944
East Is West	680	December 25, 1918
Come Blow Your Horn	677	February 22, 1961
The Most Happy Fella	676	May 3, 1956
Defending the Caveman	671	March 26, 1995
The Doughgirls	671	December 30, 1942
The Impossible Years	670	October 13, 1965
Irene	670	November 18, 1919
Boy Meets Girl	669	November 27, 1935
The Tap Dance Kid	669	December 21, 1983
Beyond the Fringe	667	October 27, 1962
Who's Afraid of Virginia Woolf?	664	October 13, 1962
Blithe Spirit	657	November 5, 1941
A Trip to Chinatown	657	November 9, 1891
The Women	657	December 26, 1936
Bloomer Girl	654	October 5, 1944
The Fifth Season	654	January 23, 1953
Rain	648	September 1, 1924
Witness for the Prosecution	645	December 16, 1954
Call Me Madam	644	October 12, 1950
Janie	642	September 10, 1942
The Green Pastures	640	February 26, 1930
Kiss Me, Kate	640	November 18, 1999
Auntie Mame (play version)	639	October 31, 1956
A Man for All Seasons	637	November 22, 1961
Jerome Robbins' Broadway	634	February 26, 1989
The Fourposter	632	October 24, 1951
The Music Master	627	September 26, 1904
Two Gentlemen of Verona (musical version)	627	December 1, 1971
The Tenth Man	623	November 5, 1959
The Heidi Chronicles	621	March 9, 1989
Is Zat So?	618	January 5, 1925
Anniversary Waltz	615	April 7, 1954
The Happy Time (play version)	614	January 24, 1950
Separate Rooms	613	March 23, 1940
Affairs of State	610	September 25, 1950
Oh! Calcutta!	610	June 17, 1969
Star and Garter	609	June 24, 1942
The Mystery of Edwin Drood	608	December 2, 1985
The Student Prince	608	December 2, 1924
Sweet Charity	608	January 29, 1966
Bye Bye Birdie	607	April 14, 1960
Irene (revival)	604	March 13, 1973
Sunday in the Park With George	604	May 2, 1984

Title	Performances	Opening Date
Adonis	603	ca. 1884
Broadway	603	September 16, 1926
Peg o' My Heart	603	December 20, 1912
Master Class	601	November 5, 1995
Street Scene (play version)	601	January 10, 1929
Art	600	March 1, 1998
Flower Drum Song	600	December 1, 1958
Kiki	600	November 29, 1921
A Little Night Music	600	February 25, 1973
Agnes of God	599	March 30, 1982
Don't Drink the Water	598	November 17, 1966
Wish You Were Here	598	June 25, 1952
Sarafina!	597	January 28, 1988
A Society Circus	596	December 13, 1905
Absurd Person Singular	592	October 8, 1974
A Day in Hollywood/A Night in the Ukraine	588	May 1, 1980
The Me Nobody Knows	586	December 18, 1970
The Two Mrs. Carrolls	585	August 3, 1943
Kismet (musical version)	583	December 3, 1953
Gypsy (musical version, revival)	582	November 16, 1989
Brigadoon	581	March 13, 1947
Detective Story	581	March 23, 1949
No Strings	580	March 14, 1962
Brother Rat	577	December 16, 1936
Blossom Time	576	September 29, 1921
Pump Boys and Dinettes	573	February 4, 1982
Show Boat	572	December 27, 1927
The Show-Off	571	February 5, 1924
Sally	570	December 21, 1920
Jelly's Last Jam	569	April 26, 1992
Golden Boy (musical version)	568	October 20, 1964
One Touch of Venus	567	October 7, 1943
The Real Thing	566	January 5, 1984
Happy Birthday	564	October 31, 1946
Look Homeward, Angel	564	November 28, 1957
Morning's at Seven (revival)	564	April 10, 1980
The Glass Menagerie	561	March 31, 1945
I Do! I Do!	560	December 5, 1966
Wonderful Town	559	February 25, 1953
The Last Night of Ballyhoo	557	February 27, 1997
Rose Marie	557	September 2, 1924
Strictly Dishonorable	557	September 18, 1929
Sweeney Todd, the Demon Barber of Fleet Street	557	March 1, 1979
The Great White Hope	556	October 3, 1968
A Majority of One	556	February 16, 1959
The Sisters Rosensweig	556	March 18, 1993
Sunrise at Campobello	556	January 30, 1958
Toys in the Attic	556	February 25, 1960
Jamaica	555	October 31, 1957
Stop the World—I Want to Get Off	555	October 3, 1962
Florodora	553	November 10, 1900
Noises Off	553	December 11, 1983
Ziegfeld Follies (1943)	553	April 1, 1943
Dial "M" for Murder	552	October 29, 1952
Good News	551	September 6, 1927
Peter Pan (revival)	551	September 6, 1979
How to Succeed in Businesswithout Really Trying (revival)	548	March 23, 1995
Let's Face It	547	October 29, 1941
Milk and Honey	543	October 10, 1961
Within the Law	541	September 11, 1912
Pal Joey (revival)	540	January 3, 1952
The Sound of Music (revival)	540	March 12, 1998
What Makes Sammy Run?	540	February 27, 1964
The Sunshine Boys	538	December 20, 1972

What a Life	538	April 13, 1938
Crimes of the Heart	535	November 4, 1981
Damn Yankees (revival)	533	March 3, 1994
The Unsinkable Molly Brown	532	November 3, 1960
The Red Mill (revival)	531	October 16, 1945
Rumors	531	November 17, 1988
A Raisin in the Sun	530	March 11, 1959
Godspell	527	June 22, 1976
Fences	526	March 26, 1987
The Solid Gold Cadillac	526	November 5, 1953
Biloxi Blues	524	March 28, 1985
Irma La Douce	524	September 29, 1960
The Boomerang	522	August 10, 1915
Follies	521	April 4, 1971
Rosalinda	521	October 28, 1942
The Best Man	520	March 31, 1960
Chauve-Souris	520	February 4, 1922
Blackbirds of 1928	518	May 9, 1928
The Gin Game	517	October 6, 1977
Sunny	517	September 22, 1925
Victoria Regina	517	December 26, 1935
Riverdance on Broadway	515	March 16, 2000
Fifth of July	511	November 5, 1980
Half a Sixpence	511	April 25, 1965
The Vagabond King	511	September 21, 1925
The New Moon	509	September 19, 1928
The World of Suzie Wong	508	October 14, 1958
The Rothschilds	507	October 19, 1970
On Your Toes (revival)	505	March 6, 1983
Sugar	505	April 9, 1972
Shuffle Along	504	May 23, 1921
Up in Central Park	504	January 27, 1945
Carmen Jones	503	December 2, 1943
Saturday Night Fever	502	October 21, 1999
The Member of the Wedding	501	January 5, 1950
Panama Hattie	501	October 30, 1940
Personal Appearance	501	October 17, 1934
Bird in Hand	500	April 4, 1929
Room Service	500	May 19, 1937
Sailor, Beware!	500	September 28, 1933
Tomorrow the World	500	April 14, 1943

A Chorus Line Ensemble (Martha Swope)

Cats Ensemble (Martha Swope)

James Naughton in *City of Angels* (Martha Swope)

Bob Gunton and Patti LuPone in *Evita*

Uta Hagen, Arthur Hill, George Grizzard in *Who's Afraid of Virginia Woolf* (Richard Atlee)

Gypsy ensemble

Mia Dillon, Beth Henley, Mary Beth Hurt, Lizbeth Mackay in *Crimes of the Heart* (Martha Swope)

Zero Mostel, Michael Granger in *Fiddler on the Roof* (Eileen Darby)

BIOGRAPHICAL DATA ON THIS SEASON'S CASTS

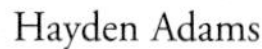

Hayden Adams

Wendy Allgaert

Michael Anderson

Todd Anthony-Jackson

Ward Asquith

James Barbour

AARON, JACK Born May 1, 1933 in New York, NY. Attended Hunter Col., Actors Workshop. OB in *Swim Low Little Goldfish*, followed by *Journey of the 5th Horse, The Nest, One Flew Over the Cuckoo's Nest, The Birds, The Pornographer's Daughter, Love Death Plays, Unlikely Heroes, Taking Steam, Mark VIII:xxxvi, Made in Heaven, No Niggers No Jews No Dogs*, Bdwy in *Sunshine Boys* (1998).

ACUÑA, ARTHUR T. Born December 11, 1961 in Manila, Philippines. Attended De La Salle U., Philippines. OB debut 1993 in *The Hounded & Possessed*, followed by *Santos & Santos, Mother Courage, Dogeater.*

ADAMS, HAYDEN Born in Northbrook, IL. Graduate IN U., U. of DE. OB debut in *Strictly Personal.*

ADAMS, MASON Born February 26, 1919 in New York, NY. Graduate U. WI. Bdwy credits include *Get Away Old Man, Public Relations, Career Angel, Violet, Shadow of the Enemy, Tall Story, Inquest, Trial of the Catonsville 9, The Sign in Sidney Brustein's Window*, OB in *Meegan's Game, Shortchanged Review, Checking Out, The Sop Touch, Paradise Lost, The Time of Your Life, Danger: Memory, The Day Room, Rose Quartet, The Ryan Interview, Last of Thorntons.*

AGUSTIN, JULIO Born October 16, 1967 in Bronx, NY. Graduate FL St. U. Bdwy debut 1997 in *Steel Pier*, followed by *Fosse, Bells Are Ringing.*

AIDEM, BETSY Born October 28, 1957 in East Meadow, NY. Graduate NYU. OB debut 1981 in *The Trading Post*, followed by *A Different Moon, Balm in Gilead, Crossing the Bar, Our Lady of the Tortilla, Steel Magnolias, Road, 5 Women Wearing the Same Dress, Pera Palas, Ghost on Fire, Tamisanfly, The Butterfly Collection.*

ALDREDGE, TOM Born February 28, 1928 in Dayton, OH. Attended Dayton U., Goodman Theatre. Bdwy debut 1959 in *Nervous Set*, followed by *UTBU, Slapstick Tragedy, Everything in the Garden, Indians, Engagement Baby, How the Other Half Loves, Sticks and Bones, Where's Charley?, Leaf People, Rex, Vieux Carré, St. Joan, Stages, On Golden Pond, The Little Foxes, Into the Woods, Two Shakespearean Actors, Inherit the Wind, Boys from Syracuse* (Encores), *1776, Tom Sawyer*, OB in *The Tempest, Between Two Thieves, Henry V, The Premise, Love's Labour's Lost, Troilus and Cressida, The Butter and Egg Man, Ergo, Boys in the Band, Twelfth Night, Colette, Hamlet, The Orphan, King Lear, The Iceman Cometh, Black Angel, Getting Along Famously, Fool for Love, Neon Psalms, Richard II, Last Yankee, Incommunicado, La Terrasse, Time of the Cuckoo.*

ALLEGAERT, WENDY Born in New York, NY. Graduate Barnard Col. Debut OB in *Saved.*

ANDERMAN, MAUREEN Born October 26, 1946 in Detroit, MI. Graduate UMI. Bdwy debut 1970 in *Othello*, followed by *Moonchildren*, for which she received a 1972 Theatre World Award, *An Evening with Richard Nixon…, The Last of Mrs. Lincoln, Seascape, Who's Afraid of Virginia Woolf?, A History of the American Film, The Lady from Dubuque, The Man Who Came to Dinner, Einstein and the Polar Bear, You Can't Take It With You, Macbeth, Benefactors, Social Security*, OB in *Hamlet, Elusive Angel, Out of Our Father's House, Sunday Runners, Ancestral Voices, The Waverly Gallery, Passion Play.*

ANDERSON, MICHAEL Born June 23, 1972 in Denver, CO. Attended Whitman Col. OB debut in *Making Peter Pope.*

ANDERSON, NANCY Born April 22, 1972 in Boston, MA. Attended Smith Col., Tufts U. OB debut in *Fables in Slang*, followed by *Jolson & Co*, Bdwy debut *A Class Act* (also OB).

ANTHONY, GERALD Born July 31, 1951 in Pittsburgh, PA. Graduate USCS, CA State. OB debut in *Uncle Jack*, followed by *Snapshots 2000.*

ANTHONY-JACKSON, TODD Born in Hartford, CT. Attended Cornell U., American Conservatory Theatre. OB in *A Lesson from Aloes.*

Brent Barrett

Becky Barta

Bryan Batt

Brian Belovitch

Shirl Bernheim

Ian Blackman

ARANAS, RAUL Born October 1, 1947 in Manila, Phillipines. Graduate Pace U. OB debut 1976 in *Savages,* followed by *Yellow is My Favorite Color, 49, Bullet Headed Birds, Tooth of the Crime, Teahouse, Shepard Sets, Cold Air, La Chunga, The Man Who Turned into a Stick, Twelfth Night, Shogun Macbeth, Boutique Living, Fairy Bones, In the Jungle of Cities, Dogeaters,* Bdwy in *Loose Ends* (1978), *Miss Saigon, King and I.*

ARI, ROBERT (BOB) Born July 1, 1949 in New York, NY. Graduate Carnegie Mellon U. OB debut 1976 in *Boys from Syracuse,* followed by *Gay Divorce, Devour the Snow, Carbondale Dreams, Show Me Where the Good Times Are, CBS Live, Picasso at the Lapin Agile, Twelfth Night, Baby Anger, Names, June Moon, Pieces of the Sky, Wish You Were Here, Jolson & Co.,* Bdwy in *Bells Are Ringing.*

ARMITAGE, ROBERT Born September 18, 1970 in Bristol, CT. Attended Central CT St. U. Bdwy debut 1996 *Victor/Victoria,* followed by *Aida,* OB in *A Connecticut Yankee in King Arthur's Court* (CC).

ASQUITH, WARD Born March 21 in Philadelphia, PA. Graduate U. PA, Columbia U. OB debut 1979 in *After the Rise,* followed by *Kind Lady, Incident at Vichy, Happy Birthday Wanda June, Another Part of the Forest, Little Foxes, Sherlock Holmes & the Hands of Othello, Macbeth, Real Inspector Hound, Uncle Vanya, Cyrano de Bergerac, What the Butler Saw, The Professional, Welcome to Our City.*

ATKINS, EILEEN Born June 16, 1934 in London, England. Attended Guildhall Schl. Bdwy debut 1966 in *The Killing of Sister George,* followed by *The Promise, Viva! Vivat Regina!, The Night of the Tribades, Indiscretions,* OB in *Prin, A Room of One's Own, Vita and Virginia, The Unexpected Man.*

BAKER, DYLAN Born in Lackey, VA. Graduate William and Mary Col., Yale U. OB debut 1985 in *Not About Heroes,* followed by *Two Gentlemen of Verona, The Common Pursuit, Much Ado About Nothing, Wolf-Man, Dearly Departed, Pride's Crossing, That Championship Season, Tartuffe, What the Butcher Saw,* Bdwy debut 1989 in *Eastern Standard* (also OB), for which he received a 1989 Theatre World Award.

BALDWIN, ALEC Born April 3, 1958 in Massapequa, NY. Attended George Washington U., NYU. Bdwy debut 1986 in *Loot,* for which he received a 1986 Theatre World Award, followed by *Serious Money, A Streetcar Named Desire,* OB in *Prelude to a Kiss, Macbeth Voices!, Arsenic and Old Lace* (CC).

BARBOUR, JAMES Born April 25, 1966 in Cherry Hill, NJ. Graduate Hofstra U. OB debut 1990 in *Class Clown,* followed by *The Merry Wives of Windsor, Tom Sawyer, Harold and the Purple Crayon, Milk and Honey,* Bdwy in *Cyrano, The Musical* (1993) followed by *Carousel, Jane Eyre, Beauty and the Beast.*

BAREIKIS, ARIJA Born July 21, 1966 in Bloomington, IN. Bdwy debut 1997 in *Last Night of Ballyhoo,* OB in *The Moment When, Hotel Universe, Alice in Bed.*

BARNETT, KEN Born July 24, 1972 in Memphis, TN. Graduate Wesleyan U. OB in *A Christmas Carol* (MSG), *Imperfect Chemistry,* Bdwy in *The Green Bird* (2000).

BARRETT, BRENT Born February 28, 1957 in Quinter, KS. Graduate Carnegie Mellon U. Bdwy debut 1980 in *West Side Story,* followed by *Dance a Little Closer, Grand Hotel, Candide* (1997), *Chicago, Annie Get Your Gun,* OB in *March of the Falsettos, Portrait of Jenny, Death of Von Richthofen, Sweethearts, What's a Nice Country Like You Doing in a State Like This?, Time of the Cuckoo, Swan Song, Closer Than Ever, Marry Me a Little, On a Clear Day You Can See Forever* (CC).

BART, ROGER Born September 29, 1962 in Norwalk, CT. Graduate Rutgers U. OB debut 1984 in *Second Wind,* followed by *Lessons, Up Against It, Henry IV Parts I and 2, Fully Committed, On A Clear Day You Can See Forever* (CC), Bdwy in *Big River* (1987), *King David, Triumph of Love, You're a Good Man, Charlie Brown, The Producers.*

BARTA, BECKY Born December 27, 1962 in Kansas City, MO. Graduate U. of KS. OB debut in *Always, Patsy Cline,* followed by *Forbidden Broadway Cleans Up It's Act.*

BARTENIEFF, GEORGE Born January 24, 1933 in Berlin, Germany. Bdwy debut 1947 in *The Whole World Over,* followed by *Venus Is, All's Well That Ends Well, Quotations from Chairman Mao Tse-Tung, Death of Bessie Smith, Cop-Out, Room Service, Unlikely Heroes,* OB in *Walking in Waldheim, Memorandum, Increased Difficulty of Concentration, Trelawny of the Wells, Charley Chestnut Rides the IRT, Radio (Wisdom): Sophia Part I, Images of the Dead, Dead End Kids, The Blonde Leading the Blonde, The Dispossessed, Growing Up Gothic, Rosetti's Apologies, On the Lam, Samuel Beckett Trilogy, Quartet, Help Wanted, Matter of Life and Death, Heart That Eats Itself, Coney Island Kid, Cymbeline, Better People, Blue Heaven, He Saw His Reflection, Sabina, Beekeeper's Daughter, Desire Under the Elms, I Love Dick, I Will Bear Witness.*

BARTLETT, PETER Born August 28, 1942 in Chicago, IL. Attended Loyola U., LAMDA. Bdwy debut 1969 in *A Patriot for Me,* followed by *Gloria and Esperanza, Beauty and the Beast, Voices in the Dark,* OB in *Boom Boom Room, I Remember the House Where I was Born, Crazy Locomotive, A Thurber Carnival, Hamlet, Buzzsaw Berkeley, Learned Ladies, Jeffrey, The Naked Truth, Mr. Charles, The Most Fabulous Story Ever Told, A Connecticut Yankee in King Arthur's Court* (CC).

BATT, BRYAN Born March 1, 1963 in New Orleans, LA. Graduate Tulane U. OB debut 1987 in *Too Many Girls,* followed by *Golden Apple, Jeffrey, Forbidden Bdwy, Forbidden Bdwy Strikes Back, Ascendancy, Forbidden Bdwy Cleans Up Its Act!,* Bdwy in *Starlight Express* (1987), *Sunset Blvd., Saturday Night Fever, Seussical.*

BEACH, DAVID Born February 20, 1964 in Dayton, OH. Attended Darmouth Col., LAMDA. OB debut 1990 in *Big Fat and Ugly with a Moustache*, followed by *Modigliani, Octoberfest, Pets, That's Life!, Message to Michael, Urinetown*, Bdwy in *Moon Over Buffalo* (1995), *Beauty and the Beast., Sweet Adeline* (Encores).

BEACH, GARY Born October 10, 1947 in Alexandria, VA. Graduate NC Sch. of Arts. Bdwy debut 1971 in *1776*, followed by *Something's Afoot, Mooney Shapiro Songbook, Annie, Doonesbury, Beauty and the Beast*, OB in *Smile Smile Smile, What's a Nice Country Like You Doing in a State Like This?, Ionescapade, By Strouse, A Bundle of Nerves.*

BELL, GLYNIS Born July 30, 1947 in London, England. Attended Oakland U., AADA. OB debut 1975 in *The Devils*, followed by *The Time of Your Life, The Robber Bridegroom, Three Sisters, Sleep Deprivation Chamber, Diana of Dobson's, Blithe Spirit*, Bdwy debut 1993 in *My Fair Lady*, followed by *Amadeus.*

BELLAMY, BRAD Born June 18, 1951 in Marshall, MO. Graduate Westminster Col. OB debut 1974 in *Little Tips*, followed by *Crocodiles in the Potomac, Man Who Shot Jesse James, Andorra, Caine Mutiny Court Marshall, Flight, District of Columbia, Proof, If It Was Easy.*

BELOVITCH, BRIAN Born April 10, 1956 in Fall River, MA. Attended RI Col. OB debut in *Boys Don't Wear Lipstick.*

BERNHEIM, SHIRL Born September 21, 1921 in New York, NY. OB debut 1967 in *A Different World*, followed by *Stage Movie, Middle of the Night, Come Back, Little Sheba, One-Act Festival, EST Marathon 93, Old Lady's Guide to Survival.*

BERTRAND, JACQUELINE Born June 1, 1939 in Quebec, Canada. Attended Neighborhood Playhouse, Actors Studio, LAMDA. OB debut 1978 in *Unfinished Woman*, followed by *Dancing for the Kaiser, Lulu, War and Peace, Nest of the Wood Grouse, Salon, When She Danced, Antigone, Bravo Ubu, In Transit.*

BINOCHE, JULIETTE Born March 9, 1964 in Paris, France. Bdwy debut 2000 in *Betrayal*, for which she received a 2001 Theatre World Award.

BIRKELUND, OLIVIA Born April 26, 1963 in New York, NY. Graduate Brown U. OB debut 1990 in *Othello*, followed by *Cowboy in His Underwear, Misanthrope, Aimee and Hope, Servicemen.*

BIRNEY, REED Born September 11, 1954 in Alexandria, VA. Attended Boston U. Bdwy debut 1977 in *Gemini*, OB in *Master and Margarita, Bella Figura, Winterplay, Flight of the Earls, Filthy Rich, Lady Moonsong, Mr. Monsoon, Common Pursuit, Zero Positive, Moving Targets, Spare Parts, Murder of Crows, 7 Blowjobs, Loose Knot, The Undertaker, An Imaginary Life, Family of Mann, Dark Ride, Minor Demons, Volunteer Man, Knee Desires the Dirt, With and Without, The Exact Center of the Universe, The Butterfly Collection.*

BITON, JOSHUA Born December 19, 1973 in Queens, NY. Graduate SUNY Albany and Rutgers U. OB debut 2000 in *The Crumple Zone.*

BLACKMAN, IAN Born September 2, 1959 in Toronto, Canada. Attended Bard Col. OB debut 1982 in *Herself as Lust*, followed by *Sister Mary Ignatius Explains It All, The Actor's Nightmare, The Bone Ring*, Bdwy debut 1986 in *The House of Blue Leaves*, followed by *The Man Who Came to Dinner.*

BLANCHARD, STEVE Born December 4, 1958 in York, PA. Attended U. MD. Bdwy debut 1984 in *The Three Musketeers*, followed by *Camelot, Christmas Carol, Beauty and the Beast*, OB in *Moby Dick.*

BLAZER, JUDITH Born October 22, 1956. OB in *Oh Boy!*, followed by *Roberta, A Little Night Music, Company, Babes in Arms, Hello Again, Jack's Holiday, Louisiana Purchase, Hurrah At Last, The Torchbearers, A Connecticut Yankee in King Arthur's Court* (CC), Bdwy in *Me and My Girl, A Change in the Heir, Titanic.*

BLOCH, SCOTTY Born January 28 in New Rochelle, NY. Attended AADA. OB debut 1945 in *Craig's Wife*, followed by *Lemon Sky, Battering Ram, Richard III, In Celebration, An Act of Kindness, The Price, Grace, Neon Psalms, Other People's Money, Walking The Dead, EST Marathon '92, The Stand-In, Unexpected Tenderness, Brutality of Fact, What I Meant Was, Scotland Road The Waverly Gallery, Saved or Destroyed*, Bdwy in *Children of a Lesser God* (1980).

BLOOM, TOM Born November 1, 1944 in Washington, D.C. Graduate Western MD Col., Emerson Col. OB debut 1989 in *Widow's Blind Date*, followed by *A Cup of Coffee, Major Barbara, A Perfect Diamond, Lips Together Teeth Apart, Winter's Tale, The Guardsman, Stray Cats, Arms and the Man*, Bdwy in *Racing Demon* (1995).

BLUM, JOEL Born May 19, 1952 in San Francisco, CA. Attended Marin Col., NYU. Bdwy debut 1976 in *Debbie Reynolds on Broadway*, followed by *42nd Street, Stardust, Radio City Easter Show, Show Boat* (1994), *Steel Pier*, OB in *And the World Goes Round, Game Show.*

BLUM, MARK Born May 14, 1950 in Newark, NJ. Graduate U. PA, U. MN. OB debut 1976 in *The Cherry Orchard*, followed by *Green Julia, Say Goodnight Gracie, Table Settings, Key Exchange, Loving Reno, Messiah, It's Only a Play, Little Footsteps, Cave of Life, Gus & Al, Laureen's Whereabouts, Mizlansky, Zilinksy, Gore Vidal's The Best Man, The Waverly Gallery*, Bdwy in *Lost in Yonkers* (1991), *My Thing of Love, A Thousand Clowns.*

BLUMENKRANTZ, JEFF Born June 3, 1965 in Long Branch, NJ. Graduate Northwestern U. OB debut 1986 in *Pajama Game*, Bdwy debut 1987 in *Into the Woods*, followed by *3 Penny Opera, South Pacific, Damn Yankees, How to Succeed in Business Without Really Trying* (1995), *A Class Act.*

BOBBY, ANNE MARIE Born December 12, 1967 in Paterson, NJ. Attended Oxford U. OB debut 1983 in *American Passion*, followed by *Class I Acts, Godspell, Progress, Groundhog, Misconceptions, Merrily We Roll Along, Strictly Personal*, Bdwy in *The Human Comedy* (1984), *The Real Thing, Hurlyburly, Precious Sons, Smile, Black Comedy.*

BOCKHORN, CRAIG Born May 30, 1961 in New York, NY. Graduate Emerson Col. OB debut 1989 in *You Can't Think of Everything*, followed by *Truth Teller, Third Millennium, As You Like It, Loveliest Afternoon of the Year, Women of Manhattan, Runyon on Wry, Bard Silly, Hope Zone, Kit Marlowe*, Bdwy debut 1990 in *Prelude to a Kiss* (also OB).

BODLE, JANE Born November 12 in Lawrence, KS. Attended U. UT. Bdwy debut 1983 in *Cats*, followed by *Les Miserables, Miss Saigon, Sunset Blvd*, OB in *Once Around the City.*

BOEVERS, JESSICA Born August 25, 1972 in Highland Park, IL. Graduate Cincinnati Cons. of Music, U. of Cincinatti. Bdwy debut 1994 in *Beauty and the Beast*, followed by *A Funny Thing Happened on the Way to the Forum*, OB in *The It Girl.*

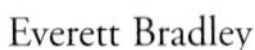

Everett Bradley

Joel Briel

Eric Martin Brown

David Burtka

Seán Campion

Len Cariou

BOSCO, PHILIP Born September 26, 1930 in Jersey City, NJ. Graduate Catholic U. Credits: *Auntie Mame, Rape of the Belt, Ticket of Leave Man, Donnybrook, A Man for All Seasons, Mrs. Warren's Profession,* with LCRep in *A Great Career, In the Matter of J. Robert Oppenheimer, The Miser, The Time of Your Life, Camino Real, Operation Sidewinder, Amphitryon, Enemy of the People, Playboy of the Western World, Good Woman of Setzuan, Antigone, Mary Stuart, Narrow Road to the Deep North, The Crucible, Twelfth Night, Enemies, Plough and the Stars, Merchant of Venice, A Streetcar Named Desire, Henry V, Threepenny Opera, Streamers, Stages, St. Joan, The Biko Inquest, Man and Superman, Whose Life Is It Anyway?, Major Barbara, A Month in the Country, Bacchae, Hedda Gabler, Don Juan in Hell, Inadmissable Evidence, Eminent Domain, Misalliance, Learned Ladies, Some Men Need Help, Ah, Wilderness!, The Caine Mutiny Court Martial, Heartbreak House, Come Back Little Sheba, Loves of Anatol, Be Happy for Me, Master Class, You Never Can Tell, Devil's Disciple, Lend Me a Tenor, Breaking Legs, Fiorello* (Encores), *An Inspector Calls, The Heiress, Moon Over Buffalo, Strike Up the Band* (Encores), *Twelfth Night, Copenhagen, Ancestral Voices, Bloomer Girl* (CC).

BOSTNAR, LISA Born July 19 in Cleveland, OH. Attended Case Western U.

BOSTON, GRETHA Born April 18, 1959 in Crossett, AR. Attended U. No. TX, U. IL. Bdwy debut 1994 in *Show Boat,* for which she received a 1995 Theatre World Award, OB in *Tea Time.*

BOURNE, BETTE Born September 22, 1939 in the United Kingdom. Graduate Central Sch. London. OB in *Resident Alien.*

BOWEN, ANDREA Born March 4, 1990 in Columbus, OH. Bdwy debut 1997 in *Les Miserables,* followed by *Sound of Music, Jane Eyre.*

BRADLEY, BRAD Born December 9, 1971 in San Diego, CA. Graduate USC. Bdwy debut 1995 in *Christmas Carol,* followed by *Steel Pier, Strike Up the Band* (Encores), *Annie Get Your Gun,* OB in *Cocoanuts.*

BRADLEY, EVERETT Born March 16, 1963 in Greenwood, SC. Graduate IN U. OB debut in *Stomp,* followed by *Bloomer Girl,* Bdwy in *Swing* (1996).

BRIEL, JOEL Born August 7, 1960 in San Francisco, CA. Graduate AZ St. U. Bdwy debut 1990 in *Cats,* OB in *That's Life,* followed by *Bearded Iris.*

BRIGHTMAN, JULIAN Born March 5 1964 in Philadelphia, PA. Graduate U. PA. OB debut 1987 in *1984,* followed by *Critic, Leaves of Grass, Songbox, Look Ma, I'm Dancing, Watch Your Step,* Bdwy in *Peter Pan* (1990/1991), *Hello, Dolly!* (1995).

BRODERICK, MATTHEW Born March 21, 1963 in New York, NY. OB debut 1981 in *Torch Song Trilogy,* followed by *The Widow Claire, A Christmas Memory,* Bdwy debut 1983 in *Brighton Beach Memoirs,* for which he received a 1983 Theatre World Award, followed by *Biloxi Blues, How to Succeed in Business Without Really Trying* (1995), *Night Must Fall, Taller Than a Dwarf, The Producers.*

BRODERICK, WILLIAM Born October 19, 1954 in Queens, NY. Graduate Hunter Col. OB debut 1986 in *Pere Goriot,* followed by *The Real Inspector Hound, Iolanthe, Teasers and Tormentors, Dorian, White Widow, Rosmersholm.*

BROOKES, JACQUELINE Born July 24, 1930 in Montclair, NJ. Graduate U. IA, RADA. Bdwy debut 1955 in *Tiger at the Gates,* followed by *Watercolor, Abelard and Heloise, A Meeting by the River,* OB debut 1954 in *The Cretan Woman,* for which she received a 1955 Theatre World Award, followed by *The Clandestine Marriage, Measure for Measure, The Duchess of Malfi, Ivanov, 8 Characters in Search of an Author, An Evening's Frost, Come Slowly Eden, The Increased Difficulty of Concentration, The Persians, Sunday Dinner, House of Blue Leaves, Owners, Hallelujah, Dream of a Black-listed Actor, Knuckle, Mama Sang the Blues, Buried Child, On Mt. Chimorazo, Winter Dancers, Hamlet, Old Flames, The Diviners, Richard II, Vieux Carre, Full Hookup, Home Sweet Home/Crack, Approaching Zanzibar, Ten Blocks on the Camino Real, Listening, Sand, Seascape, Elsa's Goodbye, Period of Adjustment, the Country Girl, All Over.*

BROWN, ANN Born December 1, 1960 in Westwood, NJ. Graduate Trinity Col. OB debut 1987 in *Pacific Overtures,* followed by *Side by Side by Sondheim, Stages, Golden Apple, 20 Fingers 20 Toes, Salute to Tom Jones and Harvey Schmidt,* Bdwy in *Once Upon a Mattress* (1996), *Sound of Music, Music Man, Tom Sawyer.*

BROWN, DAVID, JR. Born November 15, 1971 in Flushing, NY. Attended CCNY. OB debut in *Y2K,* followed by *Up Against the Wind.*

BROWN, ERIC MARTIN Born May 20 in Syracuse, NY. Graduate NYU, Yale. Debut OB in *Servicemen.*

BROWN, ROBIN LESLIE Born January 18, in Canandaigua, NY. Graduate LIU. OB debut 1980 in *Mother of Us All,* followed by *Yours Truly, Two Gentlemen of Verona, Taming of the Shrew, The Mollusc, The Contrast, Pericles, Andromache, Macbeth, Electra, She Stoops to Conquer, Berneice, Hedda Gabler, Midsummer Night's Dream, Three Sisters, Major Barbara, Fine Art of Finesse, Two by Schnitzler, As You Like It, Ghosts, Chekhov Very Funny, Beaux Strategem, God of Vengeance, Good Natured Man, Twelfth Night, Little Eyolf, Venetian Twins, King Lear, Doll's House, Antigone, Venice Preserv'd, Hard Times, The Country Wife, The Miser, Merry Wives of Windsor, The Way of the World, The Oresteia, Mirandolina, John Gabriel Borkman, The Cherry Orchard.*

BRUMMEL, DAVID Born November 1, 1942 in Brooklyn, NY. Bdwy debut 1973 in *The Pajama Game*, followed by *Music Is, Oklahoma!, Bells Are Ringing*, OB in *Cole Porter, The Fantasticks, Prom Queens Unchained, Camilla, Carmelina, Kuni-Leml.*

BUNCH, ELIZABETH Born October 23, 1975 in Huntington, WV. Graduate NYU. OB debut 1997 in *Water Children*, followed by *The Light Outside.*

BURKS, WILLIS II Born October 25, 1935 in Birmingham, AL. Attended Columbia Col. OB debut 1994 in *East Texas Hot Links*, followed by *Jitney, Saint Lucy's Eyes.*

BURRELL, FRED Born September 18, 1936. Graduate UNC, RADA. Bdwy debut 1964 in *Never Too Late*, followed by *Illya Darling, Cactus Flower, On Golden Pond, Inherit the Wind, Judgment at Nuremberg*, OB in *The Memorandum, Throckmorton, Texas, Voices in the Head, Chili Queen, The Queen's Knight, In Pursuit of the Song of Hydrogen, Unchanging Love, More Fun Than Bowling, Woman Without a Name, Sorrows of Fredrick, Voice of the Prairie, Spain, Democracy and Esther, Last Sortie, Rough/Play, Life is a Dream, Taming of the Shrew, Twelfth Night, Modest Proposal, Oedipus at Colonus, A Hamlet, 3 in the Back 2 in the Head, True Crimes, Rhinoceros, After-Dinner Joke, The Appearance of Impropriety, On the Middle Watch, God's Creatures.*

BURTKA, DAVID Born May 29, 1975 in Dearborn, MI. Graduate U. MI. OB debut 1998 in *Beautiful Thing*, followed by *The Play about the Baby.*

BURTON, ARNIE Born September 22, 1958 in Emmett, ID. Graduate U. AZ. Bdwy debut 1983 in *Amadeus*, OB in *Measure for Measure, Major Barbara, Schnitzler One Acts, Tartuffe, As You Like It, Ghosts, Othello, Moon for the Misbegotten, Twelfth Night, Little Eyolf, Mollusc, Venetain Twins, Beaux Stratagem, King Lear, Winter's Tale, When Ladies Battle, Barber of Seville, Mere Mortals, Cymbeline, A Will of His Own, Andromache, The Cherry Orchard.*

BUTLER, DAN Born December 2, 1954 in Huntington, IN. Attended IN U. Purdue, San Jose St. Bdwy debut 1982 in *The Hothouse*, followed by *Biloxi Blues*, OB in *True West* (1983), *Walk the Dog Whistle, Domino, Wrestlers, Emerald City, Lisbon Traviata, Much Ado about Nothing, Early One Evening at the Rainbow Bar & Grill, Only Thing Worse You Could Have Told Me*, which he wrote and, *Old Money.*

BUTLER, KERRY Born in Brooklyn, NY. Graduate Ithaca Col. Bdwy debut 1993 in *Blood Brothers*, followed by *Beauty and the Beast*, OB in *The "I" Word: Interns, The Folsom Head, King of Hearts, Bat Boy.*

BUTZ, NORBERT LEO Born January 30, 1967 in St. Louis, MO. Graduate Webster U., U. of AL. Bdwy debut 1996 in *Rent*, OB in *Juno and the Paycock, Saved.*

CAMP, JOANNE Born April 4, 1951 in Atlanta, GA. Graduate FL Atlantic U., George Washington U. OB debut 1981 in *The Dry Martini*, followed by *Geniuses*, for which she received a 1983 Theatre World Award, *June Moon, Painting Churches, Merchant of Venice, Lady from the Sea, The Contrast, Coastal Disturbances, The Rivals, Andromache, Electra, Uncle Vanya, She Stoops to Conquer, Hedda Gabler, Heidi Chronicles, Importance of Being Earnest, Medea, Three Sisters, Midsummer Night's Dream, School for Wives, Measure for Measure, Dance of Death, Two Schnitzler One-Acts, Tartuffe, Lips Together Teeth Apart, As You Like It, Moon for the Misbegotten, Phaedra, Little Eyolf, Beaux Strategem, King Lear, Life Is a Dream, Winter's Tale, When Ladies Battle, The Guardsman, Candida, The Country Wife, The Seagull, The Way of the World, The Oresteia, John Gabriel Borkman, Blithe Spirit, The Cherry Orchard*, Bdwy in *Heidi Chronicles* (1989), *Sisters Rosensweig, Last Night of Ballyhoo.*

CAMPION, SEÁN Born December 20, 1959 in Freshford, Co. Kilkenny, Ireland. OB debut in *Stones in His Pockets.*

CARIOU, LEN Born September 30, 1939 in Winnipeg, Canada. Bdwy debut 1968 in *House of Atrew*, followed by *Henry V, Applause*, for which he received a 1970 Theatre World Award, *Night Watch, A Little Night Music, Cold Storage, Sweeney Todd, Dance a Little Closer, Teddy and Alice, The Speed of Darkness, The Dinner Party*, OB in *A Sorrow Beyond Dreams, Up from Paradise, Master Class, Day Six, Measure for Measure, Mountain, Papa.*

CARLEY, CHRISTOPHER MURPHY Born May 31, 1978 in Suffern, NY. Attended NYU. Bdwy debut 1999 in *The Beauty Queen of Leenane, A Skull in Connemara.*

CARMELLO, CAROLEE Born in Albany, NY. Graduate SUNY Albany. Bdwy debut 1989 in *City of Angels*, followed by *Falsettos, 1776, Parade, Scarlet Pimpernel*, OB in *I Can Get it for You Wholesale* (1991), *Hello Again, Goose, The Case of the Dead Flamingo Dancer, A Class Act.*

CARTER, AARON Born December 8, 1987 in Tampa, FL. Bdwy debut 2001 in *Seussical.*

CARTER, CAITLIN Born February 1 in San Francisco, CA. Graduate Rice U., NC School of Arts. Bdwy debut 1993 in *Ain't Broadway Grand*, followed by *Chicago, Victor Victoria, Chicago, Swing, Bells Are Ringing.*

CELLI, BOB Born February 4, 1958 in Princeton, NJ. Graduate Villanova U., Rider Col. OB debut 1985 in *Vinyl*, followed by *Two Birds with One Stone, Found in the Garden, Madmen Madame and Mayhem, Jesse and the Bandit Queen, Burn This, Circle.*

CERASO, CHRIS Born September 23, 1952 in Leechburg, PA. Graduate U. Notre Dame, FL St. U. OB in *Summer Cyclone.*

CHAIFETZ, DANA Born September 1 in New York, NY. OB debut 1992 in *El Barrio*, followed by *Somewhere, Halfway There, Resurrection, The Survivor, Ghost on Fire, Sitting Pretty.*

CHALFANT, KATHLEEN Born January 14, 1945 in San Francisco, CA. Graduate Stanford U. Bdwy debut 1975 in *Dance with Me*, followed by *M. Butterfly, Angels in America, Racing Demon*, OB in *Jules Feiffer's Hold Me, Killings on the Last Line, The Boor, Blood Relations, Signs of Life, Sister Mary Ignatius Explains it All, Actor's Nightmare, Faith Healer, All the Nice People, Hard Times, Investigation of the Murder in El Salvador, 3 Poets, The Crucible, The Party, Iphigenia and Other Daughters, Cowboy Pictures, Twelve Dreams, Henry V, Endgame, When It Comes Early, Nine Armenians, Phaedra in Delirium, Wit, True History and Real Adventures, Bloomer Girl* (CC).

CHALFY, DYLAN Born June 22, 1970 in Sarasota, FL. OB debut 1994 in *Blood Guilty*, followed by *Cross Your Heart, Home of the Brave, Big Potato*, Bdwy debut 1995 in *Rose Tattoo*, followed by *Ah, Wilderness!*

CHAMBERLAIN, ANDREA Born June 5, 1972 in Fresno, CA. Bdwy debut 1998 in *Little Me*, OB in *I Love You, You're Perfect, Now Change.*

CHAMBERLIN, KEVIN Born November 25, 1963 in Baltimore, MD. Graduate Rutgers U., OB debut 1990 in *Neddy*, followed by *Smoke on the Mountain, Ziegfeld Follies of 1936, As 1000 Cheer, Dirty Blonde*, Bdwy in *My Favorite Year* (1992), *Abe Lincoln in Illinois, One Touch of Venus* (Encores), *Triumph of Love, Seussical.*

Chris Ceraso

Dana Chaifetz

Kevin Chamberlin

Tanya Clarke

Jennifer Cody

Lynn Cohen

CHANDLER, DAVID Born February 3, 1950 in Danbury, CT. Graduate Oberlin Col. Bdwy debut 1980 in *The American Clock*, followed by *Death of a Salesman, Lost in Yonkers*, OB in *Made in Heaven, Black Sea Follies, The Swan, Watbanaland, Phaedra, Slavs!, Working Title, What You Get and What You Expect, The Trestle at Pope Lick Creek, Cellini.*

CHARLES, WALTER Born April 4, 1945 in East Stroudsburg, PA. Graduate Boston U. Bdwy debut 1973 in *Grease*, followed by 1600 *Pennsylvania Avenue, Knickerbocker Holiday, Sweeney Todd, Cats, La Cage Aux Folles, Aspects of Love, Me and My Girl,* 110 *in the Shade* (NYCO), *A Christmas Carol*, OB in *Wit, Tenderloin, The Immigrant.*

CHARNEY, JORDAN Born April 1, 1937 in New York, NY. Graduate Brooklyn Col. OB in *Harry, Noon and Night, A Place for Chance, Hang Down Your Head and Die, The Pinter Plays, Telemachus Clay, Zoo Story, Viet Rock, MacBird, Red Cross, Glorious Ruler, Waiting for Godot, Slow Memories, One Flew Over the Cuckoo's Nest, Boy Who Came to Leave, Cretan Bull, Naomi Court, Sublime Lives, Waste, Code of the West, Troilus and Cressida*, Bdwy in *Slapstick Tragedy* (1966), *The Birthday Party, Talley's Folly.*

CHERNOV, HOPE Born June 13 in Philadelphia, PA. Graduate Temple U., U. CA Irvine. OB debut 1996 in *Barber of Seville*, followed by *Venice Preserv'd, As Bees in Honey Drown, Richard II, Miss Julie, School for Scandal, The Country Wife, The Seagull, Blithe Spirit.*

CHIASSON, GILLES Born November 1, 1966 in Muskegon, MI. Graduate U. MI. OB debut 1992 in *Groundhog*, followed by *Fermat's Last Tango*, Bdwy debut 1996 in *Rent*, followed by *Scarlet Pimpernel, The Civil War.*

CHRISTOPHER, THOM Born October 5, 1940 in Jackson Heights, NY. Attended Ithaca Col., Neighborhood Playhouse. OB debut 1972 in *One Flew Over the Cuckoo's Nest*, followed by *Tamara, Investigation of the Murder in El Salvador, Sublime Lives, Triumph of Love, The Changeling, Den of Thieves, Night Becoming Jasmine, Knepp*, Bdwy in *Emperor Henry IV* (1973), *Noel Coward in Two Keys*, for which he received a 1974 Theatre World Award, *Caesar and Cleopatra.*

CISSEL, CHARLES Born July 31, 1956 in Denville, NJ. Attended CT. Col. of Dance. OB in *Period of Adjustment, The Country Girl, All Over.*

CIULLA, CELESTE Born September 10, 1967 in New York, NY. Graduate Northwestem U., Harvard. OB debut 1992 in *Othello*, followed by *The Good Natured Man, Phaedra, Fair Fight, A Will of His Own, Andromache.*

CLARKE, TANYA Born February 2, 1972, in Chicago, IL. OB debut in *The Director*, followed by *Bobbi Boland.*

CLAYTON, LAWRENCE Born October 10, 1956 in Mocksville, NC. Attended NC Central U. OB debut 1980 in *Tambourines to Glory*, followed by *Skyline, Across the Universe, Two by Two, Romance in Hard Times, Juba, Tapestry, Saturn Returns*, Bdwy in *Dreamgirls* (1984), *High Rollers, Once Upon a Mattress, The Civil War, Bells Are Ringing.*

CODY, JENNIFER Born November 10, 1969 in Rochester, NY. Graduate SUNY Fredonia. OB debut 1992 in *Anyone Can Whistle, followed by The Wild Party*, Bdwy in *Cats* (1994), *Grease, Seussical.*

COFIELD, CARL JAY Born December 19 in Fulda, Germany. Attended U. of Miami, RADA. OB debut 1995 in *Henry V*, followed by *As You Like It, Mud River Stone, Desire Under the Elms, The In-Gathering.*

COHEN, LYNN Born August 10 in Kansas City, MO. Graduate Northwestern U. OB debut 1979 in *Don Juan Comes Back From the Wars*, followed by *Getting Out, The Arbor, Cat and the Canary, Suddenly Last Summer, Bella Figura, The Smash, Chinese Viewing Pavilion, Isn't It Romantic, Total Eclipse, Angelo's Wedding, Hamlet, Love Diatribe, A Couple with a Cat, XXX Love Acts, Model Apt., The Devils, Knee Desires the Dirt, Paradise Island*, Bdwy in *Orpheus Descending* (1989), *Ivanov.*

COLEMAN, ROSALYN Born July 20, 1965 in Ann Arbor, MI. Graduate Harvard U., Yale U. Bdwy debut 1990 in *Piano Lesson*, followed by *Mule Bone, Seven Guitars*, OB in *Destiny of Me* (1992), *Major Crimes, Old Settler, Flight to Freedom, Wyoming, Bitter Tears of Petra Von Kant, Breath, Boom.*

COMLEY, BONNIE Born in MA. Graduate Emerson Col. OB debut 1988 in *Noo Yawk Tawk*, followed by *Fortune's Fools, If It Was Easy.*

CONE, MICHAEL Born October 7, 1952 in Fresno, CA. Graduate U. WA. Bdwy debut 1980 in *Brigadoon*, followed by *Christmas Carol*, OB in *Bar Mitzvah Boy, The Rink, Commedia Tonite!, London Cuckolds.*

CONNELL, GORDON Born March 19, 1923 in Berkeley, CA. Graduate U. CA., NYU. Bdwy debut 1961 in *Subways are for Sleeping*, followed by *Hello, Dolly!, Lysistrata, Human Comedy* (also OB), *Big River*, OB in *Beggars Opera, Butler Did It, With Love and Laughter, Deja Review, Good Doctor, Leave It to Me.*

CONNELL, JANE Born October 27, 1925 in Berkeley, CA. Attended U. CA. Bdwy debut in *New Faces of* 1956, followed by *Drat! The Cat!, Mame* (1966/83), *Dear World, Lysistrata, Me and My Girl, Lend Me a Tenor, Crazy For You, Moon Over Buffalo, Tom Sawyer*, OB in *Shoestring Revue, Threepenny Opera, Pieces of Eight, Demi-Dozen, She Stoops to Conquer, Drat!, Real Inspector Hound, Rivals, Rise and Rise of Daniel Rocket, Laughing Stock, Singular Dorothy Parker, No No Nanette in Concert, Good Doctor, 70 Girls 70.*

Patricia Conolly

Joan Copeland

Joseph Costa

Todd Alan Crain

Joseph Culliton

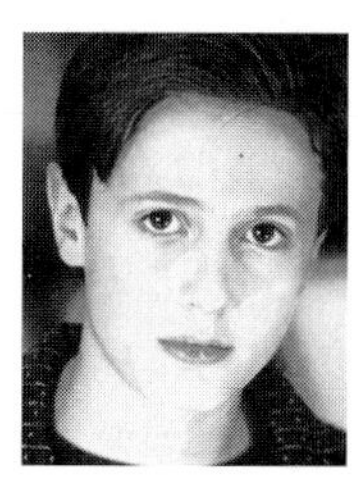
Nicholas Cutro

CONOLLY, PATRICIA Born August 29, 1933 in Tabora, East Africa. Attended U. Sydney. With APA in *You Can't Take It With You, War and Peace, School for Scandal, Wild Duck, Right You Are, We Comrades Three, Pantagleize, Exit the King, Cherry Orchard, Misanthrope, Cocktail Party, Cock-a-doodle Dandy, Streetcar Named Desire, Importance of Being Earnest, The Circle, Small Family Business, Real Inspector Hound/15 Minute Hamlet, Heiress, Tartuffe: Born Again, Sound of Music, Waiting in the Wings, Judgment at Nuremberg,* OB in *Blithe Spirit, Woman in Mind, Misalliance.*

CONROY, JARLATH Born September 30, 1944 in Galway, Ireland. Attended RADA. Bdwy debut 1976 in *Comedians,* followed by *The Elephant Man, Macbeth, Ghetto, The Visit, On the Waterfront, The Iceman Cometh,* OB in *Translations, The Wind that Shook the Barley, Gardenia, Friends, Playboy of the Western World, One-Act Festival, Abel & Bela/Architect, The Matchmaker, Henry V, Our Lady of Sligo, Bloomer Girl.*

CONROY, MARYELLEN Born August 31, 1947 in White Plains, NY. Graduate Pace U. Bdwy debut 1994 in *Inspector Calls.*

CONVERSE, FRANK Born May 22, 1938 in St. Louis, MO. Attended Carnegie Mellon U. Bdwy debut 1966 in *First One Asleep Whistle,* followed by *The Philadephia Story, Brothers, Design for Living, A Streetcar Named Desire,* OB in *House of Blue Leaves, Lady in the Dark in Concert, Thief River.*

COOK, VICTOR TRENT Born August 19, 1967 in New York, NY. OB debut 1976 in *Joseph and the Amazing Technicolor Dreamcoat,* followed by *Haggadah, Moby Dick, Romance in Hard Times, Cinderella,* Bdwy in *Don't Get God Started* (1988), *Starmites* (also OB), *Smokey Joe's Cafe, Street Corner Symphony, St. Louis Woman* (Encores).

COPELAND, JOAN Born June 1, 1922 in New York, NY. Attended Brooklyn Col., AADA. OB debut 1945 in *Romeo and Juliet,* followed by *Othello, Conversation Piece, Delightful Season, End of Summer, The American Clock, The Double Game, Isn't it Romantic? Hunting Cockroaches, Young Playwrights Festival, The American Plan, Rose Quartet, Another Time, A Dybbuk, Over the River and Through the Woods, Fishkin Touch, The Torchbearers, Second Summer,* Bdwy in *Sundown Beach, Detective Story, Not for Children, Hatful of Fire, Something More, The Price, Two by Two, Pal Joey, Checking Out, The American Clock.*

CORBO, GEORGINA Born September 21, 1965 in Havana, Cuba. Attended SUNY Purchase. OB debut 1988 in *Ariano,* followed by *Born to Rumba, Mambo Louie and the Dancing Machine, Ghost Sonata, You Can't Win, Dog Lady, The Bundle, Family Affair, The House Must be Dismantled.*

COSTA, JOSEPH Born June 8, 1946 in Ithaca, NY. Graduate Gettysburg Col., Yale U. OB debut 1978 in *The Show Off,* followed by *The Tempest, The Changeling, A Map of the World, Julius Caesar, Titus Andronicus, Love's Labor's Lost, Macbeth, The Crucible, The Way of the World, The Clearing,* Bdwy in *Gore Vidal's The Best Man.*

COVER, BRADFORD Born January 26, 1967 in New York, NY. Graduate Denison U., U. WI. OB debut 1994 in *King Lear,* followed by *Beaux Strategem, Venetian Twins, Oedipus at Colonus, Mrs. Warren's Profession, Winter's Tale, Life Is a Dream, When Ladies Battle, Antigone, Misalliance, The Forest, School for Scandal, Richard II,* Bdwy in *A Thousand Clowns.*

COWAN, EDWARDYNE Born July 23 in Queens, NY. Graduate New Rochelle Col. OB debut 1992 in *The Molly Maguires,* followed by *Anything Goes, Lakme,* Bdwy debut 1993 in *My Fair Lady,* followed by *Fermat's Last Tango.*

COX, VEANNE Born January 19, 1963 in VA. Bdwy debut 1986 in *Smile,* followed by *Company, The Dinner Party,* OB in *Nat'l Lampoon's Class of '86, Flora the Red Menace, Showing Off, Food Chain, Question of Mercy, Waiting Room, Batting Cage, Labor Day, Freedomland, The Altruists.*

COXE, HELEN P. Born October 19, 1967 in Bryn Mawr, PA. Graduate U. of Hartford, ACT. Bdwy debut 1999 in *Sideman,* OB in *My Mother's a Baby Boy.*

CRAIN, TODD ALAN Born May 16, 1972 in WI. Graduate Otterbien Col. OB debut in *Personals.*

CRAVENS, PIERCE Born January 8, 1986 in Dallas, TX. OB debut 1993 in *All's Well that Ends Well,* Bdwy debut 1994 in *Beauty and the Beast,* followed by *Tom Sawyer.*

CROFT, PADDY Born in Worthing, England. Attended Avondale Col. OB debut 1961 OB in *The Hostage,* followed by *Billy Liar, Live Like Pigs, Hogan's Goat, Long Day's Journey into Night, Shadow of a Gunman, Pygmalion, Plough and the Stars, Kill, Starting Monday, Philadelphia Here I Come!, Grandchild of Kings, Fragments, Same Old Moon, Nightingale and Not the Lark, Da, James Joyce's The Dead, A Life,* Bdwy in *Killing of Sister George, Prime of Miss Jean Brodie, Crown Matrimonial, Major Barbara, Night Must Fall, The Dead.*

CROSBY, B.J. Born November 23, 1952 in New Orleans, LA. Bdwy debut 1995 in *Smokey Joe's Café,* OB in *Tea Time.*

CRUDUP, BILLY Born July 8, 1968 in Manhasset, NY. Graduate U. NC, NYU. OB debut 1994 in *America Dreaming,* followed by *Oedipus, Measure for Measure,* Bdwy debut 1995 in *Arcadia,* for which he received a 1995 Theatre World Award, followed by *Bus Stop, Three Sisters.*

CULKIN, MACAULAY Born August 26, 1980 in New York, NY. OB debut 2001 in *Madame Melville,* for which he received a 2001 Theatre World Award.

Lisa Datz

Stephen DeRosa

Erik Devine

David DeVries

Cliff Diamond

Natascia Diaz

CULLITON, JOSEPH Born January 25, 1948 in Boston, MA. Attended CA St. U. OB debut 1982 in *Francis*, followed by *Flirtations, South Pacific* (LC), *Julius Caesar, King John, Company, On a Clear Day, Bald Soprano*, Bdwy debut 1987 in *Broadway*, followed by *Gore Vidal's The Best Man.*

CULLUM, JOHN Born March 2, 1930 in Knoxville, TN. Graduate U. TN. Bdwy debut 1960 in *Camelot*, followed by *Infidel Caesar, The Rehearsal, Hamlet, On a Clear Day You Can See Forever*, for which he received a 1966 Theatre World Award, *Man of La Mancha, 1776, Vivat! Vivat Regina!, Shenandoah* (1975/1989), *Kings, Trip Back Down, On the 20th Century, Deathtrap, Doubles, You Never Can Tell, Boys in Autumn, Aspect of Love, Show Boat*, OB in *3 Hand Reel, The Elizabethans, Carousel, In the Voodoo Parlor of Marie Leveau, King and I, Whistler, All My Sons, Urinetown, Old Money.*

CUMPSTY, MICHAEL Born in England. Graduate UNC. Bdwy debut 1989 in *Artist Descending a Staircase*, followed by *La Bete, Timon of Athens, Translations, Heiress, Racing Demon, 1776, Electra, Copenhagen, 42nd Street*, OB in *Art of Success, Man and Superman, Hamlet, Cymbeline, Winter's Tale, King John, Romeo and Juliet, All's Well That Ends Well, Timon of Athens.*

CURLESS, JOHN Born September 16 in Wigan, England. Attended Central Sch. of Speech. OB debut 1982 in *The Entertainer*, followed by *Sus, Up 'n' Under, Progress, Prin, Nightingale, Absent Friends, Owners/Traps, Comic Potential, Passion Play*, Bdwy in *A Small Family Business* (1992), *Racing Demon, King and I, Sound of Music.*

CURTIN, CATHERINE Born in New York, NY. Graduate Princeton U. Bdwy debut 1990 in *Six Degrees of Separation*, OB in *Gulf War, Making Book, Orphan Muses, Aimee and Hope, Love, Janis.*

CUTRO, NICHOLAS Born April 28, 1988 in New York, NY. Bdwy debut 2000 in *The Time of the Cuckoo* (LC), followed by *The Full Monty.*

CYR, MYRIAM Born in New Brunswick, Canada. Attended Cons. d'Art Dramatique de Montreal, Ecole Nat'l de Strasbourg, LAMDA. OB debut 1995 in *Floating Rhoda and the Glue Man*, followed by *Green Bird, Antigone, Brave Ubu, Cartas: A Nun in Love, In Transit.*

DAILY, DANIEL Born July 25, 1955 in Chicago, IL. Graduate Notre Dame U., U. WA. OB debut 1988 in *Boy's Breath*, followed by *A Ronde, Iron Bars, Chekhov Very Funny, Macbeth, As You Like It, Free Zone, Scarlet Letter, Two Nikita, The Adoption, Tenth Man, Helmut Sees America, School for Scandal, Richard II, Angel Street, The Country Wife, The Seagull, The Way of the World, The Oresteia, Merry Wives of Windsor, Mirandolina, The Cherry Orchard.*

DANIELEY, JASON Born July 13, 1971 in St. Louis, MO. Attended So. IL U. OB debut 1994 in *Hit the Lights*, followed by *Floyd Collins, Trojan Women: A Love Story*, Bdwy in *Allegro* (Encores 1994), *Candide* (1997), for which he received a 1997 Theatre World Award, *Strike Up the Band* (Encores), *The Fully Monty.*

DANNER, BLYTHE Born February 3, 1944 in Philadelphia, PA. Graduate Bard Col. OB debut 1966 in *The Infantry*, followed by *Collision Course, Summertree, Up Eden, Someone's Comin' Hungry, Cyrano, Miser*, for which she received a 1969 Theatre World Award, *Twelfth Night, New York Idea, Much Ado About Nothing, Love Letters, Sylvia, Moonlight, Ancestral Voices*, Bdwy in *Butterflies are Free, Betrayal, Philadelphia Story, Blithe Spirit, Streetcar Named Desire, Deep Blue Sea, Follies* 2001.

DANSON, RANDY Born April 30, 1950 in Plainfield NJ. Graduate Carnegie Mellon U. OB debut 1978 in *Gimme Shelter*, followed by *Big and Little, Winter Dancers, Time Steps, Casualties, Red and Blue, Resurrection of Lady Lester, Jazz Poets at the Grotto, Plenty, Macbeth, Blue Window, Cave Life, Romeo and Juliet, One-Act Festival, Mad Forest, Triumph of Love, The Treatment, Phaedra, Arts & Leisure, The Devils, The Erinyes, First Picture Show, Portia Coughlan, The Winter's Tale, Saved.*

DARLOW, CYNTHIA Born June 13, 1949 in Detroit, MI. Attended NC Sch of Arts, PA St. U. OB debut 1974 in *This Property Is Condemned*, followed by *Portrait of a Madonna, Clytemnestra, Unexpurgated Memoirs of Bernard Morgandigler, Actor's Nightmare, Sister Mary Ignatius Explains.., Fables for Friends, That's It Folks!, Baby with the Bath Water, Dandy Dick, Naked Truth, Cover of Life, Death Defying Acts, Mere Mortals, Once in a Lifetime, Til the Rapture Comes, Sex, Juno and the Paycock*, Bdwy in *Grease* (1976), *Rumors, Prelude to a Kiss* (also OB), *Sex and Longing, Taller Than a Dwarf.*

DATZ, LISA Born April 24, 1973 in Evanston, IL. Graduate U. of MI. Bdwy debut 1997 in *Titanic*, followed by *The Full Monty.*

DAVID, KEITH Born May 8, 1954 in New York, NY. Graduate Juilliard. OB debut 1979 in *Othello*, followed by *The Haggadah, Pirates of Penzance, Macbeth, Coriolanus, Titus Andronicus, The Winter's Tale, Euripides' Medea, Kit Marlowe*, Bdwy in *Jelly's Last Jam* (1992), *Seven Guitars.*

DAVIDSON, JACK Born July 17, 1936 in Worcester, MA. Graduate Boston U. OB debut 1968 OB in *Moon for the Misbegotten*, followed by *Big and Little, Battle of Angels, A Midsummer Night's Dream, Hot L Baltimore, Tribute to Lili Lamont, Ulysses in Traction, Lulu, Hey Rube!, In the Recovery Lounge, Runner Stumbles, Winter Signs, Hamlet, Mary Stuart, Ruby Ruby Sam Sam, The Diviners, Marching to Georgia, Hunting Scenes from Lower Bavaria, Richard II, Great Grandson of Jedediah Kohler, Buck, Time Framed, Love's Labour's Lost, Bing and Walker, After the Dancing in Jericho, Fair Country, Twelfth Night*, Bdwy in *Capt. Brassbound's Conversion* (1972), *Anna Christie, The Price, Shimada, Ah, Wilderness!, Judgment at Nuremberg.*

DEE, RUBY Born October 27, 1923 in Cleveland, OH. Graduate Hunter Col. Bdwy debut 1946 in *Jeb*, followed by *Anna Lucasta, Smile of the World, Long Way Home, Raisin in the Sun, Purlie Victorious, Checkmates* (1988), OB in *World of Sholom Aleichem, Boesman and Lena, Wedding Band, Hamlet, Take It from the Top, Checkmates* (1995), *My One Good Nerve, Saint Lucy's Eyes.*

DE JONG, ALEXANDER Born October 2, 1962 in Holland. Attended Amsterdam Th. Sch. Bdwy debut 1993 in *My Fair Lady*, followed by *42nd Street.*

DELANY, DANA Born March 13, 1956 in New York, NY. Graduate Wesleyan U. Bdwy debut 1980 in *A Life* (also 2000), followed by *Blood Moon, Translations*, OB in *Dinner with Friends.*

DELARIA, LEA Born 1962 in Belleville, IL. OB debut 1997 in *On the Town* (also Bdwy), for which she received a 1998 Theatre World Award, followed by *Mineola Twins*, Bdwy debut 1998 in *Li'l Abner* (Encores), followed by *The Rocky Horror Show.*

DE OCAMPO, RAMÓN Attended Carnegie Mellon U. OB debut in *The Taming of the Shrew*, followed by *Birth Marks, Middle-finger.*

DEROSA, STEPHEN Born June 10, 1968 in New York, NY. Graduate Georgetown U., Yale U. OB debut 1998 in *Love's Fire*, followed by *Mystery of Irma Vep, Do Re Mi, Wonderful Town, The It Girl, Newyorker*, Bdwy in *The Man Who Came to Dinner.*

DE SHIELDS, ANDRE Born January 12, 1946 in Baltimore, MD. Graduate U. WI. Bdwy debut 1973 in *Warp*, followed by *Rachel Lily Rosenbloom, The Wiz, Ain't Misbehavin'* (1978/1988), *Harlem Nocturne, Just So, Stardust, Play On, The Full Monty*, OB in *2008-1/2, Jazzbo Brown, Soldier's Tale, Little Prince, Haarlem Nocturne, Sovereign State of Boogedy Boogedy, Kiss Me When It's Over, Saint Tous, Ascension Day, Casino Paradise, The Wiz, Angel Levine, Ghost Cafe, Good Doctor.*

DEVINE, ERIK Born May 3, 1954 in Galveston, TX. Graduate U. Tulsa, Wayne St. U. Bdwy debut 1983 in *Cats*, followed by *Sid Caesar & Co., Allegro in Concert, Seussical*, OB in *Plain and Fancy, Lucky Stiff.*

DEVRIES, DAVID Born August 28, 1958 in Binghampton, NY. Graduate American U. Bdwy debut 1999 in *Beauty and the Beast.*

DEVRIES, JON Born March 26, 1947 in New York, NY. Graduate Bennington Col., Pasadena Playhouse. OB debut 1977 in *Cherry Orchard*, followed by *Agamemnon, Ballad of Soapy Smith, Titus Andronicus, Dreamer Examines his Pillow, Sight Unseen, Patient A, Scarlet Letter, One Flea Spare, Red Address, Kit Marlowe*, Bdwy in *Inspector General, Devour the Snow, Major Barbara, Execution of Justice.*

DEYLE, JOHN Born in Rochester, NY. Graduate NC Sch. of the Arts. OB debut 1986 in *The Pajama Game*, followed by *Pageant, Pal Joey* (Encores), *Urinetown*, Bdwy debut 1979 in *Annie*, followed by *Footloose, Camelot* (1980).

DIAMOND, CLIFF Born April 21, 1965 in New York, NY. Graduate Colby Col., Col. of William and Mary. OB Debut in *The Soul of an Intruder.*

DIAZ, NATASCIA Born January 4, 1970 in Lugano, Switzerland. Graduate Carnegie Mellon U. OB debut 1993 in *Little Prince*, followed by *I Won't Dance, Bright Lights, Big City, Saturday Night Fever*, Bdwy in *Seussical.*

DICKERMAN, DOUGLAS Born July 30, 1974 in Livingston, NJ. Graduate Ithaca Col. OB debut in *Never Swim Alone.*

DICKSON, JAMES Born January 5, 1949 in Akron, OH. Attended NYATA. OB debut 1971 in *One Flew Over the Cuckoo's Nest*, followed by *Automatic Earth, Don't Blink.*

DILLANE, STEPHEN Born March 27, 1957 in London, England. Bdwy debut 2000 in *The Real Thing.*

DILLY, ERIN Born May 12, 1972 in Royal Oak, MI. Graduate U. MI. OB debut 1999 in *Things You Shouldn't Say Past Midnight*, Bdwy in *Follies* 2001.

DIXON, ED Born September 2, 1948 in OK. Attended U. OK. Bdwy in *The Student Prince*, followed by *No, No, Nanette, Rosalie in Concert, The Three Musketeers, Les Miserables, Cyrano: The Musical, Scarlet Pimpernel, The Iceman Cometh, Gore Vidal's The Best Man*, OB in *By Bernstein, King of the Schnorrers, Rabboni, Hunchback of Notre Dame, Moby Dick, Shylock, Johnny Pye and the Foolkiller, America's Sweetheart, On a Clear Day You Can See Forever* (CC).

DIXON, MACINTYRE Born December 22, 1931 in Everett, MA. Graduate Emerson Col. Bdwy debut 1965 in *Xmas in Las Vegas*, followed by *Cop-Out, Story Theatre, Metamorphosis, Twigs, Over Here, Once in a Lifetime, Alice in Wonderland, 3 Penny Opera, A Funny Thing Happened on the Way to the Forum* (1996), *Tempest, 1776, Getting and Spending*, OB in *Quare Fellow, Plays for Bleecker Street, Stewed Prunes, The Cat's Pajamas, Three Sisters, 3 X 3, Second City, Mad Show, Meow!, Lotta, Rubbers, Conjuring an Event, His Majesty the Devil, Tomfollery, A Christmas Carol, Times and Appetites of Toulouse-Lautrec, Room Service, Sills and Company, Little Murders, Much Ado about Nothing, A Winter's Tale, Arms and the Man, Hamlet, Pericles, Luck Pluck Virtue, A Country Christmas Carol, Taming of the Shrew, Comic Potential.*

DORFMAN, ROBERT Born October 8, 1950 in Brooklyn, NY. Attended CCNY. OB debut 1979 in *Say Goodnight Gracie*, followed by *America Kicks, Winterplay, Normal Heart, Waving Goodbye, Richard II, When She Died, A Dybbuk, The Wax*, Bdwy in *Social Security* (1987).

DUELL, WILLIAM Born August 30, 1923 in Corinth, NY. Attended Wesleyan U., Yale U. OB debut 1962 in *Portrait of the Artist as a Young Man/Barroom Monks*, followed by *A Midsummer Night's Dream, Henry IV, Taming of the Shrew, The Memorandum Threepenny Opera, Loves of Cass Maguire, Romance Language, Hamlet, Henry IV (I & II), On the Bum, Arsenic and Old Lace*, Bdwy in *A Cook for Mr. General, Ballad of the Sad Cafe, Ilya Darling, 1776, Kings, Stages, Inspector General, Marriage of Figaro, Our Town, A Funny Thing Happened on the Way to the Forum* (1996), *The Man Who Came To Dinner.*

DYS, DEANNA Born April 23, 1966 in Dearborn, MI. Bdwy debut 1988 in *Legs Diamond*, followed by *Meet Me in St. Louis, Crazy for You, Candide* (1997), *Annie Get Your Gun.*

EAGAN, DAISY Born November 4, 1979 in Brooklyn, NY. Attended Neighborhood Playhouse. OB debut 1988 in *Tiny Tim's Christmas Carol*, followed by *The Little Prince, James Joyce's The Dead, Where Everything is Everything*, Bdwy debut 1989 in *Les Miserables*, followed by *The Secret Garden.*

EARLE, DOTTIE Born October 6, 1962 in Norwalk, CT. Graduate U. MA. OB debut 1989 in *Up Against It*, followed by *Radio City Christmas Spectacular*, Bdwy in *The Will Rogers Follies* (1993), *Follies* 2001.

EARLY, KATHLEEN Born October 31 in Irving, TX. Graduate U. of OK. OB debut in *The Play about the Baby.*

Douglas Dickerman

Ed Dixon

Kathleen Early

Christine Ebersole

Jennie Eisenhower

Jeremy Ellison-Gladstone

EASTON, RICHARD Born March 22, 1933 in Montreal, Canada. Bdwy debut 1957 in *The Country Wife*, for which he received a 1958 Theatre World Award, followed by *Back to Methuselah*, with APA in *Anatol, Man and Superman, The Seagull, Exit the King, Pantagleize, The Cherry Orchard, Misanthrope, Cock-a-doodle Dandy*, and *Hamlet*, OB in *Salad Days, Murderous Angels, Waste, Hotel Universe, Give Me Your Answer, Do!, The Invention of Love.*

EBERSOLE, CHRISTINE Born February 21, 1953 in Park Forest, IL. Attended AADA. Bdwy debut 1976 in *Angel Street*, followed by *I Love My Wife, On the 20th Century, Oklahoma, Camelot, Harrigan and Hart, Getting Away with Murder, Gore Vidal's The Best Man, 42nd Street*, OB in *Green Pond, Three Sisters, Geniuses, Ziegfeld Follies of 1936, Current Events, A Connecticut Yankee in King Arthur's Court* (CC).

EDELMAN, GREGG Born September 12, 1958 in Chicago, IL. Graduate Northwestern U. Bdwy debut 1982 in *Evita*, followed by *Oliver!, Cats, Cabaret, City of Angels, Falsettos, Anna Karenina, Passion, Fiorello* (Encores), *Out of This World* (Encores), *1776, Les Miserables*, OB in *Weekend, Shop on Main Street, Forbidden Broadway, She Loves Me, Babes in Arms, Make Someone Happy, Greetings, Standing By, Round About, Thief River.*

EGAN, JOHN TREACY Born July 10, 1962 in New York, NY. Graduate SUNY Purchase, Attended Westchester Comm Col. OB debut 1990 in *Whatnot, followed by When Pigs Fly, Bat Boy*, Bdwy in *Jekyll & Hyde* (1997).

EHLE, JENNIFER Born December 29, 1969 in NC. Bdwy debut 2000 in *The Real Thing.*

EISENBERG, NED Born January 13, 1957 in New York, NY. Attended Acl. Inst. of Arts. OB debut 1980 in *Time of the Cuckoo*, followed by *Our Lord of Lynchville, Dream of a Blacklisted Actor, Second Avenue, Moving Targets, Claus, Titus Adronicus, Saturday Morning Cartoons, Antigone in NY, Green Bird, Red Address, Bloomer Girl* (CC), Bdwy in *Pal Joey* (Encores, 1995).

EISENHOWER, JENNIE Born August 15, 1978 in San Clemente, CA. Graduate Northwestern U. OB debut 2000 in *Suburb.*

ELDER, DAVID Born July 7, 1966 in Houston, TX. Attended U. Houston. Bdwy debut 1992 in *Guys and Dolls*, followed by *Beauty and the Beast, Once Upon a Mattress, Titanic, Strike Up the Band* (Encores), *42nd Street.*

ELKINS, ELIZABETH Born July 24, 1967 in Ft. Lauderdale, FL. OB debut 1991 in *Blue Window*, followed by *Lion in the Streets, Never the Same Rhyme Twice, Night of Knave, Bobby Supreme, Vegetable Love, The Censor, South of No North.*

ELLISON-GLADSTONE, JEREMY Born October 20, 1976 in Concord, NH. Graduate Oberlin Col. OB debut 1999 in *Out of the Blue*, followed by *The Fantasticks, Game Show.*

EMERY, LISA Born January 29 in Pittsburgh, PA. Graduate Hollins Col. OB debut 1981 in *In Connecticut*, followed by *Talley & Son, Dalton's Back, Grownups!, The Matchmaker, Marvin's Room, Watbanaland, Monogomist, Curtains, Far East, Dinner With Friends, What the Butler Saw*, Bdwy in *Passion* (1983), *Burn This, Rumors, Present Laughter, Jackie.*

EMICK, JARROD Born July 2, 1969 in Ft. Eustas, VA. Attended SD St. U. Bdwy debut 1990 in *Miss Saigon*, followed by *Damn Yankees*, for which he received a 1994 Theatre World Award, *The Rocky Horror Show*, OB in *America's Sweetheart.*

ENDERS, CAMILLA Born September 6, 1967 in Boston, MA. Graduate Oberlin Col., U. London. Debut 1995 OB in *Sylvia*, followed by *Ivanov, Mississippi Nude, Wyoming.*

ENGEL, DAVID Born September 19, 1959 in Orange County, CA. Attended U. CA Irvine. Bdwy debut 1983 in *La Cage aux Folles*, followed by *Putting It Together, Seussical*, OB in *Forever Plaid.*

ENGLISH, ROBERT Born October 18, 1965 in Queens, NY. Graduate Northwestern U. OB debut 1995 in *Doll's House*, followed by *The Idiot, Brothers Karamazov, Antigone, Winter's Tale, The Right Way to Sue.*

EPPERSON, JOHN Born 1956 in Hazelburst, MS. OB debut 1988 in *I Could Go on Lypsynching*, followed by *The Fabulous Lypsinka Show. Lypsinka! A Day in the Life!, As I Lay Lip-Synching, Messages for Gary, Lypsinka! The Boxed Set.*

ESPARZA, RAUL Born October 24, 1970 in Wilmington, DE. Graduate NYU. Bdwy debut 2000 in *The Rocky Horror Show.*

ESTERMAN, LAURA Born April 12 in New York, NY. Attended Radcliffe Col., LAMDA. OB debut 1969 in *Time of Your Life*, followed by *Pig Pen, Carpenters, Ghosts, Macbeth, Sea Gull, Rubbers, Yankees 3 Detroit 0, Golden Boy, Out of Our Father's House, The Master and Margarita, Chinchilla, Dusa, Fish Stas and Vi, Midsummer Night's Dream, Recruiting Officer, Oedipus the King, Two Fish in the Sky, Mary Barnes, Tamara, Marvin's Room, Edith Stein, Curtains, Yiddish Trojan Women, Good as New, American Clock, Cranes, The Wax*, Bdwy in *Waltz of the Toreadors, The Show-off.*

EWIN, PAULA Born December 6, 1955 in Warwick, RI. Attended King's Col. Wilkes-Barre, PA, Graduate RI Col. OB debut 1991 in *Necktie Breakfast*, followed by *As You Like It, Lion in the Streets, Baptists, Night of Nave, Never the Same Rhyme Twice, Pig, Bobby Supreme, Vegetable Love, The Censor, South of No North.*

Camilla Enders

Raul Esparza

Katie Finneran

Thomas Michael Fiss

Eugene Fleming

Mary Fogarty

EWING, LINDA Born March 29, 1961 in Houston, TX. Graduate USC. OB debut 1996 in *Code of the West* (also 2000), followed by *Night They Burned Washington.*

FERGUSON, JESSE TYLER Born October 22, 1975 in Missoulia, MT. Graduate Amer. Musical & Dramatic Arts. OB debut 1997 in *On the Town*, followed by *The Most Fabulous Story Ever Told, Kean, This Love, Hair* (CC), *Newyorkers*, Bdwy in *On The Town.*

FIGUEROA, RONA Born March 30, 1972 in San Francisco, CA. Attended UC Santa Cruz. Bdwy debut 1993 in *Miss Saigon*, OB in *Caucasain Chalk Circle, Dogeaters.*

FINNERAN, KATIE Born January 22, 1971 in Chicago, IL. Attended Carnegie Mellon. Bdwy in *Cabaret.*

FISS, THOMAS MICHAEL Born December 7, 1986 in San Diego, CA. Bdwy debut 2000 in *The Full Monty.*

FITZPATRICK, ALLEN Born January 31, 1955 in Boston, MA. Graduate U. VA. OB debut 1977 in *Come Back Little Sheba*, followed by *Wonderful Town, Rothschilds, Group One Acts, Peephole, Jack's Holiday, Mata Hari, Carmelina, Annie Warbucks*, Bdwy debut 1991 in *Les Miserables*, followed by *Gentlemen Prefer Blondes* (1995), *Damn Yankees, Boys from Syracuse* (Encores), *Scarlet Pimpernel, 42nd Street.*

FLANAGAN, PAULINE Born June 29, 1925 in Sligo, Ireland. OB debut 1958 in *Ulysses in Nighttown*, followed by *Pictures in the Hallway, Later, Antigone, The Crucible, Plough and the Stars, Summer, Close of Play, In Celebration, Without Apologies, Yeats, A Celebration, Philadelphia Here I Come!, Grandchild of Kings, Shadow of a Gunman, Juno and the Paycock, Plough and the Stars, Portia Coughlan, A Life*, Bdwy in *God and Kate Murphy, The Living Room, The Innocents, The Father, Medea, Steaming, Corpse, Philadelphia Here I Come* (1994), *Prophets and Heroes.*

FLEMING, EUGENE Born April 26, 1961 in Richmond, VA. Attended NC Sch. of Arts. Bdwy debut in *Chorus Line*, followed by *Tap Dance Kid, Black and Blue, High Rollers, DuBarry Was a Lady* (Encores), *Swinging on a Star, Street Corner Symphony, Fosse*, OB in *Voorhas, Dutchman, Ceremonies in Dark Old Men, Freefall.*

FOGARTY, MARY Born in Manchester, NH. OB debut 1959 in *The Well of Saints*, followed by *Shadow and Substance, Nathan the Wise, Bonjour La Bonjour, Fanrih Comedy, Steel Magnolias, Dearly Departed, Filumena, Mack, The Understanding, Hard Feelings*, Bdwy in *National Health* (1974), *Watch on the Rhine* (1980), *Of the Fields Lately.*

FOOTE, HALLIE Born 1955 in New York, NY. OB in *Night Seasons, Roads to Home, Widow Claire, Courtship*, 1918, *On Valentine's Day, Talking Pictures, Laura Dennis, Young Man from Atlanta*, 900 *Oneonta, When They Speak of Rita, Last of the Thorntons.*

FOSTER, HERBERT Born May 14, 1936 in Winnipeg, Canada. Bdwy in *Ways and Means, Touch of the Poet, Imaginary Invalid, Tonight at* 8:30, *Henry V, Noises Off, Me and My Girl, Lettice and Lovage, Timon of Athens, Government Inspector, Sacrilege, Getting Away with Murder, Herbal Bed*, OB in *Afternoon Tea, Papers, Mary Stuart, Playboy of the Western World, Good Woman of Setzuan, Scenes from American Life, Twelfth Night, All's Well That Ends Well, Richard II, Gifts of the Magi, Heliotrope Bouquet, Troilus and Cressida, Sympathetic Magic, Henry VIII, Timon of Athens, Skin of Our Teeth, Cymbeline, Measure for Measure.*

FOWLER, BETH Born November 1, 1940 in NJ. Graduate Caldwell Col. Bdwy debut 1970 in *Gantry*, followed by *A Little Night Music, Over Here*, 1600 *Pennsylvania Avenue, Peter Pan, Baby, Teddy and Alice, Sweeney Todd* (1989), *Beauty and the Beast, Bells Are Ringing*, OB in *Preppies, The Blessing, Sweeney Todd.*

FOXWORTH, ROBERT Born November 1, 1941 in Houston, TX. Graduate Carnegie Tech. Bdwy debut 1969 in *Henry V*, followed by *The Crucible*, for which he received a 1972 Theatre World Award, *Candida, Ivanov, Honour, Judgment at Nuremberg*, OB in *Terra Plova.*

FRABONI, ANGELO Born September 21, 1963 in Hibbing, MN. Bdwy in *The Full Monty.*

FRANKLIN, NANCY Born in New York, NY. Debut 1959 OB in *Buffalo Skinner*, followed by *Power of Darkness, Oh Dad, Poor Dad, Mama's Hung You in the Closet and I'm Feeling So Sad, Theatre of Peretz, 7 Days of Mourning, Here Be Dragons, Beach Children, Safe Place, Innocent Pleasures, Loves of Cass McGuire, After the Fall, Bloodletters, Briar Patch, Lost Drums, Ivanov, Cat's Paw*, Bdwy in *Never Live Over a Pretzel Factory* (1964), *Happily Never After, The White House, Charlie and Algernon.*

FRANZ, JOY Born 1944 in Modesto, CA. Graduate U. MO. OB debut 1969 in *Of Thee I Sing*, followed by *Jacques Brel Is Alive is Alive and Well and Living in Paris, Out of This World Curtains, I Can't Sleep Running in Place, Tomfoolery, Penelope, Bittersuite, Assassins, New Yorkers, Bitter Tears of Petra Von Kant*, Bdwy in *Sweet Charity, Lysistrata, A Little Night Music, Pippin, Musical Chairs, Into the Woods.*

FRECHETTE, PETER Born October 3, 1956 in Warwick, RI. OB debut 1979 in *Hornbeam Maze*, followed by *Journey's End, In Cahoots, Harry Ruby's Songs My Mother Never Sang, Pontifications on Pigtails and Puberty, Scooter Thomas Makes It to the Top of the World, We're Home, Flora the Red Menace, Hyde in Hollywood, Absent Friends, And Baby Makes Seven, Destiny of Me, La Ronde, Raised in Captivity, Night and Her Stars, Hurrah at Last, What the Butler Saw*, Bdwy debut 1989 in *Eastern Standard* (also OB), for which he won a 1989 Theatre World Award, followed by *Our Country's Good, Any Given Day.*

Angelo Fraboni

Arthur French

Jan Gelberman

Joanna Glushak

Rita Glynn

Deidre Goodwin

FREED, SAM Born August 29, 1948 in York, PA. Graduate PA St. U. OB debut 1972 in *The Proposition*, followed by *What's a Nice Country Like You Doing in a State Like This?, Dance on a Country Grave, Morocco, BAFO, The Folsom Head*, Bdwy in *Candide* (1974), *Torch Song Trilogy, Brown.*

FREEMAN, JONATHAN Born February 5, 1950 in Bay Village, OH. Graduate Ohio U. OB debut 1974 in *The Miser*, followed by *Bil Baird Marionette Theatre, Babes in Arms, Confessions of Conrad Gerhardt, Bertrano, Clap Trap, In a Pig's Valise, A Class Act*, Bdwy in *Sherlock Holmes* (1974), *Platinum, 13 Days to Broadway, She Loves Me, How to Succeed in Business Without Really Trying, On the Town, Li'l Abner* (Encores), *An Empty Plate in the Café du Grand Boeuf, 42nd Street.*

FRENCH, ARTHUR Born in New York, NY. Attended Brooklyn Col. OB debut 1962 in *Raisin' Hell in the Sun*, followed by *Ballad of Bimshire, Day of Absence, Happy Ending, Brotherhood, Perry's Mission, Rosalee Pritchett, Moonlight Arms, Dark Tower, Brownsville Raid, Nevis Mountain Dew, Julius Caesar, Friends, Court of Miracles, The Beautiful LaSalles, Blues for a Gospel Queen, Black Girl, Driving Miss Daisy, The Spring Thing, George Washington Slept Here, Ascension Day, Boxing Day Parade, A Tempest, Hills of Massabielle, Treatment, As You Like It, Swamp Dwellers, Tower of Burden, Henry VI, Black Girl, Last Street Play, Out of the South, Fly, Living in the Wind*, Bdwy in *Ain't Supposed to Die a Natural Death, The Iceman Cometh, All God's Chillun Got Wings, Resurrection of Lady Lester, You Can't Take It with You, Design for Living, Ma Rainey's Black Bottom, Mule Bone, Playboy of the West Indies.*

FRUGE, ROMAIN Born March 4, 1959 in Los Angeles, CA. Graduate Allentown Col. Bdwy debut 1986 in *Big River*, followed by *Tommy, The Full Monty*, OB in *Shabbatai* (1995), *Last Sweet Days, Sam Shepard One-Acts.*

FULLER, PENNY Born 1940 in Durham, NC. Attended Northwestern U. Bdwy in *Barefoot in the Park* (1965) followed by *Cabaret, Richard II, As You Like It, Henry IV, Applause, Rex, American Daughter, The Dinner Party*, OB in *Cherry Orchard, Three Viewings, New England, A New Brain, Ancestral Voices.*

GARNER, PATRICK Born March 16, 1958 in Dearborn, MI. Graduate U. of MI, SMU. OB debut 1984 in *Found a Peanut*, followed by *Marriage of Bette & Boo, Ubu, Tartuffe, Once Around the City*, Bdwy 1986 in *Front Page* (LC), *Laughter on the 23rd Floor, A Funny Thing Happened on the Way to the Forum.*

GARRICK, BARBARA Born February 3, 1962 in New York, NY. OB debut 1986 in *Today I Am a Fountain Pen*, followed by *Midsummer Night's Dream, Rosencrantz and Guildenstern Are Dead*, Bdwy in *Eastern Standard* (1988, also OB), *Small Family Business, Stanley, A Thousand Clowns.*

GARRISON, DAVID Born June 30, 1952 in Long Branch, NJ. Graduate Boston U. OB debut 1976 in *Joseph and the Amazing Technicolor Dreamcoat*, followed by *Living at Home, Geniuses, It's Only a Play, Make Someone Happy, Family of Mann, I Do I Do* (1996), *The Torchbearers*, Bdwy in *History of the American Film* (1978), *Day in Hollywood/A Night in the Ukraine, Pirates of Penzance, Snoopy, Torch Song Trilogy, One Touch of Venus* (Encores), *Titanic, Strike Up the Band* (Encores), *Bells Are Ringing.*

GELBERMAN, JAN Born February 22, 1950 in Bronx, NY.

GELLER, MARC Born July 5, 1959 in RI. OB debut 1981 in *Butterflies are Free*, followed by *As Is, Marat/Sade, Equus, Cloud 9, Orphans, Bomber Jackets, Faustus, Box Office Poison, Unidentified Human Remains, Exit the King, Adjoining Trances, The Ballad of The Sad Café, Cloud 9, Naked Will, Dysteria.*

GIBSON, JULIA Born June 8, 1962 in Norman, OK. Graduate U. IA, NYU. OB debut 1987 in *Midsummer Night's Dream*, followed by *Love's Labor's Lost, Crucible, Man Who Fell in Love with His Wife, Learned Ladies, Machinal, Candide., Dracula, Arabian Nights, View of the Dome, Henry VIII, Da, Measure for Measure.*

GIBSON, MEG Born August 24 in Bridgeton, NJ. Graduate U. UT, Juilliard. OB debut 1983 in *Fen*, followed by *King Lear, Messiah, From Above, The Ride Down Mt. Morgan, Knepp.*

GILES, NANCY Born July 17, 1960 in Queens, NY. Graduate Oberlin Col. OB debut 1985 in *Mayor*, for which she received a 1985 Theatre World Award, followed by *Mother, Circus of Death, Pinky, Oh You Hostage, Snicker Factor, Tiny Mommy Sparks in the Park, Czar of Rock and Roll, Johnny Business, Urban Blight, Police Boys, Going To The River, The New Jack Paar Show.*

GILLETTE, ANITA Born August 16, 1938 in Baltimore, MD. OB debut 1960 in *Russell Paterson's Sketchbook*, for which she received a 1960 Theatre World Award, followed by *Rich and Famous, Dead Wrong, Road Show, Class 1-Acts, The Blessing, Moving Targets, Juno, Able-Bodied Seaman, Decline of the Middle West*, Bdwy in *Carnival, Gypsy, Gay Life, All American, Mr. President, Kelly, Don't Drink the Water, Cabaret, Jimmy, They're Playing Our Song, Brighton Beach Memoirs, Chapter Two, Bloomer Girl* (CC).

GLUSHAK, JOANNA Born May 27, 1958 in New York, NY. Attended NYU. OB debut 1983 in *Lenny and the Heartbreakers*, followed by *Lies and Legends, Miami, Unfinished Song, A Little Night Music* (NYCO), *Just as If, Big Potato*, Bdwy in *Sunday in the Park with George* (1984), *Rags, Les Miserables.*

GLYNN, RITA Born December 27, 1991 in Durham, NC. Bdwy debut 2000 in *Jane Eyre.*

Rahti Gorfien

Kathryn Graybill

Justin Greer

Sylver Gregory

Diane Grotke

Anthony Blair Hall

GOETHALS, ANGELA Born May 20, 1977 in New York, NY. Bdwy debut 1987 in *Coastal Disturbances*, followed by *Four Baboons Adoring the Sun, Picnic*, OB in *Positive Me, Approaching Zanzibar, The Good Times are Killing Me, True History and Real Adventure, Blur.*

GOETZ, PETER MICHAEL Born December 10, 1941 in Buffalo, NY. Graduate SUNY Fredonia, So. IL U. OB debut 1980 in *Jail Diary of Albie Sacks*, followed by *Before the Dawn, Comic Potential*, Bdwy in *Ned and Jack* (1981), *Beyond Therapy, Queen and the Rebels, Brighton Beach Memoirs, Government Inspector, Sex and Longing, Last Night of Ballyhoo, Macbeth.*

GOLDEN, ANNIE Born October 19, 1951 in Brooklyn, NY. Bdwy debut 1977 in *Hair*, followed by *Leader of the Pack, The Full Monty*, OB in *Dementos, Dr. Selavy's Magic Theatre, A...My Name is Alice, Little Shop of Horrors, Class of '86, Assassins, Hit the Lights!, Sugar Bean Sisters, On the Town, Broadway '68, Saturn Returns, La Terrasse, On The Town, An Empty Plate in the Café du Grand Boeuf.*

GOLDSMITH, MERWIN Born August 7, 1937 in Detroit, MI. Graduate UCLA, Old Vic. Bdwy debut 1970 in *Minnie's Boys*, followed by *The Visit, Chemin de Fer, Rex, Leda Had a Little Swan, Trelawney of the Wells, Dirty Linen, 1940's Radio Hour, Slab Boys, Me and My Girl, Ain't Broadway Grand, Bloomer Girl* (CC), OB in *Naked Hamlet, Chickencoop Chinaman, Real Life Funnies, Wanted, Rubbers and Yanks, Chinchilla, Yours Anne, Big Apple Messengers, La Boheme, Learned Ladies, An Imaginary Life, Little Prince, Beau Jest, After-Play, Louisianna Purchase, Beauty Part.*

GOODWIN, DEIDRE Born September 15, 1969 in Oklahoma City, OK. Attended Southwest MI St. U. Bdwy debut 1998 in *Chicago*, followed by *Jesus Christ Superstar, The Rocky Horror Show.*

GORFIEN, RAHTI Born April 2, 1958 in New Haven, CT. Graduate NYU. OB in *Bearded Iris.*

GRAFF, RANDY Born May 23, 1955 in Brooklyn, NY. Graduate Wagner Col. OB debut 1978 in *Pins and Needles*, followed by *Station Joy, A...My Name Is Alice, Once on a Summer's Day, Do Re Mi*, Bdwy in *Sarava, Grease, Les Miserables, City of Angels, Falsettos, Laughter on the 23rd Floor, Moon Over Buffalo, High Society, A Class Act.*

GRAHAM, ENID Born February 8 in TX. Graduate Juilliard. Bdwy debut 1998 in *Honour*, OB in *Look Back in Anger, Crimes of the Heart.*

GRANT, KATE JENNINGS Born March 23, 1970 in Elizabeth, NJ. Graduate U. of PA, Juilliard. Bdwy debut 1997 in *American Daughter*, followed by *Hard Feelings*, OB in *Wonderland, Hard Feelings.*

GRAY, CHARLES Born July 15, 1960 in Annapolis, MD. Attended Towson St. U. Bdwy debut 1995 in *Grease*, OB in *Long Road Home.*

GRAYBILL, KATHRYN Graduate SMU. OB in *King Lear.*

GREENHILL, SUSAN Born March 19 in New York, NY. Graduate U. PA., Catholic U. Bdwy debut 1982 in *Crimes of the Heart*, OB in *Hooters, Our Lord of Lynchville, September in the Rain, Seascape with Shark and Dancer, Murder of Crows, Better Days, Marathon '89, Tounges of Stone, Festival of One Acts, Watbanaland, The Increased Difficulty of Conversation, Brown.*

GREENSPAN, DAVID Born 1956 In Los Angeles, CA. OB in *Phaedra, Education of Skinny Spyz, Boys in the Band, Moose Mating, Second Hand Smoke, Sueño, Alien Boy, Small Craft Warnings, Saved or Destroyed, Lipstick Traces, The Wax.*

GREER, JUSTIN Born January 25, 1973 in Buffalo, NY. Graduate Carnegie Mellon U. Bdwy debut 1999 in *Babes in Arms* (CC/Encores), followed by *Annie Get Your Gun, Seussical.*

GREGORY, SYLVER Born October 14, 1980 in Fort-de-France, Martinique. OB debut 2000 in *Welcome to Our City.*

GRIZZARD, GEORGE Born April 1, 1928 in Roanoke, Rapids, VA. Graduate U. NC. Bdwy debut 1954 in *All Summer Long*, followed by *Desperate Hours, Happiest Millionaire*, for which he received a 1957 Theatre World Award, *The Disenchanted, Big Fish Little Fish, APA* 1961-62, *Who's Afraid of Virginia Woolf, Glass Menagerie, You Know I Can't Hear You When the Water's Running, Noel Coward's Sweet Potato, Gingham Dog, The Inquest, Country Girl, Creation of the World and Other Business, Crown Matrimonial, Royal Family, California Suite, Man and Superman, Delicate Balance* (1996), *Judgment at Nuremberg*, OB in *Beach House, Another Antigone, Ancestral Voices.*

GROTKE, DIANE Born November 15, 1953 in No. Tonawanda, NY. Attended U. FL, U. So. FL. OB debut 1987 in *Bird/Bear*, followed by *Reel to Real, Boar's Carcass, Pieces of the Sky, Horsey People.*

GUNCLER, SAM Born October 17, 1955 in Bethlehem, PA. Graduate Lehigh U. OB debut 1983 in *Her Honor the Mayor*, followed by *The Racket, Sail Away, Winning, Clash By Night, It's My Party*, Bdwy in *The Gathering.*

GURWIN, DANNY Born November 14, 1972 in Detroit, MI. Graduate U. MI. OB debut 1998 in *R & J*, followed by *Kuni-Leml, The Scarlet Pimpernel, Forbidden Broadway.*

GUTTMAN, RONALD Born August 12, 1952 in Brussels, Belgium. Graduate Brussels U. OB debut 1986 in *Coastal Disturbances*, followed by *Modigliano, Free Zone, Escurial, Liliom, Philanthropist, Funky Crazy Bugaloo Boy, No Exit, Sabina, Price of Madness, Uncle Jack, Bravo Ubu*, Bdwy in *Coastal Disturbances* (1987).

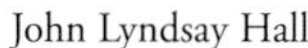
John Lyndsay Hall

Carol Halstead

Delphi Harrington

Rich Hebert

George Heslin

Conleth Hill

HADGE, MICHAEL Born June 6, 1932 in Greensboro, NC. Bdwy debut 1958 in *Cold Wind and the Warm*, followed by *Lady of the Camelias, Impossible Years*, OB in *Local Stigmata, Hunter, Night Seasons, Laura Dennis, Last of the Thorntons.*

HADLEY, JONATHAN Born May 6, 1964 in Charlotte, NC. Graduate NC Sch. of Arts. OB debut 1993 in *Theda Bara and the Frontier Rabbi*, followed by *Cincinnati Saint, Prime Time Prophet, Mayor Musicals, Sheba, Kuni-Leml, Reunion, A Class Act.*

HALL, ANTHONY BLAIR Born May 5, 1987 in Washington, D.C. Bdwy debut 1997 in *A Christmas Carol*, followed by *A Christmas Carol* (1998), *Ragtime, Seussical.*

HALL, JOHN LYNDSAY Born in Baltimore, MD. Attended Morgan St. U. OB debut 2000 in *Welcome to Our City.*

HALSTEAD, CAROL Born September 12 in Hempstead, NY. Graduate FL St. U., ACT. OB debut 1992 in *The Mask*, followed by *Bats, Margo's Party, Cucumbers*, Bdwy in *Gore Vidal's The Best Man.*

HALSTON, JULIE Born December 7, 1954 in NY. Graduate Hofstra U. OB debut 1985 in *Times Square Angel*, followed by *Vampire Lesbians of Sodom, Sleeping Beauty or Coma, The Dubliners, Lady in Question, Money Talks, Red Scare on Sunset, I'll Be the Judge of That, Lifetime of Comedy, Honeymoon Is Over, You Should Be So Lucky, This Is Not Going to Be Pretty, Saved or Destroyed*, Bdwy in *Boys from Syracuse* (Encores), *The Man Who Came to Dinner.*

HAMMEL, LORI Born in Minneapolis, MN. OB debut 1998 in *Forbidden Broadway Strikes Back*, followed by *Forbidden Broadway Cleans Up Its Act, I Love You, You're Perfect, Now Change.*

HAMMER, BEN Born December 8, 1925 in Brooklyn, NY. Graduate Brooklyn Col. Bdwy debut 1955 in *Creat Sebastians*, followed by *Diary of Anne Frank, Tenth Man, Mother Courage, The Deputy, Royal Hunt of the Sun, Colda, Broadway Bound, Three Sisters, The Gathering*, OB in *The Crucible, Murderous Angels, Richard III, Slavs!, The Gathering.*

HARADA, ANN Born February 3, 1964 in Honolulu, HI. Attended Brown U. OB debut 1987 in 1-2-3-4-5, followed by *Hit the Lights!, America Dreaming, Dog and His Master, Falsettoland, The Moment When, A Tribute to Julie and Carol*, Bdwy in *M. Butterfly* (1988), *Seussical.*

HARNER, JASON BUTLER Born October 9 in Elmira, NY. Graduate VCU, NYU. OB debut in *Henry VIII*, followed by *Macbeth, An Experiment with an Air Pump, Juno and the Paycock, Crimes of the Heart.*

HARPER, VALERIE Born August 22, 1940 in Suffern, NY. Bdwy debut in *Li'l Abner*, followed by *Destry Rides Again, Take Me Along, Wildcat, Subways are for Sleeping, Something Different, Story Theatre, Metamorphosis, Tale of the Allergist's Wife*, OB in *Death Defying Acts, All Under Heaven.*

HARRINGTON, DELPHI Born August 26 in Chicago, IL. Graduate Northwestern U. OB debut 1960 in *Country Scandal*, followed by *Moon for the Misbegotten, Baker's Dozen, The Zykovs, Character Lines, Richie, American Garage, After the Fall, Rosencrantz and Guildenstern Are Dead, Good Grief, Hay Fever, Madwoman of Chaillot, Too Clever by Half, Beauty Part, Heartbreak House, Pirate's Lullaby, Blithe Spirit, The Admirable Crichton*, Bdwy in *Thieves* (1974), *Everything in the Garden, Romeo and Juliet, Chapter Two, Sea Gull.*

HARRIS, JARED Born 1962 in London. Attended Duke U. OB in *Henry IV, Tis a Pity She's a Whore, King Lear, Ecstacy, More Lies about Jerzy,*

HARRISON, GREGORY Born May 31, 1950 on Catalina Island, CA. Graduate Actors Studio. Bdwy debut 1997 in *Steel Pier, Follies* 2001.

HARTUNG, BILLY Born June 21, 1971 in Pittsburgh, PA. Graduate Point Park Col. Bdwy debut 1997 in *Side Show* , followed by *Footloose, Minnelli on Minnelli, Hair* (CC), OB debut 1995 in *The Rink.*

HARVEY, ELLEN Born October 2 in Pomona, CA. Graduate Boston U. Bdwy debut 2000 in *Music Man.*

HAYDEN, MICHAEL Born July 28, 1963 in St. Paul, MN. Graduate Juilliard. OB debut 1991 in *The Matchmaker*, followed by *Hello Again, Off-Key, Nebraska, All My Sons, Far East*, Bdwy debut 1994 in *Carousel*, for which he received a 1994 Theatre World Award, followed by *Judgment at Nuremberg.*

HEARD, CORDIS Born July 27, 1944 in Washington, D.C. Graduate Chatham Col. Bdwy debut 1973 in *Warp*, followed by *Elephant Man, Macbeth*, OB in *Vanities, City Junket, Details without a Map, Inside Out, Jasper in Grammercy Park, Oh, My Dear Andersen.*

HEBERT, RICH Born December 14, 1956 in Quincy, MA. Graduate Boston U. OB debut 1978 in *Rimers of Eldritch*, followed by 110 *in the Shade, Dazy, Easy Money, Ballad of Sam Grey*, Bdwy in *Rock 'n' Roll: First 5000 Years* (1982), *Cats, Les Miserables, Sunset Blvd, The Life, Saturday Night Fever.*

HECHT, PAUL Born August 16, 1941 in London, England. Attended McGill U. OB in *Sjt. Musgrave's Dance, Macbird, Phaedra, Enrico IV, Coriolanus, Cherry Orchard, Androcles and the Lion, Too Clever by Half, London Suite, Moonlight, Big Potato*, Bdwy in *Rosencrantz and Guildenstern Are Dead, 1776, Rothschilds, Ride Across Lake Constance, Great God Brown, Don Juan, Emperor Henry IV, Herzl, Caesar and Cleopatra, Night and Day, Noises Off, The Invention of Love, Euripides' Medea.*

Mark Hofmaier

Mylinda Hull

Kelly Hutchinson

Bill Irwin

Jamie Jones

Jen Jones

HEREDIA, WILSON JERMAINE Born 1972 in Brooklyn, NY. OB in *New Americans, Popal Vu, The Tower, Eli's Comin',* Bdwy in *Rent* (1996—also OB).

HERRERA, JOHN Born September 21, 1955 in Havana, Cuba. Graduate Loyola U. Bdwy debut 1979 in *Grease,* followed by *Evita, Camelot, The Mystery of Edwin Drood, Shogun, Tom Sawyer,* OB in *La Boheme, Lies and Legends, Do Re Mi.*

HESLIN, GEORGE Born 1972. OB debut 2000 in *Juno and the Paycock.*

HIBBARD, DAVID Born June 21, 1965. Graduate Ohio St. U. OB debut 1989 in *Leave It to Jane,* followed by *Chess, Forbidden Bdwy Strikes Back, A Class Act,* Bdwy in *Cats* (1993), *Once Upon a Mattress* (1996).

HIDALGO, ALLEN Born December 15, 1967 in New York, NY. Attended Bard Col., NYU. OB debut 1992 in *Eating Raoul,* followed by *4 Guys Named Jose,* Bdwy in *Candide* (1997).

HILL, CONLETH Born November 24, 1964 in Ballycastle, Ireland. Attended St. MacNissis Col. Bdwy debut 2001 in *Stones in His Pockets.*

HINES, JOHN Born March 15, 1961 in Chicago, IL. Graduate U. IL, Yale U. OB debut 1998 in *Black Snow,* followed by *Arsenic and Old Lace* (CC).

HINGSTON, SEÁN MARTIN Born December 16, 1965 in Melbourne, Australia. Bdwy debut 1994 in *Crazy for You,* followed by *Boys from Syracuse* (Encores), *Promises Promises* (Encores), *A Connecticut Yankee in King Arthur's Court* (CC), OB in *Contact.*

HOCK, ROBERT Born May 20, 1931 in Phoenixville, PA. Graduate Yale U. OB debut 1982 in *Caucasian Chalk Circle,* followed by *Adding Machine, Romeo and Juliet, Edward II, Creditors, Two Orphans, Macbeth, Kitty Hawk, Heathen Valley, Comedy of Errors, Phaedra, Good Natur'd Man, Oedipus the King, Game of Love and Chance, Twelfth Night, Mrs. Warren's Profession, Oedipus at Colonus, King Lear, Beaux Stratagem, Life Is a Dream, Doll's House, Antigone, The Chairs, Venice Preserv'd, Misalliance, The Seagull, The Miser, The Country Wife, The Way of the World, The Oresteia, The Cherry Orchard,* Bdwy in *Some Americans Abroad* (1990).

HODGES, PATRICIA Born in Puyallup, WA. Graduate U. WA. OB debut 1985 in *The Normal Heart,* followed by *No End of Blame, On the Verge, Hard Times, One-Act Festival,* Bdwy in *Six Degrees of Separation* (1991), *Dancing at Lughnasa, Lion in Winter, Gore Vidal's The Best Man.*

HOFFMAN, PHILIP SEYMOUR Born July 23, 1967 in Fairport, NY. Attended NYU. OB in *Food and Shelter, The Skriker, Defying Gravity, Shopping and Fucking, All in the Timing, The Treatment, The Author's Voice, In Arabia We'd All Be Kings, The Seagull* (CC), *The Treatment, All in the Timing,* Bdwy in *True West.*

HOFHEIMER, CHARLIE Born April 17, 1981 in Detroit, MI. Bdwy debut 1995 in *On the Waterfront,* OB in *Minor Demons, Old Money.*

HOFMAIER, MARK Born July 4, 1950 in Philadelphia, PA. Graduate U. AZ. OB debut 1978 in *Midsummer Night's Dream,* followed by *Marvelous Gray, Modern Romance, Relative Values, The Racket, Come as You Are, Global Village.*

HOLLIS, TOMMY Born March 27, 1954 in Jacksonville, TX. Attended Lon Morris Col., U. Houston. OB debut 1985 in *Diamonds,* followed by *Secrets of the Lava Lamp, Paradise, Africanus Instructus, Colored Museum, Yip & Gershwin,* Bdwy debut 1990 in *Piano Lesson,* for which he received a 1990 Theatre World Award, followed by *Seven Guitars, Tom Sawyer.*

HOLM, CELESTE Born April 29, 1919 in New York, NY. Attended UCLA, U. Chicago. Bdwy debut 1938 in *Gorianna,* followed by *Time of Your Life, Another Sun, Return of the Vagabond, 8 O'Clock Tuesday, My Fair Ladies, Papa Is All, All the Comforts of Home, Damask Cheek, Oklahoma!, Bloomer Girl, She Stoops to Conquer, Affairs of State, Anna Christie, King and I, His and Hers, Interlock, Third Best Sport, Invitation to a March, Mame, Candida, Habeas Corpus, Utter Glory of Morrissey Hall, I Hate Hamlet, Allegro in Concert,* OB in *Month in the Country, Paris Was Yesterday, With Love and Laughter, Christmas Carol, The Brooch, Don Juan in Hell, Arsenic and Old Lace* (CC).

HOLMES, DENIS Born June 7, 1921 in Coventry, England. Graduate LAMDA. Bdwy debut 1955 in *Troilus and Cressida,* followed by *Homecoming, Merchant of Venice, Moliere Comedies, Hamlet, Ideal Husband, Major Barbara,* OB in *Dandy Dick* (1987).

HOPKINS, KAITLIN/KATE Born February 1, 1964 in New York, NY. Attended Carnegie Mellon U., RADA. OB debut 1984 in *Come Back Little Sheba,* followed by *Take Two, My Favorite Year, Johnny Pye and the Foolkiller, Bat Boy.*

HUFF, NEAL Born in New York, NY. Graduate NYU. OB debut 1992 in *Young Playwrights Festival,* followed by *Joined at the Head, Day the Bronx Died, Macbeth, House of Yes, Class 1-Acts, Saturday Mourning Cartoons, Troilus and Cressida, Tempest, From Above, The Seagull: 1990 The Hamptons, Other People.*

HUFFMAN, CADY Born February 2, 1965 in Santa Barbara, CA. OB debut 1983 in *They're Playing Our Song,* followed by *Festival of 1 Acts, Oh Hell!, Love Soup,* Bdwy 1985 in *La Cage aux Folles,* followed by *Big Deal, Will Rogers Follies, The Producers.*

HUGHES, JURIAN Born November 6 in Albany, NY. Graduate Williams Col., NYU. Bdwy debut 1996 in *Night of the Iguana,* followed by *Judgment at Nuremberg,* OB debut 1996 in *Grace and Glorie,* followed by *Never the Sinner, The Primary English Class.*

Catrice Joseph

Deep Katdare

Sylva Kelegian

Dennis Kelly

Michelle Kittrell

Ezra Knight

HUGHES, LAURA Born January 28, 1959 in New York, NY. Graduate Neighborhood Playhouse. OB debut 1980 in *The Diviners*, followed by *A Tale Told, Time Framed, Fables for Friends, Talley and Son, Kate's Diary, Playboy of the Western World, Missing/Kissing, The Trail of Her Inner Thighs.*

HULL, MYLINDA Born March 3 in San Diego, CA. Bdwy debut 2001 in *42nd Street*, OB in *I Love You, You're Perfect, Now Change.*

HURT, MARY BETH Born September 26, 1948 in Marshalltown, IA. Attended U. Iowa, NYU. OB debut 1972 in *More Than You Deserve*, followed by *As You Like It, Trelaway of the Wells, The Cherry Orchard, Love for Love, Member of the Wedding, Boy Meets Girl, Secret Service, Father's Day, Nest of the Wood Grouse, The Day Room, Secret Rapture, Othello, One Shoe Off, Arts and Leisure, Oblivion Postponed, Old Money*, Bdwy in *Crimes of the Heart* (1981), *The Misanthrope, Benefactors.*

HUTCHINSON, KELLY Born March 17, 1976 in New Brunswick, NJ. Graduate Boston U. Bdwy debut 2000 in *Macbeth*, followed by *Major Barbara.*

IRISH, MARK Born December 18, 1963 in Hartland, ME. Graduate Dartmouth Col. OB debut 1988 in *On Tina Tuna Walk*, followed by *Good Honest Food, The Littlest Clown, Lily Wong, Trophies, The Heidi Chronicles, Jig Saw.*

IRWIN, BILL Born April 11, 1950 in Santa Monica, CA. Attended UCLA, Clown Col. OB debut 1982 in *Regard of Flight*, followed by *The Courtroom, Waiting for Godot, Scapin*, Bdwy in *5-6-7-8 Dance* (1983), *Accidental Death of an Anarchist, Regard of Flight, Largely New York, Fool Moon, Tempest.*

IVEY, DANA Born August 12 in Atlanta, GA. Graduate Rollins Col., LAMDA. Bdwy debut 1981 in *Macbeth* (LC), followed by *Present Laughter, Heartbreak House, Sunday in the Park with George, Pack of Lies, Marriage of Figaro, Indiscretions, Last Night of Ballyhoo, Sex and Longing, Waiting in the Wings, Major Barbara*, OB in *Call from the East, Vivien, Candida, Major Barbara, Quartermaine's Terms, Baby with the Bath Water, Driving Miss Daisy, Wenceslas Square, Love Letters, Hamlet, Subject Was Roses, Beggars in the House of Plenty, Kindertransport, Li'l Abner, Tartuffe.*

IVEY, JUDITH Born September 4, 1951 in El Paso, TX. Bdwy debut 1979 in *Bedroom Farce*, followed by *Steaming, Hurlyburly, Blithe Spirit, Park Your Car in Harvard Yard, Madhouse in Goa, Voices in the Dark, Follies* 2001, OB in *Dulsa Fish Stas and Vi, Sunday Runners, Second Lady, Mrs. Dally Has a Lover, Moonshot and Cosmos, A Fair Country, Noel Coward's Suite in 2 Keys.*

JACKSON, GREG (formerly Greg Vallee) Born March 22, 1955 in NJ. Graduate Boston U. OB debut 1980 in *Times Square*, followed by *Loss of Roses, Ladies of the Odeon, Initiation Rites, Occasional Grace, Twelfth Night, Duet: A Romantic Fable, Dark of the Moon, Meanwhile, on the Other Side of Mt. Vesuvius, O Pioneers!*

JACOBY, MARK Born May 21, 1947 in Johnson City, TN. Graduate GA State U., FL. State U., St. John's U. OB debut 1984 in *Bells Are Ringing, Enter the Guardsman, Sitting Pretty*, Bdwy debut in *Sweet Charity*, for which he received a 1986 Theatre World Award, followed by *Grand Hotel, The Phantom of the Opera, Show Boat.*

JAMES, BRIAN D'ARCY Born 1968 in Saginaw, MI. Graduate Northwestern U. Bdwy in *Carousel, Blood Brothers, Titanic*, OB in *Public Enemy, Floyd Collins, Violet, The Good Thief.*

JAMES, PETER FRANCIS Born September 16, 1956 in Chicago, IL. Graduate RADA. OB debut 1979 in *Julius Caesar*, followed by *Long Day's Journey into Night, Antigone, Richard II, Romeo and Juliet, Enrico IV, Cymbeline, Hamlet, Learned Ladies, 10th Young Playwrights Festival, Measure for Measure, Amphitryon, Troilus and Cressida*, Bdwy debut 2000 in *Judgment at Nuremberg.*

JENNINGS, KEN Born October 10, 1947 in Jersey City, NJ. Graduate St. Peter's Col. Bdwy debut 1975 in *All God's Chillun Got Wings*, followed by *Sweeney Todd*, for which he received a 1979 Theatre World Award, *Present Laughter, Grand Hotel, Christmas Carol, London Assurance, Side Show*, OB in *Once on a Summer's Day, Mayor, Rabboni, Gifts of the Magi, Carmilla, Sharon, Mayor, Amphigory, Shabbatai, Urinetown.*

JOHNSTON, NANCY Born January 15, 1949 in Statesville, NC. Graduate Carson Newman Col., UNC Greensboro. OB debut 1987 in *Olympus on My Mind*, followed by *Nunsense, Living Color, White Lies, You Can Be a New Yorker Too, Splendora, Doctor Doctor*, Bdwy in *Secret Garden, Allegro* (Encores), *The Music Man.*

JONES, CHERRY Born November 21, 1956 in Paris, TN. Graduate Carnegie Mellon U. OB debut 1983 in *The Philanthropist*, followed by *He and She, The Ballad of Soapy Smith, The Importance of Being Earnest, I Am a Camera, Claptrap, Big Time, A Light Shining in Buckinghamshire, The Baltimore Waltz, Goodnight Desdemona, And Baby Makes 7, Desdemona, Pride's Crossing, A Moon for the Misbegotten*, Bdwy in *Stepping Out* (1986), *Our Country's Good, Angels in America, The Heiress, Night of the Iguana, Major Barbara.*

JONES, JAMIE Born November 11, 1959 in Sacramento, CA. Graduate Amer. Acad. of Dramatic Arts. OB debut in *Before Breakfast*, followed by *The Elephant Man.*

JONES, JEN Born March 23, 1927 in Salt Lake City, UT. OB debut 1960 in *Dreams Under the Window*, followed by *Long Voyage Home, Diff'rent, The Creditors, Look at Any Man, I Knock at the Door, Pictures in the Hallway, Grab Bag, Bo Bo, Oh Dad Poor Dad, Henhouse, Uncle Vanya, Grandma's Play, Distance from Calcutta, Good, Last of the Thorntons*, Bdwy in *Dr. Cook's Garden* (1967), *But Seriously, Eccentricities of a Nightingale, Music Man* (1980), *Octette Bridge Club.*

JONES, SIMON Born July 27, 1950 in Wiltshire, England. Attended Trinity Hall. OB debut 1984 in *Terra Nova*, followed by *Magdalena in Concert, Woman in Mind, Privates on Parade, Quick-Change Room, You Never Can Tell, Passion Play, The Admirable Crichton*, Bdwy in *The Real Thing* (1984), *Benefactors, Getting Married Private Lives, Real Inspector Hound/5 Minute Hamlet, School for Scandal, Herbal Bed, Ring Round The Moon, Waiting in the Wings.*

JONES, WALKER Born August 27, 1956 in Pensacola, FL. Graduate Boston U., Yale U. OB debut 1989 in *Wonderful Town*, followed by *Scapin, Byzantium, Merry Wives of Windsor, Merchant of Venice, Henry VI, Just As If.*

JOSEPH, CATRICE Born July 8 in New York, NY. Graduate NYU. OB debut in *Brief History of White Music*, Bdwy debut 2000 in *Seussical.*

KATDARE, DEEP Born July 4, 1970 in Buffalo, NY. Graduate MIT. Bdwy debut 2000 in *Tale of the Allergist's Wife.*

KELEGIAN, SYLVA Born February 2, 1962 in New York, NY. OB debut 2000 in *The Soul of an Intruder.*

KELLY, DENNIS Bdwy debut 1994 in *Damn Yankees*, followed by *Annie Get Your Gun*, OB in *Music in the Air, Suburb.*

KELLY, KRISTEN LEE Born 1968. OB in *Loved Less, Blaming Mom, Apollo of Bellac, After The Rain, American Passenger*, Bdwy in *Rent* (1996—also OB), *Rocky Horror Show.*

KEPROS, NICHOLAS Born November 8, 1932 in Salt Lake City, UT. Graduate U. UT, RADA. OB debut 1958 in *Golden Six*, followed by *Wars and Roses, Julius Caesar, Hamlet, Henry IV, She Stoops to Conquer, Peer Gynt, Octaroon, Endicott and the Red Cross, Judas Applause, Irish Hebrew Lesson, Judgment in Havana, The Millionairess, Androcles and the Lion, The Redempter, Othello, Times and Appetites of Toulouse-Lautrec, Two Fridays, Rameau's Nephew, Good Grief, Overtime, Measure for Measure, You Never Can Tell, Things You Shouldn't Say Past Midnight, Iphegenia Cycle, Troilus and Cressida*, Bdwy in *Saint Joan* (1968/1993), *Amadeus, Execution of Justice, Timon of Athens, Government Inspector, The Rehearsal.*

KING, NICOLAS Born July 26, 1991 in Westerly, RI. Bdwy debut 2000 in *Beauty and the Beast*, followed by *A Thousand Clowns.*

KIRK, JUSTIN Born May 28, 1969 in Salem, OR. OB debut 1990 in *The Applicant, followed by Shardston, Loose Ends, Thanksgiving, Lovequest Live, Old Wicked Songs, June Moon, Ten Unknowns*, Bdwy in *Any Given Day* (1993), *Love! Valour! Compassion!* (also OB).

KITT, EARTHA Born January 26, 1928 in North, SC. Appeared with Katherine Dunham before Bdwy debut in *New Faces of* 1952, followed by *Mrs. Patterson, Shinbone Alley, Timbuktu, Wizard of Oz* (MSG), *The Wild Party*, OB in *New Faces of* 1952, *Cinderella.*

KITTRELL, MICHELLE Born December 16, 1972 in Cocoa Beach, FL. OB debut 1993 in *Girl of My Dreams*, followed by *New Yorkers, Joseph and the Amazing Technicolor Dreamcoat*, Bdwy debut 2000 in *Seussical.*

KNIGHT, EZRA Born July 7, 1962 in Atlanta, GA. OB debut 1995 in *Othello*, followed by *King Lear, You Say What I Mean, Julius Caesar.*

KNIGHT, T.R. Born Minneapolis, MN. OB debut 1999 in *Macbeth*, followed by *This Lime Tree Bower, The Hologram Theory, The Right Way to Sue.*

KOFOED, SEANA Born in IL. Graduate Northwestern U. OB debut 1997 in *The Disputation*, followed by *The Memory of Water, Mom and the Razorblades, An Experiment with an Air Pump, Hard Feelings*, Bdwy in *Night Must Fall.*

KOLINSKI, JOSEPH Born June 26, 1953 in Detroit, MI. Attended U. Detroit. Bdwy debut 1980 in *Brigadoon*, followed by *Dance a Little Closer, The Human Comedy* (also OB), *Three Musketeers, Les Miserables, Christmas Carol, Titanic*, OB in *HiJinks!, Picking up the Pieces, Time and Again.*

KORBICH, EDDIE Born November 6, 1960 in Washington, D.C. Graduate Boston Cons. OB debut 1985 in *A Little Night Music*, followed by *Flora the Red Menace, No Frills Revue, The Last Musical Comedy, Godspell, Sweeney Todd, Assassins, Casino Paradise, Gifts of the Magi, Eating Raoul, Taking a Chance on Love*, Bdwy in *Sweeney Todd* (1989), *Singin' in the Rain, Carousel* (1994), *Seussical, Bloomer Girl* (CC).

KOREY, ALIX (formerly Alexandra) Born May 14 in Brooklyn, NY. Graduate Columbia U. OB debut 1976 in *Fiorello!*, followed by *Annie Get Your Gun, Jerry's Girls, Rosalie in Concert, America Kicks Up Its Heels, Gallery, Feathertop, Bittersuite, Romance in Hard Times, Songs You Might Have Missed, Forbidden Broadway 10th Anniversary, Camp Paradox, Cinderella* (LC), *Best of the West, Jack's Holiday, No Way to Treat a Lady, Wonderful Town, The Wild Party, Suburb*, Bdwy in *Hello, Dolly!* (1978), *Show Boat* (1983), *Ain't Broadway Grand, Triumph of Love.*

KUDISCH, MARC Born September 22, 1966 in Hackensack, NJ. Attended FL. Atlantic U. OB debut 1990 in *Tamara*, followed by *Quiet on the Set, Beauty Part*, Bdwy in *Joseph and the Amazing Technicolor Dreamcoat* (1994), *Beauty and the Beast, Chicago* (Encores), *High Society, The Wild Party, The Scarlet Pimpernel, Bells Are Ringing.*

KUHN, JUDY Born May 20, 1958 in New York, NY. Graduate Oberlin Col. OB debut 1985 in *Pearls*, followed by *Rodgers & Hart Revue, Dream True, As 1000 Cheer, Eli's Comin'*, Bdwy in *Mystery of Edwin Drood* (1985-also OB), *Rags, Les Miserables, Chess, Two Shakespearean Actors, She Loves Me, King David, Strike Up the Band* (Encores).

KURTZ, SWOOSIE Born September 6, 1944 in Omaha, NE. Attended USC, LAMDA. OB debut 1968 in *The Firebugs*, followed by *The Effect of Gamma Rays on Man-in-the-Moon Marigolds, Enter a Free Man, Children, Museum, Uncommon Women and Others, Wine Untouched, Summer, The Beach House, Lips Together Teeth Apart, The Vagina Monologues*, Bdwy in *Ah, Wilderness!* (1975), *Tartuffe, A History of the American Film, 5th of July, House of Blue Leaves, Six Degrees of Separation* (also OB).

KYBART, PETER Born December 7, 1939 in Berlin, Germany. Attended Webber-Douglas Sch. Drama. OB debut 1966 in *The Parasite*, followed by *Trials of Oz, Cymbeline*, Bdwy debut 1997 in *Diary of Anne Frank*, followed by *Judgment at Nuremberg.*

LACY, TOM Born August 30, 1933 in New York, NY. OB debut 1965 in *Fourth Pig*, followed by *The Fantasticks, Shoemakers Holiday, Love and Let Love, The Millionairess, Crimes of Passion, Real Inspector Hound, Enemies, Flying Blind, Abel & Bela/Archtruc, Kingdom of Earth, Our Lady of Sligo, Tiny Alice*, Bdwy in *Last of the Red Hot Lovers* (1971), *Two Shakesperean Actors, Timon of Athens, Government Inspector, Holiday.*

T.R. Knight

Swoosie Kurtz

Tom Lacy

Debra Laws

Joel Leffert

Zoaunne Leroy

LAGE, JORDAN Born February 17, 1963 in Palo Alto, CA. Graduate NYU. OB debut 1988 in *Boy's Life*, followed by *Three Sisters, Virgin Molly, Distant Fires, Macbeth, Yes But So What?, Blue Hour, Been Taken, The Woods, Five Very Live, Hot Keys, As Sure as You Live, The Arrangement, The Lights, Shaker Heights, Missing Persons, Blaming Mom, Night and Her Stars, Dangerous Corner, Edmond, Joy of Going Somewhere Definite, Heart of Man, Mojo, Wolf Lullaby, The Hothouse, Force Continuum,* Bdwy debut 1989 in *Our Town*, followed by *Old Neighborhood, Gore Vidal's The Best Man.*

LAMANNA, JANINE Born June 14 in Rochester, NY. Graduate Wagner Col. Bdwy debut 1998 in *Ragtime*, followed by *Seussical, Kiss Me, Kate.*

LAMB, MARY ANN Born July 4, 1959 in Seattle, WA. Attended Neighborhood Playhouse. Bdwy debut 1985 in *Song and Dance*, followed by *Starlight Express, Jerome Robbins' Broadway, Goodbye Girl, Fiorello!* (Encores), *Out of This World* (Encores), *Pal Joey* (Encores), *A Funny Thing Happened on the Way to the Forum* (1996), *Chicago, Promises Promises* (Encores), *Fosse, Seussical.*

LAMBERT, MIKEL SARAH Born in Spokane, WA. Graduate Radcliffe Col., RADA. OB debut 1996, in 900 *Oneonta*, followed by *Cyrano, Private Battles, The Way of the World, The Oresteia, Wit, Diana of Dobson's.*

LANE, NATHAN Born February 3, 1956 in Jersey City, NJ. OB debut 1978 in *A Midsummer Night's Dream*, followed by *Love, Measure for Measure, Claptrap, Common Pursuit, In a Pig's Valise, Uncounted Blessings, Film Society, Lisbon Traviata, Bad Habits, Lips Together Teeth Apart, Mizlansky/Zilensky*, Bdwy in *Present Laughter* (1982), *Merlin, Wind in the Willows, Some Americans Abroad, On Borrowed Time, Guys and Dolls, Laugher on the 23rd Floor, Love!Valour!Compassion!* (also OB), *A Funny Thing Happened on the Way to the Forum* (1996), *The Man Who Came to Dinner, The Producers.*

LANSBURY, DAVID Born February 25, 1961 in New York, NY. Attended CT Col., Circle in the Square Theatre Sch., Central Sch. of Speech/Drama, London. OB debut 1989 in *Young Playwrights Festival*, followed by *Advice from a Caterpillar, Progress, Hapgood, Principality of Sorrows, Pride's Crossing, The Invisible Hand*, Bdwy in *Heidi Chronicles* (1990), *Major Barbara.*

LAPLATNEY, MARTIN Born September 12, 1952 in Coos Bay, OR. Graduate Central WA St. U. Bdwy debut 1978 in *Crucifer of Blood, followed by Amadeus*, OB in *Passion of Dracula, Tartuffe, Private Battles, The Waverly Gallery, If It Was Easy, A Mind of It's Own, I'm Coming in Soon.*

LARSEN, LIZ Born January 16, in Philadelphia, PA. Attended Hofstra U., SUNY Purchase. Bdwy debut 1981 in *Fiddler on the Roof*, followed by *Starmites, A Little Night Music*, (NYCO/LC), *Most Happy Fella, Damn Yankees, DuBarry Was a Lady* (Encores), OB in *Kuni Leml, Hamlin, Personals, Starmites, Company, After These Messages, One Act Festival, Loman Family Picnic, Teibele and Her Demon, America's Sweetheart, The Adjustment, A New Brain, Little By Little, Newyorkers.*

LAURENT, WENDELL Born December 1, 1961 in New Orleans, LA. Graduate Loyola U. OB debut 1991 in *You're a Good Man Charlie Brown*, followed by *My Sister Eileen, Holy Ghosts, Maderati, Tis Pity She's a Whore, Chuppah, Rain from Heaven.*

LAW, MARY KATE Born September 12 in Harper, KS. Graduate Wichita St. U., Yale U. Bdwy debut 1989 in *Starmites*, followed by *Bloomer Girl* (CC), OB in *Key West.*

LAWS, DEBRA Born in Houston, TX. Attended Houston Com. Col. Bdwy debut 1999 in *It Ain't Nothin But the Blues.*

LEACH, NICOLE Born May 10, 1979 in NJ. OB debut 1994 in *Bring in the Morning*, followed by *Crumbs from the Table of Joy, UKIMWI, Starmites 2001.*

LEASK, KATHERINE Born September 2, 1957 in Munich, Germany. Graduate SMU. OB debut 1988 in *Man Who Climbed the Pecan Tree*, followed by *Cahoots, Melville Boys, Amphitryon, The Imposter, Stonewall Jackson's House, The "I" Word: Interns, The Way of the World, The Oresteia, Night Rules.*

LEAVEL, BETH Born November 1, 1955 in Raleigh, NC. Graduate Meredith Col., UNC Greensboro. OB debut 1982 in *Applause*, followed by *Promises Promises, Broadway Juke Box, Unfinished Song, The Jazz Singer*, Bdwy in *42nd Street* (1984), *Crazy for You, Civil War, 42nd Street.*

LEE, DARREN Born June 8, 1972 in Long Beach, CA. Bdwy debut 1990 in *Shogun*, followed by *Miss Saigon, Victor Victoria, Boys from Syracuse* (Encores), *On The Town, Kiss Me Kate, Seussical*, OB in *Petrified Prince* (1994), *Chang Fragments.*

LEE, KAREN TSEN Born in New York, NY. Graduate Hunter Col. OB debut 1991 in *Letters to a Student Revolutionary*, followed by *A Doll's House, Much Ado About Nothing, Macbeth, Desert Rites, Carry the Tiger to the Mountain, Fish-Eye View.*

LEEDS, JORDAN Born November 29, 1961 in Queens, NY. Graduate SUNY Binghamton. Bdwy debut 1987 in *Les Miserables*, followed by *Sunset Blvd.*, OB in *Beau Jest, Angel Levine, Jest a Second, Fishkin Touch, I Love You You're Perfect Now Change.*

Daniel C. Levine

Lorinda Lisitza

David Little

James W. Ludwig

Charles Major

David Margulies

LEFFERT, JOEL Born December 8, 1951 in New York, NY. Graduate Brown U. OB debut 1976 in *Orphee*, followed by *Heroes, Last Burning, Relatively Speaking, The Bachelor, Scaramouche, Macbeth, Don Juan in Hell, Village Wooing, Long Smoldering, Loveplay, The Straw, Richard III, Hard Times, Gardens of Frau Hess*, Bdwy debut 1999 in *Not About Nightingales*.

LEHMAN, ROSS Born September 6, 1956 in State College, PA. Graduate PA St. Bdwy debut 1995 in *Tempest*, followed by *A Funny Thing Happened on the Way to the Forum, Epic Proportions, One Flew Over the Cuckoo's Nest*, OB in *Tis a Pity She's a Whore, Wings*.

LEIBMAN, RON Born October 11, 1937 in New York, NY. Attended Ohio Wesleyan Col., Actors Studio. Bdwy debut 1963 in *Dear Me the Sky is Falling*, followed by *Bicycle Ride to Nevada, The Deputy, We Bombed in New Haven*, for which he received a 1969 Theatre World Award, *Cop-Out, I Ought to Be in Pictures, Doubles, Rumors, Angels in America*, OB in *The Academy, John Brown's Body, Scapin, The Premise, Legend of Lovers, Dead End, Poker Session, Transfers, Room Service, Love Two, Rich and Famous, Children of Darkness, Non Pasquale, Give the Bishop My Faint Regards, Merchant of Venice, A Dybbuk, Adam Baum and the Jew Movie, A Connecticut Yankee in King Arthur's Court* (CC).

LEONARD, ROBERT SEAN Born February 28, 1969 in Westwood, NJ. OB debut 1985 in *Sally's Gone She Left Her Name*, followed by *Coming of Age in Soho, Beach House, Young Playwrights Festival-And the Air Didn't Answer, When She Danced, Romeo and Juliet, Pitching to the Star, Good Evening, Great Unwashed, Principality of Sorrows, Below the Belt, You Never Can Tell*, Bdwy debut 1985 in *Brighton Beach Memoirs*, followed by *Breaking the Code, Speed of Darkness, Candida, Philadelphia Here I Come, Arcadia, The Iceman Cometh, The Music Man, The Invention of Love*.

LEROY, ZOAUNNE Born January 5, 1935 in Olympia, WA. Graduate U. of WA. OB debut 2001 in *A Skull in Connemara*.

LESTRANGE, PHILIP Born May 9, 1942 in Bronx, NY. Graduate Catholic U., Fordham U. OB debut 1970 in *Getting Married*, followed by *Erogenous Zones, Quilling of Prue, Front Page, Six Degrees of Separation*, Bdwy in *A Small Family Business* (1992), *Guys and Dolls, Rose Tattoo, Last Night of Ballyhoo, Death of a Salesman, True West, Judgment at Nuremberg*.

LEVERETT, DOYLE T. Born January 19, 1954 in Kankakee, IL. Attended IL St. U., Vienna Music Academy. Bdwy debut 1992 in *The Most Happy Fella*, OB in *King of Hearts*.

LEVINE, DANIEL C. Born July 30, 1972 in Boston, MA. Graduate Brandeis U., Tufts U. OB debut 1999 in *Naked Boys Singing!*, followed by *The Gorey Details*, Bdwy debut 2000 in *Jesus Christ Superstar*.

LINDEN, HAL Born March 20, 1931 in New York, NY. Attended CCNY, Amer. Theatre Wing. Bdwy debut 1956 in *Strip for Action*, followed by *Bells Are Ringing, Wildcat, On a Clear Day You Can See Forever, Subways are for Sleeping, Something More, The Apple Tree, Ilya Darling, The Education of H*Y*M*A*N K*A*P*L*A*N*, The Rothschilds, The Sign in Sidney Brustein's Window, Pajama Game, Three Men on a Horse, I'm Not Rappaport, The Sisters Rosensweig*, OB debut in *Anything Goes*, followed by *Visiting Mr. Green*.

LINSER, BRUCE Born November 1, 1967 in Menomonee Falls, WI. Attended UW Eau Claire, U. of MN Minneapolis. OB debut in *Naked Boys Singing*, followed by *The Performer's Confession*.

LISITZA, LORINDA Born March 8, 1970 in Porcupine Plain, Canada. Graduate U. of Saskatchewan, AMDA. OB debut 2000 in *Berlin to Broadway*.

LITTLE, DAVID Born March 21 in Wadesboro, NC. Graduate William & Mary Col., Catholic U. OB debut 1968 in *MacBird*, followed by *Iphigenia in Aulis, Antony and Cleopatra, Antigone, An Enemy of the People, The Wisteria Trees, Three Sons, Almost in Vegas, Sam and Itkeh, Bobbi Boland*, Bdwy in *Thieves* (1973), *Les Blancs, Zalmen or the Madness of God, Blood Knot, Six Degrees of Separation* (also OB).

LITZSINGER, SARAH E. Born October 22, 1971 in Indianapolis, IN. Bdwy debut 1983 in *Marilyn*, followed by *Oliver, Beauty and the Beast*, OB in *Nightmare Alley*.

LONG, JODI Born in New York, NY. Graduate SUNY Purchase. Bdwy debut 1962 in *Nowhere to Go But Up*, followed by *Loose Ends, Bacchae, Getting Away with Murder*, OB in *Fathers and Sons, Family Devotions, Rohwer, Tooth of the Crime, Dream of Kitamura, Midsummer Night's Dream, Madame de Sade, The Wash, Golden Child, Red, Old Money*.

LOPEZ, CARLOS Born May 14, 1963 in Sunnyvale, CA. Attended CA St. U. Hayward. OB debut 1987 in *Wish You Were Here*, Bdwy in *The Pajama Game* (NYCO-1989), *A Chorus Line, Grand Hotel, Guys and Dolls, Grease, Wonderful Town* (NYCO), *Annie Get Your Gun*.

LOPEZ, JONATHAN Born April 21, 1969 in Manila, Philippines. Graduate Cleveland St. U., Brooklyn Col. OB debut in *True Confessions of a Dogeater*, followed by *Dogeaters*.

LOPEZ, PRISCILLA Born February 26, 1948 in Bronx, NY. Bdwy debut 1966 in *Breakfast at Tiffany's*, followed by *Henry Sweet Henry, Lysistrata, Company, Her First Roman, Boy Friend, Pippin, Chorus Line* (also OB), *Day in HollywoodlNight in the Ukraine, Nine*, OB in *What's a Nice Country Like You Doing in a State Like This, Key Exchange, Buck, Extremites, Non Pasquak, Be Happy for Me, Times and Appetites of oulouse-Lautrec, Marathon '88, Other Peopk's Money, Antigone in NY, Newyorkers*.

Stuart Marland

Jamahl Marsh

Michael Mastro

Kathryn Meisle

Gregory Mikell

Mark Nadler

LOVEJOY, DEIRDRE Born June 30, 1962 in Abilene, TX. Graduate U. Evansville, NYU. OB debut 1988 in *Midsummer Night's Dream*, followed by *Henry IV Part 1*, *Hannah 1939*, *Machinal*, *Alice in Wonderland*, *Don Juan*, *Preservation Society*, *Water Children*, *Imperfect Chemistry*, Bdwy 1991 in *Six Degrees of Separation*, followed by *Getting and Spending*, *The Gathering*.

LUDWIG, JAMES W. Born November 16, 1967 in Subic Bay Naval Base, Phillipines. Graduate U. MI, U. WA. OB debut 1995 in *jon & jen*, followed by *Louisiana Purchase*, *After the Fair*, *Suburb*.

LUPONE, ROBERT Born July 29, 1956 in Brooklyn, NY. Graduate Juilliard. Bdwy debut 1970 in *Minnie's Boys*, followed by *Jesus Christ Superstar*, *The Rothschilds*, *Magic Show*, *A Chorus Line*, *Saint Joan*, *Late Night Comic*, *Zoya's Apartment*, *View from the Bridge*, *True West*, *A Thousand Clowns*, OB in *Charlie Was Here*, *Twelfth Night*, *In Connecticut*, *Snow Orchid*, *Lemon*, *Black Angel*, *The Quilling of Prue*, *Time Framed*, *Class 1 Acts*, *Remembrance*, *Children of Darkness*, *Kill*, *Winter Lies*, *The Able-Bodied Seamon*, *Clothes for a Summer Hotel*, *The Light Outside*.

LYLES, LESLIE Born in Plainfield, NJ. Graduate Monmouth Col., Rutgers U. OB debut 1981 in *Sea Marks*, followed by *Highest Standard of Living*, *Vanishing Act*, *I Am Who I Am*, *The Arbor*, *Terry by Terry*, *Marathon '88*, *Sleeping Dogs*, *Nebraska*, *My House Play*, *Life During Wartime*, *Angel of Death*, *Sam I Am*, *The Workroom*, *Dark Ride*, *Brutality of Fact*, *Scotland Road*, *The Perpetual Patient*, *Imperfect Love*, *Passion Play*, *Down the Garden Paths*, Bdwy in *Night and Day* (1979), *Hide and Seek*, *Real Thing*, *Garden District*, *Ah, Wilderness!*.

MA, ROSANNE Born February 22, 1974 in Stockton, CA. Graduate International Actor Training Acad., UC Santa Barbara. OB debut 1999 in *The Joy Luck Club*, followed by *Rashomon*.

MACINTYRE, MARGUERITE Born in Detroit, MI. Graduate USC, RADA. OB debut 1988 in *Some Summer Night*, followed by *Weird Romance*, *Awakening of Spring*, *Annie Warbucks*, *Mata Hari*, *No Way to Treat a Lady*, Bdwy in *City of Angels* (1991), *Jane Eyre*.

MACKAY, LIZBETH Born March 7 in Buffalo, NY. Graduate Adelphi U., Yale U. Bdwy debut 1981 in *Crimes of the Heart*, for which she received a 1982 Theatre World Award, followed by *Death and the Maiden*, *Abe Lincoln in Illinois*, *Heiress*, *The Price*, OB in *Kate's Diary*, *Tales of the Lost Formicans*, *Price of Fame*, *Old Boy*, *Durang Durang*, *The Seagull*, *Lips*, *Two-Headed More Lies About Jerzy*.

MACPHERSON, LORI Born July 23 in Albany, NY. Attended Skidmore Col. Bdwy debut 1988 in *The Phantom of the Opera*, followed by *Bloomer Girl* (CC).

MAJOR, CHARLES Born March 19 in New York, NY. Attended Bates Col, Adelphi U., Neighborhood Playhouse. Bdwy debut 1967 in *Spofford*, followed by *Sly Fox*, OB in *Gloria and Esperanza*, *The Elizabethans*, *Sports Czar*, *The Iceman Cometh*, *Othello*, *Six Characters in Search of an Author*, *An Ordinary Man*, *Tribute*, *Better Living*, *Black Hat Karma*, *Queens!*, *Sitting Pretty*.

MALONE, MICHAEL Born April 3, 1968 in Nashville, TN. Graduate Harvard U., Amer. Rep Inst. OB debut 1993 in *Orestes*, followed by *Anything Cole*, *Stonewall: Night Variations*, *Message to Michael*, *Ascendancy*, Bdwy debut 2000 in *42nd Street*.

MANN, TERRENCE Born in 1951 in KY. Graduate NC Sch. Of Arts. Bdwy debut 1980 in *Barnum*, followed by *Cats*, *Rags*, *Les Miserables*, *Jerome Robbins' Broadway*, *Beauty and the Beast*, *Christmas Carol*, *Getting Away with Murder*, *Promises Promises* (Encores), *Scarlet Pimpernel*, *Rocky Horror Show*, OB in *Night at the Fights*, *Queen's Diamond*, *Assassins*, *Arsenic and Old Lace* (CC).

MARCUM, BRIAN J. Born May 17, 1972 in Lexington, TN. Graduate OK City U. Bdwy debut 1999 in *The Gershwins' Fascinating Rhythm*, followed by *42nd Street*.

MARCUS, DANIEL Born May 26, 1955 in Redwood City, CA. Graduate Boston U. Bdwy debut 1981 in *Pirates of Penzance*, followed by 1776, OB in *La Bohême*, *Kuni Leml*, *Flash of Lightning*, *Pajama Game*, *Gunmetal Blues*, *Merchant of Venice*, *Carmelina*, *Urinetown*.

MARGULIES, DAVID Born February 19, 1937 in New York, NY. Graduate CCNY. OB debut 1958 in *Golden Six*, followed by *Six Characters in Search of an Author*, *Tragical Historie of Dr. Faustus*, *Tango*, *Little Murders*, *Seven Days of Mourning*, *La Analysis*, *An Evening with the Poet Senator*, *Kid Champion*, *The Man with the Flower in His Mouth*, *Old Tune*, *David and Paula*, *Cabal of Hypocrites*, *The Perfect Party*, *Just Say No*, *George Washington Dances*, *I'm with Ya Duke*, *The Treatment*, *Tales of I.B. Singer*, *In the Western Garden*, *Visiting Mr. Green*, *Cranes*, *Big Potato*, *In Dreams and Gimpel*, Bdwy in *Iceman Cometh* (1973), *Zalmen or the Madness of God*, *Comedians*, *Break a Leg*, *West Side Waltz*, *Brighton Beach Memoirs*, *Conversations with My Father*, *Angels in America*, *A Thousand Clowns*.

MARKS, KENNETH Born February 17, 1954 in Harwick, PA. Graduate U. PA, Lehigh U. OB debut 1978 in *Clara Bow Loves Gary Cooper*, followed by *Canadian Cothic*, *Time and the Conways*, *Savoury Meringue*, *Thrombo*, *Fun*, *1-2-3-4-5*, *Manhattan Class I Acts*, *Bright Room Called Day*, *Pix*, *Sabina*, *Easter*, *First Picture Show*, *Brutality of Fact*, *Bright Lights Big City*, *When They Speak of Rita*, *Birdseed Bundles*, *Blur*, Bdwy in *Dancing at Lughnasa* (1992).

MARLAND, STUART Born February 28, 1959 in Montreal, Canada. Attended UCLA. Bdwy debut 1993 in *Cyrano-The Musical*, followed by *Jekyll & Hyde*, OB in *Madison Avenue*, *Birdwatcher*, *The Brass Jackal*, *Scoundrel*.

MARSH, JAMAHL Born October 27, 1973 in Newark, NJ. Graduate Rutgers U. OB debut 2000 in *A Lesson Before Dying.*

MARSHALL, DONNA LEE Born February 27, 1958 in Mt. Holly, NJ. Attended AADA. OB debut 1987 in *By Strouse,* followed by *Human Comedy, Sidewalkin', Charley's Tale,* Bdwy in *Pirates of Penzance, Christmas Carol, Footloose, Tom Sawyer.*

MARTIN, LUCY Born February 8, 1942 in New York, NY. Graduate Sweet Briar Col. OB debut 1962 in *Electra,* followed by *Happy as Larry, Trojan Women, Iphigenia in Aulis, Wives, Cost of Living, Substance of Fire, Private Battles, Passion Play, Strictly Personal,* Bdwy in *Shelter* (1973) *Children of a Lesser God, Pygmalion, The Sisters Rosensweig, Major Barbara.*

MASTRO, MICHAEL (formerly Mastrototaro) Born May 17, 1962 in Albany, NY. Graduate NYU. OB debut 1984 in *Victoria Station,* followed by *Submarines, Naked Truth/Name Those Names, Darker Purpose, Hot Keys, Crows in the Cornfield, City, Escape from Happiness, Naked Faith, Alone But Not Lonely, Water Children, Tamicanfly,* Bdwy debut 1995 in *Love! Valour! Compassion!,* followed by *Side Man, Judgment at Nuremberg.*

MATHER, LEISA Born July 16, 2000 in Melbourne, Australia. OB debut 2000 in *Forbidden Broadway Cleans Up Its Act.*

MATSUSAKA, TOM Born August 8 in Wahiawa, HI. Graduate MI St. U. Bdwy debut 1968 in *Mame,* followed by *Ride the Winds, Pacific Overtures, South Pacific,* OB in *Agamemnon, Chu Chem, Jungle of Cities, Santa Anita '42, Extenuating Circumstances, Rohwer, Teahouse, Song of a Nisei Fisherman, Empress of China, Pacific Overtures* (1984), *Eat a Bowl of Tea, Shogun Macbeth, The Imposter, Privates, Lucky Come Hawaii, Caucasian Chalk Circle, Carry the Tiger to the Mountain, The Joy Luck Club, The Teahouse of the August Moon, Rashomon.*

MAU, LES J.N. Born January 8, 1954 in Honolulu, HI. Graduate U. of HI. OB debut 1983 in *Teahouse,* followed by *Empress of China, Eat a Bowl of Tea, Lucky Come Hawaii, Wilderness, Pacific Overtures, New Living Newspaper, Geniuses, Friends, Dog and His Master, The Gaol Gate/ Purgatory, Tibet Does Not Exist, The Joy Luck Club, The Poet of Columbus Ave, Rashomon.*

MAXWELL, JAN Born November 20, 1956 in Fargo, ND. Graduate Moorhead St. U. Bdwy debut 1990 in *City of Angels,* followed by *Dancing at Lughnasa, Doll's House, Sound of Music, The Dinner Party,* OB in *Everybody Everybody, Hot Feet, Light Years to Chicago, Ladies of the Fortnight, Two Gentlemen of Verona, Marriage Fool, Oedipus Private Eye, Inside Out, The Professional.*

MAXWELL, ROBERTA Born in Canada. OB debut 1968 in *Two Gentlemen of Verona,* followed by *A Whistle in the Dark, Slag, Plough and the Stars, Merchant of Venice, Ashes, Mary Stuart, Lydie Breeze, Before the Dawn, Real Estate, When I Was a Girl, Cripple of Inishmaan, June and the Paycock,* Bdwy in *Prime of Miss Jean Brodie, Henry V, House of Atreus, Resistible Rise of Arturo Ui, Othello, Hay Fever, There's One in Every Marriage, Equus, The Merchant, Our Town, Summer and Smoke.*

MAY, DEVEN Born April 3, 1971 in Whittier, CA. Attended Southern UT U. OB debut 2001 in *Bat Boy,* for which he received a 2001 Theatre World Award.

MAY, SETH MICHAEL Born April 17, 1971 in New York, NY. OB debut in *Richard II/Richard III,* followed by *Middle Finger.*

MCCALLUM, DAVID Born September 19, 1933 in Scotland. Attended Chapman Col. Bdwy debut 1968 in *Flip Side,* followed by *California Suite, Amadeus,* OB debut in *After the Prize,* followed by *The Philanthropist, Ghosts, Nasty Little Secrets, Communicating Doors, Julius Caesar, Time and Again.*

MCCARTHY, JEFF Born October 16, 1954 in Los Angeles, CA. Graduate Amer. Conservatory. Bdwy debut 1982 in *Pirates of Penzance,* followed by *Zorba* (1983), *Beauty and the Beast, Side Show,* OB in *Gifts of the Magi, On the 20th Century, Sisters Rosensweig, Urinetown.*

MCCONAHAY, LIZ Graduate U. WI, Attended Royal Nat. Theatre Sch. London. OB debut 1997 in *Secrets Every Smart Traveler Should Know,* Bdwy debut 2000 in *The Full Monty.*

MCCORMICK, CAROLYN Born September 19, 1959 in TX. Graduate Williams Col. OB debut 1988 in *In Perpetuity Throughout the Universe,* followed by *Lips Together Teeth Apart, Laureen's Whereabouts, Donahue Sisters, Oedipus, Dinner with Friends,* Bdwy in *The Dinner Party.*

MCCULLOH, BARBARA Born March 5 in Washington, D.C. Attended Col. of William & Mary, U. of MD. OB debut 1984 in *Up in Central Park,* followed by *Kuni-Leml, On the 20th Century, 1-2-3-4-5, Life Forms, Leave It to Me,* Bdwy in *King and I, Peter Pan.*

MCDONALD, DANIEL Born July 30 in Scranton, PA. OB debut 1994 in *First Night,* followed by *Chesterfield, The Personal Equation, Quartett* (BAM), Bdwy debut 1997 in *Steel Pier,* for which he won a 1997 Theatre World Award, followed by *High Society.*

MCDONALD, TANNY Born February 13 in Princeton, NJ. Graduate Vassar Col. OB debut 1961 in *American Savoyards,* followed by *All in Love, To Broadway with Love, Carricknabauna, The Beggar's Opera, Brand, Goodbye, Dan Bailey, Total Eclipse, Gorky, Don Juan Comes Back from the War, Vera with Kate, Francis, On Approval, A Definite Maybe, Temptation, Titus Andronicus, Hamlet, June, Johnny Pye and the Foolkiller, Birdseed Bundles, Sitting Pretty,* Bdwy in *Fiddler on the Roof, Come Summer, The Lincoln Mask, Clothes for a Summer Hotel, Macbeth, Man of La Mancha.*

MCDONOUGH, J.M. Born April 1, 1946 in Baltimore, MD. Graduate U. of the South. OB debut 1999 in *The Made Man,* followed by *Descent, Sweeney Todd.*

MCENTIRE, REBA Born March 28, 1955 in McAlester, OK. Graduate Southeastern St. U. Bdwy debut 2001 in *Annie Get Your Gun.*

MCGIVER, BORIS Born January 23, 1962 in Cobleskill, NY. Graduate Ithaca Col., SUNY Cobleskill, NYU. OB debut 1994 in *Richard II,* followed by *Hapgood, Troilus and Cressida, Timon of Athens, Henry VI, Anthony and Cleopatra, The Devils, Lydie Breeze, More Lies about Jerzy.*

MCGRANE, PAUL Born in Dublin, Ireland. OB debut 1994 in *Brothers of the Brush,* followed by *Whistle in the Dark, Da, Plough and the Stars, Mass Appeal. Major Barbara, Long Day's Journey into Night, The Irish...and How They Got That Way, The Shaughraun, The Picture of Dorian Gray.*

MCGRATH, MICHAEL Born September 25, 1957 in Worcester, MA. OB debut 1988 in *Forbidden Bdwy,* followed by *Cocoanuts, Forbidden Hollywood, Louisiana Purchase, Secrets Every Smart Traveler Should Know, Exactly Like You, Game Show,* Bdwy in *My Favorite Year* (1992), *Goodbye Girl, DuBarry Was a Lady* (Encores), *Swinging on a Star,* for which he received a 1996 Theatre World Award, *Boys from Syracuse* (Encores), *Little Me.*

MCROBBIE, PETER Born January 31, 1943 in Hawick, Scotland. Graduate Yale U. OB debut 1976 in *The Wobblies*, followed by *Devil's Disciple, Cinders, The Ballad of Soapy Smith, Rosmersholm, American Bagpipes, Richard III, Timon of Athens, Memory of Water*, Bdwy in *Whose Life Is It Anyway?* (1979), *Macbeth* (1981), *Mystery of Edwin Drood, Master Builder* (1992), *Saint Joan, Night Must Fall, The Invention of Love.*

MEDINA, AIXA M. ROSARIO Born July 5, 1965 in Rio Piedras, Puerto Rico. Graduate U. Puerto Rico. Bdwy debut 1995 in *Victor/Victoria*, followed by *Once Upon a Mattress* (1996), OB in *Ziegfeld Follies of* 1936, *A Connecticut Yankee in King Arthur's Court* (CC).

MEISELS, ANNIE Born in Baltimore, MD. Graduate Rutgers U. OB debut 1992 in *Things That Should Be Said*, followed by *Little Women, Caught in the Act, Pera Palas, My Mother's a Baby Boy.*

MEISLE, KATHRYN Born June 7 in Appleton, WI. Graduate Smith Col., UNC Chapel Hill. OB debut 1988 in *Dandy Dick*, followed *by Cahoots, Othello, As You Like It* (CP), *Brutality of Fact, The Most Fabulous Story Ever Told, What You Get and What You Expect, Old Money*, Bdwy in *Racing Demon* (1995), *The Rehearsal, London Assurance.*

MENZEL, IDINA Born 1972 in Long Island, NY. Graduate NYU. OB debut 1996 in *Rent* (also Bdwy), followed by *The Wild Party, Hair* (CC).

MIKELL, GREGORY Born June 18, 1966 in Statesboro, GA. Graduate Jacksonville St. U. OB debut in *Carnivore*, followed by *A Midsummer Night's Dream, Welcome to Our City.*

MILLER, ANDREW Born May 25 in Racine, WI. Attended U. of IL, Royal Nat. Theatre Studio. OB debut 1995 in *Blue Man Group: Tubes*, followed by *A Hamlet, Macbeth, Hunting Humans, In Betweens, Snapshots, The Folsom Head, The Bloomers, Sex, Troilus and Cressida.*

MILLER, BETTY Born March 27, 1925 in Boston, MA. Attended UCLA. OB in *Summer and Smoke, Cradle Song, La Ronde, Plays for Bleeker St., Desire Under the Elms, The Balcony, Power and the Glory, Beaux Stratagem, Gandhi, Girl on the Via Flammia, Hamlet, Summer, Before the Dawn, Curtains, Lake Hollywood, More Lies about Jerzy*, Bdwy in *You Can't Take It with You, Right You Are, Wild Duck, Cherry Orchard, Touch of the Poet, Eminent Domain, Queen and the Rebels, Richard III.*

MILLER, WILLIAM MARSHALL Born June 19, 1951 in Summit, NJ. OB debut 2001 in *If It Was Easy.*

MILLIGAN, (JACOB) TUCK Born March 25, 1949 in Kansas City, MO. Graduate U. Kansas City. Bdwy debut 1976 in *Equus*, followed by *Crucifer of Blood, The Kentucky Cycle, Herbal Bed, A Moon for the Misbegotten*, OB in *Beowulf, Everybody's Gettin' into the Act, Arsenic and Old Lace* (CC).

MILLS, ELIZABETH Born August 3, 1967 in San Jose, CA. Attended San Jose St. U. Bdwy debut 1993 in *Ain't Broadway Grand*, followed by *Crazy for You, DuBarry was a Lady* (Encores), *Kiss Me Kate*, OB in *A Connecticut Yankee in King Arthur's Court* (CC).

MONTANO, ROBERT Born April 22 in Queens, NY. Attended Adelphi U. Bdwy debut 1995 in *Cats*, followed by *Chita Rivera + Two, Legs Diamond, Kiss of the Spider Woman, On the Town*, OB in *The Chosen* (1987), *The Torturer's Visit, How Are Things in Costa del Fuego?, Picture Perfect, Young Playwrights Festival, On the Town, Knepp.*

MOORE, CHRISTOPHER Born May 7, 1972 in Minneapolis, MN. Graduate Juilliard, U. St. Thomas. OB debut 1997 in *Measure for Measure*, followed by *Venice Preserv'd, Richard II, School for Scandal, The Forest, Candida, The Country Wife, The Miser, The Seagull, Merry Wives of Windsor, The Way of the World, The Oresteia, John Gabriel Borkman, A Will of His Own, Andromoche, The Cherry Orchard.*

MOORE, DANA Born in Sewickley, PA. Bdwy debut 1982 in *Sugar Babies*, followed by *Dancin', Copperfield, On Your Toes, Singin' in the Rain, Sweet Charity, Dangerous Games, A Chorus Line, Will Rogers Follies, Pal Joey* (Encores), *Fosse*, OB in *Petrified Prince, Camila.*

MOORE, LEE Born February 19, 1929 in Brooklyn, NY. OB debut 1978 in *Once More with Feeling*, followed by *The Caine Mutiny Court-Martial, Christopher Blake, Cat and Canary, Shrunken Heads, Raspberry Picker, Blessed Event, Before Dawn, Small Potatoes, Alison's House, Welcome to Our City.*

MORAN, MARTIN Born December 29, 1959 in Denver, CO. Attended Stanford U., Amer. Conservatory Theatre. OB debut 1983 in *Spring Awakening*, followed by *Once on a Summer's Day, 1-2-3-4-5, Jacques Brel Is Alive* (1992), *Bed and Sofa, Floyd Collins, Fallen Angles*, Bdwy in *Oliver!* (1984), *Big River, How to Succeed in Business Without Really Trying* (1995), *Titanic, Cabaret, Bells Are Ringing.*

MORFOGEN, GEORGE Born March 30, 1933 in New York, NY. Graduate Brown U., Yale U. OB debut 1957 in *Trial of D. Karamazov*, followed by *Christmas Oratorio, Othello, Good Soldier Schweik, Cave Dwellers, Once in a Lifetime, Total Eclipse, Ice Age, Prince of Homburg, Biography: A Game, Mrs. Warren's Profession, Principia Scriptoriae, Tamara, Maggie and Misha, Country Girl, Othello, As You Like It* (CP), *Uncle Bob, Henry V, Hope Zone, The Disputation, Cyrano, Cymbeline, Hamlet, Uncle Bob*, Bdwy in *Fun Couple* (1962), *Kingdoms, Arms and the Man, An Inspector Calls.*

MORGAN, CASS Born April 15 in Rochester, NY. Attended Adelphi U. OB debut 1984 in *La Boheme*, followed by *Another Paradise, The Knife, Catfish Loves Anna, Feast Here Tonight, Can Can, Merrily We Roll Along, Inside Out, Floyd Collins, The Immigrant*, Bdwy in *Hair* (1969), *Pump Boys and Dinettes, Human Comedy, Beauty and the Beast*, 1776.

MORRIS, KENNY Born November 4, 1954 in Brooklyn, NY. Graduate UNC Chapel Hill. OB debut 1981 in *Francis*, followed by *She Loves Me, Half a World Away, Jacques Brel Is Alive and Well and Living in Paris, Quick-Change Room, Jayson, Death in England, Leave It to Me, I Married an Angel*, Bdwy debut 1983 in *Joseph and the Amazing Technicolor Dreamcoat*, followed by *Tenth Man.*

MORTON, JOE Born October 18, 1947 in New York, NY. Attended Hofstra U. OB debut 1968 in *A Month of Sundays*, followed by *Salvation, Charlie Was Here and Now He's Gone, G. R. Point, Crazy Horse, A Winter's Tale, Johnny on a Spot, A Midsummer Night's Dream, The Recruiting Officer, Oedipus the King, The Wild Duck, Rhinestone, Souvenirs, Cheapside, King John, Measure for Measure* (CP), Bdwy in *Hair, Two Gentlemen of Verona, Tricks, Raisin*, for which he received a 1974 Theatre World Award, *Oh Brother!, Honky Tonk Nights, Lady in the Dark in Concert, Art.*

MUENZ, RICHARD Born in 1948 in Hartford, CT. Attended Eastern Baptist Col. Bdwy debut 1976 in 1600 *Pennsylvania Avenue*, followed by *Most Happy Fella, Camelot, Rosalie in Concert, Chess, Pajama Game* (LC), *Nick and Nora*, 110 *in the Shade* (LC), *Wonderful Town* (LC), *42nd Street*, OB in *Leading Men Don't Dance.*

MURNEY, JULIA Born January 14, 1969 in State College, PA. Graduate Syracuse U. OB debut 2000 in *The Wild Party*, followed by *A Class Act, Time and Again, Crimes of the Heart.*

Kathy Najimy

Casey Nicholaw

Marina Nichols

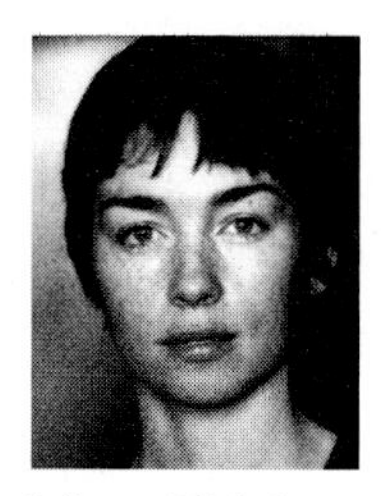

Julianne Nicholson

Bill Nolte

Ben Nordstrom

MURRAY, BRIAN Born October 9, 1939 in Johannesburg, SA. OB debut 1964 in *The Knack*, followed by *King Lear, Ashes, Jail Diary of Albie Sachs, Winter's Tale, Barbarians, The Purging, Midsummer Night's Dream, Recruiting Officer, Arcata Promise, Candide in Concert, Much Ado About Nothing, Hamlet, Merry Wives of Windsor, Travels with My Aunt, Entertaining Mr. Sloane, Molly Sweeney, The Entertainer, Da, Mud River Stone, Misalliance, Long Day's Journey into Night, Spreadeagle, The Butterfly Collection, The Play about the Baby*, Bdwy in *All in Good Time* (1965), *Rosencrantz and Guildenstern Are Dead, Sleuth, Da, Noises Off, Small Family Business, Black Comedy, Racing Demon, Little Foxes, Twelfth Nite, Uncle Vanya.*

NADLER, MARK Born October 14, 1961 in Waterloo, IA. Attended Interlochen Arts Academy. OB debut 1990 in *7 O'Clock at the Top of the Gate*, followed by *The Sheik of Avenue B, Nonstop Broadway Hootenany, Dame Edna's Royal Tour, Gershwin's American Rhapsody.*

NAJIMY, KATHY Born in San Diego, CA. Attended San Diego St. U. Bdwy debut 2001 in *Dirty Blonde.*

NAKAHARA, RON Born July 20, 1947 in Honolulu, HI. Attended U. HI, U. TN. OB debut 1981 in *Danton's Death*, followed by *Flowers and Household Gods, Rohwer, A Midsummer Night's Dream, Teahouse, Song for Nisei Fishermen, Eat a Bowl of Tea, Once Is Never Enough, Noiresque, Play Ball, Three Sisters, And the Soul Shall Dance. Earth and Sky, Cambodia Agonistes, A Doll's House, School for Wives, Ah, Wilderness!, Rashomon*, Bdwy in *A Few Good Men* (1989).

NAUFFTS, GEOFFREY Born February 3, 1961 in Arlington, MA. Graduate NYU. OB debut 1987 in *Moonchildren*, followed by *Stories from Home, Another Time Another Place, The Alarm, Jerusalem Oratorio, The Survivor, Spring Awakening, Summer Winds, Saturday Mourning Cartoons, Flyovers, June Moon, Maiden's Prayer, Snakebit, Once Around the City*, Bdwy in *A Few Good Men* (1989).

NAUGHTON, KEIRA Born June 3, 1971 in New Haven, CT. Graduate Skidmore Col., NYU. Bdwy debut in *Three Sisters*, OB debut in *All My Sons*, followed by *Tesla's Letters, Hotel Universe, Uncle Jack, Snapshots* 2000.

NICHOLAW, CASEY Born October 6, 1962. Attended UCLA. OB debut 1986 in *Pajama Game*, followed by *Petrified Prince*, Bdwy in *Crazy for You* (1992), *Best Little Whorehouse Goes Public, Victor Victoria, Steel Pier, Seussical.*

NICHOLS, MARINA Born November 20, 1972 in Lvov, Russia. OB debut 2000 in *A Taste of Honey.*

NICHOLSON, JULIANNE Born July 1, 1971 in Medford, MA. Attended Hunter Col. OB debut 2000 in *Stranger.*

NIEBANCK, PAUL Born September 22, 1964 in Philadelphia, PA. Graduate Boston U., Yale U. OB debut 1997 in *American Clock*, followed by *The Seagull, Leaving Queens.*

NOBBS, KEITH Born 1979 in Kingswood, TX. Attended Columbia U. OB in *Stupid Kids, Fuddy Meers, Four.*

NOLEN, DEAN Born October 5, 1964 in Dallas, TX. Graduate Hardin-Simmons U., Yale. OB debut 2000 in *Tabletop.*

NOLTE, BILL Born June 4, 1953 in Toledo, OH. Graduate CCCM. OB debut 1977 in *Wonderful Town*, followed by Bdwy in *Cats* (1985), *Me and My Girl, The Secret Garden, Joseph and the Amazing Technicolor Dreamcoat* (1993), *Christmas Carol* (MSG), *1776, Jane Eyre.*

NORDSTROM, BEN Born November 26, 1976 in Dallas, TX. Graduate Webster U. OB debut 2000 in *The Gorey Details.*

NORTON, JIM Born Jan 4, 1938 in Dublin, Ireland. Bdwy debut 1999 in *The Weir*, OB 2000 in *Juno and the Paycock.*

NOTH, CHRIS Born November 13, 1957 in Madison, WI. Graduate Yale U., attended Marlborough Coll, Neighborhood Playhouse. OB in *Patronage, Arms and the Man, Kentucky Cycle*, Bdwy in *The Best Man* (2000).

O'CONNOR, SUSAN Born March 11, 1975 in Las Cruces, NM. Graduate U. of FL. OB debut 2000 in *Never Swim Alone*, followed by *See Bob Run.*

OHAMA, MATSUKO OB debut 2001 in *Straight as a Line.*

O'KELLY, AIDEEN Born in Dalkey, Ireland. Member Dublin's Abbey Theatre. Bdwy debut 1980 in *A Life*, followed by *Othello*, OB in *Killing of Sister George, Man Enough, Resistance, Remembrance, Somewhere I Have Never Traveled, Same Old Moon, Da, The Libertine, Philadelphia Here I Come, The Country Boy, Red Roses and Petrol.*

O'LEARY, THOMAS JAMES Born June 21, 1956 in Windsor Locks, CT. Graduate U. CT. Bdwy debut 1991 in *Miss Saigon*, followed by *Phantom of the Opera*, OB in *Medal of Honor Rag.*

OLSSON, BJÖRN Born April 21 in Gothenburg, Sweden. OB debut 2000 in *Berlin to Broadway.*

O'NEILL, HEATHER Born in Belfast, Northern Ireland. OB debut 1999 in *Eclipsed*, followed by *The Country Boy, A Life.*

Jim Norton

Thomas James O'Leary

Björn Olsson

Kevin Pariseau

Robyne M. Parrish

Estelle Parsons

ORESKES, DANIEL Born in New York, NY. Graduate U. PA, LAMDA. OB debut 1990 in *Henry IV,* followed by *Othello, 'Tis Pity She's a Whore, Richard II, Henry VI, Troilus and Cressida, Quills, Missing/Kissing, The Devils, Mrs. Peter's Connections, Cellini,* Bdwy in *Crazy He Calls Me* (1992), *Electra, Aida.*

OSCAR, BRAD Born September 22, 1964 in Washington, D.C. Graduate Boston U. Bdwy debut 1990 in *Aspects of Love,* followed by *Jekyll & Hyde, The Producers,* OB in *Forbidden Broadway* (1993), *Do Re Mi, Jekyll & Hyde.*

O'SULLIVAN, ANNE Born February 6, 1952 in Limerick City, Ireland. OB debut 1977 in *Kid Champion,* followed by *Hello Out There, Fly Away Home, The Drunkard, Dennis, Three Sisters, Another Paradise, Living Quarters, Welcome to the Noon, Dreamer Examines His Pillow, Mama Drama, Free Fall, Magic Act, Plough and the Stars, Marathon* '88, *Bobo's Guns, Marathon* '90, *Festival of 1 Acts, Marathon* '91, *Murder of Crows, Cats and Dogs, Mere Mortals and Others, Mary McGregor, Arabian Nights.*

OVERBEY, KELLIE Born November 21, 1964 in Cincinnati, OH. Graduate Northwestern U. OB debut 1988 in *Debutante Ball,* followed by *Second Coming, Face Divided, Melville Boys, Betty's Summer Vacation, The Hologram Theory, Comic Potential,* Bdwy in *Buried Child* (1996), *Present Laughter, Judgment at Nuremberg.*

PAGE, CAROLANN Born in Odessa, TX. Graduate Curtis Inst. of Music. Bdwy debut 1974 in *Candide,* followed by *Music Is, Allegro* (Encores), OB debut 1993 in *First Lady Suite,* followed by *Sondheim Celebration at Carnegie Hall, Fishkin Touch, Blood on the Dining Room Floor, Woof.*

PANKOW, JOHN Born 1955 in St. Louis, MO. Attended St. Nichols Sch. of Arts. OB debut 1980 in *Merton of the Movies,* followed by *Slab Boys, Forty Deuce, Hunting Scenes from Lower Bovaria, Cloud 9, Jazz Poets at the Crotto, Henry V, North Shore Fish, Two Gentlemen of Verona, Italian American Reconciliation Aristocrats, Ice Cream with Hot Fudge, EST Marathon* '92, *Tempest* (CP), *Baby Anger, Measure for Measure* (CP), Bdwy in *Amadeus* (1981), *The Iceman Cometh, Serious Money.*

PAPPAS, EVAN Born August 21, 1958 in San Francisco, CA. Attended CA Jr. Col. Bdwy debut 1982 in *A Chorus Line,* followed by *My Favorite Year,* OB debut 1991 in *I Can Get It for You Wholesale,* followed by *Pera Palace, The Wound of Love, The Immigrant.*

PARISEAU, KEVIN Born January 23, 1963 in Providence, RI. Graduate Brown U. OB debut 1996 in *I Love You You're Perfect Now Change.*

PARK, JOSHUA Born November 26, 1976 in North Carolina. Attended NC Sch. of the Arts. Bdwy debut 2001 in *Tom Sawyer.*

PARK, MICHAEL Born July 20, 1968 in Canandaigua, NY. Graduate Nazareth Col. of Rochester. OB debut 1994 in *Hello Again,* followed by *Violet,* Bdwy in *Smokey Joe's Café* (1995), *Little Me, Bloomer Girl* (CC).

PARRISH, ROBYNE M. Born in Middletown, OH. Attended NC Sch. of the Arts. OB debut 2000 in *Welcome to Our City.*

PARRY, WILLIAM Born October 7, 1947 in Steubenville, OH. Graduate Mt. Union Col. Bdwy debut 1971 in *Jesus Christ Superstar,* followed by *Rockabye Hamlet, The Leaf People, Camelot* (1980), *Sunday in the Park with George, Into the Light, Passion,* OB in *Sgt. Pepper's Lonely Hearts Club Band, The Conjurer, Noah, The Misanthrope, Joseph and the Amazing Technicolor Dreamcoat, Agamemnon, Coolest Cat in Town, Dispatches, The Derby, The Knife, Cymbeline, Marathon* '90, *Den of Thieves, Once Around the City.*

PARSONS, ESTELLE Born November 20, 1927 in Lynn, MA. Attended Boston U., Actors Studio. Bdwy debut 1956 in *Happy Hunting,* followed by *Whoop Up, Beg Borrow or Steal, Mother Courage, Ready When You Are C.B., Malcolm, Seven Descents of Myrtle, And Miss Reardon Drinks a Little, Norman Conquests, Ladies at the Alamo, Miss Marguerida's Way, Pirates of Penzance, Shadow Box* (1994), OB in *DemiDozen, Pieces of Eight, Threepenny Opera, Automobile Graveyard, Mrs. Dally Has a Lover* (1963), for which she received a 1963 Theatre World Award, *Next Time I'll Sing to You, Come to the Palace of Sin, In the Summer House, Monopoly, The East Wind, Galileo, Peer Gynt, Mahagonny, People Are Living There, Barbary Shore, Oh Glorious Tintinnabulation, Mert and Paul, Elizabeth and Essex, Dialogue for Lovers, New Moon* (in concert), *Orgasmo Adulto Escapes from the Zoo, Unguided Missile, Baba Goya, Extended Forecast, Deja Revue, Grace and Gloria, The Forty-nine Years, First Picture Show, Last of the Thorntons.*

PATTERSON, EDWIN SEAN Born August 25, 1968 in Arlington, TX. Graduate U. of OK. OB debut 1998 in *A Lie of the Mind,* followed by *Loot, Cock and Bull Story, Sweeney Todd.*

PATTERSON, JEFF OB in *Horsey People.*

PATTERSON, MEREDITH Born November 24, 1975 in Concord, CA. Bdwy in *A Christmas Carol, 42nd Street,* OB in *The Increased Difficulty of Concentration.*

PATTON, CHARLOTTE Born June 12 in Danville, KY. Attended U. Cincinnati, OB in *The New Living Newspaper, The Problem, The Bad Penny, The Happy Journey from Trenton to Camden, You've Changed, Montage, Delicate Dangers, The Street, My Mother's a Baby Boy.*

PAUL, GUY Born September 12, 1949 in Milwaukee, WI. Attended U. MN. OB debut 1984 in *Flight of the Earls,* followed by *Frankenstein, The Underpants, Oresteia, Ever Afters, Oh Baby Oh Baby, Of Blessed Memory, Candida,* Bdwy in *Arms and the Man* (1985), *Wild Honey, Rumors, Private Lives, King and I* (1996), *1776, The Invention of Love.*

Jeff Patterson

Susan Pelligrino

Patti Perkins

Brocton Pierce

Ricardo Puente

John Quilty

PAWK, MICHELE Born November 16, 1961 in Pittsburgh, PA. Graduate CCCM. Bdwy debut 1988 in *Mail*, followed by *Crazy for You*, *Cabaret*, *Seussical*, OB in *Hello Again*, *Decline of the Middle West*, *john & jen*, *After the Fair*.

PEDI, CHRISTINE Born October 24 in Yonkers, NY. Graduate Fordham U. OB debut 1993 in *Forbidden Bdwy*, followed by *Forbidden Bdwy Strikes Back*, Bdwy in *Little Me*.

PELLEGRINO, SUSAN Born June 3, 1950 in Baltimore, MD. Attended CC San Francisco, CA St. U. OB debut 1982 in *Wisteria Trees*, followed by *Steel on Steel*, *Master Builder*, *Equal Wrights*, *Come as You Are*, *Painting Churches*, *Marvin's Room*, *Glory Girls*, *Minor Demons*, *Blood Orange*, *I'm Coming in Soon*, Bdwy in *Kentucky Cycle* (1994), *Present Laughter*, *View from the Bridge*.

PEREZ, ROSIE Born September 4, 1966 in Brooklyn, NY. OB debut 2001 in *The Vagina Monologues*, followed by *References to Salvador Dali Make Me Hot*.

PERKINS, PATTI Born July 9 in New Haven, CT. Attended AMDA. OB debut 1972 in *The Contrast*, followed by *Fashion*, *Tuscaloosa's Calling Me*, *Patch*, *Shakespeare's Cabaret*, *Maybe I'm Doing It Wrong*, *Fabulous LaFontaine*, *Hannah* 1939, *Free Zone*, *New Yorkers*, Bdwy in *All Over Town* (1974), *Shakespeare's Cabaret*, *The Full Monty*.

PHILLIPS, AMY JO Born November 15, 1958 in Brooklyn, NY. Graduate Ithaca Col. OB debut 1986 in *Little Shop of Horrors*, followed by *Burnscape*, *Pretty Faces*, Bdwy debut 1994 in *Show Boat*, followed *St. Louis Woman* (Encores), *Tom Sawyer*.

PIECH, JENNIFER (LYNN) Born January 25, 1967 in Camden, NJ. Graduate Col. of William and Mary. OB debut 1995 in *Lust*, followed by *After the Fair*, *As You Like It*.

PIERCE, BROCTON Born June 14 in Baltimore, MD. Graduate Frostburg St. Col. OB debut 1997 in *Grandma Sylvia's Funeral*, followed by *Welcome to Our City*.

PIETROPINTO, ANGELA Born February 4 in New York, NY. Graduate NYU. OB in *Henry IV*, *Alice in Wonderland*, *Endgame*, *Sea Gull*, *Jinx Bridge*, *The Mandrake*, *Marie and Bruce*, *Green Card Blues*, *3 by Pirandello*, *Broken Pitcher*, *Cymbeline*, *Romeo and Juliet*, *Midsummer Night's Dream*, *Twelve Dreams*, *The Rivals*, *Cap and Bells*, *Thrombo*, *Lies My Father Told Me*, *Sorrows of Stephen*, *Between the Wars*, *Hotel Play*, *Rain Some Fish No Elephants*, *Young Playwrights* 90, *Tunnel of Love*, *Thanksgiving Day*, *Vilna's Got a Golem*, *Down the Garden Paths*, Bdwy in *The Suicide* (1980), *Eastern Standard*.

PINE, LARRY Born March 3, 1945 in Tucson, AZ. Graduate NYU. OB debut 1967 in *Cyrano*, followed by *Alice in Wonderland*, *Mandrake*, *Aunt Dan and Lemon*, *Taming of the Shrew*, *Better Days*, *Dolphin Project*, *Treasure Island*, *Preservation Society*, *The Disputation*, *Mizlansky/Zilinsky*, *The Chemistry of Change*, *The Designated Mourner*, *Saved or Destroyed*, Bdwy in *End of the World* (1984), *Angels in America*, *Bus Stop*, *Wrong Mountain*.

PIRO, JACQUELYN Born January 8, 1965 in Boston, MA. Graduate Boston U. OB debut 1987 in *Company*, followed by *Suburb*, Bdwy in *Les Miserables* (1990), *Sweet Adeline* (Encores).

PITONIAK, ANNE Born March 30, 1922 in Westfield, MA. Attended U. NC Women's Col. Debut 1982 OB in *Talking With*, followed by *Young Playwrights Festival*, *Phaedra*, *Steel Magnolias*, *Pygmalion*, *The Rose Quartet*, *Batting Cage*, *Last of the Thorntons*, Bdwy debut 1983 in *'night, Mother*, for which she received a 1983 Theatre World Award, followed by *The Octette Bridge Club*, *Picnic*, *Amy's View*, *Uncle Vanya*.

PLAYTEN, ALICE Born August 28, 1947 in New York, NY. Bdwy debut 1960 in *Gypsy*, followed by *Oliver!*, *Hello Dolly!*, *Henry Sweet Henry*, for which she received a 1968 Theatre World Award, *George M.!*, *Spoils of War* (also OB), *Rumors*, *Seussical*, OB in *Promenade*, *The Last Sweet Days of Isaac*, *National Lampoon's Lemmings*, *Valentine's Day*, *Pirates of Penzance*, *Up from Paradise*, *A Visit*, *Sister Mary Ignatius Explains It All*, *An Actor's Nightmare*, *That's It Folks*, *1-2-3-4-5*, *Marathon '90 and '93*, *The Mysteries*, *First Lady Suite*, *Flea in Her Ear*.

POE, RICHARD Born January 25, 1946 in Portola, CA. Graduate U. San Francisco, UC Davis. OB debut 1971 in *Hamlet*, followed by *Seasons Greetings*, *Twelfth Night*, *Naked Rights*, *Approximating Mother*, *Jeffrey*, *View of the Dome*, *Til the Rapture Comes*, Bdwy in *Broadway* (1987), *M. Butterfly*, *Our Country's Good*, *Moon Over Buffalo*, *1776*, *Tom Sawyer*.

POTTS, MICHAEL Born September 21, 1962 in Brooklyn, NY. Graduate Columbia U., Yale U. OB debut 1993 in *Playboy of the West Indies*, followed by *America Play*, *Rent*, *Overtime*, *Mud River Stone*, *Arms and the Man*, *Once Around the City*.

PRESTON, CORLISS Born February 3 in East Chicago, IN. Graduate IN. U., Bristol Old Vic. OB debut 1988 in *Hired Man*, followed by *The Cherry Orchard*, *Alive by Night*, *A Piece of My Heart*, *The Erotica Project's Cunning Stunts*, *Boss Grady's Boys*.

PRINCE, FAITH Born August 5, 1957 in Augusta, GA. Graduate U. of Cincinnati. OB debut 1981 in *Scrambled Feet*, followed by *Olympus on My Mind*, *Groucho*, *Living Color*, *Bad Habits*, *Falsettoland*, *3 of Hearts*, *The Torchbearers*, *Ancestral Voices*, Bdwy in *Jerome Robbins' Broadway* (1989), *Nick & Nora*, *Guys and Dolls* (1992), *Fiorello* (Encores), *What's Wrong with This Picture*, *DuBarry Was a Lady* (Encores), *King and I*, *Little Me*, *James Joyce's The Dead*, *Bells Are Ringing*.

Dan Remmes

Don Richard

Derdriu Ring

James Riordan

Jana Robbins

Grant Rossenmeyer

PRUITT, RICHARD Born January 20, 1950 in New Albany, IN. Graduate IN U. OB debut 1987 in *Wicked Philanthropy*, followed by *Bat Boy*, Bdwy in *On the Waterfront* (1995).

PUENTE, RICARDO Born March 1, 1962 in Brooklyn, NY. Attended AMDA. OB debut 2000 in *Four Guys Named Jose.*

PURL, LINDA Born September 2, 1955 in Greenwich, CT. Attended Toho Geino, NYU. Bdwy debut 1998 in *Getting and Spending*, followed by *Tom Sawyer*, OB debut 1991 in *The Baby Dance.*

QUILTY, JOHN Born September 9, 1970 in Philadelphia, PA. OB debut 2000 in *The Countess.*

QUINN, PATRICK Born February 12, 1950 in Philadelphia, PA. Graduate Temple U. Bdwy debut 1976 in *Fiddler on the Roof*, followed by *Day in Hollywood/Night in the Ukraine, Oh, Coward!, Lend Me a Tenor, Damn Yankees, Beauty and the Beast, Boys from Syracuse* (Encores), *A Class Act*, OB in *It's Better with a Bank, By Strouse, Forbidden Broadway, Best of Forbidden Broadway, Raft of Medusa, Forbidden Broadway's 10th Anniversary, A Helluva Town, After the Ball, Wonderful Town.*

RAGNO, JOSEPH Born March 11, 1936 in Brooklyn, NY. Attended Allegheny Col. OB debut 1960 in *Worm in the Horseradish*, followed by *Elizabeth the Queen, Country Scandal, The Shrike, Cymbeline, Love Me Love My Children, Interrogation of Havana, The Birds, Armenians, Feedlot, Every Place in Newark, Modern Romance, Hunting Cockroaches, Just Say No, The Return, Black Marble Shoeshine Stand, Power Failure, The Vocal Lords*, Bdwy debut 1969 in *Indians*, followed by *Iceman Cometh, Sound of Music.*

RAIKEN, LAWRENCE/LARRY Born February 5, 1949 in Long Island, NY. Graduate William & Mary Col., UNC. OB debut 1979 in *Wake Up It's Time to Go to Bed*, followed by *Rise of David Levinsky, Bells Are Ringing, Pageant, Talley's Folly*, Bdwy in *Woman of the Year* (1981), *Sheik of Avenue B, Follies* 2001.

RAITER, FRANK Born January 17, 1932 in Cloquet, MN. Graduate Yale U. Bdwy debut 1958 in *Cranks*, followed by *Dark at the Top of the Stairs, J.B., Camelot, Salome, Sacrilege*, OB in *Soft Core Pornographer, Winter's Tale, Twelfth Night, Tower of Evil, Endangered Species, Bright Room Called Day, Learned Ladies, 'Tis Pity She's A Whore, Othello, Comedy of Errors, Orestes, Marathon Dancing, Sudden Devotion, The Devils, Defying Gravity, Cymbeline, Troilus and Cressida.*

RAMOS, RICHARD RUSSELL Born August 23, 1941 in Seattle, WA. Graduate U. MN. Bdwy debut 1968 in *House of Atreus*, followed by *Arturo Ui, Major Barbara*, OB in *Adaptation, Screens, Lotta, Tempest, Midsummer Night's Dream, Gorky, The Seagull, Entertaining Mr. Sloane, Largo Desolato, Henry IV Parts I and 2, Dog Opera.*

RAMSAY, REMAK Born February 2, 1937 in Baltimore, MD. Graduate Princeton U. OB debut 1964 in *Hang Down Your Head and Die*, followed by *Real Inspector Hound, Landscape of the Body, All's Well That Ends Well* (CP), *Rear Column, Winslow Boy, Dining Room, Save Grand Central, Quartermaine's Terms, Misalliance, Thief River*, Bdwy in *Half a Sixpence, Sheep on the Runway, Lovely Ladies Kind Gentlemen, On the Town, Jumpers, Private Lives, Dirty Linen, Every Good Boy Deserves Favor, The Devil's Disciple, Woman in Mind, Nick and Nora, St. Joan, Moliere Comedies, Heiress.*

REMMES, DAN Born August 19, 1966 in Stoughton, MA. Graduate AADA. OB debut 1989 in *I Love Lucy Who?*, followed by *Pvt. Wars, What Doesn't Kill Us, Waiting Women, Café Encounters, Bedlam.*

RICHARD, DON Born August 30, 1959 in Lexington, KY. Graduate U. of KY, OK U. Bdwy debut 2000 in *Jane Eyre.*

RICHARDSON, JOELY Born Jan 9, 1965 in London, England. OB debut 2001 in *Madame Melville*, for which she received a 2001 Theatre World Award.

RIGBY, TERENCE Born January 2, 1937 in Birmingham, England. Graduate RADA. Bdwy debut 1967 in *The Homecoming*, followed by *No Man's Land, Hamlet, Amadeus*, OB in *Richard III, Troilus and Cressida, Saved.*

RING, DERDRIU Born April 11, 1973 in Cahirsiveen, CO. Kerry, Ireland. Attended U. Col. Cork. OB debut 2000 in *The Hostage*, followed by *A Life.*

RIORDAN, JAMES Born February 15, 1970. Graduate Temple U. OB debut 2000 in *The Countess.*

RIPLEY, ALICE Born December 14, 1963 in San Leandro, CA. Graduate Kent St. U. Bdwy debut 1993 in *Tommy*, followed by *Sunset Blvd, King David, Side Show, Li'l Abner* (Encores), *Les Miserables, James Joyce's The Dead, Rocky Horror Show.*

RITTER, JOHN Born September 17, 1948 in Los Angeles, CA. Graduate USC. Bdwy debut 2000 in *The Dinner Party.*

RIVERA, EILEEN Born March 3, 1970 in Queens, NY. Graduate Boston U. OB debut 1995 in *Cambodia Agonistes*, followed by *Portrait of the Artist as Filipino, Shanghai Lil's, He Who Says Yes/He Who Says No, Li'l Brown Brother/Nikimalika, Dogeaters.*

ROBBINS, JANA Born April 18, 1947 in Johnstown, PA. Graduate Stephens Col. Bdwy debut 1974 in *Good News*, followed by *I Love My Wife, Crimes of the Heart, Romance/Romance, Gypsy, The Tale of the Allergist's Wife*, OB in *Tickles by Tucholsky, Tip-Toes, All Night Strut, Colette Collage, Circus Gothic, Ad Hock, So Long 174th St.*

ROBERTS, ANGELA Born October 25, 1961 in Pasadena, TX. Graduate Rice U., So. Methodist U. OB debut 1990 in *Love's Labours Lost*, followed by *Twelfth Night, Extras, Spirit of Man.*

ROBINS, LAILA Born March 14, 1959 in St. Paul, MN. Graduate U. WI, Yale U. Bdwy debut 1984 in *The Real Thing*, followed by *Herbal Bed*, OB in *Bloody Poetry, Film Society, For Dear Life, Maids of Honor, Extra Man, Merchant of Venice, Mrs. Klein, Tiny Alice.*

ROGERS, GIL Born February 4, 1934 in Lexington, KY. Attended Harvard U. OB in *Ivory Branch, Vanity of Nothing, Warrior's Husband, Hell Bent for Heaven, Gods of Lighting, Pictures in a Hallway, Rose, Memory Bank, A Recent Killing, Birth, Come Back Little Sheba, Life of Galileo, Remembrance, Mortally Fine, Frankie, History of President JFK Part I, On Deaf Ears, Second Summer*, Bdwy in *Great White Hope, Best Little Whorehouse in Texas, Corn is Green* (1983).

ROGERS, MICHAEL Born December 8, 1954 in Trinidad. Attended LIU, Yale U. OB debut 1974 in *Elena*, followed by *Chiaroscuro, Forty Deuce, Antigone, Julius Caesar, Insufficient Evidence, Othello, Young Playwrights '90, Salt, Troilus and Cressida.*

ROI, NATACHA Born December 9 in Lennoxville, Canada. Graduate Boston Conservatory, NYU. Bdwy debut in *Wait Until Dark*, followed by *Closer*, OB in *Three Birds Alighting on a Field, Passion Play.*

ROOP, RENO Born December 19 in Narva, Estonia. Graduate Goodman Theatre. OB debut 1965 in *Medea*, followed by *Hamlet, Timon of Athens, How Far Is It to Babylon?*, Bdwy in *Emperor Henry IV, Freedom of the City, Sound of Music, Judgment at Nuremberg.*

ROSENMEYER, GRANT Born July 3, 1991 in Manhasset, NY. OB debut 2000 in *Macbeth.*

ROSEN-STONE, MEKENZIE Born January 12, 1988 in Baltimore, MD. Bdwy debut 1997 in *Annie*, followed by *Tom Sawyer.*

ROSS, JAMIE Born May 4, 1939 in Markinch, Scotland. Attended RADA. Bdwy debut 1962 in *Little Moon of Alban*, followed by *Moon Besieged, Ari, Different Times, Woman of the Year, La Cage aux Folles, 42nd Street, Gypsy* (1990), *Gentlemen Prefer Blondes* (1995), OB in *Penny Friend, Oh Coward!, Approaching Zanzibar, Tale of the Allergist's Wife.*

ROTHMAN, JOHN Born June 3, 1949 in Baltimore, MD. Graduate Wesleyan U., Yale U. OB debut 1978 in *Rats Nest*, followed by *Impossible H.L. Mencken, Buddy System, Rosario and the Gypsies, Italian Straw Hat, Modern Ladies of Guanabacoa, Faith Hope Charity, Some Americans Abroad, EST Marathon '92, Death Defying Acts, Goodnight Children Everywhere, Arsenic and Old Lace* (CC), Bdwy in *End of the World...*(1984), *Some Americans Abroad.*

RUBIN-VEGA, DAPHNE Born November 18, 1968 in Panama. Bdwy debut 1996 in *Rent* (also OB), for which she received a 1996 Theatre World Award, followed by *Rocky Horror Show*, OB in *Two Sisters and a Piano, Gum.*

RUDD, PAUL Born April 6, 1969 in Passaic, NJ. Graduate U. KS, AADA/West. OB debut 1993 in *Bloody Poetry*, followed by *Alice in Bed*, Bdwy debut 1996 in *Last Night of Ballyhoo.*

RYALL, WILLIAM Born September 18, 1954 in Binghamton, NY. Graduate AADA. OB debut 1979 in *Canterbury Tales*, followed by *Elizabeth and Essex, He Who Gets Slapped, Sea Gull, Tartuffe, Little Kit*, Bdwy debut 1986 in *Me and My Girl*, followed by *Grand Hotel, Best Little Whorehouse Goes Public, How to Succeed in Business Without Really Trying* (1995), *High Society, Amadeus, Seussical.*

RYAN, AMY Born May 3, 1968 in New York, NY. OB debut 1988 in *A Shayna Maidel*, followed by *Rimers of Eldritch, Eleemosynary, Marking, Hysterical Blindness, Imaging Brad, The Stumbling Tongue, Saved, Crimes of the Heart*, Bdwy in *Sisters Rosensweig* (1993), *Uncle Vanya.*

RYAN, THOMAS JAY Born August 1, 1962 in Pittsburgh, PA. Graduate Carnegie Mellon. OB debut 1992 in *Samuel's Major Problem*, followed by *Egypt, My Head was a Sledgehammer, Robert Zucco, Dracula, Venus, South, Juno and the Paycock.*

SALAMANDYK, TIM Born February 25, 1967 in Minneapolis, MN. Graduate Wesleyan U. OB debut 1996 in *Food Chain*, followed by *Green Heart*, Bdwy in *Bloomer Girl* (CC).

SALATA, GREGORY Born July 21, 1949 in New York, NY. Graduate Queens Col. Bdwy debut 1975 in *Dance with Me*, followed by *Equus, Bent*, OB in *Piaf: A Remembrance, Sacraments, Measure for Measure, Subject of Childhood, Jacques and His Master, Androcles and the Lion, Madwoman of Chaillot, Beauty Part, Heartbreak House, Filumena, Boy Meets Girl, The Admirable Crichton.*

SAMUEL, PETER Born August 15, 1958 in Pana, IL. Graduate E. IL. U. Bdwy debut 1981 in *The First*, followed by *Joseph and His Amazing Technicolor Dreamcoat, Three Musketeers, Rags, Les Miserables, The Secret Garden, Parade, Maria Christine*, OB in *Human Comedy, 3 Guys Naked from the Waist Down, Road to Hollywood, Elizabeth and Essex, Little Eyolf, King David, Old Money.*

SANTIAGO-HUDSON, RUBEN Born 1957 in Lackawanna, NY. Attended SUNY Binghamton, Wayne St. U. OB debut in *Soldier's Play*, followed by *Measure for Measure, East Texas Hot Links, Ceremonies in Dark Old Men, Deep Down, Lackawanna Blues*, Bdwy in *Jelly's Last Jam* (1992), *Seven Guitars.*

SCHAFER, SCOTT Born August 26, 1958 in Chicago, IL. Graduate DePaul U. OB debut 1980 in *Aphrodite: The Witch Play*, followed by *Babes in Toyland, Sally, Beauty Thing, Boy Meets Girl, The Admirable Crichton*, Bdwy in *Raggedy Ann* (1986).

SCIOTTO, ERIC Born March 18, 1975 in Altoona, PA. Cinnicati's Col. Cons. of Music. Bdwy debut 1999 in *Annie Get Your Gun.*

SCOTT, MICHAEL Born January 24, 1954 in Santa Monica, CA. Attended CA St. U. Bdwy debut 1978 in *Best Little Whorehouse in Texas* (also OB), followed by *Happy New Year, Show Boat* (1994), OB in *Leave It to Me, A Country Christmas Carol.*

SEAMON, EDWARD Born April 15, 1937 in San Diego, CA. Attended San Diego St. Col. OB debut 1971 in *Life and Times of J. Walter Smintheus*, followed by *The Contractor, The Family, Fishing, Feedlot, Cabin 12, Rear Column, Devour the Snow, Buried Child, Friends, Extenuating Circumstances, Confluence, Richard II, Great Grandson of Jedediah Kohler, Marvelous Gray, Time Framed, Master Builder, Fall Hookup, Fool for Love, The Harvesting, Country for Old Men, Love's Labour's Lost, Caligula, Mound Builders, Quiet in the Land, Talley & Son, Tomorrow's Monday, Ghosts, Or Mice and Men, Beside Herself, You Can't Think of Everything, Tales of the Last Formicans, Love Diatribe, Empty Hearts, Sandbox, Winter's Tale, Cymbeline, Barber of Seville, Venice Preserv'd, The Forest, Richard II, Candida, School for Scandal, The Country Wife, The Miser, The Seagull, Merry Wives of Windsor, The Cherry Orchard*, Bdwy in *The Trip Back Down* (1977), *Devour the Snow, American Clock.*

Jamie Ross

Daphne Rubin-Vega

Amy Ryan

James Sie

Emily Skinner

Pete Starrett

SEDGWICK, KYRA Born August 19, 1965 in New York, NY. Attended USC. OB debut 1981 in *Time Was*, followed by *Dakota's Belly Wyoming, Not Waving, Thicker Than Water, Twelfth Nite, Stranger*, Bdwy debut 1989 in *Ah, Wilderness!*, for which she received a 1989 Theatre World Award.

SEGAL, HOLIDAY Born August 28, 1987 in New York, NY. Bdwy debut 1998 in *High Society*, followed by *Bobbi Boland*.

SELBY, WILLIAM Born November 22, 1961 in Melrose, MA. Graduate Emerson Col. OB debut 1987 in *Apple Tree*, followed by *Juba, Forbidden Bdwy, Forbidden Hollywood, Forbidden Bdwy Strikes Back, Forbidden Bdwy Cleans Up Its Act*.

SELDES, MARIAN Born August 23, 1928 in New York, NY. Attended Neighborhood Playhouse. Bdwy debut 1947 in *Media*, followed by *Crime and Punishment, That Lady, Town Beyond Tragedy, Ondine, On High Ground, Come of Age, Chalk Garden, Milk Train Doesn't Stop Here Anymore, The Wall, Gift of Time, Delicate Balance, Before You Go, Father's Day, Equus, The Merchant, Deathtrap, Boys from Syracuse* (Encores), *Ivanov, Ring Round the Moon*, OB in *Different, Ginger Man, Mercy Street, Isadora Duncan Sleeps with the Russian Navy, Painting Churches, Gertrude Stein and Companion, Richard II, The Milk Train Doesn't Stop…, Bright Room Called Day, Another Time, Three Tall Women, The Torchbearers, Dear Liar, The Butterfly Collection, The Play about the Baby*.

SHAKAR, MARTIN Born January 1, 1940 in Detroit, MI. Attended Wayne St. U. Bdwy debut 1969 in *Our Town*, OB in *Lorenzaccio, Macbeth, The Infantry, American Pastoral, No Place to Be Somebody, World of Mrs. Solomon, And Whose Little Boy Are You?, Investigation of Havana, Night Watch, Owners, Actors, Richard III, Transfiguration of Benno Blimpie, Jack Gelber's New Play, Biko Inquest, Second Story Sunlight, Secret Thighs of New England, After the Fall, Faith Healer, Hunting Cockroaches, Yellow Dog contract, Marathon '90, How to Sacrifice a Child, Redfest, Birth Marks, More Lies about Jerzy*.

SHIPLEY, SANDRA Born February 1 in Rainham, Kent, England. Attended New Col. of Speech and Drama, London U. OB debut 1988 in *Six Characters in Search of an Author*, followed by *Big Time, Kindertransport, Venus, Backward Glance, Phaedra in Delirium, Arms and the Man, The Clearing, Once Around the City*, Bdwy 1995 in *Indiscretions*, followed by *Deep Blue Sea*.

SIE, JAMES Born December 18, 1962 in Summit, NJ. Graduate Northwestern U. OB debut 2000 in *Straight as a Line*.

SIGNOR, TARI Born in PA. Graduate Juilliard. OB debut 1996 in *Death Defying Acts*, followed by *Trelawny of the Wells, Heartbreak House, Mr. Peter's Connections, Troilus and Cressida*.

SKINNER, EMILY Born June 29, 1970 in Richmond, VA. Graduate Carnegie Mellon U. Bdwy debut 1994 in *Christmas Carol* (MSG) followed by *Jekyll & Hyde, Side Show, The Full Monty*, OB in *Watbanaland, James Joyce's The Dead*.

SKINNER, MARGO Born January 3, 1950 in Middletown, OH. Graduate Boston U. OB debut 1980 in *Missing Persons*, followed by *The Dining Room, Mary Barnes, The Perfect Party, Spare Parts, Oedipus the King, Game of Love and Chance, Durang Durang, Mrs. Warren's Profession, Boss Grady's Boys*.

SLEZAK, VICTOR Born July 7, 1957 in Youngstown, OH. OB debut 1979 in *Electra Myth*, followed by *Hasty Heart, Ghosts, Alice and Fred, Window Claire, Miracle Worker, Talk Radio, Marathon '88, One Act Festival, Briar Patch, Appointment with a High Wire Lady, Sam I Am, White Rose, Born Guilty, Naked Truth, Ivanov, Mafia on Prozac, Tesla's Letters, 24 Years, Bacchanalia, Other People*, Bdwy in *Any Given Day* (1993), *Garden District, Jackie*.

SMIAR, BRIAN Born August 27, 1937 in Cleveland, OH. Graduate Kent State U., Emerson Col. OB debut 1982 in *Edmund*, followed by *3X3, True to Life, Young Playwrights Festival, Marathon '90, Winter's Tale, Cellini*, Bdwy in *Mixed Emotions* (1993).

SNOW, DAN Born April 24, 1951 in Pittsburgh, PA. Graduate Edinboro U. OB debut 1975 in *Salome*, followed by *Geneva, No Honey, The Cannibals, Richard III, W.E.B. DuBois Prophet in Limbo*.

SOPHIEA, CYNTHIA Born October 26, 1954 in Flint, MI. Bdwy debut 1981 in *My Fair Lady*, followed by *She Loves Me, Victor Victoria*, OB in *Lysistrata, Sufragette, Golden Apple, Winter's Tale, Petrified Prince, Leaving Queens*.

SORGE, JOEY Born July 28, 1969 in Washington, DC. Graduate U. of MD. OB debut 2000 in *Saturday Night Fever*, followed by *Follies* 2001.

SPAISMAN, ZYPORA Born January 2, 1920 in Lublin, Poland. OB debut 1955 in *Lonesome Ship*, followed by *My Father's Court, Thousand and One Nights, Eleventh Inheritor, Enchanting Melody, Fifth Commandment, Bronx Express, Melody Lingers On, Yoshke Musikant, Stempenya, Generation of Green Fields, Ship, Play for the Devil, Broome Street America, Flowering Peach, Riverside Drive, Big Winner, Land of Dreams, Father's Inheritance, At the Crossroads, Stempenyu, Mirele Efros, Double Identity, Maiden of Ludmir, Blacksmith's Folly, Green Fields*.

SPENCER, REBECCA Born April 29, 1960 in Levittown, PA. Graduate Ithaca Col. OB debut 1986 in *Desert Song*, followed by *Watch Your Step, A Connecticut Yankee in King Arthur's Court* (CC), Bdwy in *Call Me Madam* (Encores/1995), *Jekyll & Hyde*.

Cheryl Stern

Larry Swansen

Mary Testa

Clif Thorn

Jonathan Tindle

Chris Tomaino

STANLEY, DOROTHY Born November 18 in Hartford, CT. Graduate Ithaca Col., Carnegie Mellon U. OB debut 1978 in *Gay Divorce*, followed by *Dames at Sea*, Bdwy in *Sugar Babies* (1980), *Annie, 42nd Street, Broadway, Jerome Robbins' Broadway, Kiss of the Spider Woman, Show Boat* (1984), *High Society, Follies* 2001.

STARK, MOLLY Born in New York, NY. Graduate Hunter Col. OB debut 1969 in *Sacco-Vanzetti*, followed by *Riders to the Sea, Medea, One Cent Plain, Elisabeth and Essex, Principally Pinter, Toulouse, Winds of Change, The Education of Hyman Kaplan, The Land of Dreams, Beau Jest, Mamaleh!*, Bdwy in *Molly* (1973).

STARRETT, PETE Born November 4, 1970 in Fitchburg, MA. OB debut 1997 in *Blue Man Group: Tubes*, followed *by Letters From Cuba, Other People, Saved.*

STEIN, ADAM Born January 28, 1972 in Ft. Knox, KY. Graduate Yale U., NYU. OB debut 1995 in *Uncle Bob*, followed by *Skin of Our Teeth, Hotel Universe, More Lies about Jerzy*, Bdwy in *Iceman Cometh.*

STENDER, DOUG Born September 14, 1942 in Nanticoke, PA. Graduate Princeton U., RADA. Bdwy debut 1973 in *Changing Room*, followed by *Run for Your Wife, The Visit*, OB in *New England Elective, Hamlet, Second Man, How He Lied to Her Husband, Bhutan, Clothes for a Summer Hotel, The Libertine, John Gabriel Borkman, Blithe Spirit.*

STERN, CHERYL Born July 1, 1956 in Buffalo, NY. Graduate Northwestern U. OB debut 1984 in *Daydreams*, followed by *White Lies, Pets, That's Life!, I Love You You're Perfect, Now Change, Game Show.*

STEVENSON, JAMES Born November 18, 1930 in New York, NY. Graduate Vanderbilt U. Bdwy debut 1957 in *Goodbye Again*, followed by *The Wall, Don't Drink the Water, Forty Carats, Hello Dolly*, OB in *Once Upon a Mattress* (1959), *Seascape, Period of Adjustment, The Country Girl, All Over.*

STEWART, GWEN Born September 5, 1963 in Newark, NJ. OB debut 1986 in *Mama I Want to Sing*, followed by *God's Creation, Suds, Oedipus Private Eye, Starmites*, Bdwy debut 1989 in *Starmites*, followed by *Truly Blessed, Rent.*

STILLER, JERRY Born June 8, 1931 in New York, NY. Graduate Syracuse U. OB debut 1953 in *Coriolanus*, followed by *Power and the Glory, Golden Apple, Measure for Measure, Taming of the Shrew, Carefree Tree, Diary of a Scoundrel, Romeo and Juliet, As You Like It, Two Gentlemen of Verona, Passione, Prairie/Shawl, Much Ado about Nothing, After-Play, Down the Garden Paths*, Bdwy in *The Ritz* (1975), *Unexpected Guests, Passione, Hurlyburly* (also OB), 3 *Men on a Horse, What's Wrong with This Picture?, Three Sisters.*

STILLMAN, BOB (ROBERT) Born December 2, 1954 in New York, NY. Graduate Princeton U. OB debut 1981 in *The Haggadah*, followed by *Street Scene, Lola, No Frills Revue, Six Wives, Last Session, Saturn Returns*, Bdwy in *Grand Hotel* (1989), *Dirty Blonde* (and OB).

STONE, DANTON Born in Queens, NY. OB debut 1976 in *Mrs. Murray's Farm*, followed by *In This Fallen City, Say Goodnight Gracie, Angels Fall, Balm in Gilead, Fortune's Fools, Mere Mortals and Others*, Bdwy in *5th of July* (1980), *One Flew Over the Cuckoo's Nest.*

STORCH, LARRY Born January 8, 1923 in New York, NY. Bdwy debut 1958 in *Who Was That Lady I Saw You With?*, followed by *Porgy and Bess* (1983), *Arsenic and Old Lace, Annie Get Your Gun*, OB in *The Littlest Revue* (1956), *Breaking Legs, Things You Shouldn't Say Past Midnight.*

STOUT, MARY Born April 8, 1952 in Huntington, WV. Graduate Marshall U. OB debut 1980 in *Plain and Fancy*, followed by *The Sound of Music, Crisp, A Christmas Carol, Song for a Saturday, Prizes, Golden Apple, Identical Twins from Baltimore, Snapshots*, Bdwy in *Copperfield* (1981), *Change in the Heir, My Favorite Year, Jane Eyre.*

STRATTON, HANK Born in Long Beach, CA. Attended LAMDA. OB debut 1993 in *Jeffrey*, followed by *Lady in the Dark* (CC), Bdwy debut 2000 in *Man Who Came to Dinner.*

STUHLBARG, MICHAEL Born in Long Beach, CA. Attended UCLA, Juilliard. Bdwy debut 1992 in *Saint Joan*, followed by *Three Men on a Horse, Timon of Athens, The Government Inspector, Taking Sides, Cabaret, The Invention of Love*, OB in *As You Like It*, followed by *Woyzeck, All's Well That Ends Well, Richard II, Henry VIII, A Dybbuk, The Winter's Tale.*

SULLIVAN, KIM Born July 21, 1952 in Philadelphia, PA. Graduate NYU. OB debut 1972 in *Black Terror*, followed by *Legend of the West, Deadwood Dick, Big Apple Messenger, Dreams Deferred, Raisin in the Sun, The Tempest, Ground People, Celebration, In My Father's House, Hundred Penny Box, The Missing Face.*

SULLIVAN, K.T. Born October 31, 1953 in Coalgate, OK. Graduate OK U. Bdwy debut 1989 in 3 *Penny Opera*, followed by *Gentlemen Prefer Blondes* (1995), OB debut 1992 in *A...My Name Is Still Alice*, followed by *Splendora, So Long 174th St, Gershwin's American Rhapsody.*

SUTCLIFFE, STEVEN Born October 19 in Lindsay, Ontario, Canada. Attended Ryerson Theatre Sch. Bdwy debut 1998 in *Ragtime*, for which he received a 1998 Theatre World Award, OB in *A Connecticut Yankee in King Arthur's Court* (CC).

SWANSEN, LARRY Born November 10, 1930 in Roosevelt, OK. Graduate U. OK. Bdwy debut 1966 in *Those That Play the Clowns*, followed by *Great White Hope, King and I*, OB in *Dr. Faustus Lights the Lights, Thistle in My Bed, Darker Flower, Vincent, MacBird, Unknown Soldier and His Wife, Sound of Music, Conditioning of Charlie One, Ice Age, Prince of Homburg, Who's There?, Heart of a Dog, Grandma Pray for Me, Frankenstein, Knights of the Round Table, Returner, House of Mirth, On the Middle Watch, Welcome to Our City*.

TALMAN, ANN Born September 13, 1957 in Welch, WV. Graduate PA St. U. OB debut 1980 in *What's So Beautiful about a Sunset over Prairie Avenue?*, followed by *Louisiana Summer, Winterplay, Prairie Avenue, Broken Eggs, Octoberfest, We're Home, Yours Anne, Songs on a Shipwrecked Sofa, House Arrest, One Act Festival, Freud's House, Random Harvest, Cat's Paw*, Bdwy in *Little Foxes* (1981), *House of Blue Leaves, Some Americans Abroad* (also OB), *Better Days*.

TAYLOR, MYRA (LUCRETIA) Born July 9, 1960 in Ft. Motte, SC. Graduate Yale U. OB debut 1985 in *Dennis*, followed by *The Tempest, Black Girl, Marathon 86, Phantasie, Walking the Dead, I Am a Man, Marathon Dancing, Come Down Burning, American Clock, Force Continuum*, Bdwy in *A Streetcar Named Desire* (1987), *Mule Bone, Chronicle of a Death Foretold, Electra, Macbeth*.

TESTA, MARY Born June 4, 1955 in Philadelphia, PA. Attended U. RI. OB debut 1979 in *In Trousers*, followed by *Company, Life Is Not a Doris Day Movie, Not-So-New Faces of 1982, American Princess, Mandrake, 4 One-Act Musicals, Next Please!, Daughters, One-Act Festival, The Knife, Young Playwrights Festival, Tiny Mommy, Finnegan's Funeral and Ice Cream Shop, Peter Breaks Through, Lucky Stiff, 1-2-3-4-5, Scapin, Hello Muddah Hello Faddah, Broken English, On the Town, A New Brain, From Above, Ziegfeld Follies of 1936, Haile, Mary!, Tartuffe, The Wax*, Bdwy in *Barnum* (1980), *Marilyn, The Rink, A Funny Thing Happened on the Way to the Forum* (1996), *On the Town, Marie Christine*.

THOMAS, RAY ANTHONY Born December 19, 1956 in Kentwood, LA. Graduate U. TX, El Paso. OB debut 1981 in *Escape to Freedom*, followed by *Sun Gets Blue, Blues for Mr. Charlie, Hunchback of Notre Dame, Ground People, The Weather Outside, One Act Festival, Caucasian Chalk Circle, Virgin Molly, Black Eagles, Distant Fires, Shaker Heights, The Lights, Dancing on Moonlight, Volunteer Man, The Devils, Force Continuum, Saved or Destroyed, The Beginning of August*.

THOMPSON, EVAN Born September 3, 1931 in New York, NY. Graduate U. CA. Bdwy debut 1969 in *Jimmy*, followed by *1776, City of Angels, Ivanov*, OB in *Mahogonny, Treasure Island, Knitters in the Sun, HalfLife, Fasnacht Dau, Importance of Being Earnest, Under the Gaslight, Henry V, The Fantasticks, Walk the Dog Willie, Macbeth, 1984, Leave It to Me, Earth and Sky, No Conductor, Nightmare Alley, The Family Reunion, O'Neill, Buying Time*.

THOMPSON, JENNIFER LAURA Born December 5, 1969 in Southfield, MI. Graduate U. MI, AADA. OB debut 1994 in *A Doll's Life*, followed by *Urinetown*, Bdwy debut 1998 in *Strike Up the Band* (Encores).

THORN, CLIF Born August 11, 1964 in Little Rock, AK. Graduate USC. OB debut 1994 in *Forever Plaid*, followed by *Du Barry was a Lady* (CC), Bdwy 1998 in *Les Miserables*.

TINDLE, JONATHAN OB debut 2000 in *Welcome to Our City*.

TIRRELL, BARBARA Born November 24, 1953 in Nahant, MA. Graduate Temple U., Webber-Douglas Acad. OB debut 1977 in *Six Characters in Search of an Author*, followed by *Cyrano, Romeo and Juliet, Louis Quinse, Day Out of Time, King Lear, Oedipus Texas, Father West, Leaving Queens*, Bdwy in *Annie* (1997).

TITONE, THOMAS Born March 24, 1959 in Secaucus, NJ. Attended NC Sch. of Arts. with Amer. Ballet Th. before Bdwy debut 1992 in *Most Happy Fella*, followed by *My Favorite Year, Once Upon a Mattress* (1996), OB in *Hunchback of Notre Dame, A Prophet Among Them*.

TOMAINO, CHRIS Born March 8, 1967 in Long Branch, NJ. Graduate IN U., Monmouth U. OB debut 1998 in *The Jello is Always Red*, followed by *Strictly Personal*.

TONER, THOMAS Born May 25, 1928 in Homestead, PA. Graduate UCLA. Bdwy debut 1973 in *Tricks*, followed by *The Good Doctor, All Over Town, The Elephant Man, California Suite, A Texas Trilogy, The Inspector General, Me and My Girl, The Secret Garden*, OB in *Pericles, The Merry Wives of Windsor, A Midsummer Night's Dream, Richard III, My Early Years, Life and Limb, Measure for Measure, Little Footsteps, Saturday Mourning Cartoons, The Family Reunion, Boss Grady's Boys*.

TRAMMELL, SAM. Born May 15, 1971 in Los Angeles, CA. Graduate Brown U. OB debut 1997 in *Wir Spielen Seechach*, followed by *Dealers Choice, My Night with Reg, Ancestral Voices, If Memory Serves, Kit Marlowe*, Bdwy debut 1998 in *Ah, Wilderness!*, for which he won a 1998 Theatre World Award.

TUCKER, ALLYSON Born August 14 in Milwaukee, WI. Graduate Brown U. OB debut 1985 in *De Obeah Man*, Bdwy debut 1989 in *Oh Kay!*, followed by *Will Rogers Follies, Ragtime, Follies 2001*.

URBANIAK, JAMES Born September 17, 1963 in Bayonne, NJ. OB debut 1988 in *Giants of the Mountain*, followed by *The Universe, Imaginary Invalid, South, Mamba's Daughters, Lipstick Traces*.

VANDENBUSSCHE, JORRE Born April 8, 1975 in Brugge, Belgium. Attended Royal Flemish Music Cons. OB debut 2000 in *Alice in Bed*.

VAN DYCK, JENNIFER Born December 23, 1962 in St. Andrews, Scotland. Graduate Brown U. OB debut 1977 in *Gus and Al*, followed by *Marathon '88, Secret Rapture, Earth and Sky, Man in His Underwear, Cheever Evening, Arsenic and Old Lace* (CC), Bdwy in *Secret Rapture, Two Shakespearean Actors, Dancing at Lughnasa*.

VAN NOTE, JILL Born April 1, 1961 in Houlton, ME. Graduate U. of ME, attended University Col. London. OB debut 1994 in *Landscape*, followed by *Murder in the Cathedral, Measure for Measure, As You Like It, A Midsummer Night's Dream, Seascape, All Over*.

VEREEN, BEN Born October 10, 1946 in Miami, FL. OB debut 1965 in *Prodigal Son*, Bdwy in *Sweet Charity, Golden Boy, Hair, Jesus Christ Superstar*, for which he received a 1972 Theatre World Award, *Pippin, Grind, Jelly's Last Jam, Christmas Carol* (MSG).

VIVONA, JEROME Born March 7, 1967 in Bayville, NY. Attended Quinnipac Col., IN U., Nassau CC. Bdwy debut 1994 in *Guys and Dolls*, followed by *How to Succeed in Business Without Really Trying* (1995), *Kiss Me Kate, Seussical*.

WALBYE, KAY Born Ft. Collins, CO. Attended KS St U. OB debut 1984 in *Once on a Summer's Day*, followed by *Majestic Kid, Urinetown*, Bdwy in *Run for Your Wife* (1989), *Secret Garden, Rose Tattoo, Titanic*.

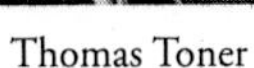

Thomas Toner

Jill Van Note

Colleen Smith Wallnau

Bob Walton

Andrew Weems

C. J. Wilson

WALLNAU, COLLEEN SMITH Born June 28, 1948 in Trenton, NJ. Graduate Emerson Col., Trenton St., Rutgers U. OB debut 1992 in *Thru Darkest Ohio*, followed by *Romeo and Juliet, On the Verge, Beggar on Horseback*, Bdwy in *Crazy for You* (1994).

WALTON, BOB Born June 25, 1960 in Marion, IN. Graduate Cincinnati Cons. of Music. OB debut 1983 in *Preppies*, followed by *Forbidden Broadway Strikes Back, I Love You, You're Perfect, Now Change, Game Show*, Bdwy debut 1990 in *City of Angels*, followed by *Once Upon a Mattress, Ziegfeld Follies of* 1936 (Encores/CC).

WARD, LAUREN Born June 19, 1970 in Lincoln, NE. Graduate NC Sch. of Arts. Bdwy debut 1994 in *Carousel*, followed by 1776, OB in *Jack's Holiday, Violet, Saturday Night Fever, Time and Again.*

WARING, WENDY Born December 7, 1960 in Melrose, MA. Attended Emerson Col. OB debut 1987 in *Wish You Were Here*, followed by *Ziegfeld Follies of* 1936, Bdwy in *Legs Diamond* (1988), *Will Rogers Follies, Crazy for You, Follies* 2001.

WASINIAK, JOHN Born June 12, 1962 in Cleveland, OH. Graduate UCCM, Xavier U. OB debut 1997 in *When Pigs Fly*, followed by *Leave It To Me.*

WATKINS, AMANDA Born August 17, 1973 in Gainesville, GA. Graduate FL St. U. Bdwy debut 1996 in *Grease*, followed by *Beauty and the Beast, Cats*, OB debut 2000 in *The Wild Party*, followed by *Imperfect Chemistry.*

WEAVER, FRITZ Born January 19, 1926 in Pittsburgh, PA. Graduate U. Chicago. Bdwy debut 1955 in *Chalk Garden*, for which he received a 1956 Theatre World Award, followed by *Protective Custody, Miss Lonelyhearts, All American, Lorenzo, The White House, Baker Street, Child's Play, Absurd Person Singular, Angels Fall, The Crucible* (1991), *A Christmas Carol, Ring Round The Moon*, OB in *The Way of the World, White Devil, Doctor's Dilemma, Family Reunion, Power and the Glory, Great God Brown, Peer Gynt, Henry IV, My Fair Lady* (CC), *Lincoln, Biko Inquest, The Price, Dialogue for Lovers, A Tale Told, Time Framed, Wrong Turn at Lungfish, The Professional, Don Juan in Hell, Ancestral Voices, A Life.*

WEBB, JEREMY Born June 10, 1972 in Ithaca, NY. Attended NC Sch. of the Arts. OB debut 2000 in *Tabletop.*

WEEMS, ANDREW Born July 18, 1961 in Seoul, S. Korea. Graduate Brown U., U. CA. OB debut 1993 in *A Quarrel of Sparrows*, followed by *Marathon Dancing, Mud Angel, Midsummer Night's Dream, Dolphin Position, Green Bird, Mere Mortals and Others*, Bdwy in *London Assurance, Troilus and Cressida, Don't Wink, Princess Turandot.*

WEISS, JEFF Born 1940 in Allentown, PA. OB debut 1986 in *Hamlet*, followed by *Front Page, Casanova, Hot Keys, Henry V, The Wallenberg Mission, Mr. Peter's Connections*, Bdwy in *Macbeth*, (1988), *Our Town, Mastergate, Face Value, Real Inspector Hound/15 Minute Hamlet, Carousel* (1994), *Present Laughter, Ivanov, Iceman Cometh, The Invention of Love.*

WHELIHAN, PAUL Born November 22, 1961 in Philadelphia, PA. Graduate Montclair St. U. OB debut 2000 in *The Flame Keeper.*

WHITE, JANE Born October 30, 1922 in New York, NY. Attended Smith Col. Bdwy debut 1942 in *Strange Fruit*, followed by *Climate of Eden, Take a Giant Step, Jane Eyre, Once Upon a Mattress* (also OB), *Cuban Thing, Follies* 2001, OB in *Razzle Dazzle, Insect Comedy, Power and Glory, Hop Signor, Trojan Women, Iphigenia in Aulis, Cymbeline, Burnt Flowerbed, Rosmersholm, Jane White Who?, Ah Men, Lola, Madwoman of Chaillot, Vivat!Vivat!Regina!, King John, Tropical Breeze Hotel, Petrified Prince, Give the Man a Fish.*

WHITTHORNE, PAUL Born February 17, 1970 in Tucson, AZ. Graduate Juilliard. Bdwy debut 1995 in *The Tempest*, OB in *Orestes: I Murdered My Mother* (1996), *Getting In, Measure for Measure, Uncle Jack, Snapshots* 2000.

WILKOF, LEE Born June 25, 1951 in Canton, OH. Graduate U. of Cincinnati. OB debut 1977 in *Present Tense*, followed by *Little Shop of Horrors, Holding Patterns, Angry Housewives, Assassins, Born Guilty, Treasure Island, Golden Boy, Names, Waiting for Lefty, Mizlansky, Zilinsky, The Stumbling Tongue, Oy!, Do Re Mi, Arsenic and Old Lace* (CC), Bdwy in *Sweet Charity* (1986), *Front Page, She Loves Me, Kiss Me Kate.*

WILLEY, CHARLES Born September 18, 1956 in Abington, PA. Graduate Syracuse U. OB debut 1991 in *Necktie Breakfast*, followed by *Battery, Single and Proud, Holy Note, The Firebugs, Blue Window, Lion in the Streets, Bobby Supreme, The Censor, South of No North.*

WILLIAMS, TREAT Born December 1, 1951 in Rowayton, CT. Bdwy debut 1974 in *Grease*, followed by *Over Here, Once in a Lifetime, Pirates of Penzance, Love Letters, Follies* 2001, OB in *Maybe I'm Doing It Wrong, Love Letters, Some Men Need Help, Oh Hell!, Oleanna, Captains Courageous.*

WILLS, RAY Born September 14, 1960 in Santa Monica, CA. Graduate Wichita St. U., Brandeis U. OB debut 1988 in *Side by Side by Sondheim*, followed by *Kiss Me Quick Before the Lava Reaches the Village, Grand Tour, The Cardigans, The Rothschilds, Hello Muddah Hello Faddah, Little Me, A Backers Audition, All in the Timing, Young Playwrights Festival/Guy World. Wonderful Town, A Class Act*, Bdwy 1993 in *Anna Karenina*, followed by *Big.*

WILLIS, RICHARD Born in Dallas, TX. Graduate Cornell U., Northwestern U. OB debut 1986 in *Three Sisters*, followed by *Nothing to Report, The Rivalry of Dolls, The Time of Your Life, Much Ado About Nothing.*

WILSON, C.J. OB debut 1994 in *The Merry Wives of Windsor*, Bdwy debut 2000 in *Gore Vidal's The Best Man*.

WILSON, PATRICK Born July 3, 1973 in Norfolk, VA. Graduate Carnegie Mellon U. OB debut 1999 in *Bright Lights Big City*, followed by *Tenderloin* (CC), Bdwy in *The Gershwins' Fascinating Rhythm, The Full Monty*.

WING, VIRGINIA Born November 9 in Marks, MS. Graduate MS Col. OB debut 1989 in *Two by Two*, followed by *Food and Shelter, Cambodia Agonistes, America Dreaming, Caucasian Chalk Circle, You Can't Take It with You, Making Tracks, Watcher*.

WINKLER, HENRY Born October 30, 1945 in New York, NY. Graduate Emerson Col., Yale U. OB debut 1973 in *42 Seconds from Broadway*, Bdwy debut 2000 in *The Dinner Party*.

WISE, WILLIAM Born May 11 in Chicago, IL. Attended Bradley U., Northwestern U. OB debut 1970 in *Adaptation/Next*, followed by *Him, Hot l Baltimore, Just the Immediate Family, 36, For the Use of the Hall, Orphans, Working Theatre Festival, Copperhead, Early One Evening at the Rainbow Bar & Grill, Special Interests, Theme and Variations, Marathon '91, Drop in the Bucket, Hysterical Blindness, Quick-Change Room, Belmont Ave. Social Club, Little Airplanes of the Heart, Moving Bodies, Summer Cyclone*.

WISEMAN, JOSEPH Born May 15, 1919 in Montreal, Canada. Attended CCNY. Bdwy in *Journey to Jerusalem, Abe Lincoln in Illinois, Candle in the Wind, The Three Sisters, Storm Operation, Joan of Lorraine, Anthony and Cleopatra, Detective Story, That Lady, King Lear, Golden Boy, The Lark, Zalmen or the Madness God, The Tenth Man, Judgment at Nuremberg*, OB in *Marco Millions, Incident at Vichy, In the Matter of J. Robert Oppenheimer, Enemies, Duchess of Malfi, Last Analysis, The Lesson, The Golem, Unfinished Stories, Slavs!, I Can't Remember Anything*.

WOLF, CATHERINE Born May 25 in Abington, PA. Attended Carnegie Tech. U., Neighborhood Playhouse. Bdwy debut 1976 in *The Innocents*, followed by *Otherwise Engaged, An Inspector Calls*, OB in *A Difficult Burning, I Can't Keep Running in Place, Cloud 9, The Importance of Being Earnest, Miami, American Plan, The Understanding, Second Summer*.

WOODS, CAROL Born November 13, 1943 in Jamaica, NY. Graduate Ithaca Col. OB debut 1980 in *One Mo' Time*, followed by *Blues in the Night, Dreamstuff*, Bdwy in *Grind* (1985), *Big River, Stepping Out, The Crucible, A Little Hotel on the Side, Goodbye Girl, One Touch of Venus* (Encores), *Follies 2001*.

WORTH, IRENE Born June 23, 1916 in Nebraska. Graduate UCLA. Bdwy debut 1943 in *The Two Mrs. Carrolls*, followed by *Cocktail Party, Mary Stuart, Toys in the Attic, King Lear, Tiny Alice, Sweet Bird of Youth, Cherry Orchard, Lady from Dubuque, John Gabriel Borkman*, OB in *Happy Days, Letters of Love and Affection, Chalk Garden, Golden Age, Coriolanus, Edith Wharton, Gypsy and the Yellow Canary, Chère Maitre, Ancestral Voices, Euripides' Medea*.

WRIGHT, VALERIE Born in Las Vegas, NV. Graduate USC. Bdwy debut 1984 in *Cats*, followed by *Song and Dance, Sally Marr & Her Escorts, Damn Yankees* (1994), *Steel Pier, Annie Get Your Gun*, OB in *Showing Off, And the World Goes Round*.

WYLIE, JOHN Born December 14, 1925 in Peacock, TX. Graduate No. TX St. U. OB debut 1987 in *Lucky Spot*, followed by *Life is a Dream, Winter's Tale, Venetian Turn, Cymbeline, Venice Preserv'd, Barber of Seville, School for Scandal, Skyscraper, Richard II, John Gabriel Borkman, Mirandolina, The Urn, The Way of the World, The Oresteia, A Will of His Own, Andromache, The Cherry Orchard*, Bdwy in *Born Yesterday* (1989), *Grand Hotel*.

YOUNG, KAREN Born September 29, 1958 in Pequonnock, NJ. Attended Douglas Col., Rutgers U. OB debut 1982 in *Three Acts of Recognition*, followed by *A Lie of the Mind, Dog Logic, Wifey, Taxicab Chronicles, The Wax*.

YOUNGSMAN, CHRISTOPHER Born October 26, 1972 in Grand Rapids, MI. Bdwy debut 1996 in *Grease!*, OB debut 2000 in *The Gorey Details*.

ZAGNIT, STUART Born March 28 in New Brunswick, NJ. Graduate Montclair St. Col. OB debut 1978 in *The Wager*, followed by *Manhattan Transference, Women in Tune, Enter Laughing, Kuni Leml, Tatterdemalion, Golden Land, Little Shop of Horrors, Lucky Stiff, Grand Tour, Majestic Kid, Made in Heaven, Encore!, A Trip to the Beach, Retribution , A Dybbuk, Good Doctor*, Bdwy in *The Wild Party, Seussical*.

ZORICH, LOUIS Born February 12, 1954 in Chicago, IL. Attended Roosevelt U. OB in *Six Characters in Search of an Author, Crimes and Crimes, Henry V, Thracian Horses, All Women Are One, The Good Soldier Schweik, Shadow of Heroes, To Clothe the Naked, A Memory of Two Mondays, They Knew What They Wanted, The Gathering, True West, The Tempest, Come Day Come Night, Henry IV Parts 1 & 2, The Size of the World, On A Clear Day You Can See Forever* (CC), Bdwy in *Becket, Moby Dick, The Odd Couple, Hadrian VII, Moonchildren, Fun City, Goodtime Charley, Herzl, Death of a Salesman, Arms and the Man, The Marriage of Figaro, She Loves Me, Follies 2001*.

OBITUARIES

Steve Allen

Victor Borge

Val Dufour

David Dukes

José Greco

Sir Alec Guinness

STEVE ALLEN (Stephen Valentine Patrick William Allen) 78, New York, NY-born comedian/composer/talk show host/author/actor, died October 30, 2000, in Los Angeles, CA, of a heart attack. He made his Broadway debut in 1953 in *Pink Elephant*, followed by *Mikado* Off-Broadway in 1995. He wrote the music and lyrics for *Sophie* in 1963, and the book, music, and lyrics for the 1982 revue *Seymour Glick is Alive but Sick*. Best known for his many years as the host of *The Tonight Show* and subsequent television appearances, he also authored over 50 books and composed over 3,000 songs. He is survived by his wife, actress Jayne Meadows sons Bill, Stephen, Jr., Brian, and David, eleven grandchildren, and three great-grandchildren.

GWEN ANDERSON 80, actress, died August 24, 2000, in Cedar Falls, Iowa, of ovarian cancer. Her Broadway credits include *Janie, The Deep Mrs. Sykes,* and *Decision*. Survivors include her husband, Henry Geerdes and daughter, Wendy Burrell Mintzer.

JEAN-PIERRE AUMONT (Jean-Pierre Salomons) 90, Paris, France-born actor/author, died January 29, 2001. He made his Broadway debut in 1942 in *Rose Burke*, followed by *My Name Is Aquilon, Heavenly Twins, Second String, Tovarich, Camino Real* (Lincoln Center), *Days in the Trees*, and *A Talent for Murder*. Off-Broadway credits include *Murderous Angels*.

LYN AUSTIN (Evelyn Austin) 78, Glen Ridge, NJ-born producer, died October 29, 2000, in New York, NY, as the result of injuries sustained by being struck by a taxi. As a producer, credits include Broadway's *Take a Giant Step* in 1953, followed by *Copper and Brass, Joyce Grenfell Requests the Pleasure, Frogs of Springs*, and as an associate of Roger L. Stevens, *Mary, Mary, The Best Man, The Chinese Prime Minister, A Far Country, In the Summer House*, and *Oh Dad, Poor Dad....* Other production credits include *Indians* and *Adaptation/Next*. In 1971, she founded the Music-Theater Group (based both in New York, NY, and in the Berkshire area of Massachusetts), dedicated to music-theater and cross-pollination of the arts. With the Music-Theater Group, she produced over 100 shows, and was a prime progenitor of new theater, producing such artists as Anne Bogart, Eve Ensler, Bill Erwin, and Julie Taymor. The Music Theater Group garnered 20 Obies, including one for sustained achievement. Diane Wondisford, her companion, and her brother, John P. Austin, survive her.

THOMAS BABE 59, playwright/director/teacher, died December 6, 2000, of lung cancer. Frequently produced at the New York Shakespeare Festival/ Public Theater, his credits there include *Kid Champion, Rebel Women, A Prayer for My Daughter*, and *Fathers and Sons*. His subsequent plays were produced by the Mark Taper Forum, the Los Angeles Theater Center, the Denver Center Theater, and the South Coast Repertory, among other venues.

SANDY BARON (Sanford Beresofsky) 63, Brooklyn, NY- born actor, died January 21, 2001, in Van Nuys, CA, of emphysema. His Broadway credits include *Second City, The Premise, Tchin-Tchin, One Flew over the Cuckoo's Nest, Arturo Ui, Generation*, and *Lenny*. Off-Broadway credits include *Muzeeka*. He is perhaps best known for his numerous roles in television and film. His sister survives him.

JONATHAN BIXBY 41, costume designer, died April 29, 2001, of complications from colon cancer. Broadway credits include *Urinetown, Street Corner Symphony, Hello, Dolly!,* and *Strike Up the Band* (Encores). Off-Broadway credits include *The Country Club, The Torch Bearers, Uncle Tom's Cabin; or, Life Among the Lowly, As Bees in Honey Drown, June Moon, Kingdom of Earth, As Thousands Cheer, "hope" is the thing with feathers, The Cocoanuts, Sheba, Advice From A Caterpillar, The Skin of Our Teeth, Man is Man, The Three Sisters, Galileo, Life is a Dream*, and *The Importance of Being Earnest*. Regional credits include *Rhinoceros* at the New Jersey Shakespeare Festival, *Merton of the Movies* at the Geffen Playhouse, *Lives of the Saints* at the Berkshire Theatre Festival, *Sayonara* (L.A. Drama Critics Circle Award), *The Illusion* and *Light Up The Sky* at Merrimack Repertory, *June Moon* at the McCarter Theater, *Man of La Mancha* and *Oklahoma!* at Birmingham Theatre, *A Streetcar Named Desire* and *Caucasian Chalk Circle* at Bloomsberg Theatre Ensemble, and the national tours of *Cirque Ingenieux, The Sound of Music, Brigadoon, The Wiz, Evita, My Fair Lady, Jesus Christ Superstar*, and *West Side Story*. A founding member of Drama Dept., he won an Emmy Award winner for his work in television.

GARY BONASORTE 45, Pittsburgh, PA-born playwright, died November 9, 2000, in New York, NY, of lymphoma. A founder of Rattlestick Theater Company, an Off-Broadway theatre company dedicated to performing new works by new American playwrights, plays which he penned include *Big Hearts, The Aunts, Killing Real Estate Women, Reinventing Big Daddy,* and *Ascendancy.* He was also a founder of the Community Research Institute on AIDS. Survivors include his companion, playwright Terrence McNally, and his father, Francis, brother Mark, and sister Kimberley, all of Pittsburgh, PA.

VICTOR BORGE (Borge Rosenbaum) 91, Danish-born comic piano virtuoso/conductor/writer/director, died December 23, 2000, in Greenwich, CT, of natural causes. Broadway credits include *Comedy of Music* in 1953, which ran for 849 performances—a record for a one-man show—and was revived in 1964 and 1977. He made numerous appearances at Carnegie Hall, and was honored by the Kennedy Center. Survivors include two sons, Ronald Borge, of Rowayton, CT, and Victor Bernhard Borge, of New York, NY; three daughters, Sanna Feirstein of New York, NY, Janet Crowle of St. Michaels, MD, and Frederikke Borge of South Egremont, MA; nine grandchildren; and one great-grandchild.

DORI BRENNER 53, New York, NY-born actress, died September 16, 2000, in Los Angeles, CA, of complications from cancer. She made her Broadway debut in *Unlikely Heroes,* followed by *Hurrah at Last* Off-Broadway. She is best known for her numerous television and film roles. Survivors include two sisters, a niece, and a nephew.

JAMES L. "JAMIE" BROWN 57, director, died June 6, 2000, in Longboat Key, FL, after being beaten and stabbed. Broadway credits include *Of the Fields, Lately* in 1983, as well as numerous regional credits, including the world premiere of Horton Foote's *Dividing the Estate* at the McCarter Theatre. He was also one of the first directors at the WPA Theatre.

JOHN BURY 75, English-born set designer, died November 12, 2000, in Gloucestershire, England, of pneumonia brought on by heart disease. Broadway credits include *Amadeus,* for which he received Tony Awards for both lighting and set design. Other New York credits include *Hedda Gabler* and *A Doll's House,* both starring Claire Bloom. He worked extensively in Great Britain with Joan Littlewood's Theatre Workshop (designing over 30 productions there), the Royal Shakespeare Company, the Royal Opera House, and the Glydenbourne Opera Festival. He also became the chief designer at the Theater Workshop in Stratford East, London, and worked with Sir Peter Hall at the National Theater, where his co-producing credits included *The Collection, The Homecoming, Landscape, Silence,* and *Betrayal.* After having left the National Theater, he concentrated on designing operas. He served as the Chairman of the Society of British Theater Designers from 1975 to 1985. Survivors include his wife, Elizabeth, sons Christopher, Adam, and Mathew, and daughter, Abigail.

VINCENT CANBY 76, Chicago, IL-born film and theater critic/playwright/author, died October 15, 2000, in New York, NY, of cancer. From 1969 through 1993, he was the senior film critic for *The New York Times,* becoming the Sunday theatre critic in 1993 and chief theater critic before returning to the Sunday column in 1996. As a playwright, Off-Broadway credits include *End of the War* and *After All.* Prior to joining *The New York Times,* he was a reporter for *Variety* from 1959 to 1965, and was the author of two novels. Survivors include his first cousin, Ann Baker Trufant, and her daughter Ridgley, both of New York.

ARTHUR CANTOR 81, Boston, MA-born producer/publicist, died April 8, 2001, in New York, NY, of a heart attack. As publicist, Broadway credits include *Goodbye My Fancy* in 1948, followed by *Anne of the Thousand Days, Miss Liberty, Lost in the Stars, Casear and Cleopatra* (1949 and 1951), *Peter Pan, Darkness at Noon, Gigi, In Any Language, Hazel Flagg, Shangri-La, Auntie Mame, Long Day's Journey Into Night, Night of the Auk, Two for the Seesaw, Handful of Fire, The Shadow of a Gunman, The Disenchanted, Rashomon, Redhead, The Rivalry, Davy Jones' Locker, The Gang's All Here, The Miracle Worker,* and *The Girls Against the Boys.* As producer, Broadway credits include Paddy Chayefsky's *The Tenth Man* in 1959, followed by *Saratoga, Toys in the Attic, All the Way Home, The Complaisant Lover, Gideon, A Thousand Clowns* (1962), *Man in the Moon, The Golden Age, The Passion of Joseph D., Follies Bergére* (1964), *The Committee, Man of La Mancha* (1965), *La Grosse Valise, The Rose Tattoo, Of Love Remembered, By George, Darling of the Day, The Venetian Twins, The House of Atreus, The Resistible Rise of Arturo Ui, Vivat! Vivat! Regina!, Promenade All!, Captain Brassbound's Conversion, The Little Black Book, 42 Seconds from Broadway, In Praise of Love, Private Lives* (1975), *The Constant Wife, The Innocents, A Party with Betty Comden and Adolph Green, St. Mark's Gospel* (1978 and 1981), *The Playboy of the Weekend World, On Golden Pond, Emylyn Williams as Charles Dickens, The Hothouse, A Little Family Business, Ian McKellen: Acting Shakespeare, Pack of Lies, Jerome Kern Goes to Hollywood, Rowan Atkinson at the Atkinson, Starlight Express, Three Sisters* and *Into the Whirlwind.* A daughter and a son survive him.

MARGUERITE CHURCHILL 90, Kansas City, KA-born actress, died January 9, 2000, in Broken Arrow, OK. Broadway credits include *House of Shadows* in 1927, followed by *The Wild Man of Borneo, Skidding, The Inside Story, Dinner at Eight,* and *And Now Good-bye,* as well as several film roles. Survivors include her daughter, Orin Ynez O'Brien.

MARY COLQUHOUN 61, London, England-born casting director, died September 10, 2000, in New York, NY, of ovarian cancer. Broadway casting credits include *Steaming, K2, 'night Mother,* and *Passion.* A Casting Society of America's Hoyt Bowers Award winner for lifetime achievement, she was best known for her work in film and television, for which she garnered two Emmy Awards. Survivors include a sister, Christina Burke, a brother, Patrick Burke, a niece, Tawny Wagner, and three nephews, Toby Wagner, Mathew Burke, and Laurence Burke, all of England.

PEGGY CONVERSE 95, Oregon City, OR-born actress, died March 2, 2001, in Los Angeles, CA. Broadway credits include *Miss Quis* and *Wuthering Heights.* Best known for her work on television and in film, she and husband Don Porter also toured nationally in *Any Wednesday, The Best Man,* and *Love and Kisses.*

FRANCES ANN CANNON DOUGHERTY 82, producer, died April 25, 2001, in East Hampton, NY. A co-founder of the National Repertory Theatre, Broadway credits with the N.R.T. include *The Seagull* (1964), *The Crucible* (1964), *The Imaginary Invalid* (1967), *A Touch of the Poet* (1967), and *Tonight at 8:30* (1967). N.R.T. touring productions include *Mary Stuart* and *The Trojan Women.* The National Repertory Theatre was awarded a Tony Award in 1965 for its work in producing classical theatre.

VAL DUFOUR (Albert Valery) 73, New Orleans, LA-born actor, died July 27, 2000, in New York, NY. Broadway credits include *High Button Shoes,* followed by *South Pacific, Picnic, Mister Roberts, Stalag 17, Electra, Frankie and Johnny, The Grass Harp,* and *Abe's Irish Rose* (1954). Off-Broadway credits include *3 by Pirandello* and *The Strange Case of Dr. Jekyll.* An Emmy Award winner for his work in television, he made numerous appearances in that medium and on film. Four brothers, Irby, Filmore, Hillman, and Allen, survive him.

DAVID DUKES 55, San Francisco, CA-born actor, died October 9, 2000, in Spanaway, WA, of a heart attack while on location for a film shoot. He lived in New York, NY. He made his Broadway debut in 1971 in *School for Wives*, followed by *Don Juan, The Play's the Thing, The Visit, Chemin de Fer, Holiday, Rules of the Game, Love for Love, Travesties, Dracula, Bent* (Tony nomination), *Amadeus, M. Butterfly, Love Letters, Someone Who'll Watch Over Me*, and *Broken Glass*. Off-Broadway credits include *Rebel Women*. A veteran of numerous film roles, he also garnered an Emmy nomination for his work in television. Survivors include his wife, the author and poetess Carol Muske-Dukes, son Shawn, and daughter Anne.

LOUIS EDMONDS 76, Baton Rouge, LA-born actor, died March 3, 2001, on Long Island, NY, of respiratory failure as a complication from cancer. Broadway credits include *Candide, Maybe Tuesday, The Killer, A Passage to India, Fire!*, and *Otherwise Engaged*. Off-Broadway credits include *Life in Louisiana, Way of the World, The Cherry Orchard, Uncle Vanya, Duchess of Malfi, Ernest in Love, The Rapists, Amoureuse, The Interview*, and *The Wisteria Trees*. He is best known for his numerous television and film roles.

ELDON ELDER 79, Atchison, KA-born set designer/teacher, died December 11, 2000, in New York, NY, of heart failure. Beginning his career with the Theatre Guild in 1951, his Broadway credits include *The Long Days, Legend of Lovers* with Richard Burton and Dorothy McGuire, *Venus Observed, Hook 'n Ladder, Time Out for Ginger, The Grey-Eyed People, Take a Giant Step, The Girl in Pink Tights, One Eye Closed, All in One, The Young and Beautiful, The Heavenly Twins, Fallen Angels, Shinbone Alley, The Affair, The Fun Couple, Mating Dance, Of Love Remembered, The Megilla of Itzik Manger, Will Rogers' USA, Music Is*, and *Hizzoner*. In 1958, he became the first resident designer for Joseph Papp's New York Shakespeare Festival, which led to his design of the Delacorte Theater in Central Park. A designer of hundreds of productions Off-Broadway, in London, and in Berlin, he also penned *Will It Make a Theater*, a guide to creating nontraditional performing space. No immediate family members survive.

DAVID ERIC actor, died December 14, 2000, of a brain tumor. Broadway credits include *Yentl, Sunset Boulevard, Shenandoah*, and *Naughty Marietta* (Lincoln Center). A Garland Award winner for *Dames at Sea*, he also served as an Actors' Equity council member.

GAIL FISHER 65, Orange, NJ-born actress, died December 2, 2000, in Los Angeles, CA, of kidney failure. She made her Broadway debut in 1961 in *Purlie Victorious*, followed by Off-Broadway credits including *Simply Heavenly, Susan Slept Here*, and *Danton's Death* (Lincoln Center). Best known as a pioneer and role model as an African-American woman in television, she garnered an Emmy Award and two Golden Globe Awards for her work in that medium. Survivors include her daughters, Samara Maxe of San Diego, and Jole Baerga of Hackensack, NJ; a brother, Herbert Fisher of Randallstown, MD; and a sister, Ona Gaither, of Alexandria, VA.

ARLENE FRANCIS (Arlene Francis Kazanjian) 93, Boston, MA-born actress/talk show personality, died May 31, 2001 in San Francisco, CA, of complications from Alzheimer's Disease. She made her Broadway debut in 1936 in *Horse Eats Hat*, followed by *The Women, All That Glitters, Michael Drops In, Journey to Jerusalem, The Doughgirls, The Overtons, The French Touch, Cup of Trembling, My Name is Aquilon, Metropole, Little Blue Light, Late Love, Once More with Feeling, Beekman Place, Mrs. Dally, Dinner at 8, Gigi*, and *Don't Call Back*. Off-Broadway credits include *Don Juan in Hell*. Her son, Peter, survives her.

PETER GENNARO 80, Metairie, LA-born dancer/choreographer, died September 28, 2000, in New York, NY. Broadway credits as a dancer include *Guys and Dolls* (1950), *The Pajama Game*, and *Bells Are Ringing*. Choreography credits include *Seventh Heaven, West Side Story* (1957, with Jerome Robbins), *Fiorello!, West Side Story* (1960), *The Unsinkable Molly Brown, Mr. President, Bajour, Jimmy, Irene, Annie* (1977, Tony Award), *The American Dance Machine, Carmelina, West Side Story* (1980), *Little Me* (1982), *Jerome Robbins' Broadway*, 3 *Penny Opera* (1989), and *Annie* (1997). He also worked on numerous productions in television and film. Survivors include his wife, dancer Jean Kinsella; daughter, Liza; son, Michael; brother, Emile, of Metairie, LA; and two grandchildren.

JOSÉ GRECO 82, Italian-born Spanish dancer/teacher, died December 31, 2000, in Lancaster, PA, of heart failure. He made his Broadway debut in 1951 in *Jose Greco Ballet*, for which he was selected as "New Broadway Personality of the Year," followed by *Jose Greco* in 1953. Numerous television and film appearances followed, and he was also a founder of the José Greco Foundation for Hispanic Dance in New York. He was awarded the Knight of Civil Merit by the Spanish government in 1962. Survivors include his wife, Ana Gorger-Reese, of Lancaster, PA; a sister, Eleaonora Greco Nobile, of Pescara, Italy; and five children: composer José, Luis, Carmela, and Lola Greco, dancers, all of Madrid; José, of Laredo, TX; and Paolo, a composer, of Liverpool, England.

SIR ALEC GUINNESS (Alec Guinness de Cuffe) 86, London, England-born actor died August 5, 2000, in West Sussex, England, of liver cancer. He made his Broadway debut in 1942 in *Flare Path*, followed by *The Cocktail Party* and *Dylan* in 1964, for which he received a Tony Award. He was the veteran of numerous West End productions including *Queer Cargo*, Tyrone Guthrie's production of *Hamlet* at the Old Vic, *Twelfth Night, The Prisoner, Hotel Paradiso, Ross, Vicious Circle, Saint Joan, Richard II*, as well as opened Canada's Shakespeare Festival in 1953 with *Richard III*. He was best known for his numerous film and television roles, and garnered two Academy Awards and an Emmy nomination for his work in those media. His wife, Merula Salaman, and son, Matthew, survive him.

ROSE HOBART (Rose Kefer) 94, actress, died August 29, 2000, in Woodland Hills, CA. Best known for her numerous television and film roles before being blacklisted by Hollywood in 1949, she made her Broadway debut in 1922 in *The Lullaby*, followed by *Caesar and Cleopatra* (1925), *John Gabriel Borkman, What Every Woman Knows, Three Sisters, Puppets of Passion, Revelry, The Fanatics, Diversion, Crashing Through, Zeppelin, A Primer for Lovers, Death Takes a Holiday, I Love You Wednesday, Girls in Uniform, Our Wife, Eight Bells, The Wind and the Rain, Siege*, and *Dear Octopus*. She also appeared on stage in London and Los Angeles, CA, was involved in USO camp shows in 1944–45, and authored *A Steady Digestion to a Fixed Point*, her autobiography.

WILLIAM HAMMERSTEIN 82, New York, NY-born director/producer/stage mgr./theatre manager, died March 9, 2001, in New York, NY. A founder of the City Center Light Opera Company for which he received a special Tony Award in 1957, Broadway credits as a director include *Do Re Mi* (1960) and *Oklahoma!* (1979). Broadway credits as a producer include *Come Blow Your Horn* (1961) and *Gift of Time* (1962), as well as numerous productions at City Center, in London, England, and regional productions. As a stage manager, Broadway credits include *Show Boat* (1946), *Mister Roberts* (1948), *The Rat Race* (1949), and *The Diary of Anne Frank* (1955). Survivors include his wife, Jane-Howard; three daughters, Patricia Benner of Durham, NC, and Martha Hammerstein and Diana Hammerstein, both of Fort Lauderdale, FL; six grandchildren; and two great-grandchildren.

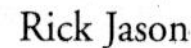
Rick Jason

Timothy Jenkins

Werner Klemperer

Jack Lemmon

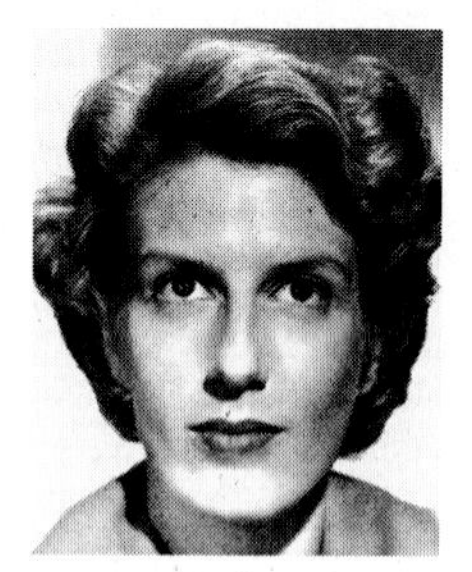
Nancy Marchand

ELINOR HARRIOT (Elinor Hirschfield Nathan) 89, Duluth, MN-born actress, died June 10, 2000, in Beverly Hills, CA. Best known as one of the first women to perform in radio on shows like *Amos 'n Andy* (for two decades), *Backstage Wife, Bachelor's Children,* and *The Couple Next Door,* her Broadway credits include *The Bonds of Interest* and *The Bride the Sun Shines On.* Survivors include her husband, Frank, two daughters, Judy Pasquinelli and Nancy Gettelman, and five grandchildren.

RADIE HARRIS 96, columnist, died February 22, 2001, at the Actors Fund Nursing Home in Englewood, NJ. As columnist of Broadway Ballyhoo in *The Hollywood Reporter* for nearly 50 years, she reported on the comings and goings of entertainment icons in New York, Hollywood, and Europe, and also regularly contributed to *Variety* and CBS Radio. She was an originator of the Stage Door Canteen in New York, NY, and was on the executive board of the American Theater Wing. Survivors include her brother-in-law, Frank Liberman.

DAVID HENEKER 94, composer/lyricist, died January 30, 2001. Broadway credits include *Irma La Douce* (1960), and *Half a Sixpence* (1965, Tony nomination).

GENJI ITO 54, New York, NY-born composer/musician/teacher, died April 23, 2001, in New York, NY, of cancer. He created scores for more than 25 productions as resident composer at LaMaMa E.T.C. He also composed 15 scores for UBU Repertory, collaborated with Great Jones Repertory Company, served as music director for the New York City Ballet on Jerome Robbins's *Watermill* (1972), was a guest artist in residence for the National Theater of the Deaf, and taught at Manhattanville College. Broadway performing credits include *Pacific Overtures* (1976). He is survived by his wife, Zishan Ugurlu; a brother, Teimoc Johnston; a daughter, Sofia Teiko Ito; and sons Ted Ito Schmidt and Teiji Orion Malkine.

JERRY JARRETT (Jerome Jaroslow) Brooklyn-born actor, died May 16, 2001, in New York, NY. He made his Broadway debut in 1949 in *At War with the Army,* followed by *Gentlemen Prefer Blondes, Stalag 17, Fiorello!,* and *Fiddler on the Roof* (1964, 1990). Off-Broadway credits include *Waiting for Lefty, Nat Turner, Me Candido, That 5 A.M. Jazz, Valentine's Day, Tickles by Tucholsky, Jazzbo Brown.* He also worked in television and film. Survivors include three daughters, Risa Jaroslow of New York, NY, Abby Jaroslow of Pennington, NJ, and Lori Jaroslow of Los Angeles, CA; brother, Fred, of Sands Point, NY; sister Ruth I. Jasoslow of Wilmington, DE; and four grandchildren.

RICK JASON 74, New York, NY born actor, died October 16, 2000, in Los Angeles, CA, of a self-inflicted gunshot wound. A Theatre World Award winner for his 1950 Broadway debut in *Now I Lay Me Down to Sleep,* he is best known for his work in television. Survivors include his wife, Cindy.

TIMOTHY JENKINS 50, Detroit, MI-born actor, died in June, 2000. Off-Broadway credits include *Room Service,* followed by *The Quilling of Prue* and *The Hasty Heart.*

MARIA KARNILOVA (Maria Dovgolenko, Maria Karniloff) 80, Hartford, CT-born actress, died April 20, 2001. She made her Broadway debut in 1938 in *Stars in Her Eyes,* followed by *Call Me Mister, High Button Shoes, Two's Company, Hollywood Pinafore, Beggar's Opera, Jerome Robbins' Ballet: USA, Gypsy* (1959), *Miss Liberty, Out of This World, Bravo Giovanni, Fiddler on the Roof* (1964, Tony Award, 1981), *Zorba* (Tony nomination), *Gigi, God's Favorite,* and *Bring Back Birdie.* Off-Broadway credits include *Kaleidescope* and *Cinderella* (New York City Opera at Lincoln Center). She was also a charter member of American Ballet Theater. Survivors include her husband, actor George S. Irving; son, Alexander, of Oceanside, CA; daughter, Katherine Irving Stark, of South Salem, NY; and three grandchildren.

HARVEY J. KLARIS (Harvey J. Klaristenfeld) 61, producer, died January 12, 2001, in New York, NY, of heart failure. Broadway credits include *Nine* (Tony Award), *The Tap Dance Kid,* and *On the Waterfront.* Off-Broadway credits include *Cloud 9.* He was also a former co-owner of *Sardi's* restaurant. Survivors include his wife, Jane; four sons, Edward, Joshua, and Alexander, all of New York, NY, and Nathan, of London, England; two daughters, Grace, of New York, NY, and Lorin, of Westport, CT; a brother, Kenneth Klaristenfeld, of West Hills, CA; father, William Klaristenfeld, of Southfield, MI; and seven grandchildren.

WERNER KLEMPERER 80, Cologne, Germany-born actor, died December 6, 2000, in New York, NY, of cancer. He made his Broadway debut in 1947 in *Heads or Tails,* followed by *Galileo, Insect Comedy, 20th Century, Dear Charles, Night of the Tribades, Cabaret* (1988 Tony nomination), *The Sound of Music* (Lincoln Center), and *Uncle Vanya.* Off-Broadway credits include *Master Class.* He is best know for his work in television, for which he garnered two Emmy Awards, and appeared in several notable films. As a narrator, he appeared with nearly every major symphony in the United States, as well as performed numerous roles as an opera singer. He served three consecutive terms on the Council of Actors' Equity and served as fourth vice president for six years. Survivors include his wife, actress Kim Hamilton Klemperer; son, Mark Klemperer, of New York, NY; daughter, Dr. Erika Klemperer Webster, of San Francisco, CA; and sister, Lotte Klemperer, of Zurich, Switzerland.

FREDERICK HENRY KOCH, JR. 88, Grand Forks, ND-born educator/theatre designer, died August 26, 2000, in Miami, FL. In 1946, he created the first Ring, or theatre in the round, at the University of Miami. Survivors include three sons, Frederick III and Christopher Alan, both of Miami, FL, and Thomas Bryant of Burnsville, NC; two brothers, Robert Alan, of Princeton, NJ, and William Julian, of Glendale, AZ; seven grandchildren; and five great-grandchildren.

JACK KROLL 74, New York, NY-born critic, died June 8, 2000, in New York, NY, from complications of colon cancer. As an editor, critic, and writer for *Newsweek* for more than 35 years, he headed the Arts sections beginning in 1963, and was named senior editor for all cultural sections in 1964. He was the author of more than 1,200 articles, including 19 cover stories, and received a George Jean Nathan Award for drama criticism in 1980, an ASCAP/Deems Taylor Award in 1981, a Page One Award in 1983, and a National Magazine Award in 1973. He also worked at *Art News* from 1960–1963. He is survived by his wife, Joan Engels, a senior photo editor at *Newsweek*; son, Lawrence, of Irvine, CA; daughter, Sue, of Los Angeles, CA; and a granddaughter.

ELIZABETH LAWRENCE 77, Huntington, WV-born actress, died June 11, 2000, of cancer. She made her Broadway debut in 1954 in *The Rainmaker*, followed by *The Lark, All the Way Home, Look Homeward Angel, The Moon Besieged, A Matter of Gravity*, and *Strange Interlude*. Off-Broadway credits include *The Misunderstanding, Rockaway, Children*, and *Beauty Marks*.

STEPHANIE LAWRENCE (Stephanie Imelda Mary Lawrence) 50, British-born actress, died November 14, 2000, in London, England. A 1993 Theatre World Award winner for her Broadway debut, *Blood Brothers* (Tony nomination), she was a veteran of many West End stage productions in London, including *Forget Me Not Lane, Marilyn!, Starlight Express, Cats*, and *Evita*. Survivors include her husband, Laurie Sautereau.

RONALD S. LEE (Ronald Lee, Ronnie Lee) 73, died May 28, 2001, following heart surgery. Broadway credits include *The King and I, Plain and Fancy, Mr. Wonderful, West Side Story, Finian's Rainbow, Wildcat, Enter Laughing, The White House, On a Clear Day You Can See Forever, Steaming, Lillian*, and *Lucifer's Child*.

JACK LEMMON 76, Boston, MA-born actor, died April 27, 2001, in Los Angeles, CA, of complications from cancer. He made his Broadway debut in 1953 in *Room Service*, followed by *Face of a Hero, Tribute*, and *Long Day's Journey into Night*. He is best known for his prolific film work, for which he garnered two Academy Awards, the American Film Institute's Life Achievement Award, the first Harvard Arts Medal, Kennedy Center Honors, the Lincoln Center Film Society Tribute, the Screen Actors Guild Life Achievement Award, and two Cannes International Film Festival Best Actor Awards.

JOSEPH LEON 82, New York, NY-born actor, died March 25, 2001. He made his Broadway debut in 1950 in *Bell, Book, and Candle*, followed by *Seven Year Itch, Pipe Dream, Fair Game, Gazebo, Julia, Jake and Uncle Joe, Beauty Part, Merry Widow, Henry Sweet Henry, Jimmy Shine, All Over Town, California Suite, The Merchant, Break a Leg, Once a Catholic, Fools, Glengary Glen Ross*, and *Social Security*. Off-Broadway credits include *Come Share My House, Dark Corners, Interrogation of Havana, Are You Now or Have You Ever, Second Avenue Rag, Buck, Ah, Wilderness!*, and *Café Crown* (also Broadway, 1989). Survivors include his longtime companion, Robin D. Litton.

DAVID LEWIS 84, Pittsburgh, PA-born actor, died December 11, 2000. He made his Broadway debut in 1943 in *Goodbye Again*, followed by *The Streets Are Guarded, Little Women* (1944), *Taming of the Shrew, The Wild Duck*, and *King of Hearts*. Off-Broadway credits include *Star Treatment*.

VERA LOCKWOOD 82, Bristol, CT-born actress, died July 28, 2000, in North Bergen, NJ. Broadway credits include *The Ritz, Goodbye Fidel, Passione, The Remarkable Mr. Pennypacker*, and *Sunrise at Campobello*. Off-Broadway credits include *Over the River and Through the Woods*. An Emmy nominee for her work in television, she is best known for her work in that medium. Four children and two grandchildren survive her.

ALLAN LOUW 84, San Francisco, CA-born actor, died in 2001. He made his Broadway debut in 1965 in *The Yearling*, followed by *Marat/Sade* (1967). Off-Broadway credits include *The Time of the Key*.

EDWARD LUDLUM 80, New York, NY-born director, died Nov. 21, 2000, of heart failure. New York credits include *Desire Under the Elms* (1951), *Inherit the Wind* (1958), and he also directed the first West Coast productions of *The Glass Menagerie* and *Compulsion*. He also worked extensively as a director in television. Survivors include two cousins, Tom Carroll, and writer Robert Ludlum.

ROBERT LUDLUM 73, New York, NY-born actor/director/writer, died March 13, 2001, in Naples, FL, of a heart attack. Broadway acting credits include *Saint Joan* (1956), among many New York theatre credits as an actor and a director, and over 200 appearances in television. He established the Playhouse-on-the-Mall Theatre in Paramus, NJ, and was a prolific and best-selling novelist. Survivors include his wife, Karen; sons Michael, of NJ, and Jonathan, of CO; and daughter, Glynis, of New England.

KERT LUNDELL 64, Swedish-born set designer/teacher, died September 11, 2000, in New York, NY, of lung cancer. A designer of more than 75 Broadway and Off-Broadway shows, Broadway credits include *The Investigation, Under the Weather, Carry Me Back to Morningside Heights, The Castro Complex, Soon, Solitaire/Double Solitaire, Ain't Supposed to Die a Natural Death, Don't Play Us Cheap!, The Lincoln Mask, The Sunshine Boys, The Enemy Is Dead, Hughie/Duet* (1975), *The Night That Made America Famous, Rockabye Hamlet, 1600 Pennsylvania Avenue, The November People, Waltz of the Stork*, and *Shenandoah*. He designed productions for Neil Simon, Arthur Kopit, and Gower Champion, and garnered a Drama Desk nomination for his work in *Contact with the Enemy* at Ensemble Studio Theatre. He was also a trustee of the Ensemble Studio Theatre. Survivors include his wife, Bretta; a son, Erik; and a daughter, Kate.

MICHAEL MAGGIO 49, Chicago, IL-born director/teacher, died August 19, 2000, in Chicago, IL, of complications from lymphoma, which he developed as a result of extensive drug treatments following a successful double lung transplant in 1991. A director in a number of productions in Chicago, he was an associate artistic director of the Goodman Theater and was recently appointed dean of the theater school at DePaul University, where he had been a professor since 1996. Productions at the Goodman included *Travesties, Arcadia*, Beckett's *Endgame* and *Waiting for Godot, Sunday in the Park with George, A Little Night Music, Romeo and Juliet, Boy Meets Girl*, and *Wings*, which transferred to the Joseph Papp Public Theater in New York in 1993. He also directed *Titus Andronicus* for the New York Shakespeare Festival in Central Park in 1989. Survivors include his wife, Rachel Kraft; parents, Carlo and Genevieve; sister, Dona Will of White Bear, MN; and son, Ben.

EDWARD MANGUM 87, theater director and founder, died January 10, 2001, in Austin, TX. A founder of Arena Stage in Washington, DC, he also directed many productions there. He also ran a theater in Honolulu, HI. His wife, Francisca, survives him.

Walter Matthau

Richard Mulligan

Renee Orin

Eugenia Rawls

Beah Richards

NANCY MARCHAND 71, Buffalo, NY-born actress, died June 18, 2000, in Stratford, CT, after suffering from lung cancer as well as chronic pulmonary disease. She made her Broadway debut in 1957 in *Miss Isobel*, followed by *Much Ado About Nothing, Tchin-Tchin, Strange Interlude, Three Bags Full, The Alchemist, Yerma, After the Rain, Cyrano de Bergerac, 40 Carats, And Miss Reardon Drinks a Little, Mary Stuart, Enemies, The Glass Menagerie* (1975), *Awake and Sing, Morning's at 7* (1980), *Octette Bridge Club, Love Letters, Cinderella* (New York City Opera at Lincoln Center), *White Liars/Black Comedy* (Tony nomination), and *Sweet Adeline* (Encores). Off-Broadway credits include *The Balcony* (Obie Award), *Children, Awake and Sing, Cocktail Hour* (Obie Award), *Love Letters, Taken in Marriage, Sister Mary Ignatius…, End of the Day, A Darker Purpose*, and *The Important of Being Earnest.* She was an original company member of the Association of Producing Artists (A.P.A.), and appeared in roles at numerous regional theatres, including the Long Wharf, Mark Taper Forum, and the Goodman Theater. Best known for her work on television, she won four Emmy Awards and a Golden Globe Award for her work in that medium, and made several appearances in films. Survivors include her daughters, actress Katie Sparer Bowe, of Stratford, CT, and Rachel Sparer Bersier, an opera singer, of New York, NY; son, David, of Madison, WI; and seven grandchildren.

MANUEL MARTÎN 66, Cuban-born playwright/director, died September 28, 2000, in New York, NY, of a heart attack. As a playwright, credits in New York include *Swallows* and *Union City Thanksgiving.* As founder and artistic director of the Duo Theater, he encouraged young Hispanic-American playwrights for over twenty years. He coordinated the Intar Theater's playwrights-in-residence laboratory in 1980 and taught drama at Boricua College, Sing Sing Correctional Facility in Ossining, NY, and the Puerto Rican Traveling Theater. Directing credits in New York include *Botanica*, and Carmen Rivera's *Julia de Burgos: Child of Water.* Survivors include two sisters, Victoria Martîn and Amanda Martîn of Havana, Cuba, and brother, Santos Martîn of San Juan, Puerto Rico.

WALTER MATTHAU (Walter Matuschankayasky) 79, New York, NY-born actor, died July 1, 2000, in Santa Monica, CA, of a heart attack. Best known for his numerous roles in television and an Academy Award winner for his work in film, he made his Broadway debut in 1948 in *Anne of the Thousand Days*, followed by *The Liar, Season in the Sun, Twilight Walk, Fancy Meeting You Again, One Bright Day, In Any Language, The Grey-Eyed People, A Certain Joy, The Burning* Glass, *The Ladies of the Corridor*, City Center revivals of *Guys and Dolls* (1953) and *Wisteria Trees* (1954), *Will Success Spoil Rock Hunter, Maiden Voyage, Once More, With Feeling, Once There Was a Russian, A Shot in the Dark* (Tony Award), *My Mother, My Father, and Me*, and *The Odd Couple* (Tony Award). Survivors include his wife, Carol, sons, director Charles Matthau and David, and daughter, Jenny.

FRANCES MERCER 85, New Rochelle, NY-born actress/model, died November 12, 2000 in Los Angeles, CA. Following a long career as a model and actress in films, she made her Broadway debut in 1939 in *Very Warm for May*, followed by *Something for the Boys* in 1943. No immediate survivors.

RUTH MITCHELL 81, Newark, NJ-born actress/producer/stage manager, died November 3, 2000. As a performer, Broadway credits include *Follow the Girls* and *Annie Get Your Gun* (1946). As a stage manager, Broadway credits include *Mister Roberts, The King and I, Pipe Dream, Bells Are Ringing, West Side Story* (1957, 1980), *Gypsy* (1959), *Fiorello!, Tenderloin, A Call on Kuprin, Take Her, She's Mine, A Funny Thing Happened on the Way to the Forum* (1962), *She Loves Me* (1963), *Fiddler on the Roof* (1964, 1976, 1981, 1990), *Poor Bitos, Baker Street*, and *It's a Bird…It's a Plane…It's Superman.* Broadway producing credits include *It's a Bird…It's a Plane…It's Superman, Cabaret* (1966, 1987), *Zorba* (1968), *Company* (1970), *A Little Night Music* (1973), *Candide* (1974), *Pacific Overtures, Side by Side by Sondheim, On the Twentieth Century, Sweeney Todd* (1979), *Merrily We Roll Along* (1981), *A Doll's Life, Play Memory, End of the World, Grind, Rosa, The Phantom of the Opera, Kiss of the Spiderwoman*, and *Show Boat.* Survivors include her companion, Florence Klotz, and a sister, Juliette Fleischer, of Fort Lauderdale, FL.

MICHAEL MEYER 79, London, England-born translator/scholar/playwright, died August 3, 2000, in London, England. With *Ibsen: A Biography*, and *Strindberg*, he established himself as a leading authority on the two playwrights, and also translated all 16 of Ibsen's plays and 18 of Strindberg's, translations which are widely used throughout the world. He was also a playwright and novelist. A daughter, Nora, survives him.

CHARLES MOORE actor, died in June, 2000. Broadway credits include *Jamaica, Kwamina, The Zulu and The Zayda*, and *Le Blancs.* Off-Broadway credits include *The Ballad for Bimshire, House of Flowers*, and *Billy Noname.*

RICHARD MULLIGAN 67, Bronx, NY-born actor, died September 26, 2000, in Los Angeles, CA, of cancer. A Theatre World Award winner for *Mating Dance* in 1967, he made his Broadway debut in *All the Way Home* in 1961, followed by *Nobody Loves an Albatross, A Thousand Clowns, Never Too Late, How the Other Half Loves, Ring Round the Bathtub, Thieves*, and *Special Occasions.* Off-Broadway credits include *Hogan's Goat.* Best known for his work in television, he garnered two Emmy Awards and a Golden Globe Award for his work in that medium, and also made numerous film appearances. Survivors include a son, James, of West Lebanon, NH, and two brothers, James, of ND, and director Robert, of CT.

N. RICHARD NASH (Nathan Richard Nasbaum) 87, Philadelphia, PA-born playwright/novelist, died December 11, 2000, in New York, NY. His Broadway debut in 1946 was *The Second Best Bed*, followed by *The Young and Fair, See the Jaguar, The Rainmaker*, and 110 *in the Shade*. As a producer, he staged *Wildcat* with Lucille Ball, *Sarava* and *The Happy Time*, the latter two for which he wrote the books. He was also a novelist and screenwriter. Survivors include two daughters, Jennifer Nash, of New York, NY, and Amanda Nash, of Cambridge, MA, and son, Cristopher, of Warrickshire, England.

HAROLD NICHOLAS 79, Winston-Salem, NC-born dancer, died July 3, 2000, in New York, NY, of heart failure. Best known in over 50 appearances in movie musicals as one of the legendary tap-dancing The Nicholas Brothers, his Broadway credits include *Ziegfeld Follies of* 1936 with Bob Hope and Fanny Brice, *Babes in Arms, St. Louis Woman*, and *Sammy*. He and his brother appeared in numerous vaudeville acts and nightclubs before they became headliners at the Cotton Club for eight years. In 1948, the movie color barrier between white and black dancers was broken when Gene Kelly danced with them in *The Pirate*. He appeared solo in numerous other films, performed on television and in tours, and appeared often with Lynn Dally's Jazz Ensemble. The brothers shared 1991 Kennedy Center Honors, the 1998 Samuel H. Scripps American Dance Festival Award, and an Academy Award tribute in 1981. Survivors include his wife, Rigmor Newman Nicholas, of New York, NY; brother, Fayard, sister, Dorothy Morrow, daughter, Harolyn, and son, Melih, all of Los Angeles, CA; and two stepchildren, Frederick Newman, of Torrington, CT, and Annie, of Los Angeles, CA.

JACK O'BRIAN 86, Buffalo, NY-born columnist, died Nov. 5, 2000, in New York, NY. Beginning his career with the Buffalo Courier-Express as a cub reporter, he joined the Associated Press as its drama and movie critic in 1943. In 1949, he moved to the *New York Journal-American* and started its television column. In 1967, he took over the Voice of Broadway column ten days after the death of its author, Dorothy Kilgallen. He continued the column at the *New York Herald Tribune*, and after its close continued a syndicated column and continued commentary on WOR-AM radio. He is survived by two daughters, Bridget and Kate O'Brian, and four grandchildren.

VIRGINIA O'BRIEN 81, actress, died January 16, 2001. Broadway credits include *The Girl Behind the Sun, The Chocolate Soldier, Jack and Jill, The Rise of Rosie O'Reilly, Princess Ida, How's Your Health*, and *Keep Off the Grass*.

JAMES O'REAR 86, Frankfurt, IN-born actor, died June 14, 2000, in Los Angeles, CA, of natural causes. A member of Orson Welles's Mercury Theatre Company, credits there include *Julius Caesar*. He also performed with the Group Theater and Westport Playhouse in CT, before making his Broadway debut in 1938 in *The Shoemakers Holiday*, followed by *My Hearts in the Highlands, Heavenly, Glamour Preferred, Eight O'Clock Tuesday, The Happy Time*, and *A Loss of Roses*. A brother survives him.

RENEE ORIN 73, Slatington, PA-born actress, died August 27, 2000, in Los Angeles, CA, of lymphoma. Broadway credits include *Plain and Fancy*, followed by *Café Crown, Slapstick Tragedy, Show Me Where the Good Times Are*, and *Plaza Suite*. Off-Broadway credits include *Good News*, followed by *The Great Magician, River-wind, Augusta*, and *Turns*. Other credits include *Pal Joey, Take Me Along, Fiddler on the Roof, Still Young and Foolish* — the cabaret tour she performed with husband, Tony-winning composer and pianist Albert Hague — and many television appearances. Survivors include her husband, daughter, Janet Hague, of Portland, OR, and son, Andrew Hague, of New York, NY.

JOSEPHINE PREMICE 74, actress, died April 13, 2001. Broadway credits include *Caribbean Carnival, Mister Johnson, Jamaica* (Tony nomination), *A Hand Is on the Gate* (Tony nomination), and *Bubbling Brown Sugar*. Off-Broadway credits include Truman Capote's *House of Flowers*. Other credits include dance study with Martha Graham and Katherine Dunham, *Blue Holiday* in 1945, an all-black production of *Electra* for the Shakespeare Festival's Mobile Theatre in 1969, and the Festival's production of *The Cherry Orchard* in 1973, as well as many television appearances. Survivors include her husband, Captain Timothy Fales of Paris, France; son, Enrico Fales; daughter, Susan Fales-Hill; and sister, Adele Premice, all of New York.

LOGAN RAMSEY 79, Long Beach, CA-born actor, died June 26, 2000, in Los Angeles, CA, of a heart attack. He made his Broadway debut in 1950 in *The Devil's Disciple*, followed by *The High Ground, In the Summer House, Sweet Bird of Youth, Marathon '33*, and *The Great Indoors*. Off-Broadway credits include *The Good Woman of Setzuan*. He also made numerous appearances in television and film. A sister survives him.

EUGENIA RAWLS 87, Macon, GA-born actress/writer, died November 8, 2000, in Denver, CO. She made her Broadway debut in 1934 in *The Children's Hour*, followed by *Pride and Prejudice, To Quito and Back, Journeyman, The Little Foxes* with Tallulah Bankhead, *Guest in the House, The Man Who Had All the Luck, Rebecca, Strange Fruit, Private Lives*, The *Shrike* with Jose Ferrer, *The Great Sebastians* with Alfred Lunt and Lynn Fontanne, *First Love, A Case of Libel, Sweet Bird of Youth*, and *The Glass Menagerie*. Off-Broadway credits include *Poker Session* and *Just the Immediate Family*, as well as three one-woman shows: *Tallulah a Memory, Affectionately Yours Fanny Kemble*, and *Women of the West*. In 1972, she became the first American actress to perform at the Abbey Theater in Dublin, Ireland, and the theatre is named for her at the Auraria Higher Education Center, home to the University of Colorado at Denver, Metropolitan State College and Denver Community College. She also played several roles on television. Survivors include her husband, Donald R. Seawell, head of the Denver Center for the Performing Arts; daughter, Brook Ashley of Santa Barbara, CA; son, Brockman Seawell, of New York, NY; brothers, Hubert F. Rawls, Jr., of Myrtle Beach, SC, and Richard Russell Rawls, of Fernandina Beach, FL; sister Dorothy Louise Rawls Tuttle, of California; a granddaughter; and two great-grandchildren.

BEAH RICHARDS 80, Vicksburg, MS-born actress, died September 14, 2000, in Vicksburg, MS, of emphysema. A Theatre World Award winner for *The Amen Corner* in 1965, other Broadway credits include *A Raisin in the Sun, The Miracle Worker, Purlie Victorious, Arturo Ui*, and *The Little Foxes*. Off-Broadway credits include *Take a Giant Step*. Regional credits include The Old Globe Theater in San Diego, CA. For her legit work, she was honored with the Paul Robeson Pioneer Award and was inducted into the NAACP Image Awards Hall of Fame. A frequent presence in television and films, she garnered two Emmy Awards and an Academy Award nomination for her work in those media.

Jason Robards

Ann Sothern

Gwen Verdon

Mary K. Wells

Marie Windsor

JASON ROBARDS (Jason Nelson Robards, Jr.) 78, Chicago, IL-born actor, died December 26, 2000, in Bridgeport, CT, of lung cancer. A Theatre World Award winner for *Long Day's Journey Into Night* (1956, also 1988) other Broadway credits include his debut in 1947 in *D'Oyly Carte Co.*, followed by *Stalag 17, The Chase, The Disenchanted* (Tony Award), *Toys in the Attic, Big Fish Little Fish, A Thousand Clowns, After the Fall, But for Whom Charlie, Hughie, The Devils, We Bombed in New Haven, The Country Girl, Moon for the Misbegotten, Touch of the Poet, You Can't Take It With You, Iceman Cometh, A Month of Sundays, Ah Wilderness!, Love Letters, A Christmas Carol,* and *Park Your Car in Harvard Yard.* Off-Broadway credits include *American Gothic* (1953), *Iceman Cometh* (Obie Award), *Hughie, The Devils, Long Day's Journey Into Night, No Man's Land, Moonlight,* and *Molly Sweeney.* Regional credits include *Henry IV, Part One* at the Stratford Festival in Ontario, Canada, and *Macbeth* in Cambridge, MA. A veteran of over 50 films, he garnered two Academy Awards for his work in that medium, and also received the National Medal of the Arts in 1997. Survivors include his wife, Lois; six children, Jason 3rd, Sarah Louise, and David from his first marriage to Eleanor Pittman, Sam from his third marriage, and Shannon and Jake from his fourth marriage.

MAUDE RUSSELL RUTHERFORD 104, TX-born dancer/actress, died March 14, 2001. Broadway credits include *Liza, Keep Shufflin', Black Rhythm,* and *Harlem Cavalcade.* Other credits include *Dixie to Broadway* and *Chocolate Sandals.*

MAX SHOWALTER (Casey Adams) 83, KS-born actor/composer, died July 30, 2000, in Middletown, CT, of cancer. He made his Broadway debut in 1938 in *Knights of Song,* followed by *Very Warm for May, My Sister Eileen, Show Boat, John Loves Mary, Make Mine Manhattan, Hello, Dolly!* (playing Horace Vandergelder 2,300 times), *Grass Harp,* and *Show Boat.* He also wrote the music for *Harrigan 'n' Hart* on Broadway in 1985. Best known for his work in television and film, he appeared in over 1,000 television programs, was a founding teacher at the Eugene O'Neill Center Cabaret Symposium, and worked in regional theatre at the Pasadena Playhouse. His sister, Ann Philpott, of Fresno, CA, survives him.

ANN SOTHERN (Harriette Lake) 92, Valley City, ND-born actress, died March 15, 2001, in Ketchum, ID. Best known for her numerous roles in television and an Academy Award nominee for her work in film, her Broadway credits include *Smiles, America's Sweetheart, Everybody's Welcome, Fatihfully Yours,* and *Of Thee I Sing,* in which she also toured. She is survived by her daughter, actress and designer Tisha Sterling; sister, Sally Adams, of Boise, ID; and a granddaughter.

NICK STEWART (Nicodemus Stewart) 90, Harlem, NY-born actor, died December 18, 2000, in Los Angeles, CA. Beginning his career as a dancer at the Hoofers Club and the Cotton Club, his Broadway credits include *Louisiana Purchase.* He worked extensively in television and film, founded the Ebony Showcase Theater in Los Angeles, CA, and garnered a NAACP lifetime achievement award "for positive portrayals of African-Americans and longevity in the theatre." Survivors include his wife, Edna, three children, and two great-grandchildren.

DR. SEYMOUR SYNA 71, director/drama critic, died August 24, 2000, in Vancouver, British Columbia, of a heart attack. A director in summer theatres and resident theatres before becoming the on-air theatre critic for WNYC-TV, he was also a freelance critic and writer for *Back Stage, New York Tribune, New York Theatre Review,* and *East Village Other.*

ALBERT TAKAZAUCKAS 56, New York, NY-born director, died July 24, 2000, in Oakland, CA, of a heart attack. New York credits include David Mamet's *Sexual Perversity in Chicago* and *Duck Variations.* Other credits include *Madame Butterfly* and *Lucia di Lammermoor* for San Francisco's Western Opera Theater, *Six Characters in Search of an Author* for Opera Festival of New Jersey, *Dinner at 8* and *Light Up the Sky* at the American Conservatory Theater, and *King Henry IV, Part I,* for the San Francisco Shakespeare Festival. He helmed the Magic Theater in San Francisco, CA, and directed numerous productions there, and founded the Allegro Theater Company. Survivors include his partner and collaborator, Hector Correa; father, Albert, of New York, NY; and sister Victoria, of Bloomfield, NJ.

PETER TURGEON 80, actor/writer/director, died October 6, 2000, at the Long Island Veterans Home at Stony Brook. Broadway credits include *The Live Wire,* followed by *A Thurber Carnival, Send Me No Flowers, Little Me* (1962), and *The Girl in the Freudian Slip.* Other credits include *Brigadoon, The Tender Trap, The Beggar's Opera* with Shirley Jones, *Inside U.S.A.* with Beatrice Lillie and Jack Haley, and the tour of *Call Me Mister* and *Life with Father.* He also worked as a writer, director, and actor at the Eugene O'Neill Theater Center in Waterford, CT, and at the John Drew Theater in East Hampton, NY, where he adapted, jointly directed, and starred with Peggy Cass in *Hail Thurber!* in 1984. Survivors include son, Paul, of New York, NY; daughter, Wendy, of St. James, NY; and five grandchildren.

HARRY TOWNES 86, Huntsville, AL-born actor, died May 23, 2001, in New York, NY. Broadway credits include *Tobacco Road* (1942), and *In the Matter of J. Robert Oppenheimer.* Other credits include *Strip for Action, Mr. Sycamore, Finian's Rainbow, Twelfth Night,* and *Gramercy Ghost.* He is perhaps best known for his work in television and film.

GWEN VERDON, 75, Culver City, CA-born dancer/actress, died October 18, 2000, in Woodstock, VT, of natural causes. A Theatre World Award and Tony Award winner for *Can-Can* in 1953, her other Broadway credits include *Alive and Kicking*, *Damn Yankees* (Tony Award), *New Girl in Town* (Tony Award), *Redhead* (Tony Award), *Sweet Charity* (Tony nomination), *Children! Children!*, and *Chicago* (Tony nomination), She also served as artistic adviser on *Dancin'* (1978), and *Fosse* (1999). At age six she was billed as the "fastest little tapper in the world," and was widely regarded as the best dancer ever to brighten the Broadway stage. Broadway dimmed its lights at 8 P.M. in her honor on October 18, 2000. She also made numerous appearances in television and film. Survivors include her son, Jimmy O'Farrell Heneghan, Jr., of Los Angeles, CA, and daughter, Nicole Providence Fosse.

RAY WALSTON 86, New Orleans, LA-born actor, died January 1, 2001, in Beverly Hills, CA, following a short illness. He made his Broadway debut in 1945 in *Hamlet*, followed by *Front Page*, *The Survivors*, *Summer and Smoke* (Clarence Derwent Award), *King Richard III*, *Mrs. Gibbons' Boys*, *The Rat Race*, *Wish You Were Here*, *South Pacific*, *Me and Juliet*, *House of Flowers*, *Damn Yankees* (Tony Award), *Who Was That Lady I Saw You With?* and *Agatha Sue, I Love You*, and also appeared in 22 productions with the Cleveland Playhouse. He is best known for his work on television, for which he garnered two Emmy Awards, and made numerous film appearances. His wife, Ruth, and daughter Kate, survive him.

CLAIRE WARING (Clara Waring) Mamaroneck, NY-born actress, died in August, 2000. Broadway credits include *Once in a Lifetime*, *A Warrior's Husband*, *Roberta*, *Kill That Story*, and *The Shrike*. Off-Broadway credits include *Young Davy Crockett* and City Center revivals of *Annie Get Your Gun*, *Show Boat*, *Guys and Dolls*, *Wonderful Town*, and *My Fair Lady*.

HENRY T. WEINSTEIN 76, Brooklyn, NY-born producer, died September 17, 2000, in Boca Raton, FL, following a long illness. Broadway credits include *The Trip to Bountiful*, *Third Best Sport* and *Triple Play*, before a long career in television and film. He also supervised the production of the filming of serious plays for subscription audiences in movie theaters, and was an executive producer of American Playhouse, which presented live dramas on public television. He is survived by two sisters, Judge Ruth Pearlman, of Jersey City, NJ, and Naomi Warren, of Boca Raton, FL.

MARY K. WELLS 79, Omaha, NE-born actress, died August 14, 2000, in New York, NY, of an infection of the colon. She made her Broadway debut in *Interlock*, followed by *Any Wednesday*, *Everything in the Garden*, *3 Men on a Horse*, and *40 Carats*. Best known for her work in television, for which she was awarded four Daytime Emmys—two for acting and two for writing—she also made several film appearances. Survivors include her son, Cameron Richardson, of New York, NY, and daughter Katherine O'Keefe, of Kent, OH.

MARIE WINDSOR (Emily Marie Bertelson) 80, Marysvale, UT-born actress, died December 10, 2000, in Beverly Hills, CA. Best known for her many film roles and over 100 appearances in television, her Broadway credits include *Follow the Girls*. She also served as a director of the Screen Actors Guild for over 25 years. Survivors include her husband, Jack Rodney Hupp; son Richard Hupp; and sister, Louise Atherley.

EDWARD WINTER 63, actor, died March 8, 2001, in Los Angeles, CA, of complications from Parkinson's disease. Broadway credits include his Broadway debut in *Cabaret* in 1966 (Tony nomination), followed by *Birthday Party*, *Promises Promises*, *Night Watch*, and *Follies*. Other credits include *Country Wife*, *Galileo*, *Danton's Death*, *The Condemned of Altona*, *The Caucasian Chalk Circle*, and *Waiting for Godot*.

JIM WISE 81, Akron, OH-born composer/teacher, died November 13, 2000, in New York, NY. Off-Broadway credits include *Dames at Sea*, and other credits include *Yankee Ingenuity*, and *Olaf*. He also taught at American Language Center at Columbia University, the Baruch School of the City of New York, and at the New Jersey Institute of Technology. No immediate family members survive.

FREDDY WITTOP (Frederico Ray) Bussum, Netherlands-born costume designer, died February 2, 2001, in Atlantis, FL. Broadway credits include *Hello Dolly!* (1964, Tony Award), *The Roar of the Greasepaint—the Smell of the Crowd* with Anthony Newley (Tony nomination), *I Do! I Do!* with Mary Martin and Robert Preston (Tony nomination), *The Happy Time* with Robert Goulet (Tony nomination), *A Patriot for Me* (Tony nomination), *Lovely Ladies, Kind Gentlemen* (Tony nomination), *Beat the Band*, *Heartbreak House*, *Carnival*, *Subways Are for Sleeping*, *Bajour*, *Kelly*, *On a Clear Day You Can See Forever*, *3 Bags Full*, *Happy Time*, *George M!*, *Dear World*, *The Three Musketeers*, *Jerry's Girls*, and *Wind in the Willows*. He created costume designs for the *Folies Bergére*, the *Théâtre de Chatelet* and the *Folies at the Alhambra* in Paris, France, and for *Judith* in London, England. He was an adjunct professor of the school of drama at the University of Georgia, and was chosen as the 2001 recipient of the Theater Development Fund's Irene Sharaff Award for lifetime achievement. He is survived by his sister, Martina Wittig Konig, of the Netherlands.

MARY HUNTER WOLF 95, Bakersfield, CA-born director, died Nov. 3, 2000, in Hamden, CT. One of the first women to direct on Broadway, her credits include *Only the Heart*, *Carib Song*, *Out of Dust*, *Ballet Ballads*, *Respectful Prostitute*, *Great to Be Alive!*, *Peter Pan*, *King Henry V* (1969), *Cat on a Hot Tin Roof* (1975), and *Othello* (1985). She co-founded the American Actors Company, and established the Professional Actor Training Program of the American Theatre Wing. In 1952, she helped found the American Shakespeare Festival in Stratford, CT, serving first as executive director, and later as associate producer. She is survived by former husband, Herman Wolf; two stepsons, David Wolf, of Ridgefield, WA, and Bill Wolf, of New Castle, VA; a stepdaughter, Louise Chandler, of Sweet Springs, WV; six grandchildren; and a great-grandson.

GEORGE WOOD 80, Forest City, AR-born actor/composer, died July 24, 2000, in Macon, GA, of heart failure. Broadway credits include his Broadway debut in 1953 in *Cyrano de Bergerac*, followed by *Richard III*, *Shangri-La*, *The Seagull*, *The Crucible*, *The Imaginary Invalid*, *A Touch of the Poet*, *Tonight at 8:30*, *King Henry V*, *Who's Who in Hell*, and *The Importance of Being Earnest*. Off-Broadway credits include *La Ronde*, *Cradle Song*, *The Lesson*, *Thor with Angels*, *A Box of Watercolors*, *Tobias and the Angels*, and *The Potting Shed*. He was an original member of the Circle in the Square Company where he composed several musicals, including *The King and the Duke* and *F. Jasmine Addams*. He also appeared regionally at the Ahmanson in Los Angeles, CA, and appeared in numerous roles in television and film. A sister survives him.

RICHARD WOODS 77, Buffalo, NY-born actor, died on January 16, 2001. Broadway credits include *Beg, Borrow, or Steal*, *Capt. Brassbound's Conversion*, *Sail Away*, *Coco*, *Last of Mrs. Lincoln*, *Gigi*, *Sherlock Holmes*, *Murder Among Friends*, *Royal Family*, *Deathtrap*, *Man and Superman*, *Man Who Came to Dinner*, *The Father*, *Present Laughter*, *Alice in Wonderland*, *You Can't Take It with You*, *Design for Living*, *Smile*, and *The Show-Off*. Off-Broadway credits include *The Crucible*, *Summer and Smoke*, *American Gothic*, *Four-in-One*, *My Heart's in the Highlands*, *Eastward in Eden*, *Long Gallery*, *Year Boston Won the Penant*, *In the Matter of J. Robert Oppenheimer*, with APA in *You Can't Take It with You*, *War and Peace*, *School for Scandal*, *Right You Are*, *Wild Duck*, *Pantagleize*, *Exit the King*, *Cherry Orchard*, *Cock-a-doodle Dandy*, and *Hamlet*, *Crimes and Dreams*, *Marathon '84*, *Much Ado About Nothing*, *Sitting Pretty in Concert*, *The Cat and the Fiddle*, and *The Old Boy*.

INDEX

B

C

D

E

F

G

H

I

L

O

P

Q

R

S

T

U

V

W

Y

Z